MAN'S BOOK

NEVER HAD
A SPANNER ON HER

James Leasor

*

THIS PERFECT DAY

Ira Levin

*

THE XYY MAN

Kenneth Royce

ODHAMS BOOKS
LONDON

MADE AND PRINTED IN GREAT BRITAIN
BY ODHAMS (WATFORD) LTD.
SBN 600778908
9·71

CONTENTS

NEVER HAD
A SPANNER ON HER

James Leasor

*'Never Had a Spanner On Her' is published
by William Heinemann Ltd.*

The Author

James Leasor has one wife, two homes—in England and Portugal—three sons and four cars. He has owned several of the rare marques mentioned in this book, and made his first successful automotive deal when he was fourteen. 'I bought a 1929 round-tank BSA motorcycle for three shillings, resprayed it by putting paint in an insecticide gun, and sold it for seven. Ideally, I should have started with more capital, but the three bob was all my money-box contained.' He is also the author of the internationally acclaimed Dr. Jason Love novels, which are published and serialized in sixteen countries.

For
ROLAND GANT
who thought of the title and
should have written
the book

CHAPTER ONE

THAT DAY BEGAN just like any other, because, if you think about it, there wasn't any other way it could possibly begin.

The sun heaved itself slowly over the roof-tops and then hung there a bit shakily, like an under-poached egg in the sky, looking down at me. I suppose it was also looking down at eight million other people in London, but I was the one it woke up.

I sat up in bed and blinked around the room which, according to your viewpoint, and whether you are advertising for a tenant, or are the tenant yourself, could be equally truthfully described as 'former groom's residence above Belgravia mews', 'delightful bachelor establishment', 'a pad', or as I call it, a pit. It's all these things, and a bit scruffy as well, with paint chipped around the edges of doors, and stuffing bursting out of the easy chairs. I bought them as a job lot in a second-hand shop in Camden Town. The man wanted six quid for them.

'Tell you what I'll do,' I told him. 'I'll give you four—and I'll take them away.'

He agreed, because he thought I was doing him a favour, until he worked it out in his midget mind that whoever bought them *had* to take them away. But by then it was too late; they were out in the back of my car, and my car was half a mile up the road.

He didn't realize then, though he may have done later, that I also buy and sell.

I live above my shop, and the shop for me is Aristo Autos, which, cut down to its infinitesimal size, is an old stables in the back of the mews in Belgravia, with a tarted-up sign outside, and three or four tarted-up old cars inside, which I buy for as little as possible, and sell for as much as I can.

People these days, in this effluent/affluent world (or out of it, for all I know), collect all kinds of things, from match-box labels to steam rollers, and because relatively few old cars have lasted for thirty or forty years—and why the hell should they?—they were only meant to last for a couple of years when they were new—they have also acquired an inflated value as antiques.

Five years ago, to buy a Bentley $4\frac{1}{2}$ litre Black Label would have set me back five hundred iron men; now, I have to pay nearly ten times this sum, and so you can be pretty sure that whoever buys one from me gets the date of his birth and his mother-in-law's age added to it for my profit.

Incidentally, the Black Label badge is another example of the mystique that surrounds old cars—and especially Bentleys. When they were made in Cricklewood up to 1931, the background colours of the big winged 'B' badges on the radiators were there to give a quick indication of the size of engine under the bonnet. Red meant the Speed Model 3 litre; blue, the ordinary standard model and the 6½ litre; green, the Speed Six; and black, the ordinary 4½ litre. Some Bentleys of those days even had the badge background painted to match the colour of the body, and so it had no significance at all, only I don't put that in my ads.

But now we have these fine cars—the world's fastest lorries as Ettore Bugatti once described them—being advertised as Green Label, or Black Label, as though they were whiskies. Snobbishness, like pre-packed TV meals and frozen foods, are the curse of the age, but it helps to make me a living, so why should I behave like a walking wayside pulpit and denounce it?

I climbed out of bed, looked in the mirror, squeezed a couple of blackheads just for the hell of it, and examined my tongue. I felt three thousand years old and I looked my age. One day nearer the grave, I thought, and wondered where and when and how it would all end. For there's only one thing I can't talk myself out of, if I've a mind to, and that's death. However, this was a gloomy thought, so I didn't think it, but tried to focus my furry mind on better things, like girls with charlies round as brandy glasses, and almost as firm, and wearing trousers so tight that when they bend down you should be able to see the line of their pants, but you can't, so you wonder, are they cheating by wearing tights, or are they wearing nothing at all?

This wasn't all that more cheerful, either, for at my time of life you don't just want to think about such things, you want to be where the action's happening, and it certainly wasn't all happening to me.

I steered my thoughts towards the three old cars in the garage beneath me, standing on the cobbles where the horses used to chew their hay only forty years ago. Business wasn't all that brisk; it never is early in the year—or sometimes, if you're honest —late, either. You have to wait for the Americans to come over for Stratford and the Lakes, and the coach tours of Bonnie Scotland, and when they are stuck for half a day, they may see my ad in their hotel foyer. Right now, even the hotels were half empty, which was one reason why I had been lumbered with these old cars for so long that I practically felt married to them. And marriage, like life insurance, is something that's never greatly attracted me: you have to die to beat them both, which took me back to my gloomy thoughts again.

I washed, shaved, mixed up a couple of eggs, half a cup of milk, and a knob of butter, poured this into a pan, threw in some salt and pepper, stirred them until they went sort of soggy, and ate them with a spoon, standing up, reading the *Daily Express* on the draining board, which is how I eat most meals when I'm on my own. Why mess about laying a table, clearing it up, washing dishes *et al* when there's no need?

Police were searching for a masked man in Hampstead, which is as good a place as any to find one, if a masked man is what (or who) you're after; a TV actress had arrived at the Old Bailey for her bankruptcy petition in a Rolls (which, unfortunately, I hadn't sold her); twin brothers, aged thirty-five had changed sex, in Pernambuco, a place I've never been to, and which I thought I'd stay from in case this could be catching.

Altogether, it seemed a pretty normal day outside in the great big world, whatever it was like for me. And, to make things par for the course, no one would turn up to buy any of my stock, a situation which would also be all too normal for my liking. What I wanted was a touch of the old abnormality, with men rushing in carrying sheaves of notes, thick as a horse's neck, all crying out to buy my cars at my prices.

I went downstairs, rolled back the entrance doors, and stood on the cobbles in the mews, wishing something like that would happen, just once in my life.

George, my mechanic, had not yet arrived. He does the real work in my business, and can spruce up an old car as well as those Mayfair beauty clinics tart up some withered old bag to make her look a little less than the hundred years old she must be.

I have had George around for quite a time now. He learned his trade in the Tanks, and we have a sort of love-hate relationship. I hate it when he spends too much of my time and my money on a car, but when he is late, as he was that day, I think how valuable he is, and where the hell would I be if I had to do the hard, hairy work myself, as well as the speaking part?

Another thing about George is that he talks in rhyming slang, which keeps my mind ticking over, for sometimes I can't understand what he means, and if I can't, how can anyone else? Sometimes, of course, I don't think he understands what he means himself, but then that can go for all of us. The great difficulty today is in communicating, as the deaf man told the dumb one.

My three cars, as I say in my old-car ads, were all 'carefully selected, all guaranteed, every worn part replaced'. I suppose that's true, so far as it goes, which isn't all that distance. I'd selected the damn things myself, mainly because I couldn't find anything else to buy at my price, and the worn parts, when they were so obviously worn that they wouldn't work, had been replaced, but only by other parts just a little less worn. Anyhow, my guarantee was carefully drawn up by a Polish lawyer in Bethnal Green, so that when I offered 'guaranteed used cars', all I really guaranteed was that they were used, and after thirty or forty years there was no doubt about that. You could have that in writing if you wanted.

The best of the three to look at was a Marendaz Special, which was quite a nice little car of the 1930s, with a radiator made to look like a little Bentley, and a bonnet with three exhaust pipes sprouting out from one side. Stirling Moss's mother used to win races in a Marendaz, so it could go fast as well as look fast, an ability not shared by all sporting cars at that time.

This car had been made in what we in the car business call The Jam Factory in Maidenhead, because it is now the home of a famous marmalade concern. From the First World War until just before the Second, several makes of car had been made there, from the G.W.K., which took its name from the initials of the three partners who produced it, Mr Grice, Mr Wood and Mr Keiller, to the Auto Electric, which had a battery and *four* engines, one for each wheel, through the rear-engined Burney, designed by Sir Dennis Burney, who pioneered the R100 airship, to one of the more successful, the Marendaz, produced by Captain D. M. K. Marendaz. In addition to the successes of Mrs Moss, Marendaz cars set a twenty-four hour record for both 1100 and 1500 cc cars at Montlhery.

Had they possessed more capital, the end might have been very different, but that's also the story of my life, and maybe yours, too, and the fact of the matter is that, having begun in small premises off the Brixton Road, next door to Bugatti's London depot, they travelled West to The Jam Factory, where they unfortunately went out of business in the late summer of 1936—about the same time as the car that stood next to the Marendaz in my garage, the little open Talbot 10, was coming on to the market .

Mine was the two-seater model, which is very rare, and although it is rather disappointing from an engineering point of view, being mainly a warmed-up Hillman Minx of that time, it *looked* fast, even standing still, and could probably top 60 downhill at full sail.

It was worth a hundred of anyone's money, which would show me a profit, for it had cost me £20. I'd have taken less, too, if I'd been pushed, but no one was around to push me, so I was not doing any business.

The third car was one of those strange sad vehicles that every dealer gets lumbered with from time to time, because they have a certain nostalgic affection for them, largely because of their ugliness. This was a 1935 Chrysler Airflow with a front like a chromium waterfall. When it was new, they said it was a car ten years ahead of its time, but ten years after its time, in 1945, it still looked ugly, because to be honest—and why not, there's no money involved?—it *was* ugly. But like some ugly things—and people—it was also interesting.

It had been built because a senior Chrysler engineer, Carl Breer, motoring home from Detroit one day, saw a flock of geese above him in the distance. As they flew nearer, he realized they weren't geese at all, but a flight of army airplanes, and he thought how close a plane was in design to a bird, how natural it looked in its own element—while car designs still harked back too much and too often to the horse and buggy days.

Breer decided to design a car that also took advantage of the air by offering the smallest possible resistance to it; and the Airflow was the result.

Well built, well thought out, it still met the stiffest resistance from a quarter more important than the air—customers. They just didn't like the look of it, and, quite honestly, neither did I. Anyhow, I hoped optimistically that some nutter would fork out £500 for this piece of misconceived modernity of the 1930s. If he wouldn't, then maybe the lead guitarist of a pop group might be persuaded that this was just what he needed for a pre-psychedelic image for himself. Everything has a buyer, if you wait long enough; the only danger is you may die before you meet him.

I was thinking about this and that and the other, but mostly about the other, when a man came round the end of the mews, and walked towards me. He couldn't very well crawl without attracting attention, even in Belgravia, but he could have come running, which might have meant I had a buyer.

When you are in my sort of business, you can tell from a stranger's tread whether he is intent on a deal or whether he just wants to fill in half an hour before his train goes, talking about cars he has never owned.

'You are Aristo Autos?' this man asked, making the thing sound more like an accusation than a question, as though I had been caught flashing it on Hampstead Heath.

'The same,' I told him. 'And you?'

'My name's Kent. Jack Kent.'

'Like the county and the cigarette. Fly your own flag. Be a trend-setter,' I said, because there was nothing else to say, and so far this fellow wasn't adding much to the sum of human knowledge, or even mine.

'Yes,' he said. 'Tell me, do you buy old cars as well as sell them?'

'Depends on the car,' I said. The last thing I wanted to buy was another ancient banger, full of dry rot and rust. I wished that the good Lord had sent me a buyer instead of a seller. Back to the prayer mats, lads. 'What have you got?' I asked him, not meaning in the way of his private parts, but the car.

'A Delahaye.'

As he spoke, he looked at me out of the ends of his eyes, wondering how I would take it.

I took it. A Delahaye has never been my favourite motor-car, but it was a very soundly built beast, although for some reason is wasn't all that easy to sell at a profit.

'What's the model?' I asked, keeping my thoughts out of my voice.

'Two-seater. Type one three five, three and a half litre, over-head valve motor.'

He'd got the facts all pat, almost as though he had learned them off from a book or a catalogue. This could be interesting; not very, but a bit. For years, Delahaye had made lorries, and then someone in the firm decided to put a lorry engine in a car chassis, and dress the whole thing up in Figoni and Falaschi bodies. We always called them 'phoney and flashy' but although they were sometimes the last, they were never the first, and a good two-seater, with enclosed front wheels, could be worth fifteen hundred nicker. Not to buy, of course, but to sell.

'Where is it?' I asked him.

'My place.'

'Where's your place?'

'Belsize Park. I rent a mews garage, Seventeen, Belsize Park West.'

'Why are you selling?'

'I'll be frank with you,' he began, and at once I knew he wasn't going to be quite that. People who talk about honesty and decency and straight-dealing are the ones to watch, prefer-ably with your back against a brick wall, although sometimes things are so rough they'll even stab you in the chest.

'I'll be frank with you. I bought it myself, thought I could make a profit doing it up, as I've read others do, but then found I just hadn't got the time, or the ability. So I want to off-load it.'

'How much?'

'Two-fifty quid,' he said. 'Notes.'

'Naturally.'

I was amazed he thought I'd deal in cheques. I'd read some-where that it costs you two and six, even to cash a cheque, assuming you have money in the bank. I like notes, because there is no record of any deal, and also you can actually claim the whole transaction as a bad debt, which is useful for putting against those deals when you have had to take a cheque against all your judgement.

'What's the condition like?' I asked him.

'Fair. A runner, anyway. You can drive it.'

This was a step in the right direction, because so many of these old cars are not even towable. Some I have bought have been so rusty that when I tried to move them, the spokes of the wheels collapsed, and they had to be carried away like mechani-cal cot cases.

'When can I see it?' I asked him, not because I particularly wanted to, but because I had nothing else to say, and for £250 I wasn't being robbed.

'Any time you like,' he said.

'Like now?' I asked.

'Like now.'

'Give me ten minutes for my man to arrive and look after the shop, and I'll be with you. You've got a car?'

'On a meter outside the mews. A grey Cortina.'

'See you there.' He held out his hand, and since he wasn't begging for money, I shook it with mine. He had the firm grip of the insurance salesman, which didn't endear me to him. Professional handshakers want watching; they have a habit of being rather less honest than they seem. Indeed, it's been my experience that their integrity runs in an inverse ratio to the strength and masculinity of their handshake. This man felt as though he were male all over, a phallus in suède brogues and a Dacron suit.

I went back into my garage, and stood for a minute looking at the faded old paintwork of the Marendaz. I always find it hard, when looking at an old car, to imagine how it must have glistened when it was new, in a showroom with potted palms, and those funny nickel ashtrays on long stalks they used to have in the nineteen-thirties. It was like looking at an old face in the mirror—mine, maybe yours—and trying to recall what it looked like when it was young, when life was still an experience to be lived, when time hadn't written its rude name all over it.

I walked into the little hutch at one side of the door, where I do the minimal paperwork my job demands, opened the safe, took out twenty tenners, because you never pay the asking price, folded them double, and buttoned them in my back trouser pocket. I had just locked the safe when George arrived.

'Sorry I'm tiddler's,' he said.

'Tiddler's?' I repeated blankly.

'Yes. Tiddler's bait. Late. Bloody tube got held up.'

'So,' I said. 'Don't lose any sleep. I'm going out to Belsize Park to see some nutter's Delahaye.'

'What about the stock here?' asked George. 'No one's exactly fighting to buy it.'

'Don't tell me,' I told him. 'But we can't keep running on the spot for ever. I've got to go through the motions of doing business.'

I was convincing myself as much as him, and not succeeding. I picked up my set of trade plates, put them in a briefcase, because if there is one person I don't want to look like, that person is a used-car dealer, and walked up the mews.

Kent was sitting in a grey Cortina, like he said. He had taken off his hat, and his hair had been cut so short on his skull that it looked like black spray dust. I wondered what his trouble was. Maybe he had lice, or perhaps he just wanted to keep his brain cool.

We sat in silence as we drove north against all the commuters driving south. The car was clean and impersonal; no little gadgets like St Christopher plaques, or chromium vases with plastic flowers, or tiny dogs that nod their head in the back shelf. I used to think that these horrors were a product of the present day, but they've actually been around ever since cars were built to appeal to a wide public.

As long ago as 1928, accessory makers marketed such Freudian monstrosities as a nickel-plated baby's teat for the radiator cap of the Baby Austin (Baby, see?) and cloth figures of a Pierrot, a Sunbonnet Girl, even a Ukulele Girl ('with small spring for suspending') to hang in the rear windows of cars.

You can tell a lot about a person's personality from a glance at their car and the rubbish with which they deck it out. The drivers I hate most have their ashtrays crammed full of sweet papers, and the carpets grey with cigarette ash.

'Had it long?' I asked him.

'Only a few months,' he said noncommittally.

'How did you find it?'

He shrugged. 'Easy to park,' he said.

That was about all we said on the drive, so the great conversationalists of our time weren't in any danger from us. He pulled off Haverstock Hill, down into a welter of streets that had once been gracious, with high gabled houses, all now reduced to hutches for single typists, young provincials up in London for the first time, eager to run in the rat race, and coloured students.

I often wonder how much resentment in coloured countries stems from leaders who once lived in digs like these, with nothing to do on Sundays except demonstrate; homesick exiles in a grey, rainy land with the gas fire out and never a shilling for the meter.

Kent stopped the car.

'We'll walk the rest,' he said. 'Easier for parking.'

I got out first, and waited for him to lock up. While he was fiddling with the keys, I put my hand in my right jacket pocket and felt for the half-inch pencil I kept there, and scribbled the car number on the back of an envelope. Then I took my hand out of my pocket as though I had just been rummaging for a cigarette.

We went up a couple of alleys to a mews rather like mine, although a bit tattier. A white Rolls, probably belonging to a pop group because it had psychedelic decorations on the doors, was being hosed down outside one garage. Farther down, some characters with cameras and lights were organizing a girl in a mini-skirt to run up an outside staircase. I guessed they were doing a TV commercial. If I'd been on my own I'd have hung about for a while, bending down, lacing my shoe or some damn thing, just to see her going up the stairs, to see what sort she'd got on, but I hadn't the chance. Business before pleasure, as the old pro told the ponce.

'In here,' said Kent. He fumbled in his pocket for a Yale key, and then leaned against the sliding door of a garage. The smell of dry rot and stale air rushed out, but luckily nothing else. Certainly, the Delahaye stayed where it was.

I walked round it, keeping all opinion out of my face. For a car of that age, it wasn't too bad. Agreed, hungry moths had made many meals on the hood, the paint was dull and the chrome pitted and rough as a bear's backside, but it was recognizable as a car, although it hadn't the body I wanted, but a reasonably smart one by Henri Chapron.

When you know people who can chromium-plate quickly, and bring up a portable spray plant to work overnight (so long as they are paid in notes) and all those other little short-cuts that can make the difference between success and failure in the old-car business, I figured I wouldn't lose on the deal. But then it is not my business to lose on any deal.

'Can you start it?' I asked Kent.

He lifted the bonnet as though to reassure himself the engine was still there, found it was, and climbed in behind the wheel and pressed the starter. When the engine fired, I put my hand casually on the radiator header tank. It was still warm. Someone must have been running the car only hours before. This is not uncommon when you're trying to sell an old car that's a swine to fire up when it's cold, and it could mean anything or nothing. It didn't mean anything to me. After all, I didn't want the car myself, and no skin fell from my nose if it was difficult to start. *Caveat emptor,* as my old Polish lawyer liked to say, which means, let the buyer beware; the seller can also be a bastard.

Kent engaged first gear and drove the nose of the car out into the mews.

'I've got the log book,' he said, as though this proved something, and took it out of the door pocket to show me.

The instruments were all there, and original; usually someone steals the clock, which leaves a sorry hole to fill. I flicked on the lights. They worked. I decided to buy the car.

'It's a difficult model to sell,' I told Kent, because it was true. I'd have told him the same if it hadn't been, of course.

He didn't say anything, but just sat looking at me, with the engine ticking away under its long louvred bonnet.

'Want's a lot of work doing on it, too,' I said. 'It's hard to get people to work on these old cars now. Only a handful of coach-trimmers are left who can do this type of job.'

'Don't make me weep,' said Kent. 'Do you want it, or don't you?'

'Not at two-fifty.'

'How much then?'

'One-fifty,' I said.

'You're joking?' He sounded hopeful.

'Not with my money. I can't afford fun.'

'This cost me four hundred,' he went on.

'I quite believe it,' I said, although I found it difficult, but why fall out with the nut? It was only his word against mine.

'Two twenty-five,' he said. 'And you're breaking my heart.'

'No good,' I told him.

I shook my head sadly, like a bishop over his favourite curate who had been found after the choirboys again. I knew my cue, now. After all, I should do. I had followed it often enough.

I gave a great sigh, ran one hand in a sort of farewell caress down the old bonnet, and turned away. I generally allow myself three paces on these occasions before I stop and put up my price —if the seller doesn't stop me first. Such is the delicate psychological balance between buying and selling that he invariably does.

Kent let me make two-and-a-half paces before he said hoarsely: 'Two hundred.'

I completed the pace, and turned and stood, head on one side, as though thinking the whole matter over very thoroughly. This was the price I had already agreed in my mind before I'd even left home, but he didn't know that. I kept him waiting, as though this was as serious a matter as General Motors merging with Ford.

'O.K.,' I said at last.

'Good,' said Kent, as though he meant it.

He backed the car into the garage, switched off the engine, climbed out.

I glanced at the log book. His name was the first entry.

'What happened to the old book?' I asked him.

'No more space,' he replied.

This is the answer I'd have given in these circumstances, for in the trade it's not unusual to provide a new book with an old car, in case the buyer tries to contact the former owner and discover the size of the mark-up or, worse, just why the last owner sold it. But, so far, Kent hadn't sounded like a car dealer.

I checked the engine and chassis numbers, and made as sure as I could with my pocket torch that they hadn't been altered from something else. You have to be as careful with old cars as with new, in case they've been stolen. Then I counted out twenty tenners, and bound the trade plates with their elastic bands around the bumpers.

'Feel like a drink?' asked Kent suddenly.

'I feel like anything,' I said. It was a bit early for drinking, but I never refuse a good offer.

'Come upstairs,' he said.

'Do you live here?' I asked him, as I followed him up the wooden, uncarpeted stairs, and a damp, musty smell poured in on me from the walls.

'If I'm in town I sometimes stay here. If like I'm with a bird.'

'I see.'

The room was not unlike mine, but rather shabbier; an old

settee in one corner, some filing cabinets, which he had probably brought from a second-hand furniture store, because they didn't match, a table and three dining-room chairs.

He opened the top drawer of his cabinet, took out two glasses and a half bottle of whisky. He measured out two of the smallest tots I'd ever seen, held them up side by side to make quite sure they were of equal size, put down the glasses and carefully screwed the cap back on the whisky bottle in case any should evaporate. Whatever else Kent was, he wasn't fighting to be the last of the big spenders, Mr Host-of-the-Year.

I glanced around the room. There was something anonymous about it, no imprint of any personality or character, not even a trade calendar on the wall to give any clue as to the occupant's business. It could be anyone's room, or no one's. It just happened to be his.

'What line of country are you in?' I asked him.

'Import, export.'

He poured some water from a beaker into our glasses. We toasted each other.

'I buy a lot of junk from Hong Kong,' he went on. 'Plastic novelties, rubbish of that kind, dress them up a bit and sell them again, mostly to the Middle East. I've an office in Cairo.'

I nodded, as though I understood this way of making a living, but I didn't, any more than he probably understood mine.

'How did you hear of me?' I asked him. It's valuable to know what advertisements are worth using.

'Someone in a pub,' he said vaguely. 'We were talking about old cars, and he gave me your address.'

'Nice of him,' I said. The man was probably lying. He'd probably read my ad somewhere; in a taxi, an hotel brochure, a newspaper. I like to have saturation coverage, as the man said, when he pee'd all over the strawberries.

'Well, I'll be off.'

I drank my drink and we shook hands. Kent watched me go down the stairs and climb into the Delahaye. Then I heard the door click shut.

I was back in my mews in under an hour. There had been no calls, and we hadn't made any money, but at least we hadn't lost any. George walked round the Delahaye, looking at it, kicking the tyres with the automatic reflex of the old-car dealer, opening and closing the doors to see whether they were sagging on their hinges.

'What are you going to ask for it?' he asked me.

'Four and a half,' I said. 'The paint's not too bad.'

It wasn't all that good, really, but when it had been compounded it would glow like new.

Compound is a mildly abrasive paste that we dealers use to take off the haze from old paint. Years ago, many car polishes contained a good percentage of this stuff, and the advertisements all stressed that although the polishing rag *would* become stained with paint from the car, this was all part of the deep cleansing action, etc. In fact, it was all part of rubbing the paint off, and if you polished the paint too often you'd eventually have no paint left. However, as my old father used to say, you believe what you want to believe, and some of us have been screwed so often that we believe in nothing, not even in ourselves.

George connected up the hose to wash the car. He'd black the tyres, buff up the chromium with some abrasive on a pad at the end of an electric drill to see if we could avoid having it all replated, shampoo the upholstery, and Kent wouldn't recognize the car by evening. I watched him work, and the day passed like any other day.

A few nutters rang up and offered me cars for sale which I didn't want to buy, and an American tourist actually came from the Ritz, where he'd had to stop over for a night on a flight from Los Angeles to Rangoon, and he'd a couple of hours to kill. He told me he owned a dozen old cars in Des Moines, but he was too cautious to make it a baker's dozen and buy another one from me.

Only one thing was different about that day. I telephoned a friend in a hire-purchase company and gave him the number of Kent's Cortina and asked him to let me know anything about it. He was back on the blower within an hour. The car wasn't Kent's at all, but a self-drive rented to him for a fortnight. So why had he lied to me about it? Did he think I'd be more impressed if he said he owned it—and this at a time when three out of four cars on the roads are owned by companies and most of the rest are rented?

I never cease to wonder at the odd ways in which people's minds work, usually activated by greed or sex, or just plain snobbery. Remember what Francis Quarles wrote about them years ago? 'Let the greatest part of the news thou hearest be the least part of what thou believest, lest the greatest part of what thou believest be the least part of what is true.'

He'd have done well in the used carriage trade, would Quarles. I could imagine his ads: 'Every carriage thoroughly restored, new hand-carved shafts, revarnished as necessary, wheels respoked, polished axle caps, leatherwork completely renovated. Never had a hammer on her. Believed former property of Elizabethan courtier.'

About five o'clock, a character turned down the mews in a Mini and stopped just behind my door. He climbed out carefully, locked his door, and came towards me. As I say, you can tell a lot from people by watching how they walk, and also how they drive, how they stop, whether they lock their car doors, or whether they don't bother. This character seemed a very

cautious type to me. He was tall, in a dark grey, double-breasted
suit, with a wide chalk stripe, carnation in button-hole, white
collar with a deep pink shirt and the two-blues of the Old Etonian
tie. He might be an accountant; he could be an hermaphrodite
so far as I was concerned. His money was the same as anyone
else's.

'I'm looking for something open and old,' he began. The way
he put it he might be looking for an old lay. One of the lays of
ancient Rome.

'How open and how old?' I countered.

'Like this car here,' he said, indicating the Delahaye. 'Haven't
seen one of those for years.'

I changed gear gracefully into my spiel.

'Very few left of this model. One of the best ever turned out
by the firm. Bound to be a collector's piece in a few years. I've
already got three people interested in it.'

This wasn't entirely a lie, either, so don't rush me. This nut
had shown some interest, George was interested because it helped
to make his living, and so was I because I hoped it would make
me a profit. That makes three people, doesn't it?

'How much?' the man asked.

'Four-fifty.'

A shadow of pain crossed his face. He must be an accountant;
or maybe he worked for the income tax.

'I can't put it any lower than that.'

I nodded to George across the bonnet. He started the engine.

'Listen to that,' I told the man. 'Everything is balanced
dynamically.'

I didn't know what this meant, really, but it sounded good.
I'd read it in someone else's advertisement, so it must be true.
I believe most things I see in print, unless they're things I put in
print myself.

'They don't make them like that any more,' I told him, in case
he didn't know. 'It would cost a fortune to get an engine like
that built today. Would you like to see it?'

He shook his head. I opened the door, but he didn't even look
inside.

'What's your lowest price you would take?' he asked me. 'For
cash.'

I signalled to George to switch off the engine. When it grew
warm, there was a knock in it like a madman beating on an anvil.
That might be serious, or again it might not. I thought it probably was.

'For cash!' I repeated, as though I'd never heard the words
before, but believe me, they were music in my ears. 'I'd take
four twenty-five.'

'I'll give you three hundred,' he said, reaching into his inside
pocket.

'For this?' I asked him in amazement. 'You must be joking.'

'Three hundred,' he said. 'Cash.'

I paused. I could keep the car and ask four-fifty, and I'd probably get it—in time. On the other hand, I'd have my own money tied up in it, and if I could make a quick £100 out of a few hours of George's time, and a trip up to Belsize Park, it seemed foolish not to do so.

But it is always psychologically wrong to give in too easily, as the virgin told the sailor. If you're going to be beaten down on a deal, the man who is doing the beating down likes to feel he's had a struggle. It's a glandular thing. So I wriggled about for five minutes, working out sums in my head, and bringing out a mass of bills which I keep filed under every conceivable make of car. They are all faked, of course, but they look convincing with details of new clutches, reconditioned rear axles, balancing of brakes, and all that crap. Finally, I let him win.

He took out his wallet.

'Cash,' I reminded him.

He counted out thirty ten-pound notes on the bonnet of the car.

'Come into my office,' I said, 'and I'll give you a receipt.'

He came in, and stood over me while I made out the printed form with his name and address, Mr G. A. Snelling, 32 Rosemary Court, Shepherds Bush, W11.

'When will you take it?' I asked him, because when you've done a deal, get rid of the actual physical vehicle as soon as possible, in case the buyer has a change of mind—or something goes wrong with the car. Some of these old motors can break down standing still.

'I'll come back later,' he told me. 'Leave the car outside here with the key in it.'

We shook hands and I watched him climb into his Mini and drive away. He was so careful he even used his flasher at the end of the mews, *and* his right hand, to show he was going to turn, and yet for a careful man he showed surprisingly little interest in the car—he hadn't even wanted to lift the bonnet. I'd have expected him to crawl all over it with a magnifying glass, shining a torch in each corner of the boot. But he hadn't done anything of this. Odd thing, human nature, I thought.

I put the money in my safe and wrote in my cash book: Cash sale, £75. So I had made an income tax loss as well as a cash profit. You couldn't have it better than that, but you could have it more often, as the psychiatrist told the nun.

I went out to the pub for lunch, and when I came back, the Delahaye had gone. Pretty soon after that it began to rain, and I stood looking out at the mews with my mind switched off, waiting for something to happen. It didn't, so I sent out a few reminders to people who owed me money, and was looking through a drawer in my desk for a book of stamps which I thought must be wedged in a crack, when I saw a bunch of keys. They didn't belong to me, and they didn't belong to George. The drawer had been jammed open a couple of inches, and they could easily have dropped in there without anyone noticing.

The only other person who had been in the office that day was Snelling, and so they must be his. I turned them over slowly; a key for a front door, a couple of small silver keys that probably fitted a suitcase, and an obvious ignition key. Snelling had been such a careful man, he must be doing his nut wondering where these were.

I looked him up in the telephone book, but there was no Snelling at that address. My good deed for the day, I thought, and the night as well; I'd take them round to him.

A thought crossed my mind, for it had nowhere else to cross. 'Did you find anything in that old Delahaye?' I asked George. I meant, apart from the usual tools, which I always keep—I must have the best selection of car tools in Belgravia—but we also look under the carpets, beneath the seats, and in all the door pockets. It's amazing the things you find—even if it's only razor blades that cut unwary fingers to the bone.

George took up a brown envelope, and shook out the contents on top of the desk. Two cinema tickets, a half wrapper for Polo mints, a cigarette, squeezed flat and unsmokable, and a small sheet of plain notepaper folded over. This I opened. It was the first page of a letter, but without any address, or date.

It began in a spidery handwriting: 'My dearest daughter. It is many weeks since I heard from you, and I have been thinking of you very much, especially over your birthday. I have only your old address to write to, and I wonder how you have been, and what news you will have to tell me when you come back. I will be here, as always, waiting for you, for . . .'

I turned over the page; it was blank on the other side. The second sheet was missing, so who was it from, and who was it to? An unknown father to an unknown daughter.

I read it through a second time. I should have thrown it away, but I didn't. I thought vaguely I should send it back to Kent; he might have written it, or maybe the daughter was his, or his wife, or maybe nothing. I pushed it into the side pocket of my jacket, and tossed all the other rubbish into the wastepaper basket.

Then I opened the doors and took out my SS100, because I am one of those nutters who believes that you should practice what you preach, and if you're flogging old cars it helps a lot if you drive one yourself, although sometimes, as you pass the Minis and Minxes with all their windows up, and a good fug flowing through the heater, you wonder if you're doing the right thing.

It was seven o'clock and the worst of the rush-hour had gone, and so I made fairly easy time down the Bayswater Road towards Shepherds Bush. Rosemary Court was a block of flats that had been modern in the late thirties, when it had been smart to live near Shepherds Bush film studios, but now the tide of fashion had long since ebbed away and the little side streets were blocked with the cars of TV executives at the B.B.C., ageless young men, with thick black hair, button-down collars and tinted glasses, and I had a hell of a job to slot mine anywhere, for the steering lock on the SS isn't fearfully good.

I managed after a time, and walked back to Rosemary Court. Close to, it looked pretentious, in that rather pathetic way of the nineteen-thirties, with a semi-circular sweep of steps, and four pillars, no doubt hollow, holding up a portico. Two swing doors opened into the building, and to make the entrance more impos-ing there was a third to the right that didn't swing. This was a telephone booth, and a couple of lovers were pressed together inside so tightly that the glass had steamed over. Whatever they were doing, they weren't phoning.

Thirty-two was on the third floor. I was just about to push through the front door when it burst open and a girl ran out. Her hair was long but tousled, and her eyes were wide with fright. She was carrying a handbag and her coat was open and blowing behind her. She rushed round me and tried the tele-phone door, but the careful lovers had wedged it closed.

'Oh, God,' she sobbed in desperation, and ran off down the road. I watched her go, past an old woman feeding pigeons from a bag of crusts, past the parked cars. Some other lover, I thought, and went upstairs. She could be the other woman, the sort of girl you see in a restaurant, with a sad-faced, middle-aged man, and she asks: 'Have you told *her* about us yet?' and the man answers carefully, not looking at her: 'Not yet. She's not been very well.'

Only thing was, this girl didn't look that type; she looked too vigorous and positive to accept that situation. But then, you never really knew with people, any more than you are ever really certain with cars.

The stair carpet was dull brown and shabby, with mud trodden into it. The smell of cabbage water and stale cooking hung over the staircase, and on each landing I caught up with snatches of music from an old film on TV. An American male was declaring: 'Honey, this thing is bigger than both of us.' Some thing, I thought, or maybe he was boasting. I went on climbing.

Thirty-two was half-way down the top corridor, on the right. Three domed bulbs burned dimly in the ceiling, one just outside the door. An illuminated bell push glowed at one side. I pressed it and listened to the chimes. There was nothing else to listen to, no creak of an inner door opening, no feet on the carpet. I rang the bell again. If no one was in, I'd just drop the keys through the letter-box.

Then I thought I'd better scribble a note to say where I'd found them. Then I discovered I hadn't even got someone else's visiting card in my pocket, and no pen, and my stub of pencil, like much of my life, had lost its point.

I rang the bell of the flat opposite to see if I could borrow some writing implement, but no one answered. The only sound of life was a dog that sniffed and snuffled along the bottom edge of the door, and then whined and gave a despairing little bark, as though it had hoped I'd open the door and let it out.

I turned back to thirty-two, and as I did so I saw that the door was about half an inch away from the jamb. I leaned against it, and it opened, as it had every right to do, because someone had fixed the Yale lock so that it could not close.

'Anyone in?' I called. 'Mr Snelling? Shop!'

There was still no answer. I would just go in, see if I could find a pencil on a table, and if not, I'd leave the keys so that Snelling would imagine they'd been there all the time. The hall was very narrow and a door opened off it to the right. I guessed this would be a sort of sitting-room cum dining-room with a bed in an alcove; I've lived in this size of flat myself.

When I opened the door I saw I'd guessed correctly. I also saw something else. All the drawers in a chest had been pulled open, clothes littered the floor—mostly slips and pants and bras. A cheap writing-desk had been smashed so that the roll-up cover could be opened. Letters, bills, magazines had been rummaged through and left in a jumble.

Sometimes I'm slow as a rheumatic snail, but it didn't take me all that long to realize that Snelling's flat had had a pretty thorough going-over. I looked for the telephone, but the wires had been torn from the wall. I turned back towards the door, and as I turned I breathed a whiff of scent, oily and rich and masculine, in a soft and pampered way. Then I heard a slight intake of breath somewhere behind my left ear; and then the room exploded, and I heard nothing else at all.

I must have been swimming or out in the rain, because I was soaking wet.

I moved my head to see where the hell I was, but my head didn't like moving and showed its disapproval by lifting off my body by several feet. When it came back on again, I saw I was sitting in the room with all the drawers and scattered clothes still on the floor. I was wet because someone appeared to have poured a bucket of water over me. At least, I saw an empty bucket on the carpet in a pool of water, and every time I moved, cold water trickled down between my shoulder blades or under my armpits.

The girl I had seen running down the stairs was sitting in a chair, looking at me intently. I tried to look at her intently, too, but this was difficult for my eyes didn't want to focus. Behind her stood two hazy figures. I shook my head again and water sprayed out from my hair.

I saw more clearly now. One man was a policeman in uniform, and the other wore a dark suit with a white open raincoat. For my money he'd be a plain-clothes cop. Why do they choose such plain clothes? They were also looking at me, not with any concern for my condition, but rather as scientists regard a specimen on a slab.

'So what happened?' I asked because I wanted to know. 'You tell us,' said the man in the raincoat. 'Who are you, anyway?'

I told him.

'Go on,' they said.

'A man called Snelling bought a car from me this afternoon,' I went on. 'He left some keys behind. He'd given me this address, so I came round with them. I couldn't get an answer at the door, and hadn't a pencil or paper to leave a note. When I saw the door was open, I came inside. Then I got hit on the head.'

'Did you see anyone?' asked the policeman in uniform.

'No one except you.'

I pointed to the girl; it was less painful than nodding to her.

'I saw this man coming into the block,' she agreed. 'I was running out to telephone the police. I'd come home and found everything in a shambles.'

'Where are these keys you mention?' the policeman asked. He seemed to have a lot to say in this show.

I put my hand in my right pocket. Nothing there at all but the lining, not even the letter. I felt in every other pocket, but although I had two five-pound notes folded in my left trouser pocket, and a handkerchief in the right, there were no keys. Like that unsigned letter, they'd gone.

'Gone,' I said.

'Anything to give you any idea who your attacker might be?'

I would have shaken my head again, but it was too sore, so I just said nothing. I didn't add that I'd smelled that strong scent, and I'd recognize it again. There couldn't be two men who smelled like that, even in Shepherds Bush. After you with that bush, shepherd.

'How did you come here?' asked the plain-clothes man.

'By car. It's parked down the road.'

I stood up slowly and water cascaded everywhere as though I were a collie dog shaking myself. Then I remembered Snelling.

'After all this, does Mr Snelling live here?' I asked all three of them.

The girl said, 'No. I do. I rent the flat furnished.'

'Maybe Mr Snelling's the landlord?' I suggested.

(This man made a certain suggestion, your worship; it all sounded like a court report.)

'Never heard of him,' she said. 'The people I pay rent to are Quendon Leaseholds Limited.'

This didn't sound like Snelling to me, but maybe if I rang them they'd tell me whether he was a tenant of another flat. Perhaps I'd mistaken the address? Perhaps anything, or perhaps nothing.

'I'm sorry about your flat,' I told the girl. 'I hope you find whoever did this.'

'We will,' said the policeman, sounding more confident than I would have been in his position.

I didn't feel like shaking hands with anyone, and they didn't offer to shake hands with me, so I just nodded very carefully so as not to disturb my head unnecessarily, and went out down the narrow corridor under the bulbs, down the stairs. No one stopped me, and I saw no one, either. The same TV programme was playing in each flat as I passed each front door. I might never have been away.

I drove back to the mews very slowly. George had gone, for it was about nine o'clock. I felt tired and had aged at least a thousand years. If Tutankamen had a spare place in his tomb I would gladly have crept in and shared it with him.

I unlocked the garage door, drove inside, shut the door again, went up the stairs, poured five fingers of the old Whyte & Mackay and drank it without adding any water. Then I sat down on the edge of the bed and tried to make sense out of what had happened. This took a lot of doing.

I checked Snelling's receipt. The address he had given me was 32 Rosemary Court. I knew I hadn't made a mistake there, but clearly I had somewhere. Could the sale of that car have anything to do with the girl's flat being ransacked? It seemed impossible, and even if it were possible I didn't know where to begin to trace the matter through.

Snelling. The name meant nothing to me, but I felt that I'd seen him somewhere in my life, or in another life if you like—for I've always had good luck with girls who are a bit mystical, and who react when you say you feel you've met them in another life, maybe they were slaves at the court of Pharaoh?

His face was as clear to me as the nude calendar on the wall. The Old Etonian tie, the bright red carnation, the dark double-breasted suit, the white collar and the deep pink shirt. A rich man or a rich man's son, or perhaps only someone wanting to appear either of these things? The last could be most likely, for the richest men I've met usually don't look at all as you'd imagine they would look.

In books and films and so on, the main character has all kinds of contacts for just this sort of problem. He'll say: 'It was at that moment that my thirteen years as chief acrobat with the Royal Albanian State Circus proved so useful: I *knew* that this man could only be Count Shagworthy, who had been a three-ball juggler when we played at the Court of King Zog, etc., etc.' And, talking about three-ball jugglers reminds me of George's limerick about that gay young man of Devizes, who owned balls of quite different sizes. The first was so small, it didn't matter at all, but the second won numerous prizes.

In real life, though, I could only think of one man who just might help me if he couldn't think of any reason against it.

I picked up the telephone and dialled old Jacko Jackson, who keeps an ear so close to the ground he's practically deformed. Jacko lives opposite me in the mews, and he's the biggest gossip since Pepys, though not so well known. I'd have gone over to see him, but I didn't think I could face the journey with the whisky churning round in my head, and my suit still damp and clammy.

Old Jacko has a strange life, but then if we're honest, don't we all? He's an actor in a small way, which means he acts out some of the simpler television commercials, as a retired ambassador, all silver-grey hair and split-arse jacket, sampling some new breakfast food, for he's a good-looking old fellow if you're not close enough to see his eyes, watery as under-poached eggs, or the tremble in his hands that a lifetime of cheap gin has given him.

His main acting parts are closely involved with the used-car trade. When a dealer takes a Rolls in part exchange that is just too old to renovate, and yet too young to write off and replace with something superior, he calls in Jacko. And Jacko, after altering the car's registration book so that the last owner appears to have been the Suffragan Bishop of Balls Pond Road, or some such other ecclesiastical dignitary, will put on a chauffeur's gear and, as the late Bishop's chauffeur, will give some innocent buyer a long spiel about the car's scheduled services, and the gentle driving he has done in it with his Grace, or his Lordship, or whoever, for the last twenty years, only carrying him to confirmation classes, or whatever.

The ringing in my ear stopped, and Jacko's voice, streaked with gin like a verbal rainbow, asked wheezily: "Who's this?'

'Me,' I said.

'Oh.'

He sounded disappointed. Maybe he'd hoped I was a client.

'I've got a bottle of gin for you,' I told him, which wasn't strictly true, but I'd buy one wholesale when a friend of mine opened his shop in Soho on the following morning.

'What have I got to do to get it? Bend down?'

He liked a touch of the old sarcasm, did Jacko, for, say what you like about me, and lots of people say plenty, I've never been one to enlarge the circle of my friends this way.

'No,' I told him. 'I want help. Do you know anyone who traders up West use when they want to bid against a genuine buyer to force him to clinch?'

We call this bidding against the wall, and it's not confined to old-car dealers. I know one estate agent in the West End who's had up to eight dummy bidders at an auction against the two or three genuine buyers. Once, the dummies overdid things and got left with a property they'd pushed up several thousand pounds beyond its real value.'

The vendor was beside himself with anger at this and sued the estate agent for malpractice. But the crafty old dealer had already discounted any risk like this. He said that he knew nothing about the dummy bidders; it was all a plot by some disloyal employees —and since he had prudently insured against dishonesty among his staff, he was as fully covered as a bush baptist in total immersion.

But, to return to our mutton, as one lustful shepherd told another.

'I know several dummies,' said Jacko. 'We use 'em for different deals. There's one who looks like a tycoon. Silvery grey hair, hundred guinea suits—he's in the Rolls and Bentley bracket. There's another with string-back gloves, sports cap and all that crap, for the E-types, and a third boyo about forty, Old Etonian tie, carnation, natty suiting, who's useful in the middle range— Daimler, Jag, Jensen—to lean on a dim buyer who can't quite make up his mind.'

This could be my man and I told Jacko so.

'What do you want him for?' he asked.

I began to *ad lib*, because here the truth would be more difficult for him to believe than fiction.

'I've got a fellow who's coming to buy a Bentley tomorrow,' I said. 'A Mark VI, in quite good nick. I may be able to squeeze him up to four-fifty quid for it, but if this old Etonian character came along and conveniently discovered that this car had belonged to his old uncle, Lord Fornicator, from new, I reckon I could push him up to five or six.'

'The bloke you need's Horatio,' said Jacko firmly. 'The old Etonian tie wallah. No doubt of it at all. Done a bit of fashion modelling in his day. Plays the part of the man about town. Beautiful suit, hand-rubbed shoes, hand-rubbed knob, too, if you ask me.'

'I'm not asking you,' I said firmly. I guessed old Jacko had been drinking, which is what he did most of the day when he wasn't sleeping off the previous day's alcoholic intake, soaking up the stuff like a great soft sponge, and sobbing softly at the sadness of it all. He wasn't my favourite man, but then who is?'

'What does he charge, this Horatio?'

'Fiver and cab fare, if it's a local job. If it's out of town, a bit more.'

'This is a local job. Where can I find him?'

'I've lost his number,' said Jacko, 'but I have his address.' Jacko gave it to me.

'What about the gin?' he asked, suddenly suspicious.

'Be at my place tomorrow at nine. I'll give you a couple of quid to buy a bottle at my cut-price bar.'

I knew he wouldn't even be awake at nine. To prise Jacko off his bed at that hour, even for a bottle of gin, was tantamount to murdering him.

'See you,' he promised, but it would be nine at night before he came; if he didn't forget all about it as soon as I rang off.

I poured myself another drink, chewed a couple of aspirins, to ease my aching head, and then went downstairs and opened the garage doors. I took out the SS, and headed towards Chelsea in search of Horatio, who if he didn't hold the bridge, could conceivably hold an answer to my question.

The address Jacko had given me was one of those old Chelsea houses in a side street off the unfashionable end of Fulham Road, with steps going up a pillared porch, and half a dozen push buttons with visiting cards against them by the side of the door. I shone my pencil torch down the names, K. Ahmed, Miss B. Jones, A. Browne (Melbourne) and then a visiting card with a fancy script that spelled out one word: Horatio. I pressed the button and waited. A voice spoke metallically through the speaker grille of the electric lock.

'Who is it?'

'Electricity meters,' I said quickly. 'Sorry it's so late, but you've been overcharged. We're making a special survey.'

'Oh, all right. Come on up. Third floor.'

I thought that if I told him who I was, he might not have asked me in. The door opened, and I was in the hall before the lock could change its mind.

It's my experience of human nature—and believe me, in selling cars you come to learn a lot about the convolutions of the human mind—that most people accept postmen, meter readers, and so on, as friendly neuters who will do them no harm.

If Horatio was just a harmless old/young/middle-aged queer, then I'd pretend to have a quick gander at the meter, and tell him that head office would be in touch with him in the morning. The fact that he'd never hear, he'd put down to general British bureaucratic inefficiency, and soon it would be forgotten, as, eventually, all is forgotten. In buying and selling and hearing all the twisted reasons people give you as to why they want to acquire or be rid of cars, you grow a bit devious yourself.

I walked up the steep, old-fashioned stairs to the third landing. The house was a hive of small rooms, all let off, each one the private world of some lonely person, either on the way up or on the way down. You could live here and die here, and the only way anyone outside would know the difference would be from milk bottles outside the front door, or the unclaimed letters in the wire cage behind it.

On the third landing the door was open a few inches, and a wedge of light shone out. I knocked gently at the door, coughed, as I imagined a genuine meter-reader would do, and went inside. A man was twiddling with the controls of a TV set. His back was towards me, so I couldn't recognize his face.

'Meter's behind the curtain,' he said, not looking round.

I closed the door behind me, and pulled aside a curtain that hung from a white book shelf. The gas and electricity meters were there all right. The man turned, and I saw he was Snelling. He also recognized me.

'What the hell?' he asked, half in anger, half in surprise.

'My little joke,' I said. 'I thought you mightn't like to see a used-car dealer after hours.'

'What's wrong?' he asked.

'Why should *anything* be wrong? You gave me an address in Rosemary Court, Mr Snelling, or Horatio, or whoever you really are. I went there with some keys you'd left behind in my office. I didn't find you at that address. In fact, you're not even known there, but someone appeared to be waiting for me. They slugged me on the head. Look.'

I bent forward so that he could see the bruise.

'My God,' he said, and his fear and surprise could have been genuine.

'Only God *can* help you now,' I said, 'because I mean to stay here until you tell me why you gave me that wrong address. And did you leave your keys behind in my garage innocently—or on purpose? Did you *expect* I'd take them on to Rosemary Court, and then maybe someone else—or maybe even you, Mr Snelling —would be waiting for me?'

'You've got it all wrong,' he said, backing away.

The picture on the screen trembled suddenly into clarity; it was a commercial for toothpaste. Snelling smiled out at me, with his striped tie and carnation, squeezing a white ribbon of paste on to an enormous brush. No wonder he'd been anxious to adjust the picture. All actors love looking at their favourite people: themselves.

'Just where have I got it wrong?' I asked him. 'Who lives at thirty-two Rosemary Court, if you don't?'

'I don't know,' he said.

'Come, come, Mr Snelling. You'll have to do better than that. Both of us can't not know.'

It wasn't very grammatical, I agree, but it made sense to him.

I took out from my trouser pocket a foot of coiled copper petrol pipe that I carry when I travel alone; this made even more sense, for there's nothing more innocent for a car dealer to carry—and nothing more useful as an instrument of persuasion, when you put your fist inside the coil, as I did now.

Snelling watched my fingers flex around the polished tube. If he had a brain, he was thinking what damage these hard ridges of copper would make to his face. If they connected, there wouldn't be any more commercials for a few weeks. Even a car dealer wouldn't want to use him if his face was all pushed in; that's how low he'd been placed.

'Who lives there, then?' I asked, taking a step towards him.

'I've told you, I don't know. A stranger rang me and asked if I'd buy the car for him. That often happens. He'd got my name from a fellow in the trade. Warren Street.

'I met him in a pub, The Goat and Compasses. I didn't know him and he didn't tell me his name. I didn't ask him—that's usual, too. The less you know the less you can louse things up.

'My fee was a fiver. He pulled out his wallet, for he was paying me in cash, and I saw a letterhead or a card—I didn't know exactly which—with that address. I didn't know who he was. He could be bent, so why get my own address involved? I simply gave you his. Hell, in this business how often do you give your real name, let alone your address?'

'What sort of man was he?'

'Thirty-five. Tall. Wore dark glasses.'

This could describe almost anyone in our business. It didn't describe anyone I know. I made a sudden lunge at Horatio as though I was going to strike him, and he screamed and backed away over the set, and the picture split into a maze of jagged edges and horizontal lines.

'Where did you take the car when you bought it?'

'To a mews,' he replied, so quickly that he didn't have time to make it up.

'Where?'

'Seventeen, Belsize Park West.'

So. That was Kent's address.

'Was the man there who'd given you the money?'

'No. The garage had been left unlocked. My instructions were to drive the car in and close the doors. They had a press padlock.'

'And you've never seen the man again? You've no address for him?'

'No. I usually don't, in these deals. People want to hire me as a front man for all sorts of things. To put up the price, to lower it, to explain why they can't go ahead with some deal. I just take my money, and don't ask questions. It's healthier that way.'

I could believe him. I know of others like him who eke out a precarious twilight existence in the half world of gambling clubs, used-car dealers and shady estate agents, men who spend their working lives pretending to be buyers, sellers, relatives; the only person they can never admit to being is themselves; they are the nothing-people.

'And you swear you know nothing about beating me up?'

'I swear it. I mean, why should I want to do that to you? We've only met once.'

This seemed a novel reason, but I believed him; he wasn't a hard-arm man.

'If I find you've been lying to me, Snelling or Horatio or whatever else you call yourself,' I said, 'I know where you live, and I'll be back. If I find you've got the slightest connection with this bruise on my head, I'll do my best to make life hard for you.'

'I swear I know nothing.'

He was trembling now, and his face was grey, with the skin stretched tight like parchment over his cheek-bones.

I went down the stairs and out into the street, and drove back to my mews. What had I learned? Simply that Kent had offered me a car, and then, through an intermediary, had apparently bought it back at £100 more. Why?

I thought about going over to see Kent, but if he was straight there was nothing I would learn, and if he was bent he'd be far too clever to tell me. Maybe he regretted selling the car so cheaply, and had unexpectedly received a fantastic offer, so that the best thing would be to buy it back. I'd done that myself once or twice in the past.

I felt like that man in George's story who feels the need for a brain transplant. He goes to the surgeon, and he's told he can have a Jew's brain for £80, or an Irishman's for only £250. All right, he says, but why the difference in price?

Because, replies the surgeon, the Irishman's brain has hardly been used.

Nor had mine. I felt as out of my depth as a girl guide in Lisle Street. I know how the boy scouts and the girl guides, but for me, I was very thankful to creep into my narrow slot of a bed and fall asleep.

CHAPTER TWO

FOR THE NEXT TWO OR THREE DAYS, nothing much happened. I agree that there was an earthquake in Peru, a man married his mother-in-law in Bangkok, three peons held up a bank in Mexico City, but in my news George and I just kept on breathing, and very quietly at that, which shows you how slow business was.

I did a bit of phoning, and answered a few calls from idiots wanting to know what I would give them for their unsaleable vehicles, and so it must have been around Wednesday the following week, when Kent stuck his head round the door, for presumably he'd nowhere better to stick it.

'Got a minute?' he asked.

'I've got more than a minute,' I said, 'and if your money's right, and your sex is right, I've got the inclination, too.'

He looked at me a bit surprised, and I wondered whether this guy might be a lay preacher or President of the League of Anti-Shafters or some such thing. I poured him a Whyte & Mackay whisky to keep him here.

He glanced around my stock; it was the same as when he'd last called.

'So you sold the Delahaye?' he said. 'Make much on it?'

I shrugged. It wasn't his business. Also, if he'd bought it, surely he should know?

'Covered my losses,' I said.

'Well, you can't grumble at that.'

I wasn't grumbling, but I thought this was going to be one of those dreary conversations when we'd start talking about the weather.

It's all right for the ducks when it's raining, and if we have an unexpected sunny day, we're going to pay for it. Mustn't grumble, though. But, why ever not? If people hadn't grumbled, we'd still be living in caves and rubbing sticks together for a flame.

Kent took out a gold cigarette case, withdrew a cigarette very slowly and carefully, lest he should lose a grain of tobacco he'd paid for, and tapped it on the side. He didn't offer me one, which didn't shorten my life span, but it reinforced my original feeling that he wasn't an over-swift man with a coin. He lit his cigarette and looked at the glowing end critically as though to check that it wasn't burning too fast. Then he came to the point of his visit.

'Would you be interested in buying any other old cars?'

'What other old cars?' I parried.

The trouble in my business, or one of the troubles, is that so many people think that an old car must be valuable simply because it is old. This just isn't so, any more than an old wardrobe is necessarily worth more than its weight in firewood, simply because it's old. But if Chippendale or Sheraton or one of those old guys made it, then that's a different deal altogether.

You may own a 1929 Austin-Seven Chummy, and I once refused one at thirty shillings in a part-exchange deal when I was buying and selling newer cars, and today it could fetch five hundred quid. But if you own an Austin Seven a few years newer, say 1934 or thereabouts, I wouldn't give you forty quid for the beast, because I don't know where I could sell it at a profit. All antiques have their fashions and their vogues, and cars are no exception.

'I don't know much about your business,' said Kent, 'but this is the sort of car I have in mind.'

He pulled an envelope from an inner pocket, and shook out

four coloured photographs. The first was of a Marmon, one of America's most expensive cars of thirty odd years ago, with the headlights built into the front wings and one of the biggest engines in the business—16 cylinders, 200 horses—at a time when big engines were far more common than they are today.

Colonel Howard Marmon, who ran a company which always made fine cars, had been facing heavy competition for years, plus sales troubles in the depression. His company was sinking in rough financial seas, and he planned this masterpiece, 'The World's Most Advanced Motor Car', as his ads called it, as a last throw.

He threw and he lost, for Cadillac brought out a V-16 first and although Marmon's was better in many ways, ten miles an hour faster *and* 150 dollars cheaper, his car was second—and who now remembers the second man to fly the Atlantic or run a four-minute mile? In this rough old world, you have to be first or not at all.

Like the Chrysler Airflow back in my mews, the Marmon was judged a failure, but it had failed majestically, and if you can't succeed, you can do worse than go down trying.

The second was of a two-seater Fiat Balilla, in bright Italian red, with its tiny vestigial fin behind the cockpit, spidery spoked wheels and minute brake drums. I could sell both easily enough.

The third interested me even more, for it was a 1930 Delage drop-head, with a spare wheel on each side of the bonnet, and big Marchal headlights. The body could be a Chapron, and probably was; this could retail at two and a half thousand iron men with no trouble whatever.

All the cars seemed to have been photographed against the same background; a sandstone wall, rather yellowish, that could look golden in the sun. They were standing on a piece of tarmac, perhaps a road, for sand had blurred its edges. They all wore white number plates with black figures, and each plate had the word 'Privé' on it.

'Where are these cars?' I asked.

'The Middle East,' said Kent, scooping up the photographs again. He tapped their edges carefully together, replaced them in the envelope, put the envelope back in an inner pocket, and buttoned down the flap. He was a cautious character, this one. I reckon he probably had two threads on that button, just in case one broke.

'What part of the Middle East?' I asked him.

'Cairo,' he said. 'I have an office there. I told you. Import, export.'

'They *could* be interesting,' I said, and they could at that, if the prices weren't too high.

'Do you know Cairo at all?' he asked.

I shook my head. I had once come down there on a flight from India, where I'd gone to try and buy a half-dozen Phantoms from a Maharajah's stable, hoping unsuccessfully for a discount for quantity. Our plane came down to refuel at Farouk Airport, which shows how long ago that was. I didn't know what they call Cairo airport now, but I'm pretty certain it's not Farouk.

'They have a lot of old cars out there,' Kent went on. 'For one thing, the climate's so dry they never seem to wear out. And if they do wear out, they're practically rebuilt, because Nasser's put a 285 per cent import duty on new cars, simply to stop them coming in. The country's too short of foreign currency to buy them.'

'So what have you in mind?' I asked, guessing the trend of his thoughts, which were about as obvious as the writing on this page.

'This. Why don't we import a few of these cars and flog them here?'

'We?'

'Well, you'd do it. You know the business. I'll help you find them and guide you through all the messing about you'd have with the Egyptian customs people if you tried it on your own. One's got to slip a bit of specie here and there to oil the wheels, and I know the people who take bribes and those who don't. Then, if you make a sale back here, maybe you'll give me a cut.'

'What would you have to pay for that Marmon?' I asked him.

'If we bought it for Egyptian pounds, they're the same as pounds sterling, at the official rate of exchange, so it would cost you a lot of dough, simply because the owner can't buy a replacement.

'But if we could help him, by putting some money for him, say, in a bank in Malta, or paying in dollars, we'd cut his asking price by 50 per cent. On the black market you can get at least a hundred and fifty piastres for a pound sterling instead of the hundred that the Gyppoes will allow you legally.

'The richer ones will do anything to get their money into another country, for then they can travel abroad, or pick up bargains in their own home town, for what everyone needs desperately is foreign currency. I reckon we could pick up that Marmon for two-fifty quid on the nose if we do things my way. What could you sell it for here?'

'Let's have another look at it.'

He brought out the photograph again and I opened the drawer, took out a magnifying glass, and examined the car closely. The paint seemed fairly good, but there were a few bent slats in the horizontal radiator, and a lamp glass was cracked. Still, if it was a runner it must be in fair mechanical order. I could probably shift it for a thousand quid to some old car museum.

So, if I paid two-fifty for it, had the bill of sale made out for, say, seventy-five, and therefore only paid import duty on that seventy-five, and then spent another hundred letting George give it a good go-over, I wouldn't be losing, even though I had to slip Kent something for his trouble.

'I might get five hundred for it,' I said cautiously. Never raise people's hopes where money is concerned; they always remember the highest figure you mention.

'It's really impossible to say. You can be lumbered with a car for weeks, and then, on the day after you drop your price and sell, you have a dozen inquiries for it.'

But I was interested, very interested, for the great difficulty in every branch of the antique trade is finding enough antiques. Only so many of anything, from Silver Ghosts to Sheraton tables, were ever made, and the rest are either complete copies or half-copies, by which I mean that they may have the original wheels or contain some bits of wood that Sheraton's chisel could have carved.

If I could find a source of old cars that somehow hadn't been tapped, then I could make a killing.

I already had advertisements running every month in *The Times of India*, and in the Calcutta and Delhi editions of *The Statesman*, informing readers that 'an English collector, wishing to augment his stable, urgently seeks pre-war motor-cars in good ccondition, preferably with open coachwork; highest prices in sterling or dollars.'

But the wily Indians were growing wise to the value of the old cars still within their shores, and they were giving nothing away cheaply.

Spain and Southern Europe had also suffered a pretty good going-over. So had Yugoslavia, where some of my rivals had found several quite extraordinary cars, but, so far as I knew, no one had tried Egypt. I suppose there was some basic resistance to Egypt after the Suez shambles, or maybe because of the Arab-Israeli war, and this could have clouded people's judgement. Yet Egypt might easily be a treasure house of old cars. There had always been rich people in Cairo, the pashas and the beys and all Farouk's hangers-on. And where you have money, you usually find expensive and interesting motor-cars.

Yes, Egypt seemed such an obvious place to look, why hadn't someone done so before? I couldn't think, but there has to be a first time for everything, and the best ideas are often the simplest; look how long it took for someone to think of the safety-pin.

'Are you sure there are no snags about getting a car out of Egypt?' I asked Kent. There might be some absurd ruling he'd never heard of, simply because he'd never tried to export a car.

'Nothing,' he said emphatically. 'I know that. I asked at the British Embassy, and I've checked with the Customs and Excise people in Cairo. It's dead easy—so long as the deal brings in foreign currency. It'd be different altogether if someone in Egypt wanted to do it without money coming in, I give you that.'

Which is about the only thing you'll ever give me, I thought, for words cost nothing and often don't mean much more.

'No strain at all,' he went on. 'Now, what do you say?'

For a moment I didn't say anything, my mind spinning like a Ferrari flywheel. This fellow should know; after all, he worked there. It could just be that I had hit the golden vein.

'It's worth a look,' I agreed cautiously, not wishing to sound too eager. 'What do you want out of the deal, if we can do any business?'

'An agent's cut,' he said. 'Say, 25 per cent.'

'Of what?'

'Your selling price.'

'After all my expenses, renovation costs, duty, and so on,' I said quickly.

'If you want it that way,' he said reluctantly.

We shook hands.

'What's the next step, then?' I asked him.

'Come out to Cairo, spend a few days there, see the cars, make it known you're in the market. I'll introduce you around. Even if you only bought one car, that should cover the cost of your trip. If you bought two, you'd be making a profit.'

'I'll think about it,' I said.

'Well, don't think too long because I'm off myself the day after tomorrow. We might fly out together.'

He poured himself another whisky. I watched him drink it. I don't think he really wanted it, but it happened to be free, and he couldn't resist it for that reason.

He pushed off and I sat down at my desk and wrote £500 for a profit on the Marmon, after all expenses, the same for the Fiat and a whacking big £2,000 profit on the Delage; total, £3,000 net. Kent needn't know I'd made quite that, so I wouldn't have to pay him entirely a quarter. It seemed too easy to be true, but it needn't be. I knew several men who'd bought and sold old beat-up bangers on bomb-sites around London after the war and then suddenly realized what the sites were worth, and so they'd sold them instead and were now millionaires. It's mostly a matter of recognizing a chance, no matter how heavily disguised your chance may be.

I don't know if you are like me, counting chickens before the hens are even pregnant, but the sum looked healthy on paper, and I couldn't see where the arithmetic went wrong. If these cars actually existed in Cairo and could be bought at this price in almost any condition, I must at the very least make this amount.

Now, if I could do it with three, I could do it with thirty, or three hundred—provided the stock was there. If we sold for cash, then we'd have no nibbling at the profits by the Income Tax boyos, and I could finance each new deal with the profits from the previous one.

I imagined how Charles Clore must have felt when the whole wonderful business of sale and leaseback suddenly hit him. This was no harder than printing my own money. Easier, because I didn't even need to buy a press. If I could find enough cars, I could be my own mint. Even so, the fact that it all seemed so easy still struck a wrong note somewhere in my cautious mind.

There are a lot of sharp boys in the car business, so why hadn't some of them tried it before? Or had they tried and run into impossible snags? I decided I would contact one of the sharpest of all, Mossy MacHarris, who'd traded from half a dozen bomb-sites fifteen years ago and now owned a steam yacht a few feet longer than the *Britannia*.

I don't know what Mossy's original name was, or where he came from, but he was so rich I'd go along with him for the journey, whatever his destination. I had known him in the great days when car dealers were making more money in notes than they knew what to do with.

He began by making a speciality of sales of Army surplus equipment, working to a set timetable. Say the Ministry of Supply advertised a sale of three-ton lorries on a Tuesday, and then 1,000 ex-W.D. motor cycles for the following day, Mossy would work out that motor cycle buyers wouldn't bother to turn up for the lorry sale, which was a reasonable enough deduction.

He'd therefore go down on the Monday, the viewing day, chat up some sergeant in charge of the dump, select half a dozen lorries that were in a lot together, and then give the sergeant a tenner to fill up each lorry with motor cycles, when everyone else had gone home, and strap down the canvas covers so that they wouldn't be seen.

Come Tuesday morning, Mossy would cheerfully outbid every-one else for these six lorries—as well he could afford to, because he was also buying fifty or sixty almost brand new motor cycles thrown in, each of which he'd sell for £40 in the trade before that evening sun went down.

You can only do this a few times before someone will split on you, possibly the sergeant, who the second time round wants £20 instead of £10 for his services, and so, having made some capital, Mossy had wisely moved out to the rather more rarefied atmosphere of property.

He still controlled a network of about forty garages round the country, but much of his time now he spent in his house in the South of France, or aboard his yacht, cruising in the Aegean.

I didn't know whether he was happy, but I did know he was rich, which was often the next best thing. Remember, there's only one thing money can't buy: poverty.

I knew Mossy pretty well, and could convince his secretary, his P.A. and so on, that I wasn't on the touch, and thus reached him on the telephone within about fifteen minutes.

'What's the matter?' he asked cautiously. 'You in trouble?'

'Nothing half a million wouldn't see me out of,' I told him. 'Just a proposition that's been put to me. I wondered if I could have a word with you about it. Now?'

'Fine,' he said. 'Come round. But don't mind if I have to dash off in a hurry. I've got a fixed time call to Nicosia that's not come through.'

I didn't mind; I wasn't paying for the call.

It was a sunny afternoon, too nice even to sit in the car, so I walked round to Curzon Street, to one of those old gracious bow-fronted houses, sleeping in the shade of the Hilton, with a metal arch over the front gate and an inverted iron cone where link-men used to snuff out their torches in the days of sedan-chairs.

Inside, it was all terribly, terribly elegant, quite different from the days when Mossy had rented a room in the Earls Court Road and we'd shared a phone box outside in the road as an office.

Here it was striped wallpaper, as thick as fur, white paint as glossy as marble, carpets up to your knees, mirrors and candelabra with real candles. Old Mossy was wearing a suit so tight it looked as though he had been poured into it, and hadn't found the way out, lizard-skin shoes, gold-strapped wristwatch, ingot cuff links. He was going through his millionaire period, and I must say I could have shared it with him. He sat at a desk topped with crimson leather, lined with gold. He looked rather like Napoleon, I thought charitably, but he was probably just that bit richer.

'Haven't seen you for years,' he said, without much regret, pressing a button on his desk, so that a bookcase in the wall revolved to show a cabinet of drinks. He poured two whiskies into gold goblets, in lieu of anything else to pour them into, and added cubes of ice. Then the bookcase turned again and showed us a lot of books. We toasted each other.

'When were you last in Cairo?' I asked him, after all the it's-so-long-since-we-met stuff had died away.

'Me?' He looked pained. 'Me? With my name? Do you mind?'

'Oh, yes. I'd forgotten that. What I meant, Mossy, was I've been offered a deal out there, and it seems such easy money I felt there must be a snag in it.'

'What sort of deal?' he asked.

He took out a gold toothpick and sawed about between his teeth, now and then looking at the end of the pick as though he expected to find the answer there, while I told him. Then he slipped the toothpick into a waistcoat pocket, and gave his opinion.

'So long as the cars are reasonable, and so long as the Gyppoes let you get them out without any frigging about, you can't lose,' he said.

'That's what I thought. But somehow it just seems too easy. Why hasn't someone thought of it before!'

'When I was a boy,' said Mossy ponderously, as though he was about a hundred and four, '*My* old man used to tell me when I put up a proposition to make money: "If it was as easy as that, Mossy boy, *everyone* would be doing it." '

'In fact, of course, everyone *was* doing it. There's no snag here. Only trouble, the profit's so small. I don't know why you mess about with these diabolical old motors for a few pounds when you can make a thousand times as much with something worth while like land, or shares, or buildings. Now, I've a development just starting in Cyprus. Those bloody Greeks and Turks can't fight for ever, and when all the Swedes and Poles and all those other dreary United Nations characters out there go home, the land values will go up quicker than a young man's fagan.'

Such crude talk sounded out of place in the surroundings, but then Mossy always liked to remind people he'd known years ago that he'd also been poor once; this was one of the ways in which he showed he was still one of us at heart.

'To each his own, Mossy,' I said, and nodded towards the bookcase. He repeated his stuff with the hidden button. I poured myself some more of his whisky, while he sat and watched me rather glumly. He was so rich he could have the stuff piped in, and if I was as rich, I'd have it piped direct from the Mackay distillery.

Then I thought of seventeen, Belsize Park West, and mentioned this to him.

He pressed a button on some complicated piece of electronic equipment on his desk, expensively and inexplicably disguised as an eighteenth-century Viennese music box, and gave his orders. Within seconds, or so it seemed, a disembodied voice was giving the answer.

'This mews is owned by one of our companies, Beechwood Freeholds. The tenant of the garage and the flat is a Mr O'Gorman, a street trader. He pays a monthly rent of £84, exclusive of rates. His lease has two years four months to run.'

'Ever heard of a man there called Kent?' I asked the box.

'We have no record of anyone of that name on this file,' the voice assured me gravely. He could have been St Peter doing a Dun and Bradstreet on a stranger at the pearly gates.

'Well, that's it, then,' said Mossy, obviously very pleased at his firm's efficiency.' Probably this character O'Gorman is sub-letting.'

'Probably,' I said, but so far as I was concerned, he meant nothing in my life.

So we left it like that, for I couldn't leave it anywhere else. I had a few more drinks, but he had none, and it was evening by the time I was back in my mews. The phone was ringing as I unlocked the door. George had gone home long since, so I scooped up the instrument and stood breathing whisky on the window, and then drew a face in the moist breath with a finger. Talk of the devil; Kent was on the line.

'Good bit of news,' he said. For you, at least. Fellow who was flying out to Cairo with me has got a slipped disc. Can't move. Flat on his back, pretty well, strapped to his bed. I've got his ticket. Wonder if you'd care to use it? Fly out with me?'

'How about paying?' I asked. He paused and I could almost hear his brain ticking like a cash register.

'Tell you what. Use it now. My firm has paid for it—comes off the tax and doesn't matter a damn. Not as though I was spending the money myself, eh? But if you do a deal, we can talk about it then. O.K.?'

'O.K.' I said. 'Where shall I see you?'

'London Airport. Nine o'clock. Day after tomorrow. Number three building. At the Air France desk.'

'What's the climate like in Cairo, this time of year?'

'Warmish. So bring a light suit. And some money.'

He rang off. I locked the door behind me and went upstairs. I felt like the cat must feel when he sees a bird on a branch, one he knows just can't get away, and he is savouring that sweet moment before the kill. This could be my lucky day, like the song says, only more so.

The next morning I spent collecting a tourist's visa from the Egyptian Embassy. Then I cabled the Ecclesiastical Bank in Malta, which is an island with certain financial advantages, the most important being that no questions are asked about income tax that you can't answer fairly easily, and where it's not impossible to exchange sterling into any other currency without shortening your life span by filling in forms.

I shifted £1,500 into dollars, and then transferred them to Cairo to await me in traveller's cheques, care of the American Express. Then I went round to my local bank and drew out my meagre £50, which was all Her Majesty's Government allowed me to take abroad legally for a holiday. I then bought three colour film packs for my Polaroid camera, because I might find more cars than Kent had known about, and could possibly buy an option on them, and photograph them and sell them on their pictures before I even had to extract them from Egypt.

On the following morning George drove me to the airport.

'I'll give you Major Stevens you're going to be done,' George told me cheerfully as we approached the International Building.

'Major Stevens?'

'Yes. Evens.'

'Oh.'

'Yes, oh, indeed. I did years out there, remember. In the Canal Zone. Lot of crafty Jerry Diddlers—fiddlers—there. Running guns, drugs, whirls—girls—anything. Old Farouk set the pace. So, watch it. I'm just giving you an old man's horning—warning.'

'Thank you very much.'

I didn't sound over-enthusiastic, but I had my own doubts, which was why I'd asked George to take me to the airport.

Things seemed to be coming my way, as the politician said when he was pelted with rotten eggs, but, being basically a cynic, I wanted to make sure that Kent was actually at the ticket desk with the ticket in his hand before I was certain.

If he wasn't, then George could drive me back to the mews again. But when we arrived, Kent was walking up and down, puffing at a cheroot, checking his watch with the clock above the gallery.

'Bags of time,' he said. 'I always like to get anywhere early. Saves rushing. Here's your ticket, then. Made out in my friend's name—Cartwright—but that's only a technical point.'

We went through into the departure lounge, where I bought a couple of newspapers. The news was so depressing, nothing but strikes at home, military coups abroad and trade figures falling like rain, that I pushed them into one of those big cylindrical ashtrays rather than read them.

The flight was as uneventful as you expect these things to be, although privately I always marvel at the way one covers prodigious distances in hours, when only a few years back they would have taken days or even weeks.

We reached Cairo airport at about seven o'clock that evening. As we walked through the building, I smelled that forgotten smell of dust, apparently soaked in oil; the scent of a warm day dying, and the arid desert all around, throwing back to the night the heat which that day had forced upon it.

We seemed to be the only people leaving the plane; the rest were going on to Karachi or wherever. An airline official wanted to press a yellow disc into our hands, thinking we must be in transit. When we said we were actually staying in Cairo, he replied in amazement, 'Welcome.'

Welcome to the customs hall like a barn, welcome to some plain-clothes policeman who asked me to fill in a form to say how much money I had brought into the country. I saw Kent look at me in anguish here. He had clearly forgotten to warn me, but I filled in my £50 honestly enough, thinking of my £1,500 at the American Express.

The great snag about being too honest here only becomes apparent when the visitor realizes that two rates of money exchange prevail, the official, at one Egyptian pound to one pound sterling, and the unofficial, which more realistically sets a value of two or even three Egyptian pounds to every English pound.

If you haven't declared all your resources at the airport you can take advantage of this arrangement and literally double your money *and* have a stay for nothing. But if you have been honest, you can only watch others do this, for you must account for every pound you brought in on the way out.

Someone appeared with a trolley to wheel our cases out to the taxi rank. There must have been a hundred cabs, each painted black with white mudguards, all waiting under the sodium lights and the dusty palm trees. A policeman shuffled up and ticked a number in a book. The local war had driven away nearly all tourists from Egypt, but the fewer there were, the fewer possible rivals, I thought, sitting back on the ancient plastic seat of the Mercedes 190D.

The cab was very old and smelled of diesel, grinding along with dim yellow headlights, braying its feeble horn at cross-roads. We ran in through Heliopolis, a long, dusty, sandstone suburb, all high walls and square buildings against the mountains of the night. Guttering oil lamps flickered over street-corner stalls. Night watchmen wrapped in blankets waited patiently out-side the gates of rich men's houses—for what or who? Enemies or friends?

'Where are we staying?' I asked Kent.

'The Hilton. It's clean and modern, and no dearer than any-where else—if you take a room at the top. If you don't want the usual American deep-fried golden batter scampi in a sea-food basket, farm-fresh, hand-tossed salad, and all that jazz we can eat out. Also, that might be cheaper.'

The Nile Hilton soared like a cliff against the lingering purple sunset, speckled here and there with lit-up windows. The taxi ran in underneath among pillars and between potted palms.

'You want me tomorrow, gentlemen?' the driver asked hope-fully. 'I give you my price. Three pounds whole day running. With this car I come here? Yes?'

He looked back at us. Trade must be terrible, I thought. Three pounds could hardly cover the cost of fuel.

Kent shook his head. 'No,' he said. 'Not tomorrow, squire, but thanks for the offer.'

We climbed out, and Kent walked ahead, leaving me to pay. He was a slow man, even with a piastre.

We were up on the ninth floor, for the rooms came cheaper the higher you went, and if we'd gone any higher we'd have been out on the roof.

I didn't know what Kent's room was like, and I didn't greatly care. Mine was done out in blue and green hessian, with a decora-tion on one wall, a sort of plastic frieze, copied from something found in a tomb or pyramid. A big, sliding window opened over Liberation Square. All cities in the Middle East have a Liberation Square, or Liberation Avenue—but what does the name mark except their progress from one tyranny to another? Who has been liberated and who were the liberators?

I hung up my spare light-weight suit in the cupboard, put my shirts into the top drawer of the chest, had a couple of Alka Seltzers for want of anything better to have, and fiddled with the knobs on the bedside table. Taped music of the thirties flooded out in a sugary tide. I slid back the picture window and stepped out on the veranda.

The evening was cool, and the trumpet-calls of car horns, plus the clanging of trams, came up only faintly. Beneath me the lawns of the hotel garden were dark; a fountain played in an ornamental lake across the square. Behind it, red and blue neons for Ethiopian Airlines and Thos. Cook's blazed against the darkening sky.

Somewhere in this city, I thought, lay the cars that were going to make me a fortune. They'd probably been here for thirty years or more; through a war, a revolution, a whole world gone. It was an intriguing thought, and I was just enjoying thinking it, when I heard a knock on the door, and Kent calling, 'Shop!'

I joined him in the corridor.

'What about a meal and then we'll see some belly dancing?' he said.

'Not for me,' I told him. 'My belly's dancing already after that flight. I just want a couple of whiskies and then to bed.'

'You must be getting old,' said Kent.

'Every day, in every way, I grow older and older,' I agreed, which is true, anyway. Every day is a day nearer the grave. You can't beat 'em, and one day we'll all join 'em.

'In that case, I'll have a drink, too, and then I'll go on down to my office and see what's been happening since I've been away.'

'Anyone be there at this hour?'

'Oh, yes,' he said. 'I've a secretary.'

'That's something,' I said. 'I've no one.'

And I hadn't, either. Just a succession of girl friends who left me to marry other men, and sometimes they sent me Christmas cards with such unlikely addresses as Pinner and Penge, and then cards to announce the birth of their various children. I'd no one who cared whether I lived or died, and sometimes I didn't know whether I was sorry or glad. This was one of those times.

We were in the lift now, going up to the roof, to that curious export of North America, the darkened bar. You can't see what you're drinking; you have to feel what's in your glass, and when it hits your stomach, you know.

In the bar, Kent and I sat perched on top of a structure of steel and glass and concrete, mathematically stressed and strained, with Cairo on one side, the ancient Nile on the other, then Gezira Island, and then the long darkness of the desert, punctured here and there by dim and flickering lights. All around us, other people were sitting close together in the gloom. If they were good Muslims they were drinking soft drinks, and if they were more broadminded, they were drinking hard ones. I thought of the indignant retort from a loyal supporter of the old Aga Khan, when someone suggested that, as a Moslem leader, the Aga Khan should not drink champagne: 'When it touches his Highness's lips, the champagne turns to water.'

Kent and I had a couple of whiskies each and they didn't turn to water, but my knees did when I saw the bill, and then I went down in the lift with him to the front hall.

'Just one thing,' he said, as we waited for the doors to open, 'our rooms are probably bugged. Nothing sinister. Simply because we're foreigners. So be careful what you say on the phone. No criticism of Colonel Nasser. It's safer to call him Mr Smith.'

'What would I say about him?' I asked. 'I've never even met the man.'

'These guys might get the idea we're trying to change some money on the side, and maybe even take out their cars at prices less than they think they're worth. If they got that idea, they might put the boot in. They're funny that way.'

'So are most people. Message received and understood. See you tomorrow, down here in the foyer, ten o'clock. O.K.?'

The pneumatic doors opened, and a crowd of package-deal tourists, ancient Americans of various sexes, faces withered and dried by years of air-conditioning, curious Canadians in store suits with wide-bottomed trousers, one actually wearing an overcoat and rubber galoshes, skins wrinkled as a tortoise's neck, thrust themselves unceremoniously on top of us. We fought our way out, through shrill voices complaining to their tour-leader, and Kent was gone.

I walked out of the back door of the hotel, across the road, on to the Nile promenade. Some poor old devil was wrapped in a white sheet like a corpse, asleep on a concrete bench; not a tourist, of course, someone who lived here, if you could call this living. The water lapped and chuckled only feet away. The Nile had seen too many centuries of poverty to show interest now. In the darkness, a number of small wooden boats, all moored at their prows, thumped and creaked against each other. Starving dogs were rooting for food in an overturned dustbin on the bank.

I walked up the street, watching the cars swing past. Apart from one or two modern ones wearing C.D. plates, they all seemed pretty old, an odd mixture of Chryslers and Chevrolets of the nineteen-thirties, with a few small Morrises and Fords of the forties, and then a rash of black and white Mercedes taxis, mostly about ten years old.

Fifty yards up the road, beside the Nile, an old Opel saloon, the one with the horizontal radiator grille, like the pre-war Cord, was pulled into the side under a street light with its bonnet up. I glanced in at the engine as I passed by. It was a bird's nest of wires and string and tubes bound up with tape. By any accepted mechanical standards it should have stopped running long ago, but with a 285 per cent tax on anything new, I knew how the owner felt.

I also felt a bit more confident myself now that I had seen these old cars actually in the streets, dragging themselves along. I had no doubt now that we would be able to pick up as many as we wanted. The only question would be the price, but then this is the biggest question all through life. Is the price of anything—a job, a girl, a deal, a career worth what is offered in return? And who can really say until they've paid it?

I went back to my room, thinking about this in lieu of anything else. The taped music was still playing, apparently the same tune. By the side of the bed lay a sheet of cardboard with a hole in it to hang on the doorknob, listing breakfast guests could order. One was called safari. This seemed symbolic of good hunting, so I chose that, marked off mango juice, coffee, two boiled eggs, toast and honey, hung it outside the door, pushed a chair up under the doorknob in case too many people had a passkey, and went to bed.

I must have slept like that fellow by the bank of the Nile, because I woke up to hear someone hammering on the door as though the place was on fire. I sprang out, pulled away the chair and opened the door.

'Welcome,' said the waiter. So, it must be morning. He was wearing a fez and a white jacket, balancing a silver tray over his right shoulder. I was wearing nothing, which is how I sleep —I like to think, ready for anything the night may offer, but it hadn't offered much so far in Cairo—so I wrapped a towel round what the old medical ads used to call coyly, the vital organs.

'Welcome to you,' I said.

I ate breakfast on the veranda, bathed, shaved, and by ten o'clock was downstairs. Kent was reading *The Egyptian Gazette*, because it is the only paper printed in English. It seemed full of gloomy news about shelling across the Canal, with statements from Arab leaders demanding this and that, with messages to and from delegates at UNO, the whole thing adding up, in my mind, to a great big nothing.

He threw it on one side, and we walked out through the swing doors, past guides and touts ('I give you special price in my brother's shop. Not to buy, only to look, just to see. You English? My very good friend, the English'), and all this ageless chat of the sellers.

'Do we take a cab?' I asked him.

'No, we'll walk,' he said. 'No need to throw money away. How have you arranged finance for the deal, by the way?'

'Through the American Express. Do I need the cash now?'

'Maybe an idea. We'll walk that way.'

I thought that if I walked that way some giant Nubian with nuts like oranges would leap on me and beat me to the ground, but I didn't think the thought was worth putting into words.

There was no one in the American Express except the clerks. I showed them my passport, but no one got very excited.

'There should be some travellers' cheques for me here,' I told a man in his shirt-sleeves behind the counter. 'Not in my name, but being cabled from Mr Utos, of Malta. Mr A. A. Utos.'

Just so that you can follow the convoluted turnings of my mind, and to confuse the fellows in Exchange Control, I sometimes send money abroad in different names. So that I won't forget the names, which is easier to do than you may think, I always use an anagram of my firm, Aristo Autos, which, cut down to a name, was, in this case, A. A. Utos.

There was a bit of coming and going and looking through files, all that crap which is inseparable from banks and travel agencies and whatever else, and then the man came up with the cheques for me to sign. I signed them, put them in my pocket, and buttoned down the flap, and we were back in the street.

It felt cold out of the sun, and the wind rattled the pages of magazines hanging by clips in a corner kiosk on the pavement. Here and there, manhole covers had been removed for some unknown purpose, and the holes were blocked with paving slabs. I thought that this would be a hell of a place to go walking around in bare feet at night.

'Are we going straight to your office?' I asked Kent.

He shook his head.

'We're going to one of my contacts first. Fellow who runs a shop. Perfume essences. There's a great trade in that here. Exported all over the world. Sometimes some of the bottles may also contain a bit of heroin or pot, but that's not our concern. He is also an expert on jewels. Sell you a diamond for twenty quid that'd cost you fifty back home.

'Just let me fill you in with a little of accepted business etiquette here before we see this character. You probably want to do a deal as quick as Speedy Gonzales and then over the hill, but, in point of fact, you can't hurry these buggers.'

'You'll have to sit about, drink coffee and chat about the political situation, his mother-in-law's corns and any other damn thing, and then only gradually will the conversation slowly steer round to the object of your visit—flogging these cars. O.K.?'

'O.K.'

We plodded on down to the centre of town. Kent seemed to know where he was going, and I followed him, past shops filled with rubbish like bridal gowns—with, oddly enough, a European dummy as the bride—and then past others selling hurricane lamps and wood carvings.

He suddenly dodged up a side alley and paused astride two swing doors. Men were squatting down on the bones of their backsides in the street, brazing together the ends of great coils of wire, for what purpose I knew not, and didn't greatly care. We went through these two swing doors like that stock Tombstone City saloon you see in every TV Western, under a sign Palace of Perfumes, into a narrow corridor, lined with benches covered in shiny black plastic. Rather modestly, they had strips of brocade tacked on to cover up their legs.

The corridor led into a round room with its ceiling concealed by dark red cloth rising to a peak, so that one had the impression of sitting in Saladin's pavilion before going out to do up Richard the Lion Heart, or grab the key of his chastity belt, or whatever else was on offer, in the great crusading days of the Middle East.

The room was ringed by shelves stacked with bottles like an old-fashioned chemist's shop. (After you with that old-fashioned chemist). There was a photograph of Nasser and a larger, highly coloured one, about three feet square, of a rather blowsy barmaid, blonde with big loose bristols, with a mild smiling man with thinning hair. I was wondering whether he had ever undone that bra and risked disturbing all that soft, loose, crinkled and unlovely flesh, when a curtain parted in the corner of the room and the character appeared.

He was slightly built and bearded, and I recognized him from his photograph on the wall, although he had more hair then. He bowed at us and smiled, showing a lot of gold in his teeth. Then he clapped his hands, and a little boy appeared, and he sent him out to bring back a lacquered tray and the tiny cups of coffee with the glasses of rather cloudy water, over which the Arabs like to talk business.

Kent said: 'This is my English friend.' He gave the man my name, which cost him nothing. The man bowed.

'It is an honour to meet you,' he said in English.

I thought that was very civil of him, so I said: 'The pleasure is mine,' which shows how unoriginal I can be when someone else isn't writing my lines.

'What is it you want to see?' said this character. 'Jewels? Scents? Essences?'

No one had told me his name so I took up a blue and red visiting card from a side table and read it for myself: Sabry Ahmed. The House of Attar, Perfumes, Scents, Musk, Unguents to make You Young Again, to Light the Fires in Your Blood. Elixirs for all Occasions.

Get away, I thought, this could be interesting, if only it were true.

'You have come here as a tourist, yes?' Sabry asked, pouring the coffee.

I nodded. I didn't want to begin a long explanation for this nut. Let's press on to the real point of our meeting. But there was no hurrying him; he had to follow the rules of a Cairo business talk.

'Then you must take back some perfumes from Egypt. You know that when Tutankamen's tomb was opened, the first thing that the explorers smelled was the perfume? Whatever perfume you buy in America, in England, in France, anywhere, it is almost certain that it has come from Egyptian flowers or herbs. I give you good price. Six bottles for eight pounds. You have any English money? If you have, I give you better price. Six bottles for four English pounds. Yes?'

'No,' I said. 'If I started wearing that stuff it wouldn't be safe to go down the King's Road.'

'Please?' he asked, mouth left open so that we could gaze at all the gold.

'Later,' I said, and looked despairingly at Kent, but he was stirring his coffee.

Sabry picked up a small phial and dabbed some perfume on the cork and then wiped the cork on the back of my hand.

'Just to smell the scent.'

The room filled with the fragrance of crushed flowers, sweet as the bloom of youth, and dying away as soon.

'Just the essence,' he said. 'You need a base to hold it. Alcohol.'

'Very interesting,' I said, and gave Kent a nudge.

Kent cleared his throat rather noisily.

'What my friend wants to discuss,' he said rather unwillingly, 'are old cars.'

'Ah. Have you seen any of the former King Farouk's old cars. Yes?'

'No,' I said. 'What were they, anyhow?'

'Almost every make,' said Sabry, sipping his coffee and straining it noisily through gaps in his teeth.

'He had a hundred and twenty cars, Rolls-Royce, Bentley, Cadillac, Alfa. When he went, the government auctioned them. Some, of course, disappeared. It was a time of disturbance, you understand.'

'I understand,' I said, wondering which sharp car dealer had got what car, and for how much. Some cars have appreciated fifty times since then.

Sabry poured more coffee.

'You like to buy some musk, yes?'

He opened a small plastic pill box, dug a match stick into the black ointment it contained, and held it at my mouth. I licked the oleaginous mess cautiously; the taste was as vile as it looked, only slightly scented.

Kent and Sabry sat watching me carefully as though I would suddenly rush out like a rutting stag, but as an aphrodisiac it did nothing to me. The oily flavour lingered like the childhood taste of castor oil.

'Make you make love like pom-pom gun,' said Sabry, full of wishful thoughts.

'Charming,' I said, but all it made me think of was George's ancient joke about the young man sent to learn the meaning of it all in Paris. So that he won't alarm his mother, the boy has a code with his dear old dad, who passes the whole thing off as a shooting trip; the boy's affairs will be called bullets. Within days he was receiving his son's urgent requests for more money: 'to bullets, 7,000 francs'; then, 'to bullets, 6,000 francs', and then a pause, followed by a third account, 'to bullets, 6,500 francs. To repairs to gun, 85,000 francs.'

Kent leaned towards Sabry: 'You gave me those photographs of old cars when I was here last,' he began conspiratorially. 'I showed them to my friend here. He wants to see the cars. He may buy them. For English pounds or American dollars.'

'Ah, so you are a man of business. Yes!'

'Yes.'

'Then you must come to my house this evening.'

He spat out some coffee-grounds rather objectionably on the floor.

'Where is your house?' I asked him.

'Mr Kent knows. On the road to the Pyramids. I have three cars there.'

'What are they?'

I wanted to get some facts as soon as possible. I didn't go much on all this chatting about, this verbal tennis. Let's get a deal and over the hill, is my motto, or it would be if I had a crest to paint it under.

'A Bugatti, a Marmon, and a Delage.'

A Bugatti was rare indeed. How had such a scarce beast found its way to Egypt? Could it be one of Farouk's cars that someone else had bought and kept? He didn't mention the Fiat I'd seen in the photo, and neither did I in case we confused the discussion. I could buy a Fiat almost any day, but a Bug was a different breed of beast.

'They are all sports cars, then?' I asked him.

'Of course,' he said.

'How much are you asking?'

'Let's not discuss business now. Let's talk like friends now, and like businessmen then. Yes?'

'Yes,' I said, regretfully, and stood up. Kent followed me out of the shop.

'How did you meet that nut?' I asked him. 'Do you work with him here?'

'He's a contact,' he explained. 'His brother is something in the Treasury. He tips me off when quotas are changing, or if there's going to be a sudden tax increase. In my business you need to have contacts.'

'What exactly is your business? What do you export and import?'

'Hong Kong toys. I told you,' he said, aggrieved.

I'd forgotten. But then why should I remember? I know so little of the real world of business that I can't begin to understand how a man in Cairo can make a living exporting plastic rubbish from Hong Kong. Who buys it? And how does he find the fellow in Hong Kong who wants to sell it to him in the first place? The whole mystique of other people's ways of making a living I've always found intriguing.

We had a drink in Groppi's, which I read about in books on the desert war. Waiters wearing tarbushes, yellow belts and robes like white nightshirts served chocolate cakes with silver tongs. There were sweet peas in silver vases on the tables, and imitation windows filled with frosted glass and lit up from behind to give the impression of sunshine, although we were right inside, at the heart of the building.

Most of the people eating there seemed to be with families, but in one corner a man in a black cloth cap was carefully eating his way through a huge fried flat fish. Maybe, like me, he was the odd man out.

If one could pick up a rarity like a Bugatti that had belonged to Farouk—or which I could say or even hint had been his— and why not? The dead can't sue—I could (and would) name my own price.

A title is always a good selling point. 'Late property of famous peer, immaculately maintained by chauffeur,' would look pretty thin against 'King's car. Unique specimen, preserved with royal disregard of cost.' I could feel the clichés multiplying like amoeba in my mind. The ads for these cars would also be collectors' pieces. But if it wasn't Farouk's? Then I should be content with what I already had. Happiness doesn't lie in the extent of a man's possessions, but in the fewness of his wants, as my old father used to tell me.

But what happens when the man's wants aren't few? Samuel Smiles or John Stuart Mill, or whoever else first produced this aphorism never dealt with that, but then most proverbs are very one-sided. 'A rolling stone gathers no moss.' Agreed, but who wants moss on his stone?

'Are you going to your office again?' I asked Kent.

He nodded.

'I'll put in an hour or so. Bound to be some letters to answer.' He sounded more hopeful than convinced.

'Were there any last night?'

'A few,' he said, non-committally.

A waiter hovered around us with a folded bill on a plate. Kent looked the other way. I unfolded the bill, put down two Egyptian pounds. The waiter salaamed me, and went off, and didn't come back. We stood up.

'I'll walk with you,' I said.

'There's no need,' he replied. 'Why don't you have a swim at the hotel?'

'I'd rather see Cairo,' I said. 'I can swim anywhere.'

We were standing at the corner of Talaat Harb Street, where the roads went off in a circle like spokes from a wheel. In the centre stood a statue of some pasha in a European frock-coat, trousers and fez, with his back to the sun, ringed in by old houses with shops at the bottom, and balconies higher up, where people had hung seedy grey lumpy mattresses, old corsets, and mercifully unidentifiable washing.

We walked up the street, on the sunny side. A man came towards us very slowly, carrying himself stiffly, as though his joints had locked and he had thrown away the key. He wore an old-fashioned grey tweed suit with wide turn-ups to the trousers, co-respondent brown-and-white shoes, a black beret and a black scarf wound round his neck, like one of a boat race crew. But the only boat he'd ever make now would be Charon's vessel over the Styx.

He held his head to one side as he walked, and I could see the growth under his right ear, huge as a roc's egg, and shining with sweat and distended skin. Every time he came to a sunny patch between the high, gloomy buildings, he stood, turning his face to the sun, warming his cancerous old bones before he shuffled on. I turned and watched him go. The very sight of the man depressed me; I wondered what it did to him.

'Here's my office,' said Kent. He had obviously not even seen the man. His thoughts were entirely on his own affairs.

We turned up some tessellated marble steps, past doors with frosted glass panels pegged apart. Inside, on the left, was a blackboard with names in Arabic script, and, underneath, the names of the firms in the building, in English.

'Which is yours?' I asked Kent; he had never told me.

'Fourth floor.'

He pulled open the lift trellis; we went up. Even on the fourth floor, sand and grit from the desert had blown in under our feet. The soles of our shoes scratched and scraped on the marble.

His office seemed to be one large room with two grey metal desks, topped with plastic. A water cooler filled one corner, with filing cabinets and a telephone on a side table. The air felt stale and old. I wondered what business he could do here. If this was all the equipment one needed, there didn't seem all that much to it. I could see no letters on the desk, no one about.

'Satisfied?' he asked me.

'With what?' I said.

'Well, you wanted to see the office, didn't you?'

'I think I'll go for that swim,' I told him.

'I'd do that thing,' he said. 'You can get a drink at the edge of the pool afterwards. I'll join you when I'm through here.'

The lift had jammed between two floors. I pressed the button, but nothing happened, so I walked down the stairs.

On the third floor, I heard the click of heels; someone was coming up slowly.

I turned the corner of the landing. A girl in sunglasses and a cotton dress was coming towards me. She was pretty in a dark way, but it wasn't her good looks that really knocked me out, it was the fact that the last time I had seen her was in that wrecked flat in Rosemary Court.

'You,' I said, and, I swear it, my voice trembled.

'I beg your pardon?' she said, as cold as iced lager.

'We've met before. In your flat. Remember?'

She looked at me as though I'd crawled out from under a flat stone, then recognition lit up her face.

'Why, the used-car man,' she said, without notable pleasure.

I felt like an uncle to the Hurdy-Gurdy Man, but all I could say was, 'Yes.'

Then, 'What brings you here?'

'I live here, that's what,' she said, and went on up the stairs.

CHAPTER THREE

I WENT ON DOWN THE STAIRS and bought a guide book to Cairo from a stall in Liberation Square. On the back was a printed list of the Embassies, with their addresses. I wasn't sure how far it was away, so I hailed a taxi and told the driver, 'The British Embassy.'

I wanted to check whether I needed any special forms before I set about exporting cars, and I thought it easiest to deal with my own countrymen, rather than risk another session with cups of coffee and inconsequential conversation in some Egyptian office. As I drove, I thought about the girl and why the hell she should be in that building and, so it seemed to me, on her way to Kent's office. Maybe she was the secretary he had mentioned? But how could she also be involved with my being beaten up? Or was she involved? In fact, was any of this really happening, or was it all in my mind?

We drove past the Hilton with its flags of many nations, down the underpass and up on the other side. The Nile ran like green oil to my right. We passed the Semiramis Hotel, then Shepheard's. They're evocative names to all who remembered school atlases with red on nearly every map, and then the British Residency on the left, dozing like an old country house that has gone to sleep in the sun, striped shades down over the windows, Queen Victoria's crown still gold on the black iron gates.

Sentry boxes outside the embassies were painted in national colours; no doubt demonstrators found them easier to recognize like that. The British box was in red, white and blue horizontal stripes. I paid off the cab, walked up the path to the crescent-shaped half-moon of a building on the right. It was very cool inside the hall, under the photograph of the Queen and Prince Philip. A man sat at a desk on my left, not English but very nearly so.

'Can I help you?' he said quietly. He might have been a floor walker in some immensely discreet shop.

'I want to export a car from Egypt,' I told him. 'I'd like a bit of advice from someone before I begin.'

'You want the Trade Secretary, then. Please follow me.'

I followed him, like he said, down the corridor into a small room piled with almanacs and trade gazettes. A young man in shirt-sleeves was writing on a foolscap pad at his desk. I introduced myself and told him my problem.

'What sort of car is it?' he asked.

'An old one,' I said. 'I collect old cars. They're my hobby.'

This is always a more promising beginning than to say one actually physically deals in cars, because then you tend to unlatch a floodgate of bitter reminiscences about cars your hearer has been swindled over, with dud clutches, worn big ends and all of the rest.

'What sort of car is it?'

'A Bugatti.' I only mentioned one; if I could export one, I could ship out a hundred.

'Now, that *is* going back a long way. And how do you propose to pay for it?'

'A bank in Malta will provide the money.'

'You are resident there?'

'Look,' I said, not liking the general trend of the conversation, 'I simply want some advice from you about exporting a car—not a discussion about exchange control. This is a perfectly legitimate commercial transaction. It doesn't matter how it's paid so long as I pay for it legally.'

'Quite so, quite so,' agreed the other man. 'Well, what is your problem?'

'Everything,' I said. 'Life is full of problems. When I've bought the car here, I want to know how I can get it out of the country. What port should it go from? Can you recommend a shipping agent?'

'It's difficult to make personal recommendations in my position. You will appreciate that. But your best port is Ismailia. You will need an export permit from the Egyptian Ministry of Trade. Where are you staying—Shepheard's?'

'No, the Hilton.'

'Send a note round by messenger. That'll save you hanging

about half the day. You should have no problem. After all, the authorities here are very anxious to have money coming into the country.'

Back in England, if I export a car, I usually hand the whole matter over to a firm that deals with this end of the business. They collect it from my garage, take it to the docks, fill in all the forms, and all that is left for me is to pay their bill, and then wait for the cry of disappointment from the overseas buyer when he finds that all the removable accessories have mysteriously disappeared between my mews and his home. There didn't seem much more to it in Cairo, either, which was comforting to discover.

We shook hands, and I walked back to the hotel. Kent was sitting in the lounge on one of the wide settees set out in a hollow square.

'Where have you been?' he asked me, suspiciously, as though he thought I'd been banging his wife, if he had a wife.

'The Embassy,' I said.

'The Embassy?' he repeated. 'What do you want to get involved there for? Lost your passport?'

'No, just checking about getting the cars out. I don't want to be loused up on the dockside because we haven't some form, and a lot of Gyppoes are screaming their nuts off, and we miss the boat.'

'But I told you,' said Kent, with all the compressed patience of a keeper addressing a lunatic, '*I'll* deal with all that. I *know* these people. It's my business to know them. I work here. Start messing about with the Embassy and all that civil service passed-to-you, up-your-pipe-in-triplicate stuff, in re-yours-of-the-fourth-ult-to-hand, and we'll never get them out. You leave the details to me. All you have to worry about is whether the cars are any good.'

This was the first time I'd seen him at all animated. I decided to give myself a second time.

'What about a drink?' I said. 'What about that treble whisky you promised me last night?'

He looked as though I had dug a spike into his vitals, and to a man of his meanness it must have hurt him about as much, or even more.

'What?' he asked hoarsely, his eyes bulging like boiled eggs at the horrible suggestion .

'Just joking,' I assured him.

'Don't make jokes like that again,' he pleaded.

I realized then, even if I hadn't before, that Kent was so touched over spending his own money, he'd rather die of thirst than spend a penny—and take that how you like.

'About those cars,' he said. 'That Bugatti Sabry was telling you about really is something. It's a Bugatti Royale.'

'Are *you* joking?' I asked him. I didn't know there was another Royale left in the world, but I did know several people who would pay my price to buy one, for the Royale is unique, a symbol of an unparalleled age that has gone for ever.

Apparently, old Ettore Bugatti had been at a dinner-party in the mid-twenties, when some woman compared his cars unfavourably with Rolls-Royces. He took umbrage at this and decided to produce a Behemoth of a Bugatti, a car built for kings, apparently on the basis that anything Royce could do, he could do bigger and better. He did the first, if not the last. His new car had a 13 litre engine, a wheelbase of 14 ft. 1 in., and tyres as large as hoops. He charged 30,000 dollars for the chassis alone, back in the 1920s, too, and he was so particular about his potential customers that he invited them—only six or seven cars were built, to my knowledge—to his castle in Molsheim, to stay as his guests, for a few days, just to make sure they were genuinely the right type to own such a car.

Bugatti drove a Royale to Spain for the 1927 San Sebastian Grand Prix, and King Alfonso XIII ordered one immediately, but was dethroned before he could take delivery, which is an occupational hazard of Royalty. Thereafter, though, the Type 41 was called the Car of Kings—La Royale—although in fact, no reigning king ever owned one. King Carol of Rumania and King Boris of Bulgaria both wanted one, but thought that such ostentation was unwise since their countries were so poor.

But while Bugatti's Royale was a commercial failure, its engine was a success. He adapted them to drive locomotives on the French railways, and sold several hundreds for this purpose. Indeed, they were still being made for some years after the war.

With each Royale, Bugatti provided a silver elephant mascot for the radiator, for even although his guarantee ran, not for the life of the car, as with lesser breeds, but for the life of the owner, it was still a mammoth mechanical white elephant.

It has been said, and I'll say it again, that if you owned one of these cars you didn't need to take the dog for a walk, you just walked round the car twice, and that was your lot. I could up the ante to £15,000 for this, and the thought of the profit I would mark up, and the write-down I'd use for tax purposes, and the whole convoluted intricacies and potentialities of the deal excited me.

'You're joking,' I repeated, in case he was.

'About money?' said Kent. 'Never. You speak of the thing I love.'

'Where the hell can you get a Royale from in Egypt? I thought the country was bankrupt?'

'Farouk,' he said. 'When Farouk went, the government took over the Abdin Palace here as a museum. Everything is preserved, just as it was on that Saturday, the 26th of July, when he sailed away in his yacht, pretty well at gun-point. A relic of what they call the bad old days. Every new dictator calls his predecessor's time, the bad old days. They have to, otherwise people get around to thinking that the present days are pretty awful, too.'

'Skip the historical and political stuff,' I told him. 'Where do we come in?'

'Now. Once Sabry was certain you were genuinely interested, he contacted some old retainer that Farouk had around him who spirited away this particular car, just to check exactly what model it was. It's a Type 41, a Royale.'

'You think it's genuine?' I asked him.

He shrugged .

'When you've been as long as I have in the Middle East, you don't talk of these things too much in hotels, in bars, because they're all bugged. Every bloody thing you say in these places is bugged. I told you,' said Kent.

'Then, why are you talking here?'

'Because you can't bug a public place like this so easily, what with people coming and going, piped music, guests being paged, and so on.'

'Thanks for the warning.'

'It didn't cost me anything,' said Kent.

'I know. That's why you gave it to me. What time do we go?'

'I've ordered a taxi for nine o'clock. In your name.'

You would, I thought, in case you had to pay cash.

'It's a bit late, isn't it?'

I don't know whether you are like me, but in some foreign countries I like to be in familiar surroundings after dark. The idea of trailing up some unknown road to the Pyramids to meet unknown people at an unknown house, said to belong to a man who owned a perfume shop, and there to pay over physical cash for three cars, maybe without being able to prove any title to their ownership, didn't entirely fill me with enthusiasm. After all, I'm in business to make money, not give it away.

'You'll be all right,' said Kent, as though he read my thoughts. He stood up.

'Well, I'll get back to the office.'

'How are things there?'

What the hell could he be doing? Banging that girl I'd passed on the stairs? I decided to find out. I said:

'Funny thing happened on my way down the stairs from your office.'

'Like what?'

'Like meeting a girl going up.'

'Dark-haired, in a flowered dress?'

'Yes.'

'Nothing funny about that. She's my secretary, Maria.'

'Nice girl.'

'Good typist, if that's what you mean.'

It wasn't, but I didn't interrupt him.

'She's half French. Was brought up here as a child, so she speaks the lingo and knows her way around. Very useful to me, I can tell you.'

'You are telling me,' I said, but I didn't tell him about the business in Rosemary Court. I don't know why, but I buttoned up my tongue; never give too much away, as one strip-tease girl told the other.

There's a time for speech and a time for silence, and somehow I thought this was a time for waiting and trying to see. After all, if Kent *had* bought the car back again, he must have *had* a reason; I'd find that out first, and then the other questions might also be answered.

'See you outside here just before nine,' Kent said. 'They eat late in Cairo, so it might be an idea to have a snack first.'

Kent didn't offer to dine with me, and I didn't ask him to. I didn't want to be lumbered with his bill; maybe he was having dinner on the free nuts and olives from the bar on the roof.

I watched him walk between the palm trees, under the centre marble staircase and away over the wide tessellated slabs. A Nubian giant in some kind of fancy dress costume opened the door for him, and he was gone, but not forgotten.

I took the lift to my room, picked up the telephone, asked the hotel operator for International, and then gave that operator the number of my garage. I wanted to speak to George. I wanted him to check on the chassis numbers of all known Royales. I didn't want to be lumbered with some fake, although it seemed quite feasible that King Farouk *might* have owned one of these gigantic mechanical extravagances.

'There's just now a delay on the line,' the operator told me. 'I will ring you back.'

I replaced the phone and slid open the windows and went out on to the veranda. A long, long way below me, cars, the size of Matchbox models, were happily going round the roundabouts in the gardens in both directions. A boy pushed a handcart, piled with a pyramid of oranges, and behind him an old man was wheeling a blind woman in a handcart. She was dressed completely in black, and even at this distance I could see her blind useless eyes, white and horrible like stones in a statue's face.

I went inside, for the telephone was ringing. I picked it up.

'The line is down,' the operator told me. 'It is impossible to make any foreign calls. Also, it is a holiday tomorrow.'

'Thank you very much,' I said. This was all I needed.

I rang room service for a Whyte & Mackay, then ordered lunch of shish kebab, some fruit and black coffee.

It was one of those days that never seems to end. I had too many hours to kill before I went off with Kent. I took out my travellers' cheques, folded them inside a shirt, put the shirt in my case and locked it. I left ten English pound notes buttoned in my back pocket, and some loose money in piastres.

I was sorry about that telephone call. There's so much faking in our business, as in all branches of the antique trade, that without knowing the chassis numbers, I felt rather like a gladiator going in naked to fight the lions.

It seemed quite feasible that Farouk or someone close to him *had* bought a Bugatti Royale, I kept assuring myself, but I couldn't be certain. It wouldn't have been impossible for a crafty Egyptian craftsman to have lengthened an earlier, smaller chassis, and made a fake Royale Bug, but would it have been worth while? After all, I had read somewhere that Farouk took 250 million dollars with him when he went into exile, so what was the odd 30,000 or 40,000 for a real Bugatti? It would only be small change to him, almost petty cash.

I lay down on the bed and read *The Egyptian Gazette* that came up with the morning coffee. Like most antique dealers, I am a bit superstitious, so I read what the stars held for me, and they weren't giving much away. I'm Sagittarius, which means I'm never satisfied, and what the astrologer had dug out didn't satisfy me much, either.

'Not everything will go your way today,' I read, 'but an inborn instinct for what the public want should enable you to be successful in the commercial world.' So there you were: you could take it either way, or leave it alone. I left it alone, kicked off my shoes and went to sleep.

When I awoke, the room was cool, and the early evening dusk had painted the sky blue outside. Because of the trouble with Israel, all neon signs had been switched off, and the buildings were black blobs against the hills and sky. A mile above Cairo, an airliner was coming in to land, its red and green wing lights flickering. Oddly enough, street lamps were still burning.

I pulled the curtains, turned on the bedside light, and the piped music. Then I looked at my watch; eight o'clock. Nearly time to meet Kent. I went into the bathroom, washed my face under the cold tap, and rinsed out my mouth to be rid of the taste of sleep.

I had a vague feeling of excitement. If what Kent said was true, this source of old cars had been completely ignored by other dealers. It was like tapping a gold vein, or finding an oil well in your backyard. If things worked out, I might contact a merchant bank on my return and borrow a million quid and buy up every damned old car in Egypt, and ship them to some safe tax haven, like Malta, and sell them from there. I might be rich, yet. It was a good feeling, but nothing like so good as being rich, only a trailer for the main event.

I put on my jacket and shoes, walked down the corridor,

waited for the lift, left the key at the desk. The lounge was crowded: another group of package-deal tourists were either arriving or leaving. The impressions of the world a package tourist has must be of too little sleep, too much constipation, too many pre-cooked meals that all taste like warmed-up white rubber, and night-time arrivals and departures in hotels that are the same in every country. They'd be far happier and healthier saving their money by staying at home and watching travelogues on the box.

A black and white taxi was waiting outside the door with the inside light on. Kent sat in the back.

'You're late,' he said accusingly.

'Only minutes,' I told him.

He seemed a bit tense. I eased myself on to the shiny, plastic seat, and the driver took off, dodging between buses with people crowded on the back bumpers and round the doors, out over the traffic lights, and away past the zoo, up the road towards the Pyramids.

It was a wide road, but badly lit. The cars, in any case, all had their headlamps painted blue because of dim-out orders, in case of air-raids, and some had no lights at all. We almost ran down one mule cart piled high with grass, and I heard the driver shouting abuse after us.

Big potholes jarred the taxi's old springs. We passed a crowd of men who were clustered round a stall lit by a dim acetylene lamp, eating cakes the shape of quoit rings; then a few night-clubs with dim signs, and then large houses, all stucco, with small lights glowing over the numbers on their gateposts.

The driver slowed near a house behind a high stone wall, with a man standing by the gate. The man waved him in. He held a long stave in his right hand, and I guessed he didn't have that to scratch himself with. For my money—and I wasn't paying any, but I like the sound of the phrase—for my money, he was guarding the place, and if he could stop people coming in, he could also stop them coming out; which was a point to remember if I had to leave hurriedly myself.

The house was like a big concrete box. No lights were showing, perhaps because of the dim-out, perhaps not, and the whole place seemed deserted and uninhabited. Le Corbusier would have done his nut if he'd seen it, for it was so ugly. Three garages were built beneath the ground floor, with roll-up doors. The driver switched off his engine, and we climbed out.

A chill wind was blowing sand, rough as a rasp, against my face. There is no rainfall at all in Cairo, nothing to hold down this pitiless, shifting sea of sand that could bury the whole city if the wind blew strong enough, and long enough, as maybe it will one day.

'Here we are,' said Kent, as though to reassure himself.

'How do you know?'

'I've been often enough before. That's how.'

This was a good start. We went up the stairs, and the door opened before we could ring the bell. The house inside had that oddly impersonal look of a furnished apartment, a shelter from the elements. Some beaten brass pots stood on the marble floor of the hall, with yellow cacti plants, and whoever had beaten them must have been a sadist, for they were covered with dents. The air felt stale and dry; a film of sand covered a table against the wall.

A servant of some kind, looking like a convict in a grey jacket and trousers with brass buttons, closed the door behind us, pulled the black-out curtains, and turned on the main lights. After the gloom, the hall blazed like a film set.

'Welcome, welcome,' said a voice, and Sabry, the man from the House of Attar—a rogue by any other name would doubtless smell as sweet—came towards us, hands outstretched in greeting. He clapped his hands together, because he had nothing else to do with them, and another man appeared with a tray of drinks. Although they weren't alcoholic, they were liquid, which helped me to get the sand out of my throat. Now, I thought, we'll have all this spiel of bitter coffee and small talk: 'What do you think of Cairo?' and 'Please, how is the Middle East position regarded in England?' and I would make my reply, 'I haven't tried the Middle East position, yet,' and they would look surprised and hurt, and I'd wish I could find a few new gags.

Sabry bowed us into the room he had left. Another man was already there, a cigar as big as a long frankfurter clamped in his face. He wore a pair of grey lightweight trousers, beautifully pressed, black crocodile skin shoes, and a short-sleeved silk shirt. His shoulders bulged under the silk, and he looked just too good to be true. In fact, he was much too good to be true, as I realized when he shook my hand, and went through that bone-squeezing technique.

Close to, his face was much older than it had appeared from the other end of the room. It was pitted by open pores and his eyes were very blue but watery, and the little dab of moustache was flecked with grey. His hair seemed black on his head, but for my money, if I was paying money, it was dyed. Dye now, pay later. As he looked at me, his left eyelid drooped in a tiny wink. I watched again and he winked again. But he wasn't trying to date me; he just had a nervous tic.

Kent introduced us.

'My good friend Hassan Sayed,' he said. 'He runs a gunsmith's shop in Alexandria.'

'Does he now?' I said. The only Sayed I had heard of had been the one in James Elroy Flecker's poem, and the only line I remembered from that was 'Some to Mecca turn to pray, and I towards thy bed, Yasmin', which didn't carry human knowledge forward very far. After you with thy bed, Yasmin.

'Who buys guns in Alexandria?' I asked to give the conversational ball a push. It was the only ball I could push decently in that room and that company.

'Not enough people,' admitted Hassan, and his voice was as I expected it to be, just too male, just too deep and throaty like an actor playing an actor playing a he-man.

'In the old days we sold many guns to noblemen. For their protection, you understand.'

'I understand.' We aristos have to hang together, or we'll all hang separately.

'And also there was much shooting. Even today, things are not too bad from the point of view of sport. I go after quail, little small birds, or doves. Very sweet birds to shoot. We wait with our guns in the gardens in the evening, and when they come to settle down to sleep, poom, poom, poom, we go!'

He raised his arms as though holding an imaginary rifle.

'Then there are pigeons. That is a fine bird. They fly in from Europe, all the way, and when they settle down to rest, we are waiting for them, poom, poom, poom!'

'I'm glad I'm not a bird,' I said, and I meant the feathered sort.

'You make the joke?' said Hassan. 'Yes?'

'Yes,' I said. 'If I can't make money or love, I make jokes. They cost nothing and don't tire me out. Show me another pleasure I can enjoy so many times a day without tiring.'

Hassan moved across the room lightly for a man of his weight. I could imagine the trouble he had keeping down his flesh; the chest expanders, the rowing machines, the cycling in some gymnasium and then the massage under steam. Ah, yes, the massage, and not only under steam. I thought of all the small boys who must have been Hassan's close and intimate friends. I thought of the weary pigeons fluttering down the evening sky, a mass of bloodied feathers.

I thought I didn't like Hassan, and when he turned his eyes on me again, small as worm-holes in wood, I thought he didn't like me, either. What the hell was Kent doing with this fellow? Maybe he was Sabry's friend? He certainly wasn't mine.

Kent might have been reading my thoughts through a hole in the side of my head, because he said: 'My good friend Hassan here is related to the Chief of Police for Northern Egypt, and as I told you, my good friend Sabry also has important relations.'

I said: 'Yes?'

After all, even the owner of a perfume palace must have relations of some kind, but if they were important to him, it didn't necessarily mean they were important to me.

'Yes. It is very necessary to have close contacts with the right people. You appreciate that. In the Middle East, things are different from back home.'

Not all that different, unfortunately, I thought, for in how many local council car-parks do you find Rover three-litres, because someone in the surveyor's department has been a useful friend to someone else who wanted to develop a couple of acres over which there had been difficulties for planning permission? But I could see how Kent was anxious to cut his expenditure, and it was obviously helpful to have two locals who would know which officials would have to be paid cash, and those who would only need to be paid compliments.

A servant came in with a silver tray of coffee. He was a midget with a squeezed-in face, and a head the size of a child's sunk on a small man's body. I was sorry for him, for his hands trembled, and he kept looking at Sabry and licking his lips as though he was afraid of him. As soon as he'd gone, Kent pulled up three chairs.

'We've got the cars,' he said, looking at each of us in turn, with me last of all.

'Where?' I asked.

'Here, in Sabry's garage.'

'What ones have you got?'

'As I said, a Bugatti, a Delage, and a Marmon.'

They sat looking at me, as though expecting me to say something, so I said, 'Let's see them.'

Sabry led us out down a steel staircase into the concrete garage that ran the whole width of the house. Two unshaded bulbs burned in the ceiling. On the right stood a pile of crates and carboys in baskets bearing labels 'Jasmine Essence', 'Oil of Attar' and so on, presumably for use in his scent shop.

I wasn't much concerned with this; what interested me were the three cars, and the first one I checked was the Bugatti. I'd never seen a Royale—not many people have—but the yellow and black beast before me was something much smaller, a Type 57, with a strange open body. Even so, it was valuable; all Bugattis are, but nothing like so valuable as a Royale. The cars had all been driven in, for I felt the bonnets and they were still warm. I examined the tax discs on the windscreen, and they were valid. I wondered who had been driving these exotic vehicles on the Cairo streets. Sabry must have seen my thoughts on my face.

'We asked the owners to leave them for tonight, so you can make any tests you need,' he said.

'Who are the owners?' I asked.

'That is immaterial. They are ordinary people who need some foreign currency.'

'Just how much foreign currency?'

'We could probably get a better price if we took the three,' said Kent. 'Each of the owners will come down a little.'

'What do they want?' I asked. 'Last price.'

'Fifteen hundred sterling,' said Sabry immediately, so I guessed he must have a good friend or relation who worked in the American Express, and who had told him the amount of money I had with me. Next time, I'd cable half to Cooks, just to confuse them; if there was a next time, of course.

'It's a lot of money,' I said, as I always do when a seller names a price.

'It is,' agreed Sabry, 'but you know what these will be worth when you get back to England. That Bugatti done up must fetch several thousand English pounds, and what would it cost to renovate—one thousand?'

I didn't say anything, because I was looking under the bonnet. The classic design of the engine, like a solid block of polished metal, looked as good as always, although it was filthy. Oil had leaked out somewhere and the dust and sand blown in and stayed, forming a crust.

'It's not a Royale,' I pointed out. It had a family resemblance, as a little boy can look like his bigger brother, but that was all. There wasn't anything like the profit here I'd hoped for, but there was still a very good profit. The Type 57 was a beautiful machine, but most that I had seen carried Van Vooren or Gangloff bodies; I had never seen one like this. It was probably an Atalante coupé.

The colour-scheme surprised me, black wings and a yellow body, like some kind of wasp on wheels. I bent down and put my nose to the door hinges, where new paint takes longest to dry. I smelled a faint whiff of cellulose. The car had recently been repainted—but why the hideous colour scheme instead of the traditional bright blue of nearly all the Bugattis I had seen?

'I'll give you twelve hundred for the lot,' I said.

'It's impossible,' said Sabry. 'The owner of the Delage, for instance, uses it to run tourists out from the Mena House Hotel to the Pyramids. They like to have their photographs taken standing by its side. It's worth keeping, rather than let it go at a low figure.'

'Five hundred is only a hundred more for each owner.'

'Of course,' agreed Sabry. 'But we have already made them cut their prices. Fifteen hundred. Last price.'

I walked round the cars again, wondering where the owner of the Bugatti could find such huge tyres. After the war, one British owner of a Royale fitted 7.50 by 21-inch Goodrich Silvertown tyres—originally intended for an American army mobile gun!

I climbed in behind the wheel of the Marmon, and started the engine. It ran easily, but a bit noisily, but this wasn't surprising for the engine must have been running for very nearly forty years. I switched it off before we poisoned ourselves with exhaust fumes.

'All right,' I said. 'Fifteen hundred. Delivered to the docks.'

I had to make one condition. Never let the seller think he's having things all his own way; that's against any religious principles, and so far as things like this are concerned, I've such strong religious principles I could practically be a bishop.

'That's our job,' said Kent. 'You drive whichever one you want, and I'll take the next, and Hassan or Sabry will have the third.'

'What about the paperwork?' I asked him. 'You said you were going to do that.'

'I've got it all fixed. We've just got to fill in the chassis and engine numbers. Do you want to look over the cars mechanically before we drive them?'

'How far is it to Ismailia, and what's the road like?'

An odd fact about antique machinery is that if you leave it alone, old engines often run for years, but once you begin to disturb them, then things start to go wrong. It's the same with old people who retire from routine jobs; break the routine and you can break them, too.

'We'll never get them out of Ismailia,' said Hassan. 'My cousin tells me that the port is on the verge of closing, because of Israeli shelling. We don't want any trouble with these things stuck on the dockside for weeks, with people stealing pieces off them, or maybe the ship itself getting seized. We'll have to go to Alexandria. That's about a hundred and forty miles, if we take the desert road.'

'We should cover that distance on a tank of petrol each,' I said, 'so long as the tyres and the radiator hoses hold up in the heat.'

All the cars were basically good engineering designs, and without weaknesses. If I'd been buying a Cord, for instance, with its electrically operated gear change that can actually select two gears at the same time, a feat that I have never known any other car achieve, I would have felt far less happy. Even so, it was only common sense to give them a quick going over, but I didn't want to make a production out of it.

I checked the oil in each sump, and although it was the colour and consistency of black treacle, the sumps were full, and there were no bad oil leaks beneath the cars, and surprisingly little play in the steering.

'We'd better have a couple of lengths of rope,' I said. 'Nylon, if possible, in case we need to tow each other. Who do I pay the money to?'

'Me,' said Sabry.

'I've brought nothing with me,' I said. 'I'll have to see you back at the hotel.'

'There's no need,' said Kent. 'We'll see you here tomorrow, at eight. We're ten miles on our way already here.'

'Best make an early start,' Sabry explained. 'It's going to be very hot driving across the desert at midday.'

'I'll be here,' I told him. 'With the money.'

I wasn't too happy about driving the cars all this way ourselves, but then I'm never too happy about anything. Fact is, I tend to look on the gloomy side of things so often that if I'm cheerful it means I've got a temperature.

Heat would be our worst enemy; although these old cars might chug around Cairo quite happily, the long desert journey would loosen the scale and rust of years in their ancient radiators, and could block their withered thermostats and make them boil.

'Eight it is,' said Kent. 'Oh, and there's one other thing. We'll want your signature on the forms. Better do that now.'

We went back upstairs. The servant had cleared away the dirty cups, and clean ones were laid on the tray. I wondered what these people's stomachs were like with all these coffee-grounds swilling about inside them. Their intestines should be the best polished in the business.

Kent opened his brief-case and took out a buff folder of papers. 'We'll need your signature here, and here,' he said, pushing forms across the table towards me. I glanced through them. They were the usual import/export declarations in Arabic script with English translations, badly printed, but quite straightforward. The years of registration of the cars seemed right—1928 for the Bugatti, 1930 for the Delage, 1933 for the Marmon. But the Bugatti was described as a Royale special-bodied roadster, which it manifestly was not. Also, it was probably a 1936 model. They didn't make Type 57's in 1928.

'What's wrong?' asked Kent, watching my face.

'The date and description of the Bug.'

'What's wrong with it?'

'It's about eight years too old here. And it's not a Royale.'

'Does that matter?'

'Only if someone in the Customs notices it.'

'So far as they're concerned, it's a Bugatti, isn't it?'

'If that's all they want, then it's all right.'

'We're very grateful to you indeed,' said Sabry carefully, 'but in my country it is better to make a mistake in a declaration and go through with it, rather than correct that mistake and cross something out. They would immediately become suspicious.'

'You know best,' I said, because maybe he did, and signed the forms. After all, it seemed an unimportant and pedantic point.

Kent took out a rubber stamp, tried it once on the back of an envelope, and banged it down on each page of the forms.

'You think of everything,' I said, and he certainly seemed to have done, for the circular stamp contained my name and the title, Managing Director, Aristo Autos, London, W1, England.

'I meant to ask you if you had a stamp for your firm,' he said apologetically, 'but I forgot. Fellow in the bazaar made this for me this morning. Doesn't mean anything, of course. Just makes it all look a bit more official. These characters in the Customs here go on stamps and seals in a big way.'

I filled in my passport number, signed the last statement, pushed the papers back to him. He read through each one carefully, returned them to his case.

'Well,' I said, standing up, 'thanks for the coffee and the sight of the cars. Are you coming back with me in the cab?'

'No,' said Kent, 'I've some business to do here. I'm not sure how long I will be. You take the taxi back.'

I guessed that this was just a way for him to avoid paying the fare.

Kent followed me out to the cab; the others stayed in the garage. It was quite dark now, and in the dim headlights I saw occasional cyclists, weaving about, then three empty donkey carts running in line, the donkeys trotting happily in the cool of the evening. We swerved for flocks of sheep, and how the driver saw his way I don't know, and didn't like to think.

I was glad when we came back past the zoo, where the eagles were perched high up on the trees in their cages, and ran up the ramp in front of the hotel. I paid off the cab and went up to my room. The telephone began to ring as I opened the door. I picked it up and kicked the door shut. There was a lot of whirring in my ears; voices asked each other questions in French which I didn't understand and then a girl spoke in English: 'You are room 927?'

'Yes.'

'Your call to London.'

'My call to London.' I had forgotten all about it. I thought the line was down, or it was a holiday. Not that it mattered now that the Bugatti wasn't what I'd hoped it would be.

George's homely voice spoke in my ear.

'Where's all the action, then?'

'I've bought three cars,' I said. 'A Marmon, a Bugatti sold as a Royale, but actually a Type 57, and an open Delage.'

'I'm doing the ads for *Motor Sport*,' said George. 'Shall I give 'em gin—put 'em in?'

'Yes,' I said, 'say they're fully restored, from a foreign collector's stable, regardless of cost, gems of old-world craftsmanship. All that crap. Expected this month.'

'It'll appear about the time you're Pope.'

'I'm Pope?' What the hell had happened to George?

'Pope of Rome—home.'

'Oh. Better insure them, too. Get on to the Midland Widows. They're best for these old things. Insure each one specifically for £5,000 agreed price for fire, theft and damage in transit.'

It had to be an agreed price, because otherwise I'd have difficulty when making a claim, for the insurance companies sometimes argue that if the car is old then it is only worth a scrap price.

'Anything else?' George asked.

'Yes. Couple of other fellows are involved out here,' I told him. 'Locals. One runs a scent and jeweller's shop. Name of Sabry Ahmed. The other seems to have been a playboy in the great days. Must be fifty-ish now. Crinkly hair. One of the lads. Runs a gun shop in Alexandria. Name of Sayed Hassan.'

'Has he a twitch in one kidney?'

'Kidney?' I repeated. George's rhyming slang was often incomprehensible to me, especially over a distance of 2,000 miles.

'Yes. Kidney pie. Eye.'

'Oh. Yes. He has. You know him?'

'Of him, at least.'

'How?'

Even as I asked, I remembered. George had served for twenty-seven years as a regular in the Royal Tank Regiment; his memory for all kinds of things, from chassis numbers to pornographic exhibitions in Bombay, was encyclopaedic.

'I told you,' he said, and indeed he had. 'I was in the Canal Zone during my last posting. They were after him on smuggling charges. Tommy Dodds, mostly. Rods. Guns to you. And some jewels. But apparently there were diplomatic difficulties. He was attached in some way to Farouk's court. No doubt a number of people got their palms crossed with banger. Banger and mash—cash. Remember that case, man in the Hillman Minx with those heavy doors?'

Indeed, I remembered the case of the Hillman with the heavy doors. A provincial bank manager had been driving it through Austria to meet his wife, who had gone on ahead by air. On the way, he picked up an English hitch-hiker, who, hearing that the manager lived in the Midlands, mentioned he had close friends living there, too.

Next day, the manager was unable to start his car, and the hotel owner recommended a garage. Some trivial fault was diagnosed, but the garage man explained he had discovered heavy wear on the steering king pins, and while he hadn't any new spares, he had made some adjustments, which might make it appear hard to steer, so he should contact his local garage as soon as he reached home.

The bank manager never had a chance to act on this advice, for the car was stolen from outside his house on the night he reached home. It was found wrecked and abandoned on its side down a ravine in the west country two weeks later—and both front doors were missing.

That might have been the end of the matter if someone hadn't found a Minx front door of the same colour thrown over a hedge a couple of miles away. Inside, welding marks gave their own explanation. While the car was in its Austrian garage, containers for drugs or jewels had been welded into the doors.

The bank manager—and no doubt other harmless tourists like him—had been a stooge. The smugglers had reckoned on their obvious respectability being good enough assurance that their car would not be searched at any frontier—and if it was, how could they explain the contraband welded into their own front doors? If Hassan had been involved here, then he was one to watch.

'Are you certain?' I asked.

'Absolutely,' said George. 'I'd watch that feather plucker. He's bent as a pin.'

'What's he look like, this Hassan?' I asked George. I had to be certain he wasn't confusing him with someone else.

'Biggish. Tough. Damn great teeth. Likes himself a lot—bags of flexing muscles. And ginger. Ginger beer—queer.'

'That's the boyo,' I agreed, because it was. The ginger man. Then the pips went, so George said goodbye.

I sat down on the edge of the bed, and superimposed that story on what was happening to me. Could *I* be the stooge in this enterprise of exporting three old cars? And if so, how? Or was I simply tired, and imagining the whole thing?

I have bought and sold old cars for long enough to know that the reasons people give for buying or selling them are rarely the true ones, although sometimes they genuinely don't realize this themselves. I have also lived long enough to know that the oddest beasts aren't always in the jungle; they walk on two legs—just like you and me.

CHAPTER FOUR

I OPENED MY SUITCASE on the spare bed, threw in my few shirts, drip-dry socks, and the second suit I hadn't even worn. I can fly around the world in one set of clothes—and often have done, for I wash them out, hang them over the rail to dry over-night, and put them on again fresh in the morning. Why carry more weight than you absolutely need to, as the thin man asked the fat man?

I had another Whyte & Mackay, set my travelling alarm for seven o'clock, wrote out on the hotel card that I wanted break-fast at seven; fruit juice, two fried eggs, honey and toast—it's marvellous what I'll eat when someone else cooks it for me—and hung this on the door.

As I came out of the bathroom with the last of the drip dries, the telephone rang. The desk clerk said a lady was waiting down-stairs to see me. I thought of one of George's gags: that was no lady, that was my brother-in-law, he just walks like that—and rejected it.

'How old?' I asked him. No point wasting your time with the sere and yellow when young meat's around.

'I would say about twenty-five, sir,' said the clerk, who had obviously considered the matter.

'You would, would you? Does she look as though she knows what it's all about?'

'Please?'

'Never mind,' I said. 'Send her up.'

Who the hell could this be? Some idiot tourist who knew someone with the same name as me on a package deal, and had confused us? I put the whisky in my case, closed the lid, brushed my hair to add a touch of class. I didn't want to disappoint this girl, whoever she was. I shall not pass this way again, and therefore any good girl I can do, let me do them now, etcetera.

There was a knock at the door. I suddenly felt like Cinderella in the pantomime when she hears knocking outside and everyone in the audience knows it's the big bad fairy or the wolf or whoever is the rascal.

Cinderella calls bravely in her high, shrill voice: 'You can't frighten *me* with that knocking.'

And the other character replies thoughtfully from the other side, in a very deep voice: 'You'd be frightened—if you knew what I was knocking on the door with!'

I opened the door, and if I'd been a jumping man, I would have jumped into the air, for standing there, smiling at me, as though she liked the sight, was the girl I had glimpsed briefly on the way into Snelling's flat when I returned his keys, the girl I had passed on the stairs on her way up to Kent's office. Maria.

'Be my guest,' I said, thinking that she might well have also been the guest of these other two, and where one has been another can also go, which was my thought for the day, and if you've got a better one, drop me a line about it.

She was wearing a light sort of dress, for the day was warm, and she had a couple of worth-while bristols which, being a tit man, interested me, even though they were doubtlessly well shielded from covetous hands. I closed the door behind her. She came into the room and threw her handbag on the bed as though she were going to stay. I decided I wouldn't stop her.

'You don't know me,' she said. 'At least we haven't been introduced formally. I'm Maria.'

'*Ave, Maria,*' I said. '*Ave atque vale,*' which shows I picked up the rudiments of something somewhere, and I don't mean something that I should go to the outpatients' clinic to see about, either. I mean a touch of the old classics. My youth wasn't wasted in bars; not all of it, anyway.

'I'm Mr Kent's secretary.'

'Get away,' I said, not meaning she should actually, but just to show I can believe all kinds of things, even the truth on occasions.

I gave her my name; I'd nothing else to give at that particular point in time.

'I tried to ring you earlier,' she went on, 'but there was no reply, so I thought I'd better come in person.'

She couldn't very well come in any other way, I thought, but didn't say so. After all, why louse up half a chance if you think you have one?

'There's something I want to ask you. About when you brought those keys back to Mr Snelling in my flat.'

'Yes?'

'Have you told Mr Kent you saw me there?'

'No. Should I have done?'

As I said this, I wondered again why I hadn't, but I hadn't. Maybe there was some subconscious reason, for I couldn't explain it otherwise; and if life has taught me anything, it's never to attempt to explain the inexplicable.

'Then please don't. I can't tell you why now. It's not really important—only to me. And I promise you I will tell you when we're safely aboard that boat, away from here.'

I looked at her a bit sharpish. Either she was having it off with Snelling or with Kent, or probably both, and didn't want Kent to know, or there was some other reason equally important to her. But women are so devious that you rarely learn the real truth about anything from them, only as much of it as they care to let go, and there was no profit in asking questions she didn't want to answer. I would have to wait until we were on that boat, like she said, and then, if she ran true to my experience of women, she'd either tell me nothing or a load of rubbish.

'You're involved in all this?' I asked, to keep the conversation ball rolling.

'All what?'

'Getting these cars out of Egypt.'

'It was my idea.'

'So. It's a good idea—if we don't run into any snags.'

'That's why I don't want you to mention about the flat.'

She paused, and so did I. How could what had happened in a cruddy flat in Shepherds Bush affect the export of three old cars from Cairo? I didn't know, but somehow I didn't greatly care for the turn the conversation was taking. Was she trying to warn me of something in a roundabout way? If so, the way was so roundabout that I couldn't follow it at all.

'Does Kent know Snelling?' I asked her.

'I don't know.'

'How well do you know Snelling?'

'I don't know him at all. I'd never heard of him until you mentioned his name.'

'Are you serious?'

If she wasn't, I was. But then she was, too—or so she said.

'Then what can my mentioning him to Kent do to louse up our deal?'

'Please,' she said. 'Don't ask me. I can't tell you yet, but I will. Can you believe me?'

'You don't make it easy.'

She didn't deny this, so I asked her: 'Are you based here or in London?'

'Here. I've worked for Kent for nearly six months. I've been over to London twice. I liked it there.'

I almost gave her my card, but then they cost three guineas a hundred to print, and I could tell her my phone number for nothing. I told her that, just in case it could ever prove useful.

'Are you driving with us to Alexandria?'

'Yes. You've seen the cars?'

I nodded. 'They should make the distance all right.'

'Do you like the Bugatti?'

'It's not my sort of car,' I told her, because it isn't. 'But it's very saleable, though I hate the colours. Kent had told me it was a Royale, and that's how it's described in the export manifests. But it's not. It's a Type 57.'

She opened her mouth as though she was going to say something interesting, but then she changed her mind; maybe Kent had also warned her about the likelihood of my room being bugged, for all she said was: 'I'll see you in the morning. Here. I can charge a taxi to the office.'

'If the office is synonymous with Kent, by all means charge it. That will be the first bill he's picked up on the whole trip. There is a first time for everything, even for that.'

She took her bag from the bed and went out. I watched her walk along the corridor, with the soft carpet and green walls and the piped music, but she didn't look back. If she had, and seen me standing there, I would have taken her up to the roof bar and who knows where it might all have ended. As it was, I couldn't have had a duller night than I had, turning and twisting in bed, wondering whether my alarm had gone off, or how the deal could possibly be crooked, and if it were whether I could lose either my money or the cars or, worst of all, both.

I woke up at about half-past six and switched off the alarm before it could ring, and sat on the edge of the bed, rubbing sleep out of my eyes and scratching my hair, and burping, all those unpleasant things men do on their own, and sometimes not just on their own, when they're only half awake.

Little things, each without any real significance on their own, seemed more important in the early morning. Kent had lied to me when he said he owned the car in which we had driven to Belsize Park, when it was only hired. Was this forgetfulness, or because he wished to impress, or for what other conceivable reason? Was it only wishful thinking that had caused the Bugatti to be described as a Royale, when it wasn't? And what the hell was Maria up to?

I shrugged away these thoughts, ate breakfast, and was down waiting in the front porch when Maria arrived. We drove in silence along the Pyramids road, past the blocks of new flats with their stucco walls all yellow ochre in the early sunshine, past night-clubs shuttered and sad in the same sun, and then green marshes and stalls of such unlikely things as sweetmeats, drainpipes and terracotta chimney pots. Two women sat under a tree, picking nits from each other's hair. Next to them was a huge bamboo cage on a wooden trolley, filled with sorry chickens in several tiers.

The road was wider than I had imagined in the dusk of the previous evening, and lined on either side by eucalyptus trees, their trunks as thick as three men locked together, if you've ever seen three men locked together which, frankly, I haven't. In the distance, to the left, we saw three grey slag-heaps. I realized with a shock that these must be the Pyramids. As with so much else in life—and maybe in death, too, for all I know—they looked far more impressive in photographs than in fact.

We turned in at the gateway of the house; it was just as deserted as it had been last night. The taxi driver seemed to know his way and blew his horn twice. The man with the stave —or someone who looked just like him—appeared and waved us in. We stopped, Maria paid off the driver and we went up the steps. The front door was open and Kent came out of a room, wiping his mouth with a table napkin.

'Good, good,' he said, as though life was. 'Would you like a coffee?'

I shook my head. I wanted to be on my way. The earlier we started, the sooner we would reach Alexandria, and the less chance of frying ourselves in the desert. I told him so, and he said 'Good,' again, and led the way down the steel stairs to the garage.

The doors were already rolled up, and dust had blown in over the cars. The Bugatti appeared even more garish in the daylight in its crude yellow and black paintwork; the other two also looked older in the merciless sunshine, nondescript old shells with tired mechanical hearts that could hardly arouse the interest of even the most inquisitive customs officer. After Sabry's and Hassan's relations had dealt with their colleagues, I hoped they would not be too concerned with questions.

'Sabry will lead with Hassan,' said Kent. 'He does the journey nearly every week from Alex to see his mother here. I'll go next with Maria, then you come behind. If you get into any trouble; break down, that sort of thing, blow the horn and we'll stop.

'Every so often, we'll pass a police post, and the drill is to get out of the car and smile at the policeman, and be pleasant, and if they speak English, say what a wonderful country this is, and how impressed you are. O.K.?'

I nodded.

'When we reach Alex, we'll go right along the front and park outside the docks. We may not clear all three cars through customs tonight, but if we can clear two of them, we'll do the third in the morning. The boat sails tomorrow at noon, by the way.'

It was all rather like being in the army again. I expected someone to shout, 'Any questions?' I had none. All I wanted to see was the colour of someone's money, preferably not my own.

Sabry came down the steps. He was smelling like a polecat with his attar of roses and musk, a rather disagreeable mixture at eight in the morning. He looked at me in a meaningful sort of way, and so I took out my travellers' cheques and signed away £1,500. If I could have beaten him down by even one pound, I would have felt better about it. As I hadn't, I made up my mind that no one in the trade must ever know I had paid three Gyppoes their asking prices for three cars.

He and Hassan had chosen the Bugatti, and it waited on its thick spoked aluminium wheels, the engine ticking over very slowly, like a metronome. Sabry climbed in beside Hassan, folded up my notes, and put them away in a button-down pocket. Kent was starting up the Marmon with Maria by his side as I threw my suitcase into the back of the Delage and then climbed in behind the wheel.

Louis Delage had been physically handicapped in that he had only one good eye, but despite this he had a natural eye for line and for engineering; he'd designed almost as many individualistic cars as Bugatti in his day, and this was one of them. The dashboard was mother-of-pearl, the instruments had pale waxy faces as though they had wilted in the sun of too many summers. The gears felt firm, and there was little side-to-side play in any of the pedals, always a sure sign that a car has been looked after.

The canvas of the hood had split with age, and dust poured in on me like flour as the wind changed. We started off, juddering on our hard springs, a strange enough convoy, but so many old vehicles were either abandoned at the roadside with broken axles, split tyres, or with the driver doing complicated repairs under the engine, for this was old-car country, that we aroused no interest.

We passed a man wheeling a huge block of ice on a sort of railway trolley. The ice was melting as he trundled it along. By the time he reached wherever he was going, he wouldn't have any ice left to deliver, which was his problem. Mine was to hope that our cars, with a combined age of about one hundred and twelve years, would reach Alexandria safely. It seemed enough to have on my mind for the moment.

The road was double-tracked, and on the roofs of some of the flats I saw soldiers and sandbags and machine-guns. Things looked a bit too warlike for my peace of mind. I'd be very glad to be away.

We curved to the right, away from the former Queen Farida's Palace, a passable imitation of a Tyrolean guest-house, and the Mena House Hotel, where Churchill and Roosevelt held a conference during the war, away from the Pyramids and the camels and the touts with Arab horses who waited for the tourists. The road was a single lane now, with a white line down the middle. Here and there, the wind had blown sand across it, completely covering the macadam, and trees stood dusty and thick on either side. Beyond them, through a haze of sand and dust, the desert shimmered like a burning glass.

We were keeping up a steady pace of about thirty miles an hour. Gradually the buildings fell behind, until the only links with the city we had left and the one we were going to were the pylons dragging the electric cables over the hard bright sand.

The desert seemed to run on endlessly, with false peaks, deep ravines, and long valleys of sand. The first police post was a hut on the left of the road. A soldier with a white flag waved us down, and we stopped obediently, climbed up and stood in a row, like naughty children, in front of an old corporal, who sat at a trestle table. His uniform was serge and must have been unbearably hot. His boots looked as though they had been stolen from the British Army dump in the Canal Zone years ago, in the days when George had been a soldier. They probably had been, and never cleaned since.

I glanced at Kent as we stood in line. He was smiling benignly, as though the corporal was a potential client, but neither Hassan nor Sabry were treating the man lightly. Hassan went into a great spiel in Egyptian to him, and then collected up our passports, and handed them over. I couldn't understand what he was saying, and I don't think that the corporal made much of it, either, but he lugubriously compared our photographs in the passports with our faces, and handed them back. The whole exercise seemed futile, about as much use as the bottom half of a mermaid, but no doubt it satisfied him or his superiors.

I didn't have a chance to plug Kent's line about this being a wonderful country, so I decided to save it for next time.

We climbed back into our cars and drove on, the hood of the Delage flapping like a flag. A strong smell of hot oil—holy smoke, we used to call it when I was a boy—drifted up from the direction of the gear box. I had forgotten to check the oil level in the box, and began to wonder whether we would make the distance. The road was completely empty for miles at a time; then the only vehicles we saw were Skoda army lorries, bright and new, driving south, presumably from the docks.

The drive would have been murder in the dark, because the road had no proper edges. Sand had blown over them, sometimes to a depth of several feet. Here and there, on the fringes of the desert, little groups of old army tents, blackened with age and use, whackered in the endless breeze, with a dry, lifeless sound.

Once or twice, we had to make a detour off the road, around a make-shift track, while engineers of some sort were working on the surface. On one of these detours my right-hand rear wheel slipped and spun uselessly in the sand. I managed, by the momentum of the car, to bring it back on the hard surface again, but the experience made me realize that if both rear wheels slid off the road, I would have to be towed out.

On either side now, the sand stretched away to a hazy blue infinity, empty of all life. I had the odd feeling, when the cars in front of me were obscured by their own dust, of being either the first or the last man in the world, with no one else, nothing else, left alive.

We slowed down for the next police post, a more sophisticated affair, with a radio set on the table and a long vertical aerial trembling in the wind. The corporal here actually wrote down our engine numbers, for what reason I didn't discover, but he appeared satisfied, and waved us on.

The wind was now far stronger than it had been near Cairo. It blew empty tins and pieces of newspaper, dropped by goodness knows who, in front of us as though they were leaves. Every few miles, on the right of the road, stood white boards with black lettering in Arabic script, and underneath a stencil of a telephone, and the figure 100, and about 100 yards farther on there was the actual, physical telephone itself, in a yellow box on a pole. I didn't know whether they worked, or whether they were even connected, but they had a reassuring look.

I tended to lose count of time. My eyes kept flickering down to the oil pressure on the dashboard, but the needle stayed firm, although the engine was nearly boiling.

Hassan, as the leader, had turned up the speed to thirty-five, and after two hours by my watch, when I reckoned that if we had nothing worse to meet than we had already passed, we should be all right, he pulled off into a kind of oasis of unexpected trees, ringed round a concrete encampment. There were bushes and advertisements for GMC trucks and Misr petrol, and a rash of big radio masts with a high brick wall round them, and a rest-house with two or three cars parked close together, as though for comfort.

We stopped. I switched off the engine and climbed out. The wind blew my trousers against my legs. It was hot, and yet, because of the wind, cool at the same time; a curious sensation. I felt gritty and in need of a bath. The old Delage engine was happily boiling away now that the fan had stopped turning.

'We'll have a drink here,' Kent explained.

We all walked into the café rather stiff-leggedly. It was a relief to be out of the wind. A juke box was playing in one corner, and some other drivers were sitting at formica-topped tables. They looked round at us, wondering who we were, then went on with their meal. A waiter came and wiped the table, produced a menu in script that meant nothing to me. Hassan ordered something which turned out to be five glasses of squeezed lemon juice and water.

Kent looked round the room in a conspiratorial way, and pulled his chair half an inch nearer the table.

'We're about forty miles from Alex,' he said. 'Hassan thought it a good idea to have a drink and a wash, for we may have to hang about for hours at the docks. Also, his car is giving a bit of trouble. One of the plugs has oiled up.'

'Do you want me to look at it?' I asked.

'No,' said Hassan, shaking his head. 'My experience of anything old and mechanical is that so long as it runs, leave it alone. That's how it is with old guns, anyhow. I'll nurse the car to Alex, and once we've reached the docks, we'll have no more driving.'

The waiter brought the bill and, as usual, I paid. This was becoming a game, to see how Kent could duck out of paying. I noticed that he managed to be going through his papers, so he pretended he didn't see the waiter. I had a slash and a wash, dried my face on my handkerchief because there wasn't any towel, and then we set off for the last lap.

The heat, the constant faint smell of exhaust, the strong smell of oil, and everywhere the shimmering dancing horizon of the desert, made me feel sleepy. More than once I dozed off, and jerked myself back to consciousness, just as the front wheel was beginning to dip itself into the sand over the edge of the road.

After about ten miles, great green stretches suddenly appeared on either side of the road, signs proclaiming 'This is a new irrigation project'. We passed a dead camel with a crowd of people standing round it, holding hands. I wondered how they would remove it.

There was probably a few hundred piastres in it for some sharp fellow, but I was glad it wasn't my problem.

About twenty miles from Alex, the road forked by a giant model of a Pepsi Cola bottle top, blue and red and white. We took the right turn, and left the desert behind us. Flowers were growing now on either side of the road, yellow flowers like buttercups, cactus plants with wide, fleshy leaves, and trees instead of sand. On the horizon I could see the fingers of factory chimneys, pouring out white smoke, and then a river, then an oil depot with a fence round it, and crates stamped 'Moscow', then a field full of baby camels. They looked just the same as the big ones, only smaller, which wasn't surprising, but the camel is such a strange anachronism of an animal, designed by a committee, so they say, and thus the only beast that never loves its master. When you see his master, you can't really wonder.

On either side of the road, lakes glittered under the sun like mirrors with clumps of reeds and grey brown dry thistles that rattled in the wind. Buffaloes stood up to their stomachs in the water. Here and there men slept at the roadside; their canoes were stuck in the reeds, half ashore, half afloat.

We were almost into Alexandria, white with domes and mosques and minarets, and the tall yellow square buildings of blocks of flats, with the chimneys pouring out their fog of smoke beyond them. The wind carried a strong smell of mud and dung from the drying salt flats. Not at all as I'd imagined Alexandria from reading Lawrence Durrell.

The road was double tracked now, pitted with holes, and grass growing in side streets.

The houses were shabby, and, from windows in blocks of flats, wooden poles pointed out at us, strung with washing. Taxis with yellow bodies and black wings and tops, looking like huge metal wasps, droned past, and men toiled like mules between the shafts of carts of bananas. Everything appeared to be broken down, and yet for centuries Alexandria had been Egypt's second city. Now it looked like a stage-set for a Middle East slum.

We came into the centre of the city, close together, travelling slowly. Boys on cycles with other boys squatting on the handlebars seemed to have a death-wish to disappear under my huge wheels, and I kept my thumb almost incessantly on the horn button.

Hassan led us under the shade of new blocks of flats, up a wide street where litter blew about, whole sheets of newspaper lifting in the wind like sails. In the distance we could see cranes, and the masts of ships, and then a funnel and masthead flags stretched tight in the wind.

We came through a street clogged with carts and old cars, and the docks were ahead of us. I don't know what I expected—water, I suppose, and ships, but here we seemed to be still in the middle of the city. Hassan stopped, and Kent jumped out of his car and ran back to me.

'There's only room inside the dock gates for two cars at a time,' he explained. 'We're leaving the Bugatti here. Another plug's oiled up and we'll have to clean the lot, otherwise I'm afraid it won't start again. Maria will stay with it, and you come with your papers. O.K.?'

I had no reason to argue the point. All I wanted was to be out of the heat and fumes. Hassan manœuvred his car behind a two-wheel cart, where a man was selling cucumbers and bottles of lemonade with glass marbles for stoppers, just as they used to sell in South East London, when I was a boy.

I threw my suitcase into the Bugatti. The doors wouldn't lock, but then it didn't matter with Maria there. Anyhow, my luggage was insured. So am I. As I always say, I'm worth more dead than alive, but to whom?

'You've got the papers?' Kent asked anxiously.

'Everything,' I assured him.

'Right. The drill here is to say nothing unless you're asked a question direct. Otherwise, let old Hassan and Sabry do the talking. That's what they're here for. What this has cost me in baksheesh is nobody's business.

'All the customs men *should* do is look at the papers, check your passport number, and maybe see that the engine and chassis numbers we've given tally with the plates under the bonnets. On no account say what you can sell these cars for in England, though, in case they want more of a cut.'

I have exported enough cars from other countries, and I couldn't see why Kent was getting so het-up and nervous. Maybe it was the thought that he had actually had to fork out some of his own money, or, if not his own, some he had hoped to make his own for bribes? Or maybe he was edgy because this wasn't really his line of country, and the first time you do anything you feel a bit nervous. Or maybe this business of Maria and Snelling, the man she said she'd never heard of, had some bearing on things, though what, I couldn't imagine.

Hassan and Sabry were waiting for me inside the dockyard gates. To the left was a small building rather like an outsize doll's house. Through a window, two men, incongruously dressed in Army great coats, sat facing each other at a table. They must have been drowning in their own sweat.

One wore a hat, the other was bare-headed. From a shelf behind them a Japanese transistor blared out Arab music. They had empty cups and saucers in front of them, and flies buzzed busily round the rims of the cups.

Sabry went up to the window, pushed aside half a dozen loafers, waved to the men inside as though they were friends from schooldays, and they might well have been, and shook hands ceremoniously with them. Behind us, I noticed a soldier in the customary wretched uniform of fustian khaki and scuffed boots, swinging an ancient Lee Enfield rifle. He was chewing betelnut, and the juice dripped through his lips like blood.

I smiled as brightly as I could, not knowing what I was meant to be doing, or who was in command. I felt rather like an actor pushed out on stage in act two of some drama with no very clear idea of what has already happened in act one. I didn't altogether like the feeling.

The man with the hat stretched out his hand towards me. I took it, thinking he wanted to shake hands, but he waved aside this pleasantry, and instead gripped my document case. I let it go. He unsnapped the case and began to thumb through the papers. Then he said something to Sabry.

Sabry turned to me.

'He wants to know why you want to take the cars out of the country?'

'Because I deal in old cars,' I said, which seemed a sufficiently good reason. After all, it was true.

Sabry translated this. The man said something else. Sabry translated again.

'He wants to know where do you deal in these old cars?'

'I've told him on the form. In London, England. Aristo Autos.'

More translation. More questions, this time between the two characters at the table.

Sabry then said: 'He wants to know why you came here from London to deal in old cars.'

'For Christ's sake,' said Kent behind me. 'What the hell has it got to do with this nut? We're paying for the bloody things, aren't we?'

I nudged him in the ribs. You never know how much English these people understand.

'I came to Egypt because I wanted to see the Pyramids, the Sphinx, and other places I had read about,' I explained, not entirely truthfully. 'Also, there are many old cars in Egypt which we do not have in England.'

As this was being translated, the man nodded and looked at me. For all his shabby appearance, he wasn't a fool. His eyes were hard and small, worm-holes in a middle-aged skull, I held his gaze because I had nothing else to hold, and also I believe childishly that if you let your eyes drop in front of someone they think you are lying, although I had hardly opened my mouth. (If you let your eyes drop right out on the deck, of course, they think you're blind, and quite right, too.)

The first set of papers dealt with the Marmon. He paused over the chassis and engine numbers, and then reached up for a paper book on the shelf behind him, and thumbed his way through with one hand, keeping the other on the papers.

'What's he doing now?' asked Kent nervously.

Before I could nudge him again to silence, Hassan turned and explained.

'He's checking that these numbers actually relate to cars that one can export.'

'What do you mean?' I asked. 'That one can export?'

'Some military vehicles might have been stolen.'

I couldn't imagine confusing that ancient Marmon with a military vehicle, and neither could the man who compiled the book, because the old fool in the hat closed it, and ticked the engine and chassis numbers to show that they had been checked. Then he signed the bottom of each page, banged it with an ancient,

battered stamp, and passed the sheaf of papers over to his colleague, who also added something in Arabic script.

The Bugatti's papers gave us a little more trouble. There was
more conversation, more searching through the book. Sabry said:
'Did you know that this car was originally registered from the
Abdin Palace in Cairo? It was apparently one of King Farouk's
cars.'

'Fancy that,' I said, glad that I hadn't been sold a pup, even
if it wasn't a Royale. 'There's no snag about exporting it, surely?'

More conversation, arms held up towards the sky as though
to catch any manna that Allah might generously cause to descend,
then heads laid on shoulders, and much chatter from the lay-
abouts gathered round us at the open window.

Sabry translated this as briefly as he could.

'No reason at all. You've paid for the car. He's just telling
you this out of interest.'

'How kind of him,' I said. 'Thank him very much.'

I beamed towards the old man to show my pleasure. He beamed
at me.

He put out his hand; this time, we shook hands properly.
He said something to Sabry, who also grinned.

'He says you've a nice face,' translated Sabry.

'Thank him very much again,' I told him. 'Tell him I'll give
him a job any time he asks. I only deal with honest men.'

Everyone laughed when this was translated, and they got
through the further nonsensical details about the make of the
tyres, the number of miles the car had covered, the tools and type
of instruments, very quickly. As the man signed the last page and
picked up the papers about the Delage, Kent pushed his way to
the window.

'Tell him we've had great trouble with that Bugatti. It's broken
down, so we won't actually be able to get it here until tomorrow
morning. But we thought we should submit all the papers in a
batch, for all the cars and then he can check the numbers against
the Bugatti, if he wants to, in the morning.'

All this was translated. The man looked up at us, his eyes cold
and stony. Kent's excuse seemed rubbish to me, but I guessed he
knew what he was doing. I hoped he did, for I had no idea. There
seemed no trouble about the Delage number, though. And after
both men had stamped and signed the form, they pushed
back their chairs on the concrete floor and came out to look at
the cars.

One of the people hanging around the window began to lift
the Delage's bonnet. I slipped him a five piastre note, and opened
it myself, for I didn't trust his little fingers on the catches. Both
men checked the numbers on the brass plate beneath the bonnet
and stamped on the chassis frame and cylinder block.

It was all over very quickly and painlessly; I've had more

trouble at Tilbury, trying to take out some beat-up pre-war Y-model Ford Eight than I had here.

The man in the hat clapped his hands and two other characters appeared in nondescript dungarees and khaki berets. The old fellow tore a strip of paper off the last page of our forms and gave one to each of these men. They climbed into the cars, fiddled with the controls, and, after several attempts, managed to start the engines.

We stood watching them drive off towards the centre of the docks. Then there were more handclasps all round, more translations, and we drifted back towards the gates. When we were outside, I turned to Kent.

'What's the point of saying the Bugatti has broken down?'

'Because it very nearly has, and because I've got an idea for a much better deal,' he said. 'That's why.'

His eyes were glistening now, partly with relief and reaction, and partly at the thought of the size of the deal.

'What is it?' I asked him.

'I'll tell you when we're away from here. I'm taking a taxi. You follow with Maria in the Bugatti. We're going about forty miles out of town. I'll take it easy so you don't drop behind. Those plugs are all fouled up so you can't go very quickly.'

'What the hell is all this about?' I asked him irritably. I'd had enough of driving across the desert. This was like entering for a hundred yards race, and then being told, when you're half way up the track, that the organizers have suddenly decided to make it a two-twenty.

'I'll tell you when we get there. It's a good deal, I promise you.'

'What about the boat that goes tomorrow?'

'We'll be on it,' he assured me.

Before I could ask anything else, he turned away to hail a cab. I walked back to the Bugatti. Maria was standing against the bonnet.

'Everything all right?' she asked.

'I don't know,' I said. 'The cars went through without any aggravation, but Kent told the man this had broken down. Now we're going forty miles out of town for some reason.'

'He has an idea for a better deal,' Maria said. Her eyes were also shining; if she wasn't excited about this deal, like Kent, then she was excited about something else—or someone else.

'He didn't give me any details,' I said. 'Can you?'

'I'd rather he did.'

I climbed in behind the wheel. She got in the other side. The engine was a bit reluctant to fire; it was so hot that the petrol had evaporated, but it growled into life eventually, missing on one and probably two cylinders. At least Kent hadn't lied about the plugs.

I did a quick, reflex-action check on the controls, ran my fingers along the wires and pipes behind the dash to feel if any were loose. They weren't. One thin pipe showed a faint gleam of copper to the right of my seat. I traced it beneath the floor. It was a petrol pipe. My fingers felt the tap, probably fitted by some previous owner as a precaution against fire when the car was left unattended.

'Let's go,' I said, and let in the clutch.

Kent's taxi, big and brown as a burnished, blown-up bumble bee, began to move. I followed it, at about fifty yards distance. We went out on to the sea front, where waves pounded against rocks behind the stone sea wall, as though angry about something. I found it difficult to realize that this was the Mediterranean which, on the opposite coast of France, has no tide whatever, and whenever I've seen it has seemed to be perpetually placid.

We passed some houses, a café, and here and there, out on streaming rocks and broken chunks of stone and concrete from old anti-invasion defences, men crouched crapping, oblivious of the flying spray. Others, equally oblivious of the crappers, stood fishing. They made a curious and unexpected sight, not the sort of thing that features in the tourist pamphlets about ancient wonders and romantic customs of the Middle East.

On the other side of the promenade, the houses were built close to the road, all shuttered and dusty, with dull, yellow walls where years of heat had burned the life out of the paint. They had English names: The Gordon Hotel, The Cecil, The Carlton, The Ivy, but no English were there now. They had all gone long since; all that they had left behind were their names.

The front doors were closed, although in some downstairs rooms I saw a face, pale and disembodied, perhaps a caretaker, looking through the glass at the angry sea, maybe remembering other years, long ago when the nannies would be out, pushing prams with pale English children under silk sun-shades with scalloped edges.

Behind the harbour wall stood a fortress, white with Moorish domes, and then we were past the town, and the road stretched itself out along the desert by the edge of the sea, so that the sand seemed like one enormous beach. A soldier at a police post waved us through, without even bothering to stop us.

Forty miles, Kent had said. I watched the mileometer turn up the distance on the dashboard, and we had gone forty-three before the right flasher of the taxi began to wink, and he turned away from the sea towards the heart of the desert. We went up a hill, and over the crest lay a gigantic building.

It looked rather like the Palace of Versailles or even the Strand Palace, and wasn't much smaller than either or both, with pillars, archways, gargoyles for water spouts to catch the non-existent rain, and all the other Byzantine archaeological extravagances that come from too much money and too little taste.

At each end of this archaeological abortion ancient cannons pointed useless hexagonal mouths at the hill. Green roller shutters on all the windows were pulled down; the red, white and black tricolour of Egypt fluttered its two green stars from a mast behind the guns. A man in a fez crouched at the base of the pole, picking his nose.

'What the hell is this?' I asked Maria, because it could be any-thing.

'A former summer palace,' she said. 'It belonged to a member of Farouk's court.'

'And what is it now?'

'Partly a museum and partly an hotel. We've booked rooms here for tonight.'

'So Kent knew all along we weren't going aboard today?'

'Yes.'

'Then why the hell couldn't he have told me?'

'He was very nervous about getting the cars through. He's afraid of his position here in Egypt. Any foreigner lives under the threat of instant expulsion, without even a reason. If he had to go, he'd lose his whole business.'

'That's why he got me to sign the forms, so if anything went wrong I'd be carrying the can?'

'If you put it like that, yes.'

I did put it like that, as the divorcee told the High Court judge, but I still didn't see why Kent had to be so secretive.

'I would have thought it was obvious,' she said, irritated at my dimness. 'If you'd known we were going to switch this old Bugatti for another car, you might have acted nervously, and then the customs people could have suspected something.'

'What do you mean, switch it for another car?' I suddenly felt dread, like indigestion, in my guts. What the hell did she mean?

'Kent will tell you,' she said, as though she had already said too much.

I remembered the lie Kent had told me about owning the Cortina when it was only hired; I remembered being beaten senseless in Maria's flat, and her request that I wouldn't say any-thing about this to him, and I had that unwelcome feeling in my stomach that things were all going wrong for me.

I didn't know where, and how, or why, but as I watched Kent get out of his taxi and hold the door open for Sabry and Hassan, the fact that there were three of them to one of me, with possibly Maria as a neutral, did nothing to cheer me up. My old mother's only son was going to be right up to his neck in it again if he didn't watch out, and the thought brought me no comfort at all.

The taxi turned in a wide arc of dust and was away; someone must have paid the driver, even if Kent hadn't. Sabry and Hassan walked up the steps of the museum, not looking back. Kent came towards me, lighting a cigarette. I cut my engine. It was very quiet out there, and the rim of hill cut off the roar of the waves, so that they seemed like the distant murmur of a crowd.

'What's all this about switching a car?' I asked Kent irritably. He looked sharply at Maria.

'I said you'd tell him,' she said quickly.

'It's a much better deal,' he said defensively.

'For whom?'

'For all of us. Sorry I had to string you along a bit, but I was scared you might give something away at the Customs if you knew what we were up to. I didn't know how good an actor you were.'

'I'm a method actor,' I said. 'And my method is always to be pleasant to anyone until I know they're heels. Where's this car you want switched?'

'In the garage of this hotel,' he said, nodding towards it. 'It's a long story. Let's book in, get a drink, and I'll see you on the terrace.'

'What's wrong with my room?' I asked. I wanted to get this nut on his own where he couldn't welch on me so easily.

'This is like Cairo. A lot of the rooms let to foreigners are bugged. We don't want to give ourselves away before we start.'

'Can't the terrace be bugged, too?'

'It's less likely. Purely from a technical point of view. Anyway, see you there in twenty minutes.'

I restarted the engine and drove up to the front of the hotel. The man who was picking his nose stopped picking and walked towards us. He was a big flabby fellow in a long brown coat, and a red belt with a huge brass buckle which still bore the Royal Arms of Egypt. He opened the door, took our suitcases out of the back.

'You have a garage?' I asked him.

'Yes, sir.'

I gave him my name. 'Put the car in the garage, then, and leave the key at the reception desk.'

He nodded.

Maria and I walked up the steps together. We might have been lovers, but we weren't. I wanted to keep my strength for whatever the night might hold, like not getting beaten up, like making sure I was aboard that boat on the following morning.

The entrance hall was gigantic. If I'd had a net and a couple of racquets and a tennis ball, we could have had a game. It was furnished in extraordinary style, with a French sideboard about forty feet long, a fireplace with a huge gilt-edge mirror above it, and an Italian ceiling picked out in panels. Red tapestries edged with gold hung from the walls. The floor was marble, and in one corner, looking incongruously insignificant, a reception clerk stood behind a glass-topped desk. Behind him were the key rings and pigeon holes for rooms. If this had been the summer palace for a member of Farouk's court, then what kind of style had Farouk commanded?

I gave the clerk my name, filled in the form, putting my profession as car exporter, which sounds more aristocratic than car coping.

'Room eleven, sir,' said the clerk.

Some webfoot picked up the key and carried my bag. I followed him down the corridor, under pictures of King Farouk as a little boy, and a calendar that stood at Saturday, 26 July, 1952, which was the day he was forced to abdicate, and so presumably a date to remember, either for good or ill, depending on which side of the social or political fence you happened to be.

The landings were thick with tapestries and marble tables, gilt chairs with round cushions embroidered with red roses in the middle of a black centre, and all edged with grey. On one wall was a De Lazlo painting of Farouk as a child, with a red fez and open shirt and jacket, and short trousers, so cunningly executed that his eyes followed me like the eyes in that Lord Kitchener recruiting poster.

The page opened a door on the left, and I was in my room. It was the strangest hotel-room I had ever seen, but then the whole set-up was as odd as a two-pound note, so I didn't fall about. The walls were panelled in pale green wood, picked out with gold. A Persian carpet covered most of the parquet floor. From each wall the Egyptian Royal crest looked down, like crown and anchor symbols. The bed was about twelve feet square. There was a fireplace with a gilt-framed mirror above it, and an ancient gold telephone with a tiny hand crank.

I slipped a handful of small change into the page's grubby fist and locked the door behind him. I had a quick glim around the room in case I could see a microphone, but I wasn't really sure what it would look like, anyhow.

I didn't see anything odd, apart from a couple of big cockroaches. I turned back the bed quilt quickly so the bugs wouldn't have time to run away, but the sheets were clean. I suppose in a former Royal palace you have different standards from a doss-house in the Earls Court Road.

I opened my suitcase, took out a packet of Alka Seltzer, ran the tap until the water turned from brown to amber, mixed them in a glass, swallowed them and felt a bit better. Then I went out, along the corridor and down the stairs to the terrace. Kent was sitting under a striped golf umbrella at the far end, as far away as he could get, without actually camping on the sand.

'I didn't order until you came,' he said.

I guessed he hadn't.

'I'll take a whisky, then,' I told him.

He frowned. 'It's very expensive here.'

'It'll come off your profits.'

'*Our* profits,' he corrected quickly.

A waiter materialized and then shuffled away and returned with two whiskies already poured out in the glasses. He did his stuff with the syphon, and went back from whence he came, and whence he came was no concern of mine.

Kent looked around in his conspiratorial way, to make sure the man was out of sight, and then jerked his head back to invite me to move a little closer. I shifted the white metal chair nearer to the edge of the table. If I was any closer, I thought, people would say we were in love, and I suddenly wondered who could love this mean man with the soul of an accountant, for so far as making money is concerned, most accountants are like eunuchs: they know how it's done, but they can't do it themselves.

'So what's it about, then?' I asked. 'Why the hell are we here when we could be aboard that boat without any problems at all? What's this better deal you spoke about, and the car you want switched?'

'It's a long story,' he said nervously.

'So you keep saying. But I've got a long time. Maybe we'll both do a long time in some Egyptian jug if your plan comes unstuck. So let's have it all and never mind about my being a good or bad actor. I'm a damn' good audience.'

He cleared his throat, rubbed his chin with his hand nervously.

'I don't know what you remember about Farouk, but it's probably not much, except he was fat and wore dark glasses and had lots of girl friends? Well, that's all true. And as Sabry told you, he had an enormous collection of fast cars. Since he was rich —he left two hundred and fifty million dollars when he died— Farouk could indulge this fancy, and any others, too.

'Well, when he got the heave, General Neguib—who had seized power—auctioned off all these cars. His government wanted rid of them as quickly as possible. They were only an embarrassment to a country trying to work out some more equable scheme of life.

'But back then, prices for old cars weren't very high. Some of them were almost given away. One, in fact, wasn't even sold at all. It wasn't in Cairo at the time, and when it was discovered some time after the sale, no one was interested.'

'Where was it?'

It seemed a good question, and it was all I could think of to say.

'Here. In this summer palace. A courtier was using it.'

He paused, as though all this should make me fall about. I sipped my whisky and sat where I was.

'The point is,' he went on, 'that car's *still* here.'

'So?'

'So I want to switch it for that Bugatti you brought along. It's a Bugatti, too, of course.'

'Of course.'

It could hardly be anything else.

'Why is it here?'

'Because it's become part of the furniture, that's why. If you're a tourist and go round the ex-King's apartments—he had a suite here, just in case he felt like a night by the sea—you'll be shown the ex-King's desk, the ex-Queen's bedroom, his lavatory, her bathroom, even his medicine cabinet with Elastoplast and his old Optrex bottle and a tube of K.Y. jelly. You may also be shown this car. It's an exhibit.'

'What's so special about it?'

'I don't know much about cars,' said Kent. 'But Maria tells me she's seen American tourists go mad when they see it. It's a Royale two-seater, with some kind of special sports body. Bloody great petrol tank which would take you half way round the world, headlamps the size of searchlights, horns as big as bugles. You know much more about all that than I do.

'Once a year, this car is removed from the public gaze, and a crowd of mechanics from Alex set about refurbishing it, putting back the little bits that tourists have stolen, painting over the scratches, and so on. This is what's happening now.'

'Well, how the hell *can* you switch cars? It doesn't seem feasible. The Royale must be too well known. It's bound to be recognized.'

'There's a risk,' he agreed. 'But not very great. Let me ask you a few questions and you'll see how little that risk really is. Tell me, have you ever been to the Tower of London?'

I shook my head. 'Never.'

Why should I go there? After all, I live in London. I can go there any day of my life and so I've never been at all.

'Windsor Castle?'

'No. Only the pub of that name in Notting Hill.'

'The Royal Mews at Buckingham Palace?'

I shook my head.

'Exactly,' said Kent smugly. 'Because you live in London. Only tourists go to places like that. It's the same here.'

'You mean to tell me that those customs men at the docks at Alex wouldn't recognize this car if they saw it?'

'Exactly. Sabry tells me that they're only paid nine pounds a month on which they have to bring up a family. That doesn't leave much over for coming forty odd miles to this Palace just to look over an old car that Farouk owned years ago, does it? How could they get here, anyhow? There are no buses, and they can't afford taxis and they don't run cars and it's too far to walk. Ten to one, they've never even heard of the car, let alone seen it.'

'The customs men aren't the only ones, though,' I pointed out. 'We'd have to drive it there. People on the road would see it.'

'Of course,' agreed Kent. 'That's where you come in.'

That's where I go out, I thought. I didn't like the sound or the smell of this. My name was on those manifests, not Kent's. I would be the one who did time in some underground Egyptian gaol, not Kent.

'You're making heavy weather of it,' he said, as though he'd read my thoughts, and maybe he had. Maybe they were what anyone else would be thinking in my position.

'When I say this is where you come in, that's exactly what I mean. This Royale is painted yellow and black—just like the Bugatti you've driven here. No one stopped me on the way to Alex, or you on the way here, did they? Right. And no one will stop us when we take the Royale to the docks tomorrow.'

I liked the way he used the Royal or editorial plural. How many of us were going to drive the bloody thing, then?

'What about the chassis numbers?'

'We've got the Type 57 here, haven't we?'

I nodded.

'Well, use your loaf. We take off the plate with the chassis and engine numbers from under the bonnet, and screw it on Farouk's car. You can fill in the number that's stamped on the engine block with a bit of putty or some paint. They'll never check that, anyhow—they didn't with the other cars, now, did they? Be fair.'

I was fair; they hadn't.

'Right. We've already established we have three cars, one a Bugatti. We've also established that the Bugatti has broken down, and we've given them the numbers.

'This will go through very easily. After all, Hassan and Sabry know these people. They've got their contacts, money's changed hands. It'll be days or even weeks before the switch is discovered. By then, we'll be back in England.'

This might be so, but it might equally well not be so.

I sat sipping my drink, thinking, watching the desert still fluid with heat in the distance, shimmering as though the sands were already liquid glass.

I knew now why they had described the car I had driven as being a Royale when it wasn't. Kent had obviously given this scheme a lot of thought and preparation. This, I didn't like. He'd probably had the idea before he contacted me in London. Maybe he'd offered me that old Delahaye so cheaply simply because he wanted to hook me—as he had succeeded in doing.

If this was so, the whole business about Snelling buying the car back for £100 more than I had given for it began to make sense. Kent was so mean he'd skin a turd for a farthing, and he just couldn't bear the thought that he was losing a potential profit, even if he could make a hundred times as much—as he would if we found a Royale.

It's not the money that's the root of evil, but, as the Good Book says, the love of money. And the love of money, the prospect of a deal, the hope of an old-car killing so big it was practically a massacre, had lured me here. Kent had held out bait and I'd bitten. I didn't like that, either, for since my name was the only one on all the manifest papers, if anything went wrong, I'd be the only one to fall in the cactus. Sabry had already taken my money, and they'd simply sail away to take the profit on the two cars aboard ship, while I stayed behind to take whatever punishment an Egyptian court decided. This, I liked least of all. I may bend the truth a little, I may turn back mileometer readings, and I do—and who doesn't, in my business?—but I have never been a ringer, substituting one car for another. This didn't seem a particularly good time to start.

'Why take the risk?' I asked. 'With the Bugatti we've already got, we'll probably make five hundred each, after all expenses, if we split down the middle.'

He looked at me. 'On this one we'll make ten times that amount. Easily. Probably more.'

He could be right, and the way he said it, his eyes narrowed so that their acquisitive gleam didn't show so plainly, I knew he'd hopes of something even higher.

'It's a lot of bread,' I agreed.

'It's a lot of car. Come and see it before you raise more objections.'

We finished our drinks and went into the hotel. Sabry was sitting on a chromium-plated tubular chair, a styling refugee from the nineteen-thirties, turning over the pages of a magazine, obviously waiting for us. He stood up as we arrived. We followed him without a word down a corridor, through a door marked 'Privé'.

It shut soundlessly behind us, and we were in the servants' world, lifted from Edwardian England, with bells hanging on curved springs; the back of the door was even covered in green baize, nailed on with brass headed tacks. A stone staircase led down to some basement. There was a metal rail, and the white-washed walls were cut and gouged where trays had scratched against them as servants had hurried to and fro on their masters' bidding. The good old days, all right; so long as you were on the right side of that door.

We went down these stairs and through another door. Someone had oiled the hinges and locks so liberally that the stuff was actually streaming down the woodwork. I wondered whether this had been Hassan or Sabry.

The garage stretched the whole length of the hotel, and beneath it; three sides were built into the sand. The fourth had the doors. The walls were concrete, and great stains and patches of crystals had formed where dampness had seeped through from the sand. The vast cellar was divided by vertical wooden partitions, each about twenty feet apart, so that a driver or mechanic could work on a car in seclusion, without any risk of being in anyone else's way. Along the far wall was a bench with shelves above it for spares, and spring clips for spanners, all in order of size. Whoever had designed this garage had been an experienced engineer.

Sabry led us past four or five empty booths, their concrete floors stained by oil that had dripped from cars of long ago. I remembered the incident of the Hispano-Suiza that had been driven in 1919 from Paris to Nice in sixteen hours—an immense achievement—and then gone on display in the local showroom, with a clean sheet of white paper under its engine to prove that Hispanos didn't leak oil.

We reached the Type 57 I had driven from Alex, and in the next booth I saw the Royale. It was so large, I would have seen it a couple of miles away.

When the Queen of Sheba visited Solomon, she reported in the Bible that, as regard to his magnificent style of life, 'The half of it had not been told me.' I felt the same when I saw this mechanical leviathan that Le Patron had created, this Brobdingnagian Bugatti.

It looked 400 feet long, but probably was about nineteen; the bonnet, from the elephant mascot to the windscreen, was exactly seven feet. It had a yellow torpedo body with two doors, and two seats so close together the driver would rub thighs with the passenger. With the sort of passenger a young man would have carried in this car when it was new, this would have been no hardship, but rather an earnest of even closer contact to come.

The wings were like black tear-drops, as on the 812 Cord, but with this difference; inside the front wings, two small lockable cupboards had been built, so concealed that you had to look carefully to see their fastenings and their hinges. These were for tools, and maybe even a couple of bottles of Brut.

The body tapered down to a sharp wedge on the tail, and the fins of the wings, sharp as many a knife, trailed slightly behind this.

The tail and the wings were ribbed with chromium beadings. I licked my thumb and then rubbed it along the chrome. The plating glittered like new.

The front of the car was imposing, with its high horseshoe-shaped radiator, its giant Marchal headlamps, with mirrored reflectors, the two Zeiss spotlights, a cluster of air horns that could have come from the brass section of an orchestra but hadn't, and on the radiator cap, that mark of luxury, the silver elephant with which the patron had endowed the Royale. Some way behind this, just in front of the windscreen, was a green glass Lalique mascot.

You don't see these now, because yobbos in car parks would smash them, or steal them, or tear them off and throw them away, but in the thirties, when these yobbos were still unborn, and their equivalents, confined in tenements and stews and hutches, hadn't the energy or the mind for the senseless destruction of beautiful things, these glass mascots were not only fashionable, but feasible.

This mascot would light up from within at night, and gliding behind that greenly illuminated Indian head, with the hiss of the big carburettor and distant drumming of the exhaust, it must have been wonderful to be alive—and rich. I'm still alive—but rich? Now that's something different altogether.

I walked round the car, examining the body. It was in good nick; rarely can such a long body have held only two people, as the gynaecologist said of the six foot five mother of twins, or, if you prefer to be classical, as Shelley wrote on another occasion altogether: 'Look on my works, ye Mighty, and despair.'

I'd have despaired of ever finding a parking space for this elephantine monster, if it had been mine. One thing puzzled me as I examined it; there should have been a dickey, with a small step behind the driver's door—for mothers-in-law and such other undesirables as the owner had been compelled reluctantly to carry—to mount up into this dickey.

I bent down and examined the curve of the metal at an angle, and could just see where the bolts had been removed and the holes soft-soldered over and rubbed down. The dickey lid had been welded shut, so the car had a completely clean sweep, without any join to mar the line.

On the back of this truly gigantic boot was a small luggage carrier, with its Vuitton travelling trunk still strapped in position, the leather oiled, the nickel buckles polished. How standards have changed, I thought, when today the owner of the most modest car demands a boot large enough to hold luggage for a month's holiday for four, while the owner of this magnificent monster had to be content with cramming his belongings into a small case under the winds and rains of heaven.

Just in front of the case was a huge petrol filler cap, the size of a saucer. If the tank was commensurate with the size of the filler, the driver could surely make a trip from Cairo to the Cape, without stopping at a petrol station, which might be useful if anyone had such a journey in mind.

Cars nowadays are designed by committees and look that way, but not this car. In the heroic days of the motor-car, when this had been designed and built, one man said how things would look and where they would go; and they went.

I have never been particularly drawn to Bugattis myself, because they are so highly strung they make a racehorse seem as untemperamental as an undertaker's mute. But they certainly have character, inherited from their creator, old Ettore, one of the greatest individualists in the whole history of the horseless carriage.

He was born in Milan, and his father sent him to an art school, where he made as little progress as his brother Rembrandt, who was studying at a technical college.

The two brothers met one holiday, compared failures—and agreed to switch careers. Within a few years, Rembrandt became a distinguished sculptor, and Ettore a manufacturer of classic cars. Father doesn't always know best.

Ettore designed the sort of cars he liked, and lived the kind of life he liked. In hot weather, he wore a beige bowler hat with holes he'd personally punched in it. Sometime he alternated this headgear with a pith helmet of the kind worn in the French colonies. Around his waist he strapped a leather belt with two holsters, not for pistols, but for carrying his measuring instruments, notebook and pencils.

At the height of his cars' acclaim, he produced fifty cars a month in an extraordinary factory at Molsheim on the fringe of the Vosges mountains.

Originally, this had been a dye works in pawn to a bank. When Bugatti had made his first car, he showed it to the banker, hoping for financial backing, and the banker was so impressed that he offered to rent this factory to Bugatti so he could start production. Here, Bugatti became virtually self-supporting. Not only did he have his own bronze and aluminium foundries, he reared pigs and poultry, prize-winning cattle, even ran a private distillery to produce his own liqueurs. He grew his own vegetables, and his table wines came from his own vineyards. For relaxation, he had a stable of thoroughbred hunters, and his own riding school.

After a dispute with the local electricity company, Bugatti built his own generating plant. He cycled round his factory on a bicycle of his own design, and knew all his employees by their first names. During the First War, he buried three of his racing cars in his factory compound in case they should be confiscated. After the war, he dug them up and entered them for the 1920 Le Mans race. Although they were seven years old, one came in twenty minutes before the next arrival. That's how far ahead the Bugatti was, and it stayed out front through the twenties and the thirties.

Then, in 1936, the twentieth century rudely caught up with him; his firm experienced its first labour troubles: Ettore Bugatti was locked out of his own factory. Mortified and humiliated, he withdrew to Paris, and never visited Molsheim again. He ran his factory by remote control—just as Sir Henry Royce ran the Rolls-Royce factory in Derby, for a generation, from Le Canadel in the South of France, after he left England on doctors' orders in 1911, following years of overwork.

When Bugatti's customers dared to complain that some Bugatti cars were hard to start on cold mornings, Ettore retorted that they should be kept in a heated garage. In fact, their engines had generally to be warmed up on one set of plugs, and then another set substituted for running on the road. Only distilled water was advised for their radiators, and an oil of specific purity was ordained for the engines. And if any customers still grumbled at the expense, and inconvenience, then they either couldn't afford to keep a Bugatti as it deserved to be kept, or they weren't the type to appreciate one, and so to hell with them.

I feel the same about some of my own customers, but only seldom do I tell them so.

I walked round the car again. The leather was good and the dashboard was inlaid with mother-of-pearl. The knobs on the switches were the original whalebone. The white faces of the dials had faded to the colour of bleached bone; or maybe they were ivory. They could have been. If they were, some old elephant had certainly not been robbed in vain.

I felt the steering wheel; the linkage had no play, and the four horn buttons were still in place, one under each slender spoke, with an eight-day clock in the centre. The switches I clicked moved with the precision of a hinge on a Fabergé box.

I looked across at Kent. He was looking at me, his face creased like a rumpled suit.

'So, what do you think?' he asked.

'I think it's worth a fortune. Correction. I don't think that. I know.'

'Will you do it?'

'It's a bloody great risk,' I said, but I was wavering. It was a bloody great car. Kent hadn't over-estimated the profit potential. We could get £15,000 in any currency for this. It was one of the real rarities, like the Larz Andersen 1906 Charron with its built-in lavatory, or the old Shah of Persia's gold-plated Pierce Arrow.

I'd like to check the engine numbers, for it could just have been a fake, using one of the later railcar engines, but then I'd easily find out, for the originals had the prefix 'W' on them—just as the numbers of engines in present-day cars often conceal their date of manufacture.

There might be difficulties about advertising this car in case someone in a local Egyptian Embassy recognized it, but this could be arranged. After all, people switch paintings and sell them for fortunes openly in auctions, don't they? There's something snobbish and O.K. about art dealing or even the wine trade, which there certainly isn't about flogging old cars.

I stood looking at the Royale, not really seeing it, wondering about our chances, wondering, odd as this may seem in an old-car dealer, about my own conscience. As I've said, I've never ringed a car before, and although there has to be a first time for everything, even death, I wasn't eager to put a foot on that slippery slope which leads so swiftly down to the dreaded hinterland of stolen cars and forged papers and the whole unpleasant involvement of lies and counter-lies.

'Well?' asked Kent anxiously.

'Let's get out in the open air,' I said. 'This place may have ears, like the hotels in Cairo.'

We went up the stairs and he followed me out on to the veranda, and then down the stone steps to the desert. As we walked, grains of sand filtered through the joints in my shoes and filled my feet. They felt like my conscience, grating on me.

'I don't like it,' I said. 'The risks are enormous for one thing, and it's dishonest for another.'

'Dishonest?' repeated Kent in amazement. '*Now* he says it. What about all those false values we put on the manifest? What about the bribes we're paying. Dishonest? *Of course* it's dishonest. But think of the money at the end, boy. Think of the deal.'

'Think of what happens if it goes wrong,' I said, for I was. 'Think of what the Good Book says. "A good name is rather to be chosen than great riches".'

'It didn't say how great the riches are,' Kent pointed out practically. 'That car must be worth fifteen grand. Think.'

'I am.'

The thought of the profit was already pressing on my mind like a heavy old man on a young girl.

'Well, we haven't got all day,' said Kent. 'If we're going to switch the cars, we'll have to get cracking soon.'

I thought how strange were the different ways in which people react to different stimuli. I've known lethargic men suddenly leap about because a young girl in tight slacks and with big charlies comes on the scene. I've seen the same thing happen when free drink flows like the fountains of Rome, and here was Kent, as mean a man as ever pinched a penny, going ecstatic, adrenalin pouring through his blood, as fast as petrol would stream through the carbs on that car, simply at the prospect of profit.

I left him and went up to my room and sat down in an easy chair, and looked at the wall. I don't want to claim credit for having principles, for maybe the real reason I was holding back was fear that perhaps I'd be left at the docks with my principles and the wrong car, while everyone else went off.

I don't know how long I was sitting there, my thoughts going round and round in my mind like snowflakes in a kaleidoscope, and then jarring up again at the prospect of what would happen if things went wrong. The door opened and Maria came in.

'He's told you?' she asked.

'Yes,' I said. 'I suppose you knew all along?'

She nodded. I wasn't paying her. There was no reason why she should have told me, but I rather wished she had. I always look for one ally when a deal grows complicated; someone I can trust. Here, I had no one I could completely trust, no one I'd like to be alone with if things went wrong. She sat down without being asked. She could have stayed standing for all I cared.

'Let me tell you about that car,' she began.

'Tell me.'

She was going to in any case, so nothing I said would make much difference.

'I had a relation in Cairo who was employed at the Palace. His job was—rather special. He bought this car for King Farouk and he had the body especially made, but he was never paid.'

'That's his problem,' I said. 'Why didn't he put in a bill?'

'He did. Frequently. But it's rather difficult when you're working for a king. You've had this trouble in England with some of your kings in the past. Royalty can be pretty slow when it comes to picking up the bill.'

'What you're really trying to tell me is that this car could conceivably be said to be yours—or your relation's?'

'Yes,' she said. 'You simplify things a bit, but that's true.'

'So, to ease my aching conscience, you give me this crumb of comfort, that if I stole this car I would actually be helping someone, apart from myself. Is that right?'

She nodded. 'Yes.'

I didn't know whether what she said was true, and I didn't greatly care. I was like the fellow on the psychiatrist's couch, or in the priest's confessional box, who wants to believe that all will be well, and who accepts assurances even when they seem against all reason. After all, you must believe something. I suppose I wanted to believe her.

'Will you do it?' she asked.

'I'll think about it,' I said, and stood up.

Maria got the message, such as it was, and stood up, too.

I watched her walk out of the room, and made up my mind, which had probably been made up more or less since the moment I saw the car, and only confirmed by what she had told me.

To hell with them all. I wouldn't do it.

CHAPTER FIVE

I WENT TO FIND KENT, to tell him, but he wasn't in his room or in the bar. Finally, I tracked him down on the veranda. He was sitting alone at one of the circular marble tables, drinking a Perrier water, which was the cheapest drink he could find, short of putting his head in the sea.

'I've been thinking it over,' I told him, 'and the answer is No.'

I sat down, facing him.

Kent didn't get up; he just looked across the table at me coldly, as though trying to decide whether I was serious, or whether I could be persuaded, but at no cost to himself, either in cash or kind.

'You're sure?' he said at last.

'Certain. I may be a bit bent, but I'm not circular. I've never switched a car, and I don't want to start now. Even though Maria has told me that legally it could even be hers because some relation was never paid for it.'

'That's true, you know.'

'Maybe. But it seems just a bit too convenient a discovery for my taste.'

Kent stood up, held up his glass in case there was a drop of water left that might escape him when he'd paid for it. There wasn't, so he put it down again.

'Then we'll do it without you,' he announced grandly. 'But, remember this. There's no cut out of this car for you when we get back to London. Right?'

'Absolutely right,' I said, 'so long as you pay me back my five hundred quid. I don't deal in hot cars.'

'The way you go on, like a bloody Sunday School teacher, you're lucky to be dealing in any cars,' said Kent irritably. Then: 'I'll tell the others.'

He went up the steps into the hotel. I didn't want to stay where his jack had been warming the seat, so I moved to another table and tapped on the top until a waiter appeared, and I ordered another whisky.

Even if I wasn't any longer personally involved, my name was still on those manifests. I could still be hauled in for questioning if anything went wrong—and I'd still be the only one not sharing any profit, if they succeeded. It was an ironic, heads-they-win, tails-I-lose situation, but there was nothing I could do about it now, so I drank the whisky and watched the sun bedding down for the night behind the hills.

It suddenly grew cold, and I shivered, for I felt that the dying sun was also watching me. I wished I was miles away, aboard that boat, out beyond the twelve-mile limit, heading for home. Most of all, I wished all this aggravation about spiriting away an old car was simply something I'd read about somewhere. I felt uneasy in my bones and my water about the turn events had taken. I had allowed myself to be manœuvred into a position of acute disadvantage, as the nun told the roué, and I didn't like it. If someone has to be pushed, I liked to do the pushing.

There was no one I wanted to talk to, and I'd nothing to read except cheque stubs, which make depressing reading when the money is all going one way—out. Suddenly, it was dark, and dogs were beginning to bark boldly in the empty distance of the desert, and the sound of the sea seemed nearer because there were so few other sounds.

I walked up into the hotel. A few waiters were pattering about in a giant hall that had once no doubt seen embassy receptions and court balls—I mean the ones where there's dancing—and that sort of thing, but it all seemed empty and faded and pointless now. They looked like actors in search of a play.

Under the crystal chandeliers, the tables had white cloths and glittering glasses; red desert flowers floated in silver bowls of water. It looked very romantic, but there was no one to be romantic with, so I sat down, ordered myself a shish kebab and a bottle of iced beer. Both came very quickly, because there were obviously far more waiters and cooks in the kitchen than guests to serve. In fact, only six or seven other people were eating, and about twice this number were standing about, waiting on them.

I hate eating alone, probably because I do so much of it, and it was about eight o'clock when I'd finished. I went up the stairs to Maria's room. A 'Do not disturb' notice was hanging on the handle, and I wondered what she was doing, whether she was having it off with someone. Whoever it might be, it wasn't me, so I didn't disturb her, but went down the stairs again to the garage.

Kent or Hassan or Sabry should be there, which shows how low I'd sunk in my search for conversation. I didn't like any of these characters much, but at least they were people to talk to.

The garage was very cold now that the sun had set. I was reminded of some sort of vault or mausoleum. The air had a chill in it. I tried to find the light switch but I couldn't, so I went down the steps very carefully. A strong smell of quick-drying cellulose hung in the air. I searched around the edge of the stall where the big car was standing until I found a switch. This lit an inspection light that hung in a wire cage on the wall.

The car had torpedo sidelights, the sort that are shaped like pears, with a litle red lens at the back, and a huge glass bulls-eye in front.

One of the other Royales, I knew, had not been fitted with any lights, and when this lack was remarked on, it was explained curtly that there was no need, since this particular owner never drove after dark!

These sidelights were ordinary enough, except that someone had picked out the tiny ruby lens, at the rear of each one, leaving a hole. I began to see why the car needed refurbishing every year. Even in this remote spot, sightseers demanded souvenirs.

I walked around the car, and to my surprise the red lens had been picked out from the other sidelight, too. The big Marchal headlamps were of the type that originally had green tell-tale lights built into their casings, though why these were needed to tell the driver his lamps were on I never have discovered, for they were large as searchlights. But from now on any driver of this Royale would have to manage without them, for these were also missing.

I looked inside the car, over the mother-of-pearl dash and the nickel plated rims of the instruments. Lamb-skin rugs still covered the floor, and the leather felt soft, as though it was waxed every month, as it probably had been. What really interested me was the fact that the little blue and amber and red tell-tale lights in the dashboard, for the ignition, main-beam and oil, had also been prised away, and from their silver sockets the bulbs looked out at me like reproachful eyes.

Usually, when people have a touch of the old kleptos, they will take anything they can remove from the car, and this includes door handles and mats and ashtrays. But here someone had apparently removed all those coloured lenses and yet left the cigar lighter, which is the easiest thing to slip into your pocket from any car.

Why?

I walked over to the other Bugatti and shone the inspection light round it. It still smelled hot from its long journey, and a little oil had dripped out from the crank-case gasket where most Bugattis leak a little, on to the concrete floor. I flashed the torch around the front of the car, and then paused. Someone—perhaps the same person?—had removed the red oval radiator badge, and its screw holes looked at me, empty as tooth sockets.

I don't know why I went back to Farouk's car to examine that radiator badge, but I did. It had greasy finger prints round it. Someone had removed the badge from the car I had driven and fixed it on Farouk's car.

I flashed the torch around the garage to see whether I could see any of the lenses, or the badge that must have been on the big Bugatti, but it was empty except for a moped on its stand and a pile of sacks and rags behind it. Sometimes, in the barns and stables of country houses, one can discover treasure troves of old horns and mascots that have been wrapped in brown paper or rags for years and then forgotten. I once found a set of Stentor air horns, a Grebel searchlight, and a kneeling Silver Lady from a Rolls in a shed in Somerset, so, like the spinster who always looks under her bed every night, I live in hope.

I thought I would just give this bunch a going-over before I left, so I kicked the sacks lightly. Nothing rattled inside them, so I kicked them again, and burrowed through the oily rags, until I found a piece of blue cloth.

The last time I'd seen this, it had been Kent's jacket, and he was wearing it on the terrace outside.

He was still wearing it, but it wasn't doing him any good, and it never would again, either, for he was as dead as the scandal in last Sunday's newspaper.

I bent down and pulled the rags away from Kent's head. He lay, face down, and I could feel no pulse on his wrist or in his neck, which wasn't surprising, because there wasn't one. I turned him over. A little saliva dribbled out of the corner of his mouth. His eyes were open, but they weren't seeing anything now, not even a chance to economize, or the prospect of a profit at the end of the deal.

What had happened to him? Had he fallen, or had he been pushed? From the fact that he was lying buried under rags, I guessed he'd been helped unwillingly over the border to that undiscovered country from whose bourne no traveller returns, and I quote Shakespeare, who died three hundred and fifty-four years ago, so he can't prevent me.

Had Kent collapsed, and then been discovered, and his body concealed by some night watchman or other web-foot who feared he might be accused of killing a foreigner? Or was there something altogether more sinister?

Could he have discovered someone stealing those coloured lenses from the car and become involved in a fight? Of course he could, but this was surely no excuse for murder—if there ever is an adequate excuse for murder.

I felt in his pockets. His wallet was still there, with his passport. I opened the wallet; the notes inside were pressed together close as sardines in a can, but with rather more value. He even had a spring clip on them in case one should slip through his fingers. So he hadn't been killed for his money, and he could carry no currency where he was now.

I covered up the body. If I were asked why in a court of law— and it worried me that I might be—I couldn't give any reason, beyond the basic one that I didn't like looking at a corpse. I hadn't liked Kent much when he was alive, but dead I liked him less.

I didn't greatly like my own situation, either. Here I was in a strange hotel, in a not notably friendly country, with a car that apparently had belonged to that country's former king, and which was now about to be stolen on papers that bore my signature—while the man who had arranged this lay dead at my feet.

I put back the inspection light on its hook and I went up to my bedroom. I washed my hands and face and a very worried me looked back out of the shaving mirror. I filled a tooth glass with whisky, drank it and felt a little more like a human being. I wondered whether the others would still go on with the switch? I thought I'd better tell Maria. Sabry and Hassan struck me as being capable of looking after themselves, but I wasn't so sure about the girl; maybe I could help to look after her? I went along the corridor to her room, wondering what this might involve. The card was still hanging on her door. I banged on the panel.

'Yes?' she said.

'Open up,' I told her.

'I'm in bed.'

'Then get out of bed. It's urgent.'

Something in my voice must have made her realize I wasn't coming in for a quick fumble, for I heard her cross the room and then the bolt slid back inside the door. She opened it a few inches, and I pushed my way in, and locked and bolted the door behind me.

'What's all this about?' she asked.

She wore a dressing-gown. I glanced at the bed; at least she'd been in it alone.

'Have you seen Kent?' I asked her.

'Of course. He's down with the car. Is that all you came to ask me?'

Her voice was edged with suspicion, as mint sauce is edged with vinegar. Surely she didn't think I'd use this just as an excuse to get into her room? Well, I hadn't, had I?

'No,' I said to her spoken question and my unspoken one, and sat down. She remained standing.

'Well?' she went on.

'Well, he's dead.'

'*Dead?*' She repeated the word as though she had never heard it before, and sat down shakily on the edge of the bed. 'What do you mean, dead?'

'What I say. Mort. Kaput. Finito. The late lamented. Dead. I went down to see how things were getting on, but the garage was deserted. I poked around a bit and found his body under a pile of rags. Dead.'

'Are you sure? Couldn't he have fainted or something?'

'Very easily. But if he did, that faint or something proved fatal. If you don't believe me, go and have a look for yourself.'

'Were there any signs of—of a struggle?'

Her voice trembled slightly. For no reason at all, I suddenly thought of her flat back in Shepherds Bush, and being beaten up, and why she hadn't wanted me to mention this to Kent. It would be no use telling him now.

'None that I could see,' I said. 'Should there have been?'

'No. I mean, I don't think so. I just wondered whether maybe someone came in and thought Kent was an intruder or something, and there was a fight. Or it could have happened the other way round. Anyway, what do we do now? Tell the hotel manager?'

'If we do,' I said, 'we'll have to stay here until the police let us go. We'll miss that boat tomorrow. And goodness knows when another one will come that can take the cars.'

'We can't leave Kent here.'

'Why not? We can't take him with us, as he is.'

'Oh, my God.'

She put her head in her hands. I saw that her shoulders were trembling, and I thought with horror that she might be going to cry, but she didn't.

'Have you told Sabry and Hassan?' she asked.

'Not yet. I thought I'd tell you first. After all, you worked with him most.'

'Yes.'

I didn't see any mileage in telling her that the lenses had been stolen from the lamps. Maybe they hadn't even been there in the first place. I couldn't swear to it either way. And they weren't even my lenses. So why should I worry? They'd cost all of five shillings to replace.

'Will you still take that car out?' I asked her.

'Of course,' she said. 'Even if *I* have to drive it myself, we'll take it.'

'All that stuff you told me about some relation of yours having paid for the car—is that true?'

'Yes.'

'Who was the relation?'

'My father.'

I looked at her right in the eyes, as though she was trying to pass me a dud cheque, and she looked right back at me. She had pretty eyes, wide and dark. I didn't know whether she was lying or not. Do you ever, with women?

'Will you help me?' she asked. 'Now?'

'Yes,' I said at once, without really meaning to, and reversing my previous decision without a thought. Hell, I wanted to be involved with that car no more than I wanted a dose of clap. Even less, for clap is curable, and that car could bring infinitely more aggravation. Yet oddly, now I was committed, I felt better, more relaxed. I couldn't think why. I must have needed my head examining, though things in this line of country aren't what they were. Life is so rough, so they say, that the psychiatrists get right down there on the couches with their patients. You don't know who's curing who.

'So what do we do now?' I asked.

'I'll tell the others.'

'What time had Kent planned to move off?'

'Four forty-five tomorrow morning. This place has a night watchman, and he hands over to a day guard then. Kent checked. He was going to settle up the bills tonight, and explain we had an early start to make, so they wouldn't be surprised to hear a car going out. It will still be dark, so even if the new guard is around, he won't be able to see the car too closely.'

This all seemed reasonable enough. Even if some peasant was awake and saw the car go, he'd only have a few seconds to recognize it from its silhouette against the horizon, and if we drove without lights, or on side-lights for the first half mile, this would cut down the risk considerably. I reckoned, too, that I could count the Egyptian *fellaheen* who could distinguish a Type 41 Bugatti Royale from a Type 57 on the fingers of the Venus de Milo.

There's a risk in anything, as the eunuch told the pansy; this was the particular one we had to run. 'I'll tell the others, then.'

'Wait,' she said. 'Had Kent been robbed?'

'His wallet seemed to be full.' In death as in life, I thought.

'I'll come down with you. I want to make sure.'

Of what? I wondered, but all I said was: 'You don't want to see the body.'

'He was kind to me,' she said. 'The least I can do is to collect his papers.'

'I'll get them for you.'

She shook her head. 'I want to come down.'

She put on some clothes. I watched her dress and she didn't mind; neither did I.

We went along the corridor, down the stone steps and through the door with the green baize on its back and then down the concrete steps to the garage. I felt I'd been making the journey here so often I'd better start thinking about taking out citizenship papers, or maybe starting a job in the kitchens. The outside garage door was still open, and the stars peered in from several million miles away and saw nothing. We couldn't see all that much either, until I fumbled round and found the inspection lamp switch. I pointed out the pile of sacks.

'Here,' I said.

Maria knelt down beside the sacks as I began to lift them away one by one. Had I been on my own I'd have kicked them to find exactly where the body lay, but this seemed a little indelicate with the girl around. The sacks came away easily enough, like artichoke leaves.

She looked at Kent in the dim light. I reached into his jacket pocket and gave her the wallet. Then I squatted on my haunches in the semi-darkness beyond the circle of light, breathing the cold sandiness of the desert, and the whiff of cellulose and the dust of the concrete.

I didn't know what the hell to do, or what was happening, and I could think of no one who could help me. What an idiot I was to have agreed to help with the car. I could think of no reasons at all for doing this except maybe an absurd wish to appear quixotic, or maybe I wanted to help Maria, or put her in my debt. Or, maybe, I just wanted her.

We stood up and I coiled the flex of the inspection lamp as we walked back to the car. She glanced at it casually, and then bent down suddenly to examine the nearest sidelight; she had seen that the red rear lens was missing. She walked round the other side to examine that light, and then she looked at the driver's helmet tail-lights.

'The red glasses have all gone,' she said slowly.

'Yes. So have the coloured tell-tales on the dash. Someone's even taken the badge off the car I drove and stuck it on the radiator.'

She shone the light on the front of the radiator, examining the red and white name-plate.

'I don't like this,' she said suddenly, and I knew from the tone of her voice, she wasn't acting; she really was scared. 'Let's get out of here. *Quickly.*'

'Why?'

She didn't answer. We went up the stairs in silence and at some speed. Somewhere in the hotel, piped music was playing a sad, soft, wailing Middle Eastern lament. I suppose it had been in the background ever since we arrived, but you grow so accustomed to piped music that you can forget it's there. We shall have Muzak wherever we go. And, sometimes, too much of it.

'You think your room's bugged?' I asked, remembering Kent's warning.

We were in the corridor outside her bedroom.

'I'll tell you here, in case it is,' she said. 'Those glasses in the lights weren't glass at all. They were jewels. Rubies. The others were emeralds and sapphires. They're worth a lot.'

'I can imagine,' I said, and I could.

'Did Kent know that?' I asked her.

She nodded.

'What about Hassan and Sabry?'

'Sabry might have. I just don't know. He was one of Farouk's hangers-on, and knew my father. He was a court jeweller, too. He *could* have known—or he'd have recognized the stones if someone else pointed them out to him.'

'And Hassan?'

She shrugged.

'I wouldn't think so. I don't really know much about him. He's a cousin of the local chief of police. Kent thought he'd be useful.'

'No wonder Kent was anxious to get the car out.'

'Yes,' she said. 'No wonder.'

Her voice sounded flat as a punctured tyre.

'Do you think Kent disturbed someone stealing those jewels —and they killed him?'

'Could be.'

'Can I trust you?' she asked suddenly.

'To do what?' I asked. 'In a crowd, or alone together?'

'I don't mean that. I need your help. I'm desperately serious.'

'So am I. Is this about Kent?'

'Partly.'

'Then don't tell me here,' I said. 'It's too risky. Come outside.'

We were near the lift door. I pressed the button and the gates opened and we went down to the edge of the terrace. The moon was now halfway up the sky and the whole scene looked unreal, as though painted on a stage backcloth. A wind was blowing in from the sea, bringing a fresh smell of salt and seaweed. It felt much colder than I'd expected, and the stars were very bright, which was a lot more than I felt.

We walked a few paces into the desert until the sand, which was trodden down near the terrace, grew soft and feathery, and we began to sink over our shoes in it. We turned round, not speaking, and walked back to the garage. The loneliness of the desert was like a pain; I hated it.

'Now,' I said. 'What's so serious?'

'You don't know who I am, really,' Maria said, 'So I'll go back and explain a few things. My father's French. His name is François. My mother was Egyptian.'

'Was?'

'Yes. She died six years ago. My father had a job in the Abdin Palace in Cairo. He'd worked for various coach-builders in France. Chapron. Figoni and Falaschi. Saoutchik. And others. Farouk liked fast cars and cars with special bodies, and so he was a good customer.

'One of the firms my father worked for in Paris sent him to Cairo to make some modifications to a car Farouk had bought. Farouk became friendly with my father and offered him a job, in charge of his cars. After all, he had a hundred and twenty.

'The two men got on well. My father would organize some special sports car for him with a one-off body, or he'd fix up tickets for Le Mans. Things like that. And as they grew closer, my father organized more intimate things.'

She paused.

'Such as girls?' I asked her.

'Yes. Girls. French. Italian. Roumanian. Even English. Although my father was several years older than Farouk, they liked the same things—excitement, girls, parties. And of course, this worked both ways. Farouk didn't pay my father much, but from time to time, he'd tell him that, say, some foreign firms were going to tender for the contract to electrify the Cairo tramways, or build new rolling stock for the railways, or some such thing.

'He'd make them slap on an extra ten or twenty or even fifty thousand pounds for what he called special contingencies. This should have covered mistakes in calculations, rises in prices and so on but, in fact, it all went into my father's pocket.'

'Nice for him,' I said.

It was certainly better than horsing around trying to flog cars. I could see the attraction very clearly. What wasn't so clear was where I came into all this, and why I should be trusted. With what—confidence or cash? If I had the option, I'd follow Omar Khayyam's advice and take the cash and let the credit go. But maybe I wouldn't have any choice?

'I was about five when we moved to Cairo,' Maria went on. 'We lived in fantastic style. We had a house with thirty indoor servants and ten gardeners. This was our seaside place.'

'*This?*'

I looked round at the hotel, which was no larger than a barracks, with its spires and balconies and shutters, and the rows of blank windows looking out to sea.

'Yes. My father was very rich.'

'So what went wrong?' I asked her, because obviously something had, otherwise she would still be living in the hotel, not as a paying guest and secretary to a dead man, but as the owner's daughter.

'Farouk was kicked out.'

'Ah, yes.'

In all this, I had forgotten the most important point. Even so, old François must have been worth a bob or two. He'd surely made enough to set himself up in a corner shop somewhere?

'What did he do with the money, apart from living so well?' I asked her. After all, you can only eat three meals a day and most years have only 365 days.

'He sent a lot of it back to France, and the rest to a Swiss numbered account.'

'Did you and your mother know he was taking bribes?'

'Not then. He was always seeing people, entertaining them, having meetings. It was just business, so far as we were concerned. And then Farouk was deposed and it all ended, and we heard what had been going on.'

'Where were you then?'

'Here. In this house. July, nineteen fifty-two. We'd come down for two months, and were actually packing a few things for a picnic. We heard on the radio that Farouk had been forced to abdicate. My mother tried to telephone Cairo, to reach my father, but all the lines were blocked. We just had to wait here and listen to the bulletins which came over each hour.'

'What about your father? He hadn't been forced to abdicate?'

'Unfortunately, no. Farouk was allowed to take a number of his staff with him into exile. My father was actually going up the gangway of the royal yacht when two police officers stopped him. They said he was wanted for questioning.'

'About his bribes?'

'Yes. They knew all about him. After all, everyone in a position of authority was taking backhanders. The new regime wanted to stop this. Their intention was to keep my father in Egypt, virtually a prisoner, as a kind of living reminder that taking bribes has no future. We had a flat in Cairo as well as this house. He was kept under arrest there for several weeks.

'We had a pretty grim time. My mother had some jewels no one knew about, and we sold these to Sabry for about a fifth of what they were worth. He cut them down and got rid of them. He made a big profit, but at least he helped us, when no one else would. Then my father was allowed to come here.

'When Colonel Nasser took over from General Neguib, things eased a bit. I was allowed to go to school in France; my father's sister kept me. After my mother died, I came back here every year to see my father. The authorities didn't interfere with me, but they opened my letters to my father—and they gave me a pretty thorough search each time I came or went through the customs.

'In the meantime, they found my father a job—as a sort of curator in the house he had once owned—a servant where he had formerly controlled so many other servants.'

'If he had so much money in France and Switzerland, couldn't he have used it for a bit of bribery to get out? After all, let's not kid ourselves, it still goes on.'

I was thinking about Kent and his arrangements with the officials in Alexandria.

'My father had told his banks long before this happened that in no circumstances was any more than a thousand pounds to be paid to anyone who asked them for money — even if they presented his cheque or brought a letter from him. Egyptians are the best forgers in the world. He was afraid someone might whip the lot.'

'Didn't he try to get away?'

'Yes. Twice. After my last visit, I smuggled out five separate letters from him to his bank in France and collected a thousand pounds on each. I couldn't bring this money into this country because, as I said, I was searched so thoroughly every time I came through, so I left it in a bank in Marseilles.

'I got to know the manager of a provision shop in Alex whose van comes here every week with food. For two thousand cash, he was willing to drive the van himself and carry my father back to Alex in a laundry basket. For another three thousand, a steward in a cruise liner calling at Alex for a day, was prepared to come ashore, change clothes with my father, give him his pass, and let my father go up the gangway. The steward would jump ship and lose his job, but he reckoned he could get another easily enough.'

'What went wrong?'

Presumably, something had, or she wouldn't be telling me about it.

'My father was discovered at the police post. They searched the van. The driver, of course, said he'd no idea how he came to be there. He couldn't very well say anything else without implicating himself. So my father was brought back here. He wasn't punished. The guards found it all highly entertaining. After all, they were promoted for being so alert.'

'And the second time?'

'I organized that from outside. I still had access to that five thousand, and I found a French pilot who had been with the

O.A.S. in Algeria. He'd been running a shuttle service with a small plane, picking up agents.

'His idea was to set out for Tripoli in Libya, flying along the international airline corridor, and then he'd cut his engine and come down here. He was to do this at night. It was a two-seater plane and he'd a dummy in flying gear in the second seat. My father would be out in the desert to meet him; they'd throw away the dummy and then they'd take off.

'Well, he came down on a deserted airfield you British used to have five miles north of here. But the plane had been picked up on radar, and they were waiting for him. They thought he was an Israeli raider, so they didn't take chances. His excuse was that he'd lost his way. They checked his papers, and let him go.'

'Did they find your father then?'

'No. I'd disguised him for the trip as a Muslim widow, in black robes. Luckily, I had an emergency signal arrangement with the pilot in case anything went wrong. He was to switch on his flashing landing lights. I could see these across the desert for a matter of miles, and so we simply turned back.'

'What did that little lot cost you?' I asked.

'Two thousand. I had to pay that before I could get him even to attempt it.'

'Did your father make any other attempts to get out?'

'No. Egypt is a very difficult country to escape from. You can either leave by boat from Alexandria or Ismailia. You can fly out from Cairo, or cross the border in the south into the Sudan, or up north-west into Tripoli.

'That makes only five ways in or out—and each of them is on the watch for my father. There's immediate promotion for anyone who stops him. Instant dismissal, and maybe imprisonment, if he gets through. The rest of the frontier is just sand. No one could cross.'

'There must be foreign tourists down here, people who'd take a risk for a large sum of money?'

'You think so? Well, imagine *you're* a tourist in a museum in a foreign country which is virtually a police state, and suddenly the curator comes up and says: "Actually, old man, I'm *really* a millionaire. If you can get me out of this country I'll give you ten thousand pounds!" You'd think he was a nutter, wouldn't you?'

I had to agree I would. Nothing like that has ever happened to me in any museum; or out of one, either.

'How much freedom does he have now?'

'During the day, he has to keep to this palace or the grounds. There's only one gate he can use, anyway, and that has a watch-man on it. At night, he's not allowed out at all. If he were, I might conceivably have organized a boat to pick him up on the beach.'

'Why haven't you tried that?' I asked.

'For God's sake,' she replied. 'Where would I begin?'

I couldn't tell her, so I didn't try.

'If I'd asked about hiring a boat in Alex, they'd be on to me at once.'

'Do the police follow you, then?'

If they did, then they could easily be following me, and with Kent dead in the basement, this thought held no comfort.

'No. Not now. After all, why should they?'

It seemed to me that she'd already given me several convincing reasons why they should, but before I could list them, she went on: 'Anyhow, the Egyptians are so afraid that the Israelis will invade, they've a radar station right here in these grounds. Not a very good one, but strong enough to pick up anything at sea.'

'Why choose this place?'

'Because it's here. That's why. And because it has a well for water and a generator for electricity. There's nothing much else along this coast for another fifty miles. Even the police posts up and down the road have to draw water from here or Alex.'

I remembered the anti-aircraft guns at Cairo airport on the roofs of the building, surrounded by sandbags, like something out of a wartime newsreel. I remembered the guns mounted on rooftops along the road into Alexandria, and the troops with binoculars, searching the sky for planes, hopefully or fearfully, according to your political viewpoint and your faith in Egyptian martial qualities.

'Where's your father now?'

'I hope, in bed.'

I wouldn't mind wishing that for myself, I thought, but preferably not alone.

'Is he under guard at night?'

'Yes. The military post here has a brick guard room.'

'I saw it.'

'Well, he's inside. Locked up until seven tomorrow morning.'

'How many troops do they have here?'

'Not many. Probably only about twenty, I'd say, at a guess. In charge of the radar equipment, and an anti-aircraft gun.'

I didn't go much on François or on anyone else who takes bribes, because once you start giving or accepting a touch of the old backhander, corruption becomes infectious. Even so, it seemed to me that he had virtually been a prisoner for the last eighteen years, and this was a long enough sentence. After all, even murderers go free nowadays in half this time. And all François had murdered was honesty.

'What was your plan to get him out?'

'It all depended on Kent.'

'Did you like Kent?' I asked.

She shrugged.

'Not in that way. He was really only a small-time operator on the fringe of other men's deals. But he was useful to me for this one thing. More than useful—essential.'

'What was in it for him if you got your father out?'

'Fifty thousand pounds. Payable in Swiss francs, on a bank in Geneva. He could have had the money anywhere in the world, but that's where he wanted it.'

I wasn't getting it anywhere, but Geneva would suit me, too, I thought. For money, or the other thing.

'Kent was a very careful man,' she went on. 'He covered himself completely. If we couldn't get my father out, if the plan was discovered, you'd have taken the blame, for your name was on all the papers. Not his.'

'I know that,' I said.

'Also, if we couldn't get him out, Kent, would still have taken half your profits on the two cars already loaded. But if we had succeeded, then he'd have been rich.'

I'm not all that bright in the top storey, but I didn't need to wear a number eight hat to realize that no matter who'd made a profit, I was the only one in this deal who stood to make a loss. And not only a loss of money, but a loss of freedom. The Gyppoes would have had me inside quicker than a chorus boy could slap a guardsman's backside.

'Why tell me all this in the middle of the night?' I asked her, for I could only think of one reason.

'Because I need your help. Like I said.'

'How?'

'I have to get my father out in Farouk's car. It's the only way. We'll never have another chance like this, for there never will *be* another chance. I'll give you ten thousand pounds in any currency you choose once we're all safely out of Egypt.'

'Why so much less than you offered Kent?'

'Because he'd worked for months on the idea. Because his risk was greater. If he'd been discovered, he'd have lost his business in Cairo. It was all or nothing for him. And I *had* to use him. There just was no one else.'

'There's no one else but me now, either. I'll not do it for ten. But I will for twenty.'

'You're serious?'

'Deadly,' I told her, and then thought I might have made a happier choice of word.

'But how can you hope to get him out?' I asked her. 'You tell me the guards at each frontier post are alerted. And we're bound to be stopped at least once on the way to Alex for a police check. And even then we still have to go through Customs. How can you possibly conceal him in this car? There's barely room for two people inside, and no room whatever underneath for him to hang on to.'

'Have you examined the car closely?' she asked.

'Sure. I've been all over it. I've never seen such a large car with so little room. There's not even any spare space under the bonnet, for the engine fills the whole thing. The cockpit's tiny, and the boot is just a joke because of that damn' great petrol tank.'

'Exactly. I'm going to put him in that tank.'

'In the tank? It'll be full of fumes. And how do you propose getting him in? Melt him down and pour him through a funnel!'

'I'm not joking,' she said. 'I told you my father had been a coachbuilder. That car's body was his design. That big petrol tank is a dummy. It was never intended for petrol. There's a tiny tank inside for that. The rest is completely empty. No fumes at all. You push forward the seats at the front and the top of the tank opens up. You'd never see the join, for it's so well made. They used it in the old days for smuggling girls in and out of the Abdin Palace, in Cairo.

'Farouk had some strange ideas, and he hated publicity, which he always seemed to attract whatever he did. It was much easier to bring girls into the Palace hidden in that car, for then no one knew they'd even arrived.'

'Do Hassan and Sabry know about this tank—or the plans for your father?'

'No. They think it's just a straight swop with two cars of the same make. That's why they had the Type 57 sprayed yellow and black, to make it look as much like this as possible.'

'How did you become involved with Kent?'

I felt I wanted to know a bit more before I involved myself too closely. This story seemed like an iceberg; the deeper you went beneath the surface, the more there was of it.

'I came back to Cairo about a year ago, determined to get my father out. I know he had been dishonest, but by the standards of Cairo at that time, he was no worse than a thousand others.'

'I'm sure,' I said quickly, to prevent any further attempt to whitewash the old man. If I didn't, I'd no doubt hear how kind he was to his cat and his budgie and how he looked after an aged spinster sister who had varicose veins, and so on.

I didn't give a fish's tit for all that chat. I wanted to know more about the man as he was now, and by learning this to learn more about my own chances of success. Twenty thousand pounds was a lot of money to pick up, and if I was ever going to pick it up, I had to recognize the risks involved.

As I turned over all this in my mind, slowly, like a man turning a pile of damp leaves with a pitchfork, I heard a tiny noise that might have been a twig creaking. The only odd thing was that an underground concrete garage isn't the place where twigs go to creak.

I jumped for the Bugatti and switched on the huge Bi-flex Marchal headlights. They took a fraction of a second to light—a sure indication of old wiring and corroded contacts—and in that moment, before their blaze turned the far wall amber, I saw the shadow of a man run for the open door. He was out before I could see who he was, but I shouted, 'Stop!'

He didn't act on this suggestion, and since I hadn't anything to throw at him, I threw myself, and sprinted over the concrete floor.

I was blinded by the blaze of lights to one side, and didn't see what tripped me. The floor suddenly whipped up to meet me, and I was down, scrabbling about on my hands and knees, out of breath, and cursing with pain, for I had cracked my shin. Maria was kneeling by my side.

'Are you all right?' she asked anxiously.

This is always a silly question, because being all right can at best be only a relative state of affairs. I sat up, shaking my head, trying to concentrate. I had tripped over a block of wood, the sort that mechanics use for putting under axles when heavy cars are up on jacks.

'Who was that?' I asked her, as though she knew; a right ridiculous question.

'Probably a beggar. They used to come in here from the desert, even in the old days. It gets very cold out there at night. They don't do any harm.'

'There's always a first time,' I told her, and levered myself to my feet. 'Why don't they lock the door?'

They do sometimes. But there's no need. They've a guard on the gate.'

So they had; I should have remembered what she'd told me only moments before. Or maybe I was just getting jumpy, as one flea told another.

Kent *could* have fallen, or had a heart attack or some such thing, but if he *had* died that way, how had he managed to pull the sacks over himself after he was dead? Perhaps one of the beggars hadn't been so harmless after all.

I glanced at my watch; a quarter to ten, on the same day that we had set out from Cairo, but so much had happened since then that I wouldn't be prepared to swear to it. It seemed to have begun years ago, one of those days I would always remember, one of those days I would far rather forget.

'What if we're stopped on the way, as we were when we drove to Alex?' I asked her. 'You believe that although the police may look over the car, they won't examine the petrol tank? Right?'

'Right.'

'But what if they *do* examine the tank? What if someone has tipped them off? Maybe someone tipped them off about your old man being in that laundry basket. My name's on the manifests. I'll be the one who goes to jail.'

'How often have you been through customs in a car, all the times you've been abroad?' she asked me.

'Dozens.'

'You've had the boot opened, maybe the carpets lifted up. But how often has anyone looked *inside* the petrol tank?'

'Never,' I had to admit.

'Well, they won't here, either.'

I only had her word for that, but I suppose it was better than no word at all. Not much, but possibly a bit.

'I'd better tell Hassan and Sabry about Kent,' I said. 'After all, Hassan's whole reason for being with us is because he's the police chief's cousin, so maybe he can smooth things over.'

'But don't mention my father. Now Kent's dead, you're the only person who knows of this plan.'

'I've never even seen François. I don't know what he looks like. I never talk about people I don't know.'

We went up the stairs to the hotel. The same music was playing; it could have been the same tune. A long row of dimmed bulbs burned in the empty corridors. There was something unreal about all this faded Edwardian splendour marooned halfway between the sand and the sea. But nothing seemed unreal about the body in the garage, or the risks I would be facing within hours.

I felt the need for a drink, and went into the bar. It was very dimly lit. Half-a-dozen Egyptians sat around a low table in the far corner chewing nuts, with soft drinks on mats. I ordered my usual Whyte & Mackay. As my eyes grew accustomed to the gloom, I recognized Sabry and Hassan among the others. They waved to me.

I went over and stood looking down at them. The reception clerk who had booked me in sat next to Sabry. I didn't know who the others were, and didn't greatly care.

'What's happened to you?' asked Sabry.

'Me? Nothing,' I said, surprised. Then I glanced down at my suit, and even in that gloom I looked like a refugee from a flour mill, for it was white with concrete dust, and I'd torn a hole in my left trouser leg at the knee.

'I fell over,' I admitted lamely.

A man at the end of the crowd said something in Arabic and they all laughed. I didn't like that. When someone is laughing, I like to share in the joke, and not feel I am the joke. I turned to Hassan.

'Could I see you outside for a moment?'

I sounded like a stage policeman, the sort of country cop in a helmet who calls at the back door of The Grange, Act II, Scene III, four weeks later.

'Now?'

Even in the dimness, Hassan seemed surprised.

'If you can spare a minute,' I said, trying to keep the irony out of my voice.

'Of course,' said Hassan. He stood up flexing his muscles, just to show he had them. His bad eyelid flickered its semaphore to no one at all.

We went out into the corridor.

'What's the trouble?' he asked, as though I were a customer who had made a complaint about bad service. Close to, he smelled strong; no wonder he liked scent. Without it, he would smell like a reptile house.

'Kent,' I said. 'He's dead.'

'*Dead?* Where? How?'

His voice stretched tight as a drum.

'He's on the garage floor under a pile of sacks, so it doesn't look as though he died of old age.'

'How did you tear your suit?'

'I went to the garage to see where you all were. Then I saw someone run.'

I didn't add that Maria had been with me.

'I went after them and tripped. That's how.'

'Ah,' he said. 'I should have been with you. With this.'

He slid his hand into the back pocket of his trousers, brought out an F.N. automatic.

'He wouldn't have got away if I'd been there.'

'Maybe,' I said, 'but you weren't. So he did. Now what do we do about Kent?'

'Does the girl know?'

'Yes.'

'Let me deal with this,' said Hassan. 'You may have to make a statement, but it'll only be a formality. After all, my cousin is chief of police. These things help.'

For the first time since I arrived at the hotel, I began to feel more cheerful. For the first time, too, I warmed to Hassan. With a bit of luck, and I could certainly use a bit of luck, or a bit of the other thing, too, we'd get away with it, even with François.

'I'll leave it to you, then,' I said to Hassan.

'You do that.'

His teeth gleamed very white under the lamplight. He looked at me almost pityingly, and I felt I wasn't measuring up to his idea of an organizer, but then what was I meant to organize except to trundle three old cars across the desert to the nearest port?

'I've changed my mind about helping you with the Royale,' I said.

'You have? Good. You drive the little Bugatti, then,' he said. 'There are four of us, and we've all got luggage, so we'll have to take them both. We can dump your car in Alex easily enough. I've a friend there who runs a garage on the sea front.'

'You've got friends everywhere,' I said.

'It comes of having a nice nature,' he assured me. 'People are like mirrors. They reflect how we treat them in the same way. Pleasantly, or, sometimes, not so pleasantly.'

It sounded like something he'd read in a religious calendar or on a Wayside Pulpit board.

'See you, then. Four forty-five in the garage. I've got the hotel manager with me and I've already told him we're leaving early. He's having our bills made out tonight. I'll fix it with the police. If you don't hear from me, take it that you won't hear from them, either. O.K.?'

'O.K.'

I went down the corridor to my own room.

It felt stuffy inside, with the curtains drawn. The heat of the day had stored itself between the heavy drapes and couldn't find a way out. I switched off the light and opened the curtains and looked out over the desert. Under the moon, sand lay white as snow. Dogs were barking somewhere, and the smell of the sea was sharp and strong.

I closed the curtains again, and turned on the light, picked a couple of blackheads on my nose, examined my tongue, which looked the same as when I had examined it less than three hours before. I felt uneasy, though why I didn't know, but the feeling of relaxation that Hassan had induced in me by his confidence was evaporating, as the dew on the moonlit desert would burn away under tomorrow's sun.

I sat down on the easy chair to consider what I always consider when I'm worried; a mental profit and loss account. On the profit side, all could go well, in which case I had no problems. On the debit side, François could be discovered, I could be charged with kidnapping him, and with being involved in Kent's death.

But if I went down on any of these charges, then Hassan and Sabry and Maria would go down with me, never mind their influential relations. Hassan and Sabry would wriggle and might probably escape, but I guessed Kent wouldn't have paid them until he was sure all the cars were aboard, so they wouldn't abandon me entirely, for otherwise they would have worked for nothing.

In fact, who would pay them? I suppose this would fall to me, unless Kent had given the cheques to Maria to pay, but remembering how slow a man he was with a dollar, I thought this unlikely.

I wondered about Hassan's reactions to my news of Kent's death; I wondered about my own. I hadn't known him well, and Hassan presumably had known him even less, so there was no question of any private grief. Also, in the Middle East, life doesn't come expensive; a death is a death is a death. We are like wheat that is cut down in the field, and all that, although it's always best to be the cutter and not the cut.

I wondered whether George had been right about Hassan. He

has a memory like a photographer's file for odd things like gear ratios and engine numbers, but was this Hassan necessarily the same man he remembered from his service years ago in the Canal Zone?

Hassan wasn't the sort of fellow I'd like to share a room with in Brighton for a week-end in a heatwave, but then no one was asking me to. After this trip, I'd never seen him again. That wasn't a threat, either; it was a promise.

Also, it's so easy to be wrong about people or about things. I remember turning down a Daimler Double-Six once because the owner assured me it had only been used to take his maiden aunt to church every Sunday, and again, a Phantom II which had supposedly barely 5,000 miles on the clock because its previous owner, an Indian Prince, had only used it in religious processions.

Trouble was, I'm too suspicious; yet both stories were true. Another dealer believed them and made a couple of thousand quid profit out of a couple of phone calls. Here, George's story could be true, and I rather thought it was.

I prised myself off the bed, opened my suitcase, and began putting in a few more things to save me packing in the early hours. As I threw in my clothes, I couldn't help wondering where I'd be when I took them out again.

I went into the bathroom, collected my electric razor, and then saw the big Dettol bottle in which I carry my emergency supply of whisky when I travel abroad, because sometimes the Customs are funny about people bringing whisky into a country unless you pay duty on it. I poured out half a tooth mug of the stuff, added some water from the tap and drank it slowly, watching my reflection in the mirror.

I finished the whisky and went back into the bedroom. I couldn't be bothered to pack anything else, so I lay down on the bed, my thoughts churning round in my mind like the blades of the Schwitzer-Cummins supercharger on the old SJ Duesenberg. What with the whisky, the reaction from a hot drive across the desert, and the worry over finding Kent's body, they must have churned to a halt, because the next thing I remember was lying with my eyes open, looking at the light burning down on me from the ceiling.

Where am I? I thought. What's happened? Where's the action?

Wherever it was, it had passed me by. I had a headache, because I don't like lying on my back, and the light had been burning for hours by my watch. Hell, I must have been tired to drop off like that. And why had I wakened so suddenly? I felt stiff and cold, and my feet were tight in my shoes. I wished I hadn't made that drink so strong.

I glanced towards the windows. The curtains were billowing out so that they looked like the brocade sails of some land-locked galleon.

There was nothing at all strange about this—except that I clearly remembered shutting the windows.

I had that sudden premonition of danger, which must have been what awakened me, and not my bursting bladder. Someone else was in the room with me, someone who wasn't a friend.

I swung up from the bed and the quick motion made me dizzy for a second, and then I shook sleep from my head. The room was empty; I was imagining things. Possibly the wind had blown the window open. I stood up, and went towards it, telling myself I was becoming altogether too melodramatic, and my nerves were bad as a result of the life I led.

I had taken exactly two paces across the carpet when the lights went out.

My head still felt fuzzy, and after the blaze of the bulbs, I saw a raw red mist instead of darkness. Then I heard the slam of the bathroom door, and I knew whoever had been in the room had been hiding there, and I jumped to the right and so missed the first blow aimed at me.

A fist punched into the plywood front of the wardrobe, and I heard a man's cry of rage and anger, and also the same scent I had smelled just before I had been attacked in Maria's flat. It was underlaid with sweat, which I had noticed when talking to Hassan earlier on, although the scent had been different then.

So now I knew who had hit me then, and who was in the room with me now. Hassan.

'Help!' I shouted, which was ridiculous, for the only fists that could help me were right at the ends of my own two arms.

No one answered. I hadn't really expected them to. I heard breathing and I slugged out with my boot in the direction of the breather. It connected with a shin bone. Suddenly, the breathing was much near to me, and I knew where he would probably be, and I brought up both my fists locked together against his face.

If the blow had connected that would have been his lot, but it didn't, and the next thing I remembered was someone on my back, and my arms being bent to my sides, and my head forced back with the crook of an elbow under my chin.

I reached down and back to where this attacker kept his cobs, and I squeezed like I was wringing water out of a Shetland wool sweater after a day in the rain.

He screamed—as I would have screamed, too, for I was reducing them to the size of wrinkled raisins—and he let me go smartly. I jabbed my elbow back in his gut to remember me by, and jumped for the bedside table. I flicked on the light, tossed it on the bed in case it fell and went out, and then threw the table, legs first, like four spears, at Hassan.

'Are you bloody mad?' I shouted at him. 'What's got into you?'
Hassan dodged the table, and half crouched, facing me, lips

drawn back over his china teeth. His right hand moved as quickly as a snake dodging the charmer in Old Bombay (or New Delhi, for that matter) and when I saw it again, he was holding the F.N.

He came towards me, and for the first time I realized how he hated me; hatred was written as large on his face as the news on that neon sign in Piccadilly. But why, for God's sake?

I picked up the lamp and threw it at him, and leapt on to the bed as he fired. I kicked out with both my feet and heard his grunt of pain, and the gun clatter to the one small square of floor not covered by carpet. Then we fought in the darkness.

Hassan's sweat, overlaid by the scent I had last smelled in Maria's bedroom in Rosemary Court, filled the room as we slugged away at each other, like two blind men in a coal cellar, fighting by ear, each aiming at the other's breathing.

I hit and hit and went on hitting, and then I paused. I couldn't even hear Hassan breathe. Either he was dead, which I doubted, or he was deliberately holding his breath—and this could mean nothing good for me.

It didn't.

I suddenly sensed someone behind me and then, as I turned, hands as hard as a King Dick wrench went around my throat. I kicked and gouged and hit nothing, only using up air in my lungs that I could have saved for a better purpose.

Against my reddened eyelids, I saw a quick run-through of nothing, and heard a loud humming in my ears. My lungs were bursting, but I had no air and I could make no noise, utter no cry, for help or mercy. I couldn't even breathe.

Then, quite suddenly, there was an end to it all; no pain, nothing at all, but a deeper darkness, soft as a Moseley Float-On-Air cushion in a 1930's car.

CHAPTER SIX

EQUALLY SUDDENLY, there was also a lot of pain, and my sweat was gluing my shirt to my body in a rather uncomfortable way, and my nose and lips were cracking with dried blood, also mine, unfortunately.

I stretched my legs and my arms—remembering that gag about the old man who recalled how, when he was young, he had four supple members and one stiff, but now he was old, he had four stiff members and one supple.

In stretching, my fingers felt the roughness of concrete. They were scratched and raw, which was also how I felt all over.

I lay where I was, because for the moment I could do nothing else, and I wasn't quite sure where the hell I was, but gradually, as consciousness returned from wherever it had been, I realized I was lying on a concrete floor. It felt very cold; wind was blowing sand in under a door that didn't fit very well, and I could see a horizontal slit of pale blue light beneath the woodwork, so the dawn couldn't be too far away, and no doubt was coming closer.

I shivered and sat up slowly, for if I moved quickly I thought my head might leave my body altogether. It stayed where it was, so I pushed my luck even further and stood up. I could make out the dim shape of a pile of sacks, then the dim glittering roundness of a car radiator. I was back in square one, in the garage beneath the hotel.

I took a few hesitant steps towards the switch, turned on the inspection light, unhung it from the wall and looked at myself in the driving mirror of the small Bugatti. My face was a mass of blood, my eyes puffed up like an adder's, and vomit had stained the front of my jacket. I shone the light around the garage.

The Royale had gone, which didn't surprise me. I'd take a lot of surprising now. I carried the light over to the pile of sacks. Kent's body hadn't gone. This didn't surprise me, either. It lay there, face down, taking no interest in anything. I glanced at my watch. The glass had smashed, but the mechanism was still working: three-thirty-five. It must be in the morning, but which morning? The morning after I found Hassan in my room, presumably.

I sat down on the running board, my head in my hands, trying to recap what had happened.

Presumably Hassan and Sabry had stolen the Royale. If so, how could they get it through the Customs? I had all the papers upstairs in my suitcase. But had I? Or had Hassan and Sabry come into the room to steal those papers? This seemed so possible that it was almost a certainty. I stood up shakily, switched off the light, and closed my eyes to accustom them to the darkness, which had turned an unhealthy red against my aching lids.

I turned the handle of the door that led to the back stairs. The handle moved easily enough, but the door didn't; it had been locked on the other side.

I crossed the garage to try the roll-up doors, but they were padlocked down.

So here was a right turn-up; locked in a garage with a dead man, both of us showing signs of having been in a fight. Whoever discovered us would understandably assume we had been in the same fight, and that I had killed Kent. And I'd be hard pushed to prove otherwise, for it was such an easy and obvious solution that I couldn't see the Egyptian police not jumping at it.

Hassan and Sabry could get the Royale through the Customs on the papers they'd no doubt taken from my room, and make a killing on the jewels in the lights, as well as the three old cars. Of course, if I ever caught up with them, I could sue—but no one but an idiot would bother to pour good money after bad in such a cause. If Hassan was related to the chief of police, no doubt he also had a good friend or relation among the judges.

Meanwhile, I was imprisoned here until someone let me out, but before that happened, I'd no doubt that Hassan would tell the hotel manager how a mad Englishman, who'd made all sorts of threats against Kent, was locked in his garage. I had to get out before that happened. But—how?

Wild ideas of driving the little Bugatti at full bore against the wooden doors and smashing my way through, of hacking a hole in the side door with the crank handle, or soaking rags in petrol behind the door and burning away the wood around the lock poured through my mind, and poured out again. They just wouldn't work.

Perhaps a spare key would be left hanging on a nail somewhere? After all, this was an hotel garage, and some other customer might innocently lock themselves in it.

I switched on the inspection light again and shielded it with my hand to direct its faint rays all round the walls. A hose hung coiled from a hook, some tins of grease and polish were piled neatly on a cobwebby wooden shelf, and two ignition keys were suspended from a piece of string on a nail; otherwise, nothing.

I pressed my hands to my head, forcing myself to think of a way out. This was a problem for George's motto, which he says he heard from a juggler: keep your balls in the air. It means, of course, that you have to keep the action going, like the three-ball juggler. Lose command of the situation for a moment and you've lost the battle.

In the great days, when this had been a private house, how would François order his chauffeur to bring the car to the door? He could send a servant, or there might be a speaking tube, as I had seen in Edwardian motor-houses in England, but more likely there would be a telephone. This gave me new heart. A telephone. If there were, I could ring Maria in her room.

I searched the walls; no telephone. I couldn't even see any wires entering the garage. Then I looked behind the Bugatti, and set into the wall I saw a small cupboard with a grey-painted door. I opened it. On a ledge stood a telephone, and behind the door was pasted a list of numbers in Arabic script, which meant nothing to me. What meant more was the fact that, to put the telephone out of action, the three wires of the flex had been neatly cut.

However, this was not an insuperable problem. I opened the Bugatti tool-box, took out a pair of wire-strippers, ripped off the red and green and yellow plastic insulation from the wires, and twisted the bare copper ends together.

Then I picked up the telephone, jaggled the rest up and down. A sleepy operator answered: 'Hello?' I gave him Maria's room

number, and heard the bell buzz, and then her voice, equally
sleepily, saying '*Oui?*'

'Never mind the French chat,' I said. 'It's me.'

'You?' she said. 'What's the time?'

'Time for you to be out of bed and down in the garage,' I
told her.

'Why? There's nearly an hour yet.'

'Not for me, there isn't. I'm locked in here.'

'Locked in? Who by?'

Disbelief touched her voice, like a frame around an old-
fashioned photograph.

'Never mind the Socratic dialogue. Come down *now*. I'll be
waiting behind the door.'

I put back the telephone, turned off the inspection light, and
waited. The gap beneath the main door showed lighter now. I
wondered where Hassan was, whether Sabry was with him. I could
picture them in that big old car, humming down the empty road,
the desert merging with the dying darkness on either side. It could
be an exciting drive. I just wished I was making it.

I heard footsteps on the stairs, and then the click and turn of
the lock. The door swung open. I let myself through.

'My God,' said Maria, when she saw me. 'What happened?'

'Hassan came into my room. We had a fight. I got knocked out,
and came to here.'

We went up to my room. All the clothes had been tossed out
of my suitcase. My passport and the car manifests had been under
them in a brown envelope. I didn't need to have Sherlock as my
middle name to see that they weren't there.

'Are you sure it was Hassan?'

'Certain. No two men could smell like him, or even look like
him.'

'But why?'

'The Royale. That's why. He's stolen it. Maybe he and Sabry
knew about those jewels, after all. Perhaps one of them was that
fellow I chased in the garage.'

'But what about my father? How can we get him away?'

'We can't,' I said. 'Without that car, it's impossible.' Anyhow,
I thought, never mind about dear old dad; what about us?

'I can't leave him here,' said Maria.

'What else can you do? If we all three pack into the little car
we'll be stopped at the first police post up the road. You told me
yourself how they all know about him.'

'We could try to move him on Kent's passport,' she said.

'Absurd. He looks nothing like Kent. Even a passport photograph can't be that bad.'

Also, for all I knew, and I knew damn-all, Hassan and Sabry
might have warned the nearest police post up the road, that if
two men and a woman *did* come past in another old car, one of

the men was François. It would be an obvious thing to do, and Hassan wasn't the sort of man who'd miss such a chance.

'Well, what are we going to do?'

'I don't know what *you're* going to do, but here's my plan. We'll get right into the Type 57 and drive to Alex ourselves—now. I've no papers for this damn' thing because Hassan's stolen them. But I'll trust my luck to get through the customs myself on Kent's passport. I'll put on a pair of dark glasses, and to these fellows one Englishman looks much the same as another. Just like Chinese all look the same to us.'

I'd had enough of this horsing about. I wanted to be out of this hotel and aboard that boat in the shortest possible time. If we delayed much longer, the boat would already have sailed.

Without money, I couldn't buy a plane ticket, and who would lend a penniless, passportless Briton the cost of a flight to London?

'But, my father. I'll never have another chance like this. It's all geared for us to leave.'

'It was,' I agreed, 'but how the hell can we possibly smuggle him out?'

'If we can only move him from the guardroom, we're halfway home. We might hide out in the desert somewhere. Maybe you could lay on a boat?'

'And what would I use for money?' I asked.

'I'll pay you what I was paying Kent if we're successful.'

'*If* we're successful, I'll earn what you were going to pay Kent. But now there's no conceivable chance of succeeding. Your whole plan hinged on moving him in the dummy petrol tank. How can I, without money or influence, possibly hire a boat big enough to sail down the Red Sea? Be your age.'

'Maybe we could hide while you had a special tank made for your car?'

'That's just not on. There's much more to it than simply having a big petrol tank made. The body on the Royale was designed specifically for the purpose. It would take weeks to have such a body made again—even *if* I knew a coachbuilder who would attempt it, and *if* I had the money. Cash. Not promises.'

'Twenty thousand,' she said. 'It's a lot of money.'

'It's a lot of talk,' I said, but I was thinking all the same, it *was* a lot of money. To keep as much in what is laughingly called legitimate business, I would have to make more than twice that amount. The ethics weren't bothering me, only the risks, for every man has his price, and no one had priced me so expensively before.

But the chance of succeeding here seemed less than minimal. I tried to cheer myself up by thinking that *if* we could spirit François out of the camp, and *if* Maria could hide up somewhere in a shack in the desert for a few days, *if* I could hire or steal a boat from Alex, it might *just* be possible to pick up dear old dad on the beach and go south after dark under sail, in case the engine was picked up by a listening post.

Allowing all these hopeful possibilities, it was then just conceivable that we could make Dar-es-Salaam with a following wind, *if* the currents were right. But as Churchill said feelingly about the catastrophic landing in Gallipoli in the First World War, 'The terrible "ifs" accumulated', and right here I could see nothing but ifs crowding in as close as sardines in a can.

I didn't know the country, and I didn't know the people, but, even so, I guessed we'd have no help at all from the locals. After all, what would be in it for them, apart from promises and the far more likely opportunity of a long stay in some Egyptian dungeon?

We'd be quite on our own, so how could Maria and her father keep alive for several days in a shack in the desert—if they could even find a shack?

Equally, Maria and her father might be prepared to ditch me if things went wrong—and I wouldn't be in that shack to know whether things were going well or badly.

Someone once said that if all the beards in the B.B.C. were stretched from end to end, they'd reach from Sodom to Gomorrah, and I wouldn't necessarily disagree with that viewpoint. Twenty-thousand pound notes, on the other hand, stretched end to end, would make a wonderful green path to a life of young girls and old wines; of sunshine, amusing conversation and, possibly, even larger ads in *Motor Sport* and *Exchange and Mart*.

Maybe it could also open the way to a chain of Aristo Autos in the more pleasant parts of the world, places where income tax was low, and where money, once made, could be kept more easily than in Belgravia.

I was weakening. Maria could see that, and so could I, but there was still the basic problem we hadn't discussed; how to get her old man out of the guardroom, past the guard, over the barbed wire and into my car—and then where to take him without being seen.

'How was Kent going to spring him?' I asked her.

'He was going to create a diversion and then spirit him out.'

'How?'

'He brought a Very pistol out from London with a couple of cartridges. He'd opened up the ends, and packed them with tiny, torn-up pieces of silver paper from cigarette packets and chocolate bars.'

'What the hell for?'

I found it hard to imagine Kent doing this in that shabby flat in the mews in Belsize Park, but then he might have been doing things even more useless; like tarting up old cars he couldn't even sell, for instance.

'He'd been a bomber pilot during the war,' she said. 'Apparently, to confuse enemy radar they'd throw out masses of these silver paper fragments. These would drift down to earth and show on radar screens as points of light—like parachutists falling, if you like. They called it window.'

This didn't sound a convincing scheme to me, transposed nearly thirty years on and substituting, for Dortmund, a desert by the Red Sea.

'Kent had worked things out on a strict time schedule,' Maria continued. 'At four-fifty, he was to drive the Royale south along the road for a couple of miles, then fire off these shots towards the hotel.

'We had a trial run with a silver paper cartridge over a field in England, and counted how long the pieces took to fall.'

'And then?'

'Then he'd hare back here. He'd switch off his engine for the last couple of hundred yards before he reached the hotel and coast along in the dark, so he wouldn't be heard.

'By then, the falling silver paper should be showing on the radar screen. The troops would be ordered to stand to.

'Kent would cut the telephone line so they wouldn't be able to alert anyone else, and the fact that they couldn't get through to Alex on the phone would heighten their fears that this was an Israeli invasion, the real thing.

'Meanwhile, I'd have taken a tin of petrol from the garage a couple of hundred yards into the desert, with a mass of old rags and a timing device Kent has also brought from London. At exactly five minutes past five, this would explode and the rags would keep burning.

'Kent worked out that the troops, already jittery, would now be absolutely certain the invasion had begun. They'd bang away with their ack-ack gun into the sky, or shoot at the flames in the desert. Under cover of all this, Kent and I would go through the back of the camp, cut the wire, kick in the door—and get my father out.'

'Wouldn't you be stopped driving away?' I asked.

'Who by? The soldiers would all be watching the south, facing the fire. We'd be going north.'

It sounded ingenious, and just feasible. I could imagine the horror in this tiny garrison of reluctant soldiers, all anticipating annihilation by parachutists. They'd keep firing away madly at anything or nothing, making as much noise as possible to conceal their own fear.

'Twenty thousand,' Maria said, seeing my thoughts in my face, as those soldiers would see the terrifying, falling flecks of light on their radar screen.

I was being an idiot, a mad, stupid nutter who should be certified and join all the other Napoleons and poached eggs and handstanders who fill our asylums, but it was a big sum, and it could just possibly be mine.

'Well, what do you think?'

'I think it's a bloody silly idea. But with some luck, it *might* work.'

'You mean, you'll try it?'

'I mean, I'll try it,' I said. 'But get this straight right from now. I'm no hero. I'm in this strictly for cash, and I want it in writing that I'm paid as soon as we reach some other country.'

Actually, it's useless having an agreement in writing, as any lawyer will tell you (for a fee), for if someone means to screw you, it doesn't matter a fish's tit whether the contract is written on vellum with crown-and-anchor seals and red ribbon and signed over five bob stamps and all that crap, they'll still screw you. But something from my lost youth or my south London background still clung pathetically to the mythical strength of the written word.

Maria pulled an old envelope out of her pocket and wrote on the back: 'I promise to pay the bearer £20,000 cash if we all reach a foreign port safely.' She signed it and gave it to me. It wasn't worth the envelope she had written on—and even that was worthless because it had been used—but it was at least some kind of promise, though I'd have an easier job skinning an amoeba than making this arrangement stick if she changed her mind.

My promised twenty grand seemed a long way off, but, even so, the promise was better than nothing, as the mother superior told the abbot—which reminded me of a terrible joke George told me just before I left, about a nun in a convent in the French vineyard country, who went to her mother superior in some dismay.

'I've discovered another case of Lesbianism in the convent,' she told her.

'Never mind,' replied the Mother Superior cheerfully. 'Let's open a bottle. It *can't* be worse than this Beaujolais we've been having.'

Things might be worse for me, but not a lot.

Anyway, I put the envelope in my back trouser pocket and buttoned down the flap.

'When do we start?' I asked her.

'Now,' she said. 'I'll get you the gun from Kent's room.'

She left me alone in the garage. I poured one can of petrol into the Bugatti's tank, dumped another behind the seats, with some sacks, then climbed in behind the wheel, drawing comfort from the now-familiar controls, trying to keep my mind off the innumerable things that could go wrong—and the horrible consequences to me if they did.

She was back before I'd succeeded.

She handed me the Very pistol. It felt rather like a small blunderbuss. The two cartridges had brass bottoms and red plastic sides; their ends were crimped in and bound over crudely with strips of Sellotape.

'If the watchman's at the gate, just wave to him,' she told me.

'Thank you very much,' I said. 'Any curfew here?'

'No. Anyhow, you're a tourist and a foreigner, and all the police and officials have orders to be pleasant to tourists.'

'I hope they carry them out,' I said. Maria glanced at her watch.

'I'll open the door,' she said. 'I took the key off its hook behind the reception desk. You start the engine.'

She crossed the garage floor and rolled up the bureau door. A cold breeze blew in from the sea, stirring the concrete dust and flapping the rags around Kent's body. I turned on the ignition and pressed the starter. The Stromberg UUR-2 carburettor hissed like a captive snake and then the engine fired. I kept down the revs to make as little noise as possible, so that the exhaust sounded like very small strips of calico being torn by a timid maiden lady instead of its usual throaty bark. I drove through the door and Maria rolled it down behind me.

She climbed in and we went down the short drive and through the gates. An old man with a stave in his hand raised up his arm in salute.

'Salaamo,' I called to him, and waved as Maria had told me. He waved back and hawked in his throat and then spat on the sand, as though the effort had been altogether too much for him.

'Get it off your chest, lad,' I said to myself and immediately felt better. The waiting was the worst; now that things were happening, even small unimportant things like driving along a coast road with a girl by my side, there was less time for doubts and dreads.

We had no lights burning, but enough reflection from the moon on the sea for me to see my way. The desert lay like lava, grey and uninviting, faintly tinged with pink in the distance as the sun struggled over the edge of the world to put in another day's warmth. I glanced behind at the hotel. Dim lights were burning at one or two of the upper windows that didn't face the sea; the early-turn staff must be going on duty soon.

I drove for about two hundred yards, and then Maria nudged me to stop. She climbed out, and I humped the petrol can and the sacks across the sand for her.

'It'll do here,' she said, after we had walked down to where the sand felt firm and damp, near the breaking waves.

I threw down the can and sacks thankfully.

'Let's set our watches,' she said.

Mine was three minutes fast. I turned back the hand.

'Everything's been timed to within thirty seconds,' she said 'I'll see you two hundred yards south of the hotel. In the car.

Don't forget to coast past the hotel, so they won't hear the engine.'

'Don't you forget that twenty thousand quid,' I told her, in case she did.

On the way back to the car I looked back once, and Maria was standing in the sand, dark against the phosphorescence of the sea. I waved to her, but she didn't wave back, so I climbed into the car and set off down the road.

I watched the mileometer clock up one and nine-tenths, and then slowed and turned carefully in case my back wheels went over the edge of the road into the sand. I stopped, loaded the pistol, and aimed it out of the window up in the air towards the hotel. I squeezed the trigger. Luckily, there was very little noise from the cartridge. I broke the pistol, reloaded it with the second cartridge and fired again. Then I threw the pistol away into the sand and hared back along the road.

I saw the glow-worm glitter of lights in the hotel windows when I was still half-a-mile away, and gave one last burst of throttle, then switched off the engine and coasted past the gate. As the car's momentum slowed, I pulled over to the right of the road and stopped. I opened the tool box, took out a pair of pliers and a hammer, shoved them into my pocket, closed the box and began to walk back to the hotel.

I climbed the first telegraph pole I saw. The first six inches were murder, as the actress told the bishop, because I had to climb with my legs wound round the rough and splintery post, but after that the Egyptian authorities had thoughtfully fitted metal steps, so I went up easily enough, to where two wires swung from their porcelain insulators. Close to, the wires sang like enormous violin strings. I snipped one of them and its song ceased. One broken wire would be an accident; two would almost certainly spell sabotage.

Down on the ground, I kept as close to the wall as I could, for there was no other cover. The only sound was the thunder of the surf and the rattle of the wind in the reeds; or maybe it was the sound of my teeth chattering.

I glanced at my watch. Two minutes to go.

By now, that falling silver paper should be showing on the radar screen. But what if no one was watching it? What if the operator was asleep? I hadn't too much faith in the soldierly qualities of the troops I'd seen. We might be going through all these complicated motions of deception without even an audience of one.

I imagined Maria also waiting out there in the darkness. I wondered what her dear old dad was thinking about in the guard house, and what was happening to Hassan and Sabry. If they knew the value of the jewels on that Royale, they'd probably be thinking about their good life ahead, or—more likely—how to double-cross each other. And me? I was thinking that if I extracted myself safely without losing either my skin or my money, I'd settle in future for a quieter life.

One minute to go.

Suddenly, I heard voices from the tents: then shouting; then shadowy figures began to mill about, climbing up into the gun emplacement. The snout of the anti-aircraft gun moved slowly round until it was pointing over the sea.

I'd wronged these Gyppoes. Someone had been watching the screen, after all.

Forty seconds to go. Out towards the sea, the darkness suddenly erupted in an orange ball of fire, so bright, so unexpected that I could see the long line of empty sand dunes, the white froth of the waves, and even the black oily smoke that ringed the flames.

The sound of the explosion followed a second later, rattling the hotel windows, and the shock wave blew my shirt hard against my body. The blaze died down slightly, but against its glare I could see soldiers rushing frantically about in the compound. Some were holding machine guns, which they began to fire wildly towards the flames, swinging their weapons as though they were hoses. This could be dangerous, for one of them was taking aim. However, so long as they kept their weapons pointed away from me, I'd be safe enough, as the young housewife told the amorous milkman.

I ran through the gate; the night watchman had prudently absented himself in the commotion, which was fortunate for me. The fence presented three strands of wire, each about a foot apart. I snipped these through easily with the pliers, and ran on, half-doubled, towards the guard house.

François should have been waiting for me, framed in the doorway, but he wasn't: the doorway was just filled with the door.

I kept back in the shadows for a moment, hoping he'd come out. Maybe he had overslept, though how he could sleep through the cacophony of noise seemed incredible to me. Soldiers had formed a line near their anti-aircraft gun, handing up shells from ammunition boxes. The gunner was aiming at nothing at all, but looking very determined about it, and firing away recklessly. I suppose each shell must have cost a fiver, but it wasn't his money, so why should he worry?

No one was looking my way, so I ran up the two steps to the door, and threw my weight against it. The door threw its weight right back at me and almost put my shoulder out. This door was meant to keep prisoners in, not to let unwanted visitors through. I took the hammer from my pocket and smashed the lock.

The door swung open. I closed it quickly with me inside. The noise of shouting and firing and the banging of the gun was fainter now. I groped for the light switch and flicked it on. The windows were blacked out, the bed was empty, the sheets pulled back as though whoever had been in it had left hurriedly and hadn't rung for room service—presumably dear old dad.

So where the hell was he? I couldn't guess, but he certainly wasn't there. I looked under the bed just in case, but two cockroaches looked back at me reproachfully, so I left them.

I switched out the light, and ran back across the compound. This time, a soldier saw me and swung his rifle towards me and fired. He was a bum shot, for he missed, and, as he tried to reload, the second bullet jammed halfway into the breech. I suppose it was blocked with the sands of the Nile, like the Sphinx's backside.*

I threw my pliers at him, and he screamed with alarm, dropped his rifle and fled.

The ack-ack gun was firing now like a pom-pom and I heard the shrapnel hissing down. I sprinted through the gate, along the road, and jumped into the car. Maria was waiting in the front seat, with the ignition already on.

I pressed the starter; the engine whirred and caught, and we were off.

'Where's dad?' she asked.

'God knows,' I said. 'I don't. He wasn't there.'

'He must have been. I saw him go in this evening.'

'Well, take my word for it. Someone else took him out, or he's made a balls of the arrangements and gone off on his own.'

Maria didn't say anything. I think she was simply beyond speech. This was the moment for which she'd been working and waiting for so long, and something had gone wrong, what and how she couldn't comprehend. She sat like a zombie, staring out of the windscreen, seeing nothing but her own failure.

I didn't know where François was, but my bet was that Hassan had loused things up for us somehow. Maybe he'd told the guard commander that I was a dangerous character, and the commander had switched François elsewhere—just in case?

The more I thought about this, the more I wished I was somewhere else. If Hassan didn't catch me on one hook, he was obviously determined to do so on another.

As we drove, not speaking, only thinking, which was worse, the sound of the firing sank to a distant crackle, like November fireworks in someone else's back garden.

---

* Another of George's rhymes:
> The sexual desires of the camel
> Are greater than anyone thinks,
> And at the height of the mating season
> He'll even fancy the Sphinx.
> Now the Sphinx's posterior passage
> Is blocked by the sands of the Nile,
> Which accounts for the hump on the camel
> And the Sphinx's inscrutable smile.

I glanced at my watch; twenty-five minutes to five. At this rate we would be in Alex by seven. I decided to drive straight to the docks.

But then I remembered I had no papers for the car, and no passport for myself. We'd stop in the café I'd seen on the sea-front on the way down and have breakfast, and ask the owner where the consulate was, and I'd tell the consul I'd lost my passport and the papers, which was true, up to a point. He'd curse me, no doubt, but he'd still help me. He'd have to, wouldn't he? That's what consuls are for, surely? I tried to convince myself, but not very successfully.

The road stretched on, grey across the desert, and without lights I couldn't make out any landmarks I remembered on the run out. I glanced at the dials on the dash for assurance; oil pressure at 30; petrol at 10 gallons; speed, 55 m.p.h., which was fast enough. Maria was sitting hunched up in her seat, staring straight ahead through the fly-spotted windscreen. I didn't know what she was thinking about, but I hoped her thoughts were more cheerful than mine.

Then I had another idea. To hell with the consul and all that horsing about—('And what was the number of your passport? Where and when was it issued? You don't *know?*'). Instead, I'd bluff my way through Immigration on Kent's passport, but I'd have to leave this car behind. What a way to make a living, and me a car dealer! Buy three cars and only collect two.

The road began to turn and twist like a tarmac corkscrew through sand-dunes, speared on either side with green reeds and rushes, now dropping between them, so that they soared twenty or thirty feet on either side of the car, then rising above, so that the full force of the wind buffeted us and made the hood flap like a punctured drum-skin.

I'm so accustomed to driving on the crowded roads of southern England, that to have no other car to pass or follow seemed some-how sinister. I wondered vaguely and irrationally whether a terrible tragedy had overtaken mankind, whether Armageddon had begun (and was over, somehow missing me)—or maybe the Chinese had exploded too large a hydrogen bomb?

There was an emptiness about everything, the quietness of death, only broken by the creak of the Bugatti's springs over occasional potholes, the flap of the canvas roof, and the muted crackle of the exhaust.

The road dipped suddenly between two dunes, and turned sharp left, away from the sea. I braked and dropped down a gear, into the hairpin bend. Then I stopped. A rock, about the size of a dustbin, had come loose from somewhere and blocked the road. I heaved the steering wheel to the right to miss it, but it still caught the hub of the front wheel and the force of the blow spun the steering wheel out of my hands.

I stopped to climb out and see what damage I'd done. At that moment I sensed rather than saw a movement from the reeds on the right, and then a policeman jumped out in front of me.

This was no ordinary Egyptian copper in tatty khaki fuzz, but a man wearing a magnificent uniform, with twill riding breeches, a smart olive-green tunic, gold epaulettes, polished Sam Browne belt and holster. This last was empty, for the .45 that usually lived in the leather was now in his hand, pointing straight at my heart. My heart didn't like being pointed at; it began to beat very rapidly indeed.

'All right,' said the policeman quietly and in English—after all, if he'd spoken in Egyptian I wouldn't have understood a word. I looked up from the mouth of his revolver. Hassan's face leered at me. Or was this his cousin, the chief of police?

'Who are you?' I asked, because I wanted to know.

'Hassan,' he replied. 'Drive right on and stop behind the car in front. It's about fifty yards away.'

'That rock?' I began.

'I put it there to stop you,' he said. 'Get moving.'

'But. . . .'

'Don't talk. Drive. And don't try anything clever.'

There was nothing clever I could think of to try; if I were clever, I wouldn't be where I was. My mouth felt dry as the desert all around, and my body was shaking with reaction. Hassan jumped up behind me and dug the muzzle of his gun into my back.

I drove on. We came through the bend and the sea was pounding only feet away on a beach scummed with driftwood and dark green strips of seaweed. A few seabirds, the first living things I'd seen since I left the hotel, apart from Hassan, floated on the water, watching us, or maybe watching fish. I didn't know. All I knew was, I envied them; they were free and I was captive.

Ahead of me, pulled half off the road, stood the big Bugatti, yellow as the yolk of an egg in the early sunshine. The bonnet was open. Sabry perched on its huge tail, smoking a cigarette. He jumped down and came towards us, hands in his pockets.

'So you came, yes?' he said, which is about as good, or as bad, an opening as any.

I half expected him to offer me a cut rate for attar of roses or musk, or some other rubbish, because even in the desert he looked what he was, a dabber of scent on the lobes of other people's ears, a ponce perfumier, or a perfumed ponce, if you like that better. I didn't like him at all; and as for Hassan, if he were burning to death I wouldn't bother to pee on him.

I had a sudden wild idea of running Sabry down, but Hassan would have fired. I know that in a film I would have ducked just before he fired, and then swung around and pitched him into the sand. I've seen this sort of thing happen on the box so many times

—and so have you—but in real life you don't write the whole script, only your own lines, so you can't guarantee the end of the action.

'Switch off your engine,' ordered Hassan, jumping down to the side of the road. 'Then get out and stand by the car with your hands behind your neck.'

'Why don't you say please?' I asked him.

'Because you're a cocky English bastard,' he said. 'And I hate the English. Why should you come and make money out of my country's old cars?'

I couldn't follow the fellow's reasoning, but this didn't seem the time to tell him so. Cocky, possibly; English, agreed; bastard, not actually—but a deal, surely that's another thing altogether?

He spat at me. I could feel his spittle cold and vile on the side of my face. I've never been spat at before, at least by anyone on target. I didn't like the feeling.

I reached out, turned the ignition key. The red warning light flickered and died. As I eased myself slowly out of the car, I put my right hand down, felt for the petrol tap by the side of my seat and pushed it to 'Off'. Waste not, want not, is as good a motto as any, and better than most. There must have been a petrol leak somewhere at sometime, or else this tap would never have been fitted. Hassan didn't see the motion, and he would have learned nothing from it if he had.

The sand felt very soft and powdery to my feet, and I immediately sank in it over the tops of my shoes, and stamped my feet and shook them, but my shoes were already full. At the other side of the car, Maria was climbing out, a forlorn figure. Sabry crossed over to her.

'I'm sorry about this,' he said. He might even have meant it, but more likely he meant he was sorry for himself, stuck by the side of the sea, on the edge of the sand in a monster car forty years old.

'We've had a breakdown. You will not be harmed in any way.'

'What the hell *is* all this?' I asked Hassan. 'Why are you dressed up in that rubbish? Hassan said nothing. He turned to Maria.

'Throw your handbag back into the car,' he told her.

He obviously thought she had a gun or some weapon. The only weapon I was carrying, I had been provided with at birth, and I could see no use for it whatever in my present situation.

Hassan jabbed his gun into my stomach. His face was very close to mine, with his too-white teeth, his thick lips and the tiny moustache. The sweat was pouring off him now; no scent in all the world could sweeten his smell. I wondered what it would be like to be a woman, and wake up every morning of your life with that face on the same pillow. I decided no woman would endure it. No wonder he was king, as George would say. King Lear—queer.

'You're the old-car expert, or so you claim,' Hassan said, 'so get this car running.'

He jerked his head towards the Royale.

'I've no tools,' I said, and I hadn't, either, apart from the one mentioned a few lines up.

'There are some in the car,' said Hassan, convincing himself as much as me. But in his pale blue eyes I could see a tiny flicker of fear and doubt, the same sort of flicker I've often seen in the eyes of someone after they've signed a cheque for one of my old cars and then belatedly wonder whether they've committed themselves to something far too expensive.

If the Royale had a broken half-shaft or a cracked distributor, or something else as serious, whatever tools were on the car would be useless; Hassan could be stuck there for hours. Virtually the only traffic would be military convoys, with drivers who wouldn't stop, or maybe a truck carrying provisions for the hotel. Add a taxi or two with foreign tourists having a quick shufti at the sea and the sand, and that would be about the lot.

We stood looking at each other. Then Hassan moved the gun from my stomach, for which my stomach was very thankful.

'Have a look at the engine,' he said, and as I started to walk towards the Royale, Sabry called: 'Wait, we'll frisk him first.'

He ran his hands down my jacket and my trouser pockets, but I was carrying nothing more lethal than a handkerchief and a few hundred-piastre notes in a money clip.

'I can't work with that gun around,' I told Hassan.

'You'll bloody work,' said Hassan and kept the gun in his hand. So, I worked.

At least, I looked under the bonnet at Ettore Bugatti's masterpiece of engine design, at the two sets of plugs to each cylinder, at all the engine-turned metal that glittered like jewels. The whole engine appeared to be a solid metal ingot; there had never been one so beautiful before, and there never would be another made like it now.

'How did it stop?' I asked Sabry. The less I had to do with Hassan, the better. I couldn't look at him without my feelings showing in my eyes.

'Hassan was driving,' said Sabry, as though this made a difference. 'The engine gave a cough, and then it began to whir inside and all the power went out of it. We just stopped.'

This sounded to me as a patient's symptoms must sound to a bored family doctor: 'I've got this strange pain, see, that starts in my left elbow and sort of goes all round my body and then gets worse here, in my right ankle.'

'Come on,' said Hassan. 'We haven't got all day. The heat will be up in an hour.'

He had command of the situation, but I also had one card to play; my mechanical knowledge, such as it was. I didn't fancy working on the engine, maybe persuading it to start, and then being shot in the back of the head for my trouble. Hassan hadn't told me he'd do this, of course, but then nations declare war on each other without informing their opponents, and I didn't trust Hassan any more than I'd trust a rattlesnake that hadn't had a good rattle in far too long.

'I know nothing about this car,' I said, which was more or less true.

'It must be the same as any other,' said Hassan, but with a welcome twinge of doubt in his voice. After all, if the Royale was twice as large as any other car, mightn't it also be twice as complicated?

'You know nothing about it,' I told him, pressing my tiny advantage, as one dwarf told the other. 'This is one of the most complicated designs in the world.'

Certainly, the engine looked so huge that it must have been unlike any engine he had seen before.

'I'll do my best,' I went on. 'But not if you're flashing that gun about. You might fall or trip, and then I'm dead.'

'I have never fallen with a gun,' said Hassan seriously. 'I was the best shot in Farouk's court.'

For shot, read shit, I thought, but didn't say the words. We stood looking at each other, and either he must have realized I was harmless, or he thought I meant what I said, because he slipped the gun into his back pocket.

'Now,' he said. 'Get going on that engine.'

From the symptoms Sabry had given me, I didn't need to be a senior wrangler or even an A.M.I.C.E. to guess that the cause of their stop was either no petrol or no spark. I turned the ignition key on and off quickly, before Hassan could see what dial I was watching, which was the petrol gauge. The needle flicked up from empty to show three-quarters full. So they had plenty of juice.

Perhaps there was a blockage in the pipe; maybe some fluff or sediment was blocking a bend after years of being unused? Then I had another think and flicked the switch again. The needle did exactly the same, as I expected it would. Hassan said irritably: 'Don't waste time. Do something mechanical.'

'I must check everything,' I told him. 'Either I do it my way or no way.'

I was stalling for time, because the longer I could spin things out, the greater my chance—not much of one, admittedly, but the only one I had—that someone might come along the road and stop to see if they could help us. And, if that happened, I could conceivably get an outsider involved, and the odds might shift a little more in my favour. As I viewed things, I was right down on the deck, so the only way I could go was up.

'Where do you keep the tools for this thing?' I went on.

I knew exactly where they were; in one of the torpedo-shaped wings, with their recessed nickel hinges and carriage locks. Hassan and Sabry looked at each other doubtfully. I pretended to make a discovery of my own.

'Are they in one of the wings?' I suggested to them both. 'Perhaps you'd like to see?'

If either bent down, I'd boot him hard right up the jack with one foot, and kick him in the side of the head with the other, executing a neat *pas de deux* meanwhile, and then try my luck with whoever was left. But Hassan didn't give me the chance.

'Open it up yourself,' he said, and put his hand into his back pocket to grip the butt of the gun.

I squatted down in front of the old-fashioned lock, pressed the button so that the lid flipped open, and took out a black leather tool roll which contained all the tools, each one nickel-plated, and stamped with the name, Bugatti. I didn't think they'd ever been used.

'Never had a spanner on her,' I thought, that old claim of so many used-car dealers, who buy a new roll of tools to drop into the tool-box of each old car they sell, so that they can open the roll and show the innocent prospective buyer how the car has never been in any mechanical trouble.

Of course, if the buyer has any sense at all, he retorts that, after thirty or forty years, a car must indeed be in a bad state if it has never had a spanner on it. But, somehow, in all my experience they never do. There's something about the statement that mesmerizes them, so remember that, next time you hear it.

I selected a plug spanner, pulled off a plug lead, slipped the spanner over the plug, gave the Tommy bar a jerk, and the plug began to turn easily. I took it out. The points were pale grey, another indication that the mixture had suddenly gone weak and died.

But how, if the tank was three-quarters full?

I loosened the union nut outside the carburettor, turned on the ignition again, pressed the rubber solenoid button on the starter motor switch to spin the engine, and watched the blue spark jump across the points of the plug. This was just play-acting. The loose join didn't even grow wet, so no petrol was passing from the pump. If the original petrol tank had been removed, so that the huge container necessary to conceal a human being could be fixed in its place, it was likely that a small petrol tank, holding only a couple of gallons, had been substituted. This would be connected to the five-inch filler, for, after all, two gallons would have been more than enough to propel even this gigantic car from a house in Cairo to the Palace, carrying a girl in the back.

The petrol gauge had probably not been altered, because this would be an unnecessarily complicated operation. If this were the case, the original unit, designed for a large tank would have a float moving up and down perhaps three feet. But the float would bottom in a tiny tank, four or five inches high, and when that happened, it would still register three-quarters full. The three-quarters it referred to would be notional, as the Income Tax people like to say about someone's profits, when they haven't had any.

I had had this experience of a false reading years ago with an old three-litre Bentley, which had been fitted with a replica body and what was apparently a forty gallon tank at the back, shielded by wire mesh grilles against an almost non-existent risk of puncture by flying stones.

The tank was just a hollow shell, and hadn't even a bottom, and inside we had fitted a much smaller tank, from a Vauxhall, with the original rheostat mechanism, so that when this replacement tank was empty the original petrol gauge still registered nearly half full.

Now that I'd satisfied myself as to the reason for their breakdown, I felt quite irrationally relieved. Maybe this was a professional thing, or maybe it was because I knew something the others didn't. The man who said knowledge was power knew a thing or two.

'Hurry up,' said Hassan. 'I can see you've a spark there. It must be a fuel blockage, for there's plenty of fuel.'

'So you know about cars?' I said. 'If you're so good, why don't you get it going?'

'I'm guessing,' he admitted.

I screwed back the plug, tightened up the union, then undid the bolts in the float chamber, slipped it down half-an-inch, peered inside. It was as dry as my own mouth. I bolted it up again.

'You're out of juice,' I said.

'We can't be. The gauge says we're three-quarters full.'

'Then why doesn't it work?'

He said nothing.

'We'll take some of your petrol,' said Sabry.

'Be my guest,' I said. 'But how are you going to manage that? I've no can.'

I guessed there was no can, no hose or other container in the big Bugatti, either. Hassan bit his lip, in lieu of anything else to try his teeth on.

'Use my hat,' he said, and pulled the peaked cap from his head.

'It'll run through that. You'll just be wasting your time. You'll need nearly ten gallons at least to get to Alex, and my car hasn't got a lot more in its tank.'

For the first time since I'd seen him, Hassan looked really worried. A shadow darkened his already dark face, and his eyes were hard as prune stones.

'Take one of the headlamps off,' he told me. 'Use the shell as a scoop.'

'Useless,' I said. 'The drain plug in my tank has been soldered.'

It hadn't, so far as I knew, but I spoke with such certainty that he believed me.

'Why not take the whole tank off, then?' suggested Sabry. 'Put it on the big car and connect it up?'

'Be your age,' I told him. 'It'll take half a day to get those nuts undone after forty years. And we'd have to empty the tank in any case before we could move it. Back in square one.'

I stood there watching them, relishing their discomfort, feeling the sun grow warm on my back and my face when I turned into it. In an hour, the desert would be like an oven.

'Have you got any water?' I asked Sabry. 'I've an idea.'

'Let's have the idea,' said Sabry.

He leaned inside the Royale, pulled out a plastic container, and filled two plastic mugs with water. He handed one to Maria and the other to me. I drank mine gratefully, swilling it round in my mouth, feeling it soak into my parched throat.

'Well,' said Hassan. 'You've had your water. What's your idea?'

'Before I tell you,' I said, trying to keep my voice calm, as though I was making a business proposition, 'What's going to happen to us?'

'That depends on whether you help us,' said Hassan, but I knew from the way he smiled, with his mouth just a muscular contraction, that it didn't depend on anything but his own whim.

'If I do get you to Alex, what then?'

Maria was looking at me with surprise in her face, and disappointment, too; almost contempt. Surely I couldn't be such an idiot as to attempt to make some deal with them, when I had no bargaining power at all?

I knew what she was thinking, and I let her think it. I'd have thought the same in her position.

'Then you can go back to England,' said Hassan smoothly.

Possibly, but dead or alive? I wondered.

'Why did you kill Kent?' I asked him. This had to come out in the open sooner or later, as the games master told the choir boy, and it was better to come out now. I didn't think that Hassan would bother to lie to me, because you only lie to someone if you want to go on dealing with them, and maybe deceiving them. You don't trouble to lie if they're no more use to you; they're simply not worth the effort of inventing an excuse or a reason. But in every life there is always at least one moment for truth. For Hassan, this was that moment.

'We didn't mean to kill him,' he said.

'We?' repeated Maria.

'Yes,' said Sabry. 'We were working on this car, cleaning it. I was polishing the lamps and I suddenly realized that the red lenses in the sidelights and the headlamps weren't red glass at all. They were rubies. So we looked at the green lights on the dash, and the red lights on the side of the tail lamps. They were emeralds and rubies. Even the radiator name plate was made of precious stones. There's a fortune in this damn' car.'

'But you left the cigar lighter?'

'Yes. The lens in that was glass.'

'And so?'

'So Kent came in when I was prising the jewels out. He must have guessed what they were. We had an argument. We struggled. He fell and hit his head.'

'Convenient,' I said. 'Maybe you pushed him?'

I turned to Hassan questioningly.

'Maybe I did, and what the hell does it matter?' he asked aggressively. 'I've a witness who'll say differently. And Kent's dead, so he can't contradict me. And you're in no position to talk, either, Englishman. Your fingerprints are all over that garage. I pressed your tiny hands in Kent's blood myself and dabbed them on all kinds of things—walls, doors, those petrol cans. So come on, fellow. How are you going to get us out of this?'

'You still haven't told me what's in this for me if I do?'

As I stood there, I suddenly—belatedly, maybe—realized why they didn't just abandon the Royale and take off in my car.

They had kidnapped François—probably imagining they were the only people to think of doing so. He'd have been waiting for Maria's signal, and when they came instead, he would have thought it was only a change of plan.

They couldn't just abandon the Royale. François was hidden inside it; and if they left him, they also forfeited their chance of a fortune. The jewels from the lights would only represent small change compared with the amount he could be forced to pay them for his freedom.

I also guessed they wouldn't give me any deal, because they didn't need to. I was expendable. I remembered the advice an American buyer of a Lorraine-Dietrich once gave me: 'Never get into an ass-kicking contest with a three-legged man.' Which means, don't play out of your league, don't fight if you've no chance of winning.

But the longer I could drag this out, the more chance I had of winning; in fact, this would give me my only chance of winning.

'What do you want?' asked Hassan.

'Safe passage for Maria and for me. My passport and the papers so I can export this Type 57. After all, I've paid you for it.'

'You get us to Alex,' said Hassan, 'And you both go free.'

'I'll have your hand on that,' I said. As I stretched out my hand, I thought that if I was a fictional superman, I'd have him over my shoulder as our hands touched. But fact is like a new river; it never runs the way you would expect it to, and I wasn't a superman. Indeed, I felt so depressed I was barely a man at all.

He shook hands, puzzled by my gesture, obviously expecting a trick, because I could see his muscles harden under the silk of his shirt.

'You don't imagine he'll keep his word, do you?' asked Maria contemptuously.

I didn't, of course, but this was no time for telling anyone. I couldn't bear to look at her. From the way she looked at me, she'd spit on the other side of my face, and I couldn't really blame her. I felt so low I could have walked under a slug's belly on stilts, and the slug wouldn't even have noticed.

'What's your plan, then?' asked Sabry.

He was the sharper of the two, but if I could fix Hassan I'd have no trouble from him. Sabry had spent too long among his scents and perfumes and pomades, too long hunched-up, peering at jewels through a magnifying glass, offering ridiculously low prices for things worth ten times as much. He was a one-punch fighter, and, if I had the chance, that one punch would be mine. For if, read when.

'I'll tow you,' I said. 'It's the only way. Outside Alex, we can stop at a petrol station, and you can fill up and buy a spare can to keep you going.'

Sabry looked at Hassan.

'It makes sense,' he said.

And, of course, it did—for them. I wouldn't know whether it did for me for some time yet.

Hassan glanced at his watch. Two minutes after six o'clock. Six hours before the boat sailed, but only four hours of useful time, for we should be there at least a couple of hours before they cast off. He nodded.

'Have you a rope?' he asked me.

'Yes.'

I still had the tow ropes I had told Kent to buy before we set off from Cairo. I lifted up the trunk lid at the back of the Type 57, pulled one out, and looped one end round the nearside spring shackle.

'Drive the car in front of the Royale,' Hassan ordered Maria.

He took out his gun and held it about a foot away from my stomach, so close that a blind man couldn't miss, and with his skill he'd give me a second navel in no time. As if I needed such a thing.

'Don't try anything,' Sabry warned Maria, as though she might. 'Hassan just wants an excuse to fire.'

She shook her head. She looked so miserable, so disappointed in me and my pathetic showing, that she had no words left to express her feelings. She started the engine, drove in front of the Royale and then slowly backed up to it.

'Switch off,' I called to her. I'd turned off the petrol, and it could only run for a few minutes on what was already in the carburettor. I didn't want them to find out about that tap. I bent down, tied the rope to the front dumb iron of the Bugatti. Maria moved over to the passenger seat, still not looking at anybody, simply staring straight ahead.

'I'll drive,' I told Hassan as he came towards me to order me out. 'I know this car. I drove it up from Cairo, and you've got to nurse it.'

'Then I'll ride in the back,' said Hassan. 'And don't get any ideas about putting us off the road, because I'll shoot. It's a long time since I shot a man.'

'I thought your thing was birds,' I said. 'Feathered birds.'

He hit me across the mouth with the back of his hand, luckily not with the one that held the gun, but I felt my lips split against my teeth, and my blood tasted salt on my tongue.

Another debt to pay, I thought. He was the only creditor with whom I'd looked forward to settling accounts in a long, long time.

'Get moving,' said Hassan. 'And only stop if Sabry blows his horn twice.'

Sabry could do what he liked with his horn, for my money.

I gripped the serrated rim of the steering wheel, sitting low in the now familiar leather seat, looking out through the faintly tinted windscreen, down the long narrow bonnet to the radiator cap. My heart was thumping like an S.U. pump with an air lock. I felt tired, and desperate for a way out. Hassan climbed in behind me and sat with his gun pressed into the nape of my neck.

'There's no need for all that crap,' I said, moving my head.

'You just drive,' said Hassan coldly, but he took the pistol out of my flesh, although I guessed it was still aimed at me. I hoped he hadn't a twitch in his trigger finger, but then if he had, I'd know nothing about it.

I switched on the engine, put my right hand down carefully under the seat and pushed over the petrol tap to 'On'. Then I pressed the starter button. The engine fired. I let in the clutch gently and the rope took up the strain. The car jerked as the other Bugatti began to move, and then we were off.

Every few hundred yards I pushed over the petrol tap with my hand, and the engine coughed and spluttered and we stopped, and Hassan cursed us. I shrugged my shoulders, waited for a few moments, and then turned on the tap again and we started off. If I had to explain in a court of law why I did this, I couldn't give a rational answer. But then isn't that true of an awful lot of things in life?

I had a customer once, a psychiatrist, who bought, of all things, a Bean, a car about as dull as its name, and he told me that every time he rode alone in a lift, just as he was leaving, he'd press all the buttons for the other floors, plus the 'up' and 'down' buttons. He'd no clear idea why, he just liked to do it. So if he can't say, when it's his living why we do the odd things we do, how can I? I suppose I wanted to bitch things for Hassan, and this was the only way in which I could annoy him. There was also another reason: the longer we took on the journey, the longer we stayed alive—and the greater chance that someone would stop and offer to help.

'We haven't all day,' complained Hassan, at the fifth stop.

'I know that,' I said. 'But I can't help this damn' car. It wasn't built to tow something twice its weight. If you can do better, you drive it.'

'I've a bloody good mind to,' said Hassan.

'All right,' I said, opening the door and climbing out.

He covered me with the gun. For a moment I thought he really would take my place, and then he'd soon discover my trick with the petrol tap, so I said hastily, and quite slanderously, 'If you let the clutch in too quickly you'll snap the half-shafts like sticks. They're a weak point on this model.'

'Get in again,' said Hassan, believing me. 'And take it gently.'

By a quarter past seven, we had covered fifteen miles. One or two Skoda trucks were coming towards us now, being driven down from the docks of Alexandria, part of an Iron Curtain consignment of military equipment. They blew their horns impatiently and roared past, enveloping us in dust so that I had to stop until it had settled, and I could see the way ahead again.

We drew near to a railway that ran alongside the road for a few miles. A train overtook us, crowded with soldiers, some of them hanging outside, some even sitting, legs wide apart to keep their balance, on the roofs of the carriages. They waved to us as though we were in some kind of a race, and I suppose in a sense we were. I wondered uneasily whether their movement north was anything to do with our attempts at a diversion a few hours earlier.

We passed road blocks, giant squares of concrete with rusty metal loops, that had been dragged up, ready to be rolled across the road in the event of an Israeli invasion, and a few hutches at the edge of the beach, dried black skins stretched over driftwood boards. I don't know who lived there, but even if the shacks didn't look like split-level, gracious living as advertised in the home section of Sunday newspapers, at least their tenants were free, which was more than I could claim to be.

We were nearer the sea now, and the spray was rising, and the waves pounded other blocks of concrete, like the foundations of submerged citadels. One of the wasp-coloured taxis, black and yellow, came surging down the road from Alexandria, and I had a brief glimpse of two middle-aged tourists, unmistakably American, in horn-rimmed glasses, flowered shirts and nylon sun-hats.

One of them waved to us and Maria waved back, but they didn't stop. I wondered what they made of our two old cars roped together, grinding along on the side of the road in their dust. I wondered what they would have said if they had known the truth. Obviously, they wouldn't have believed it, because truth of this kind would be far beyond the frontiers of their comfortable, air-conditioned, package-deal world, and I wished to hell it was outside mine.

I glanced down at the mileometer. We were only eleven or twelve miles out of town. In the long, dim distance, now, I could see a few faint jagged shapes on the rim of the shimmering desert —Alexandria. Even at our pace, we would be there within an hour. Then either Hassan would keep his word, or he wouldn't. There were no other options, but I didn't feel optimistic about the matter, for every turn of our wheels diminished our use to him.

He must have been thinking along those lines himself, because he suddenly jabbed the muzzle of the automatic into my neck.

'Pull off the road,' he ordered.

'Why?' I asked. 'We're miles away yet.'

'You talk too much. Do as you're told.'

I did.

'Get out,' he ordered, as the wheels stopped turning. I did that, too.

It was hotter now in the sun than under the old tattered hood, which was bad enough. My shirt was stained dark with perspiration. I saw my face in the outside driving mirror; lips swollen, dried blood down my chin, dark shadows under my eyes, and in them a look of resignation and defeat. I must say, if I'd been in a competition for salesmen and how they could influence new clients, I wouldn't have made first base.

'Undo the tow rope,' Hassan ordered.

I went round to the back of the car, crouched down in the sand, and wrestled with the knot. It came undone finally, with reluctance and at the cost of several torn finger nails. I saw a beetle crawl across the sand, and bombed it with drops of my own sweat. I spun out the job as long as I could, but nothing lasts forever, and this didn't last more than seven or eight minutes.

I stood up, and the desert looked so hot that it shimmered in the distance, sand melting into sky. The sea was blue as melting glass and looked as warm. I had a vague idea I might use the rope as a lasso or a stock whip, but Sabry stopped that. He took it from me, threw it into the back of the Royale, then poured himself a mug of water from a canister, handed one to Hassan and another to Maria. When she finished drinking, he poured some more in it for me. I drank it gratefully and perspiration poured out of my forehead and forearms. But I felt better, not quite so parched. I hadn't won yet, but also I hadn't entirely lost.

'Throw the rest away,' Hassan told Sabry.

Obediently, he turned the canister upside down. The water glug-glugged into the sand. It made a tiny pool, then there was nothing but a darker stain where it had been, and then even that disappeared. Within minutes there might have been no water at all. The desert was also thirsty.

Sabry handed me the empty container. I shook a few drops out into my mouth. Some ran down my chin, and I licked at them greedily.

'We'll use that can for petrol,' said Hassan. 'Drain some off from your car's tank.'

'I told you, the plug's jammed,' I said.

'Punch a hole with a screwdriver. And hurry. That can will hold enough for us to reach Alex now.'

I didn't really know that the plug was jammed, but when I looked, I found that it had been soldered over. They often do that in old cars, because the plugs weep petrol. I suppose the threads become distorted; after all, most cars are built to last for two or three years, not forty or more, in the nineteen-twenties as today.

I went back to the Royale, opened the tool box, took out a screwdriver and a hammer, and started to walk towards the smaller car. I walked slowly, for my legs under Hassan's gaze felt like logs, and my feet sank into the sand. I once read of a wartime spy who had been captured by the Nazis and made to dig his own grave; I was beginning to understand how he must have felt.

I was certain now that neither Maria nor I would go free. We knew too much, and our knowledge was the only thing that kept Hassan and Sabry from a fortune. This was our bad luck, but it didn't make the thought of approaching death any easier. My mind spun uselessly round the problem as a slipping clutch on a one in four hill. And then I had an idea; the clutch gripped; I went back to the Royale with a little more alacrity.

'What's wrong?' asked Hassan suspiciously.

'Thought I saw a funnel in there,' I said. 'It would save us wasting half the juice.'

I'd seen nothing in there, but I wanted to look behind the front seats to see whether there was a control lever to release the lid of the dummy tank. There must be something somewhere. There was. I saw a small nickel-plated lever, like an old-fashioned motor-cycle throttle control, before they thought of twist-grips. It was connected by a Bowden cable to the dark recesses of the car. I moved down the lever as far as it would go and scrabbled noisily about, as though looking for a funnel.

'No good,' I told Hassan, my head still down, for I've an old-world idea that it's easier to make someone believe a lie if you don't have to look at them while you tell it.

I walked back to the Type 57, crouched down under the tank at the back, and scooped out a hole in the sand for the base of the container, to hold it steady. Then I put the end of the screw-driver blade against the tank and tapped it gently with the hammer. The metal was thin and old, and at the third blow the point went through it and petrol gushed out.

I filled the container, then screwed one corner of my handkerchief into a spill and stuffed this up into the hole. It would still leak, but it wouldn't leak so quickly, and if Hassan was, by any unthinkable chance, going to keep his part of the bargain, I would need some petrol to reach Alexandria.

The smell of leaking petrol was very strong, and I wondered about the danger of fire, but that was the least of my problems. I picked up the container, took it back to the Bugatti, opened the filler cap and poured it in. Not entirely to my surprise, the couple of gallons or so in the can filled the tank completely. So I had been right; they *had* run out of fuel because of the smallness of the tank. Not that this confirmation did me any good at that particular moment in my life, but if you're a pro it's always cheering to know your diagnosis is correct.

'Now get back in your own car,' said Hassan. He had his pistol out in his hand which, in some quarters, would be considered better than having something else out in his hand, but I wasn't in those quarters or even halves; I was in the hell of a mess, and the sight of that blue barrel did nothing to slow my heartbeats to a healthier speed.

'Turn your car round,' he said.

'Why?' I asked, watching his eyes for that tiny flicker towards the pistol that would mean he was going to fire. 'Alex is this way.'

'You're not going to Alex,' he said. 'You're going somewhere else.'

'Where?'

I leaned against the door and felt the warmth of the metal through my thin damp shirt, and I knew where I was going : to the graveyard. I was suddenly cold all over; cohorts of men could be walking over my grave, and if I didn't do something to help myself at once, or sooner, that's just what they would be doing. The long day seemed nearly done, and so was I.

'All right,' I said hoarsely, 'I'll turn it.' I moved towards Maria.

'You wait there,' I called to her. 'Guide me if the wheels are too near the sand.'

I started the engine, moved the car forward a few yards, turned and then backed so that I was facing Hassan. He stood about eight feet away from the radiator, gun pointing at me. On the floor, halfway under the seat, was the crank handle. I carefully put my left foot on the clutch, pushed the gear into second and brought up the crank handle until one end was resting on the accelerator pedal. This had a rubber cover, so it didn't slip. I pushed the crank slightly; the engine began to rev.

'Come on,' called Hassan. 'Park over to my left. Then get out.'

He wants all the work done for him, I thought. Then, when I'm out of the car, he'll kill me. That way, there would be no bullet-holes through the doors, no messy bloodstains on the seats. Just a body on the sand; a mad Englishman who'd killed one of his countrymen, stolen a car and then shot himself.

As Hassan spoke, I jammed the crank handle hard against the accelerator, and at the same time threw myself down under the dashboard.

The car bounded forward. Above the scream of the hundred odd horses under the bonnet, I heard a crack like a stock whip, and then a splutter as the engine died, and then another crack, and then silence, broken only by the distant thunder of the sea on the shore. The car rolled slowly to a stop. I had failed again.

Hassan had fired at the radiator, and by some incredibly lucky chance for him—or maybe because he really was as good a shot as he claimed—the bullet must have shattered the distributor, or the coil or the main lead or one of the other vulnerable and vital parts that a single well-aimed bullet could destroy.

Well, I'd tried. I still held the crank in my right hand. I had lost everything now except the last battle, and no bookie would have given me any odds on that.

I lay where I was for a moment, for I'd nowhere else to lie, and then slowly I levered myself up. I'd be in a better position to ward off a counter-attack sitting up than lying down.

As I moved, I half expected a bullet to splinter the windscreen. I could feel it in advance, boring through my shoulder, puncturing the bone, shattering the muscle, tearing apart the tendons. Imagining it was nearly as bad as having it happen; what did Shakespeare say about cowards dying many times before their death? I was practically part of my own instant funeral kit—the corpse part.

Finally, I was sitting upright behind the wheel, still alive, and gripping the crank, and looking at Hassan. He was standing only feet away, bewilderment on his face, holding his right wrist in his left hand. His pistol lay on the sand near his feet.

I climbed out of the car, watching him. We were like characters in one of those pictures with which they used to illustrate the adventure stories of my schooldays; everyone would stand staring at everyone else, arms half bent, but nothing actually happening, because the artist hadn't got the gift of action. If he had, of course, he wouldn't have been drawing such deplorable pictures.

I saw Sabry standing up in the passenger seat of the other car, both hands carefully above his head as though he'd been frantically waving to someone and they had suddenly frozen like that. Just behind him, I saw that the lid of the tank had opened, like the turret top of a tank. An old man stood there, a plastic mug in one hand, sipping from it. In his other hand he held a toy pistol with an ivory butt.

Good for dad, I thought, if this was Maria's dad. He certainly wasn't mine. Good for someone. He called to me in English.

'I'll deal with this—person.'

He spat out the word, so I gathered that he wasn't exactly a fully paid-up member of the Sabry supporters' club.

As the old man spoke, Sabry took a swing to the right with both his hands gripped together like a flail. He hit the old man in the stomach. The mug of water flew over the side of the car, and his pistol arm went up into the air, but he didn't drop the pistol.

Sabry started to run, taking great steps, but not covering much ground because of the sand, like a man running in a nightmare. It was all happening in slow motion, which made it worse for him, although not for me. I liked to see him run, and so far as I was concerned, the slower and longer he ran the better, for there was nowhere in all the world he could run to now. He was running to eternity.

He held out his hands in front of him, as though he could drag himself along by will power only, desperate to be out of range of that tiny gun.

The old man steadied himself with his left hand against the open lid of the tank, and then, taking his time and his aim, he fired twice. Then he put away his pistol. I suppose it only held three shots. The pistol was a toy unless you knew how to use it, but like the man with the twelve-inch hampton, François knew how to use it.

Sabry ran on for a few more paces, but his legs had turned to rubber, and his knees folded, and his whole body rolled forward, and he fell on the hard road and slipped sideways. He lay where he fell, and I didn't need a coroner's qualifications to know he would never get up again, because whoever moved Sabry would have to carry him off in a box with handles on its sides.

'I've left Hassan to you,' said the old man casually. 'I expect you'd like to deal with him yourself.'

He climbed out over the back of the car and jumped down on to the sand. He might be a bit long in the tooth, but he was no arthritic bathchair boyo.

Hassan made a sudden dive for his F.N., near his feet, and I threw the crank at him. It hit him across the top of the head as he bent down, and he staggered back and fell. I picked up his pistol and put it in my own jacket pocket. If anyone was going to use it, I was going to.

'You bastard,' I said, and as his face came up, I hit him hard, right on those china teeth. Maybe what George would call his Hampstead Heath—his teeth—were the best china, for he kept grinning at me. But this was only a muscular reaction, for his lips were drawn back like an animal's over those firm gums that must have gammed many a game young Egyptian boy.

He stood now, bent forward, his arms out, fingers hooked. As we faced each other, he kicked out with his right foot and tapped at my left kneecap. I don't know what this was supposed to do, except to throw me off balance, which it might well have done had my kneecap been where he aimed at. But years in the old-car trade have taught me some crude cunning, if nothing else, for you never know how customers can react when they feel a deal's going against them. I stepped smartly to one side as I saw his foot approaching.

I seized his shoe as his foot came up and twisted it as though I wanted to break it off at the ankle, and so, like that character in the Old Testament who digged a pit and then fell into the midst of it himself, Hassan, the thrower, became Hassan the thrown. This time, as he jumped up, I clobbered him on the side of the head, and as he reeled, I hit him twice hard, left and right, in the guts.

They wouldn't have stood for those blows at the National Sporting Club, and neither did Hassan. He dropped on his hands and knees, and I trod on his fingers and ground them into the sharp hot sand before he could grip my ankles and try to bring me down.

The Marquess of Queensberry wouldn't have liked that, but then I wasn't asking him to. I must be honest and add that Hassan didn't like it, either, but he was tough and he knew, as I did very clearly, that, on his feet, he could cripple me in seconds. I was therefore determined to keep him off his feet, and at mine, as much as possible, for I was tiring. I'd have to finish him soon, or he would finish me.

Hassan lay for a second as though out, and then, unexpectedly, for he'd taken more punishment than I'd have liked to receive, he jumped up and came at my throat. My hands went up between his and then out, breaking his stranglehold, and then, body to body, I brought up my right knee hard in his groin.

He gave a whimper of pain and in his giant agony, his mouth opened like a gargoyle, and he sank rather than fell, and scrabbled in the sand, half turning like the bent spoke of a living wheel.

'Get up,' I told him.

He scooped up handfuls of sand as he struggled to his knees. I kicked him in the crotch to make him move more quickly, thinking as I did so, of George's old adage, 'Never kick a man when he's down—he may get up.'

Maybe Hassan had heard it, too, for he crawled to a squatting position and crouched there. I'd never trusted him, but now I didn't have to. I took out his automatic, blew the dust off it, fired once into the sand to see that it hadn't been damaged. It hadn't, so I pointed it at Hassan's stomach.

'Get up,' I repeated.

This time, he unwound himself and stood up shakily, his face matted with sand and blood, streaks of sweat running down from his hair. It could run where it liked so far as I was concerned. My own running days were over.

I kept him covered, and called over my shoulder to Maria, because I wasn't sure whether her dear old dad, François, was still around. 'Has your father reloaded?' I asked her.

François replied: 'No. I only carry three bullets.'

'They're enough,' I told him. 'Put all Hassan's and Sabry's stuff in the little Bugatti. And quickly, before someone comes.'

I felt like that fellow in the story who's screwing a young girl and she suddenly gets agitated and asks: 'Ooh, what if my mother comes?' And her lover sternly replies: 'Apart from you, the only one who's coming round here is me.'

I was in charge now, and I was staying that way because that's the best way to be; more, it's the only way.

François pulled two suitcases, a brief-case, and an airline bag with the neck of a bottle sticking out, from the Royale. I fired into the bag and the bottle splintered and lime juice poured across the sand.

'Ever heard of the first Rockefeller?' I asked Hassan, only rhetorically, you understand. I didn't care whether he had heard of him, but he was going to hear about him now. He was what one might call a captive audience.

Hassan said nothing.

'Well, I'll tell you about him,' I went on generously. 'He was very rich, very hard, very tough. One day, he realized his associates were trying to screw him, so he called them all together, and he said: "Gentlemen, you have conspired to swindle me. I won't sue you, the law takes too long. Instead, I'll ruin you!" And he did.'

I don't know whether Hassan absorbed the message, which was that what was good enough for Rockefeller, was good enough for me. Hassan and Sabry had tried, and very nearly succeeded not only in swindling me, but in landing me on a possible murder charge. Sabry was now where I didn't want to go for a while yet, but Hassan I could handle.

'I'm going to leave you here in your uniform with Sabry's body,' I told him. 'You can talk your way out of that one—as you wanted to make me talk my way out of being found with Kent's body.

'Just to even the score, I'll also leave you a gun.'

François had moved up to my side. Out of the edge of my eyes. I could sense rather than see he was grinning, the poetic justice of the thing must have appealed to him, as keeping him a poor man had no doubt appealed to the Egyptians. Odd what a kick we can all get from making life hard for other people, isn't it?

I put out my right hand, still keeping Hassan covered, and took François's empty pistol from him, and threw it in the sand at Hassan's feet.

'When people want to know how Sabry died—if anyone cares— you can tell them that two shells from this gun are in his body.

Or perhaps they'll find out for themselves if they do a post mortem. The empties are still in the breech.

'But then again, maybe no one will want to know. There's not much traffic that comes along here, so you have a fighting chance. Now, take off your shoes.'

He bent down, and began to unlace them.

'Throw them into the back of my car,' I told him.

He did so. They landed in the front seat.

'Now, all your money and identity papers.'

He unbuttoned an inner pocket and pulled out a yellow wash-leather wallet.

'Throw them one by one into the car, too.'

'But I must keep my identity card,' he protested. 'Otherwise, no one will know who I am.'

'I know,' I told him. 'And I wouldn't want to change you, darling. Chuck them in the car or I'll do it for you.'

I jerked the gun slightly. Hassan opened the wallet as quickly as a spinster opening her arms to a night intruder. He threw the car's papers, my passport, then a cheque book, then some currency notes clipped together, finally, the empty wallet.

'Now,' I said. 'I'll tell you how you sprang François here. You borrowed or stole that uniform from your cousin, the chief of police, and you simply told the guards you were taking him out. It was very simple, no strain at all. They thought you were the chief of police, and, of course, they released him at once. Right?'

'Right,' said François.

Hassan said nothing. I threw him a few more lines of dialogue. I liked the sound of my own voice. It made a change from being ordered about.

'First, you killed Kent, though.'

'It was an accident,' Hassan insisted.

'So you told me. But now your only witness, Sabry, is dead, too. So we've only your word for that accident. The court will only have your word, too.'

'What do you mean?'

Hassan seemed genuinely puzzled, or maybe the genuine look of concern he gave me was as phoney as anything else he'd given me.

'Just what I say. We're leaving you here to explain to your good Egyptian friends how you came to be wearing the uniform of the chief of police—without any shoes or any identity papers, and with a man dead here, shot by two bullets from this gun.'

He stood staring at me, his eyes as big as onions in his head. I stared right back at him. He hadn't told me why he had beaten me up in Rosemary Court, so long ago it seemed now it was practically out of this century, and yet it was less than a week ago. If I didn't find out now I never would, because I hoped I would never see Hassan again this side of Jordan, and I didn't mean the river or the country, but this side of the tomb. The fact is, I wasn't so keen on seeing him the other side, either, so before we said goodbye, I had to know the reason for his roughness.

'You never told me why you clobbered me in that flat in London,' I said. 'The one Maria was using. I'll give you three to talk.'

'And if I won't,' said Hassan.

'I'll shoot you first through the left knee-cap, then the right, then where the bullet falls.' It sounded kinder to use George's rhyming slang.

'What do you say?'

'I'll talk,' said Hassan.

I was relieved, for this saved me three bullets, and there was no guarantee that I would have hit him, even at that distance.

'I had to get to London,' he said. 'I deal in guns, and there are no guns here any more, except the ones we buy and sell among ourselves, but they're not enough. I needed new stock, but I had no currency.'

He paused. I threw a couple of lines into the pause.

'So you went to your cousin, the chief of police, and gave him a long spiel about doing a job for him, and so he let you have some official currency. Right?'

'Yes. I saw that Maria had a job with Kent. I knew who her father was. I told my cousin she was planning to smuggle him out. I needed to watch her. He'd get all the praise if we caught them both just going over the border. But first of all I had to go to London.

'He gave me the authority to take out some money. When I got to London I thought I'd go over Maria's flat first to see if I could pick up anything like a letter, even any cash. She came back unexpectedly, and when I heard the key in the door, I jumped into the cupboard. She ran out again before I could escape, and then you came.'

This made sense to me. The letter in the Delahaye had obviously been from Maria's father. If Hassan had found that in her flat, then he would have realized that what he had imagined and invented was actually happening.

If he'd discovered this, then he could have helped smuggle François out himself with Maria; but then if we all had different turns of mind we wouldn't be where we are.

I felt sorry for him in a way, but not that sorry. I was glad I wasn't in his stockinged feet.

'Get in the Royale,' I told Maria. François was already behind the wheel.

'You can't leave me here,' protested Hassan.

'Why not?' I asked him. 'You've a sporting chance. More chance than all those birds you used to shoot.'

I handed Hassan's gun to François; he was a better shot than me, and there was a special reason why I wanted him to fire, which

I'll come to later. 'Shoot,' I told him, and nodded in the direction I wanted him to fire.

'No!' shouted Hassan. 'No, I beg of you!'

He closed his eyes as he prepared for death.

François fired once, twice, not at Hassan, but into the petrol tank of the small Bugatti. For a second, nothing happened, and I thought nothing would. Hassan opened his eyes and with a roar like thunder, the rear of the car erupted into a ball of flame.

The petrol, leaking out of the tank, past my handkerchief, had vaporized in the heat. As any schoolboy will tell you, if you can grab an articulate one for long enough, a mixture of petrol and air is heavier than air alone, and so the petrol vapour hung beneath the car like a dangerous and invisible fog.

Hassan would have a long walk on his bare feet—and some interesting explanations to make at the end of the trail.

I heard a crackle of exhaust as François started up the Royale's engine, and I vaulted over the back of the car.

'Drive,' I told him, as he must so often have commanded his own chauffeur in years long past.

He drove, with me sitting astride the tail, like a split-arse mechanic. Behind us, a column of thick oily smoke grew taller in the sky, the funeral pyre of Hassan's dream. He ran after us in his stockinged feet, screaming with rage, and then, as we drew away, he bent down and hurled handfuls of sand after us. I gave him the old V-sign. It cost me nothing, and aren't we told somewhere that it is more blessed to give than to receive?

I felt blessed all right as François coaxed fifty out of the old Royale, and we trundled along for a couple of miles. Then he pulled to the side of the road and switched off the engine.

'What's wrong?' I asked him. I couldn't believe that he was simply stopping to admire the scenery, which wasn't worth a postcard home.

'Nothing,' he said, 'But don't forget I'm still the most wanted man in Egypt. And there's a police post only a mile ahead.'

'Once more into the tank, dear friend,' I said, and leaned down behind the seat and pulled the release lever. We lifted up the lid. The dummy tank was lined with felt, and had a strip of thick sorbo rubber on the floor. A plastic water bottle and a mug were clipped to one side of the wall. He might be hot in there, but he'd survive until we were aboard ship and well beyond the twelve-mile limit.

Maria and I locked the tank lid shut, and I drove. The car felt heavy at slow speeds, but as the speedometer needle climbed round the dial, the steering grew lighter—not that I worried much so long as the thing would carry us to the docks. I never wanted to drive it again.

We stopped at the police post with its radio aerial, the trestle table covered by the inevitable army blanket. Two shabby soldiers stood up as we approached. One had a rifle over his shoulder. The other waved us down with a cigarette in his hand.

'I'll do the talking,' said Maria, as I cut the engine to save petrol, and we coasted the last hundred yards.

'Do that,' I agreed, because I can't speak a word of Arabic. 'But make it clear that if these two guys want promotion, then they can arrest an impostor—doubtless an alien spy—disguised as the chief of police.

'Tell them he's only a few miles behind us in the desert with a burned-out car and a dead man. Don't spare the details. Give it to them rich and thick, just like the soup mother used to make.'

'Whose mother?'

'Everyone's.'

Both men looked around the car as though they'd never seen one like it before, and no doubt they hadn't. After all, why should they have done? I hadn't seen one myself, and I'm in the business.

Maria climbed out and began a long spiel to the character with the rifle. He didn't appear greatly interested. Maybe he wasn't promotion-orientated. She held out her hand, and I saw the pink edge of a thousand-piastre note between her fingers. The soldier saw it, too, and shook hands with a bit more enthusiasm, palming the note with a practised ease that any head waiter would have envied.

Here, I was sure, stood no upright fighter for the worthy cause of Egyptian solidarity. Here was a man like me, who wanted to do a deal, and who now saw his chance. Even so, he went through the motions of examining the car. He peered under the bonnet, patted the huge tail appreciatively, and then waved us on.

'Did you tell him?' I asked Maria.

'Everything. Just as you said.'

I pressed the starter button, and the motor gave a sad whine and died.

I pressed the button again, and nothing happened except that the petrol gauge needle swung down its dial, and I didn't have to be a paid-up member of the Motor Trader's Association to realize we had a dud battery.

Heaven knows how long the battery had been in the car when it was on show, and this business of starting the gigantic engine a number of times in the baking heat of the desert, had made it realize its age. It also made me realize mine, and what an awkward spot we were in, for I didn't under-estimate Hassan's powers of survival, or his tennis-ball ability to bounce back.

'What's wrong?' asked Maria.

'Battery's down. They'll have to push us.'

It was impossible to think of swinging that engine on a crank, even if I had one, which I hadn't. Maria spoke to the guard, who listened gravely and then shrugged his shoulders. However, he called to his companions, and together they leaned against the body of the car. It didn't budge an inch. They were old soldiers, of course, and only leaning, not actually pushing.

Maria spoke sharply to them, and they called out two other men from inside the post. They also leaned on the car, without much enthusiasm, but at least it did begin to roll forward very slowly. I put my foot on the clutch, engaged third, and then let out the clutch sharply. The engine fired, and I kept it running while we shouted mutual congratulations at each other.

The soldiers crowded round Maria. She handed out a hundred-piastre note to the nearest, who saluted her, as well he might. He looked more intelligent than his companions. Maria thought so, too, for she began to talk to him urgently, pointing back at the desert behind us I had no idea what the hell she was saying, and so I asked her when we were on our way.

'I gave him a revised version of what I'd told his companion with so little effect. There's been an Israeli raid back up the road. Our people had been engaging them with heavy anti-aircraft fire. A plane had been shot down and burned itself out. And only a few miles away was a traitor, wearing Egyptian police uniform, with a burned-out car and an Egyptian patriot he'd shot.'

'Hassan,' I said approvingly, hoping we'd be well away and out of sight of land before any of these characters learned the truth. 'Hassan.'

'Who else?' she asked.

Who else, indeed, I thought. It might have been me. I beat on the petrol tank.

'You all right down there, dad?' I asked. 'François, art thou sleeping there below?'

He certainly wasn't sleeping, but whatever he said I couldn't understand it. He sounded as though he were speaking from the middle of a gasometer, and, frankly, I didn't care how he sounded so long as he was near me, for the thought that I would soon have twenty thousand pounds was growing ever more rosy in my mind.

Alexandria in the morning was like Alexandria in the evening, but a bit busier, with more cars and masses of bicycles, and a whole string of camels walking in line. Each held in its mouth the tail of the camel in front, which was one way of keeping together.

I would have liked a coffee or some breakfast, but there was no time. We had to reach the docks first; business, as I've said earlier, before pleasure. Maria knew the back streets away from the sea front where we'd pass fewer people. I rather missed the hotel names, The Gordon, The Cecil, The Ivy, but I felt that maybe my conduct had not been quite up to their high aristocratic standards.

We came into the docks behind a crowd of workers arriving on bicycles, all showing their passes, which was better than showing anything else, but no doubt they did that, too, when the mood overtook them. They looked a villainous lot.

The same man with the hat was in the little house with the window by the gate. He might never have gone home; perhaps that was his home. He came out when he saw me, and we shook hands. I handed over the papers, and Maria did her spiel in Egyptian.

Up went the Royale's bonnet. He checked each digit of the chassis and engine numbers on the plates and on the papers. Luckily, he didn't glance too closely at the engine, and the dust of the desert, caked on the oil leaks, had effectively concealed Hassan's handiwork with paint and putty on the previous evening. He stamped the papers, examined Kent's passport which I offered as my own, and called up the same man who had driven the other cars into the docks.

We'd made it. All that remained now was for the ship's captain to cast off or pull his anchor out or whatever else he'd got in, and we'd be away. François would be free and I'd be richer by twenty thousand little green men. It was a happy thought and I enjoyed thinking it.

'What now?' I asked Maria.

'All the cars are being loaded immediately,' she said. 'We can go aboard any time.'

'The sooner the better,' I said.

With a bit of luck, Kent's body would still be undiscovered, and even if we hadn't that bit of luck, I'd cut the telephone line, so how could they contact the police here? And even if they did contact the police by semaphore, runner, pigeon, flag or heliograph, or even by any other unexpected means, how could they trace us to the docks so quickly? The answer seemed reassuring enough. They damn' well couldn't.

I walked with Maria to our ship, between wooden crates just unloaded from Russia. The blue peter was already fluttering at the masthead, and a wisp of steam grew like a beard from the exhaust behind the funnel. Only minutes now, and we would be away—and suddenly I remembered something.

My mind must have been slipping, or maybe it was the change of life, or a change of sex or heart, for I'd forgotten one most important thing I had to do before I boarded the ship—the real reason why I'd asked François to set the Type 57 alight rather than do it myself.

'One minute,' I said to Maria.

'There's a lavatory aboard,' she said.

'No, I don't want that,' I told her. I knew exactly what I wanted, for I'd seen a sign in English above a small hut: *Telegraph Office*. I ran towards it, hoping it was open. Inside the wooden room, a clerk sat at a table surrounded by sheets of telegrams held down by crystal balls. I counted three of them.

He could have been going into the pawnbroking business.

'Please?' he asked, looking at me with the pained irritation of all Post Office servants when a member of the public approaches.

'I want to send a telegram,' I told him.

He pushed a form towards me.

'You have a pen?'

Yes, I had a pen. I wrote out the telegram, handed it back. He read it aloud suspiciously in case it contained a code.

It was to: MIDLAND WIDOWS INSURANCE CO. FEN-CHURCH STREET LONDON STOP ATTENTION CAR INSURANCE DEPARTMENT STOP MUST INFORM YOU THAT BUGATTI CAR INSURED WITH YOU AGREED VALUE 5,000 POUNDS THROUGH ARISTO AUTOS BEL-GRAVIA TOTAL LOSS IN EGYPTIAN DESERT STOP AM INFORMING LOCAL POLICE STOP.

'That will be three hundred piastres,' he said.

'Cheap at the price,' I told him, and sent another telegram to the Chief of Police to tell him where the car was now.

'A total loss?' asked the clerk sympathetically.

'Absolutely total,' I agreed.

'But it was insured?' he went on hopefully.

'To the full amount,' I assured him thankfully, which was why I couldn't very well have set fire to the thing myself, I mean, could I? That would have been arson. We must have some standards, that's what I always say. That's what's so wrong with everything today: no moral code, no sense of honour.

I walked back towards the gangway. Maria was waiting for me, standing in the sun. I could see she hadn't a slip beneath her dress, and I wondered what else she'd be wearing, or not wearing. Well, I'd have time enough and money enough to find out.

I thought about that, too, and about the voyage through the warm wine-dark Mediterranean to Marseilles—a touch of the old Homer there. And once we were at sea there'd be a touch of the old this-and-that, too.

I was also thinking of my old family motto, or what I'd have chosen if I'd had either an old family or a motto.

For too long it had been business before pleasure. Well, I'd had the business. I'd collect £5,000 on the insurance, and at least as much again on these three cars, and half as much on the jewels, and then there was also the prospect of Maria's £20,000.

Moneywise, as the financial writers in newspapers like to say, it hadn't been an entirely unproductive trip. But otherwise, how would I rate it? That remained to be seen; the journey was not over yet. So much for business, I thought. Now for pleasure. Maria's pleasure. And mine.

We went up the gangway together.

London—Cairo—Alexandria.

THIS PERFECT DAY
Ira Levin

'This Perfect Day' is published by
Michael Joseph Ltd.

The Author

Ira Levin was born in 1929 in New York City and is a graduate of the Horace Mann School and New York University. *This Perfect Day* is his third novel; the first was the suspense classic *A Kiss Before Dying*, never out of print since its publication seventeen years ago, and the second, the world-renowned *Rosemary's Baby*. He has also written plays, short stories, and song lyrics. He lives in New York and has three sons.

Christ, Marx, Wood, and Wei
  Led us to this perfect day.
Marx, Wood, Wei, and Christ;
  All but Wei were sacrificed.
Wood, Wei, Christ, and Marx
  Gave us lovely schools and parks.
Wei, Christ, Marx, and Wood
  Made us humble, made us good.

—child's rhyme for
  bouncing a ball

PART ONE: GROWING UP

1

A CITY'S BLANK WHITE CONCRETE SLABS, the giant ones ringed by the less giant, gave space in their midst to a broad pink-floored plaza, a playground in which some two hundred young children played and exercised under the care of a dozen supervisors in white coveralls. Most of the children, bare, tan, and black-haired, were crawling through red and yellow cylinders, swinging on swings, or doing group calisthenics; but in a shadowed corner where a hopscotch grid was inlaid, five of them sat in a close, quiet circle, four of them listening and one speaking.

'They catch animals and eat them and wear their skins,' the speaker, a boy of about eight, said. 'And they—they do a thing called "fighting". That means they hurt each other, on purpose, with their hands or with rocks and things. They don't love and help each other at all.'

The listeners sat wide-eyed. A girl younger than the boy said, 'But you *can't* take off your bracelet. It's impossible.' She pulled at her own bracelet with one finger, to show how safely-strong the links were.

'You can if you've got the right tools,' the boy said. 'It's taken off on your linkday, isn't it?'

'Only for a second.'

'But it's taken off, isn't it?'

'Where do they live?' another girl asked.

'On mountaintops,' the boy said. 'In deep caves. In all kinds of places where we can't find them.'

The first girl said, 'They must be sick.'

'Of course they are,' the boy said, laughing. 'That's what "incurable" *means*, sick. That's why they're called incurables, because they're very, very sick.'

The youngest child, a boy of about six, said, 'Don't they get their treatments?'

The older boy looked at him scornfully. 'Without their bracelets?' he said. 'Living in caves?'

'But how do they *get* sick?' the six-year-old asked. 'They get their treatments *until* they run away, don't they?'

'Treatments,' the older boy said, 'don't always work.'

The six-year-old stared at him. 'They do,' he said.

'No they don't.'

'My goodness,' a supervisor said, coming to the group with

volley balls tucked one under each arm, 'aren't you sitting too close together? What are you playing, Who's Got the Rabbit?'

The children quickly hitched away from one another, separating into a larger circle—except the six-year-old boy, who stayed where he was, not moving at all. The supervisor looked at him curiously.

A two-note chime sounded on loudspeakers. 'Shower and dress,' the supervisor said, and the children hopped to their feet and raced away.

'Shower and dress!' the supervisor called to a group of children playing passball nearby.

The six-year-old boy stood up, looking troubled and unhappy. The supervisor crouched before him and looked into his face with concern. 'What's wrong?' she asked.

The boy, whose right eye was green instead of brown, looked at her and blinked.

The supervisor let drop her volley balls, turned the boy's wrist to look at his bracelet, and took him gently by the shoulders. 'What is it, Li?' she asked. 'Did you lose the game? Losing's the same as winning; you know that, don't you?'

The boy nodded.

'What's important is having fun and getting exercise, right?'

The boy nodded again and tried to smile.

'Well, that's better,' the supervisor said. 'That's a little better. Now you don't look like such a sad old sad-monkey.'

The boy smiled.

'Shower and dress,' the supervisor said with relief. She turned the boy around and gave him a pat on his bottom. 'Go on,' she said, 'skedaddle.'

The boy, who was sometimes called Chip but more often Li—his nameber was Li RM35M4419—said scarcely a word while eating, but his sister Peace kept up a continuous jabbering and neither of his parents noticed his silence. It wasn't until all four had seated themselves in the TV chairs that his mother took a good look at him and said, 'Are you feeling all right, Chip?'

'Yes, I feel fine,' he said.

His mother turned to his father and said, 'He hasn't said a word all evening.'

Chip said, 'I feel fine.'

'Then why are you so quiet?' his mother asked.

'Shh,' his father said. The screen had flicked on and was finding its right colors.

When the first hour was over and the children were getting ready for bed, Chip's mother went into the bathroom and watched him finish cleaning his teeth and pull his mouthpiece from the tube. 'What is it?' she said. 'Did somebody say something about your eye?'

'No,' he said, reddening.

'Rinse it,' she said.

'I did.'

'*Rinse it.*'

He rinsed his mouthpiece and, stretching, hung it in its place on the rack. 'Jesus was talking,' he said. 'Jesus DV. During play.'

'About what? Your eye?'

'No, not my *eye*. Nobody says anything about my *eye*.'

'Then what?'

He shrugged. 'Members who—get sick and—leave the Family. Run away and take off their bracelets.'

His mother looked at him nervously. 'Incurables,' she said.

He nodded, her manner and her knowing the name making him more uneasy. 'It's true?' he said.

'No,' she said. 'No, it isn't. No. I'm going to call Bob. He'll explain it to you.' She turned and hurried from the room slipping past Peace, who was coming in closing her pajamas.

In the living room Chip's father said, 'Two more minutes. Are they in bed?'

Chip's mother said, 'One of the children told Chip about the incurables.'

'Hate,' his father said.

'I'm calling Bob,' his mother said, going to the phone.

'It's after eight.'

'He'll come,' she said. She touched her bracelet to the phone's plate and read out the nameber red-printed on a card tucked under the screen rim: 'Bob NE20G3018.' She waited, rubbing the heels of her palms tightly together. 'I knew something was bothering him,' she said. 'He didn't say a single word all evening.'

Chip's father got up from his chair. 'I'll go talk to him,' he said, going.

'Let Bob do it!' Chip's mother called. 'Get Peace into bed; she's still in the bathroom!'

Bob came twenty minutes later.

'He's in his room,' Chip's mother said.

'You two watch the program,' Bob said. 'Go on, sit down and watch.' He smiled at them. 'There's nothing to worry about,' he said. 'Really. It happens every day.'

'*Still?*' Chip's father said.

'Of course,' Bob said. 'And it'll happen a hundred years from now. Kids are kids.'

He was the youngest adviser they had ever had—twenty-one, and barely a year out of the Academy. There was nothing diffident or unsure about him though; on the contrary, he was more relaxed and confident than advisers of fifty or fifty-five. They were pleased with him.

He went to Chip's room and looked in. Chip was in bed, lying on an elbow with his head in his hand, a comic book spread open before him.

'Hi, Li,' Bob said.

Chip said, 'Hi, Bob.'

Bob went in and sat down on the side of the bed. He put his telecomp on the floor between his feet, felt Chip's forehead and ruffled his hair. 'Whatcha readin'?' he said.

'*Wood's Struggle,*' Chip said, showing Bob the cover of the comic book. He let it drop closed on the bed and, with his forefinger, began tracing the wide yellow *W* of 'Wood's'.

Bob said, 'I hear somebody's been giving you some cloth about incurables.'

'Is that what it is?' Chip asked, not looking from his moving finger.

'That's what it is, Li,' Bob said. 'It used to be true, a long, long time ago, but not any more; now it's just cloth.'

Chip was silent, retracing the *W*.

'We didn't always know as much about medicine and chemistry as we do today,' Bob said, watching him 'and until fifty years or so after the Unification, members used to get sick sometimes, a very few of them, and feel that they *weren't* members. Some of them ran away and lived by themselves in places the Family wasn't using, barren islands and mountain peaks and so forth.'

'And they took off their bracelets?'

'I suppose they did,' Bob said. 'Bracelets wouldn't have been much use to them in places like that, would they, with no scanners to put them to?'

'Jesus said they did something called "fighting".'

Bob looked away and then back again. ' "Acting aggressively" is a nicer way of putting it,' he said. 'Yes, they did that.'

Chip looked up at him. 'But they're dead now?' he said.

'Yes, all dead,' Bob said. 'Every last one of them.' He smoothed Chip's hair. 'It was a long, long time ago,' he said. 'Nobody gets that way today.'

Chip said, 'We know more about medicine and chemistry today. Treatments *work.*'

'Right you are,' Bob said. 'And don't forget there were five separate computers in those days. Once one of those sick members had left his home continent, he was completely unconnected.'

'My grandfather helped to build UniComp.'

'I know he did, Li. So next time anyone tells you about the incurables, you remember two things: one, treatments are much more effective today than they were a long time ago; and two, we've got UniComp looking out for us everywhere on Earth. Okay?'

'Okay,' Chip said, and smiled.

'Let's see what it says about *you,*' Bob said, picking up his telecomp and opening it on his knees.

Chip sat up and moved close, pushing his pajama sleeve clear of his bracelet. 'Do you think I'll get an extra treatment?' he asked.

'If you need one,' Bob said. 'Do you want to turn it on?'

'Me?' Chip said. 'May I?'

'Sure,' Bob said.

Chip put his thumb and forefinger cautiously to the telecomp's on-off switch. He clicked it over, and small lights came on—blue, amber, amber. He smiled at them.

Bob, watching him, smiled and said, 'Touch.'

Chip touched his bracelet to the scanner plate, and the blue light beside it turned red.

Bob tapped the input keys. Chip watched his quickly moving fingers. Bob kept tapping and then pressed the answer button; a line of green symbols glowed on the screen, and then a second line beneath the first. Bob studied the symbols. Chip watched him.

Bob looked at Chip from the corners of his eyes, smiling. 'Tomorrow at 12.25,' he said.

'Good!' Chip said. 'Thank you!'

'Thank Uni,' Bob said, switching off the telecomp and closing its cover. 'Who told you about the incurables?' he asked. 'Jesus who?'

'DV 33-something,' Chip said. 'He lives on the twenty-fourth floor.'

Bob snapped the telecomp's catches. 'He's probably as worried as you were,' he said.

'Can he have an extra treatment too?'

'If he needs one; I'll alert his adviser. Now to *sleep*, brother; you've got school tomorrow.' Bob took Chip's comic book and put it on the night table.

Chip lay down and snuggled smilingly into his pillow, and Bob stood up, tapped off the lamp, ruffled Chip's hair again, and bent and kissed the back of his head.

'See you Friday,' Chip said.

'Right,' Bob said. 'Good night.'

''Night, Bob.'

Chip's parents stood up anxiously when Bob came into the living room.

'He's fine,' Bob said. 'Practically asleep already. He's getting an extra treatment during his lunch hour tomorrow, probably a bit of tranquilizer.'

'Oh, what a relief,' Chip's mother said, and his father said, 'Thank's Bob.'

'Thank Uni,' Bob said. He went to the phone. 'I want to get some help to the other boy,' he said, 'the one who told him'— and touched his bracelet to the phone's plate.

* * *

The next day, after lunch, Chip rode the escalators down from his school to the medicenter three floors below. His bracelet, touched to the scanner at the medicenter's entrance, produced a winking green *yes* on the indicator, and another winking green *yes* at the door of the therapy section; and another winking green *yes* at the door of the treatment room.

Four of the fifteen units were being serviced, so the line was fairly long. Soon enough, though, he was mounting children's steps and thrusting his arm, with the sleeve pushed high, through a rubber-rimmed opening. He held his arm grownuply still while the scanner inside found and fastened on his bracelet and the infusion disc nuzzled warm and smooth against his upper arm's softness. Motors burred inside the unit, liquids trickled. The blue light overhead turned red and the infusion disc tickled-buzzed-stung his arm; and then the light turned blue again.

Later that day, in the playground, Jesus DV, the boy who had told him about the incurables, sought Chip out and thanked him for helping him.

'Thank Uni,' Chip said. 'I got an extra treatment; did you?'

'Yes,' Jesus said. 'So did the other kids and Bob UT. He's the one who told *me*.'

'It scared me a little,' Chip said, 'thinking about members getting sick and running away.'

'Me too a little,' Jesus said. 'But it doesn't happen any more; it was a long, long time ago.'

'Treatments are better now than they used to be,' Chip said.

Jesus said, 'And we've got UniComp watching out for us everywhere on Earth.'

'Right you are,' Chip said.

A supervisor came and shooed them into a passball circle, an enormous one of fifty or sixty boys and girls spaced out at fingertip distance, taking up more than a quarter of the busy playground.

2

CHIP'S GRANDFATHER was the one who had given him the name Chip. He had given all of them extra names that were different from their real ones: Chip's mother, who was his daughter, he called 'Suzu' instead of Anna; Chip's father was 'Mike' not Jesus (and thought the idea foolish); and Peace was 'Willow', which she refused to have anything at all to do with. 'No! Don't call me that; I'm Peace! I'm Peace KD37T5002!'

Papa Jan was odd. Odd-*looking*, naturally; all grandparents had their marked peculiarities—a few centimeters too much or too little of height, skin that was too light or too dark, big ears, a bent nose. Papa Jan was both taller and darker than normal, his eyes were big and bulging, and there were two reddish patches in his graying hair. But he wasn't only odd-*looking*, he was odd-*talking;* that was the real oddness about him. He was always saying things vigorously and with enthusiasm and yet giving Chip the feeling that he didn't mean them at all, that he meant in fact their exact opposites. On that subject of names, for instance: 'Marvelous! Wonderful!' he said. 'Four names for boys, four names for girls! What could be more friction-free, more everyone-the-same? Everybody would name boys after Christ, Marx, Wood, or Wei anyway, wouldn't they?'

'Yes,' Chip said.

'Of course!' Papa Jan said. 'And if Uni gives out four names for boys it has to give out four names for girls too, right? Obviously? Listen.' He stopped Chip and, crouching down, spoke face to face with him, his bulging eyes dancing as if he was about to laugh. It was a holiday and they were on their way to the parade, Unification Day or Wei's Birthday or whatever; Chip was seven, 'listen, Li RM35M26J449988WXYZ,' Papa Jan said. 'Listen, I'm going to tell you something fantastic, incredible. In my day—are you listening?—in my day there were *over twenty different names for boys alone!* Would you believe it? Love of Family, it's the truth. There was "Jan", and "John", and "Amu", and "Lev". "Higa" and "Mike!" "Tonio!" And in my father's time there were even more, maybe forty or fifty! Isn't that ridiculous? All those different names when members themselves are exactly the same and interchangeable? Isn't that the silliest thing you ever heard of?'

And Chip nodded, confused, feeling that Papa Jan meant the opposite, that somehow it *wasn't* silly and ridiculous to have forty or fifty different names for boys alone.

'Look at them!' Papa Jan said, taking Chip's hand and walking on with him—through Unity Park to the Wei's Birthday parade. 'Exactly the same! Isn't it marvelous? Hair the same, eyes the same, skin the same the same; boys, girls, all the same. Like peas in a pod. Isn't it fine? Isn't it top speed?'

Chip, flushing (not his green eye, not the same as *anybody's*), said, 'What does "peezinapod" mean?'

'I don't know,' Papa Jan said. 'Things members used to eat before totalcakes. Sharya used to say it.'

He was a construction supervisor in EUR55131, twenty kilometers from '55128, where Chip and his family lived. On Sundays and holidays he rode over and visited them. His wife, Sharya, had drowned in a sightseeing-boat disaster in '135, the same year Chip was born; he hadn't remarried. Chip's other grandparents, his father's mother and father, lived in MEX10405, and the only time he saw them was when they phoned on birthdays. They were odd, but not nearly as odd as Papa Jan.

*   *   *

School was pleasant and play was pleasant. The Pre-U Museum was pleasant although some of the exhibits were a bit scary—the 'spears' and 'guns', for instance, and the 'prison cell' with its striped-suited 'convict' sitting on the cot and clutching his head in motionless month-to-month woe. Chip always looked at him—he would slip away from the rest of the class if he had to—and having looked, he always walked quickly away.

Ice cream and toys and comic books were pleasant too. Once when Chip put his bracelet and a toy's sticker to a supply-center scanner, its indicator red-winked *no* and he had to put the toy, a construction set, in the turnback bin. He couldn't understand why Uni had refused him; it was the right day and the toy was in the right category. 'There *must* be a reason, dear,' the member behind him said. 'You go call your adviser and find out.'

He did, and it turned out that the toy was only being withheld for a few days, not denied completely; he had been teasing a scanner somewhere, putting his bracelet to it again and again, and he was being taught not to. That winking red *no* was the first in his life for a claim that mattered to him, not just for starting into the wrong classroom or coming to the medicenter on the wrong day; it hurt him and saddened him.

Birthdays were pleasant, and Christmas and Marxmas and Unification Day and Wood's and Wei's Birthdays. Even more pleasant, because they came less frequently, were his linkdays. The new link would be shinier than the others, and would stay shiny for days and days and days; and then one day he would remember and look and there would be only old links, all of them the same and indistinguishable. Like peezinapod.

In the spring of 145, when Chip was ten, he and his parents and Peace were granted the trip to EUR00001 to see UniComp. It was over an hour's ride from carport to carport and the longest trip Chip remembered making, although according to his parents he had flown from Mex to Eur when he was one and a half, and from EUR20140 to '55128 a few months later. They made the UniComp trip on a Sunday in April, riding with a couple in their fifties (someone's odd-looking grandparents, both of them lighter than normal, she with her hair unevenly clipped) and another family, the boy and girl of which were a year older than Chip and Peace. The other father drove the car from the EUR00001 turnoff to the carport near UniComp. Chip watched with interest as the man worked the car's lever and buttons. It felt funny riding slowly on wheels again after shooting along on air.

They took snapshots outside UniComp's white marble dome—whiter and more beautiful than it was in pictures or on TV, as the snow-tipped mountains beyond it were more stately, the Lake of Universal Brotherhood more blue and far-reaching—and then they joined the line at the entrance, touched the admission scanner, and went into the blue-white curving lobby. A smiling member in pale blue showed them toward the elevator line. They joined it, and Papa Jan came up to them, grinning with delight at their astonishment.

'What are *you* doing here?' Chip's father asked as Papa Jan kissed Chip's mother. They had told him they had been granted the trip and he had said nothing at all about claiming it himself.

Papa Jan kissed Chip's father. 'Oh, I just decided to surprise you, that's all,' he said. 'I wanted to tell my friend here'—he laid a large hand across Chip's shoulder—'a little more about Uni than the earpiece will. Hello, Chip.' He bent and kissed Chip's cheek, and Chip, surprised to be the reason for Papa Jan's being there, kissed him in return and said, 'Hello, Papa Jan.'

'Hello, Peace KD37T5002,' Papa Jan said gravely, and kissed Peace. She kissed him and said hello.

'When did you claim the trip?' Chip's father asked.

'A few days after you did,' Papa Jan said, keeping his hand on Chip's shoulder. The line moved up a few meters and they all moved with it.

Chip's mother said, 'But you were here only five or six years ago, weren't you?'

'Uni knows who put it together,' Papa Jan said, smiling. 'We get special favors.'

'That's not so,' Chip's father said. 'No one gets special favors.'

'Well, here I am, anyway,' Papa Jan said, and turned his smile down toward Chip. 'Right?'

'Right,' Chip said, and smiled back up at him.

Papa John had helped build UniComp when he was a young man. It had been his first assignment.

The elevator held about thirty members, and instead of music it had a man's voice—'Good day, brothers and sisters; welcome to the site of UniComp'—a warm, friendly voice that Chip recognized from TV. 'As you can tell, we've started to move,' it said, 'and now we're descending at a speed of twenty-two meters per second. It will take us just over three and a half minutes to reach Uni's five-kilometer depth. This shaft down which we're traveling . . .' The voice gave statistics about the size of UniComp's housing and the thickness of its walls, and told of its safety from all natural and man-made disturbances. Chip had heard this information before, in school and on TV, but hearing it now, while on the very verge of *seeing* UniComp, made it seem new and exciting. He listened attentively, watching the speaker disc over the elevator door. Papa Jan's hand still held his shoulder, as if to restrain him. 'We're slowing now,' the voice said. 'Enjoy your visit, won't you?'—and the elevator sank to a cushiony stop and the door divided and slid to both sides.

There was another lobby, smaller than the one at ground level, another smiling member in pale blue, and another line, this one extending two by two to double doors that opened on a dimly lit hallway.

'Here we are!' Chip called, and Papa Jan said to him, 'We don't all have to be together.' They had become separated from Chip's parents and Peace, who were farther ahead in the line and looking back at them questioningly—Chip's parents; Peace was too short to be seen. The member in front of Chip turned and offered to let them move up, but Papa Jan said, 'No, this is all right. Thank you, brother.' He waved a hand at Chip's parents and smiled, and Chip did the same. Chip's parents smiled back, then turned around and moved forward.

Papa Jan looked about, his bulging eyes bright, his mouth keeping its smile. His nostrils flared and fell with his breathing. 'So,' he said, 'you're finally going to see UniComp. Excited?'

'Yes, very,' Chip said.

They followed the line forward.

'I don't blame you,' Papa Jan said. 'Wonderful! Once-in-a-lifetime experience, to see the machine that's going to classify you and give you your assignments, that's going to decide where you'll live and whether or not you'll marry the girl you want to marry; and if you do, whether or not you'll have children and what they'll be named if you have them—of course you're excited; who wouldn't be?'

Chip looked at Papa Jan, disturbed.

Papa Jan, still smiling, clapped him on the back as they passed in their turn into the hallway. 'Go look!' he said. 'Look at the displays, look at Uni, look at everything! It's all here for you—look at it!'

There was a rack of earpieces, the same as in a museum; Chip took one and put it in. Papa Jan's strange manner made him nervous, and he was sorry not to be up ahead with his parents and Peace. Papa Jan put in an earpiece too. 'I wonder what interesting new facts I'm going to hear!' he said, and laughed to himself. Chip turned away from him.

His nervousness and feeling of disturbance fell away as he faced a wall that glittered and skittered with a thousand sparkling minilights. The voice of the elevator spoke in his ears, telling him, while the lights showed him, how UniComp received from its round-the-world relay belt the microwave impulses of all the uncountable scanners and telecomps and telecontrolled devices; how it evaluated the impulses and sent back its answering impulses to the relay belt and the sources of inquiry.

Yes, he was excited. Was anything quicker, more clever, more everywhere than Uni?

The next span of wall showed how the memory banks worked; a beam of light flicked over a crisscrossed metal square, making parts of it glow and leaving parts of it dark. The voice spoke of electron beams and superconductive grids, of charged and un-charged areas becoming the yes-or-no carriers of different bits of information. When a question was put to UniComp, the voice said, it scanned the relevant bits ...

He didn't understand it, but that made it *more* wonderful, that Uni could know all there was to know so magically, so *un*-understandably!

And the next span was glass not wall, and there it was Uni-Comp: a twin row of different-colored metal bulks, like treat-ment units only lower and smaller, some of them pink, some brown, some orange; and among them in the large, rosily lit room, ten or a dozen members in pale blue coveralls, smiling and chatting with one another as they read meters and dials on the thirty-or-so units and marked what they read on handsome pale blue plastic clipboards. There was a gold cross and sickle on the far wall, and a clock that said *11.08 Sun 12 Apr 145 Y.U.* Music crept into Chip's ear and grew louder: 'Outward, Outward,' played by an enormous orchestra, so movingly, so majestically, that tears of pride and happiness came to his eyes.

He could have stayed there for hours, watching those busy cheerful members and those impressively gleaming memory banks, listening to 'Outward, Outward' and then 'One Mighty Family'; but the music thinned away (as *11.10* became *11.11*) and the voice, gently, aware of his feelings, reminded him of other members waiting and asked him to move on please to the next display farther down the hallway. Reluctantly he turned himself from UniComp's glass wall, with other members who were wiping at the corners of their eyes and smiling and nodding. He smiled at them, and they at him.

Papa Jan caught his arm and drew him across the hallway to a scanner-posted door. 'Well, did you like it?' he asked.

Chip nodded.

'That's not Uni,' Papa Jan said.

Chip looked at him.

Papa Jan pulled the earpiece out of Chip's ear. 'That's not UniComp!' he said in a fierce whisper. 'Those aren't real, those pink and orange boxes in there! Those are *toys*, for the Family to come look at and feel cozy and warm with!' His eyes bulged close to Chip's; specks of his spit hit Chip's nose and cheeks. 'It's down below!' he said. 'There are three levels under this one, and that's where it is! Do you want to see it? Do you want to see the *real* UniComp?'

Chip could only stare at him.

'Do you, Chip?' Papa Jan said. 'Do you want to see it? I can show it to you!'

Chip nodded.

Papa Jan let go of his arm and stood up straight. He looked around and smiled. 'All right,' he said, 'let's go this way,' and taking Chip's shoulder he steered him back the way they had come, past the glass wall thronged with members looking in, and the flicking light-beam of the memory banks and the skittering wall of minilights, and—'Excuse us, please'—through the line of incoming members and down to another part of the hallway that was darker and empty, where a monster telecomp lolled broken away from its wall display and two blue stretchers lay side by side with pillows and folded blankets on them.

There was a door in the corner with a scanner beside it, but as they got near it Papa Jan pushed down Chip's arm.

'The scanner,' Chip said.

'No,' Papa Jan said.

'Isn't this where we're——'

'Yes.'

Chip looked at Papa Jan, and Papa Jan pushed him past the scanner, pulled open the door, thrust him inside, and came in after him, dragging the door shut against its hissing slow-closer.

Chip stared at him, quivering.

'It's all right,' Papa Jan said sharply; and then, not sharply, kindly, he took Chip's head in both his hands and said, 'It's all right, Chip. Nothing will happen to you. I've done it lots of times.'

'We didn't *ask*,' Chip said, still quivering.

'It's all *right*,' Papa Jan said. 'Look: who does UniComp belong to?'

'Belong to?'

'Whose is it? Whose computer?'

'It's—it's the whole Family's.'

'And you're a member of the Family, aren't you?'

'Yes . . .'

'Well then, it's partly your computer, isn't it? *It* belongs to *you*, not the other way around; *you* don't belong to *it*.'

'No, we're supposed to *ask* for things!' Chip said.

'Chip, please trust me,' Papa Jan said. 'We're not going to take anything, we're not even going to touch anything. We're only going to look. That's the reason I came here today, to show you the real UniComp. You want to see it, don't you?'

Chip, after a moment, said, 'Yes.'

'Then don't worry; it's all right.' Papa Jan looked reassuringly into his eyes, and then let go of his head and took his hand.

They were on a landing, with stairs going down. They went down four or five of them—into coolness—and Papa Jan stopped, and stopped Chip. 'Stay right here,' he said, 'I'll be back in two seconds. Don't move.'

Chip watched anxiously as Papa Jan went back up to the landing, opened the door to look, and then went quickly out. The door swung back toward closing.

Chip began to quiver again. He had passed a scanner without

touching it, and now he was alone on a chilly silent stairway—
and Uni didn't know where he was!

The door opened again and Papa Jan came back in with blue
blankets over his arm. 'It's very cold,' he said.

They walked together, wrapped in blankets, down the just-wide-
enough aisle between two steel walls that stretched ahead of them
convergingly to a faraway cross-wall and reared up above their
heads to within half a meter of a glowing white ceiling—not
walls, really, but rows of mammoth steel blocks set each against
the next and hazed with cold, numbered on their fronts in eye-
level black stencil-figures: $H46$, $H48$ on this side of the aisle;
$H49$, $H51$ on that. The aisle was one of twenty or more; narrow
parallel crevasses between back-to-back rows of steel blocks, the
rows broken evenly by the intersecting crevasses of four slightly
wider cross-aisles.

They came up the aisle, their breath clouding from their
nostrils, blurs of near-shadow staying beneath their feet. The
sounds they made—the paplon rustle of their coveralls, the slapping of their sandals—were the only sounds there were, edged
with echoes. 'Well?' Papa Jan said, looking at Chip.

Chip hugged his blanket more tightly around him. 'It's not as
nice as upstairs,' he said.

'No,' Papa Jan said. 'No pretty young members with pens and
clipboards down here. No warm lights and friendly pink
machines. It's empty down here from one year to the next. Empty
and cold and lifeless. Ugly.'

They stood at the intersection of two aisles, crevasses of steel
stretching away in one direction and another, in a third direction
and a fourth. Papa Jan shook his head and scowled. 'It's wrong,'
he said. 'I don't know why or how, but it's wrong. Dead plans
of dead members. Dead ideas, dead decisions.'

'Why is it so cold?' Chip asked, watching his breath.

'Because it's dead,' Papa Jan said, then shook his head. 'No,
I don't know,' he said. 'They don't work if they're not freezing
cold; I don't know; all I knew was getting the things where they
were supposed to be without smashing them.'

They walked side by side along another aisle: $R20$, $R22$, $R24$.
'How many are there?' Chip asked.

'Twelve hundred and forty on this level, twelve hundred and
forty on the level below. And that's only for *now;* there's twice
as much space cut out and waiting behind that east wall, for
when the Family gets bigger. Other shafts, another ventilating
system already in place . . .'

They went down to the next lower level. It was the same as
the one above except that there were steel pillars at two of the
intersections and red figures on the memory banks instead of
black ones. They walked past $J65$, $J63$, $J61$. 'The biggest excava-

tion there ever was,' Papa Jan said. 'The biggest *job* there ever was, making one computer to obsolete the old five. There was news about it every night when I was your age. I figured out that it wouldn't be too late to help when I was twenty, provided I got the right classification. So I asked for it.'

'You asked for it?'

'That's what I said,' Papa Jan said, smiling and nodding. 'It wasn't unheard of in those day. I asked my adviser to ask Uni— well, it wasn't Uni, it was EuroComp—anyway I asked her to ask, and she did, and Christ, Marx, Wood, and Wei, I got it— 042C; construction worker, third class. First assignment, here.' He looked about, still smiling, his eyes vivid. 'They were going to lower these hulks down the shafts one at a time,' he said, and laughed. 'I sat up all one night and figured out that the job could be done eight months earlier if we tunneled in from the other side of Mount Love'—he thumbed over his shoulder—'and rolled them in on wheels. EuroComp hadn't thought of that simple idea. Or maybe it was in no rush to have its memory siphoned away!' He laughed again.

He stopped laughing; and Chip, watching him, noticed for the first time that his hair was all gray now. The reddish patches that he'd had a few years earlier were completely gone.

'And here they are,' he said, 'all in their places, rolled down my tunnel and working eight months longer than they would have been otherwise.' He looked at the banks he was passing as if he disliked them.

Chip said, 'Don't you—like UniComp?'

Papa Jan was silent for a moment. 'No, I don't,' he said, and cleared his throat. 'You can't argue with it, you can't explain things to it . . .'

'But it knows *everything*,' Chip said. 'What's there to explain or argue about?'

They separated to pass a square steel pillar and came together again. 'I don't know,' Papa Jan said. 'I don't know.' He walked along, his head lowered, frowning, his blanket wrapped around him. 'Listen,' he said, 'is there any classification that *you* want more than any other? Any assignment that *you're* especially hoping for?'

Chip looked uncertainly at Papa Jan and shrugged. 'No,' he said. 'I want the classification I'll get, the one I'm right for. And the assignments I'll get, the ones that the Family needs me to do. There's only one assignment anyway, helping to spread the——'

' "Helping to spread the Family through the universe," ' Papa Jan said. 'I know. Through the unified UniComp universe. Come on,' he said, 'let's get back up above. I can't take this brother-fighting cold much longer.'

Embarrassed, Chip said, 'Isn't there another level? You said there——'

'We can't,' Papa Jan said. 'There are scanners there, and members around who'd see us not touching them and rush to "help" us. There's nothing special to see there anyway; the receiving and transmitting equipment and the refrigerating plants.'

They went to the stairs. Chip felt let down. Papa Jan was disappointed with him for some reason; and worse, he wasn't well, wanting to argue with Uni and not touching scanners and using bad language. 'You ought to tell your adviser,' he said as they started up the stairs. 'About wanting to argue with Uni.'

'I don't want to argue with Uni,' Papa Jan said. 'I just want to be able to argue *if* I want to argue.'

Chip couldn't follow that at all. 'You ought to tell him anyway,' he said. 'Maybe you'll get an extra treatment.'

'Probably I would,' Papa Jan said; and after a moment, 'All right, I'll tell him.'

'Uni knows everything about everything,' Chip said.

They went up the second flight of stairs, and on the landing outside the display hallway, stopped and folded the blankets. Papa Jan finished first. He watched Chip finish folding his.

'There,' Chip said, patting the blue bundle against his chest.

'Do you know why I gave you the name "Chip"?' Papa Jan asked him.

'No,' Chip said.

'There's an old saying, "a chip off the old block". It means that a child is like his parents or his grandparents.'

'Oh.'

'I didn't mean you were like your father or even like me,' Papa Jan said. 'I meant you were like *my* grandfather. Because of your eye. He had a green eye too.'

Chip shifted, wanting Papa Jan to be done talking so they could go outside where they belonged.

'I know you don't like to talk about it,' Papa Jan said, 'but it's nothing to be ashamed of. Being a little different from everyone else isn't such a terrible thing. Members used to be so different from each other, you can't imagine. Your great-great-grandfather was a very brave and capable man. His name was Hanno Rybeck —names and numbers were separate then—and he was a cosmonaut who helped build the first Mars colony. So don't be ashamed that you've got his eye. They fight around with the genes today, excuse my language, but maybe they missed a few of yours; maybe you've got more than a green eye, maybe you've got some of my grandfather's bravery and ability too.' He started to open the door but turned to look at Chip again. 'Try wanting something, Chip,' he said. 'Try a day or two before your next treatment. That's when it's easiest; to want things, to worry about things . . .'

When they came out of the elevator into the ground-level lobby,

Chip's parents and Peace were waiting for them. 'Where have you been?' Chip's father asked. Peace, holding a miniature orange memory bank (not really), said, 'We've been waiting so long!'

'We were looking at Uni,' Papa Jan said.

Chip's father said, 'All this time?'

'That's right.'

'You were supposed to move on and let other members have their turn.'

'*You* were, Mike,' Papa Jan said, smiling. '*My* earpiece said "Jan old friend, it's good to see you! You and your grandson can stay and look as long as you like!"'

Chip's father turned away, not smiling.

They went to the canteen, claimed cakes and cokes—except Papa Jan, who wasn't hungry—and took them out to the picnic area behind the dome. Papa Jan pointed out Mount Love to Chip and told him more about the drilling of the tunnel, which Chip's father was surprised to hear about—a tunnel to bring in thirty-six not-so-big memory banks. Papa Jan told him that there were more banks on a lower level, but he didn't say how many or how big they were, or how cold and how lifeless. Chip didn't either.

It gave him an odd feeling, knowing there was something that he and Papa Jan knew and weren't telling the others; it made the two of them *different* from the others, and the same as each other, at least a little . . .

When they had eaten, they walked to the carport and got on the claim line. Papa Jan stayed with them until they were near the scanners; then he left, explaining that he would wait and go home with two friends from Riverbend who were visiting Uni later in the day. 'Riverbend' was his name for '55131, where he lived.

The next time Chip saw Bob NE, his adviser, he told him about Papa Jan; that he didn't like Uni and wanted to argue with it and explain things to it.

Bob, smiling, said, 'that happens sometimes with members your grandfather's age, Li. It's nothing to worry about.'

'But can't you tell Uni?' Chip said. 'Maybe he can have an extra treatment, or a stronger one.'

'Li,' Bob said, leaning forward across his desk, 'the different chemicals we get in our treatments are very precious and hard to make. If older members got as much as they sometimes need, there might not be enough for the younger members, who are really more important to the Family. And to make enough chemicals to satisfy everyone, we might have to neglect the more important jobs. Uni knows what has to be done, how much of everything there is, and how much of everything everyone needs. Your grandfather isn't really unhappy, I promise you. He's just a bit crotchety, and we will be too when we're in our fifties.'

'He uses that word,' Chip said; 'F-blank-blank-blank-T.'

'Old members sometimes do that too,' Bob said. 'They don't really mean anything by it. Words aren't in themselves "dirty"; it's the actions that the so-called dirty words represent that are offensive. Members like your grandfather use only the words, not the actions. It's not very nice, but it's no real sickness. How about you? Any friction? Let's leave your grandfather to his own adviser for a while.'

'No, no friction,' Chip said, thinking about having passed a scanner without touching it and having been where Uni hadn't said he could go and now suddenly not wanting to tell Bob about it. 'No friction at all,' he said. 'Everything is top speed.'

'Okay,' Bob said. 'Touch. I'll see you next Friday, right?'

A week or so later Papa Jan was transferred to USA60607. Chip and his parents and Peace drove to the airport at EUR55130 to see him off.

In the waiting room while Chip's parents and Peace watched through glass the members boarding the plane, Papa Jan drew Chip aside and stood looking at him, smiling fondly. 'Chip green-eye,' he said—Chip frowned and tried to undo the frown—'you asked for an extra treatment for me, didn't you?'

'Yes,' Chip said. 'How did you know?'

'Oh, I guessed, that's all,' Papa Jan said. 'Take good care of yourself, Chip. Remember who you're a chip off of, and remember what I said about trying to want something.'

'I will,' Chip said.

'The last ones are going,' Chip's father said.

Papa Jan kissed them all good-by and joined the members going out. Chip went to the glass and watched; and saw Papa Jan walking through the growing dark toward the plane, an unusually tall member, his take-along kit swinging at the end of a gangling arm. At the escalator he turned and waved—Chip waved back, hoping Papa Jan could see him—then turned again and put his kit-hand wrist to the scanner. Answering green sparked through dusk and distance, and he stepped on to the escalator and was taken smoothly upward.

In the car going back Chip sat silently, thinking that he would miss Papa Jan and his Sunday-and-holiday visits. It was strange, because he was such an odd and different old member. Yet that was exactly why he *would* miss him, Chip suddenly realized: because he was odd and different, and nobody else would fill his place.

'What's the matter, Chip?' his mother asked.

'I'm going to miss Papa Jan,' he said.

'So am I,' she said, 'but we'll see him on the phone once in a while.'

'It's a good thing he's going,' Chip's father said.

'I want him not to go,' Chip said. 'I want him to be transferred back here.'

'He's not very likely to be,' his father said, 'and it's a good thing. He was a bad influence on you.'

'Mike,' Chip's mother said.

'Don't *you* start that cloth,' Chip's father said. 'My name is Jesus, and his is Li.'

'And mine is Peace,' Peace said.

3

CHIP REMEMBERED what Papa Jan had told him, and in the weeks and months that followed, thought often about wanting something, wanting *to do* something, as Papa Jan at ten had wanted to help build Uni. He lay awake for an hour or so every few nights, considering all the different assignments there were, all the different classifications he knew of—construction supervisor like Papa Jan, lab technician like his father, plasmaphysicist like his mother, photographer like a friend's father; doctor, adviser, dentist, cosmonaut, actor, musician. They all seemed pretty much the same, but before he could really want one he had to pick one. It was a strange thought to think about—to pick, to choose, to decide. It made him feel small, yet it made him feel big too, both at the same time.

One night he thought it might be interesting to plan big buildings, like the little ones he had built with a construction set he had had a long time before (winking red *no* from Uni). That was the night before a treatment, which Papa Jan had said was a good time for wanting things. The next night big-building planner didn't seem any different from any other classification. In fact, the whole idea of wanting one particular classification seemed silly and pre-U that night, and he went straight to sleep.

The night before his next treatment he thought about planning buildings again—buildings of all different shapes, not just the three usual ones—and he wondered why the interestingness of the idea had disappeared the month before. Treatments were to prevent diseases and to relax members who were tense and to keep women from having too many babies and men from having hair on their faces; why should they make an interesting idea seem not interesting? But that was what they did, one month, and the next month, and the next.

Thinking such thoughts might be a form of selfishness, he suspected; but if it was, it was such a minor form—involving only an hour or two of sleep time, never of school or TV time—that he didn't bother to mention it to Bob NE, just as he wouldn't have mentioned a moment's nervousness or an occasional dream.

Each week when Bob asked if everything was okay, he said yes it was: top speed, no friction. He took care not to 'think wanting' too often or too long, so that he always got all the sleep he needed, and mornings, while washing, he checked his face in the mirror to make sure he still looked right. He did—except of course for his eye.

In 146 Chip and his family, along with most of the members in their building, were transferred to AFR71680. The building they were housed in was a brand-new one, with green carpet instead of gray in the hallways, larger TV screens, and furniture that was upholstered though non-adjustable.

There was much to get used to in '71680. The climate was somewhat warmer, and the coveralls lighter in weight and color; the monorail was old and slow and had frequent breakdowns; and the totalcakes were wrapped in greenish foil and tasted salty and not quite right.

Chip's and his family's new adviser was Mary CZ14L8584. She was a year older than Chip's mother, though she looked a few years younger.

Once Chip had grown accustomed to life in '71680—school, at least, was no different—he resumed his pastime of 'thinking wanting'. He saw now that there were considerable differences between classifications, and began to wonder which one Uni would give him when the time came. Uni, with its two levels of cold steel blocks, its empty echoing hardnesses . . . He wished Papa Jan had taken him down to the bottom level, where members were. It would be pleasanter to think of being classified by Uni and some members instead of by Uni alone; if he were to be given a classification he didn't like, and members were involved, maybe it would be possible to explain to them . . .

Papa Jan called twice a year; he claimed more, he said, but that was all he was granted.

He looked older, smiled tiredly. A section of USA60607 was being rebuilt and he was in charge.

Chip would have liked to tell him that he was trying to want something, but he couldn't with the others standing in front of the screen with him. Once, when a call was nearly over, he said, 'I'm trying,' and Papa Jan smiled like his old self and said, 'That's the boy!'

When the call was over, Chip's father said, 'What are you trying?'

'Nothing,' Chip said.

'You must have meant *something*,' his father said.

Chip shrugged.

Mary CZ asked him too, the next time Chip saw her. 'What did you mean when you told your grandfather you were trying?' she said.

'Nothing,' Chip said.

'Li,' Mary said, and looked at him reproachfully. 'You said you were trying. Trying what?'

'Trying not to miss him,' he said. 'When he was transferred to Usa I told him I would miss him, and he said I should try not to, that members were all the same and anyway he would call whenever he could.'

'Oh,' Mary said, and went on looking at Chip, now uncertainly. 'Why didn't you say so in the first place?' she asked.

Chip shrugged.

'And *do* you miss him?'

'Just a little,' Chip said. 'I'm trying not to.'

Sex began, and that was even better to think about than wanting something. Though he'd been taught that orgasms were extremely pleasurable, he had had no idea whatsoever of the all-but-unbearable deliciousness of the gathering sensations, the ecstasy of the coming, and the drained and boneless satisfaction of the moments afterward. *Nobody* had had any idea, none of his classmates; they talked about nothing else and would gladly have devoted themselves to nothing else as well. Chip could hardly think about mathematics and electronics and astronomy, let alone the differences between classifications.

After a few months, though, everyone calmed down, and accustomed to the new pleasure, gave it its proper Saturday-night place in the week's pattern.

One Saturday evening when Chip was fourteen, he bicycled with a group of his friends to a fine white beach a few kilometers north of AFR71680. There they swam—jumped and pushed and splashed in waves made pink-foamed by the foundering sun—and built a fire on the sand and sat around it on blankets and ate their cakes and cokes and crisp sweet pieces of a bashed-open coconut. A boy played songs on a recorder, not very well, and then, the fire crumbling to embers, the group separated into five couples, each on its own blanket.

The girl Chip was with was Anna VF, and after their orgasm—the best one Chip had ever had, or so it seemed—he was filled with a feeling of tenderness toward her, and wished there was something he could give her as a conveyor of it, like the beautiful shell that Karl GG had given Yin Ap, or Li OS's recorder-song, softly cooing now for whichever girl he was lying with. Chip had nothing for Anna, no shell, no song; nothing at all, except, maybe, his thoughts.

'Would you like something interesting to think about?' he asked, lying on his back with his arm about her.

'Mm,' she said, and squirmed closer against his side. Her head was on his shoulder, her arm across his chest.

He kissed her forehead. 'Think of all the different classifications there are——' he said.

'Mm?'

'And try to decide which one you would pick if you had to pick one.'

'To pick one?' she said.

'That's right.'

'What do you mean?'

'To pick one. To *have*. To *be in*. Which classification would you like best? Doctor, engineer, adviser . . .'

She propped her head up on her hand and squinted at him. 'What do you mean?' she said.

He gave a little sigh and said, 'We're going to be classified, right?'

'Right.'

'Suppose we *weren't* going to be. Suppose we had to classify ourselves.'

'That's silly,' she said, finger-drawing on his chest.

'It's interesting to think about.'

'Let's fuck again,' she said.

'Wait a minute,' he said. 'Just think about all the different classifications Suppose it were up to us to——'

'I don't want to,' she said, stopping drawing. 'That's silly. And sick. We *get* classified; there's nothing to think about. Uni knows what we're——'

'Oh, fight Uni,' Chip said. 'Just pretend for a minute that we're living in——'

Anna flipped away from him and lay on her stomach, stiff and unmoving, the back of her head to him.

'I'm sorry,' he said.

'*I'm* sorry,' she said. 'For you. You're sick.'

'No I'm not,' he said.

She was silent.

He sat up and looked despairingly at her rigid back. 'It just slipped out,' he said. 'I'm sorry.'

She stayed silent.

'It's just a *word*, Anna,' he said.

'You're sick,' she said.

'Oh, hate,' he said.

'You see what I mean?'

'Anna,' he said, 'look. Forget it. Forget the whole thing, all right? Just forget it.' He tickled between her thighs, but she locked them, barring his hand.

'Ah, Anna,' he said. 'Ah, come on. I said I was sorry, didn't I? Come on, let's fuck again. I'll suck you first if you want.'

After a while she relaxed her thighs and let him tickle her.

Then she turned over and sat up and looked at him. '*Are* you sick, Li?' she asked.

'No,' he said, and managed to laugh. 'Of course I'm not,' he said.

'I never heard of such a thing,' she said. ' "Classify ourselves". How could we do it? How could we possibly know enough?'

'It's just something I think about once in a while,' he said. 'Not very often. In fact, hardly ever.'

'It's such a—a funny idea,' she said. 'It sounds—I don't know—pre-U.'

'I won't think about it any more,' he said, and raised his right hand, the bracelet slipping back. 'Love of Family,' he said. 'Come on, lie down and I'll suck you.'

She lay back on the blanket, looking worried.

The next morning at five of ten Mary CZ called Chip and asked him to come to see her.

'When?' he asked.

'Now,' she said.

'All right,' he said. 'I'll be right down.'

His mother said, 'What does she want to see you on a Sunday for?'

'I don't know,' Chip said.

But he knew. Anna VF had called her adviser.

He rode the escalators down, down, down, wondering how much Anna had told, and what he should say; and wanting suddenly to cry and tell Mary that he was sick and selfish and a liar. The members on the upgoing escalators were relaxed, smiling, content, in harmony with the cheerful music of the speakers; no one but he was guilty and unhappy.

The advisory offices were strangely still. Members and advisers conferred in a few of the cubicles, but most of them were empty, the desks in order, the chairs waiting. In one cubicle a green-coveralled member leaned over the phone working a screwdriver at it.

Mary was standing on her chair, laying a strip of Christmas bunting along the top of *Wei Addressing the Chemotherapists*. More bunting was on the desk, a roll of red and a roll of green, and Mary's open telecomp with a container of tea beside it. 'Li?' she said, not turning. 'That was quick. Sit down.'

Chip sat down. Lines of green symbols glowed on the telecomp's screen. The answer button was held down by a souvenir paperweight from RUS81655.

'Stay,' Mary said to the bunting and, watching it, backed down off her chair. It stayed.

She swung her chair around and smiled at Chip as she drew it into her and sat. She looked at the telecomp's screen, and while she looked, picked up the container of tea and sipped from it. She put it down and looked at Chip and smiled.

'A member says you need help,' she said. 'The girl you fucked last night, Anna'—she glanced at the screen—'VH35H6143.'

Chip nodded. 'I said a dirty word,' he said.

'Two,' Mary said, 'but that's hardly important. At least not relatively. What *is* important are some of the other things you said, things about deciding which classification you would pick if we didn't have UniComp to do the job.'

Chip looked away from Mary, at the rolls of red and green Christmas bunting.

'Is that something you think about often, Li?' Mary asked.

'Just sometimes,' Chip said. 'In the free hour or at night; never in school or during TV.'

'Nighttime counts too,' Mary said. 'That's when you're supposed to be sleeping.'

Chip looked at her and said nothing.

'When did it start?' she asked.

'I don't know,' he said, 'a few years ago. In Eur.'

'Your grandfather,' she said.

He nodded.

She looked at the screen, and looked at Chip again, ruefully. 'Didn't it ever dawn on you,' she said, 'that "deciding" and "picking" are manifestations of selfishness? *Acts* of selfishness?'

'I thought, maybe,' Chip said, looking at the edge of the desktop, rubbing a fingertip along it.

'Oh, Li,' Mary said. 'What am I here for? What are *advisers* here for? To help us, isn't that so?'

He nodded.

'Why didn't you tell me? Or your adviser in Eur? Why did you wait, and lose sleep, and worry this Anna?'

Chip shrugged, watching his fingertip rubbing the desktop, the nail dark. 'It was—interesting, sort of,' he said.

' "Interesting, sort of",' Mary said. 'It might also have been interesting, sort of, to think about the kind of pre-U chaos we'd have if we actually *did* pick our own classifications. Did you think about that?'

'No,' Chip said.

'Well, do. Think about a hundred million members deciding to be TV actors and not a single one deciding to work in a crematorium.'

Chip looked up at her. 'Am I very sick?' he asked.

'No,' Mary said, 'but you might have ended up that way if not for Anna's helpfulness.' She took the paperweight from the telecomp's answer button and the green symbols disappeared from the screen. 'Touch,' she said.

Chip touched his bracelet to the scanner plate, and Mary began tapping the input keys. 'You've been given hundreds of tests since your first day of school,' she said, 'and UniComp's been fed the results of every last one of them.' Her fingers darted over the dozen black keys. 'You've had hundreds of adviser meetings,' she said, 'and UniComp knows about those too. It knows what jobs have to be done and who there is to do them. It knows *every-*

thing. Now who's going to make the better, more efficient classification, you or UniComp?'

'UniComp, Mary,' Chip said. 'I know that. I didn't really want to do it myself; I was just—just thinking *what if,* that's all.'

Mary finished tapping and pressed the answer button. Green symbols appeared on the screen. Mary said, 'Go to the treatment room.'

Chip jumped to his feet. 'Thank you,' he said.

'Thank Uni,' Mary said, switching off the telecomp. She closed its cover and snapped the catches.

Chip hesitated. 'I'll be all right?' he asked.

'Perfect,' Mary said. She smiled reassuringly.

'I'm sorry I made you come in on a Sunday,' Chip said.

'Don't be,' Mary said. 'For once in my life I'm going to have my Christmas decorations up before December twenty-fourth.'

Chip went out of the advisory offices and into the treatment room. Only one unit was working, but there were only three members in line. When his turn came, he plunged his arm as deep as he could into the rubber-rimmed opening, and gratefully felt the scanner's contact and the infusion disc's warm nuzzle. He wanted the tickle-buzz-sting to last a long time, curing him completely and forever, but it was even shorter than usual, and he worried that there might have been a break in communication between the unit and Uni or a shortage of chemicals inside the unit itself. On a quiet Sunday morning mightn't it be carelessly serviced? He stopped worrying, though, and riding up the escalators he felt a lot better about everything—himself, Uni, the Family, the world, the universe.

The first thing he did when he got into the apartment was call Anna VF and thank her.

At fifteen he was classified 663D—genetic taxonomist, fourth class—and was transferred to RUS41500 and the Academy of the Genetic Sciences. He learned elementary genetics and lab techniques and modulation and transplant theory; he skated and played soccer and went to the pre-U Museum and the Museum of the Family's Achievements; he had a girlfriend named Anna from Jap and then another named Peace from Aus. On Thursday, 18 October 151, he and everyone else in the Academy sat up until four in the morning watching the launching of the *Altaira,* then slept and loafed through a half-day holiday.

One night his parents called unexpectedly. 'We have bad news,' his mother said. 'Papa Jan died this morning.'

A sadness gripped him and must have shown on his face.

'He was sixty-two, Chip,' his mother said. 'He had his life.'

'Nobody lives forever,' Chip's father said.

'Yes,' Chip said. 'I'd forgot how old he was. How are you? Has Peace been classified yet?'

When they were done talking he went out for a walk, even though it was a rainy night and almost ten. He went into the park. Everyone was coming out. 'Six minutes,' a member said, smiling at him.

He didn't care. He wanted to be rained on, to be drenched. He didn't know why but he wanted to.

He sat on a bench and waited. The park was empty; everyone else was gone. He thought of Papa Jan saying things that were the opposite of what he meant, and then saying what he really meant down in the inside of Uni, with a blue blanket wrapped around him.

On the back of the bench across the walk someone had red-chalked a jagged FIGHT UNI. Someone else—or maybe the same sick member, ashamed—had crossed it out with white. The rain began, and started washing it away; white chalk, red chalk, smearing pinkly down the benchback.

Chip turned his face to the sky and held it steady under the rain, trying to feel as if he was so sad he was crying.

4

EARLY IN HIS THIRD and final year at the Academy, Chip took part in a complicated exchange of dormitory cubicles worked out to put everyone involved closer to his or her girlfriend or boyfriend. In his new location he was two cubicles away from one Yin DW; and across the aisle from him was a shorter-than-normal member named Karl WL, who frequently carried a green-covered sketch pad and who, though he replied to comments readily enough, rarely started a conversation on his own.

This Karl WL had a look of unusual concentration in his eyes, as if he were close on the track of answers to difficult questions. Once Chip noticed him slip out of the lounge after the beginning of the first TV hour and not slip in again till before the end of the second; and one night in the dorm, after the lights had gone out, he saw a dim glow filtering through the blanket of Karl's bed.

One Saturday night—early Sunday morning, really—as Chip was coming back quietly from Yin DW's cubicle to his own, he saw Karl sitting in his. He was on the side of the bed in pajamas, holding his pad tilted toward a flashlight on the corner of the desk and working at it with brisk chopping hand movements. The flashlight's lens was masked in some way so that only a small beam of light shone out.

Chip went closer and said, 'No girl this week?'

Karl started, and closed the pad. A stick of charcoal was in his hand.

'I'm sorry I surprised you,' Chip said.

'That's all right,' Karl said, his face only faint glints at chin and cheekbones. 'I finished early. Peace KG. Aren't you staying all night with Yin?'

'She's snoring,' Chip said.

Karl made an amused sound. 'I'm turning in now,' he said. 'What are you doing?'

'Just some gene diagrams,' Karl said. He turned back the cover of the pad and showed the top page. Chip went close and bent and looked—at cross sections of genes in the B3 locus, carefully drawn and shaded, done with a pen. 'I was trying some with charcoal,' Karl said, 'but it's no good.' He closed the pad and put the charcoal on the desk and switched off the flashlight. 'Sleep well,' he said.

'Thanks,' Chip said. 'You too.'

He went into his own cubicle and groped his way into bed, wondering whether Karl had in fact been drawing gene diagrams, for which charcoal hardly even seemed worth a trial. Probably he should speak to his adviser, Li YB, about Karl's secretiveness and occasional unmemberlike behaviour, but he decided to wait awhile, until he was sure that Karl needed help and that he wouldn't be wasting Li YB's time and Karl's and his own. There was no point in being an alarmist.

Wei's birthday came a few weeks later, and after the parade Chip and a dozen or so other students railed out to the Amusement Gardens for the afternoon. They rowed boats for a while and then strolled through the zoo. While they were gathered at a water fountain, Chip saw Karl WL sitting on the railing in front of the horse compound, holding his pad on his knees and drawing. Chip excused himself from the group and went over.

Karl saw him coming and smiled at him, closing his pad. 'Wasn't that a great parade?' he said.

'It was really top speed,' Chip said. 'Are you drawing the horses?'

'Trying to.'

'May I see?'

Karl looked him in the eye for a moment and then said, 'Sure, why not?' He riffled the bottom of the pad and, opening it partway through, turned back the upper section and let Chip look at a rearing stallion that crammed the page, charcoaled darkly and vigorously. Muscles bulked under its gleaming hide; its eye was wild and rolling; its forelegs quivered. The drawing surprised Chip with its vitality and power. He had never seen a picture of a horse that came anywhere near it. He sought words, and could only come up with, 'This is—great, Karl! Top speed!'

'It's not accurate,' Karl said.

'It is!'

'No it isn't,' Karl said. 'If it were accurate I'd be at the Academy of Art.'

Chip looked at the real horses in the compound and at Karl's drawing again; at the horses again, and saw the greater thickness of their legs, the lesser width of their chests.

'You're right,' he said, looking at the drawing again. 'It's not accurate. But it's—it's somehow *better* than accurate.'

'Thanks,' Karl said. 'That's what I'd like it to be. I'm not finished yet.'

Looking at him, Chip said, 'Have you done others?'

Karl turned down the preceding page and showed him a seated lion, proud and watchful. In the lower right-hand corner of the page there was an *A* with a circle around it. 'Marvelous!' Chip said. Karl turned down other pages; there were two deer, a monkey, a soaring eagle, two dogs sniffing each other, a crouching leopard.

Chip laughed. 'You've got the whole fighting zoo!' he said.

'No I haven't,' Karl said.

All the drawings had the *A* with the circle around it in the corner. 'What's that for?' Chip asked.

'Artists used to sign their pictures. To show whose work it was.'

'I know,' Chip said, 'but why an *A*?'

'Oh,' Karl said, and turned the pages back one by one. 'It stands for Ashi,' he said. 'That's what my sister calls me.' He came to the horse, added a line of charcoal to its stomach, and looked at the horses in the compound with his look of concentration, which now had an object and a reason.

'I have an extra name too,' Chip said. 'Chip. My grandfather gave it to me.'

'Chip?'

'It means "chip off the old block". I'm supposed to be like my grandfather's grandfather.' Chip watched Karl sharpen the lines of the horse's rear legs, and then moved from his side. 'I'd better get back to the group I'm with,' he said. 'Those are top speed. It's a shame you weren't classified an artist.'

Karl looked at him. 'I wasn't, though,' he said, 'so I only draw on Sundays and holidays and during the free hour. I never let it interfere with my work or whatever else I'm supposed to be doing.'

'Right,' Chip said. 'See you at the dorm.'

That evening, after TV, Chip came back to his cubicle and found on his desk the drawing of the horse. Karl, in his cubicle, said, 'Do you want it?'

'Yes,' Chip said. 'Thanks. It's great!' The drawing had even more vitality and power than before. An *A*-in-a-circle was in a corner of it.

Chip tabbed the drawing to the bulletin board behind the

desk, and as he finished, Yin DW came in, bringing back a copy of *Universe* she had borrowed. 'Where'd you get that?' she asked.

'Karl WL did it,' Chip said.

'That's very nice, Karl,' Yin said. 'You draw well.'

Karl, getting into pajamas, said. 'Thanks, I'm glad you like it.'

To Chip, Yin whispered, 'It's all out of proportion. Keep it there, though. It was kind of you to put it up.'

Once in a while, during the free hour, Chip and Karl went to the Pre-U together. Karl made sketches of the mastodon and the bison, the cavemen in their animal hides, the soldiers and sailors in their countless different uniforms. Chip wandered among the early automobiles and dictypes, the safes and handcuffs and TV 'sets'. He studied the models and pictures of the old buildings: the spired and buttressed churches, the turreted castles, the large and small houses with their windows and lock-fitted doors. Windows, he thought, must have had their good points. It would be pleasant, would make one feel bigger, to look out at the world from one's room or working place; and at night, from outside, a house with rows of lighted windows must have been attractive, even beautiful.

One afternoon Karl came into Chip's cubicle and stood beside the desk with his hands fisted at his sides. Chip, looking up at him, thought he had been stricken by a fever or worse; his face was flushed and his eyes were narrowed in a strange stare. But no, it was anger that held him, anger such as Chip had never seen before, anger so intense that, trying to speak, Karl seemed unable to work his lips.

Anxiously Chip said, 'What is it?'

'Li,' Karl said. 'Listen. Will you do me a favor?'

'Sure! Of course!'

Karl leaned close to him and whispered, 'Claim a pad for me, will you? I just claimed one and was denied. Five fighting hundred of them, a pile this high, and I had to turn it back in!'

Chip stared at him.

'Claim one, will you? Karl said. 'Anyone can try a little sketching in his spare time, right? Go on down, okay?'

Painfully Chip said, 'Karl——'

Karl looked at him, his anger retreated, and he stood up straight. 'No,' he said. 'No, I—I just lost my temper, that's all. I'm sorry. I'm sorry, brother. Forget it.' He clapped Chip's shoulder. 'I'm okay now,' he said. 'I'll claim again in a week or so. Been doing too much drawing anyway, I suppose. Uni knows best.' He went off down the aisle toward the bathroom.

Chip turned back to the desk and leaned on his elbows and held his head, shaking.

That was Tuesday. Chip's weekly adviser meetings were on Woodsday mornings at 10.40, and this time he would tell Li YB about Karl's sickness. There was no longer any question of being an alarmist; there was faulted responsibility, in fact, in having waited as long as he had. He ought to have said something at the first clear sign, Karl's slipping out of TC (to draw, of course), or even when he had noticed the unusual look in Karl's eyes. Why in hate had he waited? He could hear Li YB gently reproaching him: 'You haven't been a very good brother's keeper, Li.'

Early on Woodsday morning, though, he decided to pick up some coveralls and the new *Geneticist*. He went down to the supply center and walked through the aisles. He took a *Geneticist* and a pack of coveralls and walked some more and came to the art-supplies section. He saw the pile of green-covered sketch pads; there weren't five hundred of them, but there were seventy or eighty and no one seemed in a rush to claim them.

He walked away, thinking that he must be going out of his mind. Yet if Karl were to promise not to draw when he wasn't supposed to . . .

He walked back again—'*Anyone can try a little sketching in his spare time, right?*'—and took a pad and a packet of charcoal. He went to the shortest checkout line, his heart pounding in his chest, his arms trembling. He drew a deep-as-possible breath; another, and another. He put his bracelet to the scanner, and the stickers of the coveralls, the *Geneticist*, the pad, and the charcoal. Everything was *yes*. He gave way to the next member.

He went back up to the dorm. Karl's cubicle was empty, the bed unmade. He went into his own cubicle and put the coveralls on the shelf and the *Geneticist* on the desk. On the top page of the pad he wrote, his hand still trembling, *Free time only. I want your promise.* Then he put the pad and the charcoal on his bed and sat at the desk and looked at the *Geneticist*.

Karl came, and went into his cubicle and began making his bed. 'Are those yours?' Chip asked. Karl looked at the pad and charcoal on Chip's bed. Chip said, 'They're not mine.'

'Oh, yes. Thanks,' Karl said, and came over and took them. 'Thanks a lot,' he said.

'You ought to put your nameber on the first page,' Chip said, 'if you're going to leave it all over like that.'

Karl went into his cubicle, opened the pad, and looked at the first page. He looked at Chip, nodded, raised his right hand, and mouthed, 'Love of Family'.

They rode down to the classrooms together. 'What did you have to waste a page for?' Karl said.

Chip smiled.

'I'm not joking,' Karl said. 'Didn't you ever hear of writing a note on a piece of scrap paper?'

'Christ, Marx, Wood, and Wei,' Chip said.

*   *   *

In December of that year, 152, came the appalling news of the Gray Death, sweeping through all the Mars colonies except one and completely wiping them out in nine short days. In the Academy of the Genetic Sciences, as in all the Family's establishments, there was helpless silence, then mourning, and then a massive determination to help the Family overcome the staggering setback it had suffered. Everyone worked harder and longer. Free time was halved; there were classes on Sundays and only a half-day Christmas holiday. Genetics alone could breed new strengths in the coming generations; everyone was in a hurry to finish his training and get on to his first real assignment. On every wall were the white-on-black posters: *MARS AGAIN!*

The new spirit lasted several months. Not until Marxmas was there a full day's holiday, and then no one quite knew what to do with it. Chip and Karl and their girlfriends rowed out to one of the islands in the Amusement Gardens lake and sunbathed on a large flat rock. Karl drew his girlfriend's picture. It was the first time, as far as Chip knew, that he had drawn a living human being. In June, Chip claimed another pad for Karl.

Their training ended, five weeks early, and they received their assignments: Chip to a viral genetics research laboratory in USA90058; Karl to the Institute of Enzymology in JAP50319.

On the evening before they were to leave the Academy they packed their take-along kits. Karl pulled green-covered pads from his desk drawers—a dozen from one drawer, half a dozen from another, more pads from other drawers; he threw them into a pile on his bed. 'You're never going to get those all into your kit,' Chip said.

'I'm not planning to,' Karl said. 'They're done; I don't need them.' He sat on the bed and leafed through one of the pads, tore out one drawing and another.

'May I have some?' Chip asked.

'Sure,' Karl said, and tossed a pad over to him.

It was mostly Pre-U Museum sketches. Chip took out one of a man in chain mail holding a crossbow to his shoulder, and another of an ape scratching himself.

Karl gathered most of the pads and went off down the aisle towards the chute. Chip put the pad on Karl's bed and picked up another one.

In it were a nude man and woman standing in parkland outside a blank-slabbed city. They were taller than normal, beautiful and strangely dignified. The woman was quite different from the man, not only genitally but also in her longer hair, protrusive breasts, and overall softer convexity. It was a great drawing, but something about it disturbed Chip, he didn't know what.

He turned to other pages, other men and women; the pictures grew surer and stronger, done with fewer and bolder lines. They were the best drawings Karl had ever made, but in each there was that disturbing something, a lack, an imbalance that Chip was at a loss to define.

It hit him with a chill. They had no bracelets.

He looked through to check, his stomach knotting sicktight. No bracelets. No bracelets on any of them. And there was no chance of the drawings being unfinished; in the corner of each of them was an *A with a circle around it.*

He put down the pad and went and sat on his bed; watched as Karl came back and gathered the rest of the pads and, with a smile, carried them off.

There was a dance in the lounge but it was brief and subdued because of Mars. Later Chip went with his girlfriend into her cubicle. 'What's the matter?' she asked.

'Nothing,' he said.

Karl asked him too, in the morning while they were folding their blankets. 'What's the matter, Li?'

'Nothing.'

'Sorry to be leaving?'

'A little.'

'Me too. Here, give me your sheets and I'll chute them.'

'What's his nameber?' Li YB asked.

'Karl WL35S7497,' Chip said.

Li YB jotted it down. 'And what specifically seems to be the trouble?' he asked.

Chip wiped his palms on his thighs. 'He's drawn some pictures of members,' he said.

'Acting aggressively?'

'No, no,' Chip said. 'Just standing and sitting, fucking, playing with children.'

'Well?'

Chip looked at the desk. 'They don't have bracelets,' he said.

Li YB didn't speak. Chip looked at him; he was looking at Chip. After a moment Li YB said, 'Several pictures?'

'A whole padful.'

'And no bracelets at all.'

'None.'

Li YB breathed in, and then pushed out the breath between his teeth in a series of rapid hisses. He looked at his note pad. 'KWL35S7497,' he said.

Chip nodded.

He tore up the picture of the man with the crossbow, which was aggressive, and tore up the one of the ape too. He took the pieces to the chute and dropped them down.

He put the last few things into his take-along kit—his clippers and mouthpiece and a framed snapshot of his parents and Papa Jan—and pressed it closed.

Karl's girlfriend came by with her kit slung on her shoulder. 'Where's Karl?' she asked.

'At the medicenter.'

'Oh,' she said. 'Tell him I said good-by, will you?'

'Sure.'

They kissed cheeks. 'Good-by,' she said.

'Good-by.'

She went away down the aisle. Some other students, no longer students, went past. They smiled at Chip and said good-by to him.

He looked around the barren cubicle. The picture of the horse was still on the bulletin board. He went to it and looked at it; saw again the rearing stallion, so alive and wild. Why hadn't Karl stayed with the animals in the zoo? Why had he begun to draw living humans?

A feeling formed in Chip, formed and grew; a feeling that he had been wrong to tell Li YB about Karl's drawings, although he knew of course that he had been right. How could it be wrong to help a sick brother? *Not* to tell would have been wrong, to keep quiet as he had done before, letting Karl go on drawing members without bracelets and getting sicker and sicker. Eventually he might even have been drawing members acting aggressively. Fighting.

Of course he had been right.

Yet the feeling that he had been wrong stayed and kept growing, grew into guilt, irrationally.

Someone came near, and he whirled, thinking it was Karl coming to thank him. It wasn't; it was someone passing the cubicle, leaving.

But that was what was going to happen: Karl was going to come back from the medicenter and say, 'Thanks for helping me, Li. I was really sick but I'm a whole lot better now,' and *he* was going to say, 'Don't thank *me*, brother; thank Uni,' and Karl was going to say, 'No, no,' and insist and shake his hand.

Suddenly he wanted not to be there, not to get Karl's thanks for having helped him; he grabbed his kit and hurried to the aisle—stopped short, uncertainly, and hurried back. He took the picture of the horse from the board, opened his kit on the desk, pushed the drawing in among the pages of a notebook, closed the kit, and went.

He jogged down the downgoing escalators, excusing himself past other members, afraid that Karl might come after him; jogged all the way down to the lowest level, where the rail station was, and got on the long airport line. He stood with his head held still, not looking back.

Finally he came to the scanner. He faced it for a moment, and touched it with his bracelet. *Yes,* it green-winked.

He hurried through the gate.

PART TWO: COMING ALIVE

1

BETWEEN JULY OF 153 and Marx of 162, Chip had four assignments: two at research laboratories in Usa; a brief one at the Institute of Genetic Engineering in Ind, where he attended a series of lectures on recent advances in mutation induction; and a five-year assignment at a chemo-synthetics plant in Chi. He was upgraded twice in his classification and by 162 was a genetic taxonomist, second class.

During those years he was outwardly a normal and contented member of the Family. He did his work well, took part in house athletic and recreational programs, had weekly sexual activity, made monthly phone calls and bi-yearly visits to his parents, was in place and on time for TV and treatments and adviser meetings. He had no discomfort to report, either physical or mental.

Inwardly, however, he was far from normal. The feeling of guilt with which he had left the Academy had led him to withhold himself from his next adviser, for he wanted to retain that feeling, which, though unpleasant, was the strongest feeling he had ever had and an enlargement, strangely, of his sense of being; and withholding himself from his adviser—reporting no discomfort, playing the part of a relaxed, contented member—had led over the years to a withholding of himself from everyone around him, a general attitude of guarded watchfulness. Everything came to seem questionable to him: totalcakes, coveralls, the sameness of members' rooms and thoughts, and especially the work he was doing, whose end, he saw, would only be to solidify the universal sameness. There were no alternatives, of course, no imaginable alternatives to anything, but still he withheld himself, and questioned. Only in the first few days after treatments was he really the member he pretended to be.

One thing alone in the world was indisputably right: Karl's drawing of the horse. He framed it—not in a supply-center frame but in one he made himself, out of wood strips ripped from the back of a drawer and scraped smooth—and hung it in his rooms in Usa, his room in Ind, his room in Chi. It was a lot better to look at than *Wei Addressing the Chemotherapists* or *Marx Writing* or *Christ Expelling the Money Changers*.

In Chi he thought of getting married, but he was told that he wasn't to reproduce and so there didn't seem much point in it.

*   *   *

In mid-Marx of 162, shortly before his twenty-seventh birthday, he was transferred back to the Institute of Genetic Engineering in IND26110 and assigned to a newly established Genic Sub-classification Center. New microscopes had found distinctions between genes that until then had appeared identical, and he was one of forty 663B's and C's put to defining subclassifications. His room was four buildings away from the Center, giving him a short walk twice a day, and he soon found a girlfriend whose room was on the floor below his. His adviser was a year younger than he, Bob RO. Life apparently was going on as before.

One night in April, though, as he made ready to clean his teeth before going to bed, he found a small white something lodged in his mouthpiece. Perplexed, he picked it out. It was a triple bend of tightly rolled paper. He put down the mouthpiece and un-rolled a thin rectangle filled with typing. *You seem to be a fairly unusual member,* it said. *Wondering about which classification you would choose, for instance. Would you like to meet some other unusual members? Think about it. You are only partly alive. We can help you more than you can imagine.*

The note surprised him with its knowledge of his past and disturbed him with its secrecy and its 'You are only partly alive.' What did it mean—that strange statement and the whole strange message? And who had put it in his mouthpiece, of all places? But there was no better place, it struck him, for making certain that he and he alone should find it. Who then, not so foolishly, had put it there? Anyone at all could have come into the room earlier in the evening or during the day. At least two other members had done so; there had been notes on his desk from Peace SK, his girlfriend, and from the secretary of the house photography club.

He cleaned his teeth and got into bed and reread the note. Its writer or one of the other 'unusual members' must have had access to UniComp's memory of his boyhood self-classification thoughts, and that seemed to be enough to make the group think he might be sympathetic to them. Was he? They were abnormal; that was certain. Yet what was *he*? Wasn't he abnormal too? *We can help you more than you can imagine.* What did *that* mean? Help him how? Help him do what? And what if he decided he wanted to meet them; what was he supposed to do? Wait, apparently, for another note, for a contact of some kind. *Think about it,* the note said.

The last chime sounded, and he rolled the piece of paper back up and tucked it down into the spine of his night-table *Wei's Living Wisdom.* He tapped off the light and lay and thought about it. It was disturbing, but it was different too, and interesting. *Would you like to meet some other unusual members?*

He didn't say anything about it to Bob RO. He looked for another note in his mouthpiece each time he came back to his room, but didn't find one. Walking to and from work, taking a seat in the lounge for TV, standing on line in the dining hall or the supply center, he searched the eyes of the members around him, alert for a meaningful remark or perhaps only a look and a head movement inviting him to follow. None came.

Four days went by and he began to think that the note had been a sick member's joke, or worse, a test of some kind. Had Bob RO himself written it, to see if he would mention it? No, that was ridiculous; he was *really* getting sick.

He had been interested—excited even, and hopeful, though he hadn't known of what—but now, as more days went by with no note, no contact, he became disappointed and irritable.

And then, a week after the first note, it was there: the same triple bend of rolled paper in the mouthpiece. He picked it out, excitement and hope coming back instantaneously. He unrolled the paper and read it: *If you want to meet us and hear how we can help you, be between buildings J16 and J18 on Lower Christ Plaza tomorrow night at 11.15. Do not touch any scanners on the way. If members are in sight of one you have to pass, take another route. I'll wait until 11.30.* Beneath was typed, as a signature, *Snowflake.*

Few members were on the walkways, and those hurrying to their beds with their eyes set straight ahead of them. He had to change his course only once, walked faster, and reached Lower Christ Plaza exactly at 11.15. He crossed the moonlit white expanse, with its turned-off fountain mirroring the moon, and found J16 and the dark channel that divided it from J18.

No one was there—but then, meters back in shadow, he saw white coveralls marked with what looked like a medicenter red cross. He went into the darkness and approached the member, who stood by J16's wall and stayed silent.

'Snowflake?' he said.

'Yes.' The voice was a woman's. 'Did you touch any scanners?'

'No.'

'Funny feeling, isn't it?' She was wearing a pale mask of some kind, thin and close-fitting.

'I've done it before,' he said.

'Good for you.'

'Only once, and somebody pushed me,' he said. She seemed older than he, how much he couldn't tell.

'We're going to a place that's a five-minute walk from here,' she said. 'It's where we get together regularly, six of us, four women and two men—a terrible ratio that I'm counting on you to improve. We're going to make a certain suggestion to you; if you decide to follow it you might eventually become one of us; if you don't, you won't, and tonight will be our last contact. In that case, though, we can't have you knowing what we look like

or where we meet.' Her hand came out of her pocket with white-
ness in it. 'I'll have to bandage your eyes,' she said. 'That's why
I'm wearing these medicenter cuvs, so it'll look all right for me
to be leading you.'

'At this hour?'

'We've done it before and had no trouble,' she said. 'You don't
mind?'

He shrugged. 'I guess not,' he said.

'Hold these over your eyes.' She gave him two wads of cotton.
He closed his eyes and put the wads in place, holding them with
a finger each. She began winding bandage around his head and
over the wads; he withdrew his fingers, bent his head to help her.
She kept winding bandage, around and around, up onto his forehead, down onto his cheeks.

'Are you sure you're really not medicenter?' he said.

She chuckled and said, 'Positive'. She pressed the end of the
bandage, sticking it tight; pressed all over it and over his eyes,
then took his arm.

She turned him—toward the plaza, he knew—and started him
walking.

'Don't forget your mask,' he said.

She stopped short. 'Thanks for reminding me,' she said. Her
hand left his arm, and after a moment, came back. They walked
on.

Their footsteps changed, became muted by space, and a breeze
cooled his face below the bandage; they were in the plaza. 'Snowflake's hand on his arm drew him in a diagonal leftward course,
away from the direction of the Institute.

'When we get where we're going,' she said, 'I'm going to put a
piece of tape over your bracelet; over mine too. We avoid knowing one another's namebers as much as possible. I know yours—
I'm the one who spotted you—but the others don't; all they
know is that I'm bringing a promising member. Later on, one or
two of them may have to know it.'

'Do you check the history of everyone who's assigned here?'

'No. Why?'

'Isn't that how you "spotted" me, by finding out that I used
to think about classifying myself?'

'Three steps down here,' she said. 'No, that was only confirmation. And two and three. What I spotted was a look you have,
the look of a member who isn't one-hundred-per-cent in the
bosom of the Family. You'll learn to recognize it too, if you join
us. I found out who you were, and then I went to your room and
saw that picture on the wall.'

'The horse?'

'No, *Marx Writing*,' she said. 'Of course the horse. You draw
the way no normal member would even think of drawing. I
checked your history *then*, after I'd seen the picture.'

They had left the plaza and were on one of the walkways west of it—K or L, he wasn't sure which.

'You've made a mistake,' he said. 'Someone else drew that picture.'

'You drew it,' she said; 'you've claimed charcoal and sketch pads.'

'For the member who drew it. A friend of mine at academy.'

'Well *that*'s interesting,' she said. 'Cheating on claims is a better sign than anything. Anyway, you liked the picture well enough to keep it and frame it. Or did your friend make the frame too?'

He smiled. 'No, I did,' he said. 'You didn't miss a thing.'

'We turn here, to the right.'

'Are you an adviser?'

'Me? Hate, no.'

'But you can pull histories?'

'Sometimes.'

'Are you at the Institute?'

'Don't ask so many questions,' she said. 'Listen, what do you want us to call you? Instead of Li RM.'

'Oh,' he said. 'Chip.'

' "Chip?" No,' she said, 'don't just say the first thing that comes into your mind. You ought to be something like "Pirate" or "Tiger". The others are King and Lilac and Leopard and Hush and Sparrow.'

'Chip's what I was called when I was a boy,' he said. 'I'm used to it.'

'All right,' she said, 'but it's not what *I* would have chosen. Do you know where we are?'

'No.'

'Fine. Left now.'

They went through a door, up steps, through another door, and into an echoing hall of some kind, where they walked and turned, walked and turned, as if by-passing a number of irregularly placed objects. They walked up a stopped escalator and along a corridor that curved toward the right.

She stopped him and asked for his bracelet. He raised his wrist, and his bracelet was pressed tight and rubbed. He touched it; there was smoothness instead of his nameber. That and his sightlessness made him suddenly feel disembodied; as if he were about to drift from the floor, drift right out through whatever walls were around him and up into space, dissolve there and become nothing.

She took his arm again. They walked farther and stopped. He heard a knock and two more knocks, a door opening, voices stilling. 'Hi,' she said, leading him forward. 'This is Chip. He insists on it.'

Chairs scuffed against the floor, voices gave greetings. A hand took his and shook it. 'I'm King,' a member said, a man. 'I'm glad you decided to come.'

'Thanks,' he said.

Another hand gripped his harder. 'Snowflake says you're quite an artist'—an older man than King. 'I'm Leopard.'

Other hands came quickly, women: 'Hello, Chip; I'm Lilac.' 'And I'm Sparrow. I hope you'll become a regular.' 'I'm Hush, Leopard's wife. Hello.' The last one's hand and voice were old; the other two were young.

He was led to a chair and sat in it. His hands found table-top before him, smooth and bare, its edge slightly curving; an oval table or a large round one. The others were sitting down; Snowflake on his right, talking; someone else on his left. He smelled something burning, sniffed to make sure. None of the others seemed aware of it. 'Something's burning,' he said.

'Tobacco,' the old woman, Hush, said on his left.

'Tobacco?' he said.

'We smoke it,' Snowflake said. 'Would you like to try some?'

'No,' he said.

Some of them laughed. 'It's not really deadly,' King said, farther away on his left. 'In fact, I suspect it may have some beneficial effects.'

'It's very pleasing,' one of the young women said, across the table from him.

'No, thanks,' he said.

They laughed again, made comments to one another, and one by one grew silent. His right hand on the tabletop was covered by Snowflake's hand; he wanted to draw it away but restrained himself. He had been stupid to come. What was he doing, sitting there sightless among those sick false-named members? His own abnormality was nothing next to theirs. Tobacco! The stuff had been extincted a hundred years ago; where the hate had they got it?

'We're sorry about the bandage, Chip,' King said. 'I assume Snowflake's explained why it's necessary.'

'She has,' Chip said, and Snowflake said, 'I did.' Her hand left Chip's; he drew his from the tabletop and took told of his other in his lap.

'We're abnormal members, which is fairly obvious,' King said. 'We do a great many things that are generally considered sick. We think they're not. We *know* they're not.' His voice was strong and deep and authoritative; Chip visualized him as large and powerful, about forty. 'I'm not going to go into too many details,' he said, 'because in your present condition you would be shocked and upset, just as you're obviously shocked and upset by the fact that we smoke tobacco. You'll learn the details for yourself in the future, if there *is* a future as far as you and we are concerned.'

'What do you mean,' Chip said, ' "in my present condition"?'

There was silence for a moment. A woman coughed. 'While you're dulled and normalized by your most recent treatment,' King said.

Chip sat still, facing in King's direction, stopped by the irrationality of what he had said. He went over the words and answered them: 'I'm not dulled and normalized.'

'But you are,' King said.

'The whole Family is,' Snowflake said, and from beyond her came 'Everyone, not just you'—in the old man's voice of Leopard.

'What do you think a treatment consists of?' King asked.

Chip said, 'Vaccines, enzymes, the contraceptive, sometimes a tranquilizer——'

'*Always* a tranquilizer,' King said. 'And LPK, which minimizes aggressiveness and also minimizes joy and perception and every other fighting thing the brain is capable of.'

'And a sexual depressant,' Snowflake said.

'That too,' King said. 'Ten minutes of automatic sex once a week is barely a fraction of what's possible.'

'I don't believe it,' Chip said. 'Any of it.'

They told him it was true. 'It's true, Chip.' 'Really, it's true!'

'You're in genetics,' King said, 'isn't that what genetic engineering is working toward?—removing aggressiveness, controlling the sex drive, building in helpfulness and docility and gratitude? Treatments are doing the job in the meantime, while genetic engineering gets past size and skin color.'

'Treatments help us,' Chip said.

'They help Uni,' the woman across the table said.

'And the Wei-worshippers who programmed Uni,' King said. 'But they don't help *us*, at least not as much as they hurt us. They make us into machines.'

Chip shook his head, and shook it again.

'Snowflake told us'—it was Hush, speaking in a dry quiet voice that accounted for her name—'that you have abnormal tendencies. Haven't you ever noticed that they're stronger just before a treatment and weaker just after one?'

Snowflake said, 'I'll bet you made that picture frame a day or two *before* a treatment, not a day or two after one.'

He thought for a moment. 'I don't remember,' he said, 'but when I was a boy and thought about classifying myself after treatments it seemed stupid and pre-U, and before treatments it was—exciting.'

'There you are,' King said.

'But it was *sick* excitement!'

'It was healthy,' King said, and the woman across the table said, 'You were alive, you were feeling something. *Any* feeling is healthier than no feeling at all.'

He thought about the guilt he had kept secret from his advisers since Karl and the Academy. He nodded. 'Yes,' he said, 'yes, that could be.' He turned his face toward King, toward the woman, toward Leopard and Snowflake, wishing he could open his eyes and see them. 'But I don't understand this,' he said. '*You* get treatments, don't you? Then aren't *you*——'

'Reduced ones,' Snowflake said.

'Yes, we get treatments,' King said, 'but we've managed to have them reduced, to have certain components of them reduced, so that we're a little more than the machines Uni thinks we are.'

'And that's what we're offering *you*,' Snowflake said; 'a way to see more and feel more and do more and enjoy more.'

'And to be more unhappy; tell him that too.' It was a new voice, soft but clear, the other young woman. She was across the table and to Chip's left, close to where King was.

'That isn't so,' Snowflake said.

'Yes it is,' the clear voice said—a girl's voice almost; she was no more than twenty, Chip guessed. 'There'll be days when you'll *hate* Christ, Marx, Wood, and Wei,' she said, 'and want to take a torch to Uni. There'll be days when you'll want to tear off your bracelet and run to a mountain-top like the old incurables, just to be able to do what you want to do and make your own choice and live your own life.'

'Lilac,' Snowflake said.

'There'll be days when you'll hate *us*,' she said, 'for waking you up and making you *not* a machine. Machines are at home in the universe; people are aliens.'

'Lilac,' Snowflake said, 'we're trying to get Chip to join us; we're not trying to scare him away.' To Chip she said, 'Lilac is *really* abnormal.'

'There's truth in what Lilac says,' King said. 'I think we all have moments when we wish there were someplace we could go, some settlement or colony where we could be our own master——'

'Not me,' Snowflake said.

'And since there isn't such a place,' King said, 'yes, we're sometimes unhappy. Not you, Snowflake; I know. With rare exceptions like Snowflake, being able to feel happiness seems to mean being able to feel *un*happiness as well. But as Sparrow said, any feeling is better and healthier than none at all; and the unhappy moments aren't that frequent, really.'

'They are,' Lilac said.

'Oh, cloth,' Snowflake said. 'Let's *stop* all this talk about unhappiness.'

'Don't worry, Snowflake,' the woman across the table, Sparrow, said, 'if he gets up and runs you can trip him.'

'Ha, ha, hate, hate,' Snowflake said.

'Snowflake, Sparrow,' King said. 'Well, Chip, what's your answer? Do you want to get your treatments reduced? It's done by steps; the first one is easy, and if you don't like the way you feel a month from now, you can go to your adviser and tell him you were infected by a group of very sick members who you unfortunately can't identify.'

After a moment Chip said, 'All right. What do I do?' His arm was squeezed by Snowflake. 'Good,' Hush whispered.

'Just a moment, I'm lighting my pipe,' King said.

'Are you all smoking?' Chip asked. The burning smell was intense, drying and stinging his nostrils.

'Not right now,' Hush said. 'Only King, Lilac, and Leopard.'

'We've all *been* doing it though,' Snowflake said. 'It's not a continuous thing; you do it awhile and then stop awhile.'

'Where do you get the tobacco?'

'We grow it,' Leopard said, sounding pleased. 'Hush and I. In parkland.'

'In *parkland*?'

'That's right,' Leopard said.

'We have two patches,' Hush said, 'and last Sunday we found a place for a third.'

'Chip?' King said, and Chip turned toward him and listened. 'Basically, step one is just a matter of acting as if you're being *overtreated*,' King said; 'slowing down at work, at games, at everything—slowing down *slightly*, not conspicuously. Make a small mistake at your work, and another one a few days later. And don't do well at sex. The thing to do there is masturbate before you meet your girlfriend; that way you'll be able to fail convincingly.'

'Masturbate?'

'Oh, fully treated, fully satisfied member,' Snowflake said.

'Bring yourself to an orgasm with your hand,' King said. 'And then don't be too concerned when you don't have one later. Let your girlfriend tell *her* adviser; don't tell yours. Don't be too concerned about anything, the mistakes you make, lateness for appointments or whatever; let others do the noticing and reporting.'

'Pretend to doze off during TV,' Sparrow said.

'You're ten days from your next treatment,' King said. 'At your next week's adviser meeting, if you've done what I've told you, your adviser will sound you out about your general torpor. Again, no concern on your part. Apathy. If you do the whole thing well, the depressants in your treatment will be slightly reduced, enough so that a month from now you'll be anxious to hear about step two.'

'It sounds easy enough,' Chip said.

'It is,' Snowflake said, and Leopard said, 'We've all done it; you can too.'

'There's one danger,' King said. 'Even though your treatment may be slightly weaker than usual, its effects in the first few days will be strong. You'll feel a revulsion against what you've done and an urge to confess to your adviser and get stronger treatments than ever. There's no way of telling whether or not you'll be able to resist the urge. We did, but others haven't. In the past year we've given this talk to two other members; they did the slowdown but then confessed within a day or two after being treated.'

'Then won't my adviser be suspicious when I do the slowdown? He must have heard about those others.'

'Yes,' King said, 'but there are legitimate slowdowns, when a member's need for depressants has lessened, so if you do the job convincingly you'll get away with it. It's the urge to confess that you have to worry about.'

'Keep telling yourself'—it was Lilac speaking—'that it's a chemical that's making you think you're sick and in need of help, a chemical that was infused into you without your consent.'

'My consent?' Chip said.

'Yes,' she said. 'Your body is yours, not Uni's.'

'Whether you'll confess or hold out,' King said, 'depends on how strong your mind's resistance is to chemical alteration, and there's not much you can do about it one way or the other. On the basis of what we know of you, I'd say you have a good chance.'

They gave him some more pointers on slowdown technique—to skip his midday cake once or twice, to go to bed before the last chime—and then King suggested that Snowflake take him back to where they had met. 'I hope we'll be seeing you again, Chip,' he said. 'Without the bandage.'

'I hope so,' Chip said. He stood and pushed back his chair. 'Good luck,' Hush said; Sparrow and Leopard said it too. Lilac said it last: 'Good luck, Chip.'

'What happens,' he asked, 'if I resist the urge to confess?'

'We'll know,' King said, 'and one of us will get in touch with you about ten days after the treatment.'

'How will you know?'

'We'll know.'

His arm was taken by Snowflake's hand. 'All right,' he said. 'Thank you, all of you.'

They said, 'Don't mention it,' and 'You're welcome, Chip,' and 'Glad to be of help.' Something sounded strange, and then—as Snowflake led him from the room—he realized what it was: the not-being-said of 'Thank Uni'.

They walked slowly, Snowflake holding his arm not like a nurse but like a girl walking with her first boyfriend.

'It's hard to believe,' he said, 'that what I can feel now and see now—isn't all there is.'

'It isn't,' she said. 'Not even half. You'll find out.'

'I hope so.'

'You will. I'm sure of it.'

He smiled and said, 'Were you sure about those two who tried and didn't make it?'

'No,' she said. Then, 'Yes, I was sure of one, but not of the other.'

'What's step two?' he asked.

'First get through step one.'

'Are there more than two?'

'No. Two, if it works, gets you a major reduction. That's when you *really* come alive. And speaking of steps, there are three right ahead of us, going up.'

They went up the three steps and walked on. They were back in the plaza. It was perfectly silent, with even the breeze gone.

'The fucking's the best part,' Snowflake said. 'It gets much better, much more intense and exciting, and you'll be able to do it almost every night.'

'It's incredible.'

'And please remember,' she said, 'that I'm the one who found you. If I catch you even *looking* at Sparrow I'll kill you.'

Chip started, and told himself not to be foolish.

'Excuse me,' she said; 'I'll act aggressively toward you. Maxi-aggressively.'

'It's all right,' he said. 'I'm not shocked.'

'Not much.'

'What about Lilac?' he said. 'May I look at her?'

'All you want; she loves King.'

'Oh?'

'With a pre-U passion. He's the one who started the group; first her, then Leopard and Hush, then me, then Sparrow.'

Their footsteps became louder and resonant. She stopped him. 'We're here,' she said. He felt her fingers picking at the side of the bandage; he lowered his head. She began unwinding, peeling bandage from margins of skin that turned instantly cool. She unwound more and more and finally took the cotton from his eyes. He blinked them and stretched them wide.

She was close to him and moonlit, looking at him in a way that seemed challenging while she thrust the bandage into her medicenter coveralls. Somehow he had got her pale mask back on—but it wasn't a mask, he saw with a shock; it was her face. She was light. Lighter than any member he had ever seen, except a few near-sixty ones. She was almost white. Almost as white as snow.

'Mask neatly in place,' she said.

'I'm sorry,' he said.

'That's all right,' she said, and smiled. 'We're all odd in one way or another. Look at that eye.' She was thirty-five or so, sharp-featured and intelligent-looking, her hair freshly clipped.

'I'm sorry,' he said again.

'I said it's all right.'

'Are you supposed to let me see what you look like?'

'I'll tell you something,' she said. 'If you don't come through I don't give a fight if the whole bunch of us get normalized. In fact, I think I'd prefer it.' She took his head in both hands and kissed him, her tongue prying at his lips. It slid in and flickered in his mouth. She held his head tight, pushed her groin against his, and rubbed circularly. He felt a responsive stiffening and put his hands to her back. He worked his tongue tentatively against hers.

She withdrew her mouth. 'Considering that it's the middle of the week,' she said, 'I'm encouraged.'

'Christ, Marx, Wood, and Wei,' he said. 'Is that how you *all* kiss?'

'Only me, brother,' she said, 'only me.'

They did it again.

'Go on home now,' she said. 'Don't touch scanners.'

He backed away from her. 'I'll see you next month,' he said.

'You fighting well better had,' she said. 'Good luck.'

He went out into the plaza and headed toward the Institute. He looked back once. There was only empty passageway between the blank moon-white buildings.

2

BOB RO, seated behind his desk, looked up and smiled. 'You're late,' he said.

'I'm sorry,' Chip said. He sat down.

Bob closed a white folder with a red file tab on it. 'How are you?' he asked.

'Fine,' Chip said.

'Have a good week?'

'Mm-hmm.'

Bob studied him for a moment, his elbow on his chair arm, his fingers rubbing the side of his nose. 'Anything in particular you want to talk about?' he asked.

Chip was silent, and then shook his head. 'No,' he said.

'I hear you spent half of yesterday afternoon doing somebody else's work.'

Chip nodded. 'I took a sample from the wrong section of the IC box,' he said.

'I see,' Bob said, and smiled and grunted.

Chip looked questioningly at him.

'Joke,' Bob said. 'IC, I see.'

'Oh,' Chip said, and smiled.

Bob propped his jaw on his hand, the side of a finger lying against his lips. 'What happened Friday?' he asked.

'Friday?'

'Something about using the wrong microscope.'

Chip looked puzzled for a moment. 'Oh,' he said. 'Yes. I didn't really use it. I just went into the chamber. I didn't change any of the settings.'

Bob said, 'It looks like it *wasn't* such a good week.'

'No, I guess it wasn't,' Chip said.

'Peace SK says you had trouble Saturday night.'

'Trouble?'

'Sexually.'

Chip shook his head. 'I didn't have any trouble,' he said. 'I just wasn't in the mood, that's all.'

'She says you tried and couldn't erect.'

'Well I felt I *ought* to do it, for *her* sake, but I just wasn't in the mood.'

Bob watched him, not saying anything.

'I was tired,' Chip said.

'It seems you've been tired a lot lately. Is that why you weren't at your photography club meeting Friday night?'

'Yes,' he said. 'I turned in early.'

'How do you feel now? Are you tired now?'

'No. I feel fine.'

Bob looked at him, then straightened in his chair and smiled. 'Okay, brother,' he said, 'touch and go.'

Chip put his bracelet to the scanner of Bob's telecomp and stood up.

'See you next week,' Bob said.

'Yes.'

'On time.'

Chip, having turned away, turned back and said, 'Beg pardon?'

'On time next week,' Bob said.

'Oh,' Chip said. 'Yes.' He turned and went out of the cubicle.

He thought he had done it well but there was no way of knowing, and as his treatment came nearer he grew increasingly anxious. The thought of a significant rise in sensation became more intriguing by the hour, and Snowflake, King, Lilac, and the others became more attractive and admirable. So what if they smoked tobacco? They were happy and healthy members—no, *people,* not members!—who had found an escape from sterility and sameness and universal mechanical efficiency. He wanted to see them and be with them. He wanted to kiss and embrace Snowflake's unique lightness; to talk with King as an equal, friend to friend; to hear more of Lilac's strange but provocative ideas. 'Your body is yours, not Uni's—what a disturbing pre-U thing to say! If there were any basis for it, it could have implications that might lead him to—he couldn't think what; a jolting change of some sort in his attitude toward everything!

That was the night before his treatment. He lay awake for hours, then climbed with bandaged hands up a snow-covered mountaintop, smoked tobacco pleasurably under the guidance of a friendly smiling King, opened Snowflake's coveralls and found her snow-white with a throat-to-groin red cross, drove an early wheel-steered car through the hallways of a huge Genetic Suffocation Center, and had a new bracelet inscribed *Chip* and a window in his room through which he watched a lovely nude girl watering a lilac bush. She beckoned impatiently and he went to her—and woke feeling fresh and energetic and cheerful, despite those dreams, more vivid and convincing than any of the five or six he had had in the past.

That morning, a Friday, he had his treatment. The tickle-buzz-sting seemed to last a fraction of a second less than usual, and when he left the unit, pushing down his sleeve, he still felt good and himself, a dreamer of vivid dreams, a cohort of unusual people, an outwitter of Family and Uni. He walked falsely-slowly to the Center. It struck him that this of all times was when he should go on with the slowdown, to justify the even greater reduction that step two, whatever it was and whenever he took it, would be aimed at achieving. He was pleased with himself for having realized this, and wondered why King and the others hadn't suggested it. Perhaps they had thought he wouldn't be able to do anything after his treatment. Those other two members had apparently fallen apart completely, unlucky brothers.

He made a good small mistake that afternoon, started to type a report with the mike held wrong-side up while another 663B was looking. He felt a bit guilty about doing it, but he did it anyway.

That evening, to his surprise, he really dozed off during TV, although it was something fairly interesting, a tour of a new radio telescope in Isr. And later, during the house photography meeting, he could hardly keep his eyes open. He excused himself early and went to his room. He undressed without bothering to chute his used coveralls, got into bed without putting on pajamas, and tapped out the light. He wondered what dreams he would have.

He woke feeling frightened, suspecting that he was sick and in need of help. What was wrong? Had he done something he shouldn't have?

It came to him, and he shook his head, scarcely able to believe it. Was it real? Was it possible? Had he been so—so contaminated by the group of pitiably sick members that he had purposely made mistakes, had tried to deceive Bob RO (and maybe succeeded!), had thought thoughts hostile to his entire loving Family? Oh, Christ, Marx, Wood, and Wei!

He thought of what the young one, 'Lilac', had told him: to

remember that it was a chemical that was making him think he was sick, a chemical that had been infused into him without his consent. His consent! As if *consent* had anything to do with a treatment given to preserve one's health and well-being, an integral part of the health and well-being of the entire Family! Even before the Unification, even in the chaos and madness of the twentieth century, a member's consent wasn't asked before he was treated against typhic or typho or whatever it was. Consent! And he had listened without challenging her!

The first chime sounded and he jumped from his bed, anxious to make up for his unthinkable wrongs. He chuted the day before's coveralls, urined, washed, cleaned his teeth, evened up his hair, put on fresh coveralls, made his bed. He went to the dining hall and claimed his cake and tea, sat among other members and wanted to help them, to give them something, to demonstrate that he was loyal and loving, not the sick offender he had been the day before. The member on his left ate the last of his cake.

'Would you like some of mine?' Chip asked.

The member looked embarrassed. 'No, of course not,' he said. 'But thanks, you're very kind.'

'No I'm not,' Chip said, but he was glad the member had said he was.

He hurried to the Center and got there eight minutes early. He drew a sample from his own section of the IC box, not somebody else's, and took it into his own microscope; put on his glasses the right way and followed the OMP to the letter. He drew data from Uni respectfully (*Forgive my offenses, Uni who knows everything*) and fed it new data humbly (*Here is exact and truthful information about gene sample NF5049*).

The section head looked in. 'How's it going?' he asked.

'Very well, Bob.'

'Good.'

At midday he felt worse, though. What about *them*, those sick ones? Was he to leave them to their sickness, their tobacco, their reduced treatments, their pre-U thoughts? He had no choice. They had bandaged his eyes. There was no way of finding them.

But that wasn't so; there *was* a way. Snowflake had shown him her face. How many almost-white members, women of her age, could there be in the city? Three? Four? Five? Uni, if Bob RO asked it, could output their namebers in an instant. And when she was found and properly treated, she would give the namebers of some of the others; and they, the namebers of the ones remaining. The whole group could be found and helped within a day or two.

The way he had helped Karl.

That stopped him. He had helped Karl and felt guilt—guilt he had clung to for years and years, and now it persisted, a part of him. Oh Jesus Christ and Wei Li Chun, how sick beyond imagining he was!

'Are you all right, brother?'

It was the member across the table, an elderly woman. 'Yes,' he said, 'I'm fine,' and smiled and put his cake to his lips.

'You looked so *troubled* for a second,' she said.

'I'm fine,' he said. 'I thought of something I forgot to do.'

'Ah,' she said.

To help them or not to help them? Which was wrong, which was right? He *knew* which was wrong: not to help them, to abandon them as if he weren't his brother's keeper at all.

But he wasn't sure that helping them wasn't wrong too, and how could both be wrong?

He worked less zealously in the afternoon, but well and without mistakes, everything done properly. At the end of the day he went back to his room and lay on his back on his bed, the heels of his hands pressing into his shut eyes and making pulsing auroras there. He heard the voices of the sick ones, saw himself taking the sample from the wrong section of the box and cheating the Family of time and energy and equipment. The supper chime sounded but he stayed as he was, too tangled in himself for eating.

Later Peace SK called. 'I'm in the lounge,' she said. 'It's ten of eight. I've been waiting twenty minutes.'

'I'm sorry,' he said. 'I'll be right down.'

They went to a concert and then to her room.

'What's the *matter*?' she said.

'I don't know,' he said. 'I've been—upset the last few days.'

She shook her head and plied his slack penis more briskly. 'It doesn't make sense,' she said. 'Didn't you tell your adviser? I told mine.'

'Yes, I did. Look'—he took her hand away—'a whole group of new members came in on sixteen the other day. Why don't you go to the lounge and find somebody else?'

She looked unhappy. 'Well I think I ought to,' she said.

'I do too,' he said. 'Go ahead.'

'It just doesn't make any sense,' she said, getting up from the bed.

He dressed and went back to his room and undressed again. He thought he would have trouble falling asleep but he didn't.

On Sunday he felt even worse. He began to hope that Bob would call, would see that he wasn't well and draw the truth out of him. That way there would be no guilt or responsibility, only relief. He stayed in his room, watching the phone screen. Someone on the soccer team called; he said he wasn't feeling well.

At noon he went to the dining hall, ate a cake quickly, and returned to his room. Someone from the Center called, to find out if he knew someone else's nameber.

Hadn't Bob been told by now that he wasn't acting normally? Hadn't Peace said anything? Or the caller from the soccer team? And that member across the table at lunch yesterday, hadn't she been smart enough to see through his excuse and get his nameber? (Look at him, expecting others to help *him;* who in the Family was he helping?) Where *was* Bob? What kind of adviser was he?

There were no more calls, not in the afternoon, not in the evening. The music stopped once for a starship bulletin.

Monday morning, after breakfast, he went down to the medi-center. The scanner said *no,* but he told the attendant that he wanted to see his adviser; the attendant telecomped, and then the scanners said *yes, yes, yes,* all the way into the advisory offices, which were half empty. It was only 7.50.

He went into Bob's empty cubicle and sat down and waited for him, his hands on his knees. He went over in his mind the order in which he would tell: first about the intentional slow-down; then about the group, what they said and did and the way they could all be found through Snowflake's lightness; and finally about the sick and irrational guilt-feeling he had concealed all the years since he had helped Karl. One, two, three. He would get an extra treatment to make up for anything he mightn't have got on Friday, and he would leave the medicenter sound in mind and sound in body, a healthy contented member.

Your body is yours, not Uni's.

Sick, pre-U. Unit was the will and wisdom of the entire Family. It had *made* him; had granted him his food, his clothing, his housing, his training. It had granted even the permission for his very conception. Yes, it had made him, and from now on he would be——

Bob came in swinging his telecomp and stopped short. 'Li,' he said. 'Hello. Is anything wrong?'

He looked at Bob. The *name* was wrong. He was Chip, not Li. He looked down at his bracelet: *Li RM35M4419.* He had expected it to say *Chip.* When had he had one that said *Chip?* In a dream, a strange happy dream, a girl beckoning . . .

'Li?' Bob said, putting his telecomp on the floor.

Uni had made him *Li.* For Wei. But he was Chip, chip off the old block. Which one was he? Li? Chip? Li?

'What is it, brother?' Bob asked, leaning close, taking his shoulder.

'I wanted to see you,' he said.

'About what?'

He didn't know what to say. 'You said I shouldn't be late,' he said. He looked at Bob anxiously. 'Am I on time?'

'On time?' Bob stepped back and squinted at him. 'Brother, you're a day early,' he said. 'Tuesday's your day, not Monday.'

He stood up. 'I'm sorry,' he said. 'I'd better get over to the Center'—and started to go.

Bob caught his arm. 'Hold on,' he said, his telecomp falling on its side, slamming the floor.

'I'm all right,' Chip said. 'I got mixed up. I'll come to-morrow.' He went from Bob's hand, out of the cubicle.

'Li,' Bob called.

He kept going.

He watched TV attentively that evening—a track meet in Arg, a relay from Venus, the news, a dance program, and *Wei's Living Wisdom*—and then he went to his room. He tapped the light button but something was covering it and it didn't work. The door closed sharply, had been closed by someone who was near him in the dark, breathing.

'Who is it?' he asked.

'King and Lilac,' King said.

'What happened this morning?' Lilac asked, somewhere over by the desk . 'Why did you go to your adviser?'

'To tell,' he said.

'But you didn't.'

'I should have,' he said. 'Get out of here, please.'

'You see?' King said.

'We have to try,' Lilac said.

'Please go,' Chip said. 'I don't want to get involved with you again, with any of you. I don't know what's right or wrong any more. I don't even know who I am.'

'You've got about ten hours to find out,' King said. 'Your adviser's coming here in the morning to take you to Medicenter Main. You're going to be examined there. It wasn't supposed to happen for three weeks or so, after some more slowing down. It would have been step two. But it's happening tomorrow, and it'll probably be step minus-one.'

'It doesn't have to be, though,' Lilac said. 'You can still make it step two if you do what we tell you.'

'I don't want to hear,' he said. 'Just go, please.'

They didn't say anything. He heard King make a movement.

'Don't you understand?' Lilac said. If you do what we tell you your treatments will be reduced as much as ours are. If you don't they'll be put back to where they were. In fact, they'll prob-ably be increased beyond that, won't they, King?'

'Yes,' King said.

'To "protect" you,' Lilac said. 'So that you'll never again even *try* to get out from under. Don't you see, Chip?' Her voice came closer. 'It's the only chance you'll ever have. For the rest of your life you'll be a machine.'

'No, not a machine, a member,' he said. 'A healthy member doing his assignment; *helping* the Family, not cheating it.'

'You're wasting your breath, Lilac,' King said. 'If it were a few days later you might be able to get through, but it's too soon.'

'Why didn't you tell this morning?' Lilac asked him. 'You went to your adviser; why didn't you tell? Others have.'

'I was going to,' he said.

'Why didn't you?'

He turned away from her voice. 'He called me Li,' he said. 'And I thought I was Chip. Everything got—unsettled.'

'But you *are* Chip,' she said, coming still closer. 'Someone with a name different from the nameber Uni gave him. Someone who thought of picking his own classification instead of letting Uni do it.' He moved away, perturbed, then turned and faced their dim coverall shapes—Lilac, small, opposite him and a couple of meters away; King to his right against the light-outlined door.

'*How can you speak against Uni?*' he asked. 'It's granted us everything!'

'Only what we've given it to grant us,' Lilac said. 'It's denied us a hundred times more.'

'It let us be born!'

'How many,' she said, 'will it *not* let be born? Like your children. Like mine.'

'What do you mean?' he said. 'That anyone who *wants* children —should be allowed to have them?'

'Yes,' she said. 'That's what I mean.'

Shaking his head, he backed to his bed and sat down. She came to him; crouched and put her hands on his knees. 'Please, Chip,' she said, 'I shouldn't say such things when you're still the way you are, but please, please, believe me. Believe *us*. We are not sick, we are *healthy*. It's the world that's sick—with chemistry, and efficiency, and humility, and helpfulness. Do what we tell you. Become healthy. Please, Chip.'

Her earnestness held him. He tried to see her face. 'Why do you care so much?' he asked. Her hands on his knees were small and warm, and he felt an impulse to touch them, to cover them with his own. Faintly he found her eyes, large and less slanted than normal, unusual and lovely.

'There are so few of us,' she said, 'and I think that maybe, if there were more, we could do something; get away somehow and make a place for ourselves.'

'Like the incurables,' he said.

'That's what we learn to call them,' she said. 'Maybe they were really the unbeatables, the undruggables.'

He looked at her, trying to see more of her face.

'We have some capsules,' she said, 'that will slow down your reflexes and lower your blood pressure, put things in your blood that will make it look as if your treatments are too strong. If you take them tomorrow morning, before your adviser comes, and if you behave at the medicenter as we tell you and answer certain questions as we tell you—then tomorrow will be step two, and you'll take it and be healthy.'

'And unhappy,' he said.

'Yes,' she said, a smile coming into her voice, 'unhappy, too, though not as much as I said. I sometimes get carried away.'

'About every five minutes,' King said.

She took her hands from Chip's knees and stood up. 'Will you?' she asked.

He wanted to say yes to her, but he wanted to say no, too. He said, 'Let me see the capsules.'

King, coming forward, said, 'You'll see them after we leave. They're in here.' He put into Chip's hand a small smooth box. 'The red one has to be taken tonight and the other two as soon as you get up.'

'Where did you get them?'

'One of the group works in a medicenter.'

'Decide,' Lilac said. 'Do you want to hear what to say and do?'

He shook the box but it made no sound. He looked at the two dim figures waiting before him.

He nodded. 'All right,' he said.

They sat and spoke to him, Lilac on the bed beside him, King on the drawn-over desk chair. They told him about a trick of tensing his muscles before the metabolic examination and one of looking above the objective during the depth-perception test. They told him what to say to the doctor who had charge of him and the senior adviser who interviewed him. They told him about tricks that might be played on him: sudden sounds behind his back; being left all alone, but not really, with the doctor's report form conveniently at hand. Lilac did most of the talking. Twice she touched him, once on his leg and once on his forearm; and once, when her hand lay by his side, he brushed it with his own. Hers moved away in a movement that might have begun before the contact.

'That's terrifically important,' King said.

'I'm sorry, what was that?'

'Don't ignore it completely,' King said. 'The report form.'

'Notice it,' Lilac said. 'Glance at it and then act as if it really isn't worth the bother of picking up and reading. As if you don't care much one way or the other.'

It was late when they finished; the last chime had sounded half an hour before. 'We'd better go separately,' King said. 'You go first. Wait by the side of the building.'

Lilac stood up and Chip stood, too. Her hand found his. 'I know you're going to make it, Chip,' she said.

'I'll try,' he said. 'Thanks for coming.'

'You're welcome,' she said, and went to the door. He thought he would see her by the light in the hallway as she went out, but King got up and was in the way and the door closed.

They stood silently for a moment, he and King, facing each other.

'Don't forget,' King said. 'The red capsule now and the other two when you get up.'

'Right,' Chip said, feeling for the box in his pocket.

'You shouldn't have any trouble.'

'I don't know; there's so much to remember.'

They were silent again.

'Thank you very much, King,' Chip said, holding out his hand in the darkness.

'You're a lucky man,' King said. 'Snowflake is a very passionate woman. You and she are going to have a lot of good times together.'

Chip didn't understand why he had said that. 'I hope so,' he said. 'It's hard to believe it's possible to have more than one orgasm a week.'

'What we have to do now,' King said. 'is find a man for Sparrow. Then everyone will have someone. It's better that way. Four couples. No friction.'

Chip lowered his hand. He suddenly felt that King was telling him to stay away from Lilac, was defining who belonged with whom and telling him to obey the definition. Had King somehow seen him touching Lilac's hand?

'I'm going now,' King said. 'Turn around, please.'

Chip turned around and heard King moving away. The room appeared dimly as the door was opened, a shadow swept across it, and it disappeared again with the door's closing.

Chip turned. How strange it was to think of someone loving one member in particular so much as to want no one else to touch her! Would he be that way, too, if his treatments were reduced? It was—like so many other things—hard to believe.

He went to the light button and felt what was covering it: tape, with something square and flat underneath. He picked at the tape, peeled it away, and tapped the button. He shut his eyes against the ceiling's glare.

When he could see he looked at the tape; it was skin-colored, with a square of blue cardboard stuck to it. He dropped it down the chute and took the box from his pocket. It was white plastic with a hinged lid. He opened it. A red capsule, a white one, and one that was half white and half yellow lay bedded on a cotton filling.

He took the box into the bathroom and tapped on the light. Setting the open box on the edge of the sink, he turned on the water and pulled a cup from the slot and filled it. He turned the water off.

He started to think, but before he could think too much he picked up the red capsule, put it far back on his tongue, and drank the water.

Two doctors, not one, had charge of him. They led him in a pale blue smock from examination room to examination room, conferred with the examining doctors, conferred with each other, and made checks and notations on a clipboarded report form that they handed back and forth between them. One was a woman in her forties, the other a man in his thirties. The woman sometimes walked with her arm around Chip's shoulders, smiling and calling him 'young brother'. The man watched him impassively, with eyes that were smaller and set closer together than normal. He had a fresh scar on his cheek, running from the temple to the corner of his mouth and dark bruises on his cheek and his forehead. He never took his eyes off Chip except to look at the report form. Even when conferring with doctors he kept watching him. When the three of them walked to the next examination room he usually dropped behind Chip and the smiling woman doctor. Chip expected him to make a sudden sound, but he didn't.

The interview with the senior adviser, a young woman, went well, Chip thought, but nothing else did. He was afraid to tense his muscles before the metabolic examination because of the doctor watching him, and he forgot about looking above the objective in the depth-perception test until it was too late.

'Too bad you're missing a day's work,' the watching doctor said.

'I'll make it up,' he said, and realized as he said it that it was a mistake. He should have said *It's all for the best* or *Will I be here all day?* or simply a dull overtreated *Yes.*

At midday he was given a glass of bitter white liquid to drink instead of a totalcake and then there were more tests and examinations. The woman doctor went away for half an hour but not the man.

Around three o'clock they seemed to be finished and went into a small office. The man sat down behind the desk and Chip sat opposite him. The woman said, 'Excuse me, I'll be back in two seconds.' She smiled at Chip and went out.

The man studied the report form for a minute or two, running a fingertip back and forth along his scar, and then he looked at the clock and put down the clipboard. 'I'll go get her,' he said, and got up and went out, closing the door part-way.

Chip sat still and sniffed and looked at the clipboard. He leaned over, twisted his head, read on the report form the words *cholinesterase absorption factor, unamplified,* and sat back in his chair again. Had he looked too long?—he wasn't sure. He rubbed his thumb and examined it, then looked at the room's pictures, *Marx Writing* and *Wood Presenting the Unification Treaty.*

They came back in. The woman doctor sat down behind the desk and the man sat in a chair near her side. The woman looked at Chip. She wasn't smiling. She looked worried.

'Young brother,' she said, 'I'm worried about you. I think you've been trying to fool us.'

Chip looked at her. 'Fool you?' he said.

'There are sick members in this town,' she said: 'do you know that?'

He shook his head.

'Yes,' she said. 'As sick as can be. They cover members' eyes and take them someplace, and tell them to slow down and make mistakes and pretend they've lost their interest in sex. They try to make other members as sick as they are. Do you know any such members?'

'No,' Chip said.

'Anna,' the man said, 'I've *watched* him. There's no reason to think there's anything wrong beyond what showed on the tests.' He turned to Chip and said, 'Very easily corrected; nothing for you to think about.'

The woman shook her head. 'No,' she said. 'No, it doesn't *feel* right. Please, young brother, you want us to help you, don't you?'

'Nobody told me to make mistakes,' Chip said. 'Why? Why should I?'

The man tapped the report form. 'Look at the enzymological rundown,' he said to the woman.

'I've looked at it, I've looked at it.'

'He's been badly OT'ed there, there, there, and there. Let's give the data to Uni and get him fixed up again.'

'I want Jesus HL to see him.'

'Why?'

'Because I'm *worried*.'

'I don't know any sick members,' Chip said. 'If I did I would tell my adviser.'

'Yes,' the woman said, 'and why did you want to see him yesterday morning?'

'Yesterday?' Chip said. 'I thought it was my day. I got mixed up.'

'Please, let's go,' the woman said, standing up holding the clipboard.

They left the office and walked down the hallway outside it. The woman put her arm around Chip's shoulders but she didn't smile. The man dropped behind.

They came to the end of the hallway, where there was a door marked *600A* with a brown white-lettered plaque on it: *Chief, Chemotherapeutics Division*. They went in, to an ante-room where a member sat behind a desk. The woman doctor told her that they wanted to consult Jesus HL about a diagnostic problem, and the member got up and went out through another door.

'A waste of time all around,' the man said.

The woman said, 'Believe me, I hope so.'

There were two chairs in the anteroom, a bare low table, and *Wei Addressing the Chemotherapists*. Chip decided that if they made him tell he would try not to mention Snowflake's light skin and Lilac's less-slanted-than-normal eyes.

The member came back and held the door open.

They went into a large office. A gaunt gray-haired member in his fifties—Jesus HL—was seated behind a large untidy desk. He nodded to the doctors as they approached, and looked absently at Chip. He waved a hand toward a chair facing the desk. Chip sat down in it.

The woman doctor handed Jesus HL the clipboard. 'This doesn't feel right to me,' she said. 'I'm afraid he's malingering.'

'Contrary to the enzymological evidence,' the other doctor said.

Jesus HL leaned back in his chair and studied the report form. The doctors stood by the side of the desk, watching him. Chip tried to look curious but not concerned. He watched Jesus HL for a moment, and then looked at the desk. Papers of all sorts were piled and scattered on it and lay drifted over an old-style telecomp in a scuffed case. A drink container jammed with pens and rulers stood beside a framed snapshot of Jesus HL, younger, smiling in front of Uni's dome. There were two souvenir paper-weights, an unusual square one from CH161332 and a round one from ARG20400, neither of them on paper.

Jesus HL turned the clipboard end for end and peeled the form down and read the back of it.

'What I would like to do, Jesus,' the woman doctor said, 'is keep him here overnight and run some of the tests again to-morrow.'

'Wasting——' the man said.

'Or better still,' the woman said, louder, 'question him now under TP.'

'Wasting time and supplies,' the man said.

'What are we, doctors or efficiency analyzers?' the woman asked him sharply.

Jesus HL put down the clipboard and looked at Chip. He got up from his chair and came around the side of the desk, the doctors stepping back quickly to let him pass. He came and stood directly in front of Chip's chair, tall and thin, his red-crossed coveralls stained with yellow spots.

He took Chip's hands from the chair arms, turned them over, and looked at the palms, which glistened with sweat.

He let one hand go and held the wrist of the other, his fingers at the pulse. Chip made himself look up, unconcernedly. Jesus HL looked quizzically at him for a moment and then suspected—no, *knew*—and smiled his knowledge contemptuously. Chip felt hollow, beaten.

Jesus HL took hold of Chip's chin, bent over, and looked closely at his eyes. 'Open your eyes as wide as you can,' he said. His voice was King's. Chip stared at him.

'That's right,' he said. 'Stare at me as if I've said something shocking.' It was *King's voice,* unmistakable. Chip's mouth opened. 'Don't speak, please.' King = Jesus HL said, squeezing Chip's jaw painfully. He stared into Chip's eyes, turned his head to one side and then the other, and then released it and stepped back. He went back around the desk and sat down again. He picked up the clipboard, glanced at it, and handed it to the woman doctor, smiling. 'You're mistaken, Anna,' he said. 'You can put your mind at rest. I've seen many members who were malingering; this one isn't. I commend you on your concern, though.' To the man he said, 'She's right, you know, Jesus; we mustn't be efficiency analyzers. The Family can afford a little waste where a member's health is involved. What *is* the Family, after all, except the sum of its members?'

'Thank you, Jesus,' the woman said, smiling. 'I'm glad I was wrong.'

'Give that data to Uni,' King said, turning and looking at Chip, 'so our brother here can be properly treated from now on.'

'Yes, right away.' The woman beckoned to Chip. He got up from the chair.

They left the office. In the doorway Chip turned. 'Thank you,' he said.

King looked at him from behind his littered desk—only looked, with no smile, no glimmer of friendship. 'Thank Uni,' he said.

Less than a minute after he got back to his room Bob called. 'I just got a report from Medicenter Main,' he said. 'Your treatments have been slightly out of line but from now on they're going to be exactly right.'

'Good,' Chip said.

'This confusion and tiredness you've been feeling will gradually pass away during the next week or so, and then you'll be your old self.'

'I hope so.'

'You will. Listen, do you want me to squeeze you in tomorrow, Li, or shall we let it go till next Tuesday?'

'Next Tuesday's all right.'

'Fine,' Bob said. He grinned. 'You know what?' he said. 'You look better already.'

'I feel a little better,' Chip said.

3

HE FELT A LITTLE BETTER every day, a little more awake and alert, a little more sure that sickness was what he had had and health was what he was growing toward. By Friday—three days after the examination—he felt the way he usually felt on the day before a treatment. But his last treatment was only a week behind him; three weeks and more lay ahead, spacious and unexplored, before the next one. The slowdown had worked; Bob had been fooled and the treatment reduced. And the next one, on the basis of the examination, would be reduced even further. What wonders of feeling would he be feeling in five, in six weeks' time?

That Friday night, a few minutes after the last chime, Snowflake came into his room. 'Don't mind me,' she said, taking off her coveralls. 'I'm just putting a note in your mouthpiece.'

She got into bed with him and helped him off with his pajamas. Her body to his hands and lips was smooth, pliant, and more arousing than Peace SK's or anyone else's; and his own, as she stroked and kissed and licked it, was more shudderingly reactive than ever before, more strainingly in want. He eased himself into her—deeply, snugly in—and would have driven them both to immediate orgasm, but she slowed him, stopped him, made him draw out and come in again, putting herself into one strange but effective position and then another. For twenty minutes or more they worked and contrived together, keeping as noiseless as they could because of the members beyond the wall and on the floor below. When they were done and apart she said, 'Well?'

'Well it was top speed, of course,' he said, 'but frankly, from what you said, I expected even more.'

'Patience, brother,' she said. 'You're still an invalid. The time will come when you'll look back on this as the night we shook hands.'

He laughed.

'Shh.'

He held her and kissed her. 'What does it say?' he asked. 'The note in my mouthpiece.'

'Sunday night at eleven, the same place as last time.'

'But no bandage.'

'No bandage,' she said.

He would see them all, Lilac and all the others. 'I've been wondering when the next meeting would be,' he said.

'I hear you whooshed through step two like a rocket.'

'Stumbled through it, you mean. I wouldn't have made it at all if not for——' Did she know who King really was? Was it all right to speak of it?

'If not for what?'

'If not for King and Lilac,' he said. 'They came here the night before and prepped me.'

'Well of course,' she said. '*None* of us would have made it if not for the capsules and all.'

'I wonder where they get them.'

'I think one of them works in a medicenter.'

'Mm, that would explain it,' he said. She didn't know. Or she knew but didn't know that *he* knew. Suddenly he was annoyed by the need for carefulness that had come between them.

She sat up. 'Listen,' she said, 'it pains me to say this, but don't forget to carry on as usual with your girlfriend. Tomorrow night, I mean.'

'She's got someone new,' he said. 'You're my girlfriend.'

'No I'm not,' she said. 'Not on Saturday nights anyway. Our advisers would wonder why we took someone from a different house. I've got a nice normal Bob down the hall from me, and you find a nice normal Yin or Mary. But if you give her more than a little quick one I'll break your neck.'

'Tomorrow night I won't even be able to give her that.'

'That's all right,' she said, 'you're still supposed to be recovering.' She looked sternly at him. 'Really,' she said, 'you have to remember not to get too passionate, except with me. And to keep a contented smile in place between the first chime and the last. And to work hard at your assignment but not *too* hard. It's just as tricky to *stay* undertreated as it is to get that way.' She lay back down beside him and drew his arm around her. 'Hate,' she said, 'I'd give anything for a smoke now.'

'Is it really so enjoyable?'

'Mm'hmm. Especially at times like this.'

'I'll have to try it.'

They lay talking and caressing each other for a while, and then Snowflake tried to rouse him again—'Nothing ventured, nothing gained,' she said—but everything she did proved unavailing. She left around twelve or so. 'Sunday at eleven,' she said by the door. 'Congratulations.'

Saturday evening in the lounge Chip met a member named Mary KK whose boyfriend had been transferred to Can earlier in the week. The birth-year part of her nameber was 38, making her twenty-four.

They went to a pre-Marxmas sing in Equality Park. As they sat waiting for the amphitheater to fill, Chip looked at Mary closely. Her chin was sharp but otherwise she was normal: tan skin, upslanted brown eyes, clipped black hair, yellow coveralls on her slim spare frame. One of her toenails, half covered by sandal strap, was discolored a bluish purple. She sat smiling, watching the opposite side of the amphitheater.

'Where are you from?' he asked her.

'Rus,' she said.

'What's your classification?'

'One-forty B.'

'Ophthalmologic technician.'

'What do you do?'

She turned to him. 'I attach lenses,' she said. 'In the children's section.'

'Do you enjoy it?'

'Of course.' She looked uncertainly at him. 'Why are you

asking me so many questions?' she asked. 'And why are you looking at me so—as if you've never seen a member before?'

'I've never seen *you* before,' he said. 'I want to know you.'

'I'm no different from any other member,' she said. 'There's nothing unusual about me.'

'Your chin is a little sharper than normal.'

She drew back, looking hurt and confused.

'I didn't mean to hurt you,' he said. 'I just meant to point out that there *is* something unusual about you, even if it isn't something important.'

She looked searchingly at him, then looked away, at the opposite side of the amphitheater again. She shook her head. 'I don't understand you,' she said.

'I'm sorry,' he said. 'I was sick until last Tuesday. But my adviser took me to Medicenter Main and they fixed me up fine. I'm getting better now. Don't worry.'

'Well *that's* good,' she said. After a moment she turned and smiled cheerfully at him. 'I forgive you,' she said.

'Thank you,' he said, suddenly feeling sad for her.

She looked away again. 'I hope we sing "The Freeing of the Masses",' she said.

'We will,' he said.

'I love it,' she said, and smiling she began to hum it.

He kept looking at her, trying to do so in a normal-seeming way. What she had said was true: she was no different from any other member. What did a sharp chin or a discolored toenail signify? She was exactly the same as every Mary and Anna and Peace and Yin who had ever been his girlfriend: humble and good, helpful and hard-working. Yet she made him feel sad. Why? And could all the others have done so, had he looked at them as closely as he was looking at her, had he listened as closely to what they said?

He looked at the members on the other side of him, at the scores in the tiers below, the scores in the tiers above .They were all like Mary KK, all smiling and ready to sing their favorite Marxmas songs, and all saddening; everyone in the amphitheater, the hundreds, the thousands, the tens of thousands. Their faces lined the mammoth bowl like tan beads strung away in immeasurable close-laid ovals.

Spotlights struck the gold cross and red sickle at the bowl's center. Four familiar trumpet notes blasted, and everybody sang:

> One mighty Family,
> A single perfect breed,
> Free of all selfishness,
> Aggressiveness and greed,
>> Each member giv-ing all he has to give
>> And get-ting all he needs to live!

But they weren't a mighty Family, he thought. They were a

weak Family, a saddening and pitiable one, dulled by chemicals and dehumanized by bracelets. It was Uni that was mighty.

> One mighty Family,
> A single noble race,
> Sending its sons and daughters
> Bravely into space . . .

He sang the words automatically, thinking that Lilac had been right: reduced treatments brought new unhappiness.

Sunday night at eleven he met Snowflake between the buildings on Lower Christ Plaza. He held her and kissed her gratefully, glad of her sexuality and humor and pale skin and bitter tobacco taste—all the things that were she and nobody else. 'Christ and Wei, I'm glad to see you,' he said.

She gave him a tighter hug and smiled happily at him. 'It gets to be a shut-off being with normals, doesn't it?' she said.

'And how,' he said. 'I wanted to kick the soccer team instead of the ball this morning.' She laughed.

He had been depressed since the sing; now he felt released and happy and taller. 'I found a girlfriend,' he said, 'and guess what; I fucked her without the least bit of trouble.'

'Hate.'

'Not as extensively or as satisfyingly as we did, but with no trouble at all, not twenty-four hours later.'

'I can live without the details.'

He grinned and ran his hands down her sides and clasped her hipbones. 'I think I might even manage to do it again tonight,' he said, teasing her with his thumbs.

'Your ego is growing by leaps and bounds.'

'My everything is.'

'Come on, brother,' she said, prying his hands away and holding onto one, 'we'd better get you indoors before you start singing.'

They went into the plaza and crossed it diagonally. Flags and sagging Marxmas bunting hung motionless above it, dim in the glow of distant walkways. 'Where are we going anyway?' he asked, walking happily. 'Where's the secret meeting place of the diseased corrupters of healthy young members?'

'The Pre-U,' she said.

'The *Museum*?'

'That's right. Can you think of a better place for a group of Uni-cheating abnormals? It's exactly where we belong. Easy,' she said, tugging at his hand; 'don't walk so energetically.'

A member was coming into the plaza from the walkway they were going toward. A briefcase or telecomp was in his hand.

Chip walked more normally alongside Snowflake. The member, coming closer—it was a telecomp he had—smiled and nodded. They smiled and nodded in return as they passed him.

They went down the steps and out of the plaza.

'Besides,' Snowflake said, 'it's empty from eight to eight and it's an endless source of pipes and funny costumes and unusual beds.'

'You take things?'

'We leave the beds,' she said. 'But we make use of them now and again. Meeting solemnly in the staff conference room was just for your benefit.'

'What else do you do?'

'Oh, sit around and complain a little. That's Lilac's and Leopard's department mostly. Sex and smoking is enough for me. King does funny versions of some of the TV programs; wait till you find out how much you can laugh.'

'The making use of the beds,' Chip said; 'is it done on a group basis?'

'Only by two's, dear; we're not *that* pre-U.'

'Who did *you* use them with?'

'Sparrow, obviously. Necessity is the mother of et cetera. Poor girl, I feel sorry for her now. '

'Of course you do.'

'I do! Oh well, there's an artificial penis in Nineteenth Century Artifacts. She'll survive.'

'King says we should find a man for her.'

'We should. It would be a much better situation, having four couples.'

'That's what King said.'

As they were crossing the ground floor of the museum—lighting their way through the strange-figured dark with a flashlight that Snowflake had produced—another light struck them from the side and a voice nearby said, 'Hello there!' They started. 'I'm sorry,' the voice said. 'It's me, Leopard.'

Snowflake swung her light onto the twentieth-century car, and a flashlight inside it went off. They went over to the glinting metal vehicle. Leopard, sitting behind the steering wheel, was an old round-faced member wearing a hat with an orange plume. There were several dark brown spots on his nose and cheeks. He put his hand, also spotted, through the car's window frame. 'Congratulations, Chip,' he said. 'I'm glad you came through.'

'Going for a ride?' Snowflake asked.

'I've been for one,' he said. 'To Jap and back. Volvo's out of fuel now. And thoroughly wet, too, come to think of it.'

They smiled at him and at each other.

'Fantastic, isn't it?' he said, turning the wheel and working a lever that projected from its shaft. 'The driver was in complete control from start to finish, using both hands and both feet.'

'It must have been awfully bumpy,' Chip said, and Snowflake said, 'Not to mention dangerous.'

'But fun, too,' Leopard said. 'It must have been an adventure, really; choosing your destination, figuring out which roads to take to get there, gauging your movements in relation to the movements of other cars——'

'Gauging wrong and dying,' Snowflake said.

'I don't think that really happened as often as we're told it did,' Leopard said. 'If it had, they would have made the front parts of the cars much thicker.'

Chip said, 'But that would have made them heavier and they would have gone even slower.'

'Where's Hush?' Snowflake asked.

'Upstairs with Sparrow,' Leopard said. He opened the car's door, and coming out of it with a flashlight in his hand, said, 'They're setting things up. Some more stuff was put in the room.' He cranked the window of the door halfway up and closed the door firmly. A wide brown belt decorated with metal studs was fastened about his coveralls.

'King and Lilac?' Snowflake asked.

'They're around someplace.'

Chip thought, *Making use of one of the beds*—as the three of them went on through the museum.

He had thought about King and Lilac a good deal since seeing King and seeing how old he was—fifty-two or -three or even more. He had thought about the difference between the ages of the two—thirty years, surely, at the very least—and about the way King had told him to stay away from Lilac; and about Lilac's large less-slanted-than-normal eyes and her hands that had rested small and warm on his knees as she crouched before him urging him toward greater life and awareness.

They went up the steps of the unmoving central escalator and across the museum's second floor. The two flashlights, Snowflake's and Leopard's, danced over the guns and daggers, the bulbed and wired lamps, the bleeding boxers, the kings and queens in their jewels and fur-trimmed robes, and the three beggars, filthy and crippled, parading their disfigurements and thrusting out their cups. The partition behind the beggars had been slid aside, opening a narrow passageway that extended farther into the building, its first few meters lit by a light from a doorway in the left-hand wall. A woman's voice spoke softly. Leopard went on ahead and through the doorway, while Snowflake, standing beside the beggars, sprung pieces of tape from a first-aid-kit cartridge. 'Snowflake's here with Chip,' Leopard said inside the room. Chip laid a piece of tape over his bracelet plaque and rubbed it down firmly.

They went to the doorway and into a tobacco-smelling stuffiness where an old woman and a young one sat close together on pre-U chairs, with two knives and a heap of brown leaves on a table before them. Hush and Sparrow; they shook Chip's hand and congratulated him. Hush was crinkle-eyed and smiling;

Sparrow, large-limbed and embarrassed-looking, her hand hot and moist. Leopard stood by Hush, holding a heat coil in the bowl of a curved black pipe and blowing out smoke around the sides of its stem.

The room, a fairly large one, was a storeroom, its farther reaches filled with a ceiling-high mass of pre-U relics, late and early: machines and furniture and paintings and bundles of clothing; swords and wood-handled implements; a statue of a member with wings, an 'angel'; half a dozen crates, opened, unopened, stenciled IND26110 and pasted at their corners with square yellow stickers. Looking around, Chip said, 'There are enough things here for another museum.'

'All genuine, too,' Leopard said. 'Some of the things on display aren't, you know.'

'I didn't.'

A varied lot of chairs and benches had been set about the forward part of the room. Paintings leaned against the walls, and there were cartons of smaller relics and piles of moldering books. A painting of an enormous boulder caught Chip's eye. He moved a chair to get a full view of it. The boulder, a mountain almost, floated above the earth in blue sky, meticulously painted and jarring to senses. 'What an odd picture,' he said.

'A lot of them are odd,' Leopard said.

'The ones of Christ,' Hush said, 'show him with a light around his head, and he doesn't look human at all.'

'I've seen those,' Chip said, looking at the boulder, 'but I've never seen anything like this. It's fascinating; real and unreal at the same time.'

'You can't take it,' Snowflake said. 'We can't take anything that might be missed.'

Chip said, 'There's no place I could put it anyway.'

'How do you like being undertreated?' Sparrow asked.

Chip turned. Sparrow looked away, at her hands holding a roll of leaves and a knife. Hush was at the same task, chopping rapidly at a roll of leaves, cutting it into thin shreds that piled before her knife. Snowflake was sitting with a pipe in her mouth; Leopard was holding the heat coil in the bowl of it. 'It's wonderful,' Chip said. 'Literally. Full of wonders. More of them every day. I'm grateful to all of you.'

'We only did what we're told to,' Leopard said, smiling. 'We helped a brother.'

'Not exactly in the approved way,' Chip said.

Snowflake offered him her pipe. 'Are you ready to try a puff?' she asked.

He went to her and took it. The bowl of it was warm, the tobacco in it gray and smoking. He hesitated for a moment, smiled at them watching him, and put the stem to his lips. He sucked briefly at it and blew out smoke. The taste was strong but pleasant, surprisingly so. 'Not bad,' he said. He did it again with more assurance. Some of the smoke went into his throat and he coughed.

Leopard, going smiling to the doorway, said, 'I'll get you one of your own,' and went out.

Chip returned the pipe to Snowflake and, clearing his throat, sat down on a bench of dark worn wood. He watched Hush and Sparrow cutting the tobacco. Hush smiled at him. He said, 'Where do you get the seeds?'

'From the plants themselves,' she said.

'Where did you get the ones you started with?'

'King had them.'

'What did I have?' King asked, coming in, tall and lean and bright-eyed, a gold medallion chain-hung on his coveralled chest. He had Lilac behind him, his hand holding hers. Chip stood up. She looked at him, unusual, dark, beautiful, young.

'The tobacco seeds,' Hush said.

King offered his hand to Chip, smiling warmly. 'It's good to see you here,' he said. Chip shook his hand; its grip was firm and hearty. 'Really good to see a new face in the group,' King said. 'Especially a male one, to help me keep these pre-U women in their proper place!'

'Huh,' Snowflake said.

'It's good to be here,' Chip said, pleased by King's friendliness. His coldness when Chip left his office must have been only a pretense, for the sake, of course, of the onlooking doctors. 'Thank you,' Chip said. 'For everything. Both of you.'

Lilac said, 'I'm very glad, Chip.' Her hand was still held by King's. She was darker than normal, a lovely near-brown touched with rose. Her eyes were large and almost level, her lips pink and soft-looking. She turned away and said, 'Hello, Snowflake.' She drew her hand from King's and went to Snowflake and kissed her cheek. She was twenty or twenty-one, no more. The upper pockets of her coveralls had something in them, giving her the breasted look of the women Karl had drawn. It was a strange, mysteriously alluring look.

'Are you beginning to feel different now,' Chip?' King asked. He was at the table, bending and putting tobacco into the bowl of a pipe.

'Yes, enormously,' Chip said. 'It's everything you said it would be.'

Leopard came in and said, 'Here you are, Chip.' He gave him a yellow thick-bowled pipe with an amber stem. Chip thanked him and tried the feel of it; it was comfortable in his hand and comfortable to his lips. He took it to the table, and King, his gold medallion swinging, showed him the right way to fill it.

Leopard took him through the staff section of the museum, showing him other storerooms, the conference room, and various offices and workrooms. 'It's a good idea,' he said, 'for someone to keep rough track of who goes where during these get-togethers, and then check around later and make sure nothing is conspicuously out of place. The girls could be a little more careful than they are. I generally do it, and when I'm gone perhaps you'll take over the job. Normals aren't quite as unobservant as we'd like them to be.'

'Are you being transferred?' Chip asked.

'Oh no,' Leopard said. 'I'll be dying soon. I'm over sixty-two now, by almost three months. So is Hush.'

'I'm sorry,' Chip said.

'So are we,' Leopard said, 'but nobody lives forever. Tobacco ashes are a danger, of course, but everyone's good about that. You don't have to worry about the smell; the air conditioning goes on at seven-forty and whips it right out; I stayed one morning and made sure. Sparrow's going to take over the tobacco growing. We dry the leaves right here, in back of the hot-water tank; I'll show you.'

When they got back to the storeroom, King and Snowflake were sitting opposite each other astride a bench, playing intently at a mechanical game of some kind that lay between them. Hush was dozing in her chair and Lilac was crouched at the verge of a mass of relics, taking books one at a time from a carton, looking at them, and putting them in a pile on the floor. Sparrow wasn't there.

'What's that?' Leopard asked.

'New game that came in,' Snowflake said, not looking up.

There were levers that they pressed and released, one for each hand, making little paddles hit a rusted ball back and forth on a rimmed metal board. The paddles, some of them broken, squeaked as they swung. The ball bounded this way and that and came to a stop in a depression at King's end of the board. 'Five!' Snowflake cried. 'There you are, brother!'

Hush opened her eyes, looked at them, and closed them again.

'Losing's the same as winning,' King said, lighting his pipe with a metal lighter.

'Like hate it is,' Snowflake said. 'Chip? Come on, you're next.'

'No, I'll watch,' he said, smiling.

Leopard declined to play, too, and King and Snowflake began another match. At a break in the play, when King had scored a point against Snowflake, Chip said, 'May I see the lighter?' and King gave it to him. A bird in flight was painted on the side of it; a duck, Chip thought. He had seen lighters in museums but had never worked one. He opened the hinged top and pushed his thumb against the ridged wheel. On the second try the wick flamed. He closed the lighter, looked at it all over, and at the next break handed it back to King.

He watched them play for another few moments and then moved away. He went over to the mass of relics and looked at it, and then moved nearer to Lilac. She looked up at him and smiled, putting a book on one of several piles beside her. 'I keep hoping to find one in the language,' she said, 'but they're always in the old ones.'

He crouched and picked up the book she had just put down. On the spine of it were small letters: *Bädda för död.* 'Hmm,' he said, shaking his head. He glanced through the old brown pages, at strange words and phrases: *allvarlig, lögnerska, dök ner på brickorna.* The double dots and little circles were over many of the letters.

'Some of them are enough like the language so that you can understand a word or two,' she said, 'but some of them are—well look at this one.' She showed him a book on which backward *N*'s and rectangular open-bottomed characters were mixed in with ordinary *P*'s and *E*'s and *O*'s. 'Now what does *that* mean?' she said, putting it down.

'It would be interesting to find one we could read,' he said, looking at her cheek's rose-brown smoothness.

'Yes, it would,' she said, 'but I think they were screened before they were sent here and that's why we can't.'

'You think they were screened?'

'There ought to be lots of them in the language,' she said. 'How could it have *become* the language if it wasn't the one most widely used?'

'Yes, of course,' he said. 'You're right.'

'I keep hoping, though,' she said, 'that there was a slip in the screening.' She frowned at a book and put it on a pile.

Her filled pockets stirred with her movements, and suddenly they looked to Chip like empty pockets lying against round breasts, breasts like the ones Karl had drawn; the breasts, almost, of a pre-U woman. It was possible, considering her abnormal darkness and the various physical abnormalities of the lot of them. He looked at her face again, so as not to embarrass her if she really had them.

'I thought I was double-checking this carton,' she said, 'but I have a funny feeling I'm triple-checking it.'

'But *why* should the books have been screened?' he asked her.

She paused, with her dark hands hanging empty and her elbows on her knees, looking at him gravely with her large, level eyes. 'I think we've been taught things that aren't true,' she said. 'About the way of life before the Unification. In the *late* pre-U, I mean, not the early.'

'What things?'

'The violence, the aggressiveness, the greed, the hostility. There was some of it, I suppose, but I can't believe that there was nothing else, and that's what we're taught, really. And the "bosses" punishing the "workers", and all the sickness and alcohol=drinking and starvation and self-destruction. Do *you* believe it?'

He looked at her. 'I don't know,' he said. 'I haven't thought much about it.'

'I'll tell you what *I* don't believe,' Snowflake said. She had risen from the bench, the game with King evidently finished. '*I* don't believe that they cut off the baby boys' foreskins,' she said. 'In the early pre-U, maybe—in the early, *early* pre-U—but not in the late; it's just too incredible. I mean, they had *some* kind of intelligence, didn't they?'

'It's incredible, all right,' King said, hitting his pipe against his palm, 'but I've seen photographs. Alleged photographs, anyway.'

Chip shifted around and sat on the floor. 'What do you mean?' he said. 'Can photographs be—not genuine?'

'Of course they can,' Lilac said. 'Take a close look at some of the ones inside. Parts of them have been drawn in. And parts have been drawn out.' She began putting books back into the carton.

'I had no idea that was possible,' Chip said.

'It is with the flat ones,' King said.

'What we're probably given,' Leopard said—he was sitting in a gilded chair, toying with the orange plume of the hat he had worn—'is a mixture of truth and untruth. It's anybody's guess as to which part is which and how much there is of each.'

'Couldn't we study these books and learn the languages?' Chip asked. 'One would be all we'd really need.'

'For what?' Snowflake asked.

'To find out,' he said. 'What's true and what isn't.'

'I tried it,' Lilac said.

'She certainly did,' King said to Chip, smiling. 'A while back she wasted more nights than I care to remember beating her pretty head against one of those nonsensical jumbles. Don't *you* do it, Chip; I beg you.'

'Why not?' Chip asked. 'Maybe I'll have better luck.'

'And suppose you do?' King said. 'Suppose you decipher a language and read a few books in it and find out that we *are* taught things that are untrue. Maybe *everything's* untrue. Maybe life in A.D. 2000 was one endless orgasm, with everyone choosing the right classification and helping his brothers and loaded to the ears with love and health and life's necessities. So what? You'll still be right here, in 162 Y.U., with a bracelet and an adviser and a monthly treatment. You'll only be unhappier. We'll *all* be unhappier.'

Chip frowned and looked at Lilac. She was packing books into the carton, not looking at him. He looked back at King and sought words. 'It would still be worth knowing,' he said. 'Being happy or unhappy—is that really the most important thing? Knowing the truth would be a different kind of happiness—a more satisfying kind, I think, even if it turned out to be a sad kind.'

'A sad kind of happiness?' King said, smiling. 'I don't see that at all.'

Leopard looked thoughtful.

Snowflake, gesturing to Chip to get up, said, 'Come on, there's something I want to show you.'

He climbed to his feet. 'But we'd probably only find that things have been exaggerated,' he said; 'that there was hunger but not so *much* hunger, aggressiveness but not so *much* aggressiveness. Maybe some of the minor things have been made up, like the foreskin-cutting and the flag-worship.'

'If you feel that way, then there's *certainly* no point in bothering,' King said. 'Do you have any idea what a job it would be? It would be staggering.'

Chip shrugged. 'It would be good to *know*, that's all,' he said. He looked at Lilac; she was putting the last few books into the carton.

'Come on,' Snowflake said, and took his arm. 'Save us some tobacco, you mems.'

They went out and into the dark of the exhibit hall. Snowflake's flashlight lit their way. 'What is it?' Chip asked. 'What do you want to show me?'

'What do you think?' she said. 'A bed. Certainly not more books.'

They generally met two nights a week, Sundays and Woods or Thursdays. They smoked and talked and idled with relics and exhibits. Sometimes Sparrow sang songs that she wrote, accompanying herself on a lap-held instrument whose strings at her fingers made pleasing antique music. The songs were short and sad, about children who lived and died on starships, lovers who were transferred, the eternal sea. Sometimes King reenacted the evening's TV, comically mocking a lecturer on climate control or a fifty-member chorus singing 'My Bracelet'. Chip and Snowflake made use of the seventeenth-century bed and the nineteenth-century sofa, the early pre-U farm wagon and the late pre-U plastic rug. On nights between meetings they sometimes went to one or the other's room. The nameber on Snowflake's door was Anna PY24A9155; the 24, which Chip couldn't resist working out, made her thirty-eight, older than he had thought her to be.

Day by day his senses sharpened and his mind grew more alert and restless. His treatment caught him back and dulled him, but only for a week or so; then he was awake again, alive again. He went to work on the language Lilac had tried to decipher. She showed him the books she had worked from and the lists she had made. *Momento* was moment; *silenzio*, silence. She had several pages of easily recognized translations; but there were words in the books' every sentence that could only be guessed at and the guesses tried elsewhere. Was *allora* 'then' or 'already'? What were *quale* and *sporse* and *rimanesse*? He worked with the books for an hour or so at every meeting. Sometimes she leaned over his shoulder and looked at what he was doing—said, 'Oh, of course!' or 'Couldn't that be one of the days of the week?'—but most of the time she stayed near King, filling his pipe for him and listening while he talked. King watched Chip working and, reflected in glass panes of pre-U furniture, smiled at the others and raised his eyebrows.

Chip saw Mary KK on Saturday nights and Sunday afternoons. He acted normal with her, smiled through the Amusement Gardens and fucked her simply and without passion. He acted normal at his assignment, slowly following the established procedures. Acting normal began to irritate him, more and more as week followed week.

In July, Hush died. Sparrow wrote a song about her, and when Chip returned to his room after the meeting at which she had sung it, she and Karl (Why hadn't he thought of him sooner?) suddenly came together in his mind. Sparrow was large and awkward but lovely when she sang, twenty-five or so and lonely. Karl presumably had been 'cured' when Chip 'helped' him, but might he not have had the strength or the genetic capacity or the whatever-it-was to resist the cure, at least to a degree? Like Chip he was a 663; there was a chance that he was right there at the Institute somewhere, an ideal prospect for being led into the group and an ideal match for Sparrow. It was certainly worth a try. What a pleasure it would be to *really* help Karl! Undertreated, he would draw—well what *wouldn't* he draw?—pictures such as no one had ever imagined! As soon as he got up the next morning he got his last nameber book out of his take-along kit, touched the phone, and read out Karl's nameber. But the screen stayed blank and the phone voice apologized; the member he had called was out of reach.

Bob RO asked him about it a few days later, just as he was getting up from the chair. 'Oh, say,' Bob said, 'I meant to ask you; how come you wanted to call this Karl WL?'

'Oh,' Chip said, standing by the chair. 'I wanted to see how he was. Now that *I'm* all right, I guess I wanted to be sure that everyone else is.'

'Of course he is,' Bob said. 'It's an odd thing to do, after so many years.'

'I just happened to think of him,' Chip said.

He acted normal from the first chime to the last and met with the group twice a week. He kept working at the language—Italiano, it was called—although he suspected that King was right and there was no point in it. It was something to do, though, and seemed more worthwhile than playing with mechanical toys.

And once in a while it brought Lilac to him, leaning over to look, with one hand on the leather-topped table he worked at and the other on the back of his chair. He could smell her—it wasn't his imagination; she actually smelled of flowers—and he could look at her dark cheek and neck and the chest of her coveralls pushed taut by two mobile round protrusions. They were breasts. They were definitely breasts.

4

ONE NIGHT LATE IN AUGUST, while looking for more books in Italiano, he found one in a different language whose title, *Vers l'avenir*, was similar to the Italiano words *verso* and *avvenire* and apparently meant *Toward the Future*. He opened the book and thumbed its pages, and *Wei Li Chun* caught his eye, printed at the tops of twenty or thirty of them. Other names were at the tops of other clusters of pages, *Mario Sofik*, *A. F. Liebman*. The book, he realized, was a collection of short pieces by various writers, and two of the pieces were indeed by Wei. The title of one of them, *Les pas prochain en avant*, he recognized (*pas* would be *passo*; *avant*, *avanti*) as 'The Next Step Forward', in Part One of *Wei's Living Wisdom*.

The value of what he had found, as he began to perceive it, held him motionless. Here in this small brown book, its cover clinging by threads, were twelve or fifteen pre-U-language pages of which he had an exact translation waiting in his night-table drawer. Thousands of words, of verbs in their baffling changing forms; instead of guessing and groping as he had done for his near-useless fragments of Italiano, he could gain a solid footing in this second language in a matter of hours!

He said nothing to the others; slipped the book into his pocket and joined them; filled his pipe as if nothing were out of the ordinary. *Le pas*-whatever-it-was-*avant* might not be 'The Next Step Forward' after all. But it *was*, it had to be.

It was; he saw it as soon as he compared the first few sentences. He sat up in his room all that night, carefully reading and comparing, with one finger at the lines in the pre-U-language and another at the lines translated. He worked his way twice through the fourteen-page essay, and then began making alphabetical word lists.

The next night he was tired and slept, but the following night, after a visit from Snowflake, he stayed up and worked again.

He began going to the museum on nights between meetings. There he could smoke while he worked, could look for other Français books—Français was the language's name; the hook below the *C* was a mystery—and could roam the halls by flash-

light. On the third floor he found a map from 1951, artfully
patched in several places, where Eur was 'Europe', with the
division called 'France' where Français had been used, and all
its strangely and appealingly named cities: 'Paris' and 'Nantes'
and 'Lyon' and 'Marseille'.

Still he said nothing to the others. He wanted to confound
King with a language fully mastered, and delight Lilac. At meetings he no longer worked at Italiano. One night Lilac asked him
about it, and he said, truthfully that he had given up trying to
unravel it. She turned away, looking disappointed, and he was
happy, knowing the surprise he was preparing for her.

Saturday nights were wasted, lying by Mary KK, and meeting
nights were wasted too; although now, with Hush dead, Leopard
sometimes didn't come, and when he didn't, Chip stayed on at
the museum to straighten up and stayed still later to work.

In three weeks he could read Français rapidly, with only a word
here and there that was indecipherable. He found several Français
books. He read one whose title, translated, was *The Purple Sickle
Murders;* and another, *The Pygmies of the Equatorial Forest;* and
another, *Father Goriot.*

He waited until a night when Leopard wasn't there, and then he
told them. King looked as if he had heard bad news. His eyes
measured Chip and his face was still and controlled, suddenly
older and more gaunt. Lilac looked as if she had been given a
longed-for gift. 'You've read *books* in it?' she said. Her eyes were
wide and shining and her lips stayed parted. But neither one's
reaction could give Chip the pleasure he had looked forward to.
He was grave with the weight of what he now knew.

'Three of them,' he said to Lilac. 'And I'm halfway through a
fourth.'

'That's marvellous, Chip!' Snowflake said. 'What did you keep
it a secret for?' And Sparrow said, 'I didn't think it was possible.'

'Congratulations, Chip,' King said, taking out his pipe. 'It's an
achievement, even with the help of the essay. You've really put
me in my place.' He looked at his pipe, working the stem of it to
get it straight. 'What have you found out so far?' he asked. 'Anything interesting?'

Chip looked at him. 'Yes,' he said. 'A lot of what we're told is
true. There was crime and violence and stupidity and hunger.
There was a lock on every door. Flags were important, and the
borders of territories. Children waited for their parents to die so
they could inherit their money. The waste of labour and material
was fantastic.'

He looked at Lilac and smiled consolingly at her; her longed-
for gift was breaking. 'But with it all,' he said, 'members seem to
have felt stronger and happier than we do. Going where they
wanted, doing what they wanted, "earning" things, "owning"

things, choosing, always choosing—it made them somehow more *alive* than members today.'

King reached for tobacco. 'Well that's pretty much what you expected to find, isn't it?' he said.

'Yes, pretty much,' Chip said. 'And there's one thing more.'

'What's that?' Snowflake asked.

Looking at King, Chip said, 'Hush didn't have to die.'

King looked at him. The others did too. 'What are you talking about?' King said, his fingers stopped in pipe-filling.

'Don't you know?' Chip asked him.

'No,' he said. 'I don't understand.'

'What do you mean?' Lilac asked.

'Don't you know, King?' Chip said.

'*No,*' King said. 'What are—I haven't the faintest idea of what you're getting at. How could pre-U books tell you anything about *Hush*? And why should I be expected to know what it is if they could?'

'Living to the age of sixty-two,' Chip said, 'is no marvel of chemistry and breeding and totalcakes. Pygmies of the equatorial forests, whose life was hard even by pre-U standards, lived to be fifty-five and sixty. A member named Goriot lived to seventy-three and nobody thought it was terribly unusual, and that was in the early nineteenth century. Members lived to their eighties, even to their nineties!'

'That's impossible,' King said. 'The body wouldn't last that long; the heart, the lungs——'

'The book I'm reading now,' Chip said, 'is about some members who lived in 1991. One of them has an artificial heart. He gave money to doctors and they put it into him in place of his own.'

'Oh for——' King said. 'Are you sure you really understand that Frandaze?'

'Fran*çais,*' Chip said. 'Yes, I'm positive. Sixty-two isn't a long life; it's a relatively short one.'

'But that's when we *die,*' Sparrow said. 'Why *do* we if it isn't ——when we have to?'

'We *don't* die . . .' Lilac said, and looked from Chip to King.

'That's right,' Chip said. 'We're *made* to die. By Uni. It's programmed for efficiency, for efficiency first, last, and always. It's scanned all the data in its memory bank—which aren't the pretty pink toys you've seen if you've made the visit; they're ugly steel monsters—and it's decided that sixty-two is the optimum dying time, better than sixty-one or sixty-three and better than bothering with artificial hearts. If sixty-two isn't a new high in longevity that we're lucky to have reached—and it *isn't*, I *know* it isn't—then that's the only answer. Our replacements are trained and waiting, and off we go, a few months early or late so that everything isn't too suspiciously tidy. Just in case anyone is sick enough to be able to *feel* suspicion.'

'Christ, Marx, Wei,' Snowflake said.

'Yes,' Chip said. 'Especially Wood and Wei.'

'King?' Lilac said.

'I'm staggered,' King said. 'I see now, Chip, why you thought I'd know.' To Snowflake and Sparrow he said, 'Chip knows that I'm in chemotherapy.'

'And don't you know?' Chip said.

'I don't.'

'Is there or is there not a poison in the treatment units?' Chip asked. 'You *must* know *that*.'

'Gently, brother, I'm an old member,' King said. 'There's no poison as such, no; but almost any compound in the setup *could* cause death if too much of it were infused.'

'And you don't know how much of the compounds are infused when a member hits sixty-two?'

'No,' King said. 'Treatments are formulated by impulses that go directly from Uni to the units, and there's no way of monitoring them. I can *ask* Uni, of course, what any particular treatment consisted of, or is going to consist of, but if what you're saying is true'—he smiled—'it's going to lie to me, isn't it?'

Chip drew a breath, and let it go.

'Yes,' he said.

'And when a member dies,' Lilac said, 'the symptoms are the ones of old age?'

'They're the ones I was *taught* are of old age,' King said. 'They could very well be the ones of something entirely different.' He looked at Chip. 'Have you found any medical books in that language?' he asked.

'No,' Chip said.

King took out his lighter and thumbed it open. 'It's possible,' he said. 'It's very possible. It never even crossed my mind. Members live to sixty-two; it used to be less, some day it'll be more; we have two eyes, two ears, one nose. Established facts.' He lit the lighter and put the flame to his pipe.

'It *must* be true,' Lilac said. 'It's the final logical end of Wood's and Wei's thinking. Control everyone's life and you eventually get around to controlling everyone's death.'

'It's awful,' Sparrow said. 'I'm glad Leopard's not here. Can you imagine how he'd feel? Not only Hush, but he himself any day now. We mustn't say anything to him; let him think it's going to happen naturally.'

Snowflake looked bleakly at Chip. 'What did you have to tell *us* for?' she said.

King said, 'So that we can experience a happy kind of sadness. Or was it a sad kind of happiness, Chip?'

'I thought you would want to know,' he said.

'Why?' Snowflake said. 'What can we do about it? Complain to our advisers?'

'I'll tell you one thing we can do,' Chip said. 'Start getting more members into this group.'

'Yes!' Lilac said.

'And where do we find them?' King said. 'We can't just grab any Karl or Mary off the walkways, you know.'

Chip said, 'Do you mean to say that in your assignment you can't pull a print-out on local members with abnormal tendencies?'

'Not without giving Uni a good reason, I can't,' King said. 'One fuzzy note, brother, and the doctors will be examining *me*. Which would also mean, incidentally, that they'd be *re*examining *you*.'

'Other abnormals are around,' Sparrow said. '*Somebody* writes "Fight Uni" on the backs of buildings.'

'We've got to figure out a way to get *them* to find *us*,' Chip said. 'A signal of some kind.'

'And then what?' King said. 'What do we do when we're twenty or thirty strong? Claim a group visit and blow Uni to pieces?'

'The idea has occurred to me,' Chip said.

'Chip!' Snowflake said. Lilac stared at him.

'First of all,' King said, smiling, 'It's impregnable. And second of all, most of us have already been there, so we wouldn't be granted another visit. Or would we *walk* from here to Eur? And what would we do with the world once everything was uncontrolled—once the factories were clogged and the cars had crashed and the chimes had all stopped chiming—get really pre-U and say a prayer for it?'

'If we could find members who know computer and microwave theory,' Chip said, 'members who know *Uni*, maybe we could work out a way to change its programming.'

'*If* we could find those members,' King said. '*If* we could get them with us. *If* we could get to Eur-zip-one. Don't you see what you're asking for? The impossible, that's all. *This* is why I told you not to waste time with those books. There's nothing we can do about *anything*. This is *Uni's world*, will you get that through your head? It was handed over to it fifty years ago, and it's going to do its assignment—spread the fighting Family through the fighting universe—and *we're* going to do *our* assignments, including dying at sixty-two and not missing TV. This is it right here, brother: all the freedom we can hope for—a pipe and a few jokes and some extra fucking. Let's not lose what we've got, all right?'

'But if we get other——'

'Sing a song, Sparrow,' King said.

'I don't want to,' she said.

'Sing a song!'

'All right, I will.'

Chip glared at King and got up and strode from the room. He

strode into the dark exhibit hall, banged his hip against hardness, and strode on, cursing. He went far from the passageway and the storeroom; stood rubbing his forehead and rocking on the balls of his feet before the jewel-glinting kings and queens, mute darker-than-darkness watchers. 'King,' he said. 'Think he really *is*, the brother-fighting . . .'

Sparrow's singing came faintly, and the string-tinkle of her pre-U instrument. And footsteps, coming closer. 'Chip?' It was Snowflake. He didn't turn. His arm was touched. 'Come on back,' she said.

'Leave me alone, will you?' he said. 'Just leave me alone for a couple of minutes.'

'Come on,' she said. 'You're being childish.'

'Look,' he said, turning to her. 'Go listen to Sparrow, will you? Go smoke your pipe.'

She was silent, and then said, 'All right,' and went away.

He turned back to the kings and queens, breathing deeply. His hip hurt and he rubbed it. It was infuriating the way King cut off his every idea, made everyone do exactly as he——

She was coming back. He started to tell her to get the hate away but checked himself. He took a clenched-teeth breath and turned around.

It was King coming toward him, his gray hair and coveralls catching the dim glow from the passageway. He came close and stopped.

They looked at each other, and King said, 'I didn't intend to speak quite that sharply.'

'How come you haven't taken one of these crowns?' Chip asked. 'And a robe. Just that medallion—hate, that's not enough for a real pre-U king.'

King stayed silent for a moment, and then said, 'My apologies.'

Chip drew a breath and held it, then let it go. 'Every member we can get to join us,' he said, 'would mean new ideas, new information we can draw on, possibilities that maybe we haven't thought of.'

'New risks too,' King said. 'Try to see it from my viewpoint.'

'I can't,' Chip said. 'I'd rather go back to full treatments than settle for just this.'

' "Just this" seems very nice to a member my age.'

'You're twenty or thirty years closer to sixty-two than I am; *you* should be the one who wants to change things.'

'If change were possible, maybe I would be,' King said. 'But chemotherapy plus computerization equals no change.'

'Not necessarily,' Chip said.

'It does,' King said, 'and I don't want to see "just this" go down the drain. Even your coming here on off nights is an added risk. But don't take offense—he raised a hand—I'm not telling you to stay away.'

'I'm not going to,' Chip said; and then, 'Don't worry, I'm careful.'

'Good,' King said. 'And we'll go on carefully looking for abnormals. Without signals.' He held out his hand.

After a moment Chip shook it.

'Come on back in now,' King said. 'The girls are upset.'

Chip went with him toward the passageway.

'What was that you said before, about the memory banks being "steel monsters"?' King asked.

'That's what they are,' Chip said. 'Enormous frozen blocks, thousands of them. My grandfather showed them to me when I was a boy. He helped build Uni.'

'The brother-fighter.'

'No, he was sorry. He wished he hadn't. Christ and Wei, if he were alive he'd be a marvelous member to have with us.'

The following night Chip was sitting in the storeroom reading and smoking when 'Hello, Chip,' Lilac said, and was standing in the doorway with a flashlight at her side.

Chip stood up, looking at her.

'Do you mind my interrupting you?' she asked.

'Of course not, I'm glad to see you,' he said. 'Is King here?'

'No,' she said.

'Come on in,' he said.

She stayed in the doorway. 'I want you to teach me that language,' she said.

'I'd like to,' he said. 'I was going to ask you if you wanted the lists. Come on in.'

He watched her come in, then found his pipe in his hand, put it down, and went to the mass of relics. Catching the legs of one of the chairs they used, he tossed it right side up and brought it back to the table. She had pocketed the flashlight and was looking at the open pages of the book he had been reading. He put the chair down, moved his chair to the side, and put the second chair next to it.

She turned up the front part of the book and looked at its cover.

'It means *A Motive for Passion*,' he said. 'Which is fairly obvious. Most of it isn't.'

She looked at the open pages again. 'Some of it looks like Italiano,' she said.

'That's how I got on to it,' he said. He held the back of the chair he had brought for her.

'I've been sitting all day,' she said. 'You sit down. Go ahead.'

He sat and got his folded lists out from under the stacked Français books. 'You can keep these as long as you want,' he said, opening them and spreading them out on the table. 'I know it all pretty well by heart now.'

He showed her the way the verbs fell into groups, following different patterns of change to express time and subject, and the way the adjectives took one form or another depending on the nouns they were applied to. 'It's complicated,' he said, 'but once you get the hang of it, translation's fairly easy.' He translated a page of *A Motive for Passion* for her. Victor, a trader in shares of various industrial companies—the member who had had the artificial heart put into him—was rebuking his wife, Caroline, for having been unfriendly to an influential lawmaker.

'It's fascinating,' Lilac said.

'What amazes me,' Chip said, 'is how many non-productive members there were. These share-traders and lawmakers; the soldiers and policemen, bankers, tax-gatherers . . .'

'They weren't non-productive,' she said. 'They didn't produce *things* but they made it possible for members to live the way they did. They produced the *freedom*, or at least they maintained it.'

'Yes,' he said. 'I suppose you're right.'

'I am,' she said, and moved restlessly from the table.

He thought for a moment, 'Pre-U members,' he said, 'gave up efficiency—in exchange for freedom. And we've done the reverse.'

'*We* haven't done it,' Lilac said. 'It was done *for* us.' She turned and faced him, and said, 'Do you think it's possible that the incurables are still alive?'

He looked at her.

'That their descendants have survived somehow,' she said, 'and have a—a society somewhere? On an island or in some area that the Family isn't using?'

'Wow,' he said, and rubbed his forehead. 'Sure it's possible,' he said. 'Members survived on islands *before* the Unification; why not after?'

'That's what *I* think,' she said, coming back to him. 'There have been five generations since the last ones——'

'Battered by disease and hardship——'

'But reproducing at will!'

'I don't know about a *society*,' he said, 'but there might be a colony——'

'A city,' she said. 'They were the smart ones, the strong ones.'

'What an idea,' he said.

'It's possible, isn't it?' She was leaning toward him, hands on the table, her large eyes questioning, her cheeks flushed to a rosier darkness.

He looked at her. 'What does King think?' he asked. She drew back a bit and he said, 'As if I can't guess.'

She was angry suddenly, fierce-eyed. 'You were *terrible* to him last night!' she said.

'Terrible? I *was*? To *him*?'

'Yes!' She whirled from the table. 'You questioned him as if you were—— How could you even *think* he would know about Uni killing us and not tell us?'

'I still think he knew.'

She faced him angrily. 'He didn't!' she said. 'He doesn't keep secrets from me!'

'What are you, his adviser?'

'Yes!' she said. 'That's *exactly* what I am, in case you want to know.'

'You're not,' he said.

'I am.'

'Christ and Wei,' he said. 'You really are? You're an adviser? That's the *last classification* I'd have thought of. How *old* are you?'

'Twenty-four.'

'And you're *his*?'

She nodded.

He laughed. 'I decided that you worked in the gardens,' he said. 'You smell of flowers, do you know that? You really do.'

'I wear perfume,' she said.

'You *wear* it?'

'The perfume of flowers, in a liquid. King made it for me.'

He stared at her. 'Parfum!' he said, slapping the open book before him. 'I thought it was some kind of germicide; she put it in her bath. Of course!' He groped among the lists, took up his pen, crossed out and wrote. 'Stupid,' he said. '*Parfum* equals *perfume*. Flowers in a liquid. How did he do *that*?'

'Don't accuse him of deceiving us.'

'All right, I won't.' He put the pen down.

'Everything we've got,' she said, 'we owe to him.'

'What is it though?' he said. 'Nothing—unless we use it to try for more. And he doesn't seem to want us to.'

'He's more sensible than we are.'

He looked at her, standing a few meters away from him before the mass of relics.

'What would you do,' he asked, 'if we somehow found that there *is* a city of incurables?'

Her eyes stayed on his. 'Get to it,' she said.

'And live on plants and animals?'

'If necessary.' She glanced at the book, moved her head toward it. 'Victor and Caroline seem to have enjoyed their dinner.'

He smiled and said, 'You really are a pre-U woman, aren't you?'

She said nothing.

'Would you let me see your breasts?' he asked.

'What for?' she said.

'I'm curious, that's all.'

She pulled open the top of her coveralls and held the two sides apart. Her breasts were rose-brown soft-looking cones that stirred with her breathing, taut on their upper surfaces and rounded below. Their tips, blunt and pink, seemed to contract and grow darker as he looked at them. He felt oddly aroused, as if he were being caressed.

'They're nice,' he said.

'I know they are,' she said, closing her coveralls and pressing the closure. 'That's something else I owe King. I used to think I was the ugliest member in the entire Family.'

'You?'

'Until he convinced me I wasn't.'

'All right,' he said, 'you owe King very much. We all do. What have you come to *me* for?'

'I *told* you,' she said. 'To learn that language.'

'Cloth,' he said, getting up. 'You want me to start looking for places the Family isn't using, for signs that your "city" exists. Because I'll do it and he won't; because *I'm* not "sensible", or old, or content to make fun of TV.'

She started for the door but he caught her by the shoulder and pushed her around. 'Stay here!' he said. She looked frightenedly at him and he took hold of her jaw and kissed her mouth; clamped her head in both his hands and pushed his tongue against her shut teeth. She pressed at his chest and wrenched her head. He thought she would stop, give in and take the kiss, but she didn't; she kept struggling with increasing vigor, and finally he let go and she pushed away from him.

'That's—that's *terrible*!' she said. 'Forcing me! That's— I've never been *held* that way!'

'I love you,' he said.

'Look at me, I'm shaking,' she said. 'Wei Li Chun, is *that* how you love, by becoming an animal? That's *awful*!'

'A human,' he said, 'like you.'

'No,' she said. 'I wouldn't hurt anyone, hold anyone that way!' She held her jaw and moved it.

'How do you think incurables kiss?' he said.

'Like humans, not like animals.'

'I'm sorry,' he said. 'I love you.'

'Good,' she said. 'I love you too—the way I love Leopard and Snowflake and Sparrow.'

'That's not what I mean,' he said.

'But it's what *I* mean,' she said, looking at him. She went sideways to the doorway and said, 'Don't do that again. That's terrible!'

'Do you want the lists?' he asked.

She looked as if she was going to say no, hesitated, and then said, 'Yes. That's what I came for.'

He turned and gathered the lists on the table, folded them together, and took *Père Goriot* from the stack of books. She came over and he gave them to her.

'I didn't mean to hurt you,' he said.

'All right,' she said. 'Just don't do it again.'

'I'll look for places the Family isn't using,' he said. 'I'll go over the maps at the MFA and see if——'

'I've done that,' she said.

'Carefully?'

'As carefully as I could.'

'I'll do it again,' he said. 'It's the only way to begin. Millimeter by millimeter.'

'All right,' she said.

'Wait a second, I'm going now too.'

She waited while he put away his smoking things and got the room back the way it belonged, and then they went out together through the exhibit hall and down the escalator.

'A city of incurables,' he said.

'It's possible,' she said.

'It's worth looking for anyway,' he said.

They went out on to the walkway.

'Which way do you go?' he asked.

'West,' she said.

'I'll go a few blocks with you.'

'No,' she said. 'Really, the longer you're out, the more chances there are for someone to see you not touching.'

'I touch the rim of the scanner and block it with my body. Very tricky.'

'No,' she said. 'Please, go your own way.'

'All right,' he said. 'Good night.'

'Good night.'

He put his hand on her shoulder and kissed her cheek.

She didn't move away; she was tense and waiting under his hand.

He kissed her lips. They were warm and soft, slightly parted, and she turned and walked away.

'Lilac,' he said, and went after her.

She turned and said, 'No. Please, Chip, go,' and turned and walked away again.

He stood uncertainly. Another member was in the distance, coming toward them.

He watched her go, hating her, loving her.

5

EVENING AFTER EVENING he ate quickly (but not *too* quickly), then railed to the Museum of the Family's Achievements and studied its maze of ceiling-high illuminated maps until the ten-of-TV closing. One night he went there after the last chime—an hour-and-a-half walk—but found that the maps were un-readable by flashlight, their markings lost in glare; and he hesitated to put on their internal lights, which, tied in as they seemed to be with the lighting of the entire hall, might have produced a Uni-alerting overdraft of power. One Sunday he took Mary KK there, sent her off to see the Universe of Tomorrow exhibit, and studied the maps for three hours straight.

He found nothing: no island without its city or industrial installation; no mountaintop that wasn't spacewatch or climat-onomy center; no square kilometer of land—or of ocean floor, for that matter—that wasn't being mined or harvested or used for factories or houses or airports or parkland by the Family's eight billion. The gold-lettered legend suspended at the entrance of the map area—*The Earth Is Our Heritage; We Use It Wisely and Without Waste*—seemed true, so true that there was no place left for even the smallest non-Family community.

Leopard died and Sparrow sang. King sat silently, picking at the gears of a pre-U gadget, and Snowflake wanted more sex.

Chip said to Lilac, 'Nothing. Nothing at all.'

'There must have been hundreds of little colonies to begin with,' she said. 'One of them *must* have survived.'

'Then it's half a dozen members in a cave somewhere,' he said.

'Please keep looking,' she said. 'You can't have checked *every* island.'

He thought about it, sitting in the dark in the twentieth-century car, holding its steering wheel, moving its different knobs and levers; and the more he thought about it, the less possible a city or even a colony of incurables came to seem. Even if he had over-looked an unused area on the maps, could a community exist without Uni learning of it? People made marks on their environ-ment; a thousand people, even a hundred, would raise an area's temperature, soil its streams with their wastes, and its air perhaps with their primitive fires. The land or sea for kilometers around would be affected by their presence in a dozen detectable ways.

So Uni would have long since known of the theoretical city's existence, and having known, would have—done what? Dis-patched doctors and advisers and portable treatment units; would have 'cured' the incurables and made them into 'healthy' members.

Unless, of course, they had defended themselves . . . Their ancestors had fled the Family soon after the Unification, when treatments were optional, or later, when they were compulsory but not yet at present-day effectiveness; surely some of *those* incurables must have defended their retreats by force, with deadly weapons. Wouldn't they have handed on the practice, and the weapons too, to succeeding generations? What would Uni do today, in 162, facing an armed, defensive community with an unarmed, unaggressive Family? What would it have done five or twenty-five years ago, detecting the signs of it? Let it be? Leave its inhabitants to their 'sickness' and their few square kilometers of the world? Spray the city with LPK? But what if the city's weapons could bring down planes. Would Uni decide in its cold steel blocks that the cost of the 'cure' outweighed its usefulness?

He was two days from a treatment, his mind as active as it ever got. He wished it could get still more active. He felt that there was something he wasn't thinking of, just beyond the rim of his awareness.

If Uni let the city be, rather than sacrifice members and time and technology to the 'helping' of it—then *what*? There was *something else*, a next idea to be picked and pried out of that one.

He called the medicenter on Thursday, the day before his treatment, and complained of a toothache. He was offered a Friday-morning appointment, but he said that he was coming in on Saturday morning for his treatment and couldn't he catch two birds with one net? It wasn't a severe toothache, just a slight throb.

He was given an appointment for Saturday morning at 8.15.

Then he called Bob RO and told him that he had a dental appointment at 8.15 on Saturday. Did he think it would be a good idea if he got his treatment then too? Catch two birds with one net.

'I guess you might as well,' Bob said. 'Hold on'—and switched on his telecomp. 'You're Li RM——'

'Thirty-five M4419.'

'Right,' Bob said, tapping keys.

Chip sat and watched unconcernedly.

'Saturday morning at 8.05,' Bob said.

'Fine,' Chip said. 'Thanks.'

'Thank Uni,' Bob said.

Which gave him a day longer between treatments than he'd had before.

That night, Thursday, was a rain night, and he stayed in his room. He sat at his desk with his forehead on his fists, thinking, wishing he were in the museum and able to smoke.

If a city of incurables existed, and Uni knew about it and was leaving it to its armed defenders—then—then—

Then Uni wasn't letting the Family know—and be troubled or in some instances tempted—*and it was feeding concealing data to the mapmaking equipment*.

Of course! How could supposedly unused areas be shown on beautiful Family maps? 'But look at that place there, Daddy!' a child visiting the MFA exclaims. 'Why aren't we Using Our Heritage Wisely and Without Waste?' And Daddy replies, 'Yes, that is odd . . .' So the city would be labeled IND99999 or Enormous Desk Lamp Factory, and no one would ever be passed within five kilometers of it. If it were an island it wouldn't be shown at all; blue ocean would replace it.

And looking at maps was therefore useless. There could be cities of incurables here, there, everywhere. Or—there could be none at all. The maps proved or disproved nothing.

Was this the great revelation he had racked his brain for—that his map-examining had been stupidity from the beginning? That there was no way at all of finding the city, except possibly by walking everywhere on Earth?

Fight Lilac, with her maddening ideas!

No, not really.

Fight *Uni*.

For half an hour he drove his mind against the problem—how do you find a theoretical city in an untravelable world?—and finally he gave up and went to bed.

He thought then of Lilac, of the kiss she had resisted and the kiss she had allowed, and the strange arousal he had felt when she showed him her soft-looking conical breasts . . .

On Friday he was tense and on edge. Acting normal was unendurable; he held his breath all day long at the Center, and through dinner, TV, and Photography Club. After the last chime he walked to Snowflake's building—'Ow,' she said, 'I'm not going to be able to *move* tomorrow!' and then to the Pre-U. He circled the halls by flashlight, unable to put the idea aside. The city might exist, it might even be somewhere near. He looked at the money display and the prisoner in his cell (*The two of us, brother*) and the locks and the flat-picture cameras.

There was *one* answer that he could see, but it involved getting dozens of members into the group. Each could then check out the maps according to his own limited knowledge. He himself, for instance, could verify the genetics labs and research centers and the cities he had seen or heard spoken of by other members. Lilac could verify the advisory establishments and other cities . . . But it would take forever, and an army of undertreated accomplices. He could hear King raging.

He looked at the 1951 map, and marveled as he always did at the strange names and the intricate networks of borders. Yet members then could go where they wanted, more or less! Thin shadows moved in response to his light at the edges of the map's neat patches, cut to fit precisely into the crosslines of the grid. If not for the moving flashlight the blue rectangles would have been com——

Blue rectangles . . .

If the city were an island it wouldn't be shown; blue ocean would replace it.

And would have to replace it on pre-U maps as well.

He didn't let himself get excited. He moved the flashlight slowly back and forth over the glass-covered map and counted the shadow-moving patches. There were eight of them, all blue. All in the oceans, evenly distributed. Five of them covered single rectangles of the grid, and three covered pairs of rectangles. One of the one-rectangle patches was right there off Ind, in 'Bay of Bengal'—Stability Bay.

He put the flashlight on a display case and took hold of the wide map by both sides of its frame. He lifted it free of its hook, lowered it to the floor, leaned its glassed face against his knee and took up the flashlight again.

The frame was old, but its gray-paper backing looked relatively new. The letters *EV* were stamped at the bottom of it.

He carried the map by its wire across the hall, down the escalator, across the second-floor hall, and into the storeroom. Tapping on the light, he brought the map to the table and laid it carefully face-down.

With the corner of a fingernail he tore the taut paper backing along the bottom and sides of the frame, pulled it out from under the wire, and pressed it back so that it stayed. White cardboard lay in the frame, pinned down by ranks of short brads.

He searched in the cartons of smaller relics until he found a rusted pair of pincers with a yellow sticker around one handle. He used the pincers to pull the brads from the frame, then lifted out the cardboard and another piece of cardboard that lay beneath it.

The back of the map was brown-blotched but untorn, with no holes that would have justified the patching. A line of brown writing was faintly visible: *Wyndham, MUS—2161*—some kind of early namebar.

He picked at the map's edges and lifted it from the glass, turned it over and raised it sagging above his head against the white light of the ceiling. Islands showed through all the patches: here a large one. 'Madagascar'; here a cluster of small ones, 'Azores'. The patch in Stability Bay showed a line of four small ones. 'Andaman Islands'. He remembered none of the patch-covered islands from the maps at the MFA.

He put the map back down in the frame, face-up, and leaned his hands on the table and looked at it, grinned at its pre-U oddity, its eight blue almost-invisible rectangles. *Lilac!* he thought. *Wait till I tell you!*

With the head of the frame propped on piles of books and his flashlight standing under the glass, he traced on a sheet of paper the four small 'Andaman Islands' and the shoreline of 'Bay of Bengal'. He copied down the names and locations of the other islands and traced the map's scale, which was in 'miles' rather than kilometers.

One pair of medium-sized islands, 'Falkland Islands,' was off the coast of Arg ('Argentina') opposite 'Santa Cruz', which seemed to be ARG20400. Something teased his memory in that, but he couldn't think what.

He measured the Andaman Islands; the three that were closest together were about a hundred and twenty 'miles' in overall length—somewhere around two hundred kilometers, if he remembered correctly; big enough for several cities! The shortest approach to them would be from the other side of Stability Bay, SEA77122, if he and Lilac (and King? Snowflake? Sparrow?) were to go there. *If* they were to go? Of course they would go, now that he had found the islands. They'd manage it somehow; they *had* to.

He turned the map face-down in the frame, put back the pieces of cardboard, and pushed the brads back into their holes with a handle-end of the pincers—wondering as he did so why ARG20400 and the 'Falkland Islands' kept poking at his memory.

He slipped the frame's backing in under the wire—Sunday night he would bring tape and make a better job of it—and carried the map back to the third floor. He hung it on its hook and made sure the loose backing didn't show from the sides.

ARG20400 . . . A new zinc mine being cut underneath it had been shown recently on TV; was that why it seemed significant? He'd certainly never been there . . .

He went down to the basement and got three tobacco leaves from behind the hot-water tank. He brought them up to the storeroom, got his smoking things from the carton he kept them in, and sat down at the table and began cutting the leaves.

Could there possibly be another reason why the islands were covered and unmapped? And who did the covering?

Enough. He was tired of thinking. He let his mind go—to the knife's shiny blade, to Hush and Sparrow cutting tobacco the first time he'd seen them. He had asked Hush where the seeds had come from, and she'd said that King had had them.

And he remembered where he had seen *ARG20400*—the name-ber, not the city itself.

A screaming woman in torn coveralls was being led into Medicenter Main by red-cross-coveralled members on either side of her. They held her arms and seemed to be talking to her, but she kept on screaming—short sharp screams, each the same as the others, that screamed again from building walls and screamed again from farther in the night. The woman kept on screaming and the walls and the night kept screaming with her.

He waited until the woman and the members leading her had gone into the building, waited longer while the far-off screams lessened to silence, and then he slowly crossed the walkway and went in. He lurched against the admission scanner as if off balance, clicking his bracelet below the plate on metal, and went slowly and normally to an up-gliding escalator. He stepped on to it and rode with his hand on the rail.

Somewhere in the building the woman still screamed, but then she stopped.

The second floor was lighted. A member passing in the hallway with a tray of glasses nodded to him. He nodded back.

The third and fourth floors were lighted too, but the escalator to the fifth floor wasn't moving and there was darkness above. He walked up the steps, to the fifth floor and the sixth.

He walked by flashlight down the sixth-floor hallway—quickly now, not slowly—past the doors he had gone through with the two doctors, the woman who had called him 'young brother' and the scar-cheeked man who had watched him. He walked to the end of the hallway, shining his light on the door marked *600A* and *Chief, Chemotherapeutics Division*.

He went through the anteroom and into King's office. The large desk was neater than before: the scuffed telecomp, a pile of folders, the container of pens—and the two paperweights, the unusual square one and the ordinary round one. He picked up the round one—*ARG20400* was inscribed on it—and held its cool plated-metal weight on his palm for a moment. Then he put it down, next to King's young smiling snapshot at Uni's dome.

He went around behind the desk, opened the center drawer, and searched in it until he found a plastic-coated section roster. He scanned the half column of Jesuses and found Jesus HL09E6290. His classification was 080A; his residence, G35, room 1744.

He paused outside the door for a moment, suddenly realizing that Lilac might be there too, dozing next to King under his outstretched possessing arm. *Good!* he thought. *Let her hear it at first hand!* He opened the door, went in, and closed it softly behind him. He aimed his flashlight towards the bed and switched it on.

King was alone, his gray head encircled by his arms.

He was glad and sorry. More glad, though. He would tell her later, come to her triumphantly and tell her all he had found.

He tapped on the light, switched off the flashlight, and put it in his pocket. 'King,' he said.

The head and the pajamaed arms stayed unmoving.

'King,' he said, and went and stood beside the bed. 'Wake up, Jesus HL,' he said.

King rolled on to his back and laid a hand over his eyes. Fingers chinked and an eye squinted between them.

'I want to speak to you,' Chip said.

'What are you doing here?' King asked. 'What time is it?'

Chip glanced at the clock. 'Four-fifty,' he said.

King sat up, palming at his eyes. 'What the hate's going on?' he said. 'What are you doing here?'

Chip got the desk chair and put it near the foot of the bed and sat down. The room was untidy, coveralls caught in the chute, tea stains on the floor.

King coughed into the side of a fist, and coughed again. He kept the fist at his mouth, looking red-eyed at Chip, his hair pressed to his scalp in patches.

Chip said, 'I want to know what it's like on the Falkland Islands.'

King lowered his hand. 'On what islands?' he said.

'Falkland,' Chip said. 'Where you got the tobacco seeds. And the perfume you gave Lilac.'

'I made the perfume,' King said.

'And the tobacco seeds? Did you make them?'

King said, 'Someone gave them to me.'

'In ARG20400?'

After a moment King nodded.

'Where did *he* get them?'

'I don't know.'

'You didn't ask?'

'No,' King said, 'I didn't. Why don't you get back where you're supposed to be? We can talk about this tomorrow night.'

'I'm staying,' Chip said. 'I'm staying here until I hear the truth. I'm due for a treatment at 8.05. If I don't take it on time, everything's going to be finished—me, you, the group. You're not going to be king of anything.'

'You brother-fighter,' King said, 'get out of here.'

'I'm staying,' Chip said.

'I've *told* you the truth.'

'I don't believe it.'

'Then go fight yourself,' King said, and lay down and turned over on to his stomach.

Chip stayed as he was. He sat looking at King and waiting.

After a few minutes King turned over again and sat up. He threw aside the blanket, swung his legs around, and sat with his bare feet on the floor. He scratched with both hands at his pajamaed thighs. ' "Americanueva," ' he said, 'not "Falkland". They come ashore and trade. Hairy-faced creatures in cloth and leather.' He looked at Chip. 'Diseased, disgusting savages,' he said, 'who speak in a way that's barely understandable.'

'They exist, they've survived.'

'That's *all* they've done. Their hands are like wood from working. They steal from one another and go hungry.'

'But they haven't come back to the Family.'

'They'd be better off if they did,' King said. 'They've still got religion going. And alcohol-drinking.'

'How long do they live?' Chip asked.

King said nothing.

'Past sixty-two?' Chip asked.

King's eyes narrowed coldly. 'What's so magnificent about living,' he said, 'that it has to be prolonged indefinitely? What's so fantastically beautiful about life here or life there that makes sixty-two not enough of it instead of too fighting much? Yes, they live past sixty-two. One of them claimed to be eighty, and looking at him, I believed it. But they die *younger*, too, in their thirties, even in their twenties—from work and filth and defending their "money".'

'That's only one group of islands,' Chip said. 'There are seven others.'

'They'll all be the same,' King said. 'They'll all be the same.'

'How do you know?'

'How can they *not* be?' King asked. 'Christ and Wei, if I'd thought a halfway-human life was possible I'd have said something!'

'You should have said something anyway,' Chip said. 'There are islands right here in Stability Bay. Leopard and Hush might have got to them and still be living.'

'They'd be dead.'

'Then you should have let them choose where they died,' Chip said. 'You're not Uni.'

He got up and put the chair back by the desk. He looked at the phone screen, reached over the desk, and took the adviser's-nameber card from under the rim of it: *Anna SG38P2823.*

'You mean you don't know her nameber?' King said. 'What do you do, meet in the dark? Or haven't you worked your way out to her extremities yet?'

Chip put the card into his pocket. 'We don't meet at all,' he said.

'Oh come on,' King said, 'I know what's been going on. What do you think I am, a dead body?'

'Nothing's been going on,' Chip said. 'She came to the museum once and I gave her the word lists for Français, that's all.'

'I can just imagine,' King said. 'Get out of here, will you? I need my sleep.' He lay back on the bed, put his legs in under the blanket, and spread the blanket up over his chest.

'Nothing's been going on,' Chip said. 'She feels that she owes you too much.'

With his eyes closed, King said, 'But we'll soon take care of that, won't we?'

Chip said nothing for a moment, and then he said, 'You should have told us. About Americanova.'

'Americanueva,' King said, and then said nothing more. He lay with his eyes closed, his blanketed chest rising and falling rapidly.

Chip went to the door and tapped off the light. 'I'll see you tomorrow night,' he said.

'I hope you get there,' King said. 'The two of you. To Americanueva. You deserve it.'

Chip opened the door and went out.

King's bitterness depressed him, but after he had been walking for fifteen minutes or so he began to feel cheerful and optimistic, and elated with the results of his night of extra clarity. His right-hand pocket was crisp with a map of Stability Bay and the Andaman Islands, the names and locations of the other incurable strongholds, and Lilac's red-printed nameber card. Christ, Marx, Wood, and Wei, what would he be capable of with no treatments at all?

He took the card out and read it as he walked. *Anna SG38P2823*. He would call her after the first chime and arrange to meet her —during the free hour that evening. Anna SG. Not she, not an 'Anna'; a Lilac she was, fragrant, delicate, beautiful. (Who had picked the name, she or King? Incredible. The hater thought they had been meeting and fucking. If only!) *Thirty*-eight P, twenty-*eight* twenty-*three*. He walked to the swing of the nameber for a while, then realized he was walking too briskly and slowed himself, pocketing the card again.

He would be back in his building before the first chime, would shower, change, call Lilac, eat (he was starving), then get his treatment at 8.05 and keep his 8.15 dental appointment ('It feels much better today, sister. The throbbing's almost completely gone'). The treatment would dull him, fight it, but not so much that he wouldn't be able to tell Lilac about the Andaman Islands and start planning with her—and with Snowflake and Sparrow if they were interested—how they would try to get there. Snowflake would probably choose to stay. He hoped so; it would simplify things tremendously. Yes, Snowflake would stay with King, laugh and smoke and fuck with him, and play that mechanical paddle-ball game. And he and Lilac would go.

Anna SG, *thirty*-eight P, twenty-*eight* twenty-*three* . . .

He got to the building at 6.22. Two up-early members were coming down his hallway, one naked, one dressed. He smiled and said, 'Good morning, sisters.'

He went into his room, tapped on the light, and Bob was on the bed, lifting himself up on his elbows and blinking at him. His telecomp lay open on the floor, its blue and amber lights gleaming.

6

HE CLOSED THE DOOR behind him.

Bob swung his legs off the bed and sat up, looking at him anxiously. His coveralls were partway open. 'Where've you been, Li?' he asked.

'In the lounge,' Chip said. 'I went back there after Photography Club—I'd left my pen there—and I suddenly got very tired. From being late on my treatment, I guess. I sat down to rest and'—he smiled—'all of a sudden it's morning.'

Bob looked at him, still anxiously, and after a moment shook his head. 'I checked the lounge,' he said. 'And Mary KK's room, and the gym, and the bottom of the pool.'

'You must have missed me,' Chip said. 'I was in the corner behind——'

'I *checked* the *lounge*, Li,' Bob said. He pressed closed his coveralls and shook his head despairingly.

Chip moved from the door, walked a slow away-from-Bob curve toward the bathroom. 'I've got to ure,' he said.

He went into the bathroom and opened his coveralls and urined, trying to find the extra mental clarity he had had before, trying to think of an explanation that would satisfy Bob or at worst seem like only a one-night aberration. Why had Bob come there anyway? How long had he been there?

'I called at eleven-thirty,' Bob said, 'and there was no answer. Where have you been between then and now?'

He closed his coveralls. 'I was walking around,' he said— loudly, to reach Bob in the room.

'Without touching scanners?' Bob said.

Christ and Wei.

'I must have forgot,' he said, and turned on the water and rinsed his fingers. 'It's this toothache,' he said. 'It's gotten worse. The whole side of my head aches.' He wiped his fingers, looking in the mirror at Bob on the bed looking back at him. 'It was keeping me awake,' he said, 'so I went out and walked around. I told you that story about the lounge because I know I should have gone right down to the——'

'It was keeping *me* awake, too,' Bob said, 'that "toothache" of yours. I saw you during TV and you looked tense and abnormal. So finally I pulled the nameber of the dental-appointment clerk. You were offered a Friday appointment but you said your treatment was on Saturday.'

Chip put the towel down and turned and stood facing Bob in the doorway.

The first chime sounded, and 'One Mighty Family' began to play.

Bob said, 'It was all an act, wasn't it, Li—the slowdown last spring, the sleepiness and overtreatedness.'

After a moment Chip nodded.

'Oh, brother,' Bob said. 'What have you been doing?'

Chip didn't say anything.

'Oh, brother,' Bob said, and bent over and switched his tele-comp off. He closed its cover and snapped the catches. 'Are you going to forgive me?' he asked. He stood the telecomp on end and steadied the handle between the fingers of both hands, trying to get it to stay standing up. 'I'll tell you something funny,' he said. 'I have a streak of vanity in me. I do. Correction, I did. I thought I was one of the two or three best advisers in the house. In the house, hate; in the *city*. Alert, observant, *sensitive* . . .

"Comes the rude awakening." ' He had the handle standing, and slapped it down and smiled drily at Chip. 'So you're not the only sick one,' he said 'if that's any consolation.'

'I'm not sick, Bob,' Chip said. 'I'm healthier than I've been in my entire life.'

Still smiling, Bob said, 'That's kind of contrary to the evidence, isn't it?' He picked up the telecomp and stood up.

'You can't see the evidence,' Chip said. 'You've been dulled by your treatments.'

Bob beckoned with his head and moved toward the door. 'Come on,' he said, 'let's go get you fixed up.'

Chip stayed where he was. Bob opened the door and stopped, looking back.

Chip said, 'I'm perfectly healthy.'

Bob held out his hand sympathetically. 'Come on, Li,' he said.

After a moment Chip went to him. Bob took his arm and they went out into the hallway. Doors were open and members were about, talking quietly, walking. Four or five were gathered at the bulletin board, reading the day's notices.

'Bob,' Chip said, 'I want you to listen to what I'm going to say to you.'

'Don't I always listen?' Bob said.

'I want you to try to open your mind,' Chip said. 'Because you're not a stupid member, you're bright, and you're good hearted and you want to help me.'

Mary KK came toward them from the escalators, holding a pack of coveralls with a bar of soap on top of it. She smiled and said, 'Hi,' and to Chip, 'Where were you?'

'He was in the lounge,' Bob said.

'In the middle of the night?' Mary said.

Chip nodded and Bob said, 'Yes,' and they went on to the escalators, Bob keeping his hand lightly on Chip's arm.

They rode down.

'I know you think your mind is open already,' Chip said, 'but will you try to open it even more, to listen and think for a few minutes as if I'm just as healthy as I say I am?'

'All right, Li, I will,' Bob said.

'Bob,' Chip said, 'we're not free. None of us is. Not one member of the Family.'

'How can I listen as if you're healthy,' Bob said, 'when you say something like that? Of course we're free. We're free of war and want and hunger, free of crime, violence, aggressiveness, sel——'

'Yes, yes, we're free *of* things,' Chip said, 'but we're not free to *do* things. Don't you see that, Bob? Being "free of" really has nothing to do with being free at all.'

Bob frowned. 'Being free to do what?' he said.

They stepped off the escalator and started around toward the next one. 'To choose our own classifications,' Chip said, 'to have children when we want, to go where we want and do what we want, to refuse treatments if we want . . .'

Bob said nothing.

They stepped onto the next escalator. 'Treatments really do dull us, Bob,' Chip said. 'I know that from my own experience. There are things in them that "make us humble, make us good" —like in the rhyme, you know? I've been undertreated for half a year now?—the second chime sounded—'and I'm more awake and alive than I've *ever* been. I think more clearly and feel more deeply. I fuck four or five times a week, would you believe that?'

'No,' Bob said, looking at his telecomp riding on the handrail.

'It's true,' Chip said. 'You're more sure than ever that I'm sick now, aren't you? Love of Family, I'm not. There are others like me, thousands, maybe millions. There are islands all over the world, there may be cities on the mainland, too'—they were walking around to the next escalator—'where people live in true freedom. I've got a list of the islands right here in my pocket. They're not on maps because Uni doesn't want us to know about them, because they're *defended* against the Family and the people there won't *submit* to being treated. Now, you want to help me, don't you? To *really* help me?'

They stepped onto the next escalator. Bob looked grievingly at him. 'Christ and Wei,' he said, 'can you doubt it, brother?'

'All right, then,' Chip said, 'this is what I'd like you to do for me: when we get to the treatment room tell Uni that I'm okay, that I fell asleep in the lounge the way I told you. Don't input anything about my not touching scanners or the way I made up the toothache. Let me get just the treatment I would have got yesterday, all right?'

'And that would be helping you?' Bob said.

'Yes, it would,' Chip said. 'I know you don't think so, but I ask you as my brother and my friend to—to respect what I think and feel. I'll get away to one of these islands somehow and I won't harm the Family in any way. What the Family has given me, I've given back to it in the work I've done, and I didn't ask for it in the first place, and I had no choice about accepting it.'

They walked around to the next escalator.

'All right,' Bob said when they were riding down, 'I listened to *you*, Li; now *you* listen to *me*.' His hand above Chip's elbow tightened slightly. 'You're very, very sick,' he said, 'and it's entirely my fault and I feel miserable about it. There are no islands that aren't on maps; and treatments don't dull us; and if we had the kind of "freedom" you're thinking about we'd have disorder and overpopulation and want and crime and war. Yes, I'm going to help you, brother. I'm going to tell Uni everything, and you'll be cured and you'll thank me.'

They walked around to the next escalator and stepped onto it. *Third floor—Medicenter*, the sign at the bottom said. A red-cross-coveralled member riding toward them on the up escalator smiled and said, 'Good morning, Bob.'

Bob nodded to him.

Chip said, 'I don't *want* to be cured.'

'That's proof that you need to be,' Bob said. 'Relax and trust me, Li. No, why the hate should you? Trust Uni, then; will you do that? Trust the members who programmed Uni.'

After a moment Chip said, 'All right, I will.'

'I feel awful,' Bob said, and Chip turned to him and struck away his hand. Bob looked at him, startled, and Chip put both hands at Bob's back and swept him forward. Turning with the movement, he grasped the handrail—hearing Bob tumble, his telecomp clatter—and climbed out onto the up-moving central incline.

It wasn't moving once he was on it; he crept sideways, clinging with fingers and knees to metal ridges; crept sideways to the up-escalator handrail, caught it, and flung himself over and down into the sharp-staired trench of humming metal. He got quickly to his feet—'Stop him!' Bob shouted below—and ran up the upgoing steps taking two in each stride. The red-crossed member at the top, off the escalator, turned. 'What are you——' and Chip took him by the shoulders—elderly wide-eyed member —and swung him aside and pushed him away.

He ran down the hallway. 'Stop him!' someone shouted, and other members: 'Catch that member!' 'He's sick; stop him!'

Ahead was the dining hall, members on line turning to look. He shouted, 'Stop that member!' running at them and pointing; 'Stop him!' and ran past them. 'Sick member in there!' he said, pushing past the ones at the doorway, past the scanner. ''Needs help in there! Quickly!'

In the dining hall he looked, and ran to one side, through a swing-door to the behind-the-dispensers section. He slowed, walked quickly, trying to still his breathing, past members loading stacks of cakes between vertical tracks, members looking down at him while dumping tea powder into steel drums. A cart filled with boxes marked *Napkins*; he took the handle of it, swung it around, and pushed it before him, past two members standing eating, two more gathering cakes from a broken carton.

Ahead was a door marked *Exit*, the door to one of the corner stairways. He pushed the cart toward it, hearing raised voices behind him. He rammed the cart against the door, butted it open, and went with the cart out onto the landing; closed the door and brought the cart handle back against it. He backed down two steps and pulled the cart sideways to him, wedged it tight between the door and the stair-rail post with one black wheel turning in air.

He hurried down the stairs.

He had to get out, out of the building and onto the walkways and plazas. He would walk to the museum—it wouldn't be open yet—and hide in the storeroom or behind the hot-water tank until tomorrow night, when Lilac and the others would be there. He should have grabbed some cakes just now. Why hadn't he thought of it? Hate!

He left the stairway at the ground floor and walked quickly along the hallway, nodded at an approaching member. She looked at his legs and bit her lip worriedly. He looked down and stopped. His coveralls were torn at the knees and his right knee was bruised, with blood in small beads on the surface.

'Can I do anything?' the member asked.

'I'm on my way to the medicenter now,' he said. 'Thanks, sister.' He went on. There was nothing he could do about it; he would have to take his chances. When he got outside, away from the building, he would tie a tissue around the knee and fix the coveralls as best he could. The knee began to sting, now that he knew about it. He walked faster.

He turned into the back of the lobby and paused, looked at the escalators planing down on either side of him and, up ahead, the four glass scanner-posted doors with the sunny walkway beyond them. Members were talking and going out, a few coming in. Everything looked ordinary; the murmur of voices was low, unalarmed.

He started toward the doors, walking normally, looking straight ahead. He would do his scanner trick—the knee would be an excuse for the stumbling if anyone noticed—and once he was out on—The music stopped, and 'Excuse me,' a woman's voice loudspeakered, 'would everyone please stay exactly where he is for a moment? Would everyone please stop moving?'

He stopped, in the middle of the lobby.

Everyone stopped, looked around questioningly and waited. Only the members on the escalators kept moving, and then they stopped, too, and looked down at their feet. One member walked down steps. 'Don't move!' several members called to her, and she stopped and blushed.

He stood motionless, looking at the huge stained-glass faces above the doors: bearded Christ and Marx, hairless Wood, smiling slit-eyed Wei. Something slipped down his shin: a drop of blood.

'Brothers, sisters,' the woman's voice said, 'an emergency has arisen. There's a member in the building who's sick, very sick. He's acted aggressively and ran away from his adviser'—members drew breath—'and he needs every one of us to help find him and get him to the treatment room as quickly as possible.'

'Yes!' a member behind Chip said, and another said, 'What do we do?'

'He's believed to be somewhere below the fourth floor,' the woman said; 'a twenty-seven-year-old——' A second voice spoke

to her, a man's voice, quick and unintelligible. A member about
to step on the nearest escalator was looking at Chip's knees. Chip
looked at the picture of Wood. 'He'll probably try to leave the
building,' the woman said, 'so the two members nearest each
exit will move to it and block it, please. No one else move; only
the two members nearest each exit.'

The members near the doors looked at one another, and two
moved to each door and put themselves uneasily side by side in
line with the scanners. 'It's awful!' someone said. The member
who had been looking at Chip's knees was looking now at his face.
Chip looked back at him, a man of forty or so; he looked away.

'The member we're looking for,' a man's voice on the speaker
said, 'is a twenty-seven-year-old male, nameber Li RM35M4419.
That's Li, RM, 35M, 4419. First we'll check among ourselves and
then we'll search the floors we're on. Just a minute, just a minute,
please. UniComp says the member is the only Li RM in the
building, so we can forget the rest of his nameber. All we have to
look for is Li RM. Li RM. Look at the bracelets of the members
around you. We're looking for Li RM. Be sure that every member within your sight is checked by at least one other member.
Members who are in their rooms will come out now into the
hallways. Li RM. We're looking for Li RM.'

Chip turned to a member near him, took his hand and looked
at his bracelet. 'Let me see yours,' the member said. Chip raised
his wrist and turned away, went towards another member. 'I
didn't see it,' the member said. Chip took the other member's
hand. His arm was touched by the first member, saying, 'Brother,
I didn't see.'

He ran for the doors. He was caught and arm-pulled around
—by the member who had been looking at him. He clenched
his hand to a fist and hit the member in the face and he fell away.

Members screamed. 'It's him!' they cried. 'There he is!' 'Help
him!' 'Stop him!'

He ran to a door and fist-hit one of the members there. His
arm was grabbed by the other, saying in his ear, 'Brother, brother!'
His other arm was caught by other members; he was clutched
around the chest from behind.

'We're looking for Li RM,' the man on the speaker said. 'He
may act aggressively when we find him but we mustn't be afraid.
He's depending on us for our help and our understanding.'

'Let go of me!' he cried, trying to pull himself free of the arms
tightly holding him.

'Help him!' members cried. 'Get him to the treatment room!
Help him!'

'Leave me alone!' he cried. 'I don't *want* to be helped! Leave
me *alone*, you brother-fighting haters!'

He was dragged up escalator steps by members panting and
flinching, one of them with tears in his eyes. 'Easy, easy,' the

said, 'we're helping you. You'll be all right, we're helping you.'
He kicked, and his legs were caught and held.

'I don't *want* to be helped!' he cried. 'I want to be left alone!
I'm healthy! I'm healthy! I'm not sick!'

He was dragged past members who stood with hands over ears,
with hands pressed to mouths below staring eyes.

'*You're* sick,' he said to the member whose face he had hit.
Blood was leaking from his nostrils, and his nose and cheek
were swollen; Chip's arms were locked under his. 'You're dulled
and you're drugged,' Chip said to him. 'You're dead. You're a
dead man. You're *dead!*'

'Shh, we love you, we're helping you,' the member said.

'*Christ and Wei, let GO of me!*'

He was dragged up more steps.

'He's been found,' the man on the speaker said. 'Li RM has
been found, members. He's being brought to the medicenter.
Let me say that again: Li RM has been found, and is being
brought to the medicenter. The emergency is over, brothers and
sisters, and you can go on now with what you were doing. Thank
you; thank you for your help and co-operation. Thank you on
behalf of the Family, thank you on behalf of Li RM.'

He was dragged along the medicenter hallway.

Music started in mid-melody.

'You're all dead,' he said. 'The whole Family's dead. Uni's
alive, only Uni. But there are islands where *people* are living!
Look at the map! Look at the map in the Pre-U Museum!'

He was dragged into the treatment room. Bob was there, pale
and sweating, with a bleeding cut over his eyebrow; he was
jabbing at the keys of his telecomp, held for him by a girl in a
blue smock.

'Bob,' he said, 'Bob, do me a favor, will you? Look at the map
in the Pre-U Museum. Look at the map from 1951.'

He was dragged to a blue-lighted unit. He grabbed the edge of
the opening, but his thumb was pried up and his hand forced
in; his sleeve torn back and his arm shoved in all the way to the
shoulder.

His cheek was soothed—by Bob, trembling. 'You'll be all *right,*
Li,' he said. 'Trust Uni.' Three lines of blood ran from the cut
into his eyebrow hairs.

His bracelet was caught by the scanner, his arm touched by
the infusion disc. He clamped his eyes shut. *I will not be made
dead!* he thought. *I will not be made dead! I'll remember the
islands, I'll remember Lilac! I will not be made dead! I will not
be made dead!* He opened his eyes, and Bob smiled at him. A
strip of skin-colored tape was over his eyebrow. 'They *said* three
o'clock and they *meant* three o'clock,' he said.

'What do you mean?' he asked. He was lying in a bed and
Bob was sitting beside it.

'That's when the doctor's said you'd wake up,' Bob said. 'Three o'clock. And that's what it is. Not 2.29, not 3.01, but three o'clock. These mems are so clever it scares me.'

'Where am I?' he asked.

'In Medicenter Main.'

And then he remembered—remembered the things he had thought and said, and worst of all, the things he had done. 'Oh Christ,' he said. 'Oh, Marx. Oh, Christ and Wei.'

'Take it easy, Li,' Bob said, touching his hand.

'Bob,' he said, 'oh, Christ and Wei, Bob, I—I pushed you down the——'

'Escalator,' Bob said. 'You certainly did, brother. That was the most surprised moment in my life. I'm fine though.' He tapped the tape above his eyebrow. 'All closed up and good as new, or will be in a day or two.'

'I *hit* a member! With my hand!'

'He's fine, too,' Bob said. 'Two of those are from him.' He nodded across the bed, at red roses in a vase on a table. 'And two from Mary KK, and two from the members in your section.'

He looked at the roses, sent to him by the members he had hit and deceived and betrayed, and tears came into his eyes and he began to tremble.

'Hey, easy there, come on,' Bob said.

But Christ and Wei, he was thinking only of himself! 'Bob, listen,' he said, turning to him, getting up on an elbow, back-handing at his eyes.

'Take it easy,' Bob said.

'Bob, there are *others*,' he said, 'others who're just as sick as I was! We've got to find them and help them!'

'We know.'

'There's a member called "Lilac", Anna SG38 P2823, and an-other one——'

'We know, we know,' Bob said. 'They've already been helped. They've all been helped.'

'They have?'

Bob nodded. 'You were questioned while you were out,' he said. 'It's Monday. Monday afternoon. They've already been found and helped—Anna SG; and the one you called "Snowflake", Anna PY; and Yin GU, "Sparrow".'

'And King,' he said. 'Jesus HL; he's right here in this build-ing; he's——'

'No,' Bob said, shaking his head. 'No, we were too late. That one—that one is dead.'

'He's dead?'

Bob nodded.

'He hung himself,' he said.

Chip stared at him.

'From his shower, with a strip of blanket,' Bob said.

'Oh, Christ and Wei,' Chip said, and lay back on the pillow. Sickness, sickness, sickness; and he had been part of it.

'The others are all fine though,' Bob said, patting his hand. 'And you'll be fine, too. You're going to a rehabilitation center, brother. You're going to have yourself a week's vacation. Maybe even more.'

'I feel so ashamed, Bob,' he said, 'so fighting ashamed of myself . . .'

'Come on,' Bob said, 'You wouldn't feel ashamed if you'd slipped and broken an ankle, would you? It's the same thing. *I'm* the one who should feel ashamed, if anyone should.'

'I *lied* to you!'

'I let myself be lied to,' Bob said. 'Look, nobody's really responsible for anything. You'll see that soon.' He reached down, brought up a take-along kit, and opened it on his lap. 'This is yours,' he said. 'Tell me if I missed anything. Mouthpiece, clippers, snapshots, nameber books, picture of a horse, your——'

'That's sick,' he said. 'I don't want it. Chute it.'

'The picture?'

'Yes.'

Bob drew it from the kit and looked at it. 'It's nicely done,' he said. 'It's not accurate, but it's—nice in a way.'

'It's sick,' he said, 'It was done by a sick member. Chute it.'

'Whatever you say,' Bob said. He put the kit on the bed and got up and crossed the room; opened the chute and dropped the picture down.

'There are islands full of sick members,' Chip said. 'All over the world.'

'I know,' Bob said. 'You told us.'

'Why can't we help them?'

'That I *don't* know,' Bob said. 'But Uni does. I told you before, Li: trust Uni.'

'I will,' he said, 'I will,' and tears came into his eyes again.

A red-cross-coveralled member came into the room. 'How are we feeling?' he asked.

Chip looked at him.

'He's pretty low,' Bob said.

'That's to be expected,' the member said. 'Don't worry; we'll get him evened up.'

He went over and took Chip's wrist.

'Li, I have to go now,' Bob said.

'All right,' Chip said.

Bob went over and kissed his cheek. 'In case you're not sent back here, good-by, brother,' he said.

'Good-by, Bob,' Chip said. 'Thanks. Thanks for everything.'

'Thank Uni,' Bob said, and squeezed his hand and smiled. He nodded at the red-crossed member and went out.

The member took an infusion syringe from his pocket and

snapped off its cap. 'You'll be feeling perfectly normal in no time at all,' he said.

Chip lay still and closed his eyes, wiped with one hand at tears while the member pushed up his other sleeve. 'I was so sick,' he said. 'I was so sick.'

'Shh, don't think about it,' the member said, gently infusing him. 'It's nothing to think about. You'll be fine in no time.'

PART THREE: GETTING AWAY

1

OLD CITIES WERE DEMOLISHED; new cities were built. The new cities had taller buildings, broader plazas, larger parks, monorails whose cars flew faster though less frequently.

Two more starships were launched, toward Sirius B and 61 Cygni. The Mars colonies, repopulated and safeguarded now against the devastation of 152, were expanding daily; so, too, were the colonies on Venus and the Moon, the outposts on Titan and Mercury.

The free hour was extended by five minutes. Voice-input telecomps began to replace key-input ones, and totalcakes came in a pleasant second flavor. Life expectancy increased to 62.4.

Members worked and ate, watched TV and slept. They sang and went to museums and walked in amusement gardens.

On the two-hundredth anniversary of Wei's birth, in the parade in a new city, a huge portrait banner of smiling Wei was carried at one of its poles by a member of thirty or so who was ordinary in every respect except that his right eye was green instead of brown. Once long ago this member had been sick, but now he was well. He had his assignment and his room, his girlfriend and his adviser. He was relaxed and content.

A strange thing happened during the parade. As this member marched along, smiling, holding the banner pole, he began to hear a nameber saying itself over and over in his head: Anna SG, *thirty*-eight P, twenty-*eight* twenty-*three*; Anna SG, *thirty*-eight P, twenty-*eight* twenty-*three*. It kept repeating itself to him, in time with his marching. He wondered who the nameber belonged to, and why it should be repeating itself in his head that way .

Suddenly he remembered: it was from his sickness! It was the nameber of one of the other sick ones, the one called 'Lovely'— no, 'Lilac'. Why, after so long, had her nameber come back to him? He stamped his feet down harder, trying not to hear it, and was glad when the signal to sing was given.

He told his adviser. 'It's nothing to think about,' she said. 'You probably saw something that reminded you of her. Maybe you even saw *her*. There's nothing to be afraid of in remembering— unless, of course, it becomes bothersome. Let me know if it happens again.'

But it didn't happen again. He was well, thank Uni.

One Christmas Day, when he had another assignment, was living in another city, he bicycled with his girlfriend and four other members to the outlying parkland. They brought cakes and cokes with them, and lunched on the ground near a grove of trees.

He had set his coke container on an almost-level stone and, reaching for it while talking, knocked it over. The other members refilled his container from theirs.

A few minutes later, while folding his cake wrapper, he noticed a flat leaf lying on the wet stone, drops of coke shining on its back, its stem curled upward like a handle. He took the stem and lifted the leaf, the stone underneath it was dry in the leaf's oval shape. The rest of the stone was wet-black, but where the leaf had been it was dry-gray. Something about the moment seemed significant to him, and he sat silently, looking at the leaf in his one hand, the folded cake wrapper in his other, and the dry leaf shape on the stone. His girlfriend said something to him and he took himself away from the moment, put the leaf and the wrapper together and gave them to the member who had the litter bag.

The image of the dry leaf shape on the stone came into his mind several times that day, and on the next day too. Then he had his treatment and he forgot about it. In a few weeks, though, it came into his mind again. He wondered why. Had he lifted a leaf from a wet stone that way sometime before? If he had, he didn't remember it . . .

Every now and then, while he was walking in a park or, oddly enough, waiting on line for his treatment, the image of the dry leaf shape came into his mind and made him frown.

There was an earthquake. (His chair flung him off it; glass broke in the microscope and the loudest sound he had ever heard roared from the depths of the lab.) A seismovalve half the continent away had jammed and gone undetected, TV explained a few nights later. It hadn't happened before and it wouldn't happen again. Members must mourn, of course, but it was nothing to think about in the future.

Dozens of buildings had collapsed, hundreds of members had died. Every medicenter in the city was overloaded with the injured, and more than half the treatment units were damaged; treatments were delayed up to ten days.

A few days after he was to have had his, he thought of Lilac and how he had loved her differently and more—more *excitingly* —than he loved everyone else. He had wanted to tell her something. What was it? Oh yes, about the islands. The islands he had found hidden on the Pre-U map. The islands of incurables . . .

His adviser called him. 'Are you all right?' he asked.

'I don't think so, Karl,' he said. 'I need my treatment.'

'Hold on a minute,' his adviser said, and turned away and spoke softly to his telecomp. After a moment he turned back. 'You can get it tonight at seven-thirty,' he said, 'but you'll have to go to the medicenter in T24.'

He stood on a long line at seven-thirty, thinking about Lilac, trying to remember exactly what she looked like. When he got near the treatment units, the image of a dry leaf shape on a stone came into his mind.

Lilac called him (she was right there in the same building) and he went to her room, which was the storeroom in the Pre-U. Green jewels hung from her earlobes and glittered around her rose-brown throat; she was wearing a gown of gleaming green cloth that exposed her pink-tipped soft-cone breasts. 'Bon soir, Chip,' she said, smiling. 'Comment vas-tu? Je m'ennuyais telle-ment de toi.' He went to her and took her in his arms and kissed her—her lips were warm and soft, her mouth opening—and he awoke to darkness and disappointment; it was a dream, it had only been a dream.

But strangely, frighteningly, everything was in him: the smell of her perfume (parfum) and the taste of tobacco and the sound of Sparrow's songs, and desire for Lilac and anger at King and re-sentment of Uni and sorrow for the Family and happiness in feel-ing, in being alive and awake.

And in the morning he would have a treatment and it would all be gone. At eight o'clock. He tapped on the light, squinted at the clock: 4.54. In a little more than three hours . . .

He tapped the light off again and lay open-eyed in the dark. He didn't want to lose it. Sick or not, he wanted to keep his memories and the capacity to explore and enjoy them. He didn't want to think about the *islands*—no, never; that was *real* sickness—but he wanted to think about Lilac, and the meetings of the group in the relic-filled storeroom, and once in a while, maybe, to have an-other dream.

But the treatment would come in three hours and everything would be gone. There was nothing he could do—except hope for another earthquake, and what chance was there of that? The seis-movalves had worked perfectly in the years since and they would go on working perfectly in the years ahead. And what short of an earthquake could postpone his treatment? Nothing. Nothing at all. Not with Uni knowing that he had lied for a postponement once before.

A dry leaf shape on stone came into his mind but he chased it away to think of Lilac, to see her as he had seen her in the dream not to waste his three short hours of aliveness. He had forgotten how large her eyes were, how lovely her smile and her rose-brown skin, how moving her earnestness. He had forgotten so fighting much: the pleasure of smoking, the excitement of deciphering Français . . .

The dry leaf shape came back, and he thought about it, irrita-ted, to find out why his mind hung on to it, to get rid of it once and for all. He thought back to the ridiculously meaningless moment; saw again the leaf, with the drops of coke shining on it; saw his fingers lifting it by its stem, and his other hand holding the folded foil cake wrapper, and the dry gray oval on the black coke-wet stone. He had spilled the coke, and the leaf had been lying there, and the stone underneath it had——

He sat up in bed and clasped his hand to his pajamaed right arm. 'Christ and Wei,' he said, frightened.

He got up before the first chime and dressed and made the bed.

He was the first one in the dining room; ate and drank, and went back to his room with a cake wrapper folded loosely in his pocket.

He opened the wrapper, put it on the desk, and smoothed it down flat with his hand. He folded the square of foil neatly in half, and the half into thirds. He pressed the packet flat and held it; it was thin despite its six layers. Too thin? He put it down again.

He went into the bathroom and, from the cabinet's first-aid kit, got cotton and the cartridge of tape. He brought them back to the desk.

He put a layer of cotton on the foil packet—a layer smaller than the packet itself—and began covering the cotton and the packet with long overlapping strips of skin-coloured tape. He stuck the tape ends lightly to the desktop.

The door opened and he turned, hiding what he was doing and putting the tape cartridge into his pocket. It was Karl TK from next door.

'Ready to eat?' he asked.

'I already have,' he said.

'Oh,' Karl said. 'See you later.'

'Right,' he said, and smiled.

Karl closed the door.

He finished the taping and then peeled the tape ends from the desk and carried the bandage he had made into the bathroom. He laid it foil-side up on the edge of the sink and pushed up his sleeve.

He took the bandage and put the foil carefully against the inner surface of his arm, where the infusion disc would touch him. He clasped the bandage and pressed its tape border tightly to his skin.

A leaf. A shield. Would it work?

If it did, he would think only of Lilac, not of the islands. If he found himself thinking of the islands, he would tell his adviser.

He drew down his sleeve.

At eight o'clock he joined the line in the treatment room. He stood with his arms folded and his hand over the sleeve-covered bandage—to warm it in case the infusion disc was temperature-sensitive.

I'm sick, he thought. *I'll get all the diseases: cancer, small-pox, cholera, everything. Hair will grow on my face!*

He would do it just this once. At the first sign of anything wrong he would tell his adviser.

Maybe it wouldn't work.

His turn came. He pushed his sleeve to his elbow, put his hand wrist-deep into the unit's rubber-rimmed opening, and then pushed his sleeve to his shoulder and in the same moment slid his arm all the way in.

He felt the scanner finding his bracelet, and the infusion disc's slight pressure against the cotton-packed bandage . . . Nothing happened.

'You're done,' a member said behind him.

The unit's blue light was on.

'Oh,' he said, and pushed down his sleeve as he drew out his arm.

He had to go right to his assignment.

After lunch he went back to his room and, in the bathroom, pushed up his sleeve and pulled the bandage from his arm. The foil was unbroken. but so was skin after a treatment. He tore the foil packet from the tape.

The cotton was grayish and matted. He squeezed the bandage over the sink, and a trickle of waterlike liquid ran from it.

Awareness came, more of it each day. Memory came, in sharper, more anguishing detail.

Feeling came. Resentment of Uni grew into hatred; desire for Lilac grew into hopeless hunger.

Again he played the old deceptions; was normal at his assignment, normal with his adviser; normal with his girlfriend. But day by day the deceptions grew more irritating to maintain, more infuriating.

On his next treatment day he made another bandage of cake wrapper, cotton, and tape; and squeezed from it another trickle of waterlike liquid.

Black specks appeared on his chin and cheeks and upper lip— the beginnings of hair. He took apart his clippers, wired the cutter blade to one of the handles, and before the first chime each morning, rubbed soap on his face and shaved the specks away.

He dreamed every night. Sometimes the dreams brought orgasms.

More and more maddening it became, to pretend relaxation and contentment, humility, goodness. On Marxmas Day, at a beach, he trotted along the shore and then ran, ran from the members trotting with him, ran from the sunbathing, cake-eating Family. He ran till the beach narrowed into tumbled stone, and ran on through surf and over slippery ancient abutments. Then he stopped, and alone and naked between ocean and soaring cliffs, clenched his hands into fists and hit at the cliffs; cried 'Fight it!' at the clear blue sky and wrenched and tore at the untearable chain of his bracelet.

It was 169, the fifth of May. Six and a half years he had lost. *Six and a half years!* He was thirty-four. He was in USA90058.

And where was she? Still in Ind, or was she somewhere else? Was she on Earth or on a starship?

And was she alive, as he was, or was she dead, like everyone else in the Family?

2

IT WAS EASIER NOW, now that he had bruised his hands and shouted; easier to walk slowly with a contented smile, to watch TV and the screen of his microscope, to sit with his girlfriend at amphitheater concerts.

Thinking all the while of what to do . . .

'Any friction?' his adviser asked.

'Well, a little,' he said.

'I thought you didn't look right. What is it?'

'Well, you know, I was pretty sick a few years ago——"

'I know.'

'And now one of the members I was sick with, the one who got me sick, in fact, is right here in the building. Could I possibly be moved somewhere else?'

His adviser looked doubtfully at him. "I'm a little surprised,' he said, 'that UniComp's put the two of you together again.'

'So am I,' Chip said. 'But she's here. I saw her in the dining hall last night and again this morning.'

'Did you speak to her?'

'No.'

'I'll look into it,' his adviser said. 'If she *is* here and it makes you uncomfortable, of course we'll get you moved. Or get *her* moved. What's her nameber?'

'I don't remember all of it,' Chip said. 'Anna ST38P.'

His adviser called him early the next morning. 'You were mistaken, Li,' he said. 'It wasn't that member you saw. And by the way, she's Anna SG, not ST.'

'Are you sure she's not here?'

'Positive. She's in Afr.'

'That's a relief,' Chip said.

'And Li, instead of having your treatment Thursday, you're going to have it today.'

'I am?'

'Yes. At one-thirty.'

'All right,' he said. 'Thank you, Jesus.'

Thank Uni.'

He had three cake wrappers folded and hidden in the back of his desk drawer. He took one out, went into the bathroom, and began making a bandage.

She was in Afr. It was nearer than Ind but still an ocean away. And the width of Usa besides.

His parents were there, in '71334; he would wait a few weeks and then claim a visit. It was a little under two years since he had seen them last; there was a fair chance that the claim would be granted. Once in Afr he could call her—pretend to have an injured arm, get a child to touch the plate of an outdoor phone for him—and find out her exact location. *Hello, Anna SG. I hope you're as well as I am. What city are you in?*

And then what? Walk there? Claim a car ride to someplace near, an installation involved with genetics in one way or another? Would Uni realize what he was up to?

But even if it all happened, even if he got to her, what would he do *then*? It was too much to hope that she too had lifted a leaf from a wet stone one day. No, fight it, she would be a normal member, as normal as he himself had been until a few months ago. And at his first abnormal word she would have him in a medicenter. Christ, Marx, Wood and Wei, what could he *do*?

He could forget about her, that was one answer; strike out on his own, now, for the nearest free island. There would be women there, probably a lot of them, and some of them would probably have rose-brown skin and large less-slanted-than-normal eyes and soft-looking conical breasts. Was it worth risking his own aliveness on the slim chance of awakening hers?

Though *she* had awakened *his,* crouching before him with her hands on his knees . . .

Not at the risk of her own, though. Or at least not at as *great* a risk.

He went to the Pre-U Museum; went the old way, at night, without touching scanners. It was the same as the one in IND 26110. Some of the exhibits were slightly different, standing in different places.

He found another pre-U map, this one made in 1937, with the same eight blue rectangles pasted to it. Its backing had been cut and crudely taped; someone else had been at it before him. The thought was exciting; someone else had found the islands, was maybe on the way to one at that very moment.

In another storeroom—this one with only a table and a few cartons and a curtained boothlike machine with rows of small levers—he again held a map to the light, again saw the hidden islands. He traced on paper the nearest one. 'Cuba,' off Usa's southeast tip. And in case he decided to risk seeing Lilac he traced the shape of Afr and the two islands near it, 'Madagascar' to the east and the little 'Majorca' to the north.

One of the cartons held books; he found one in Français, *Spinoza et ses contemporains*. Spinoza and his contemporaries. He looked through it and took it.

He put the reframed map in its place and browsed through the museum. He took a wrist-strap compass that still seemed to be working, and a bone-handled 'razor' and the stone for sharpening it.

'We're going to be reassigned soon,' his section head said at lunch one day. 'GL4 is taking over our work.'

'I hope I go to Afr,' he said. 'My parents are there.'

It was a risky thing to say, slightly unmemberlike, but maybe the section head had an indirect influence on who went where.

His girlfriend was transferred and he went with her to the airport to see her off—and to see whether it was possible to get aboard a plane without Uni's permission. It didn't seem to be; the close single line of boarding members would allow no false touching of the scanner, and by the time the last member in the line was touching, a member in orange coveralls was at his side ready to stop the escalator and sink it in its pit. Getting off a plane presented the same difficulty: the last member out touched the scanner, while two orange-coveralled members looked on; they reversed the escalator, touched, and went aboard with steel containers for the cake and drink dispensers. He might manage to get on a plane waiting in the hangar area—and hide in it, although he didn't recall any hiding place in planes—but how could he know where it would eventually go?

Flying was impossible, till Uni said he could fly.

He claimed the visit to his parents. It was denied.

New assignments were posted for his section. Two 66's were sent to Afr, but not he; he was sent to USA36104. During the flight he studied the plane. There was no hiding place. There was only the long seat-filled hull, the bathroom at the front, the cake and drink dispensers at the back, and the TV screens, with an actor playing Marx on all of them.

USA36104 was in the southeast, close to Usa's tip and Cuba beyond it. He could go bicycling one Sunday and keep bicycling; go from city to city, sleeping in the parkland between them and going into the cities at night for cakes and drinks; it was twelve hundred kilometres by the MFA map. At '33037 he could find a boat, or traders coming ashore like the ones in ARG20400 that King had spoken of.

Lilac, he thought, *what else can I do?*

He claimed the visit to Afr again, and again it was denied.

He began bicycling on Sundays and during the free hour, to ready his legs. He went to the '36104 Pre-U and found a better compass and a tooth-edged knife he could use for cutting branches in the parkland. He checked the map there; this one's backing was intact, unopened. He wrote on it, *Yes, there are islands where members are free. Fight Uni!*

Early one Sunday morning he set out for Cuba, with the compass and a map he had drawn in one of his pockets. In the bike's basket, *Wei's Living Wisdom* lay on a folded blanket along with a container of coke and a cake; within the blanket was his take-along kit, and in that were his razor and its sharpening stone, a bar of soap, his clippers, two cakes, the knife, a flashlight, cotton, a cartridge of tape, a snapshot of his parents and Papa Jan, and an extra set of coveralls. Under his right sleeve there was a bandage on his arm, though if he were taken for treatment it would almost certainly be found. He wore sunglasses and smiled, pedalling southeast among other cyclists on the path toward '36081. Cars skimmed past in rhythmic sequence over the roadway that paralleled the path. Pebbles kicked by the car's airjets pinged now and then against the metal divider.

He stopped every hour or so and rested for a few minutes. He ate half a cake and drank some of the coke. He thought about Cuba, and what he would take from '33037 to trade there. He thought about the women on Cuba. Probably they would be attracted by a new arrival. They would be completely untreated, passionate beyond imagining, as beautiful as Lilac or even more beautiful...

He rode for five hours, and then he turned around and rode back.

He forced his mind to his assignment. He was the staff 663 in a medicenter's pediatrics division. It was boring work, endless gene examinations with little variation, and it was the sort of assignment from which one was seldom transferred. He would be there for the rest of his life.

Every four or five weeks he claimed a visit to his parents in Afr. In February of 170 the claim was granted.

He got off the plane at four in the morning Afr time and went into the waiting room, holding his right elbow and looking uncomfortable, his kit slung on his left shoulder. The member who had got off the plane behind him, and who had helped him up when he had fallen, put her bracelet to a phone for him. 'Are you sure you're all right?' she asked.

'I'm fine,' he said, smiling. 'Thanks, and enjoy your visit.' To the phone he said, 'Anna SG38P2823.' The member went away.

The screen flashed and patterned as the connection was made, and then it went dark and stayed dark. *She's been transferred*, he thought; *she's off the continent.* He waited for the phone to tell him. But she said, 'Just a second, I can't——' and was there, blurry-close. She sat back down on the edge of her bed, rubbing

her eyes, in pajamas. 'Who is it?' she asked. Behind her a member
turned over. It was Saturday night. Or was she married?

'Who?' she asked. She looked at him and leaned closer, blinking. She was more beautiful. Were there ever such eyes?

'Li RM,' he said, making himself be only courteous, memberlike. 'Don't you remember? From IND26110, back in 162.'

Her brow contracted uneasily for an instant. 'Oh yes, of course,'
she said, and smiled. 'Of course I remember. How are you, Li?'

'Very well,' he said. 'How are you?'

'Fine,' she said, and stopped smiling.

'Married?'

'No,' she said. 'I'm glad you called, Li. I want to thank you.
You know, for helping me.'

'Thank Uni,' he said.

'No, no,' she said, 'Thank you. Belatedly.' She smiled again.

'I'm sorry to call at this hour,' he said. 'I'm passing through
Afr on a transfer.'

'That's all right,' she said. 'I'm glad you did.'

'Where are you?' he asked.

'In '14509.'

'That's where my sister lives.'

'Really?' she said.

'Yes,' he said. 'Which building are you in?'

'P51.'

'She's in A-something.'

The member behind her sat up and she turned and said
something to him. He smiled at Chip. She turned and said, 'This
is Li XE.'

'Hello,' Chip said, thinking '14509, P51; '14509, P51.

'Hello, brother,' Li XE's lips said; his voice didn't reach the
phone.

'Is something wrong with your arm?' Lilac asked.

He was still holding it. He let it go. 'No,' he said. 'I fell getting
off the plane.'

'Oh, I'm sorry,' she said. She glanced beyond him. 'There's a
member waiting,' she said. 'We'd better say good-by now.'

'Yes,' he said. 'Good-by. It was nice seeing you. You haven't
changed at all.'

'Neither have you,' she said. 'Good-by, Li.' She rose and reached
forward and was gone.

He tapped off and gave way to the member behind him.

She was dead; a normal healthy member lying down now beside
her boyfriend in '14509, P51. How could he risk talking to her of
anything that wasn't as normal and healthy as she was? He should
spend the day with his parents and fly back to Usa; go bicycling
next Sunday and this time not turn back.

He walked around the waiting room. There was an outline
map of Afr on one wall, with lights at the major cities and thin

orange lines connecting them. Near the north was '14510, near where she was. Half the continent from '71330, where he was. An orange line connected the two lights.

He watched the flight-schedule signboard flashing and blinking, revising the *Sunday 18 Feb* schedule. A plane for '14510 was leaving at 8.20 in the evening, forty minutes before his own flight for USA33100.

He went to the glass that faced the field and watched members single-filing onto the escalator of the plane he had left. An orange-coveralled member came and waited by the scanner.

He turned back to the waiting room. It was nearly empty. Two members who had been on the plane with him, a woman holding a sleeping infant and a man carrying two kits, put their wrists and the infant's wrist to the scanner at the door to the carport—*yes*, it greened three times—and went out. An orange-coveralled member, on his knees by a water fountain, unscrewed a plate at its base; another pushed a floor polisher to the side of the waiting room, touched a scanner—*yes*—pushed the polisher out through a swing-door.

He thought for a moment, watching the member working at the fountain, and then he crossed the waiting room, touched the carport-door scanner—*yes*—and went out. A car for '71334 was waiting, three members in it. He touched the scanner—*yes*—and got into the car, apologizing to the members for having kept them waiting. The door closed and the car started. He sat with his kit in his lap, thinking.

When he got to his parents' apartment he went in quietly, shaved, and then woke them. They were pleased, even happy to see him.

The three of them talked and ate breakfast and talked more. They claimed a call to Peace, in Eur, and it was granted; they talked with her and her Karl, her ten-year-old Bob and her eight-year-old Yin. Then, at his suggestion, they went to the Museum of the Family's Achievements.

After lunch he slept for three hours and they railed to the Amusement Gardens. His father joined a volleyball game, and he and his mother sat on a bench and watched. 'Are you sick again?' she asked him.

He looked at her. 'No,' he said. 'Of course not. I'm fine.'

She looked closely at him. She was fifty-seven now, gray-haired, her tan skin wrinkled. 'You've been thinking about something,' she said. 'All day.'

'I'm well,' he said. 'Please. You're my mother; believe me.'

She looked into his eyes with concern.

After a moment she said, 'All right, Chip.'

Love for her suddenly filled him; love, and gratitude, and a boylike feeling of oneness with her. He clasped her shoulder and kissed her cheek. 'I love you, Suzu,' he said.

She laughed. 'Christ and Wei,' she said, 'what a memory you have!'

'That's because I'm healthy,' he said. 'Remember that, will you? I'm healthy and happy. I want you to remember that.'

'Why?'

'Because,' he said.

He told them that his plane left at eight. 'We'll say good-by at the carport,' he said. 'The airport will be too crowded.'

His father wanted to come along anyway, but his mother said no, they would stay in '334; she was tired.

At seven-thirty he kissed them good-by—his father and then his mother, saying in her ear, 'Remember'—and got on line for a car to the '71330 airport.

The scanner, when he touched it, said *yes*.

The waiting room was even more crowded than he had hoped it would be. Members in white and yellow and pale blue walked and stood and sat and waited in line, some with kits and some without. A few members in orange moved among them.

He looked at the signboard; the 8.20 flight for '14510 would load from lane two. Members were in line there, and beyond the glass, a plane was swinging into place against a rising escalator. Its door opened and a member came out, another behind him.

Chip made his way through the crowd to the swing-door at the side of the room, false-touched its scanner, and pushed through: into a depot area where crates and cartons stood ranked under white light, like Uni's memory banks. He unslung his kit and jammed it between a carton and the wall.

He walked ahead normally. A cart of steel containers crossed his path, pushed by an orange-coveralled member who glanced at him and nodded.

He nodded back, kept walking, and watched the member push the cart out through a large open portal onto the floodlit field.

He went in the direction from which the member had come, into an area where members in orange were putting steel containers on the conveyor of a washing machine and filling other containers with coke and steaming tea from the taps of giant drums. He kept walking.

He false-touched a scanner and went into a room where coveralls, ordinary ones, hung on hooks, and two members were taking off orange ones. 'Hello,' he said.

'Hello,' they both said.

He went to a closet door and slid it open; a floor polisher and bottles of green liquid were inside. 'Where are the cuvs?' he asked.

'In there,' one of the members said, nodding at another closet.

He went to it and opened it. Orange coveralls were on shelves; orange toeguards, pairs of heavy orange gloves.

'Where did you come from?' the member asked.

'RUS50937,' he said, taking a pair of coveralls and a pair of toeguards. 'We kept the cuvs in there.'

'They're supposed to be in *there*,' the member said, closing white coveralls.

'I've been in Rus,' the other member, a woman, said. 'I had two assignments there; first four years and then three years.'

He took his time putting on the toeguards, finishing as the two members chuted their orange coveralls and went out.

He pulled the orange coveralls on over his white ones and closed them all the way to his throat. They were heavier than ordinary coveralls and had extra pockets. He looked in other closets, found a wrench and a good-sized piece of yellow paplon.

He went back to where he had left his kit, got it out, and wrapped the paplon around it. The swing-door bumped him. 'Sorry,' a member said, coming in. 'Did I hurt you?'

'No,' he said, holding the wrapped kit.

The orange-coveralled member went on.

He waited for a moment, watching him, and then he tucked the kit under his left arm and got the wrench from his pocket. He gripped it in his right hand, in a way that he hoped looked natural.

He followed after the member, then turned and went to the portal that opened onto the field.

The escalator leaning against the flank of the lane-two plane was empty. A cart, probably the one he had seen pushed out, stood at the foot of it, beside the scanner.

Another escalator was sinking into the ground, and the plane it had served was on its way toward the runways. There was an 8.10 flight to Chi, he recalled.

He crouched on one knee, put his kit and the wrench down on concrete, and pretended to have trouble with his toe-guard. Everyone in the waiting room would be watching the plane for Chi when it lifted; that was when he would go onto the escalator. Orange legs rustled past him, a member walking toward the hangars. He took off his toeguard and put it back on, watching the plane pivot . . .

It raced forward. He gathered his kit and the wrench, stood up, and walked normally. The brightness of the floodlights unnerved him, but he told himself that no one was watching him, everyone was watching the plane. He walked to the escalator, false-touched the scanner—the cart beside it helped, justifying his awkwardness—and stepped onto the upgoing stairs. He clutched his paplon-wrapped kit and the damp-handled wrench as he rose quickly toward the open plane door. He stepped off the escalator and into the plane.

Two members in orange were busy at the dispensers. They looked at him and he nodded. They nodded back. He went down the aisle toward the bathroom.

He went into the bathroom, leaving the door open, and put his kit on the floor. He turned to a sink, worked its faucets, and tapped them with the wrench. He got down on his knees and tapped the drainpipe. He opened the jaws of the wrench and put them around the pipe.

He heard the escalator stop, and then start again. He leaned over and looked out the door. The members were gone.

He put down the wrench, got up, closed the door, and pulled open the orange coveralls. He took them off, folded them lengthwise, and rolled them into as compact a bundle as he could. Kneeling, he unwrapped his kit and opened it. He squeezed in the coveralls, and folded the yellow paplon and put that in too. He took the toeguards off his sandals, nested them together, and tucked them into one of the kit's corners. He put the wrench in, stretched the cover tight, and pressed it closed.

With the kit slung on his shoulder, he washed his hands and face with cold water. His heart was beating quickly but he felt good, excited, alive. He looked in the mirror at his one-green-eyed self. *Fight Uni!*

He heard the voices of members coming aboard the plane. He stayed at the sink, wiping his already-dry hands.

The door opened and a boy of ten or so came in.

'Hi,' Chip said, wiping his hands. 'Did you have a nice day?'

'Yes,' the boy said.

Chip chuted the towel. 'First time you've flown?'

'*No,*' the boy said, opening his coveralls. 'I've done it lots of times.' He sat down on one of the toilets.

'See you inside,' Chip said, and went out.

The plane was about a third filled, with more members filing in. He took the nearest empty aisle seat, checked his kit to make sure it was securely closed, and stowed it below.

It would be the same at the other end. When everyone was leaving the plane he would go into the bathroom and put on the orange coveralls. He would be working at the sink when the members came aboard with the refill containers and he would leave after they left. In the depot area behind a crate or in a closet, he would get rid of the coveralls, the toeguards, and the wrench; and then he would false-touch out of the airport and walk to '14509. It was eight kilometers east of '510; he had checked on a map at the MFA that morning. With luck he would be there by midnight or half past.

"Isn't that odd,' the member next to him said.

He turned to her.

She was looking toward the back of the plane. 'There's no seat for that member,' she said.

A member was walking slowly up the aisle, looking to one side and then the other. All the seats were taken. Members were looking about, trying to be of help to him.

'There *must* be one,' Chip said, lifting himself in his seat and looking about. 'Uni couldn't have made a mistake.'

'There isn't,' the member next to him said. 'Every seat is filled.'

Conversation rose in the plane. There was indeed no seat for the member. A woman took a child onto her lap and called to him.

The plane began moving and the TV screens went on, with a program about Afr's geography and resources.

He tried to pay attention to it, thinking there might be information in it that would be useful to him, but he couldn't. If he were found and treated now, he would never get alive again. This time Uni would make certain that he would see no meaning in even a thousand leaves on a thousand wet stones.

He got to '14509 at twenty past midnight. He was wide awake, still on Usa time, with afternoon energy.

First he went to the Pre-U, and then to the bike station on the plaza nearest building P51. He made two trips to the bike station, and one to P51's dining hall and its supply center.

At three o'clock he went into Lilac's room. He looked at her by flashlight while she slept—looked at her cheek, her neck, her dark hand on the pillow—and then he went to the desk and tapped on the lamp.

'Anna,' he said, standing at the foot of the bed. 'Anna, you have to get up now.'

She mumbled something.

'You have to get up now, Anna,' he said. 'Come on, get up.'

She raised herself with a hand at her eyes, making little sounds of complaint. Sitting, she drew the hand away and peered at him; recognized him and frowned bewilderedly.

'I want you to come for a ride with me,' he said. 'A bike ride. You mustn't talk loud and you mustn't call for help.' He reached into his pocket and took out a gun. He held it the way it seemed meant to be held, with his first finger across the trigger, the rest of his hand holding the handle, and the front of it pointed at her face. 'I'll kill you if you don't do what I tell you,' he said. 'Don't shout now, Anna.'

3

SHE STARED at the gun, and at him.

'The generator's weak,' he said, 'but it made a hole a centimeter deep in the wall of the museum and it'll make a deeper one in you. So you'd better obey me. I'm sorry to frighten you, but eventually you'll understand why I'm doing it.'

'This is terrible!' she said. 'You're still sick!'

'Yes,' he said, 'and I've gotten worse. So do as I say or the Family will lose two valuable members; first you, and then me.'

'How can you *do* this, Li?' she said. 'Can't you see yourself—with a *weapon* in your hand, *threatening* me?'

'Get up and get dressed,' he said.

'Please, let me call——'

'Get dressed,' he said. 'Quickly!'

'All right,' she said, turning aside the blanket. 'All right, I'll do exactly as you say.' She got up and opened her pajamas.

He backed away, watching her, keeping the gun pointed at her. She took off her pajamas, let them fall, and turned to the shelf for a set of coveralls. He watched her breasts and the rest of her body, which in subtle ways—a fullness of the buttocks, a round-ness of the thighs—was different too from the normal. How beautiful she was!

She stepped into the coveralls and put her arms into the sleeves. 'Li, I beg you,' she said, looking at him, 'let's go down to the medicenter and——'

'Don't talk,' he said.

She closed the coveralls and put her feet into her sandals. 'Why do you want to go *bicycling*?' she said. 'It's the middle of the night.'

'Pack your kit,' he said.

'My take-along?'

'Yes,' he said. 'Put in another set of cuvs and your first-aid kit and your clippers. And anything that's important to you that you want to keep. Do you have a flashlight?'

'What are you planning to *do*?' she asked.

'Pack your kit,' he said.

She packed her kit, and when she had closed it he took it and slung it on his shoulder. 'We're going to go around behind the building,' he said. 'I've got two bikes there. We're going to walk side by side and I'll have the gun in my pocket. If we pass a member and you give any indication that anything's wrong, I'll kill you *and* the member, do you understand?'

'Yes,' she said.

'Do whatever I tell you. If I say stop and fix your sandal, stop and fix your sandal. We're going to pass scanners without touching them. You've done that before; you're going to do it again.'

'We're not coming back here?' she said.

'No. We're going far away.'

'Then there's a snapshot I'd like to take.'

'Get it,' he said. 'I told you to take whatever you wanted to keep.'

She went to the desk, opened the drawer, and rummaged in it. *A snapshot of King?* he wondered. No, King was part of her 'sickness'. Probably one of her family. 'It's in here somewhere,' she said, sounding nervous, not right.

He hurried to her and pushed her aside. *Li RM gun 2 bicy* was written on the bottom of the drawer. A pen was in her hand. 'I'm trying to help you,' she said.

He felt like hitting her but stopped himself; but stopping was wrong, she would know he wouldn't hurt her; he hit her face with his open hand, stingingly hard. 'Don't try to trick me!' he said. 'Don't you realize how sick I am? *You'll* be dead and maybe a dozen *other* members will be dead if you do something like this again!'

She stared wide-eyed at him, trembling, her hand at her cheek.

He was trembling too, knowing he had hurt her. He snatched the pen from her hand, made zigzags over what she had written, and covered it with papers and a nameber book. He threw the pen in the drawer and closed it, took her elbow and pushed her toward the door.

They went out of her room and down the hallway, walking side by side. He kept his hand in his pocket, holding the gun. 'Stop shaking,' he said. 'I won't hurt you if you do what I tell you.'

They rode down escalators. Two members came toward them, riding up. 'You and them,' he said. 'And anyone else who comes along.'

He smiled at the members. They smiled back. She nodded at them.

'This is my second transfer this year,' he said to her.

They rode down more escalators, and stepped onto the one leading to the lobby. Three members, two with telecomps, stood talking by the scanner at one of the doors. 'No tricks now,' he said.

They rode down, reflected at a distance in dark-outside glass. The members kept talking. One of them put his telecomp on the floor.

They stepped off the escalator. 'Wait a minute, Anna,' he said. She stopped and faced him, 'I've got an eyelash in my eye,' he said. 'Do you have a tissue?'

She reached into her pocket and shook her head.

He found one under the gun and took it out and gave it to her. He stood facing the members and held his eye wide open, his other hand in his pocket again. She held the tissue to his eye. She was still trembling. 'It's only an eyelash,' he said. 'Nothing to be nervous about.'

Beyond her the member had picked up his telecomp and the three were shaking hands and kissing. The two with telecomps touched the scanner. *Yes*, it winked, *yes*. They went out. The third member came toward them, a man in his twenties.

Chip moved Lilac's hand away. 'That's it,' he said, blinking. 'Thanks, sister.'

'Can I be of help?' the member asked. 'I'm a 101.'

'No, thanks, it was just an eyelash,' Chip said. Lilac moved. Chip looked at her. She put the tissue in her pocket.

The member, glancing at the kit, said, 'Have a good trip.'

'Thanks,' Chip said. 'Good night.'

'Good night,' the member said, smiling at them.

'Good night,' Lilac said.

They went toward the doors and saw in them the reflection of the member stepping onto an upgoing escalator. 'I'm going to lean close to the scanner,' Chip said. 'Touch the side of it, not the plate.'

They went outside.

'Please, Li,' Lilac said, 'for the sake of the Family, let's go back in and go up to the medicenter.'

'Be quiet,' he said.

They turned into the passageway between the building and the next one. The darkness grew deeper and he took out his flashlight.

'What are you going to do to me?' she asked.

'Nothing,' he said, 'unless you try to trick me again.'

'Then what do you want me for?' she asked.

He didn't answer.

There was a scanner at the cross-passage behind the buildings. Lilac's hand went up; Chip said, 'No!' They passed it without touching, and Lilac made a distressed sound and said under her breath, 'Terrible.'

The bikes were leaning against the wall where he had left them. His blanket-wrapped kit was in the basket of one, with cakes and drink containers squeezed in with it. A blanket was draped over the basket of the other; he put Lilac's kit down into it, closed the blanket around it and tucked it snugly. 'Get on,' he said, holding the bike upright for her.

She got on and held the handlebars.

'We'll go straight along between the buildings to the East Road,' he said. 'Don't turn or stop or gear up unless I tell you to.'

He got astride the other bike. He pushed the flashlight down into the side of the basket, with the light shining out through the mesh at the pavement ahead..

'All right, let's go,' he said.

They pedaled side by side down the straight passage that was all darkness except for columns of lesser darkness between buildings, and far above a narrow strip of stars, and far ahead the pale blue spark of a single walkway light.

'Gear up a little,' he said.

They rode faster.

'When are you due for your next treatment?' he asked.

She was silent, and then said, 'Marx eighth.'

Two weeks, he thought. Christ and Wei, why couldn't it have

been tomorrow or the next day? Well, it could have been worse; it could have been *four* weeks.

'Will I be able to get it?' she asked.

There was no point in disturbing her more than he had already. 'Maybe,' he said. 'We'll see.'

He had intended to go a short distance every day, during the free hour when cyclists would attract no attention. They would go from parkland to parkland, passing one city or perhaps two, and make their way by small steps to '12082 on Afr's north coast, the city nearest Majorca.

That first day, though, in the parkland north of '14509, he changed his mind. Finding a hiding place was harder than he expected; not until long after sunrise—around eight o'clock, he guessed—were they settled under a rock-ledge canopy fronted by a thicket of saplings whose gaps he had filled with cut branches. Soon after, they heard a copter's hum; it passed and repassed above them while he pointed the gun at Lilac and she sat motionless, watching him, a half-eaten cake in her hands. At midday they heard branches cracking, leaves slashing, and a voice no more than twenty meters away. It spoke unintelligibly, in the slow flat way one addressed a telephone or a voice-input telecomp.

Either Lilac's desk-drawer message had been found, or, more likely, Uni had put together his disappearance, her disappearance, and two missing bicycles. So he changed his mind and decided that having been looked for and missed, they would stay where they were all week and ride on Sunday. They would make a sixty- or seventy-kilometer hop—not directly to the north but to the northeast—then settle and hide for another week. Four or five Sundays would bring them in a curving path to '12082, and each Sunday Lilac would be more herself and less Anna SG, more helpful or at least less anxious to see him 'helped'.

Now, though, she was Anna SG. He tied and gagged her with blanket strips and slept with the gun at his hand till the sun went down. In the middle of the night he tied and gagged her again, and carried away his bike. He came back in a few hours with cakes and drinks and two more blankets, towels and toilet paper, a 'wristwatch' that had already stopped ticking, and two Français books. She was lying awake where he had left her, her eyes anxious and pitying. Held captive by a sick member, she suffered his abuses forgivingly. She was sorry for him.

But in daylight she looked at him with revulsion. He touched his cheek and felt two days' stubble. Smiling, slightly embarrassed, he said, 'I haven't had a treatment in almost a year.'

She lowered her head and put a hand over her eyes. 'You've made yourself into an animal,' she said.

'That's what we are, really,' he said. 'Christ, Marx, Wood, and Wei made us into something dead and unnatural.'

She turned away when he began to shave, but she glanced over her shoulder, glanced again, and then turned and watched distastefully.

'Don't you cut your skin?' she asked.

'I did in the beginning,' he said, pressing taut his cheek and working the razor easily, watching it in the side of his flashlight propped on a stone. 'I had to keep my hand at my face for days.'

'Do you always use tea?' she asked.

He laughed. 'No,' he said. 'It's a substitute for water. Tonight I'm going to go looking for a pond or a stream.'

'How often do you—do that?' she asked.

'Every day,' he said. 'I missed yesterday. It's a nuisance, but it's only for a few more weeks. At least I hope so.'

'What do you mean?' she said.

He said nothing, kept shaving.

She turned away.

He read one of the Français books, about the causes of a war that had lasted thirty years. Lilac slept, and then she sat on a blanket and looked at him and at the trees and at the sky.

'Do you want me to teach you this language?' he asked.

'What for?' she said.

'Once you wanted to learn it,' he said. 'Do you remember? I gave you lists of words.'

'Yes,' she said, 'I remember. I learned them, but I've forgotten them. I'm well now; what would I want to learn it now for?'

He did calisthenics and made her do them too, so that they would be ready for Sunday's long ride. She followed his directions unprotestingly.

That night he found, not a stream, but a concrete-banked irrigation channel about two meters wide. He bathed in its slow-flowing water, then brought filled drink containers back to the hiding place and woke Lilac and untied her. He led her through the trees and stood and watched while she bathed. Her wet body glistened in the faint light of the quarter moon.

He helped her up onto the bank, handed her a towel, and stayed close to her while she dried herself. 'Do you know why I'm doing this?' he asked her.

She looked at him.

'Because I love you,' he said.

'Then let me go,' she said.

He shook his head.

'Then how can you say you love me?'

'I do,' he said.

She bent over and dried her legs. 'Do you want me to get sick again?' she asked.

'Yes,' he said.

'Then you *hate* me,' she said, 'you don't love me.' She stood up straight.

He took her arm, cool and moist, smooth. 'Lilac,' he said.
'Anna.'

He tried to kiss her lips but she turned her head and drew away. He kissed her cheek.

'Now point your gun at me and "rape" me,' she said.

'I won't do that,' he said. He let go of her arm.

'I don't know why not,' she said, getting into her coveralls. She closed them fumblingly. 'Please, Li,' she said, 'let's go back to the city. I'm *sure* you can be cured, because if you were really sick, *incurably* sick, you *would* "rape" me. You'd be much less kind than you are.'

'Come on,' he said, 'let's get back to the place.'

'Please, Li——' she said.

'*Chip*,' he said. '*My* name is *Chip*. Come on.' He jerked his head and they started through the trees.

Toward the end of the week she took his pen and the book he wasn't reading and drew pictures on the inside of the book's cover—near-likenesses of Christ and Wei, groups of buildings, her left hand, and a row of shaded crosses and sickles. He looked to make sure she wasn't writing messages that she would try to give to someone on Sunday.

Later he drew a building and showed it to her.

'What is it?' she asked.

'A building,' he said.

'No it isn't.'

'It is,' he said. 'They don't all have to be blank and rectangular.'

'What are the ovals?'

'Windows.'

'I've never seen a building like this one,' she said. 'Not even in the Pre-U. Where is it?'

'Nowhere,' he said. 'I made it up.'

'Oh,' she said. 'Then it *isn't* a building, not really. How can you draw things that aren't real?'

'I'm sick, remember?' he said.

She gave the book back to him, not looking at his eyes. 'Don't joke about it,' she said.

He hoped—well, didn't *hope*, but thought it might possibly happen—that Saturday night, out of custom or desire or even only memberlike kindness, she would show a willingness for him to come close to her. She didn't, though. She was the same as she had been every other night, sitting silently in the dusk with her arms around her knees, watching the band of purpling sky between the shifting black treetops and the black rock ledge overhead.

'It's Saturday night,' he said.

'I know,' she said.

They were silent for a few moments, and then she said, 'I'm not going to be able to have my treatment, am I?'

'No,' he said.

'Then I might get pregnant,' she said. 'I'm not supposed to have children and neither are you.'

He wanted to tell her that they were going someplace where Uni's decisions were meaningless, but it was too soon; she might become frightened and unmanageable. 'Yes, I suppose you're right,' he said.

When he had tied her and covered her, he kissed her cheek. She lay in the darkness and said nothing, and he got up from his knees and went to his own blankets.

Sunday's ride went well. Early in the day a group of young members stopped them, but it was only to ask their help in repairing a broken drive chain, and Lilac sat on the grass away from the group while Chip did the job. By sundown they were in the parkland north of '14266. They had gone about seventy-five kilometers.

Again it was hard to find a hiding place, but the one Chip finally found—the broken walls of a pre-U or early-U building, roofed with a sagging mass of vines and creepers—was larger and more comfortable than the one they had used the week before. The same night, despite the day's riding, he went into '266 and brought back a three-day supply of cakes and drinks.

Lilac grew irritable that week. 'I want to clean my *teeth*,' she said, 'and I want to take a shower. How long are we going to go on this way? Forever? *You* may enjoy living like an animal but I don't; I'm a human being. And I can't sleep with my hands and feet tied.'

'You slept all right last week,' he said.

'Well I can't now!'

'Then lie quietly and let *me* sleep,' he said.

When she looked at him it was with annoyance, not with pity. She made disapproving sounds when he shaved and when he read; answered curtly or not at all when he spoke. She balked at doing calisthenics, and he had to take out the gun and threaten her.

It was getting close to Marx eighth, her treatment day, he told himself, and this irritability, a natural resentment of captivity and discomfort, was a sign of the healthy Lilac who was buried in Anna SG. It ought to have pleased him, and when he thought about it, it did. But it was much harder to live with than the previous week's sympathy and memberlike docility.

She complained about insects and boredom. There was a rainy night and she complained about the rain.

One night Chip woke and heard her moving. He shone his flashlight at her. She had untied her wrists and was untying her ankles. He retied her and struck her.

That Saturday night they didn't speak to each other.

On Sunday they rode again. Chip stayed close to her side and watched her carefully when members came toward them. He reminded her to smile, to nod, to answer greetings, to act as if nothing was wrong. She rode in grim silence, and he was afraid that despite the threat of the gun she might call out for help at any moment or stop and refuse to go on. 'Not just you,' he said, 'everyone in sight. I'll kill them all, I swear I will.' She kept riding. She smiled and nodded resentfully. Chip's gearshift jammed and they went only forty kilometers.

Toward the end of the third week her irritation subsided. She sat frowning, picking at blades of grass, looking at her fingertips, turning her bracelet around and around her wrist. She looked at Chip curiously, as if he were someone strange whom she hadn't seen before. She followed his instructions slowly, mechanically.

He worked on his bike, letting her awaken in her own time.

One evening in the fourth week she said, 'Where are we going?'

He looked at her for a moment—they were eating the day's last cake—and said, 'To an island called Majorca. In the Sea of Eternal Peace.'

' "Majorca"?' she said.

'It's an island of incurables,' he said. 'There are seven others all over the world. More than seven, really, because some of them are groups. I found them on a map in the Pre-U, back in Ind. They were covered over and they're not shown on MFA maps. I was going to tell you about them the day I was—"cured".'

She was silent, and then she said, 'Did you tell King?'

It was the first time she had mentioned him. Should he tell her that King hadn't needed to be told, that he had known all along and withheld it from them? What for? King was dead; why diminish her memory of him? 'Yes, I did,' he said. 'He was amazed, and very excited. I don't understand why he—did what he did. You know about it, don't you?'

'Yes, I know,' she said. She took a small bite of cake and ate it, not looking at him. 'How do they live on this island?' she asked.

'I have no idea,' he said. 'It might be very rough, very primitive. Better than this, though.' He smiled. 'Whatever it's like,' he said, 'it's a free life. It might be highly civilized. The first incurables must have been the most independent and resourceful members.'

'I'm not sure that I want to go there,' she said.

'Just think about it,' he said. 'In a few days you'll be sure. You're the one who had the idea that incurable colonies might exist, do you remember? You asked me to look for them.'

She nodded. 'I remember,' she said.

Later in the week she took a new Français book that he had found and tried to read it. He sat beside her and translated it for her.

That Sunday, while they were riding along, a member pedaled up on Chip's left and stayed even with them. 'Hi,' he said.

'Hi,' Chip said.

'I thought all the old bikes had been phased out,' he said.

'So did I,' Chip said, 'but these are what was there.'

The member's bike had a thinner frame and a thumb-knob gear control.

'Back in '935?' he asked.

'No, '939,' Chip said.

'Oh,' the member said. He looked at their baskets, filled with their blanket-wrapped kits.

'We'd better speed up, Li,' Lilac said. 'The others are out of sight.'

'They'll wait for us,' Chip said. 'They have to; we have the cakes and blankets.'

The member smiled.

'No, come on, let's go faster,' Lilac said. 'It's not fair to make them wait around.'

'All right,' Chip said, and to the member, 'Have a good day.'

'You too,' he said.

They pedaled faster and pulled ahead.

'Good for you,' Chip said. 'He was just going to ask why we're carrying so much.'

Lilac said nothing.

They went about eighty kilometers that day and reached the parkland northwest of '12471, within another day's ride of '082. They found a fairly good hiding place, a triangular cleft between high rock spurs overhung with trees. Chip cut branches to close off the front of it.

'You don't have to tie me any more,' Lilac said. 'I won't run away and I won't try to attract anyone. You can put the gun in your kit.'

'You want to go?' Chip said. 'To Majorca?'

'Of course,' she said. 'I'm anxious to. It's what I've always wanted—when I've been myself, I mean.'

'All right,' he said. He put the gun in his kit and that night he didn't tie her.

Her casual matter-of-factness didn't seem right to him. Shouldn't she have shown more enthusiasm? Yes, and gratitude, too; that was what he had expected, he admitted to himself: gratitude, expressions of love. He lay awake listening to her soft slow breathing. Was she really asleep or was she only pretending? Could she be tricking him in some unimaginable way? He shone his flashlight at her. Her eyes were closed, her lips parted, her arms together under the blanket as if she were still tied.

It was only Marx twentieth, he told himself. In another week or two she would show more feeling. He closed his eyes, When he woke she was picking stones and twigs from the ground. 'Good morning,' she said pleasantly.

They found a narrow trickle of stream nearby, and a green-fruited tree that he thought was an 'olivier'. The fruit was bitter and strange-tasting. They both preferred cakes.

She asked him how he had avoided his treatments, and he told her about the leaf and the wet stone and the bandages he had made. She was impressed. It was clever of him, she said.

They went into '12471 one night for cakes and drinks, towels, toilet paper, coveralls, new sandals; and to study, as well as they could by flashlight, the MFA map of the area.

'What will we do when we get to '082?' she asked the next morning.

'Hide by the shore,' he said, 'and watch every night for traders.'

'Would they do that?' she asked. 'Risk coming ashore?'

'Yes,' he said, 'I think they would, away from the city.'

'But wouldn't they be more likely to go to Eur? It's nearer.'

'We'll just have to hope they come to Afr, too,' he said. 'And I want to get some things from the city for *us* to trade, when we get *there*, things that they're likely to put a value on. We'll have to think about that.'

'Is there any chance that we can find a boat?' she asked.

'I don't think so,' he said. 'There aren't any offshore islands, so there aren't likely to be any powerboats around. Of course, there are always amusement-garden rowboats, but I can't see us rowing two hundred and eighty kilometers; can you?'

'It's not impossible,' she said.

'No,' he said, 'if worse comes to worst. But I'm counting on traders, or maybe even some kind of organized rescue operation. Majorca has to defend itself, you see, because Uni knows about it; it knows about all the islands. So the members there might keep a lookout for newcomers, to increase their population, increase their strength.'

'I suppose they might,' she said.

There was another rain night, and they sat together with a blanket around them in the inmost narrow corner of their place, tight between the high rock spurs. He kissed her and tried to work open the top of her coveralls, but she stopped his hand with hers. 'I know it doesn't make sense,' she said, 'but I still have a little of that only-on-Saturday-night feeling. Please? Could we wait till then?'

'It *doesn't* make sense,' he said.

'I know,' she said, 'but please? Could we wait?'

After a moment he said, 'Sure, if you want to.'

'I do, Chip,' she said.

They read, and decided on the best things to take from '082 for trading. He checked over the bikes and she did calisthenics, did them longer and more purposefully than he did.

On Saturday night he came back from the stream and she stood holding the gun, pointing it at him, her eyes narrowed hatingly. 'He called me before he did it,' she said.

He said, 'What are you——' and 'King!' she cried. 'He called me! You lying, hating——' She squeezed the gun's trigger. She squeezed again, harder. She looked at the gun and looked at him.

'There's no generator,' he said.

She looked at the gun and looked at him, drawing a deep breath through flaring nostrils.

'Why the hate do you——' he said, and she swept back the gun and threw it at him; he raised his hands and it hit him in the chest, making pain and no air in him.

'*Go* with you?' she said, '*Fuck* with you? After you killed him? Are you—are you *fou*, you green-eyed cochon, chien, bâtard!'

He held his chest, found breath. 'Didn't kill him!' he said. 'He killed *himself*, Lilac! Christ and——'

'Because you lied to him! Lied about us! Told him we'd been——'

'That was *his* idea; I *told* him it wasn't true! I told him and he wouldn't believe me!'

'You *admitted* it,' she said. 'He said he didn't care, we deserved each other, and then he tapped off and——'

'Lilac,' he said, 'I swear by my love of the Family, *I told him it wasn't true!*'

'*Then why did he kill himself?*'

'Because he knew!'

'Because you told him!' she said, and turned and grabbed up her bike—its basket was packed—and rammed it against the branches piled at the place's front.

He ran and caught the back of the bike, held it with both hands. 'You stay here!' he said.

'Let go of it!' she said, turning.

He took the bike at its middle, wrenched it away from her, and flung it aside. He grabbed her arm. She hit at him but he held her. 'He knew about the *islands*!' he said. 'The *islands*! He'd *been* near one, traded with the members! That's how I know they come ashore!'

She stared at him. 'What are you talking about?' she said.

'He'd had an assignment near one of the islands,' he said. 'The Falklands, off Arg. And he'd met the members and traded with them. He hadn't told us because he knew we would want to go, and *he didn't* want to! That's why he killed himself! He knew you were going to find out, from me, and he was ashamed of himself, and tired, and he wasn't going to be "King" any more.'

'You're lying to me the way you lied to him,' she said, and tore her arm free, her coveralls splitting at the shoulder.

'That's how he got the perfume and tobacco seeds,' he said.

'I don't want to hear you,' she said. 'Or see you. I'm going by myself.' She went to her bike, picked up her kit and the blanket trailing from it.

'Don't be stupid,' he said.

She righted the bike, dumped the kit in the basket, and
jammed the blanket in on top of it. He went to her and held
the bike's seat and handlebar. 'You're not going alone,' he said.

'Oh yes I am,' she said, her voice quavering. They held the bike
between them. Her face was blurred in the growing darkness.

'I'm not going to let you,' he said.

'I'll do what *he* did before I go with *you*.'

'You listen to me, you——' he said. 'I could have been on one
of the islands half a year ago! I was on my way and I turned
back, because I didn't want to leave you dead and brainless!' He
put his hand on her chest and pushed her hard, sent her back
flat against rock wall and slung the bike rolling and bumping
away. He went to her and held her arms against the rock. 'I came
all the way from Usa,' he said, 'and I haven't enjoyed this animal
life any more than you have. I don't give a fight whether you
love me or hate me'—'I hate you,' she said—'you're going to
stay with me! The gun doesn't work but other things do, like
rocks and hands. You won't have to kill yourself because——'
Pain burst in his groin—her knee—and she was away from him
and at the branches, a pale yellow shape, thrashing, pushing.

He went and caught her by the arm, swung her around, and
threw her shrieking to the ground. '*Bâtard!*' she shrieked. '*You
sick aggressive*——' and he dived onto her and clapped his hand
over her mouth, clamped it down as tight as he could. Her teeth
caught the skin of his palm and bit it, bit it harder. Her legs
kicked and her fisted hands hit his head. He got a knee on her
thigh, a foot on her other ankle; caught her wrist, let the other
hand hit him, her teeth go on biting. 'Someone might be here!'
he said. 'It's Saturday night! Do you want to get us *both* treated,
you stupid garce?' She kept hitting him, biting his palm.

The hitting slowed and stopped; her teeth parted, let go. She
lay panting, watching him. 'Garce!' he said. She tried to move the
leg under his foot, but he bore down harder against it. He kept
holding her wrist and covering her mouth. His palm felt as if
she had bitten flesh out of it.

Having her under him, having her subdued, with her legs
held apart, suddenly excited him. He thought of tearing off her
coveralls and 'raping' her. Hadn't she said they should wait till
Saturday night? And maybe it would stop all the cloth about
King, and her hating him; stop the fighting—that was what they
had been doing, *fighting*—and the Français hate-names.

Her eyes looked at him.

He let go of her wrist and took her coveralls where they were
split at the shoulder. He tore them down across her chest and she
began hitting him again and straining her legs and biting his
palm.

He tore the coveralls away in stretching splitting pieces until
her whole front was open, and then he felt her; felt her soft

fluid breasts and her stomach's smoothness, her mound with a few close-lying hairs on it, the moist lips below. Her hands hit his head and clutched at his hair; her teeth bit his palm. He kept feeling her with his other hand—breasts, stomach, mound, lips; stroking, rubbing, fingering, growing more excited—and then he opened his coveralls. Her leg wrenched out from under his foot and kicked. She rolled, trying to throw him off her, but he pressed her back down, held her thigh, and threw his leg over hers. He mounted squarely atop her, his feet on her ankles locking her legs bent outward around his knees. He ducked his loins and thrust himself at her; caught one of her hands and fingers of the other. 'Stop,' he said, 'stop,' and kept thrusting. She bucked and squirmed, bit deeper into his palm. He found himself partway inside her; pushed, and was all the way in. 'Stop,' he said, 'stop.' He moved his length slowly; let go of her hands and found her breasts beneath him. He caressed their softness, and stiffening nipples. She bit his hand and squirmed. 'Stop,' he said, 'stop it, Lilac.' He moved himself slowly in her, then faster and harder.

He got up onto his knees and looked at her. She lay with one arm over her eyes and the other thrown back, her breasts rising and falling.

He stood up and found one of his blankets, shook it out and spread it over her up to her arms. 'Are you all right?' he asked, crouching beside her.

She didn't say anything.

He found his flashlight and looked at his palm. Blood was running from an oval of bright wounds. 'Christ and Wei,' he said. He poured water over it, washed it with soap, and dried it. He looked for the first-aid kit and couldn't find it. 'Did you take the first-aid kit?' he asked.

She didn't say anything.

Holding his hand up, he found her kit on the ground and opened it and got out the first-aid kit. He sat on a stone and put the kit in his lap and the flashlight on another stone.

'Animal,' she said.

'I don't bite,' he said. 'And I also don't try to kill. Christ and Wei, you thought the gun was working.' He sprayed healer on his palm; a thin coat and then a thicker one.

'Cochon,' she said.

'Oh come on,' he said, 'don't start that again.'

He unwrapped a bandage and heard her getting up, heard her coveralls rustling as she took them off. She came over nude and took the flashlight and went to her kit, took out soap, a towel, and coveralls, and went to the back of the place, where he had piled stones between the spurs, making steps leading out toward the stream.

He put the bandage on in the dark and then found her flashlight on the ground near her bike. He put the bike with his, gathered blankets and made the two usual sleeping places, put her kit by hers, and picked up the gun and the pieces of her coveralls. He put the gun in his kit.

The moon slid over one of the spurs behind leaves that were black and motionless.

She didn't come back and he began to worry that she had gone away on foot.

Finally, though, she came. She put the soap and towel into her kit and switched off the flashlight and got between her blankets.

'I got excited having you under me that way,' he said. 'I've always wanted you, and these last few weeks have been just about unbearable. You know I love you, don't you?'

'I'm going alone,' she said.

'When we get to Majorca,' he said, 'if we get there, you can do what you want; but *until* we get there we're staying together. That's *it*, Lilac.'

She didn't say anything.

He woke hearing strange sounds, squeals and pained whimpers.

He sat up and shone the light on her; her hand was over her mouth, and tears were running down her temple from her closed eyes.

He hurried to her and crouched beside her, touching her head. 'Oh Lilac, don't,' he said. 'Don't cry, Lilac, please don't.' She was doing it, he thought, because he had hurt her, maybe internally.

She kept crying.

'Oh Lilac, I'm sorry!' he said. 'I'm sorry, love! Oh Christ and Wei, I wish the gun *had* been working!'

She shook her head, holding her mouth.

'Isn't that why you're crying?' he said. 'Because I hurt you? Then why? If you don't want to go with me, you don't really have to.'

She shook her head again and kept crying.

He didn't know what to do. He stayed beside her, caressing her head and asking her why she was crying and telling her not to, and then he got his blankets, spread them alongside her, and lay down and turned her to him and held her. She kept crying, and he woke up and she was looking at him, lying on her side with her head propped on her hand. 'It doesn't make sense for us to go separately,' she said, 'so we'll stay together.'

He tried to recall what they had said before sleeping. As far as he could remember, nothing; she had been crying. 'All right,' he said, confused.

'I feel awful about the gun,' she said. 'How could I have done that? I was sure you had lied to King.'

'I feel awful about what *I* did,' he said.

'Don't,' she said. 'I don't blame you. It was perfectly natural. How's your hand?'

He took it out from under the blanket and flexed it; it hurt badly. 'Not bad,' he said.

She took it in her hand and looked at the bandage. 'Did you spray it?' she asked.

'Yes,' he said.

She looked at him, still holding his hand. Her eyes were large and brown and morning-bright. 'Did you really start for one of the islands and turn back?' she asked.

He nodded.

She smiled. 'You're très fou,' she said.

'No I'm not,' he said.

'You are,' she said, and looked at his hand again. She took it to her lips and kissed his fingertips one by one.

4

THEY DIDN'T GET STARTED until mid-morning, and then they rode quickly for a long while to make up for their laxness. It was an odd day, hazy and heavy-aired, the sky greenish gray and the sun a white disc that could be looked at with fully opened eyes. It was a freak of climate control; Lilac remembered a similar day in Chi when she was twelve or thirteen. ('Is that where you were born?' 'No, I was born in Mex.' 'You were? I was, too!') There were no shadows, and bikes coming toward them seemed to ride above the ground like cars. Members glanced at the sky apprehensively, and coming nearer, nodded without smiling.

When they were sitting on grass, sharing a container of coke, Chip said, 'We'd better go slowly from now on. There are liable to be scanners in the path and we want to be able to pick the right moment for passing them.'

'Scanners because of us?' she said.

'Not necessarily,' he said. 'Just because it's the city nearest to one of the islands. Wouldn't *you* set up extra safeguards if you were Uni?'

He wasn't as much afraid of scanners as he was that a medical team might be waiting ahead.

'What if there are members watching for us?' she said. 'Advisers or doctors, with pictures of us.'

'It's not very likely after all this time,' he said. 'We'll have to take our chances. I've got the gun, and the knife, too.' He touched his pocket.

After a moment she said, 'Would you use it?'

'Yes,' he said. 'I think so.'

'I hope we don't have to,' she said.

'So do I.'

'You'd better put your sunglasses on,' she said.

'Today?' He looked at the sky.

'Because of your eye.'

'Oh,' he said. 'Of course.' He took his glasses out and put them on, looked at her and smiled. 'There's not much that you can do,' he said, 'except exhale.'

'What do you mean?' she said, then flushed and said, 'They're not noticeable when I'm dressed.'

'First thing I saw when I looked at you,' he said. 'First *things* I saw.'

'I don't believe you,' she said. 'You're lying. You are. Aren't you?'

He laughed and poked her on the chin.

They rode slowly. There were no scanners in the path. No medical team stopped them.

All the bicycles in the area were new ones, but nobody remarked on their old ones.

By late afternoon they were in '12082. They rode to the west of the city, smelling the sea, watching the path ahead carefully.

They left their bikes in parkland and walked back to a canteen where there were steps leading down to the beach. The sea was far below them, spreading away smooth and blue, away and away into greenish-gray haze.

'Those members didn't touch,' a child said.

Lilac's hand tightened on Chip's. 'Keep going,' he said. They walked down concrete steps jutting from rough cliff-face.

'Say, you there!' a member called, a man. 'You two members!'

Chip squeezed Lilac's hand and they turned around. The member was standing behind the scanner at the top of the steps, holding the hand of a naked girl of five or six. She scratched her head with a red shovel, looking at them.

'Did you touch just now?' the member asked.

They looked at each other and at the member. 'Of course we did,' Chip said. 'Yes, of course,' Lilac said.

'It didn't say yes,' the girl said.

'It did, sister,' Chip said gravely. 'If it hadn't we wouldn't have gone on, would we?' He looked at the member and let a smile show. The member bent and said something to the girl.

'No I *didn't*,' she said.

'Come on,' Chip said to Lilac, and they turned and walked downward again.

'Little hater,' Lilac said, and Chip said, 'Just keep going.'

They went all the way down and stopped at the bottom to take off their sandals. Chip, bending, looked up: the member and the girl were gone; other members were coming down.

The beach was half empty under the strange hazy sky. Members sat and lay on blankets, many of them in their coveralls.

They were silent or talked softly, and the music of the speakers—
'Sunday, Fun Day'—sounded loud and unnatural. A group of
children jumped rope by the water's edge: 'Christ, Marx, Wood,
and Wei, lead us to this perfect day; Marx, Wood, Wei, and
Christ——'

They walked westward, holding hands and holding their sandals. The narrow beach grew narrower, emptier. Ahead a scanner
stood flanked by cliff and sea. Chip said, 'I've never seen one on
a beach before.'

'Neither have I,' Lilac said.

They looked at each other.

'This is the way we'll go,' he said. 'Later.'

She nodded and they walked closer to the scanner.

'I've got a fou impulse to touch it,' he said. ' "Fight you, Uni;
here I am." '

'Don't you dare,' she said.

'Don't worry,' he said, 'I won't.'

They turned around and walked back to the center of the
beach. They took their coveralls off, went into the water, and
swam far out. Treading with their backs to the sea, they studied
the shore beyond the scanner, the gray cliffs lessening away into
greenish-gray haze. A bird flew from the cliffs, circled, and flew
back. It disappeared, gone in a hairline cranny.

'There are probably caves where we can stay,' Chip said.

A lifeguard whistled and waved at them. They swam back to
the beach.

'It's five of five, members,' the speakers said. 'Litter and towels
in the baskets, please. Be mindful of the members around you
when you shake out your blankets.'

They dressed, went back up the steps, and walked to the grove
of trees where they had left their bikes. They carried them
farther in and sat down to wait. Chip cleaned the compass and
the flashlights and the knife, and Lilac packed the other things
they had into a single bundle.

An hour or so after dark they went to the canteen and gathered
a carton of cakes and drinks and went down to the beach again.
They walked to the scanner and beyond it. The night was moonless and starless; the haze of the day was still above. In the water's
lapping edge phosphorescent sparks glittered now and then;
otherwise there was only darkness. Chip held the carton of cakes
and drinks under his arm and shone his flashlight ahead of them
every few moments. Lilac carried the blanket-bundle.

'Traders won't come ashore on a night like this,' she said.

'Nobody else will be on the beach either,' Chip said. 'No sex-
wild twelve-year-olds. It's a good thing.'

But it wasn't, he thought; it was a bad thing. What if the haze
remained for days, for nights, blocking them at the very brink of

freedom? Was it possible that Uni had *created* it, intentionally, for just that purpose? He smiled at himself. He was très fou, exactly as Lilac had said.

They walked until they guessed themselves to be midway between '082 and the next city to the west, and then they put down the carton and the bundle and searched the cliff face for a usable cave. They found one within minutes; a low-roofed sand-floored burrow littered with cake wrappers and, intriguingly, two pieces—a green 'Egypt', a pink 'Ethip'—torn from a pre-U map. They brought the carton and the bundle into the cave, spread their blankets, ate, and lay down together.

'Can you?' Lilac said. 'After this morning and last night?'

'Without treatments,' Chips said, 'all things are possible.'

'It's fantastic,' Lilac said.

Later Chip said, 'even if we don't get any farther than this, even if we're caught and treated five minutes from now, it'll have been worth it. We've been ourselves, alive, for a few hours at least.'

'I want all of my life, not just a little of it,' Lilac said.

'You'll have it,' Chip said. 'I promise you.' He kissed her lips, caressing her cheek in the darkness. 'Will you stay with me?' he asked. 'On Majorca?'

'Of course,' she said. 'Why shouldn't I?'

'You weren't going to,' he said. 'Remember? You weren't even going to come this far with me.'

'Christ and Wei, that was *last night*,' she said, and kissed him. 'Of course I'm going to stay,' she said. 'You woke me up and now you're stuck with me.'

They lay holding each other and kissing each other.

'Chip!' she cried—in reality, not in his dream.

She was beside him. He sat up and banged his head on stone, groped for the knife he had left stuck in the sand. 'Chip! Look!' —as he found it and threw himself over onto knees and one hand. She was a dark shape crouched at the cave's blinding blue opening. He raised the knife, ready to slash whoever was coming.

'No, no,' she said, laughing. 'Come look! Come on! You won't believe it!'

Squinting at the brilliance of sky and sea, he crawled over to her. 'Look,' she said happily, pointing up the beach.

A boat sat on the sand about fifty meters away, a small two-rotor launch, old, with a white hull and a red skirting. It sat just clear of the water, tipped slightly forward. There were white splatters on the skirting and the windscreen, part of which seemed to be missing.

'Let's see if it's good!' Lilac said. With her hand on Chip's shoulder she started to rise from the cave; he dropped the knife, caught her arm, and pulled her back. 'Wait a minute,' he said.

'What for?' She looked at him.

He rubbed his head where he had bumped it, and frowned at the boat—so white and red and empty and convenient in the bright morning haze-free sun. 'It's a trick of some kind,' he said. 'A trap. It's too convenient. We go to sleep and wake up and a boat's been delivered for us. You're right, I *don't* believe it.'

'It wasn't "delivered" for us,' she said. 'It's been here for weeks. Look at the bird stuff on it, and how deep in the sand the front of it is.'

'Where did it come from?' he asked. 'There are no islands nearby.'

'Maybe traders brought it from Majorca and got caught on shore,' she said. 'Or maybe they left it behind on purpose, for members like us. You said there might be a rescue operation.'

'And nobody's seen it and reported it in the time it's been here?'

'Uni hasn't let anyone onto this part of the beach.'

'Let's wait,' he said. 'Let's just watch and wait a while.'

Reluctantly she said, 'All right.'

'It's too convenient,' he said.

'Why must everything be *in*convenient?'

They stayed in the cave. They ate and rebundled the blankets, always watching the boat. They took turns crawling to the back of the cave, and buried their wastes in sand.

Wave edges slipped under the back of the boat's skirting, then fell away toward low tide. Birds circled and landed on the windscreen and handrail, four that were sea gulls and two smaller brown ones.

'It's getting filthier every minute,' Lilac said. 'And what if it's *been* reported and today's the day it's going to be taken away?'

'Whisper, will you?' Chip said. 'Christ and Wei, I wish I'd brought a telescope.'

He tried to improvise one from the compass lens, a flashlight lens, and a rolled flap of the food carton, but he couldn't make it work.

'How long are we going to wait?' she asked.

'Till after dark,' he said.

No one passed on the beach, and the only sounds were the waves' lapping and the wingbeats and cries of the birds.

He went to the boat alone, slowly and cautiously. It was older than it had looked from the cave; the hull's flaking white paint showed repair scars, and the skirting was dented and cracked. He walked around it without touching it, looking with his flashlight for signs—he didn't know what form they would take—of deception, of danger. He didn't see any; he saw only an old boat that had been inexplicably abandoned, its center seats gone, a third of its windscreen broken away, and all of it spattered with dried white birdwaste. He switched his light off and looked at the cliff—touched the boat's handrail and waited for an alarm. The cliff stayed dark and deserted in pale moonlight.

He stepped on to the skirting, climbed into the boat, and shone his light on its controls. They seemed simple enough: on-off switches for the propulsion rotors and the lift rotor, a speed-control knob calibrated to 100 KPH, a steering lever, a few gauges and indicators, and a switch marked *Controlled* and *Independent* that was set in the independent position. He found the battery housing on the floor between the front seats and unlatched its cover; the battery's fade-out date was April 171, a year away.

He shone his light at the rotor housings. Twigs were piled in one of them. He brushed them out, picked them all out, and shone the light on the rotor within; it was new, shiny. The other rotor was old, its blades nicked and one missing.

He sat down at the controls and found the switch that lighted them. A miniature clock said 5.11 *Fri 27 Aug* 169. He switched on one propulsion rotor and then the other; they scraped but then hummed smoothly. He switched them off, looked at the gauges and indicators, and switched the control lights off.

The cliff was the same as before. No members had sprung from hiding. He turned to the sea behind him; it was empty and flat, silvered in a narrowing path that ended under the nearly full moon. No boats were flying toward him.

He sat in the boat for a few minutes, and then he climbed out of it and walked back to the cave.

Lilac was standing outside it. 'Is it all right?' she asked.

'No, it's not,' he said. 'It wasn't left by traders because there's no message or anything in it. The clock stopped last year but it has a new rotor. I didn't try the lift rotor because of the sand, but even if it works, the skirting is cracked in two places and it may just wallow and get nowhere. On the other hand it may take us directly into '082—to a little seaside medicenter—even though it's supposed to be off telecontrol.'

Lilac stood looking at him.

'We might as well try it though,' he said. 'If traders didn't leave it, they're not going to come ashore while it's sitting here. Maybe we're just two very lucky members.' He gave the flashlight to her.

He got the carton and the blanket-bundle from the cave and held one under each arm. They started walking toward the boat. 'What about the things to trade?' she said.

'We'll have *it*,' he said. 'A boat must be worth a hundred times more than cameras and first-aid kits.' He looked toward the cliff. 'All right, doctors!' he called. 'You can come out now!'

'Shh, *don't*!' she said.

'We forgot the sandals,' he said.

'They're in the carton.'

He put the carton and the bundle into the boat and they scraped the birdwaste from the broken windscreen with pieces of shell.

They lifted the front of the boat and hauled it around toward the sea, then lifted the back and hauled again.

They kept lifting and hauling at either end and finally they had the boat down in the surf, bobbing and veering clumsily. Chip held it while Lilac climbed aboard, and then he pushed it farther out and climbed in with her.

He sat down at the controls and switched on their lights. She sat in the seat beside him, watching. He glanced at her—she looked anxiously at him—and he switched on the propulsion rotors and then the lift rotor. The boat shook violently, flinging them from side to side. Loud clankings banged from beneath it. He caught the steering lever, held it, and turned the speed-control knob. The boat splashed forward and the shaking and clanging lessened. He turned the speed higher, to twenty, twenty-five. The clanking stopped and the shaking subsided to a steady vibration. The boat scuffed along on the water's surface.

'It's not lifting,' he said.

'But it's moving,' she said.

'For how long though? It's not built to hit the water this way and the skirting's cracked already.' He turned the speed higher and the boat splashed through the crests of swells. He tried the steering lever; the boat responded. He steered north, got out his compass, and compared its reading with the direction indicator's. 'It's not taking us into '082,' he said. 'At least not yet.'

She looked behind them, and up at the sky. 'No one's coming,' she said.

He turned the speed higher and got a little more lift, but the impact when they scraped the swells was greater. He turned the speed back down. The knob was at fifty-six. 'I don't think we're doing more than forty,' he said. 'It'll be light when we get there, *if* we get there. It's just as well, I suppose; I won't get us on to the wrong island. I don't know how much this is throwing us off course.'

Two other islands were near Majorca: EUR91766, forty kilometers to the northeast, the site of a copper-production complex; and EUR91603, eighty-five kilometers to the southwest, where there was an algae-processing complex and a climatonomy sub-center.

Lilac leaned close to Chip, avoiding the wind and spray from the broken part of the windscreen. Chip held the steering lever. He watched the direction indicator and the moonlit sea ahead and the stars that shone above the horizon.

The stars dissolved, the sky began to lighten, and there was no

Majorca. There was only the sea, placid and endless all around them.

'If we're doing forty,' Lilac said, 'it should have taken seven hours. It's been more than that, hasn't it?'

'Maybe we haven't been doing forty,' Chip said.

Or maybe he had compensated too much or too little for the eastward drift of the sea. Maybe they had passed Majorca and were heading toward Eur. Or maybe Majorca didn't exist—had been blanked from pre-U maps because pre-U members had 'bombed' it to nothing and why should the Family be reminded again of folly and barbarism?

He kept the boat headed a hairline west of north, but slowed it down a little.

The sky grew lighter and still there was no island, no Majorca. They scanned the horizon silently, avoiding each other's eyes.

One final star glimmered above the water in the northeast. No, glimmered *on* the water. No—'There's a light over there,' he said.

She looked where he pointed, held his arm.

The light moved in an arc from side to side, then up and down as if beckoning. It was a kilometer or so away.

'Christ and Wei,' Chip said softly, and steered toward it.

'Be careful,' Lilac said. 'Maybe it's——'

He changed hands on the steering lever and got the knife from his pocket, laid it in his lap.

The light went out and a small boat was there. Someone sat waving in it, waving a pale thing that he put on his head—a hat—and then waving his empty hand and arm.

'One member,' Lilac said.

'One *person*,' Chip said. He kept steering toward the boat—a rowboat, it looked like—with one hand on the lever and the other on the speed-control knob.

'Look at him!' Lilac said.

The waving man was small and white-bearded, with a ruddy face below his broad-brimmed yellow hat. He was wearing a blue-topped white-legged garment.

Chip slowed the boat, steered it near the rowboat, and switched all three rotors off.

The man—old past sixty-two and blue-eyed, fantastically blue-eyed—smiled with brown teeth and gaps where teeth were missing and said, 'Running from the dummies, are you? Looking for liberty?' His boat bobbed in their sidewaves. Poles and nets shifted in it—fish-catching equipment.

'Yes,' Chip said. 'Yes, we are! We're trying to find Majorca.'

'Majorca?' the man said. He laughed and scratched his beard. 'Myorca,' he said. 'Not Majorca, Myorca! But *Liberty* is what it's called now. It hasn't been called Myorca for—God knows, a hundred years, I guess! Liberty, it is.'

'Are we near it?' Lilac asked, and Chip said, 'We're friends. We haven't come to—interfere in any way, to try to "cure" you or anything.'

'We're incurables ourselves,' Lilac said.

'You wouldn't be coming this way if you wasn't,' the man said. 'That's what I'm here for, to watch for folks like you and help them into port. Yes, you're near it. That's it over there.' He pointed to the north.

And now on the horizon a dark green bar lay low and clear. Pink streaks glowed above its western half—mountains lit by the sun's first rays.

Chip and Lilac looked at it, and looked at each other, and looked again at Majorca-Myorca-Liberty.

'Hold fast,' the man said, 'and I'll tie on to your stern and come aboard.'

They turned in their seats and faced each other. Chip took the knife from his lap, smiled, and tossed it to the floor. He took Lilac's hands.

They smiled at each other.

'I thought we'd gone past it,' she said.

'So did I,' he said. 'Or that it didn't even exist any more.'

They smiled at each other, and leaned forward and kissed each other.

'Hey, give me a hand here, will you?' the man said, looking at them over the back of the boat, clinging with dirty-nailed fingers.

They got up quickly and went to him. Chip kneeled on the back seat and helped him over.

His clothes were made of cloth, his hat woven of flat strips of yellow fibre. He was half a head shorter than they and smelled strangely and strongly. Chip grasped his hard-skinned hand and shook it. 'I'm Chip,' he said, 'and this is Lilac.'

'Glad to meet you,' the bearded blue-eyed old man said, smiling his ugly-toothed smile. 'I'm Darren Costanza.' He shook Lilac's hand.

'Darren Costanza?' Chip said.

'That's the name.'

'It's beautiful!' Lilac said.

'You've got a good boat here,' Darren Costanza said, looking about.

'It doesn't lift,' Chip said, and Lilac said, 'But it got us here. We were lucky to find it.'

Darren Costanza smiled at them 'And your pockets are filled with cameras and things?' he said.

'No,' Chip said, 'we decided not to take anything. The tide was in and——'

'Oh, that was a mistake,' Darren Costanza said. 'Didn't you take *anything*?'

'A gun without a generator,' Chip said, taking it from his pocket. 'And a few books and a razor in the bundle there.'

'Well, this is worth something,' Darren Costanza said, taking the gun and looking at it, thumbing its handle.

'We'll have the boat to trade,' Lilac said.

'You should have taken more,' Darren Costanza said, turning from them and moving away. They glanced at each other and looked at him again, about to follow, but he turned, holding the gun. He pointed it at them and put Chip's gun into his pocket. 'This old thing shoots bullets,' he said, backing farther away to the front seats. 'Doesn't need a generator,' he said. 'Bang, bang. Into the water now, real quick. Go on. Into the water.'

They looked at him.

'*Get in the water, you dumb steelies!*' he shouted. 'You want a bullet in your head?' He moved something at the back of the gun and pointed it at Lilac.

Chip pushed her to the side of the boat. She clambered over the rail and on to the skirting—saying 'What is he doing this for?'—and slipped down into the water. Chip jumped in after her.

'Away from the boat!' Darren Costanza shouted. 'Clear away! Swim!'

They swam a few meters, their coveralls ballooning around them, then turned, treading water.

'What are you *doing* this for?' Lilac asked.

'Figure it out for yourself, steely!' Darren Costanza said, sitting at the boat's controls.

'We'll drown if you leave us!' Chip cried. 'We can't swim that far!'

'Who told you to come here?' Darren Costanza said, and the boat rushed splashing away, the rowboat dragging from its back carving up fins of foam.

'You fighting brother-hater!' Chip shouted. The boat turned toward the eastern tip of the far-off island.

'He's taking it himself!' Lilac said. '*He's* going to trade it!'

'The sick selfish pre-U——' Chip said. 'Christ, Marx, Wood, and Wei, I had the knife in my hand and I threw it on the floor! "Waiting to help us into port"! He's a *pirate*, that's what he is, the fighting——'

'Stop! Don't!' Lilac said, and looked at him despairingly.

'Oh Christ and Wei,' he said.

They pulled open their coveralls and squirmed themselves out of them. 'Keep them!' Chip said. 'They'll hold air if we tie the openings!'

'Another boat!' Lilac said.

A speck of white was speeding from west to east, midway between them and the island.

She waved her coveralls.

'Too far!' Chip said. 'We've got to start swimming!'

They tied the sleeves of their coveralls around their necks and swam against the chilly water. The island was impossibly far away—twenty or more kilometers.

If they could take short rests against the inflated coveralls, Chip thought, they could get far enough in so that another boat might see them. But who would be on it? Members like Darren Costanza? Foul-smelling *pirates* and *murderers*? Had King been right? *'I hope you get there,'* King said, lying in his bed with his eyes closed. *'The two of you. You deserve it.'* Fight that brother-hater!

The second boat had got near their pirated one, which was heading farther east as if to avoid it.

Chip swam steadily, glimpsing Lilac swimming beside him. Would they get enough rest to go on, to make it? Or would they drown, choke, slide languidly downward through darkening water . . . He drove the image from his mind; swam and kept swimming.

The second boat had stopped; their own was farther from it than before. But the second boat seemed bigger now, and bigger still.

He stopped and caught Lilac's leg. She looked around, gasping, and he pointed.

The boat hadn't stopped; it had turned and was coming toward them.

They tugged at the coverall sleeves at their throats, loosed them and waved the light blue, the bright yellow.

The boat turned slightly away, then back, then away in the other direction.

'Here!' they cried, 'Help! Here! Help!'—waving the coveralls, straining high in the water.

The boat turned back and away again, then sharply back. It stayed pointed at them, enlarging, and a horn sounded—loud, loud, loud, loud.

Lilac sank against Chip, coughing water. He ducked his shoulder under her arm and supported her.

The boat came skimming to full-size white closeness—*I.A.* was painted large and green on its hull; it had one rotor—and splatted to a stop with a wave that washed over them. 'Hang on!' a member cried, and something flew in the air and splashed beside them: a floating white ring with a rope. Chip grabbed it and the rope sprang taut, pulled by a member, young, yellow-haired.

He drew them through the water. 'I'm all right.' Lilac said in Chip's arm. 'I'm all right.'

The side of the boat had rungs going up it. Chip pulled Lilac's coveralls from her hand, bent her fingers around a rung, and put her other hand to the rung above. She climbed. The member, leaning over and stretching, caught her hand and helped her. Chip guided her feet and climbed up after her.

They lay on their backs on warm firm floor under scratchy blankets, hand in hand, panting. Their heads were lifted in turn and a small metal container was pressed to their lips. The liquid in it smelled like Darren Costanza. It burned in their throats, but once it was down it warmed their stomachs surprisingly.

'Alcohol?' Chip said.

'Don't worry,' the young yellow-haired man said, smiling down at them with normal teeth as he screwed the container on to a flask, 'one sip won't rot your brain.' He was about twenty-five, with a short beard that was yellow too, and normal eyes and skin. A brown belt at his hips held a gun in a brown pocket; he wore a white cloth shirt without sleeves and tan cloth trousers patched with blue that ended at his knees. Putting the flask on a seat, he unfastened the front of his belt. 'I'll get your coveralls,' he said. 'Catch your breath.' He put the gun-belt with the flask and climbed over the side of the boat. A splash sounded and the boat swayed.

'At least they're not all like that other one,' Chip said.

'He has a gun,' Lilac said.

'But he left it here,' Chip said. 'If he were—sick, he would have been afraid to.'

They lay silently hand in hand under the scratchy blankets, breathing deeply, looking at the clear blue sky.

The boat tilted and the young man climbed back aboard with their dripping coveralls. His hair, which hadn't been clipped in a long time, clung to his head in wet rings. 'Feeling better?' he asked, smiling at them.

'Yes,' they both said.

He shook the coveralls over the side of the boat. 'I'm sorry I wasn't here in time to keep that lunky away from you,' he said. 'Most immigrants come from Eur, so I generally stay to the north. What we need are *two* boats, not one. Or a longer-range spotter.'

'Are you a—policeman?' Chip asked.

'*Me?*' The young man smiled. 'No,' he said, 'I'm with Immigrants' Assistance. That's an agency we've been generously allowed to set up, to help new immigrants get oriented. And get ashore without being drowned.' He hung the coveralls over the boat's railing and pulled apart their clinging folds.

Chip raised himself on his elbows. 'Does this happen often?' he asked.

'Stealing immigrants' boats is a popular local pastime,' the young man said. 'There are others that are even more fun.'

Chip sat up, and Lilac sat up beside him. The young man faced them, pink sunlight gleaming on his side.

'I'm sorry to disappoint you,' he said, 'but you haven't come to any paradise. Four fifths of the island's population is descended from the families who were here before the Unification or who came here right after; they're inbred, ignorant, mean, self-satisfied —and they despise immigrants. "Steelies", they call us. Because of the bracelets. Even after we take them off.'

He took his gun-belt from the seat and put it around his hips. '*We* call *them* "lunkies",' he said, fastening the belt's buckle. 'Only don't ever say it out loud or you'll find five or six of them stamping on your ribs. That's another of their pastimes.'

He looked at them again. 'The island is run by a General Costanza,' he said, 'with the——'

'That's who took the boat!' they said. 'Darren Costanza!'

'I doubt it,' the young man said, smiling. 'The General doesn't get up this early. Your lunky must have been pulling your leg.'

Chip said, 'the *brother*-hater!'

'General Costanza,' the young man said, 'has the Church and the Army behind him. There's very little freedom even for lunkies, and for us there's virtually none. We have to live in specified areas, "Steelytowns", and we can't step outside them without a good reason. We have to show identity cards to every lunky cop, and the only jobs we can get are the lowest, most back-breaking ones.' He took up the flask. 'Do you want some more of this?' he asked. 'It's called "whiskey".'

Chip and Lilac shook their heads.

The young man unscrewed the container and poured amber liquid into it. 'Let's see, what have I left out?' he said. 'We're not allowed to own land or weapons. I turn in my gun when I set foot on shore.' He raised the container and looked at them. 'Welcome to Liberty,' he said, and drank.

They looked disheartenedly at each other, and at the young man.

'That's what they call it,' he said. 'Liberty.'

'We thought they would welcome newcomers,' Chip said. 'To help keep the Family away.'

The young man, screwing the container back on to the flask, said, 'Nobody comes here except two or three immigrants a month. The last time the Family tried to treat the lunkies was back when there were five computers. Since Uni went into operation not one attempt has been made.'

'Why not?' Lilac asked.

The young man looked at them. 'Nobody knows,' he said. 'There are different theories. The lunkies think that either "God" is protecting them or the Family is afraid of the Army, a bunch of drunken incapable louts. Immigrants think—well, some of them think that the island is so depleted that treating everyone on it simply isn't worth Uni's while.'

'And others think——' Chip said.

The young man turned away and put the flask on a shelf below the boat's controls. He sat down on the seat and turned to face them. 'Others,' he said, 'and I'm one of them, think that Uni is *using* the island, *and* the lunkies, and *all* the hidden islands all over the world.'

'*Using* them?' Chip said, and Lilac said, 'How?'

'As prisons for *us*,' the young man said.

They looked at him.

'Why is there always a boat on the beach?' he asked. '*Always*, in Eur and in Afr—an old boat that's still good enough to get here. And why are there those handy patched-up maps in museums? Wouldn't it be easier to make *fake ones* with the islands *really* omitted?'

They stared at him.

'What do you do,' he said, looking at them intently, 'when you're programming a computer to maintain a perfectly efficient, perfectly stable, perfectly cooperative society? How do you allow for biological freaks, "incurables", possible troublemakers?'

They said nothing, staring at him.

He leaned closer to them. 'You leave a few "un-unified" islands all round the world,' he said. 'You leave maps in museums and boats on beaches. The computer doesn't have to weed out your bad ones; *they do the weeding themselves*. They wiggle their way happily into the nearest isolation ward, and *lunkies* are waiting, with a General Costanza in charge, to take their boats, jam them into Steelytowns, and keep them helpless and harmless—in ways that high-minded disciples of Christ, Marx, Wood, and Wei would never *dream* of stooping to.'

'It can't *be*,' Lilac said.

'A lot of us think it can,' the young man said.

Chip said, 'Uni *let us* come here?'

'No.' Lilac said. 'It's too—twisted.'

The young man looked at Chip.

Chip said, 'I thought I was being so fighting clever!'

'So did I,' the young man said, sitting back. 'I know just how you feel.'

'No, it can't be,' Lilac said.

There was silence for a moment, and then the young man said. 'I'll take you in now. I.A. will take off your bracelets and get you registered and lend you twenty-five bucks to get started.' He smiled. 'As bad as it is,' he said, 'it's better than being with the Family. Cloth is more comfortable than paplon—really—and even a rotten fig tastes better than total-cakes. You can have children, a drink, a cigarette—a couple of rooms if you work hard. Some steelies even get rich—entertainers, mostly. If you "sir" the lunkies and stay in Steelytown, it's all right. No scanners, no advisers, and not one "Life of Marx" in a whole year's TV.'

Lilac smiled. Chip smiled too.

'Put the coveralls on,' the young man said. 'Lunkies are horri-
fied by nakedness. It's "ungodly".' He turned to the boat's
controls.

They put aside the blankets and got into their moist coveralls,
then stood behind the young man as he drove the boat toward
the island. It spread out green and gold in the radiance of the
just-risen sun, crested with mountains and dotted with bits of
white, yellow, pink, pale blue.

'It's beautiful,' Lilac said determinedly.

Chip, with his arm about her shoulders, looked ahead with
narrowed eyes and said nothing.

5

THEY LIVED in a city called Pollensa, in half a room in a cracked
and crumbling Steelytown building with intermittent power and
brown water. They had a mattress and a table and a chair, and
a box for their clothing that they used as a second chair. The
people in the other half of the room, the Newmans—a man and
woman in their forties with a nine-year-old daughter—let them
use their stove and TV and a shelf in the 'fridge' where they
stored their food. It was the Newmans' room; Chip and Lilac paid
four dollars a week for their half of it.

They earned nine dollars and twenty cents a week between
them. Chip worked in an iron mine, loading ore into carts with
a crew of other immigrants alongside an automatic loader that
stood motionless and dusty, unrepairable. Lilac worked in a
clothing factory, attaching fasteners to shirts. There too a machine
stood motionless, furred with lint.

Their nine dollars and twenty cents paid for the week's rent
and food and railfare, a few cigarettes, and a newspaper called
the *Liberty Immigrant*. They saved fifty cents toward clothing
replacement and emergencies that might arise, and gave fifty
cents to Immigrants' Assistance as partial repayment of the
twenty-five-dollar loan they had been given on their arrival. They
ate bread and fish and potatoes and figs. At first these foods gave
them cramps and constipation, but they soon came to like them,
to relish the different tastes and consistencies. They looked forward to meals, although the preparation and the cleaning up
afterward became a bother.

Their bodies changed. Lilac's bled for a few days, which the
Newmans assured them was natural in untreated women, and
it grew more rounded and supple as her hair grew longer. Chip's
body hardened and strengthened from his work in the mine. His
beard grew out black and straight, and he trimmed it once a
week with the Newmans' scissors.

They had been given names by a clerk at the Immigration Bureau. Chip was named Eiko Newmart, and Lilac, Grace Newbridge. Later, when they married—with no application to Uni, but with forms and a fee and vows to 'God'—Lilac's name was changed to Grace Newmark. They still called themselves Chip and Lilac, however.

They got used to handling coins and dealing with shopkeepers, and to traveling on Pollensa's rundown overcrowded monorail. They learned how to sidestep natives and avoid offending them; they memorized the Vow of Loyalty and saluted Liberty's red-and-yellow flag. They knocked on doors before opening them, said *Wednesday* instead of Woodsday, *March* instead of Marx. They reminded themselves that *fight* and *hate* were acceptable words but *fuck* was a 'dirty' one.

Hassan Newman drank a great deal of whiskey. Soon after coming home from his job—in the island's largest furniture factory—he would be playing loud games with Gigi, his daughter, and fumbling his way through the room's dividing curtain with a bottle clutched in his three-fingered saw-damaged hand. 'Come on, you sad steelies,' he would say, 'where the hate are your glasses? Come on, have a little cheer.' Chip and Lilac drank with him a few times, but they found that whiskey made them confused and clumsy and they usually declined his offer. 'Come on,' he said one evening. 'I know I'm the landlord, but I'm not exactly a lunky, am I? Or what is it? Do you think I'll expect you to receep—to reci*p*rocate? I know you like to watch the plinnies.'

'It's not that,' Chip said.

'Then what is it?' Hassan asked. He swayed and steadied himself.

Chip didn't say anything for a moment, and then he said, 'Well, what's the point in getting away from treatments if you're going to dull yourself with whiskey? You might as well be back in the Family.'

'Oh,' Hassan said. 'Oh sure, I get you.' He looked angrily at them, a broad, curly-bearded, bloodshot-eyed man. 'Just wait,' he said. 'Wait till you've been here a little longer. Just wait till you've been here a little longer, that's all.' He turned around and groped his way through the curtain, and they heard him muttering, and his wife, Ria, speaking placatingly.

Almost everyone in the building seemed to drink as much whiskey as Hassan did. Loud voices, happy or angry, sounded through the walls at all hours of the night. The elevator and the hallways smelled of whiskey, and of fish, and of sweet perfumes that people used against the whiskey and fish smells.

Most evenings, after they had finished whatever cleaning had to be done, Chip and Lilac either went up to the roof for some fresh air or sat at their table reading the *Immigrant* or books they

had found on the monorail or borrowed from a small collection
at Immigrants' Assistance. Sometimes they watched TV with the
Newmans—plays about foolish misunderstandings in native
families, with frequent stops for announcements about different
makes of cigarettes and disinfectants. Occasionally there were
speeches by General Costanza or the head of the Church, Pope
Clement—disquieting speeches about shortages of food and space
and resources, for which immigrants alone weren't to be blamed.
Hassan, belligerent with whiskey, usually switched them off before they were over; Liberty TV, unlike the Family's, could be
switched on and off at one's choosing.

One day in the mine, toward the end of the fifteen-minute
lunch break, Chip went over to the automatic loader and began
examining it, wondering whether it was in fact unrepairable or
whether some part of it that couldn't be replaced might not be
by-passed or substituted for in some way. The native in charge
of the crew came over and asked him what he was doing. Chip
told him, taking care to speak respectfully, but the native got
angry. 'You fucking steelies all think you're so God-damned
smart!' he said, and put his hand on his gun handle. 'Get over
there where you belong and stay there!' he said. 'Try to figure
out a way to eat less food if you've got to have something to think
about!'

All natives weren't quite that bad. The owner of their building
took a liking to Chip and Lilac and promised to let them have
a room for five dollars a week as soon as one became available.
'You're not like some of these others,' he said. 'Drinking, walking
around the hallways stark naked—I'd rather take a few cents less
and have your kind.'

Chip, looking at him, said, 'There are reasons why immigrants
drink, you know.'

'I know, I know,' the owner said. 'I'm the first one to say it;
it's terrible the way we treat you. But still and all, do *you* drink?
Do *you* walk around stark naked?'

Lilac said, 'Thank you, Mr Corsham. We'll be grateful if you
can get a room for us.'

They caught 'colds' and 'the flu'. Lilac lost her job at the
clothing factory but found a better one in the kitchen of a native
restaurant within walking distance of the house. Two policemen
came to the room one evening, checking identity cards and looking for weapons. Hassan muttered something as he showed his
card and they clubbed him to the floor. They stuck knives into
the mattresses and broke some of the dishes.

Lilac didn't have her 'period', her monthly few days of vaginal
bleeding, and that meant she was pregnant.

One night on the roof Chip stood smoking and looking at the
sky to the northeast, where there was a dull orange glow from
the copper-production complex on EUR91766. Lilac, who had

been taking washed clothes from a line where she had hung them to dry, came over to him and put her arm around him. She kissed his cheek and leaned against him. 'It's not so bad,' she said. 'We've got twelve dollars saved, we'll have a room of our own any day now, and before you know it we'll have a baby.'

'A steely,' Chip said.

'No,' Lilac said. 'A baby.'

'It stinks,' Chip said. 'It's rotten. It's inhuman.'

'It's all there is,' Lilac said. 'We'd better get used to it.'

Chip said nothing. He kept looking at the orange glow in the sky.

The *Liberty Immigrant* carried weekly articles about immigrant singers and athletes, and occasionally scientists, who earned forty or fifty dollars a week and lived in good apartments, who mixed with influential and enlightened natives, and who were hopeful about the chances of a more equitable relationship developing between the two groups. Chip read these articles with scorn—they were meant by the newspaper's native owners to lull and pacify immigrants, he felt—but Lilac accepted them at face value, as evidence that their own lot would ultimately improve.

One week in October, when they had been on Liberty for a little over six months, there was an article about an artist named Morgan Newgate, who had come from Eur eight years before and who lived in a four-room apartment in New Madrid. His paintings, one of which, a scene of the Crucifixion, had just been presented to Pope Clement, brought him as much as a hundred dollars each. He signed them with an *A*, the article explained, because his nickname was Ashi.

'Christ and Wei,' Chip said.

Lilac said, 'What is it?'

'I was at academy with this "Morgan Newgate",' Chip said, showing her the article. 'We were good friends. His name was Karl. You remember that picture of the horse I had back in Ind?'

'No,' she said, reading.

'Well, he drew it,' Chip said. 'He used to sign everything with an *A* in a circle.' And yes, he thought, 'Ashi' seemed like the name Karl had mentioned. Christ and Wei, so he had got away too!—had 'got away', if you could call it that, to Liberty, to Uni's isolation ward. At least he was doing what he'd always wanted; for him Liberty really *was* liberty.

'You ought to call him,' Lilac said, still reading.

'I will,' Chip said.

But maybe he wouldn't. Was there any point, really, in calling 'Morgan Newgate', who painted Crucifixions for the Pope and assured his fellow immigrants that conditions were getting better every day? But maybe Karl hadn't said that; maybe the *Immigrant* had lied.

'Don't just say it,' Lilac said. 'He could probably help you get a better job.'

'Yes,' Chip said, 'he probably could.'

She looked at him. 'What's the matter?' she said. 'Don't you want a better job?'

'I'll call him tomorrow, on the way to work,' he said.

But he didn't. He swung his shovel into ore and lifted and heaved, swung and lifted and heaved. *Fight them all,* he thought: *the steelies who drink, the steelies who think things are getting better; the lunkies, the dummies; fight Uni.*

On the following Sunday morning Lilac went with him to a building two blocks from theirs where there was a working telephone in the lobby, and she waited while he paged through the tattered directory. *Morgan* and *Newgate* were names commonly given to immigrants, but few immigrants had phones; there was only one *Newgate, Morgan* listed, and that one in New Madrid.

Chip put three tokens into the phone and spoke the number. The screen was broken, but it didn't make any difference since Liberty phones no longer transmitted pictures anyway.

A woman answered, and when Chip asked if Morgan Newgate was there, said he was, and then nothing more. The silence lengthened, and Lilac, a few meters away beside a Sani-Spray poster, waited and then came close. 'Isn't he there?' she asked in a whisper. 'Hello?' a man's voice said.

'Is this Morgan Newgate?' Chip asked.

'Yes. Who's this?'

'It's Chip,' Chip said. 'Li RM, from the Academy of the Genetic Sciences.'

There was silence, and then, 'My God,' the voice said, 'Li! You got pads and charcoal for me!'

'Yes,' Chip said. 'And I told my adviser you were sick and needed help.'

Karl laughed. 'That's right, you did, you bastard!' he said. 'This is great! When did you get over?'

'About six months ago,' Chip said.

'Are you in New Madrid?'

'Pollensa.'

'What are you doing?'

'Working in a mine,' Chip said.

'Christ, that's a shut-off,' Karl said, and after a moment, 'It's hell here, isn't it?'

'Yes,' Chip said, thinking *He even uses their words. Hell. My God I'll bet he says prayers.*

'I wish these phones were working so I could get a look at you,' Karl said.

Suddenly Chip was ashamed of his hostility. He told Karl about Lilac and about her pregnancy; Karl told him that he had been married in the Family but had come over alone. He wouldn't let Chip congratulate him on his success. 'The things I sell are awful,' he said, 'Appealing little lunky children. But I manage to do my own work three days a week, so I can't complain. Listen, Li—no, what is it, Chip? Chip, listen, we've got to get together. I've got a motorbike; I'll come down there one evening. No, wait,' he said, 'are you doing anything next Sunday, you and your wife?'

Lilac looked anxiously at Chip. He said, 'I don't think so. I'm not sure.'

'I'm having some friends over,' Karl said. 'You come too, all right? Around six o'clock.'

With Lilac nodding at him, Chip said, 'We'll try. We'll probably be able to make it.'

'See that you do,' Karl said. He gave Chip his address. 'I'm glad you got over,' he said. 'It's better than *there* anyway, isn't it?'

'A little,' Chip said.

'I'll expect you next Sunday,' Karl said. 'So long, brother.'

'So long,' Chip said, and tapped off.

Lilac said, 'We're going, aren't we?'

'Do you have any idea what the railfare's going to be?' Chip said.

'Oh, Chip . . .'

'All right,' he said. 'All right, we'll go. But I'm not taking any favours from him. And you're not *asking* for any. You remember that.'

Every evening that week Lilac worked on the best of their clothes, taking off the frayed sleeves of a green dress, remending a trouser leg so that the mend was less noticeable.

The building, at the very edge of New Madrid's Steelytown, was in no worse condition than many native buildings. Its lobby was swept, and smelled only slightly of whiskey and fish and perfume, and the elevator worked well.

A pushbutton was set in new plaster next to Karl's door: a bell to be rung. Chip pressed it. He stood stiffly, and Lilac held his arm.

'Who is it?' a man's voice asked.

'Chip Newmark,' Chip said.

The door was unlocked and opened, and Karl—a thirty-five-year-old bearded Karl with the long-ago Karl's sharp-focused eyes —grinned and grabbed Chip's hand and said, 'Li! I thought you weren't coming!'

'We ran into some good-natured lunkies,' Chip said.

'Oh Christ,' Karl said, and let them in.

He locked the door and Chip introduced Lilac. She said, 'Hello, Mr Newgate,' and Karl, taking her held-out hand and looking at her face, said, 'It's Ashi. Hello, Lilac.'

'Hello, Ashi,' she said.

To Chip, Karl said, 'Did they hurt you?'

'No,' Chip said. 'Just "recite the Vow" and that kind of cloth.

'Bastards,' Karl said. 'Come on, I'll give you a drink and you'll forget about it.' He took their elbows and led them into a narrow passage walled with frame-to-frame paintings. 'You look great, Chip,' he said.

'So do you,' Chip said. 'Ashi.'

They smiled at each other.

'Seventeen years, brother,' Karl-Ashi said.

Men and women were sitting in a smoky brown-walled room, ten or twelve of them, talking and holding cigarettes and glasses. They stopped talking and turned expectantly.

'This is Chip and this is Lilac,' Karl said to them. 'Chip and I were at academy together; the Family's two worst genetics students.'

The men and women smiled, and Karl began pointing to them in turn and saying their names. 'Vito, Sunny, Ria, Lars . . .' Most of them were immigrants, bearded men and long-haired women with the Family's eyes and colouring. Two were natives: a pale erect beak-nosed woman of fifty or so, with a gold cross hanging against her black empty-looking dress ('Julia', Karl said, and she smiled with closed lips); and an overweight red-haired younger woman in a tight dress glazed with silvery beads. A few of the people could have been either immigrants or natives: a gray-eyed beardless man named Bob, a blond woman, a young blue-eyed man.

'Whiskey or wine?' Karl asked. 'Lilac?'

'Wine, please,' Lilac said.

They followed him to a small table set out with bottles and glasses, plates holding a slice or two of cheese and meat, and packets of cigarettes and matches. A souvenir paperweight sat on a pile of napkins. Chip picked it up and looked at it; it was from AUS21989. 'Make you homesick?' Karl asked, pouring wine.

Chip showed it to Lilac and she smiled. 'Not very,' he said, and put it down.

'Chip?'

'Whiskey.'

The red-haired native woman in the silvery dress came over smiling and holding an empty glass in a ring-fingered hand. To Lilac she said, 'You're absolutely beautiful. Really,' and to Chip, 'I think *all* you people are beautiful. The Family may not have any freedom but it's way ahead of us in physical appearance. I'd give anything to be lean and tan and slant-eyed.' She talked on—about the Family's sensible attitude toward sex—and Chip found himself with a glass in his hand and Karl and Lilac talking to other people and the woman talking to him. Lines of black paint edged and extended her brown eyes. 'You people are so much more *open* than we are,' she said. 'Sexually, I mean, You *enjoy* it more.'

An immigrant woman came over and said, 'Isn't Heinz coming, Marge?'

'He's in Palama,' the woman said, turning. 'A wing of the hotel collapsed.'

'Would you excuse me, please?' Chip said, and sidestepped away. He went to the other end of the room, nodded at people sitting there, and drank some of his whiskey, looking at a painting on the wall—slabs of brown and red on a white background. The whiskey tasted better than Hassan's. It was less bitter and searing; lighter and more pleasant to drink. The painting with its brown and red slabs was only a flat design, interesting to look at for a moment but with nothing in it connected to life. Karl's (no, Ashi's!) *A*-in-a-circle was in one of its bottom corners. Chip wondered whether it was one of the bad paintings he sold or, since it was hanging there in his living room, part of his 'own work' that he had spoken of with satisfaction. Wasn't he still doing the beautiful unbraceleted men and women he had drawn back at the Academy?

He drank some more of the whiskey and turned to the people sitting near him: three men and a woman, all immigrants. They were talking about furniture. He listened for a few minutes, drinking, and moved away.

Lilac was sitting next to the beak-nosed native woman—Julia. They were smoking and talking, or rather Julia was talking and Lilac was listening.

He went to the table and poured more whiskey into his glass. He lit a cigarette.

A man named Lars introduced himself. He ran a school for immigrant children there in New Madrid. He had been brought to Liberty as a child, and had been there for forty-two years.

Ashi came, holding Lilac by the hand. 'Chip, come see my studio,' he said.

He led them from the room into the passage walled with paintings. 'Do you know who you were speaking to?' he asked Lilac.

'Julia?' she said.

'Julia *Costanza*,' he said. 'She's the General's cousin. Despises him. She was one of the founders of Immigrants' Assistance.'

His studio was large and brilliantly lighted. A half-finished painting of a native woman holding a kitten stood on an easel; on another easel stood a canvas painted with slabs of blue and green. Other paintings stood against the walls: slabs of brown and orange, blue and purple, purple and black, orange and red.

He explained what he was trying to do, pointing out balances, and opposing thrusts, and subtle shadings of colour.

Chip looked away and drank his whiskey.

*   *   *

'Listen, you steelies!' he said, loudly enough so they all could hear him. 'Stop talking about *furniture* for a minute and listen! You know what we've got to do? Fight Uni! I'm not being *rude*, I mean it literally. Fight Uni! Because it's Uni who's to blame—for everything! For lunkies, who're what they are because they don't have enough food, or space, or *connection with any outside world*; and for dummies, who're what they are because they're LPK'ed that way and tranquilized that way; and for *us*, who're what *we* are because Uni put us here to get rid of us! It's *Uni* who's to blame—it's frozen the world so there's no more change —and we've got to fight it! We've got to get up off our stupid beaten behinds and FIGHT IT!'

Ashi, smiling, slapped at his cheek. 'Hey, brother,' he said, 'you've had a little too much, you know that? Hey, Chip, you hear me?'

Of course he'd had too much; of course, of course, of course. But it hadn't dulled him, it had freed him. It had opened up everything that had been closed inside him for months and months. Whiskey was *good*! Whiskey was *marvelous*!

He stopped Ashi's slapping hand and held it. 'I'm okay, Ashi,' he said. 'I know what I'm talking about.' To the others, sitting and swaying and smiling, he said, 'We can't just give up and accept things, *adjust ourselves* to this prison! Ashi, you used to draw members without bracelets, and they were so beautiful! And now you're painting color, slabs of *color*!'

They were trying to get him to sit down, Ashi on one side of him and Lilac on the other, Lilac looking anxious and embarrassed. 'You, too, love,' he said. 'You're accepting, adjusting.' He let them seat him, because standing hadn't been easy and sitting was better, more comfortable and sprawly. 'We've got to fight, not adjust,' he said. 'Fight, fight, fight. We've got to fight,' he said to the gray-eyed beardless man sitting next to him.

'By God, you're right!' the man said. 'I'm with you all the way! Fight Uni! What'll we do? Go over in boats and take the Army along for good measure? But maybe the sea is monitored by satellite and doctors'll be waiting with clouds of LPK. I've got a better idea; we'll get a plane—I hear there's one on the island that actually flies—and we'll——'

'Don't tease him, Bob,' someone said. 'He just came over.'

'That's obvious,' the man said, getting up.

'There's a way to do it,' Chip said. 'There has to be. There's a way to do it.' He thought about the sea and the island in the middle of it, but he couldn't think as clearly as he wanted. Lilac sat where the man had been and took his hand. 'We've got to fight,' he said to her.

'I know, I know,' she said, looking at him sadly.

Ashi came and put a warm cup to his lips. 'It's coffee,' he said. 'Drink it.'

It was very hot and strong; he swallowed a mouthful, then pushed the cup away. 'The copper complex,' he said. 'On '91766. The copper must get ashore. There must be boats or barges; we could——'

'It's been done before,' Ashi said.

Chip looked at him, thinking he was tricking him, making fun of him in some way, like the gray-eyed beardless man.

'Everything you're saying,' Ashi said, 'everything you're thinking—"fight Uni"—it's been said before and thought before. And tried before. A dozen times.' He put the cup to Chip's lips. 'Take some more,' he said.

Chip pushed the cup away, staring at him, and shook his head. 'It's not true,' he said.

'It is, brother. Come on, take a——'

'It isn't!' he said.

'It is,' a woman said across the room. 'It's true.'

Julia. It was Julia, General's-cousin-Julia, sitting erect and alone in her black dress with her little gold cross.

'Every five or six years,' she said, 'a group of people like you—sometimes only two or three, sometimes as many as ten—sets out to destroy UniComp. They go in boats, in submarines that they spend years building; they go on board the barges you just mentioned. They take guns, explosives, gas masks, gas bombs, gadgets; they have plans that they're sure will work. They never come back. I financed the last two parties and am supporting the families of men who were in them, so I speak with authority. I hope you're sober enough to understand, and to spare yourself useless anguish. Accepting and adjusting is all that's possible. Be grateful for what you have: a lovely wife, a child on the way, and a small amount of freedom that we hope in time will grow larger. I might add that in no circumstances whatsoever will I finance another such party. I am not as rich as certain people think I am.'

Chip sat looking at her. She looked back at him with small black eyes above her pale beak of nose.

'They never come back, Chip,' Ashi said. Chip looked at him.

'Maybe they get to shore,' Ashi said; 'maybe they get to '001. Maybe they even get into the dome. But that's as *far* as they get, because they're gone, every one of them. And Uni is still working.'

Chip looked at Julia. She said, 'Men and women exactly like you. As far back as I can remember.'

He looked at Lilac, holding his hand. She squeezed it, looking compassionately at him.

He looked at Ashi, who held the cup of coffee toward him.

He blocked the cup and shook his head. 'No, I don't want coffee,' he said. He sat motionless, with sudden sweat on his forehead, and then he leaned forward and began vomiting.

*   *   *

He was in bed, and Lilac was lying beside him sleeping. Hassan was snoring on the other side of the curtain. A sour taste was in his mouth, and he remembered vomiting. Christ and Wei! And on carpet—the first he'd seen in half a year!

Then he remembered what had been said to him by that woman, Julia, and by Karl—by Ashi.

He lay still for a while, and then he got up and tiptoed around the curtain and past the sleeping Newmans to the sink. He got a drink of water, and because he didn't want to go all the way down the hall, urined quietly in the sink and rinsed it out thoroughly.

He got back down beside Lilac and drew the blanket over him. He felt a little drunk again and his head hurt, but he lay on his back with his eyes closed, breathing lightly and slowly, and after a while he felt better.

He kept his eyes closed and thought about things.

After half an hour or so Hassan's alarm clock jangled. Lilac turned.

He stroked her head and she sat up.

'Are you all right?' she asked.

'Yes, sort of,' he said.

The light went on and they winced. They heard Hassan grunting and getting up, yawning, farting. 'Get up, Ria,' he said. 'Gigi? It's time to get up.'

Chip stayed on his back with his hand on Lilac's cheek. 'I'm sorry, darling,' he said. 'I'll call him today and apologize.'

She took his hand and turned her lips to it. 'You couldn't help it,' she said. 'He understood.'

'I'm going to ask him to help me find a better job,' Chip said.

Lilac looked at him questioningly.

'It's all out of me,' he said. 'Like the whiskey. All out. I'm going to be an industrious, optimistic steely. I'm going to accept and adjust. We're going to have a bigger apartment than Ashi some day.'

'I don't want that,' she said. 'I would love to have two rooms, though.'

'We will,' he said. 'In two years. Two rooms in two years; that's a promise.'

She smiled at him.

He said, 'I think we ought to think about moving to New Madrid where our rich friends are. That man Lars runs a school, did you know that? Maybe you could teach there. And the baby could go there when it's old enough.'

'What could I teach?' she said.

'Something,' he said. 'I don't know.' He lowered his hand and stroked her breasts. 'How to have beautiful breasts, maybe,' he said.

Smiling, she said, 'We've got to get dressed.'

'Let's skip breakfast,' he said, drawing her down. He rolled onto her and they embraced and kissed.

'Lilac?' Ria called. 'How was it?'

Lilac freed her mouth. 'Tell you later!' she called.

While he was walking down the tunnel into the mine he remembered the tunnel into Uni, Papa Jan's tunnel down which the memory banks had been rolled.

He stopped still.

Down which the *real* memory banks had been rolled. And above them were the false ones, the pink and orange toys that were reached through the dome and the elevators, and which everyone thought was Uni itself; everyone including—it had to be!—all those men and women who had gone out to fight it in the past. But Uni, the real Uni, was on the levels below, and could be reached through the tunnel, through Papa Jan's tunnel from behind Mount Love.

It would still be there—closed at its mouth probably, maybe even sealed with a meter of concrete—but it would still be there; because nobody fills in all of a long tunnel, especially not an efficient computer. And there was space cut out below for more memory banks—and Papa Jan had said so—so the tunnel would be needed again some day.

It was there, behind Mount Love.

A tunnel into Uni.

With the right maps and charts, someone who knew what he was doing could probably work out its exact location, or very nearly.

'You there! Get moving!' someone shouted.

He walked ahead quickly, thinking about it, thinking about it.

It was there. The tunnel.

6

'IF IT'S MONEY, the answer is no,' Julia Costanza said, walking briskly past clattering looms and immigrant women glancing at her. 'If it's a job,' she said, 'I might be able to help you.'

Chip, walking along beside her, said, 'Ashi's already got me a job.'

'Then it's money,' she said.

'Information first,' Chip said, 'then maybe money.' He pushed open a door.

'No,' Julia said, going through. 'Why don't you go to I.A.? That's what it's there for. What information? About what?' She glanced at him as they started up a spiral stairway that shifted with their weight.

Chip said, 'Can we sit down somewhere for five minutes?'

'If I sit down,' Julia said, 'half this island will be naked tomorrow. That's probably acceptable to you but it isn't to me. What information?'

He held in his resentment. Looking at her beak-nosed profile, he said, 'Those two attacks on Uni you——'

'No,' she said. She stopped and faced him, one hand holding the stairway's centerpost. 'If it's about *that* I really won't listen,' she said. 'I knew it the minute you walked into that living room, the disapproving air you had. No. I'm not interested in any more plans and schemes. Talk to somebody else.' She went up the stairs.

He went quickly and caught up with her. 'Were they planning to use a tunnel?' he asked. 'Just tell me that; were they going in through a tunnel from behind Mount Love?'

She pushed open the door at the head of the stairway; he held it and went through after her, into a large loft where a few machine parts lay. Birds rose fluttering to holes in the peaked roof and flew out.

'They were going in with the other people,' she said, walking straight through the loft toward a door at its far end. 'The sightseers. At least that was the plan. They were going to go down in the elevators.'

'And then?'

'There's no *point* in——'

'Just answer me, will you, please?' he said.

She glanced at him, angrily, and looked ahead. 'There's supposed to be a large observation window,' she said. 'They were going to smash it and throw in explosives.'

'Both groups?'

'Yes.'

'They may have succeeded,' he said.

She stopped with her hand on the door and looked at him, puzzled.

'That's not really Uni,' he said. 'It's a display for the sightseers. And maybe it's also meant as a false target for attackers. They could have blown it up and nothing would have happened except that they would have been grabbed and treated.'

She kept looking at him.

'The real thing is farther down,' he said. 'On three levels. I was in it once when I was ten or eleven years old.'

She said, 'Digging a tunnel is the most ri——'

'It's there already,' he said. 'It doesn't have to be dug.'

She closed her mouth, looked at him, and turned quickly away and pushed open the door. It led to another loft, brightly lit, where a row of presses stood motionless with layers of cloth on their beds. Water was on the floor, and two men were trying to lift the end of a long pipe that had apparently fallen from the wall and lay across a stopped conveyor belt piled with cut cloth pieces. The wall end of the pipe was still anchored, and the men were trying to lift its other end and get it off the belt and back up against the wall. Another man, an immigrant, waited on a ladder to receive it.

'Help them,' Julia said, and began gathering pieces of cloth from the wet floor.

'If that's how I spend my time, nothing's going to be changed,' Chip said. 'That's acceptable to you, but it isn't to me.'

'Help them!' Julia said. 'Go on! We'll talk later! You're not going to get anywhere by being cheeky!'

Chip helped the men get the pipe secured against the wall, and then he went out with Julia onto a railed landing on the side of the building. New Madrid stretched away below them, bright in the mid-morning sun. Beyond it lay a strip of blue-green sea dotted with fishing boats.

'Every day it's something else,' Julia said, reaching into the pocket of her gray apron. She took out cigarettes, offered Chip one, and lit them with ordinary cheap matches.

They smoked, and Chip said, 'The tunnel's there. It was used to bring in the memory banks.'

'Some of the groups I wasn't involved with may have known about it,' Julia said.

'Can you find out?'

She drew on her cigarette. In the sunlight she was older-looking, the skin of her face and neck netted with wrinkles. 'Yes,' she said. 'I suppose so. How do *you* know about it?'

He told her. 'I'm sure it's not filled in,' he said. 'It must be fifteen kilometers long. And besides, it's going to be used again. There's space cut out for more banks for when the Family gets bigger.'

She looked questioningly at him. 'I thought the colonies had their own computers,' she said.

'They do,' he said, not understanding. And then he understood. It was only in the colonies that the Family was growing; on Earth, with two children per couple and not every couple allowed to reproduce, the Family was getting smaller, not bigger. He had never connected that with what Papa Jan had said about the space for more memory banks. 'Maybe they'll be needed for more telecontrolled equipment,' he said.

'Or maybe,' Julia said, 'your grandfather wasn't a reliable source of information.'

'He was the one who had the idea for the tunnel,' Chip said. 'It's there; I know it is. And it may be a way, the *only* way, that Uni can be gotten at. I'm going to try it, and I want your help, as much of it as you can give me.'

'You want my *money*, you mean,' she said.

'Yes,' he said. 'And your help. In finding the right people with the right skills. And in getting information that we'll need, and equipment. And in finding people who can teach us skills that we don't have. I want to take this very slowly and carefully. I want to come back.'

She looked at him with eyes narrowed against her cigarette smoke. 'Well, you're not an absolute imbecile,' she said. 'What kind of job has Ashi found for you?'

'Washing dishes at the Casino.'

'God in heaven!' she said. 'Come here tomorrow morning at a quarter to eight.'

'The Casino leaves my mornings free,' he said.

'Come here!' she said. 'You'll get the time you need.'

'All right,' he said, and smiled at her. 'Thanks,' he said.

She turned away and looked at her cigarette. She crushed it against the railing. 'I'm not going to pay for it,' she said. 'Not all of it. I can't. You have no idea how expensive it's going to be. Explosives for instance: last time they cost over two thousand dollars, and that was five years ago; God knows what they'll be today.' She scowled at her cigarette stub and threw it away over the railing. 'I'll pay what I can,' she said, 'and I'll introduce you to people who'll pay the rest if you flatter them enough.'

'Thank you,' Chip said. 'I couldn't ask for more. Thank you.'

'God in heaven, here I go again,' Julia said. She turned to Chip. 'Wait, you'll find out,' she said: 'the older you get, the more you stay the same. I'm an only child who's used to having her way, that's my trouble. Come on, I've got work to do.'

They went down stairs that led from the landing. 'Really,' Julia said. 'I have all kinds of noble reasons for spending my time and money on people like you—a Christian urge to help the Family, love of justice, freedom, democracy—but the truth of the matter is, I'm an only child who's used to having her way. It *maddens* me, it absolutely *maddens* me, that I can't go anywhere I please on this planet! Or *off* it, for that matter! You have no idea how I *resent* that damned computer!'

Chip laughed. 'I *do*!' he said. 'That's just the way *I* feel.'

'It's a monster straight out of hell,' Julia said.

They walked around the building. 'It's a monster, all right,' Chip said, throwing away his cigarette. 'At least the way it is now. One of the things I want to try to find out is whether, if we got the chance, we could change its programme instead of destroying it. If the *Family* were running *it*, instead of vice versa, it wouldn't be so bad. Do you really believe in heaven and hell?'

'Let's not get into religion,' Julia said, 'or you're going to find yourself washing dishes at the Casino. How much are they paying you?'

'Six-fifty a week.'

'Really?'

'Yes.'

'I'll give you the same,' Julia said, 'but if anyone around here asks, say you're getting five.'

He waited until Julia had questioned a number of people without learning of any attack party that had known about the tunnel, and then, confirmed in his decision, he told his plans to Lilac.

'You *can't*!' she said. 'Not after all those other people went!'

'They were aiming at the wrong target,' he said.

She shook her head, held her brow, looked at him. 'It's—I don't know what to *say*,' she said. 'I thought you were—done with all this. I thought we were *settled*.' She threw her hands out at the room around them, their New Madrid room, with the walls they had painted, the bookshelf he had made, the bed, the refrigerator, Ashi's sketch of a laughing child.

Chip said, 'Honey, I may be the only person on any of the islands who knows about the tunnel, about the real Uni, I *have* to make use of that. How can I *not* do it?'

'All right, *make* use of it,' she said, 'Plan, help *organize* a party—fine! I'll help you! But why do you have to *go*? *Other* people should do it, people without families.'

'I'll be here when the baby's born,' he said. 'It's going to take longer than that to get everything ready. And then I'll only be gone for—maybe as little as a week.'

She stared at him. 'How can you *say* that?' she said. 'How can you say you'll—you could be gone forever! You could be caught and treated!'

'We're going to learn how to fight,' he said. 'We're going to have guns and——'

'Others should go!' she said.

'How can I ask them, if I'm not going myself?'

'Ask them, that's all. Ask them.'

'No,' he said. '*I've* got to go, too.'

'You *want* to go, that's what it is,' she said. 'You don't *have* to go; you *want* to.'

He was silent for a moment, and then he said, 'All right, I want to. Yes. I can't think of not being there when Uni is beaten. I want to throw the explosive myself, or pull the switch myself, or do whatever it is that's finally done—myself.'

'You're sick,' she said. She picked up the sewing in her lap and found the needle and started to sew. 'I mean it,' she said. 'You're sick on the subject of Uni. It didn't *put* us here; we're lucky to have *got* here. Ashi's right: it would have killed us the way it kills people at sixty-two; it wouldn't have wasted boats and islands. We got away from it; it's *already* been beaten; and you're sick to want to go back and beat it again.'

'It put us here,' Chip said, 'because the programmers couldn't justify killing people who were still young.'

'Cloth,' Lilac said. 'They justified killing old people, they'd have justified killing *infants*. We got away. And now you're going back.'

'What about our parents?' he said. '*They're* going to be killed in a few more years. What about Snowflake and Sparrow—the whole Family, in fact?'

She sewed, jabbing the needle into green cloth—the sleeves from her green dress that she was making into a shirt for the baby. 'Others should go,' she said. 'People without families.'

Later, in bed, he said, 'If anything *should* go wrong, Julia will take care of you. And the baby.'

'That's a great comfort,' she said. 'Thanks. Thanks very much. Thank Julia, too.'

It stayed between them from that night on: resentment on her part and refusal to be moved by it on his.

PART FOUR: FIGHTING BACK

1

HE WAS BUSY, busier than he'd been in his entire life: planning, looking for people and equipment, traveling, learning, explaining, pleading, devising, deciding. And working at the factory, too, where Julia, despite the time off she allowed him, made sure she got her six-fifty-a-week's worth out of him in machinery repair and production speed-up. And with Lilac's pregnancy advancing, he was doing more of the at-home chores, too. He was more exhausted than he'd ever been, and more wide awake; more sick of everything one day and more sure of everything the next; more alive.

It, the plan, the project, was like a machine to be assembled, with all the parts to be found or made, and each dependent for its shape and size on all the others.

Before he could decide on the size of the party, he had to have a clearer idea of its ultimate aim; and before he could have that, he had to know more about Uni's functioning and where it could be most effectively attacked.

He spoke to Lars Newman, Ashi's friend who ran a school. Lars sent him to a man in Andrait, who sent him to a man in Manacor.

'I knew those banks were too small for the amount of insulation they seemed to have,' the man in Manacor said. His name was Newbrook and he was near seventy; he had taught in a technological academy before he left the Family. He was minding a baby granddaughter, changing her diaper and annoyed about it. 'Hold *still,* will you?' he said. 'Well, assuming you can get in,' he said to Chip, 'the power source is what you've obviously got to go for. The reactor or, more likely, the rea*ctors.*'

'But they could be replaced fairly quickly, couldn't they?' Chip said. 'I want to put Uni out of commission for a good long time, long enough for the Family to wake up and decide what it wants to do with it.'

'Damn it, hold *still!*' Newbrook said. 'The refrigerating plant, then.'

'The refrigerating plant?' Chip said.

'That's right,' Newbrook said. 'The internal temperature of the banks has to be close to absolute zero; raise it a few degrees and the grids won't—there, *you see* what you've done?—the grids won't be superconductive any more. You'll erase Uni's memory.' He picked up the crying baby and held her against his shoulder, patting her back. 'Shh, shh,' he said.

'Erase it permanently?' Chip asked.

Newbrook nodded, patting the crying baby. 'Even if the refrigeration's restored,' he said, 'all the data will have to be fed in again. It'll take years.'

'That's exactly what I'm looking for,' Chip said.

The refrigerating plant.

And the stand-by plant.

And the second stand-by plant, if there was one.

Three refrigeration plants to be put out of operation. Two men for each, he figured; one to place the explosives and one to keep members away.

Six men to stop Uni's refrigeration and then hold its entrances against the help it would summon with its thawing faltering brain. Could six men hold the elevators and the tunnel? (And had Papa Jan mentioned other shafts in the other cut-out space?) But six was the minimum, and the minimum was what he wanted, because if any man was caught while they were on their way, he would tell the doctors everything and Uni would be expecting them at the tunnel. The fewer the men, the less the danger.

He and five others.

The yellow-haired young man who ran the I.A. patrol boat—Vito Newcome, but he called himself Dover—painted the boat's railing while he listened, and then, when Chip spoke about the tunnel and the real memory banks, listened without painting; crouched on his heels with the brush hanging in his hand, squinted up at Chip with flecks of white in his short beard and on his chest. 'You're sure of it?' he asked.

'Positive,' Chip said.

'It's about time somebody took another crack at that brother-fighter.' Dover Newcome looked at his thumb, white-smeared, and wiped it on his trouser thigh.

Chip crouched beside him. 'Do you want to be in on it?' he asked.

Dover looked at him and, after a moment, nodded. 'Yes,' he said. 'I certainly do.'

Ashi said no, which was what Chip had expected; he asked him only because not asking, he thought, would be a slight. 'I just don't feel it's worth the risk,' Ashi said. 'I'll help you out in any way I can, though. Julia's already hit me for a contribution and I've promised a hundred dollars. I'll make it more than that if you need it.'

'Fine,' Chip said. 'Thanks. Ashi. You *can* help. You can get into the Library, can't you? See if you can find any maps of the area around EUR-zip-one, U or pre-U. The larger the better: maps with topographical details.'

When Julia heard that Dover Newcome was to be in the group, she objected. 'We need him here, on the boat,' she said.

'You won't once we're finished,' Chip said.

'God in heaven,' Julia said. 'How do you get by with so little confidence?'

'It's easy,' Chip said. 'I have a friend who says prayers for me.'

Julia looked coldly at him. 'Don't take anyone else from I.A.,' she said. 'And don't take anyone from the factory. And don't take anyone with a family that *I* may wind up supporting!'

'How do you get by with so little faith?' Chip said.

He and Dover between them spoke to some thirty or forty immigrants without finding any others who wanted to take part in the attack. They copied names and addresses from the I.A. files, of men and women over twenty and under forty who had come to Liberty within the previous few years, and they called on seven or eight of them every week. Lars Newman's son wanted to be in the group, but he had been born on Liberty, and Chip wanted only people who had been raised in the Family, who were accustomed to scanners and walk-ways, to the slow pace and the contented smile.

He found a company in Pollensa that would make dynamite bombs with fast or slow mechanical fuses, provided they were ordered by a native with a permit. He found another company, in Calvia, that would make six gas masks, but they wouldn't guarantee them against LPK unless he gave them a sample for testing. Lilac, who was working in an immigrant clinic, found a doctor who knew the LPK formula, but none of the island's chemical companies could manufacture any; lithium was one of its chief constituents, and there hadn't been any lithium available for over thirty years.

He was running a weekly two-line advertisement in the *Immigrant,* offering to buy coveralls, sandals, and take-along kits. One day he got an answer from a woman in Andrait, and a few evenings later he went there to look at two kits and a pair of sandals. The kits were shabby and outdated, but the sandals were good.

The woman and her husband asked why he wanted them. Their name was Newbridge and they were in their early thirties, living in a tiny wretched rat-infested cellar. Chip told them, and they asked to join the group—insisted on joining it, actually. They were perfectly normal-looking, which was a point in their favor, but there was a feverishness about them, a keyed-up tension, that bothered Chip a little.

He went to see them again a week later, with Dover, and that time they seemed more relaxed and possibly suitable. Their names were Jack and Ria. They had had two children, both of whom had died in their first few months. Jack was a sewer worker and Ria worked in a toy factory. They said they were healthy and seemed to be.

Chip decided to take them—provisionally, at least, and he told them the details of the plan as it was taking shape.

'We ought to blow up the whole fucking thing, not just the refrigerating plants,' Jack said.

'One thing has to be very clear,' Chip said. 'I'm going to be in charge. Unless you're prepared to do exactly as I say every step of the way, you'd better forget the whole thing.'

'No, you're absolutely right,' Jack said. 'There *has* to be one man in charge of an operation like this; it's the only way it can work.'

'We can offer suggestions, can't we?' Ria said.

'The more the better,' Chip said. 'But the decisions are going to be mine, and you've got to be ready to go along with them.'

Jack said, 'I am,' and Ria said, 'so am I.'

Locating the entrance of the tunnel turned out to be more difficult than Chip had anticipated. He collected three large-scale maps of central Eur and a highly detailed pre-U topographic one of 'Switzerland' on which he carefully transcribed Uni's site, but everyone he consulted—former engineers and geologists, native mining engineers—said that more data was needed before the tunnel's course could be projected with any hope of accuracy. Ashi became interested in the problem and spent occasional hours in the Library copying references to 'Geneva' and 'Jura Mountains' out of old encyclopedias and works on geology.

On two consecutive moonlit nights Chip and Dover went out in the I.A. boat to a point west of EUR91766 and watched for the copper barges. These passed, they found, at precise intervals of four hours and twenty-five minutes. Each low flat dark shape moved steadily toward the northwest at thirty kilometers an hour, its rolling afterwaves lifting the boat and dropping it, lifting it and dropping it. Three hours later a barge would come from the opposite direction, riding higher in the water, empty.

Dover calculated that the Eur-bound barges, if they maintained their speed and direction, would reach EUR91772 in a little over six hours.

On the second night he brought the boat alongside a barge and slowed to match its speed while Chip climbed aboard. Chip rode on the barge for several minutes, sitting comfortably on its flat compacted load of copper ingots in wood cribs, and then he climbed back aboard the boat.

Lilac found another man for the group, an attendant at the clinic named Lars Newstone who called himself Buzz. He was thirty-six, Chip's age, and taller than normal; a quiet and capable-seeming man. He had been on the island for nine years and at the clinic for three, during which he had picked up a certain amount of medical knowledge. He was married but living apart from his wife. He wanted to join the group, he said, because he had always felt that 'somebody ought to do something, or at least try. It's wrong,' he said, 'to let Uni—*have* the world without trying to get it back.'

'He's fine, just the man we need,' Chip said to Lilac after Buzz had left their room. 'I wish I had two more of him instead of the Newbridges. Thank you.'

Lilac said nothing, standing at the sink washing cups. Chip went to her, took her shoulders, and kissed her hair. She was in the seventh month of her pregnancy, big and uncomfortable.

At the end of March, Julia gave a dinner party at which Chip, who had by then been working four months on the plan, presented it to her guests—natives with money who could each be counted on, she had said, for a contribution of at least five hundred dollars. He gave them copies of a list he had prepared of all the cost that would be involved, and passed around his 'Switzerland' map with the tunnel drawn in in its approximate position.

They weren't as receptive as he had thought they would be.

'Thirty-six hundred for explosives?' one asked.

'That's right, sir,' Chip said. 'If anyone knows where we can get them cheaper, I'll be glad to hear about it.'

'What's this "kit reinforcing"?'

'The kits we're going to carry; they're not made for heavy loads. They have to be taken apart and remade around metal frames.'

'You people can't buy guns and bombs, can you?'

'I'll do the buying,' Julia said, 'and everything will stay on my property until the party leaves. I have the permits.'

'When do you think you'll go?'

'I don't know yet,' Chip said. 'The gas masks are going to take three months from when they're ordered. And we still have one more man to find, and training to go through. I'm hoping for July or August.'

'Are you sure this is where the tunnel actually is?'

'No, we're still working on that. That's just an approximation.'

Five of the guests gave excuses and seven gave checks that added up to only twenty-six hundred dollars, less than a quarter of the eleven thousand that was needed.

'Lunky bastards,' Julia said.

'It's a beginning, anyway,' Chip said. 'We can start ordering things. And take on Captain Gold.'

'We'll do it again in a few weeks,' Julia said. 'What were you so nervous for? You've got to speak more forcefully!'

The baby was born, a boy, and they named him Jan. Both his eyes were brown.

On Sundays and Wednesday evenings, in an unused loft in Julia's factory, Chip, Dover, Buzz, Jack, and Ria studied various forms of fighting. Their teacher was an officer in the Army, Captain Gold, a small smiling man who obviously disliked them and seemed to take pleasure in having them hit one another and throw one another to the thin mats spread on the floor. 'Hit!

Hit! Hit!' he would say, bobbing before them in his undershir
and army trousers. 'Hit! Like this! *This* is hitting, not *this*
This is waving at someone! God almighty, you're hopeless, yo
steelies! Come on, Green-eye *hit him!*'

Chip swung his fist at Jack, and was in the air and on his bacl
on a mat.

'Good, you!' Captain Gold said. 'That looked a little human
Get up, Green-eye, you're not dead! What did I tell you abou
keeping low?'

Jack and Ria learned most quickly; Buzz, most slowly.

Julia gave another dinner, at which Chip spoke more force
fully, and they got thirty-two hundred dollars.

The baby was sick—had a fever and a stomach infection—bu
he got better and was fine-looking and happy, sucking hungril
at Lilac's breasts. Lilac was warmer than before, pleased witl
the baby and interested in hearing Chip tell about the money
raising and the gradual coming-into-being of the plan.

Chip found a sixth man, a worker on a farm near Santany
who had come over from Afr shortly before Chip and Lilac had
He was a little older than Chip would have liked, forty-three, bu
he was strong and quick-moving, and sure that Uni could be
beaten. He had worked in chromatomicrography in the Family
and his name was Morgan Newmark, though he still called him
self by his Family name, Karl.

Ashi said, 'I think I could find the damned tunnel myself now,
and handed Chip twenty pages of notes that he had copied from
books in the Library. Chip brought them, along with the maps
to each of the people he had consulted before, and three of them
were now willing to hazard a projection of the tunnel's likeliest
course. They came up, not unexpectedly, with three different
places for the tunnel's entrance. Two were within a kilometer of
each other and one was six kilometers away? 'This is enough if
we can't do better,' Chip said to Dover.

The company that was making the gas masks went out of
business—without returning the eight-hundred-dollar advance
Chip had given them—and another maker had to be found.

Chip talked again with Newbrook, the former technological
academy teacher, about the type of refrigerating plants Uni
would be likely to have. Julia gave another dinner and Ashi gave
a party; three thousand dollars more were collected. Buzz had a
run-in with a gang of natives and, though he surprised them by
fighting effectively, came out of it with two cracked ribs and a
fractured shinbone. Everyone began looking for another man in
case he wasn't able to go.

Lilac woke Chip one night.

'What's wrong?' he said.

'Chip?' she said.

'Yes?' He could hear Jan breathing, asleep in his cradle.

'If you're right,' she said, 'and this island is a prison that Uni has put us on——'

'Yes?'

'And attacks have made from here before——'

'Yes?' he said.

She was silent—he could see her lying on her back with her eyes open—and then she said, 'Wouldn't Uni put *other* people here, "healthy" members, to warn it of other attacks?'

He looked at her and said nothing.

'Maybe to—take part in them?' she said. 'And get everyone "helped" in Eur?'

'No,' he said, and shook his head. 'It's—no. They would have to get treatments, wouldn't they? To *stay* "healthy"?'

'Yes,' she said.

'You think there's a secret medicenter somewhere?' he asked, smiling.

'No,' she said.

'No,' he said. 'I'm sure there aren't any—"espions" here. Before Uni would go to those lengths, it *would* simply kill incurables the way you and Ashi say it would.'

'How do you *know*?' she said.

'Lilac, there *are* no espions,' he said. 'You're just looking for things to worry about. Go to sleep now. Go on. Jan's going to be up in a little while. Go on.'

He kissed her and she turned over. After a while she seemed to be asleep.

He stayed awake.

It couldn't be. They would need treatments . . .

How many people had he told about the plan, the tunnel, the real memory banks? There was no counting. Hundreds! And each must have told others . . .

He'd even put the ad in the *Immigrant: Will buy kits, cuvs, sandals . . .*

Someone who was *in the group*? No. Dover?—impossible. Buzz?—no, never. Jack or Ria?—no. Karl? He didn't really know Karl that well yet—pleasant, talked a lot, drank a little more than he should have but not enough to worry about—no, Karl *couldn't* be anything but what he seemed, working on a farm out in the middle of nowhere . . .

Julia? He was out of his head. Christ and Wei! God in heaven! Lilac was just worrying too much, that was all.

There couldn't be any espions, any people around who were secretly on Uni's side, because they would need treatments to stay that way.

He was going ahead with it no matter what.

He fell asleep.

The bombs came: bundles of thin brown cylinders taped around a central black one. They were stored in a shed behind the factory. Each had a small metal handle, blue or yellow, lying taped against its side. The blue handles were thirty-second fuses; the yellow, four-minute ones.

They tried one in a marble quarry at night; wedged it in a cleft and pulled its fuse handle, blue, with fifty meters of wire from behind a pile of cut blocks. The explosion when it came was thunderous, and where the cleft had been they found a hole the size of a doorway, running with rubble, churning with dust.

They hiked in the mountains—all except Buzz—wearing kits weighted with stones. Captain Gold showed them how to load a bullet-gun and focus an L-beam; how to draw, aim, and shoot—at planks propped against the factory's rear wall.

'Are you giving another dinner?' Chip asked Julia.

'In a week or two,' she said.

But she didn't. She didn't mention money again, and neither did he.

He spent some time with Karl, and satisfied himself that he wasn't an 'espion'.

Buzz's leg healed almost completely, and he insisted he would be able to go.

The gas masks came, and the remaining guns, and the tools and the shoes and the razors; and the plastic sheeting, the remade kits, the watches, the coils of strong wire, the inflatable raft, the shovel, the compasses, the binoculars.

'Try to hit me,' Captain Gold said, and Chip hit him and split his lip.

It took till November to get everything done, almost a year, and then Chip decided to wait and go at Christmas, to make the move to '001 on the holiday, when bike paths and walkways, carports and airports, would be at their busiest; when members would move a little less slowly than normal and even a 'healthy' one might miss the plate of a scanner.

On the Sunday before they were to go, they brought everything from the shed into the loft and packed the kits and the secondary kits they would unpack when they landed. Julia was there, and Lars Newman's son John, who was going to bring back the I.A. boat, and Dover's girlfriend Nella—twenty-two and yellow-haired as he, excited by it all. Ashi looked in and so did Captain Gold. 'You're nuts, you're all nuts,' Captain Gold said, and Buzz said, 'Scram, you lunky.' When they were done, when all the kits were plastic-wrapped and tied, Chip asked everyone not in the group to go outside. He gathered the group in a circle on the mats.

'I've been thinking a lot about what happens if one of us gets caught,' he said, 'and this is what I've decided. If anyone, even *one*, gets caught—the rest of us will turn around and go back.'

They looked at him. Buzz said, 'After all this?'

'Yes,' he said. 'We won't have a chance, once anyone's treated and telling a doctor that we're going in through the tunnel. So we'll go back, quickly and quietly, and find one of the boats. In fact, I want to try to spot one when we land, before we start traveling.'

'Christ and Wei!' Jack said. 'Sure, if three or *four* get caught, but *one*?'

'That's the decision,' Chip said. 'It's the right one.'

Ria said, 'What if *you* get caught?'

'Then Buzz is in charge,' Chip said, 'and it's up to him. But meanwhile that's the way it's going to be: if anyone gets caught we all turn back.'

Karl said, 'So let's nobody get caught.'

'Right,' Chip said. He stood up. 'That's all,' he said. 'Get plenty of sleep. Wednesday at seven.'

'Woodsday,' Dover said.

'Woodsday, Woodsday, Woodsday,' Chip said. 'Woodsday at seven.'

He kissed Lilac as if he were going out to see someone about something and would be back in a few hours. 'By, love,' he said.

She held him and kept her cheek against his and didn't say anything.

He kissed her again, took her arms from around him, and went to the cradle. Jan was busy reaching for an empty cigarette box hanging on a string. Chip kissed his cheek and said good-by to him.

Lilac came to him and he kissed her. They held each other and kissed, and then he went out, not looking back at her.

Ashi was waiting downstairs on his motorbike. He drove Chip to Pollensa and the pier.

They were all in the I.A. office by a quarter of seven, and while they were clipping one another's hair the truck came. John Newman and Ashi and a man from the factory loaded the kits and the raft on to the boat, and Julia unpacked sandwiches and coffee. The men clipped their hair and shaved their faces bare.

They put bracelets on and closed links that looked like ordinary ones. Chip's bracelet said Jesus AY31G6912.

He said good-by to Ashi, and kissed Julia. 'Pack your kit and get ready to see the world,' he said.

'Be careful,' she said. 'And try praying.'

He got on the boat, sat on the deck in front of the kits with John Newman and the others—Buzz and Karl, Jack and Ria; strange-looking and Family-like with their clipped hair, their beardless similar faces.

Dover started the boat and steered it out of the harbor, then turned it toward the faint orange glow that came from '91766.

2

IN PALLID PRE-DAWN LIGHT they slipped from the barge and pushed the kit-loaded raft away from it. Three of them pushed and three swam along beside, watching the black high-cliffed shore. They moved slowly, keeping about fifty meters out. Every ten minutes or so they changed places; the ones who had been swimming pushed, the ones who had been pushing swam.

When they were well below '91772 they turned and pushed the raft in. They beached it in a small sandy cove with towering rock walls, and unloaded the kits and unwrapped them. They opened the secondary kits and put on coveralls; pocketed guns, watches, compasses, maps; then dug a hole and packed into it the two emptied kits and all the plastic wrappings, the deflated raft, their Liberty clothing, and the shovel they had used for digging. They filled the hole and stamped it level, and with kits slung on their shoulders and sandals in their hands, began walking in single file down the narrow strip of beach. The sky lightened and their shadows appeared before them, sliding in and out over rocky cliff-base. Near the back of the line Karl started whistling 'One Mighty Family'. The others smiled, and Chip, at the front, joined in. Some of the others did too.

Soon they came to a boat—an old blue boat lying on its side, waiting for incurables who would think themselves lucky. Chip turned, and walked backward, said, 'Here it is, if we need it,' and Dover said, 'We won't,' and Jack, after Chip had turned and they had passed it, picked up a stone, turned, threw it at the boat, and missed.

They switched their kits from one shoulder to the other as they walked. In a little less than an hour they came to a scanner with its back to them. 'Home again,' Dover said, and Ria groaned, and Buzz said, 'Hi, Uni, how are you?'—patting the scanner's top as he passed it. He was walking without limping; Chip had looked around a few times to check.

The strip of beach began to widen, and they came to a litter basket and more of them, and then lifeguard platforms, speakers and a clock—6.54 Thu 25 Dec 171 Y.U.—and a stairway zigzagging up the cliff with red and green bunting wound around some of its railing supports.

They put their kits down, and their sandals, and took their coveralls off and spread them out. They lay down on them and rested under the sun's growing warmth. Chip mentioned things that he thought they should say when they spoke to the Family —afterwards—and they talked about that and about the extent to which Uni's stopping would block TV and how long the restoring of it would take.

Karl and Dover fell asleep.

Chip lay with his eyes closed and thought about some of the problems the Family would face as it awakened, and different ways of dealing with them.

'Christ, Who Taught Us' began on the speakers at eight o'clock, and two red-capped lifeguards in sunglasses came walking down the zigzag stairs.

One of them came to a platform near the group. 'Merry Christmas,' he said.

'Merry Christmas,' they said to him.

'You can go in now if you want,' he said, climbing up on to the platform.

Chip and Jack and Dover got up and went into the water. They swam around for a while, watching members come down the stairs, and then they went out and lay down again.

When there were thirty-five or forty members on the beach, at 8.22, the six got up and began putting on their coveralls and shouldering their kits.

Chip and Dover went up the stairs first. They smiled and said 'Merry Christmas' to members coming down, and easily false-touched the scanner at the top. The only members nearby were at the canteen with their backs turned.

They waited by a water fountain, and Jack and Ria came up, and then Buzz and Karl.

They went to the bike racks, where twenty or twenty-five bikes were lined up in the nearest slots. They took the last six, put their kits in the baskets, mounted, and rode to the entrance of the bike path. They waited there, smiling and talking, until no cyclists and no cars were going by, and then they passed the scanner in a group, touching their bracelets to the side of it in case someone could see them from a distance.

They rode toward EUR91770 singly and in twos, spaced out widely along the path. Chip went first, with Dover behind him. He watched the cyclists who approached them and the occasional cars that rushed past. *We're going to do it,* he thought. *We're going to do it.*

They went into the airport separately and gathered near the flight-schedule signboard. Members pressed them close together; the red-and-green-streamered waiting room was densely crowded, and so voice-filled that Christmas music could only intermittently be heard. Beyond the glass, large planes turned and moved ponderously, took members on from three escalators at once, let lines of members off, rolled to and from the runways.

It was 9.35. The next flight to EUR00001 was at 11.48.

Chip said, 'I don't like the idea of staying here so long. The barge either used extra power or came in late, and if the difference was conspicuous, Uni may have figured out what caused it.'

'Let's go now,' Ria said, 'and get as close to '001 as we can and then bike again.'

'We'll get there a lot sooner if we wait,' Karl said. 'This isn't such a bad hiding place.'

'No,' Chip said, looking at the signboard, 'let's go—on the 10.06 to '00020. That's the soonest we can manage it, and it's only about fifty kilometers from '001. Come on, the door's over that way.'

They made their way through the crowd to the swing-door at the side of the room and clustered around its scanner. The door opened and a member in orange came out. Excusing himself, he reached between Chip and Dover to touch the scanner—*yes*, it winked—and went on.

Chip slipped his watch from his pocket and checked it against a clock. 'It's lane six,' he said. 'If there's more than one escalator, be on line for the one at the back of the plane; and make sure you're near the end of the line but with at least six members behind you. Dover?' He took Dover's elbow and they went through the door into the depot area. A member in orange standing there said, 'You're not supposed to be in here.'

'Uni okayed it,' Chip said. 'We're in airport design.'

'Three-thirty-seven A,' Dover said.

Chip said, 'This wing is being enlarged next year.'

'I see what you meant about the ceiling,' Dover said, looking up at it.

'Yes,' Chip said. 'It could easily go up another meter.'

'Meter and a half,' Dover said.

'Unless we run into trouble with the ducts,' Chip said.

The member left them and went out through the door.

'Yes, all the ducts,' Dover said. 'Big problem.'

'Let me show you where they lead,' Chip said. 'It's interesting.'

'It certainly is,' Dover said.

They went into the area where members in orange were readying cake and drink containers, working more quickly than members usually did.

'Three-thirty-seven A?' Chip said.

'Why not?' Dover said, and pointed at the ceiling as they separated for a member pushing a cart, 'You see the way the ducts run?' he said.

'We're going to have to change the whole setup,' Chip said. 'In here too.'

They false-touched and went into the room where coveralls hung on hooks. No one was in it. Chip closed the door and pointed to the closet where the orange coveralls were kept.

They put orange coveralls on over their yellow ones, and toe-guards on their sandals. They tore openings inside the pockets of the orange coveralls so that they could reach into the pockets of the inner ones.

A member in white came in. 'Hello,' he said. 'Merry Christmas.'
'Merry Christmas,' they said.

'I was sent up from '765 to help out,' he said. He was about thirty.

'Good, we can use it,' Chip said.

The member, opening his coveralls, looked at Dover, who was closing him. 'What have you got the other ones on underneath for?' he asked.

'It's warmer that way,' Chip said, going to him.

He turned to Chip, puzzled. 'Warmer?' he said. 'What do you want to be warmer for?'

'I'm sorry, brother,' Chip said, and hit him in the stomach. He bent forward, grunting, and Chip swung his fist up under his jaw. The member straightened and fell backward; Dover caught him under the arms and lowered him to the floor. He lay with his eyes closed, as if sleeping.

Chip, looking down at him, said, 'Christ and Wei, it works.'

They tore up a set of coveralls and tied the member's wrists and ankles and knotted a sleeve between his teeth; then lifted him and put him into the closet where the floor polisher was.

The clock's *9.51* became *9.52*.

They wrapped their kits in orange coveralls and went out of the room and past the members working at the cake and drink containers. In the depot area they found a half-empty carton of towels and put the wrapped kits into it. Carrying the carton between them, they went out through the portal on to the field. A plane was opposite lane six, a large one, with members leaving it on two escalators. Members in orange waited at each escalator with a container cart.

They went away from the plane, toward the left; crossed the field diagonally with the carton between them, skirting a slow-moving maintenance truck and approaching the hangars that lay in a flat-roofed wing extending towards the runways.

They went into a hangar. A smaller plane was there, with members in orange underneath it, lowering a square black housing from it. Chip and Dover carried the carton to the back of the hangar where there was a door in the side wall. Dover opened it, looked in, and nodded to Chip.

They went in and closed the door. They were in a supply room: racks of tools, rows of wood crates, black metal drums marked *Lub Oil SG*. 'Couldn't be better,' Chip said as they put the carton on the floor.

Dover went to the door and stood at its hinge side. He took out his gun and held it by its barrel.

Chip, crouching, unwrapped a kit, opened it, and took out a bomb, one with a yellow four-minute handle.

He separated two of the oil drums and put the bomb on the floor between them, with its taped-down handle facing up. He took his watch out and looked at it. Dover said, 'How long?' and he said, 'Three minutes.'

He went back to the carton and, still holding the watch, closed the kit and rewrapped it and closed the carton's leaves.

'Is there anything we can use?' Dover asked, nodding at the tool racks.

Chip went to one and the door of the room opened and a member in orange came in. 'Hello,' Chip said, and took a tool from the rack and put the watch in his pocket. 'Hello,' the member said, coming to the other side of the rack. She glanced over it at Chip. 'Who're you?' she asked.

'Li RP,' he said. 'I was sent up from '765 to help.' He took another tool from the rack, a pair of calipers.

'It's not as bad as Wei's Birthday,' the member said.

Another member came to the door. 'We've got it, Peace,' he said. 'Li had it.'

'I asked him and he said he didn't,' the first member said.

'Well he did,' the second member said, and went away.

The first member went after him. 'He was the first one I asked,' she said.

Chip stood and watched the door as it slowly closed. Dover, behind it, looked at him and closed it all the way, softly. Chip looked back at Dover, and then at his hand holding the tools. It was shaking. He put the tools down, let his breath out, and showed his hand to Dover, who smiled and said, 'Very unmember-like.'

Chip drew a breath and got the watch from his pocket. 'Less than a minute,' he said, and went to the drums and crouched. He pulled the tape from the bomb's handle.

Dover put his gun into his pocket—poked it into the inner one—and stood with his hand on the doorknob.

Chip, looking at the watch and holding the fuse handle, said, 'Ten seconds.' He waited, waited, waited—and then pulled the handle up and stood as Dover opened the door. They picked up the carton and carried it from the room and pulled the door closed.

They walked with the carton through the hangar—'Easy, easy,' Chip said—and across the field toward the plane opposite lane six. Members were filing onto the escalators, riding up.

'What's that?' a member in orange with a clipboard asked, walking along with them.

'We were told to bring it over there,' Chip said.

'Karl?' another member said at the other side of the one with the clipboard. He stopped and turned, saying 'Yes?' and Chip and Dover kept walking.

They brought the carton to the plane's rear escalator and put it down. Chip stayed opposite the scanner and looked at the escalator controls; Dover slipped through the line and stood at the scanner's back. Members passed between them, touching their bracelets to the green-winking scanner and stepping onto the escalator.

A member in orange came to Chip and said, 'I'm on this escalator.'

'Karl just told me to take it,' Chip said. 'I was sent up from '765 to help.'

'What's wrong?' the member with the clipboard asked, coming over. 'Why are there three of you here?'

'I thought I was on this escalator,' the other member said. The air shuddered and a loud roar clapped from the hangars.

A black pillar, vast and growing, stood on the wing of hangars, and rolling orange fire was in the black. A black and orange rain fell on the roof and the field, and members in orange came running and slowing and looking back up at the fiery pillar on the roof.

The member with the clipboard stared, and hurried forward. The other member hurried after him.

The members on line stood motionless, looking upward toward the hangars. Chip and Dover caught at their arms and drew them forward. 'Don't stop,' they said. 'Keep moving, please. There's no danger. The plane is waiting. Touch and step on. Keep moving, please.' They herded the members past the scanner and onto the escalator and one was Jack—'Beautiful,' he said, gazing past Chip as he false-touched; and Ria, who looked as excited as she had the first time Chip had seen her; and Karl, looking awed and somber; and Buzz, smiling. Dover moved to the escalator after Buzz; Chip thrust a wrapped kit to him and turned to the other members on line, the last seven or eight, who stood looking toward the hangars.

'Keep moving, please,' he said. 'The plane is waiting for you. Sister!'

'There is no cause for alarm,' a woman's voice loudspeakered. 'There has been an accident in the hangars but everything is under control.'

Chip urged the members to the escalator. 'Touch and step on,' he said. 'The plane's waiting.'

'Departing members, please resume your places in line,' the voice said. 'Members who are boarding planes, continue to do so. There will be no interruption of service.'

Chip false-touched and stepped onto the escalator behind the last member. Riding upward with his wrapped kit under his arm, he glanced toward the hangars: the pillar was black and smudging; there was no more fire. He looked ahead again, at pale blue coveralls. 'All personnel except forty-sevens and forty-nines, resume your assigned duties,' the woman's voice said. 'All personnel except forty-sevens and forty-nines, resume your assigned duties. Everything is under control.' Chip stepped into the plane and the door slid down behind him. 'There will be no interruption of——' Members stood confusedly, looking at filled seats.

'There are extra passengers because of the holiday,' Chip said. 'Go forward and ask members with children to double up. It can't be helped.'

The members moved down the aisle, looking from one side of the plane to the other.

The five were sitting in the last row, next to the dispensers. Dover took his wrapped kit from the aisle seat and Chip sat down. Dover said, 'Not bad.'

'We're not up yet,' Chip said.

Voices filled the plane: members telling members about the explosion, spreading the news from row to row. The clock said *10.06* but the plane wasn't moving.

The *10.06* became *10.07*.

The six looked at one another, and looked forward, normally.

The plane moved; swung gently to the side and then pulled forward. It moved faster. The light dimmed and the TV screens flicked on.

They watched *Christ's Life* and a years-old *Family at Work*. They drank tea and coke but couldn't eat; there were no cakes on the plane, because of the hour, and though they had foil-wrapped rounds of cheese in their kits, they would have been seen eating them by the members who came to the dispensers. Chip and Dover sweated in their double coveralls. Karl kept dozing off, and Ria and Buzz on either side of him nudged him to keep him awake and watching.

The flight took forty minutes.

When the location sign said *EUR00020*, Chip and Dover got up from their seats and stood at the dispensers, pressing the buttons and letting tea and coke flow down the drains. The plane landed and rode and stopped, and members began filing off. After a few dozen had gone through the doorway nearby, Chip and Dover lifted the emptied containers from the dispensers, set them on the floor and raised their covers, and Buzz put a wrapped kit into each. Then Buzz, Karl, Ria, and Jack got up and the six went to the doorway. Chip, carrying a container against his chest, said, 'Would you excuse us, please?' to an elderly member and went out. The others followed close behind him. Dover, carrying the other container, said to the member, 'You'd better wait till I'm off the escalator,' and the member nodded, looking confused.

At the bottom of the escalator Chip leaned his wrist toward the scanner and then stood opposite it, blocking it from the members in the waiting room. Buzz, Karl, Ria, and Jack passed in front of him, false-touching, and Dover leaned against the scanner and nodded to the member waiting above.

The four went toward the waiting room, and Chip and Dover

crossed the field to the portal and went through it into the depot area.

Setting down the containers, they took the kits out of them and slipped between two rows of crates. They found a cleared space near the wall and took off the orange coveralls and pulled the toeguards from their sandals.

They left the depot area through the swing-door, their kits slung on their shoulders. The others were waiting around the scanner. They went out of the airport by twos—it was almost as crowded as the one in '91770—and gathered again at the bike racks.

By noon they were north of '00018. They ate their rounds of cheese between the bike path and the River of Freedom, in a valley flanked by mountains that rose to awesome snow-streaked heights. While they ate they looked at their maps. By nightfall, they calculated, they could be in parkland a few kilometers from the tunnel's entrance.

A little after three o'clock, when they were nearing '00013, Chip noticed an approaching cyclist, a girl in her early teens, who was looking at the faces of the northbound cyclists—his own as she passed him—with an expression of concern, of memberlike wanting-to-help. A moment later he saw another approaching cyclist looking at faces in the same slightly anxious way, an elderly woman with flowers in her basket. He smiled at her as she passed, then looked ahead. There was nothing out of the ordinary in the path and the road beside it; a few hundred meters ahead both path and road turned to the right and disappeared behind a power station.

He rode onto grass, stopped, and looking back, signaled to the others as they came along.

They pushed their bikes farther onto the grass. They were on the last stretch of parkland before the city: a span of grass, then picnic tables and a rising slope of trees.

'We're never going to make it if we stop every half hour,' Ria said.

They sat down on the grass.

'I think they're checking bracelets up ahead,' Chip said. 'Telecomps and red-crossed coveralls. I noticed two members coming this way who looked as if they were trying to spot the sick one. They had that how-can-I-help look.'

'Hate,' Buzz said.

Jack said, 'Christ and Wei, Chip if we're going to start worrying about members' *facial expressions,* we might as well just turn around and go home.'

Chip looked at him and said, 'A bracelet check isn't so unlikely, is it? Uni must know by now that the explosion at '91770 was no accident, and it might have figured out exactly why it happened. This is the shortest route from '020 to Uni—and we're coming to the first sharp turn in about twelve kilometers.'

'All right, so they're checking bracelets,' Jack said. 'What the hate are we carrying guns for?'

'Yes!' Ria said.

Dover said, 'If we shoot our way through we'll have the whole bike path after us.'

'So we'll drop a bomb behind us,' Jack said. 'We've got to move fast, not sit on our asses as if we're in a chess game. These dummies are half dead anyway; what difference does it make if we kill a few of them? We're going to help all the rest, aren't we?'

'The guns and bombs are for when we need them,' Chip said, 'not for when we can avoid using them.' He turned to Dover. 'Take a walk in the woods there,' he said. 'See if you can get a look at what's past the turn.'

'Right,' Dover said. He got up and crossed the grass, picked something up and brought it to a litter basket, and went in among the trees. His yellow coveralls became bits of yellow that vanished up the slope.

They turned from watching him. Chip took out his map.

'Shit,' Jack said.

Chip said nothing. He looked at the map.

Buzz rubbed his leg and took his hand from it abruptly.

Jack tore bits of grass from the ground. Ria, sitting close to him, watched him. 'What's your suggestion,' Jack said, 'if they *are* checking bracelets?'

Chip looked up from the map and, after a moment, said, 'We'll go back a little way and cut east and by-pass them.'

Jack tore up more grass and then threw it down. 'Come on,' he said to Ria, and stood up. She sprang up beside him, bright-eyed.

'Where are you going?' Chip said.

'Where we planned to go,' Jack said, looking down at him. 'The parkland near the tunnel. We'll wait for you until it gets light.'

'Sit down, you two,' Karl said.

Chip said, 'You'll go with all of us when I say we'll go. You agreed to that at the beginning.'

'I've changed my mind,' Jack said. 'I don't like taking orders from *you* any more than I like taking them from Uni.'

'You're going to ruin everything,' Buzz said.

Ria said, '*You* are! Stopping, turning back, by-passing—if you're going to do a thing, *do* it!'

'Sit down and wait till Dover gets back,' Chip said.

Jack smiled. 'You want to make me?' he said. 'Right out here in front of the Family?' He nodded to Ria and they picked up their bikes and steadied the kits in the baskets.

Chip got up, putting the map in his pocket. 'We can't break

the group in two this way,' he said. 'Stop and think for a minute, will you, Jack? How will we know if——'

'You're the stopper-and-thinker,' Jack said. 'I'm the one who's going to walk down that tunnel.' He turned and pushed his bike away. Ria pushed hers along with him. They went toward the path.

Chip took a step after them and stopped, his jaw tight, his hands fisted. He wanted to shout at them, to take his gun out and force them back—but there were cyclists passing, members on the grass nearby.

'There's nothing you can do, Chip,' Karl said, and Buzz said, 'The brother-fighters.'

At the edge of the path Jack and Ria mounted their bikes. Jack waved. 'So long!' he called. 'See you in the lounge at TV!' Ria waved too and they pedaled away.

Buzz and Karl waved after them.

Chip snatched up his kit from his bike and slung it on his shoulder. He took another kit and tossed it in Buzz's lap. 'Karl, you stay here,' he said. 'Buzz, come on with me.'

He went into the woods and realized he had moved quickly, angrily, abnormally, but thought *Fight it!* He went up the slope in the direction Dover had taken. *God DAMN them!*

Buzz caught up with him 'Christ and Wei,' he said, 'don't *throw* the kits!'

'God *damn* them!' Chip said. 'The first time I saw them I knew they were no good! But I shut my eyes because I was so fighting —God damn *me*!' he said. 'It's *my* fault. Mine.'

'Maybe there's no bracelet check and they'll be waiting in the parkland,' Buzz said.

Yellow flickered among the trees ahead: Dover coming down. He stopped, then saw them and came on. 'You're right,' he said. 'Doctors on the ground, doctors in the air——'

'Jack and Ria have gone on,' Chip said.

Dover looked at him wide-eyed and said, 'Didn't you stop them?'

'How?' Chip said. He caught Dover's arm and turned him around. 'Show us the way,' he said.

Dover led them quickly up the slope through the trees. 'They'll never get through,' he said. 'There's a whole medicenter, and barriers to prevent the bikes from turning.'

They came out of the trees onto an incline of rock, Buzz last and hurrying.

Dover said, 'Get down or we'll be seen.'

They dropped to their stomachs and crawled up the incline to its rim. Beyond lay the city, '00013, its white slabs standing clean and bright in the sunlight, its interweaving rails glittering, its border of roadways flashing with cars. The river curved before it and continued to the north, blue and slender, with sightseeing

boats drifting slowly and a long line of barges passing under
bridges.

Below, they looked into a rock-walled half bowl whose floor
was a semicircular plaza where the bike path branched; it came
down from the north around the power station, and half of it
turned, passed over the car-rushing road, and bridged to the city,
while the other half went on across the plaza and followed the
river's curving eastern bank with the road coming up to rejoin
it. Before it branched, barriers channeled the oncoming cyclists
into three lines, each of them passing before a group of red-cross-
coveralled members standing beside a short unusual-looking
scanner. Three members in antigrav gear hovered face-down in
the air, one over each group. Two cars and a copter were in the
nearer part of the plaza, and more members in red-crossed coveralls stood by the line of cyclists who were leaving the city, hurrying them along when they slowed to look at the ones who were
touching the scanners.

'Christ, Marx, Wood, and Wei,' Buzz said.

Chip, while he looked, pulled his kit open at his side. 'They
must be in the line somewhere,' he said. He found his binoculars
and put them to his eyes and focused them.

'They are,' Dover said. 'See the kits in the baskets?'

Chip swept the line and found Jack and Ria; they were pedal-
ing slowly, side by side in wood-barriered lanes. Jack was looking
ahead and his lips were moving. Ria nodded.

They were steering with their left hands only; their right hands
were in their pockets.

Chip passed the binoculars to Dover and turned to his kit.
'We've got to help them get through,' he said. 'If they make it
over the bridge they may be able to lose themselves in the city.'

'They're going to shoot when they get to the scanners,' Dover
said.

Chip gave Buzz a blue-handled bomb and said, 'Take off the
tape and pull when I tell you. Try to get it near the copter; two
birds with one net.'

'Do it before they start shooting,' Dover said.

Chip took the binoculars back from him and looked through
them and found Jack and Ria again. He scanned the lines ahead
of them; about fifteen bikes were between them and the groups
at the scanners.

'Do they have bullets or L-beams?' Dover asked.

'Bullets,' Chip said. 'Don't worry, I'll time it right.' He watched
the lines of slow-moving bikes, gauging their speed.

'They'll probably shoot anyway,' Buzz said. 'Just for fun. Did
you see that look in Ria's eyes?'

'Get ready,' Chip said. He watched until Jack and Ria were
five bikes from the scanners. 'Pull,' he said.

Buzz pulled the handle and threw the bomb underhanded to

the side. It hit stone, tumbled downward, bounded off a projection, and landed near the side of the copter. 'Get back,' Chip said. He took another look through the binoculars, at Jack and Ria two bikes from the scanners looking tense but confident, and slipped back between Buzz and Dover. 'They look as if they're going to a party,' he said.

They waited, their cheeks on stone, and the explosion roared and the incline shuddered. Metal crashed and grated below. There was silence, and the bomb's bitter smell; and then voices, murmuring and rising louder. 'Those two!' someone shouted.

They edged forward to the rim.

Two bikes were racing onto the bridge. All the others had stopped, their riders standing one-footed, facing toward the copter—tipped to its side below and smoking—and turning now toward the two bikes speeding and the red-cross-coveralled members running after them. The three members in the air veered and flew towards the bridge.

Chip raised the binoculars—to Ria's bent back and Jack's ahead of her. They pedaled rapidly in depthless flatness seeming to get no farther away. A glittering mist appeared, partly obscuring them.

Above, a hovering member downpointed a cylinder gushing thick white gas.

'He's got them!' Dover said.

Ria stood astride her bike; Jack looked over his shoulder at her.

'Ria, not Jack,' Chip said.

Jack stopped and turned with his gun aimed upward. It jerked, and jerked again.

The member in the air went limp (*crack* and *crack*, the shots sounded), the white-gushing cylinder falling from his hand.

Members fleeing the bridge bicycled in both directions, ran wide-eyed on the flanking walkways.

Ria sat by her bike. She turned her head, and her face was moist and glittering. She looked troubled. Red-crossed-coveralls blurred over her.

Jack stared, holding his gun, and his mouth opened big and round, closed and opened again in glittering mist. ('Ria!' Chip heard, small and far away.) Jack raised his gun ('Ria!') and fired, fired, fired.

Another member in the air (*crack, crack, crack*) went limp and dropped his cylinder. Red spattered on the walkway below him, and more red.

Chip lowered the binoculars.

'Your *gas mask!*' Buzz said. He had binoculars too.

Dover was lying with his face in his arms.

Chip sat up and looked with only his eyes: at the narrow emptied bridge with a faraway cyclist in pale blue wobbling down the middle of it and a member in the air following him at a distance; at the two dead or dying members, turning slowly in the air, drifting; at the red-cross-coveralled members, walking now in a bridge-wide line, and one of them helping a member in yellow by a fallen bike, taking her about the shoulders and leading her back toward the plaza.

The cyclist stopped and looked back toward the red-cross-coveralled members, then turned and bent forward over the front of his bike. The member in the air flew quickly closer and pointed his arm; a thick white feather grew from it and brushed the cyclist.

Chip raised the binoculars.

Jack, gray-snouted in his gas mask, leaned to his left in glittering mist and put a bomb on the bridge. Then he pedaled, skidded, sideslipped, and fell. He raised himself on one arm with the bike lying between his legs. His kit, spilled from the bike's basket, lay by the bomb.

'Oh Christ and Wei,' Buzz said.

Chip took down the binoculars, looked at the bridge, and then wound the binoculars' neckstrap tightly around their middle.

'How many?' Dover asked, looking at him.

Chip said, 'Three.'

The explosion was bright, loud, and long. Chip watched Ria, walking from the bridge with the red-cross-coveralled member leading her.

She didn't turn around.

Dover, up on his knees and looking, turned to Chip.

'His whole kit,' Chip said. 'He was sitting next to it.' He put the binoculars into his kit and closed it. 'We've got to get out of here,' he said. 'Put them away, Buzz. Come on.'

He meant not to look, but before they left the incline he did.

The middle of the bridge was black and rubbled, and its sides were burst outward. A bicycle wheel lay outside the blackened area, and there were other smaller things toward which the red-cross-coveralled members slowly moved. Pieces of pale blue were on the bridge and floating on the river.

They went back to Karl and told him what had happened, and the four of them got on their bikes and rode south for a few kilometers and went into parkland. They found a stream and drank from it and washed.

'And now we turn back?' Dover said.

'No,' Chip said, 'not all of us.'

They looked at him.

'I said that we would,' he said, 'because if anyone got caught, I wanted him to believe it, and say it when he was questioned. The way Ria's probably saying it right now.' He took a cigarette that they were passing around—despite the risk of the smoke smell traveling—and drew on it and passed it to Buzz. 'One of us is going to go back,' he said. 'At least I hope only one will go—to set off a bomb or two between here and the coast and take a boat, to make it look as if we've stuck to the plan. The rest of us will hide in parkland, work our way closer to '001, and go for the tunnel in two weeks or so.'

'Good,' Dover said, and Buzz said, 'I never thought it made sense to give up so easily.'

'Will three of us be enough?' Karl asked.

'We won't know till we try,' Chip said. 'Would six have been enough; Maybe it can be done by one, and maybe it can't be done by a dozen. But after coming this far, I fighting well mean to find out.'

'I'm with you; I was just asking,' Karl said. Buzz said, 'I'm with you too,' and Dover said, 'So am I.'

'Good,' Chip said. 'Three stand a better chance than one, that I *do* know. Karl, you're the one who goes back.'

Karl looked at him. 'Why me?' he asked.

'Because you're forty-three,' Chip said. 'I'm sorry, brother, but I can't think of any other basis for deciding.'

'Chip,' Buzz said, 'I think I'd better tell you: my leg has been hurting me for the past few hours. I can make it back or I can go on, but—well, I thought you ought to know.'

Karl gave Chip the cigarette. It was down to a couple of centimeters; he snuffed it into the ground. 'All right, Buzz, you'd better be the one,' he said. 'Shave first. We'd all better shave, in case we run into anyone.'

They shaved, and then Chip and Buzz worked out a route for Buzz to the nearst part of the coast, about three hundred kilometers away. He would set off a bomb at the airport at '00015 and another when he was near the sea. He kept two extra in case he needed them and gave his others to Chip. 'With luck you'll be on a boat by tomorrow night,' Chip said. 'Make sure there's nobody counting heads when you take it. Tell Julia, and Lilac too, that we'll be hiding for at least two weeks, maybe longer.'

Buzz shook hands with all of them, wished them luck, and took his bike and left.

'We'll stay right here for a while and take turns getting some sleep,' Chip said. 'Tonight we'll go into the city for cakes and cuvs.'

'Cakes,' Karl said, and Dover said, 'It's going to be a long two weeks.'

'No it isn't,' Chip said. 'That was in case *he* gets caught. We're going to do it in four or five days.'

'Christ and Wei,' Karl said, smiling, 'you're really being cagey.'

3

THEY STAYED where they were for two days—slept and ate and shaved and practised fighting, played children's word games, talked about democratic government and sex and the pygmies of equatorial forests—and on the third day, Sunday, they bicycled north. Outside of '00013 they stopped and went up onto the incline overlooking the plaza and the bridge. The bridge was partly repaired and closed off by barriers. Lines of cyclists crossed the plaza in both directions; there were no doctors, no scanners, no copter, no cars. Where the copter had been, there was a rectangle of fresh pink paving.

Early in the afternoon they passed '001 and glimpsed at a distance Uni's white dome beside the Lake of Universal Brotherhood. They went into the parkland beyond the city.

The following evening, at dusk, with their bikes hidden in a branch-covered hollow and their kits on their shoulders, they passed a scanner at the parkland's farther border and went out onto the grassy slopes that approached Mount Love. They walked briskly, in shoes and green coveralls, with binoculars and gas masks hung about their necks. They held their guns, but as the darkness grew deeper and the slope more rocky and irregular, they pocketed them. Now and then they paused, and Chip put a hand-covered flashlight to his compass.

They came to the first of the three presumed locations of the tunnel's entrance, and separated and looked for it, using their flashlight, guardedly. They didn't find it.

They started for the second location, a kilometer to the northeast. A half moon came over the shoulder of the mountain, wanly lighting it, and they searched its base carefully as they crossed the rock-slope before it.

The slope became smooth, but only in the strip where they were walking—and they realized that they were on a road, old and scrub-patched. Behind them it curved away toward the parkland; ahead it led into a fold in the mountain.

They looked at one another, and took out their guns. Leaving the road, they moved close to the side of the mountain and edged along slowly in single file—first Chip, then Dover, then Karl—holding their kits to keep them from bumping, holding their guns.

They came to the fold, and waited against the mountainside, listening.

No sound came from within.

They waited and listened, and then Chip looked back at the others and raised his gas mask and fastened it.

They did the same.

Chip stepped out into the opening of the fold, his gun before him. Dover and Karl stepped out beside him.

Within was a deep and level clearing; and opposite, at the base of sheer mountain wall, the black round flat-bottomed opening of a large tunnel.

It appeared to be completely unprotected.

They lowered their masks and looked at the opening through their binoculars. They looked at the mountain above it and, taking a few steps forward, looked at the fold's out-curving walls and the oval of sky that roofed it.

'Buzz must have done a good job,' Karl said.

'Or a bad one and got caught,' Dover said.

Chip swung his binoculars back to the opening. Its rim had a glassy sheen, and pale green scrub lay along its bottom. 'It feels like the boats on the beaches,' he said. 'Sitting there wide open . . .'

'Do you think it leads back to Liberty?' Dover asked, and Karl laughed.

Chip said, 'There could be fifty traps that we won't see until it's too late.' He lowered his binoculars.

Karl said, 'Maybe Ria didn't say anything.'

'When you're questioned at a medicenter you say *everything*,' Chip said. 'But even if she didn't, wouldn't it at least be closed? That's what we've got the tools for.'

Karl said, 'It must still be in use.'

Chip stared at the opening.

'We can always go back,' Dover said.

'Sure, let's,' Chip said.

They looked all around them, and raised their masks into place, and walked slowly across the clearing. No gas jetted, no alarms sounded, no members in antigrav gear appeared in the sky.

They walked to the opening of the tunnel and shone their flashlights into it. Light shimmered and sparked in high plastic-lined roundness, all the way to the place where the tunnel seemed to end, but no, was bending to its downward angle. Two steel tracks reached into it, wide and flat, with a couple of meters of unplasticked black rock between them.

They looked back at the clearing and up at the opening's rim. They stepped inside the tunnel, looked at one another, lowered their masks and sniffed.

'Well,' Chip said. 'Ready to walk?'

Karl nodded, and Dover, smiling, said, 'Let's go.'

They stood for a moment, and then walked ahead of the smooth black rock between the tracks.

'Will the air be all right?' Karl asked.

'We've got masks if it isn't,' Chip said. He shone his flashlight on his watch. 'It's a quarter of ten,' he said. 'We should be there around one.'

'Uni'll be up,' Dover said.

'Till we put it to sleep,' Karl said.

The tunnel bent to a slight incline, and they stopped and looked—at plastic roundness glimmering away and away and away into blackest black.

'Christ and Wei,' Karl said.

They started walking again, at a brisker pace, side by side between the tracks. 'We should have brought the bikes,' Dover said. 'We could have coasted.'

'Let's keep the talk to a minimum,' Chip said. 'And just one light at a time. Yours now, Karl.'

They walked without talking, behind the light of Karl's flashlight. They took their binoculars off and put them in their kits.

Chip felt that Uni was listening to them, was recording the vibrations of their footsteps or the heat of their bodies. Would they be able to overcome the defenses it surely was readying, outfight its members, resist its gases? (Were the gas masks any good? Had Jack fallen because he had got his on too late, or would getting it on sooner have made no difference?)

Well, the time for questioning was over, he told himself. This was the time for going ahead. They would meet whatever was waiting for them and do their best to get to the refrigerating plants and blast them.

How many members would they have to hurt, to kill? Maybe none, he thought; maybe the threat of their guns would be enough to protect them. (Against helpful unselfish members seeing Uni in danger? No, never.)

Well, it had to be; there was no other way.

He turned his thoughts to Lilac—to Lilac and Jan and their room in New Madrid.

The tunnel grew cold but the air stayed good.

They walked on, into plastic roundness that glimmered away into blackest black with the tracks reaching into it. *We're here*, he thought. *Now. We're doing it.*

At the end of an hour they stopped to rest. They sat on the tracks and divided a cake among them and passed a container of tea around. Karl said, 'I'd give my arm for some whiskey.'

'I'll buy you a case when we get back,' Chip said.

'You heard him,' Karl said to Dover.

They sat for a few minutes and then they got up and started walking again. Dover walked on a track. 'You look pretty confident,' Chip said, flashing his light at him.

'I am,' Dover said. 'Aren't you?'

'Yes,' Chip said, shining his light ahead again.

'I'd feel better if there were six of us,' Karl said.

'So would I,' Chip said.

It was funny about Dover: he had hidden his face in his arms when Jack had started shooting, Chip remembered, and now, when *they* would soon be shooting, perhaps killing, he seemed cheerful and carefree. But maybe it was a cover-up, to hide anxiety. Or maybe it was just being twenty-five or twenty-six, however old he was.

They walked, shifting their kits from one shoulder to the other.

'Are you sure this thing ends?' Karl said.

Chip flicked the light at his watch. 'It's eleven-thirty,' he said. 'We should be past the halfway mark.'

They kept walking into the plastic roundness. It grew a little less cold.

They stopped again at a quarter of twelve, but they found themselves restless and got up in a minute and went on.

Light glinted far away in the center of the blackness, and Chip pulled out his gun. 'Wait,' Dover said, touching his arm, 'it's *my* light. Look!' He switched his flashlight off and on, off and on, and the glint in the blackness went and came back with it. 'It's the end,' he said. 'Or something on the tracks.'

They walked on, more quickly. Karl took his gun out too. The glint, moving slightly up and down, seemed to stay the same distance from them, small and faint.

'It's moving away from us,' Karl said.

But then, abruptly, it grew brighter, was nearer.

They stopped and raised their masks, fastened them, and walked on.

Toward a disc of steel, a wall that sealed the tunnel to its rim.

They went close to it but didn't touch it. It would slide upward, they saw; bands of fine vertical scratches ran down it and its bottom was shaped to fit over the tracks.

They lowered their masks and Chip put his watch to Dover's light.

'Twenty of one,' he said. 'We made good time.'

'Or else it goes on on the other side,' Karl said.

'You would think of that,' Chip said, pocketing his gun and unslinging his kit. He put it down on the rock, got on one knee beside it, and pulled it open. 'Come closer with the light, Dover,' he said. 'Don't touch it, Karl.'

Karl, looking at the wall, said, 'Do you think it's electrified?'

'Dover?' Chip said.

'Hold on,' Dover said.

He had backed a few meters into the tunnel and was shining his light at them. The tip of his L-beam protruded into it. 'Don't panic, you're not going to be hurt,' he said. 'Your guns don't work. Drop yours, Karl. Chip, let me see your hands, then put them on your head and stand up.'

Chip stared above the light. There was a glistening line: Dover's clipped blond hair.

Karl said, 'Is this a joke or what?'

'Drop it, Karl,' Dover said. 'Put down your kit too. Chip, let me see your hands.'

Chip showed his empty hands and put them on his head and stood up. Karl's gun clattered on the rock, and his kit bumped 'What *is* this?' he said, and to Chip, 'What's he *doing*?'

'He's an espion,' Chip said.

'A what?'

Lilac had been right. An espion in the group. But *Dover*? It was impossible. It couldn't be.

'Hands on your head, Karl,' Dover said. 'Now turn around, both of you, and face the wall.'

'You brother-fighter,' Karl said.

They turned around and faced the steel wall with their hands on their heads.

'Dover,' Chip said. 'Christ and Wei—'

'You little bastard,' Karl said.

'You're not going to be hurt,' Dover said. The wall slid upward—and a long concrete-walled room extended before them, with the tracks going halfway into it and ending. A pair of steel doors were at the room's far end.

'Six steps forward and stop,' Dover said. 'Go on. Six steps.'

They walked six steps forward and stopped.

Kit-strap fittings clinked behind them. 'The gun is still on you,' Dover said—from lower down; he was crouching. They glanced at each other. Karl's eyes questioned; Chip shook his head.

'All right,' Dover said, his voice coming from his standing height again. 'Straight ahead.'

They walked through the concrete-walled room, and the steel doors at the end of it slid apart. White-tiled wall stood beyond.

'Through and to the right,' Dover said.

They went through the doorway and turned to the right. A long white-tiled corridor stretched before them, ending at a single steel door with a scanner beside it. The right-hand wall of the corridor was solid tile; the left was broken by evenly spaced steel doors, ten or twelve of them, each with its scanner, about ten meters apart.

Chip and Karl walked side by side down the corridor with their hands on their heads. *Dover!* Chip thought. The first person he had gone to! And why not? So bitterly anti-Uni he had sounded, that day on the I.A. boat! It was Dover who had told him and Lilac that Liberty was a prison, that Uni had let them get to it! 'Dover!' he said. 'How the hate can you—'

'Just keep walking,' Dover said.

'You're not dulled, you're not treated!'

'No.'

'Then—*how? Why?*'

'You'll see in a minute,' Dover said.

They neared the door at the end of the corridor and it slid abruptly open. Another corridor stretched beyond it: wider, less brightly lit, dark-walled, not tiled.

'Keep going,' Dover said.

They went through the doorway and stopped, staring.

'Go ahead,' Dover said.

They walked on.

What kind of corridor was this? The floor was carpeted, with a gold-colored carpet thicker and softer than any Chip had ever seen or walked on. The walls were lustrous polished wood, with numbered gold-knobbed doors (*12*, *11*) on both sides. Paintings hung between the doors, beautiful paintings that were surely pre-U: a woman sitting with folded hands smiling knowingly; a hillside city of windowed buildings under a strange black-clouded sky; a garden; a woman reclining; a man in armor. A pleasant odor spiced the air; tangy, dry, impossible to name.

'Where *are* we?' Karl asked.

'In Uni,' Dover said.

Ahead of them double doors stood open; a red-draped room lay beyond.

'Keep going,' Dover said.

They went through the doorway and into the red-draped room; it spread away on both sides, and members, people, were sitting and smiling and starting to laugh, were laughing and rising and some were applauding; young people, old people, were rising from chairs and sofas, laughing and applauding; applauding, applauding, *they all were applauding!*; and Chip's arm was pulled down—by Dover, laughing—and he looked at Karl, who looked at him, stupefied; and still they were applauding, men and women, fifty, sixty of them, alert- and alive-looking, in coveralls of silk not paplon, green-gold-blue-white-purple; a tall and beautiful woman, a black-skinned man, a woman who looked like Lilac, a man with white hair who must have been over ninety; applauding, applauding, laughing, applauding . . .

Chip turned, and Dover, grinning, said, 'You're awake,' and to Karl, 'It's real, it's happening.'

'*What* is?' Chip said. 'What the hate *is* this? Who *are* they?'

Laughing, Dover said, 'They're the *programmers*, Chip! And that's what *you're* going to be! Oh if you could only see your faces!'

Chip stared at Karl, and at Dover again. 'Christ and Wei, what are you *talking* about?' he said. 'The programmers are *dead*! Uni's—it goes on by *itself*, it doesn't have—'

Dover was looking past him, smiling. Silence had spread through the room.

Chip turned around.

A man in a smiling mask that looked like Wei (was this really happening?) was coming to him, moving springily in red silk high-collared coveralls. 'Nothing goes on by itself,' he said in a voice that was high-pitched but forceful, his smiling mask-lips moving like real ones. (But *was* it a mask—the yellow skin shrunken tight over the sharp cheekbones, the glinting slit-eyes, the wisps of white hair on the shining yellow head?) 'You must be "Chip" with the one green eye,' the man said, smiling and holding out his hand. 'You'll have to tell me what was wrong with the name "Li" that inspired you to change it.' Laughter lifted around them.

The outstretched hand was normal-colored and youthful. Chip took it (*I'm going mad*, he thought), and it gripped his hand strongly, squeezed his knucklebones to an instant's pain.

'And you're Karl,' the man said, turning and holding out his hand again. 'Now if *you* had changed your name I could understand it.' Laughter rose louder. 'Shake it,' the man said smiling. 'Don't be afraid.'

Karl, staring, shook the man's hand.

Chip said, 'You're——'

'Wei,' the man said, his slit-eyes twinkling. 'From here up, that is.' He touched his coveralls' high collar. 'From here down,' he said, 'I'm several other members, principally Jesus RE who won the decathlon in 163.' He smiled at them. 'Didn't you ever bounce a ball when you were a child?' he asked. 'Didn't you ever jump rope? "Marx, Wood, Wei and Christ; all but Wei were sacrificed." It's still true, you see. "Out of the mouths of babes." Come, sit down, you must be tired. Why couldn't you use the elevators like everyone else? Dover, it's good to have you back. You've done very well, except for that awful business at the '013 bridge.'

They sat in deep and comfortable red chairs, drank pale yellow tart-tasting wine from sparkling glasses, ate sweetly stewed cubes of meat and fish and who-knew-what brought on delicate white plates by young members who smiled at them admiringly—and as they sat and drank and ate, they talked with Wei.

With *Wei!*

How old was that tight-skinned yellow head, living and talking on its lithe red-coveralled body that reached easily for a cigarette, crossed its legs casually? The last anniversary of his birth had been what—the two-hundred-and-sixth, the two-hundred-and-seventh?

Wei died when he was sixty, twenty-five years after the Unification. Generations before the building of Uni, which was programmed by his 'spiritual heirs'. Who died, of course, at sixty-two. So the Family was taught.

And there he sat, drinking, eating, smoking. Men and women stood listening around the group of chairs; he seemed not to notice them. 'The islands have been all those things,' he said. 'At first they were the strongholds of the original incurables; and then, as you put it, "isolation wards" to which we let later incurables "escape", although we weren't so kind as to supply boats in those days.' He smiled and drew on his cigarette. 'Then, however,' he said,' I found a better use for them, and now they serve as, forgive me, wildlife preserves, where natural leaders can emerge and prove themselves exactly as you have done. Now we supply boats and maps, rather obliquely, and "shepherds" like Dover who accompany returning members and prevent as much violence as they can. And prevent, of course, the final intended violence, Uni's destruction—although the visitors' display is the usual target, so there's no real danger whatsoever.'

Chip said, 'I don't know where I am.' Karl, spearing a cube of meat with a small gold fork, said, 'Asleep in the parkland,' and the men and women nearby laughed.

Wei, smiling, said, 'Yes, it's a disconcerting discovery, I'm sure. The computer that you thought was the Family's changeless and uncontrolled master is in fact the Family's servant, controlled by members like yourselves—enterprising, thoughtful, and concerned. Its goals and procedures change continually, according to the decisions of a High Council and fourteen sub-councils. We enjoy luxuries, as you can see, but we have responsibilities that more than justify them. Tomorrow you'll begin to learn. Now, though'—he leaned forward and pressed his cigarette into an ashtray—'it's very late, thanks to your partiality to tunnels. You'll be shown to your rooms; I hope you find them worth the walk.' He smiled and rose, and they rose with him. He shook Karl's hand—'Congratulations, Karl,' he said—and Chip's. 'And congratulations to you, Chip,' he said. 'We suspected a long time ago that sooner or later you would be coming. We're glad you haven't disappointed us. *I'm* glad, I mean; it's hard to avoid talking as if Uni has feelings too.' He turned away and people crowded around them, shaking their hands and saying, 'Congratulations, I never thought you'd make it before Unification Day . . . it's awful isn't it when you come in and everyone's sitting here . . . congratulations . . . you'll get used to things before you . . . congratulations. . . .'

The room was large and pale blue, with a large pale-blue silken bed with many pillows, a large painting of floating water lilies, a table of covered dishes and decanters, dark green armchairs, and a bowl of white and yellow chrysanthemums on a long low cabinet.

'It's beautiful,' Chip said. 'Thank you.'

The girl who had led him to it, an ordinary-looking member

of sixteen or so in white paplon, said, 'Sit down and I'll take off your——' She pointed at his feet.

'Shoes,' he said, smiling. 'No. Thanks, sister; I can do it myself.'

'Daughter,' she said.

'Daughter?'

'The programmers are our Fathers and Mothers,' she said. 'Oh,' he said. 'All right. Thanks, daughter. You can go now.'

She looked surprised and hurt. 'I'm supposed to stay and take care of you,' she said. 'Both of us.' She nodded toward a doorway beyond the bed. Light and the sound of running water came from it.

Chip went to it.

A pale-blue bathroom was there, large and gleaming; another young member in white paplon kneeled by a filling tub, stirring her hand in the water. She turned and smiled and said, 'Hello, Father.'

'Hello,' Chip said. He stood with his hand on the jamb and looked back at the first girl—drawing the cover from the bed— and back again at the second girl.

She smiled up at him, kneeling. He stood with his hand on the jamb. 'Daughter,' he said.

<h2 style="text-align:center">4</h2>

HE WAS SITTING IN BED—had finished his breakfast and was reaching for a cigarette—when a knock at the door sounded. One of the girls went to answer it and Dover came in, smiling and clean and brisk in yellow silk. 'How you doing, brother?' he asked.

'Pretty well,' Chip said, 'pretty well.' The other girl lit his cigarette, took the breakfast tray, and asked him if he wanted more coffee. 'No, thanks,' he said. 'Do you want some coffee?'

'No, thanks,' Dover said. He sat in one of the dark green chairs and leaned back, his elbows on the chair arms, his hands meshed across his middle, his legs outstretched. Smiling at Chip, he said, 'Over the shock?'

'Hate, no,' Chip said.

'It's a long-standing custom,' Dover said. 'You'll enjoy it when the next group comes in.'

'It's cruel, really cruel,' Chip said.

'Wait, you'll be laughing and applauding with everyone else.'

'How often do groups turn up?'

'Sometimes not for years,' Dover said, 'sometimes a month apart. It averages out to one-point-something people a year.'

'And you were in contact with Uni the whole time, you brother-fighter?'

Dover nodded and smiled. 'A telecomp the size of a matchbox,' he said. 'In fact, that's what I kept it in.'

'Bastard,' Chip said.

The girl with the tray had taken it out, and the other girl changed the ashtray on the night table and took her coveralls from a chairback and went into the bathroom. She closed the door.

Dover looked after her, then looked at Chip quizzically. 'Nice night?' he asked.

'Mm-hmm,' Chip said. 'I gather they're not treated.'

'Not in all departments, that's for sure,' Dover said. 'I hope you're not sore at me for not dropping a hint somewhere along the way. The rules are ironclad: no help beyond what's asked of you, no suggestions, no nothing; stay on the sidelines as much as you can and try to prevent bloodshed. I shouldn't have even been doing that routine on the boat—about Liberty being a prison—but I'd been there for two years and nobody was even *thinking* of trying anything. You can see why I wanted to move things along.'

'Yes, I certainly can,' Chip said. He tipped ashes from his cigarette into the clean white tray.

'I'd just as soon you didn't say anything to Wei about it,' Dover said. 'You're having lunch with him at one o'clock.'

'Karl too?'

'No, just you. I think he's got you pegged as High Council material. I'll come by at ten-of and take you to him. You'll find a razor inside there—a thing that looks like a flashlight. This afternoon we'll go to the medicenter and start dewhiskerizing.'

'There's a medicenter?'

'There's everything,' Dover said. 'A medicenter, a library, a gym, a pool, a theater—there's even a garden that you'd swear was up on top. I'll show you around later.'

Chip said, 'And this is where we—stay?'

'All except us poor shepherds,' Dover said. 'I'll be going out to another island, but not for at least six months, thank Uni.'

Chip put his cigarette out. He pressed it out thoroughly. 'What if I don't want to stay?' he said.

'Don't *want* to?' Dover said.

'I've got a wife and a baby, remember?'

'Well so do lots of the others,' Dover said. 'You've got a bigger obligation here, Chip; an obligation to the whole Family, *including* the members on the islands.'

'Nice obligation,' Chip said. 'Silk coveralls and two girls at once.'

'That was for last night only,' Dover said. 'Tonight you'll be lucky to get one.' He sat up straight. 'Look,' he said, 'I know there are—surface attractions here that make it all look—questionable. But the Family *needs* Uni. Think of the way things

were on Liberty! And it needs untreated programmers to run
Uni and—well, Wei'll explain things better than I can. And one
day a week we wear paplon anyway. And eat cakes.'

'A whole day?' Chip said. 'Really?'

'All right, all right,' Dover said, getting up. He went to a chair
where Chip's green coveralls lay and picked them up and felt
their pockets. 'Is everything here?' he asked.

'Yes,' Chip said. 'Including some snapshots I'd like to have.'

'Sorry, nothing you came in with,' Dover said. 'More rules.'
He took Chip's shoes from the floor and stood and looked at him.
'Everyone's a little unsure at first,' he said. 'You'll be proud to
stay once you've got the right slant on things. It's an obligation.'

'I'll remember that,' Chip said.

There was a knock at the door, and the girl who had taken the
tray came in with blue silk coveralls and white sandals. She put
them on the foot of the bed.

Dover, smiling, said, 'If you want paplon it can be arranged.'

The girl looked at him.

'Hate, no,' Chip said. 'I guess I'm as worthy of silk as anyone
else around here.'

'You are,' Dover said. 'You are, Chip. I'll see you at ten of one,
right?' He started to the door with the green coveralls over his
arm and the shoes in his hand. The girl hurried ahead to open the
door for him.

Chip said, 'What happened to Buzz?'

Dover stopped and turned, regretful-looking. 'He was caught
in '015,' he said.

'And treated?'

Dover nodded.

'More rules,' Chip said.

Dover nodded again and turned and went out.

There were thin steaks cooked in a lightly spiced brown sauce,
small browned onions, a sliced yellow vegetable that Chip hadn't
seen on Liberty—'Squash,' Wei said—and a clear red wine that
was less enjoyable than the yellow of the night before. They ate
with gold knives and forks, from plates with wide gold borders.

Wei, in gray silk, ate quickly, cutting his steak, forking it into
his wrinkle-lipped mouth, and chewing only briefly before
swallowing and raising his fork again. Now and then he paused,
sipped wine, and pressed his yellow napkin to his lips.

'These things existed,' he said. 'Would there have been any
point in destroying them?'

The room was large and handsomely furnished in pre-U style:
white, gold, orange, yellow. At a corner of it, two white-coveralled
members waited by a wheeled serving table.

'Of course it seems wrong at first,' Wei said, 'but the ultimate
decisions *have* to be made by untreated members and untreated

members can't and shouldn't live their lives on cakes and TV and *Marx Writing*.' He smiled. 'Not even on *Wei Addressing the Chemotherapists*,' he said, and put steak into his mouth.

'Why can't the Family make its decisions itself?' Chip asked.

Wei chewed and swallowed. 'Because it's incapable of doing so,' he said. 'That is, of doing so reasonably. Untreated it's—well, you had a sample on your island; it's mean and foolish and aggressive, motivated more often by selfishness than by anything else. Selfishness and fear.' He put onions into his mouth.

'It achieved the Unification,' Chip said.

'Mmm, yes,' Wei said, 'but after what a struggle! And what a fragile structure the Unification was until we buttressed it with treatments! No, the Family has to be helped to full humanity—by treatments today, by genetic engineering tomorrow—and decisions have to be made for it. Those who have the means and the intelligence have the duty as well. To shirk it would be treason against the species.' He put steak into his mouth and raised his other hand and beckoned.

'And part of the duty,' Chip said, 'is to kill members at sixty-two?'

'Ah, *that*,' Wei said, and smiled. 'Always a principal question, sternly asked.'

The two members came to them, one with a decanter of wine and the other with a gold tray that he held at Wei's side. 'You're looking at only part of the picture,' Wei said, taking a large fork and spoon and lifting a steak from the tray. He held it with sauce dripping from it. 'What you're neglecting to look at,' he said, 'is the immeasurable number of members who would die far *earlier* than sixty-two if not for the peace and stability and well-being we give them. Think of the mass for a moment, not of individuals within the mass.' He put the steak on his plate. 'We add many more years to the Family's total life than we take away from it,' he said. 'Many, many more years.' He spooned sauce onto the steak and took onions and squash. 'Chip?' he said.

'No, thanks,' Chip said. He cut a piece from the half-steak before him. The member with the decanter refilled his glass.

'Incidentally,' Wei said, cutting steak, 'the actual time of dying is closer now to sixty-three than sixty-two. It will grow still higher as the population on Earth is gradually reduced.' He put steak into his mouth.

The members withdrew.

Chip said, 'Do you include the members who don't get born in your balance of years added and taken away?'

'No,' Wei said, smiling. 'We're not that unrealistic. If those members *were* born, there would be no stability, no wellbeing, and eventually no Family.' He put squash into his mouth and chewed and swallowed. 'I don't expect your feelings to change in one lunch,' he said. 'Look around, talk with everyone, browse in the library—particularly in the history and sociology banks. I hold informal discussions a few evenings a week—once a teacher, always a teacher—sit in on some of them, argue, discuss.'

'I left a wife and a baby on Liberty,' Chip said.

'From which I deduce,' Wei said, smiling, 'that they weren't of overriding importance to you.'

Chip said, 'I expected to be coming back.'

'Arrangements can be made for their care if necessary,' Wei said. 'Dover told me you had already done so.'

'Will I be allowed to go back?' Chip asked.

'You won't want to,' Wei said. 'You'll come to recognize that we're right and your responsibility lies here.' He sipped wine and pressed his napkin to his lips. 'If we're wrong on minor points you can sit on the High Council some day and correct us,' he said. 'Are you interested in architecture or city planning, by any chance?'

Chip looked at him and, after a moment, said, 'I've thought once or twice about designing buildings.'

'Uni thinks you should be on the Architectural Council at present,' Wei said. 'Look in on it. Meet Madhir, the head of it.' He put onions into his mouth.

Chip said, 'I really don't *know* anything . . .'

'You can learn if you're interested,' Wei said, cutting steak. 'There's plenty of time.'

Chip looked at him. 'Yes,' he said. 'Programmers seem to live past sixty-two. Even past sixty-three.'

'Exceptional members have to be preserved as long as possible,' Wei said. 'For the Family's sake.' He put steak into his mouth and chewed, looking at Chip with his slit-eyes. 'Would you like to hear something incredible?' he said. 'Your generation of programmers is almost certain to live indefinitely. Isn't that fantastic? We old ones are going to die sooner or later—the doctors say maybe not, but Uni says we will. You younger ones though, in all probability you *won't* die. Ever.'

Chip put another piece of the steak into his mouth and chewed it slowly.

Wei said, 'I suppose it's an unsettling thought. It'll grow more attractive as you get older.'

Chip swallowed what was in his mouth. He looked at Wei, glanced at his gray-silk chest, and looked at his face again. 'That member,' he said. 'The decathlon winner. Did he die naturally or was he killed?'

'He was killed,' Wei said. 'With his permission, given freely, even eagerly.'

'Of course,' Chip said. 'He was treated.'

'An athlete?' Wei said. 'They take very little. No, he was proud that he was going to become—allied to me. His only concern was whether I would keep him "in condition"—a concern that I'm afraid was justified. You'll find that the children, the ordinary members here, vie with one another to give parts of themselves for transplant. If you wanted to replace that eye, for instance, they'd be slipping into your room and begging you for the honor.' He put squash into his mouth.

Chip shifted in his seat. 'My eye doesn't bother me,' he said. 'I like it.'

'You shouldn't,' Wei said. 'If nothing could be done about it, then you would be justified in accepting it. But an imperfection that can be remedied? That we must *never* accept.' He cut steak. '"One goal, one goal only, for all of us—perfection,"' he said. 'We're not there yet, but some day we will be: a Family improved genetically so that treatments no longer are needed; a corps of ever-living programmers so that the islands too can be unified; perfection, on Earth and moving "outward, outward, outward to the stars".' His fork, with steak on it, stopped before his lips. He looked ahead of him and said, 'I dreamed of it when I was young: a universe of the gentle, the helpful, the loving, the unselfish. I'll live to see it. I shall live to see it.'

Dover led Chip and Karl through the complex that afternoon—showed them the library, the gym, the pool, and the garden ('Christ and Wei.' 'Wait till you see the sunsets and the stars'); the music room, the theater, the lounges; the dining room and the kitchen ('I don't know, from somewhere,' a member said, watching other members taking bundles of lettuce and lemons from a steel carrier. 'Whatever we need comes in,' she said smiling. 'Ask Uni'). There were four levels, passed through by small elevators and narrow escalators. The medicenter was on the bottom level. Doctors named Boroviev and Rosen, young-moving men with shrunken faces as old-looking as Wei's, welcomed them and examined them and gave them infusions. 'We can replace that eye one-two-three, you know,' Rosen said to Chip, and Chip said, 'I know. Thanks, but it doesn't bother me.'

They swam in the pool. Dover went to swim with a tall and beautiful woman Chip had noticed applauding the night before, and he and Karl sat on the edge of the pool and watched them. 'How do you feel?' Chip asked.

'I don't know,' Karl said. 'I'm pleased, of course, and Dover says it's all necessary and it's our duty to help, but—I don't know. Even if they're running Uni, it's Uni anyway, isn't it?'

'Yes,' Chip said. 'That's how I feel.'

'There would have been a mess up above if we'd done what we planned,' Karl said, 'but it would have been straightened out eventually, more or less.' He shook his head. 'I honestly don't know, Chip,' he said. 'Any system the Family set up on its own would certainly be a lot less *efficient* than Uni is, than these people are; you can't deny that.'

'No, you can't,' Chip said.

'Isn't it fantastic how long they live?' Karl said. 'I still can't get over the fact that—look at those breasts, will you? Christ and Wei.'

A light-skinned round-breasted woman dived into the pool from the other side.

Karl said, 'Let's talk some more later on, all right?' He slipped down into the water.

'Sure, we've got plenty of time,' Chip said.

Karl smiled at him and kicked off and swam arm-over-arm away.

The next morning Chip left his room and walked down a green-carpeted painting-hung corridor toward a steel door at the end of it. He hadn't gone very far when 'Hi, brother,' Dover said and came along and walked beside him. 'Hi,' Chip said. He looked ahead again and, walking, said, 'Am I being guarded?'

'Only when you go in this direction,' Dover said.

Chip said, 'I couldn't do anything with my bare hands even if I wanted to.'

'I know,' Dover said. 'The old man's cautious. Pre-U mind.' He tapped his temple and smiled. 'Only for a few days,' he said.

They walked to the end of the corridor and the steel door slid open. White-tiled corridor stretched beyond it; a member in blue touched a scanner and went through a doorway.

They turned and started back. The door whispered behind them. 'You'll get to see it,' Dover said. 'He'll probably give you the tour himself. Want to go to the gym?'

In the afternoon Chip looked in at the offices of the Architectural Council. A small and cheerful old man recognized him and welcomed him—Madhir, the Council's head. He looked to be over a hundred; his hands too—all of him apparently. He introduced Chip to other members of the Council: an old woman named Sylvie, a reddish-haired man of fifty or so whose name Chip didn't catch, and a short but pretty woman called Gri-gri. Chip had coffee with them and ate a piece of pastry with a cream filling. They showed him a set of plans they were discussing, lay-outs that Uni had made for the rebuilding of 'G-3 cities'. They talked about whether or not the layouts should be redone to different specifications, asked questions of a telecomp and disagreed on the significance of its answers. The old woman Sylvie gave a point-by-point explanation of why she felt the layouts were needlessly monotonous. Madhir asked Chip if he had an opinion; he said he didn't. The younger woman, Gri-gri, smiled at him invitingly.

There was a party in the main lounge that night—'Happy new Year!' 'Happy U year!'—and Karl shouted in Chip's ear, 'I'll tell you one thing I don't like about this place! No whiskey! Isn't that a shut-off? If wine is okay, why not whiskey?' Dover was dancing with the woman who looked like Lilac (not really, not half as pretty), and there were people Chip had sat with at meals and met in the gym and the music room, people he had seen in one part of the complex or another, people he hadn't seen before; there were more than had been there the other night when he and Karl had come in—almost a hundred of them, with white-paploned members channeling trays among them. 'Happy U year!' someone said to him, an elderly woman who had been at his lunch table, Hera or Hela. 'It's almost 172!' she said. 'Yes,' he said, 'half an hour.' 'Oh, there he is!' she said, and moved forward. Wei was in the doorway, in white, with people crowding around him. He shook their hands and kissed their cheeks, his shriveled yellow face grin-split and gleaming, his eyes lost in wrinkles. Chip moved back farther into the crowd and turned away. Gri-gri waved, jumping up to see him over the people between them. He waved back at her and smiled and kept moving.

He spent the next day, Unification Day, in the gym and the library.

He went to a few of Wei's evening discussions. They were held in the garden, a pleasant place to be. The grass and the trees were real, and the stars and the moon were near reality, the moon changing phase but never position. Bird warblings sounded from time to time and a gentle breeze blew. Fifteen or twenty programmers were usually at the discussions, sitting on chairs and on the grass. Wei, in a chair, did most of the talking. He expanded on quotations from the *Living Wisdom* and deftly traced the particulars of questions to their encompassing generalities. Now and then he deferred to the head of the Educational Council, Gustafsen, or to Boroviev, the head of the Medical Council, or to another of the High Council members.

At first Chip sat at the edge of the group and only listened, but then he began to ask questions—why parts, at least, of treatments couldn't be put back on a voluntary basis; whether human perfection might not include a degree of selfishness and aggressiveness; whether selfishness, in fact, didn't play a considerable part in their own acceptance of alleged 'duty' and 'responsibility'. Some of the programmers near him seemed affronted by his questions, but Wei answered them patiently and fully; seemed even to welcome them, heard his 'Wei?' over the askings of the others. He moved a little closer in from the group's edge.

One night he sat up in bed and lit a cigarette and smoked in the dark.

The woman lying beside him stroked his back. 'It's right, Chip,' she said. 'It's what's best for everyone.'

'You read minds?' he said.

'Sometimes,' she said. Her name was Deirdre and she was on

the Colonial Council. She was thirty-eight, light-skinned, and not especially pretty, but sensible, shapely, and good company.

'I'm beginning to think it *is* what's best,' Chip said, 'and I don't know whether I'm being convinced by Wei's logic or by lobsters and Mozart and you. Not to mention the prospect of eternal life.'

'That scares me,' Deirdre said.

'Me too,' Chip said.

She kept stroking his back. 'It took me two months to cool down,' she said.

'Is that how you thought of it?' he said. 'Cooling down?'

'Yes,' she said. 'And growing up. Facing reality.'

'So why does it feel like giving in?' Chip said.

'Lie down,' Deirdre said.

He put out his cigarette, put the ashtray on the table, and turned to her, lying down. They held each other and kissed. 'Truly,' she said. 'It's best for everybody, in the long run. We'll improve things gradually, working in our own councils.'

They kissed and caressed each other, and then they kicked down the sheet and she threw her leg over Chip's hip and his hardness slipped easily into her.

He was sitting in the library one morning when a hand took his shoulder. He looked around, startled, and Wei was there. He bent, pushing Chip aside, and put his face down to the viewer hood.

After a moment he said, 'Well, you've gone to the right man.' He kept his face at the hood another moment, and then stood up and let go of Chip's shoulder and smiled at him. 'Read Liebman too,' he said. 'And Okida and Marcuse. I'll make a list of titles and give it to you in the garden this evening. Will you be there?'

Chip nodded.

His days fell into a routine: mornings at the libary, afternoons at the Council. He studied construction methods and environment planning; examined factory flow charts and circulation patterns of residential buildings. Madhir and Sylvie showed him drawings of buildings under construction and buildings planned for the future, of cities as they existed and (plastic overlay) cities as they might some day be modified. He was the eighth member of the Council; of the other seven, three were inclined to challenge Uni's designs and change them, and four, including Madhir, were inclined to accept them without question. Formal meetings were held on Friday afternoons; at other times seldom more than four or five of the members were in the offices. Once only Chip and Gri-gri were there, and they wound up locked together on Madhir's sofa.

After Council, Chip used the gym and the pool. He ate with

Deirdre and Dover and Dover's woman-of-the-day and whoever else joined them—sometimes Karl, on the Transportation Council and resigned to wine.

One day in February, Chip asked Dover if it was possible to get in touch with whoever had replaced him on Liberty and find out if Lilac and Jan were all right and whether Julia was providing for them as she had said she would.

'Sure,' Dover said. 'No problem at all.'

'Would you do it then?' Chip said. 'I'd appreciate it.'

A few days later Dover found Chip in the library. 'All's well,' he said. 'Lilac is staying home and buying food and paying rent, so Julia must be coming through.'

'Thanks, Dover,' Chip said. 'I was worried.'

'The man there'll keep an eye on her,' Dover said. 'If she needs anything, money can come in the mail.'

'That's fine,' Chip said. 'Wei told me.' He smiled. 'Poor Julia,' he said, 'supporting all those families when it isn't really necessary. If she knew she'd have a fit.'

Dover smiled. 'She would,' he said. 'Of course, everyone who set out didn't get here, so in some cases it *is* necessary.'

'That's right,' Chip said. 'I wasn't thinking.'

'See you at lunch,' Dover said.

'Right,' Chip said. 'Thanks.'

Dover went, and Chip turned to the viewer and bent his face to the hood. He put his finger on the next-page button and, after a moment, pressed it.

He began to speak up at Council meetings and to ask fewer questions at Wei's discussions. A petition was circulated for the reduction of cake days to one a month; he hesitated but signed it. He went from Deirdre to Blackie to Nina and back to Deirdre; listened in the smaller lounges to sex gossip and jokes about High Council members; followed crazes for paper-airplane making and speaking in pre-U languages ('Français' was pronounced 'Fransay', he learned).

One morning he woke up early and went to the gym. Wei was there, jumping astride and swinging dumbbells, shining with sweat, slab-muscled, slim-hipped; in a black supporter and something white tied around his neck. 'Another early bird, good morning,' he said, jumping his legs out and in, out and in, swinging the dumbbells out and together over his white-wisped head.

'Good morning,' Chip said. He went to the side of the gym and took off his robe and hung it on a hook. Another robe, blue, hung a few hooks away.

'You weren't at the discussion last night,' Wei said.

Chip turned. 'There was a party,' he said, toeing off his sandals. 'Patya's birthday.'

'It's all right,' Wei said, jumping, swinging the dumbbells. 'I just mentioned it.'

Chip walked onto a mat and began trotting in place. The white thing around Wei's neck was a band of silk, tightly knotted.

Wei stopped jumping and tossed down the dumbbells and took a towel from one of the parallel bars. 'Madhir's afraid you're going to be a radical,' he said smiling.

'He doesn't know the half of it,' Chip said.

Wei watched him, still smiling, wiping the towel over his big-muscled shoulders and under his arms.

'Do you work out every morning?' Chip asked.

'No, only once or twice a week,' Wei said. 'I'm not athletic by nature.' He rubbed the towel behind him.

Chip stopped trotting. 'Wei, there's something I'd like to speak to you about,' he said.

'Yes?' Wei said. 'What is it?'

Chip took a step toward him. 'When I first came here,' he said, 'and we had lunch together—'

'Yes?' Wei said.

Chip cleared his throat and said, 'You said that if I wanted to I could have my eye replaced. Rosen said so too.'

'Yes, of course,' Wei said. 'Do you want to have it done?'

Chip looked at him uncertainly. 'I don't know, it seems like such—vanity,' he said. 'But I've always been aware of it——'

'It's not vanity to correct a flaw,' Wei said. 'It's negligence not to.'

'Can't I get a lens put on?' Chip said. 'A brown lens?'

'Yes,' Wei said, 'if you want to cover it and not correct it.'

Chip looked away and then back at him. 'All right,' he said, 'I'd like to do it, have it done.'

'Good,' Wei said, and smiled. 'I've had eye changes twice,' he said. 'There's blurriness for a few days, that's all. Go down to the medicenter this morning. I'll tell Rosen to do it himself, as soon as possible.'

'Thank you,' Chip said.

Wei put his towel around his white-banded neck, turned to the parallel bars, and lifted himself straight-armed onto them. 'Keep quiet about it,' he said, hand-walking between the bars, 'or the children will start pestering you.'

It was done, and he looked in his mirror and both his eyes were brown. He smiled, and stepped back, and stepped close again. He looked at himself from one side and the other, smiling.

When he had dressed he looked again.

Deirdre, in the lounge, said, 'It's a tremendous improvement! You look wonderful! Karl, Gri-gri, look at Chip's eye!'

Members helped them into heavy green coats, thickly quilted

and hooded. They closed them and put on thick green gloves, and a member pulled open the door. The two of them, Wei and Chip, went in.

They walked together along an aisle between steel walls of memory banks, their breath clouding from their nostrils. Wei spoke of the banks' internal temperature and of the weight and number of them. They turned into a narrower aisle where the steel wall stretched ahead of them convergingly to a faraway crosswall.

'I was in here when I was a child,' Chip said.

'Dover told me,' Wei said.

'It frightened me then,' Chip said. 'But it has a kind of—majesty to it; the order and precision . . .'

Wei nodded, his eyes glinting. 'Yes,' he said. 'I look for excuses to come in.'

They turned into another cross-aisle, passed a pillar, and turned into another long narrow aisle between back-to-back rows of steel memory banks.

In coveralls again, they looked into a vast railed pit, round and deep, where steel and concrete housings lay, linked by blue arms and sending thicker blue arms branching upward to low brightly glowing ceilings. ('I believe you had a special interest in the refrigerating plants,' Wei said, smiling, and Chip looked uncomfortable.) A steel pillar stood beside the pit; beyond it lay a second railed and blue-armed pit, and another pillar, another pit. The room was enormous, cool and hushed. Transmitting and receiving equipment lined its two long walls, with red pinpoint lights gleaming; members in blue drew out and replaced two-handled vertical panels of speckled black and gold. Four red-dome reactors stood at one end of the room, and beyond them, behind glass, half a dozen programmers sat at a round console reading into microphones, turning pages.

'There you are,' Wei said.

Chip looked around at it all. He shook his head and blew out breath. 'Christ and Wei,' he said. Wei laughed happily.

They stayed a while, walking about, looking, talking with some of the members, and then they left the room and walked through white-tiled corridors. A steel door slid open for them, and they went through and walked together down the carpeted corridor beyond.

5

EARLY IN SEPTEMBER OF 172, a party of seven men and women accompanied by a 'shepherd' named Anna set out from the Andaman Islands in Stability Bay to attack and destroy Uni. Announcements of their progress were made in the programmers' dining room at each mealtime. Two members of the party 'failed' in the airport at SEA77120 (head-shakings and sighs of disappointment), and two more the following day in a carport in EUR46209 (head-shakings and sighs of disappointment). On the evening of Thursday, September tenth, the three others—a young man and woman and an older man—came single-file into the main lounge with their hands on their heads, looking angry and frightened. A stocky woman behind them, grinning, pocketed a gun.

The three stared foolishly, and the programmers rose, laughing and applauding, Chip and Deirdre among them. Chip laughed loud, applauded hard. All the programmers laughed loud and applauded hard as the newcomers lowered their hands and turned to one another and to their laughing applauding shepherd.

Wei in gold-trimmed green went to them, smiling, and shook their hands. The programmers hushed one another. Wei touched his collar and said, 'From here up, at any rate. From here down . . .' The programmers laughed and hushed one another. They moved closer, to hear, to congratulate.

After a few minutes the stocky woman slipped out of the crush and left the lounge. She turned to the right and went toward a narrow upgoing escalator. Chip came after her. 'Congratulations,' he said.

'Thanks,' the woman said, glancing back at him and smiling tiredly. She was about forty, with dirt on her face and dark rings under her eyes.

'When did you come in?' she asked.

'About eight months ago,' Chip said.

'Who with?' The woman stepped onto the escalator.

Chip stepped on behind her. 'Dover,' he said.

'Oh,' she said. 'Is he still here?'

'No,' Chip said. 'He was sent out last month. Your people didn't come in empty-handed, did they?'

'I wish they had,' the woman said. 'My shoulder is killing me. I left the kits by the elevator. I'm going to get them now.' She stepped off the escalator and walked back around it.

Chip went with her. 'I'll give you a hand with them,' he said.

'It's all right, I'll pick up one of the boys,' the woman said, turning to the right.

'No, I don't mind doing it,' Chip said.

They walked down the corridor past the glass wall of the pool. The woman looked in and said, 'That's where I'm going to be in fifteen minutes.'

'I'll join you,' Chip said.

The woman glanced at him. 'All right,' she said.

Boroviev and a member came into the corridor toward them 'Anna! Hello!' Boroviev said, his eyes sparkling in his withered face. The member, a girl, smiled at Chip.

'Hello!' the woman said, shaking Boroviev's hand. 'How are you?'

'Fine!' Boroviev said. 'Oh, you look exhausted!'

'I am.'

'But everything's all right?'

'Yes,' the woman said. 'They're downstairs. I'm on my way to get rid of the kits.'

'Get some rest!' Boroviev said.

'I'm going to,' the woman said, smiling. 'Six months of it.'

Boroviev smiled at Chip, and taking the member's hand, went past them and down the corridor. The woman and Chip went ahead toward the steel door at the corridor's end. They passed the archway to the garden, where someone was singing and playing a guitar.

'What kind of bombs did they have?' Chip asked.

'Crude plastic ones,' the woman said. 'Throw and boom. I'll be glad to get them into the can.'

The steel door slid open; they went through and turned to the right. White-tiled corridor stretched before them with scanner-posted doors in the left-hand wall.

'Which council are you on?' the woman asked.

'Wait a second,' Chip said, stopping and taking her arm.

She stopped and turned and he punched her in the stomach. Catching her face in his hand, he smashed her head back hard against the wall. He let it come forward, smashed it back again, and let go of her. She slid downward—a tile was cracked—and sank heavily to the floor and fell over sideways, one knee up, eyes closed.

Chip stepped to the nearest door and opened it. A two-toilet bathroom was inside. Holding the door with his foot, he reached over and took hold of the woman under her arms. A member came into the corridor and stared at him, a boy of about twenty.

'Help me,' Chip said.

The boy came over, his face pale. 'What happened?' he asked.

'Take her legs,' Chip said. 'She passed out.'

They carried the woman into the bathroom and set her down on the floor. 'Shouldn't we take her to the medicenter?' the boy asked.

'We will in a minute,' Chip said. He got on one knee beside the woman, reached into the pocket of her yellow-paplon coveralls, and took out her gun. He aimed it at the boy. 'Turn around and face the wall,' he said. 'Don't make a sound.'

The boy stared wide-eyed at him, and turned around and faced the wall between the toilets.

Chip stood up, passed the gun between his hands, and holding it by its taped barrel, stepped astride the woman. He raised the gun and quickly swung its butt down hard on the boy's close-clipped head. The blow drove the boy to his knees. He fell forward against the wall and then sideways, his head stopping against the wall and toilet pipe, red gleaming in its short black hair.

Chip looked away and at the gun. He passed it back to a shooting grip, thumbed its safety catch aside, and turned it toward the bathroom's back wall: a red thread, gone, shattered a tile and drilled dust from behind it. Chip put the gun into his pocket, and holding it, stepped over the woman and moved to the door.

He went into the corridor, pulled the door tightly closed, and walked quickly, holding the gun in his pocket. He came to the end of the corridor and followed its left turn.

A member coming toward him smiled and said, 'Hello Father.'

Chip nodded, passing him. 'Son,' he said.

A door was ahead in the right-hand wall. He went to it, opened it, and went through. He closed the door behind him and stood in the dark hallway. He took out the gun.

Opposite, under a ceiling that barely glowed, were the pink, brown, and orange memory-banks-for-visitors, the gold cross and sickle, the clock on the wall—*9.33 Thu 10 Sep 172 Y.U.*

He went to the left, past the other displays, unlighted, dormant, increasingly visible in the light from an open door to the lobby.

He went to the open door.

On the floor in the center of the lobby lay three kits, a gun, and two knives. Another kit lay near the elevator doors.

Wei leaned back, smiling, and drew on his cigarette. 'Believe me,' he said, 'that's how everybody feels at this point. But even the most stubbornly disapproving come to see that we're wise and we're right.' He looked at the programmers standing around the group of chairs. 'Isn't that so, Chip?' he said. 'Tell them.' He looked about, smiling.

'Chip went out,' Deirdre said, and someone else said 'After Anna.' Another programmer said, 'Too bad, Deirdre,' and Deirdre, turning, said, 'He didn't go out after Anna, he went out; he'll be right back.'

'A little tired, of course,' someone said.

Wei looked at his cigarette and leaned forward and pressed it out. 'Everyone here will confirm what I'm saying,' he said to the newcomers, and smiled. 'Excuse me, will you?' he said. 'I'll be back in a little while. Don't get up.' He rose, and the programmers parted for him.

Straw filled half the kit, held in place by a wood divider; on the other side, wires, tools, papers, cakes, whatnot. He brushed straw away—from more dividers that formed square straw-filled compartments. He fingered in one and found only straw and hollowness; in another, though, there was something soft-surfaced but firm.

He pulled away straw and lifted out a heavy whitish ball, a claylike handful with straw sticking to it. He put it on the floor and took out two more—another compartment was empty—and a fourth one. He ripped the wood framework from the kit, put it aside, and dumped out straw, tools, everything; put the four bombs close together in the kit, opened the other two kits and took out their bombs and put them in with the four—five from one kit, six from the other. Room for three more remained.

He got up and went for the fourth kit by the elevators. A sound in the hallway spun him around—he had left the gun by the bombs—but the doorway was empty-dark and the sound (whisper of silk?) was no more. If it had been at all. His own sound, it might have been, reflected back at him.

Watching the doorway, he backed to the kit, caught up its strap, and brought it quickly to the other kits; kneeled again and brought the gun close to his side. He opened the kit, pulled out straw, and lifted out three bombs and fitted them in with the others. Three rows of six. He covered them and pressed the kit closed, then put his arm through the strap and lodged it on his shoulder. He raised the kit carefully against his hip. The bombs in it shifted heavily.

The gun with the kits was an L-beam too, newer-looking than the one he had. He picked it up and opened it. A stone was in the generator's place. He put the gun down, took one of the knives—black-handled, pre-U, its blade worn thin but sharp—and slipped it into his right-hand pocket. Taking the working gun and holding the kit with his fingers under its bottom, he got up from his knees, stepped over an empty kit, and went quietly to the doorway.

Darkness and silence were outside it. He waited till he could see more clearly, then walked to the left. A giant telecomp clung to the display wall (it had been broken, hadn't it, when he had been there before?); he passed it and stopped. Someone lay near the wall ahead, motionless.

But no, it was a stretcher, two stretchers, with pillows and blankets. The blankets Papa Jan and he had wrapped around them. They very same two, conceivably.

He stood for a moment, remembering.

Then he went on. To the door. The door that Papa Jan had pushed him through. And the scanner beside it, the first he had ever passed without touching. How frightened he had been!

This time you don't have to push me, Papa Jan, he thought.

He opened the door a bit, looked in at the landing—brightly lit, empty—and went in.

And down the stairs into coolness. Quickly now, thinking of

the boy and the woman upstairs, who might soon be coming to crying an alarm.

He passed the door to the first level of memory banks.

And the second.

And came to the end of the stairs, the bottom-level door.

He put his right shoulder against it, held the gun ready, and turned the knob with his left hand.

He eased the door slowly open. Red lights gleamed in dimness, one of the walls of transmitting-receiving equipment. The low ceiling glowed faintly. He opened the door wider. A railed refrigerator pit lay ahead of him, blue arms upreaching; beyond it, a pillar, a pit, a pillar, a pit. The reactors were at the other end of the room, red domes doubled in the glass of the dimly lit programming room. Not a member in sight, closed doors, silence —except for a whining sound, low and steady. He opened the door wider, stepping into the room with it, and saw the second wall of equipment sparked with red lights.

He went farther into the room, caught the door edge behind him and let it pull itself away toward closing. He lowered the gun, thumbed the strap up off his shoulder, and let the kit down gently to the floor. His throat was clamped, his head torn back. A green silk elbow was under his jaw, the arm crushing his neck, choking him. His gun-wrist was locked in a powerful hand and 'You liar, liar,' Wei whispered in his ear, 'what a pleasure to kill you.'

He pulled at the arm, punched it with his free left hand; it was marble, a statue's arm in silk. He tried to back his feet into a stance for throwing Wei off him, but Wei moved backward too, keeping him arched and helpless, dragging him beneath the turning glowing ceiling; and his hand was bent around and smashed, smashed, smashed against hard railing, and the gun was gone, clanging into the pit. He reached back and grabbed Wei's head, found his ear and wrenched at it. His throat was crushed tighter by the hard-muscled arm and the ceiling was pink and pulsing. He thrust his hand down into Wei's collar, squeezed his fingers under a band of cloth. He wound his hand in it, driving his knuckles as hard as he could into tough ridged flesh. His right hand was freed, his left seized and pulled at. With his right he caught the wrist at his neck, pulled the arm open. He gasped air down his throat.

He was flung away, thrown flat against red-lit equipment, the torn band wound around his hand. He grabbed two handles and pulled out a panel, turned and flung it at Wei coming at him.

Wei struck it aside with an arm and kept coming, both his hands raised to chop. Chip crouched, his left arm up ('Keep *low*, Green-eye!' Captain Gold shouted.) Blows hit his arm; he punched at Wei's heart. Wei backed off, kicking at him. He got away from the wall, circled outward stuffed his numbed hand down into his pocket and found the knife handle. Wei rushed at him and chopped at his neck and shoulders. With his left arm raised, he cut the knife up out of his pocket and stuck it into Wei's middle—partway in, then hard, all the way, hilt into silk. Blows kept hitting him. He pulled the knife out and backed away.

Wei stayed where he was. He looked at Chip, at the knife in his hand, looked down at himself He touched his waist and looked at his fingers. He looked at Chip.

Chip circled, watching him, holding the knife.

Wei lunged. Chip knifed, slashed Wei's sleeve, but Wei caught his arm in both hands and drove him back against the railing, kneeing at him. Chip caught Wei's neck and squeezed as hard as he could inside the torn green-and-gold collar. He forced Wei off him, turned from the railing, and squeezed, kept squeezing while Wei held his knife-arm. He forced Wei back around the pit. Wei struck with one hand at his wrist, knocked it downward; he pulled his arm free and knifed at Wei's side. Wei dodged and spilled over the railing, fell into the pit and fell flat on his back on a cylindrical steel housing. He slid off it and sat leaning against blue pipe, looking up at Chip with his mouth open, gasping, a black-red stain in his lap.

Chip ran to the kit. He picked it up and walked back quickly down the side of the room, holding the kit on his arm. He put the knife in his pocket—it fell through but he let it—ripped the kit open and tucked its cover back under it He turned and walked backward toward the end of the equipment wall, stopped and stood facing the pits and the pillars between them,

He backhanded sweat from his mouth and forehead, saw blood on his hand and wiped it on his side.

He took one of the bombs from the kit, held it back behind his shoulder, aimed, and threw it. It arched into the center pit. He put his hand on another bomb. A *thunk* sounded from the pit, but no explosion came. He took out the second bomb and threw it harder into the pit.

The sound it made was flatter and softer than the first bomb's. The railed pit stayed as it was, blue arms reaching up from it.

Chip looked at it, and looked at the rows of white straw-stuck bombs in the kit.

He took out another one and hurled it as hard as he could into the nearer pit.

A *thunk* again.

He waited, and went cautiously toward the pit; went closer, and saw the bomb on the cylindrical steel housing, a blob of white, a white clay breast.

A high-pitched gasping sound came sifting from the farthest pit. Wei. He was laughing.

These three were her *bombs, the shepherd's,* Chip thought.

Maybe she did something to them. He went to the middle of the equipment wall and stood squarely facing the center pit. He hurled a bomb. It hit a blue arm and stuck to it, round and white.

Wei laughed and gasped. Scrapings, sounds of movement, came from the pit he was in.

Chip hurled more bombs. *One of them may work, one of them will work!* ('Throw and boom,' she had said. 'Glad to get them into the can.' She wouldn't have lied to him. What had gone wrong with them?) He hurled bombs at the blue arms and the pillars, plastered the square steel pillars with flat white overlapping discs. He hurled all the 'bombs', hurled the last one clean across the room; it splattered wide on the opposite equipment wall.

He stood with the empty kit in his hand.

Wei laughed loud.

He was sitting astride the pit railing, holding the gun in both hands, pointing it at Chip. Black-red smears ran down his clinging coverall legs; red leaked over his sandal straps. He laughed more. 'What do you think?' he asked. 'Too cold? Too damp? Too dry? Too old? Too what?' He took one hand from the gun, reached back behind him, and eased down off the railing. Lifting his leg over it, he winced and drew in breath hissingly. 'Ooh Jesus Christ,' he said, 'you really hurt this body. Ssss! You really did it damage.' He stood and held the gun with both hands again, facing Chip. He smiled. 'Idea,' he said. 'You give me yours, right? You hurt a body, you give me another one. Fair? And—neat, *economical!* What we have to do now is shoot you in the head, very carefully, and then between us we'll give the doctors a long night's work.' He smiled more broadly. 'I promise to keep you "in condition", Chip,' he said, and walked forward with slow stiff steps, his elbows tight to his sides, the gun clasped before him chest high, aimed at Chip's face.

Chip backed to the wall.

'I'll have to change my speech to newcomers,' Wei said. ' "From here down I'm Chip, a programmer who almost fooled me with his talk and his new eye and his smiles in the mirror." I don't think we'll have any more newcomers though; the risk has begun to outweigh the amusement.'

Chip threw the kit at him and lunged, leaped at Wei and threw him backward to the floor. Wei cried out, and Chip lying on him, wrestled for the gun in his hand. Red beams shot from it. Chip forced the gun to the floor. An explosion roared. He tore the gun from Wei's hand and got off him, got up to his feet and backed away and turned and looked.

Across the room, a cave, crumbling and smoking, hollowed the middle of the wall of equipment—where the bomb he had thrown had been splattered. Dust shimmered in the air and a wide arc of black fragments lay on the floor.

Chip looked at the gun and at Wei. Wei, on an elbow, looked across the room and up at Chip.

Chip backed away, toward the end of the room, toward its corner, looking at the white-plastered pillars, the white-hung blue arms over the center pit. He raised the gun.

'Chip!' Wei cried. 'It's *yours!* It'll be *yours* some day! We *both* can live! Chip, listen to me,' he said, leaning forward, 'there's *joy* in having it, in controlling, in being the only one. That's the absolute truth, Chip. You'll see for yourself. There's *joy* in having it.'

Chip fired the gun at the farther pillar. A red thread hit above the white discs; another hit directly on one. An explosion flashed and roared, thundered and smoked. It subsided and the pillar was bent slightly toward the other side of the room.

Wei moaned grievingly. A door beside Chip started to open; he pushed it closed and stood back against it. He fired the gun at the bombs on the blue arms. Explosion roared, flame erupted, and a louder explosion blasted from the pit, mashing him against the door, breaking glass, flinging Wei to the swaying wall of equipment, slamming doors that had opened at the other side of the room. Flame filled the pit, a huge shuddering cylinder of yellow-orange, railed around and drumming at the ceiling. Chip raised his arm against the heat of it.

Wei climbed to all fours and onto his feet. He swayed and started stumblingly forward. Chip shot a red thread to his chest, and another, and he turned away and stumbled toward the pit. Flames feathered his coveralls, and he dropped to his knees, fell forward on the floor. His hair caught fire, his coveralls burned.

Blows shook the door and cries came from behind it. The other doors opened and members came in. 'Stay back!' Chip shouted, and aimed the gun at the nearer pillar and fired. Explosion roared, and the pillar was bent.

The fire in the pit lowered, and the bent pillars slowly turned, screeching.

Members came into the room. 'Get back!' Chip shouted, and they retreated to the doors. He moved into the corner, watching the pillars, the ceiling. The door beside him opened. 'Stay back!' he shouted, pressing against it.

The steel of the pillars split and rolled open; a chunk of concrete slid from the nearer one. The blackened ceiling, cracked, groaned, sagged, dropped fragments.

The pillars broke and the ceiling fell. Memory banks crashed into the pits; mammoth steel blocks smashed down on one another and slid thunderously, butted into the walls of equipment. Explosions roared in the nearest and farthest pits, lifting blocks and cushioning them in flames.

Chip raised his arm against the heat. He looked where Wei had been. A block was there, its edge above the cracked floor.

More groaning and cracking sounded—from the blackness above, framed by the ceiling's broken fire-lit borders. And more banks fell, pounded down on the ones below, crushing and bursting them. Memory banks filled the opening, sliding, rumbling.

And the room, despite the fires, cooled.

Chip lowered his arm and looked—at the dark shapes of fire-gleaming steel blocks piled through the broken border of ceiling. He looked and kept looking, and then he moved around the door and pushed his way out through the members staring in.

He walked with the gun at his side through members and programmers running toward him down white-tiled corridors, and through more programmers running down carpeted corridors hung with paintings. 'What is it?' Karl shouted, stopping and grabbing his arm.

Chip looked at him and said, 'Go see.'

Karl let go of him, glanced at the gun and at his face, and turned and ran.

Chip turned and kept walking.

6

HE WASHED, sprayed the bruises on his hand and some cuts on his face, and put on paplon coveralls. Closing them, he looked around at the room. He had planned to take the bedcover, for Lilac to use for dressmaking, and a small painting or something for Julia; now, though, he didn't want to. He put cigarettes and the gun in his pockets. The door opened and he pulled the gun out again. Deirdre stared at him, looking frantic.

He put the gun back in his pocket.

She came in and closed the door behind her. 'It *was* you,' she said.

He nodded.

'Do you *realize* what you've *done*?'

'What you didn't do,' he said. 'What you came here to do and talked yourself out of.'

'I came here to stop it so it could be reprogrammed,' she said, 'not to destroy it completely!'

'It was *being* reprogrammed, remember?' he said. 'And if I'd stopped it and forced a *real* reprogramming—I don't know how, but if I had—it would still have wound up the same way sooner or later. The same *Wei*. Or a new one—me. "There's joy in having it;" those were his last words. Everything else was rationalization. And self-deception.'

She looked away, angrily, and back at him. 'The whole place is going to cave in,' she said.

'I don't feel any tremors,' he said.

'Well everyone's going. The ventilation may stop. There's danger of radiation.'

'I wasn't planning to stay,' he said

She opened the door and looked at him and went out.

He went out after her. Programmers hurried along the corridor in both directions, carrying paintings, pillowcase bundles, dictypes, lamps. ('Wei was in it! He's dead!' 'Stay away from the kitchen, it's a madhouse!') He walked among them. The walls were bare except for large frames hanging empty. ('Sirri says it was Chip, not the new ones!' '—twenty-five years ago, Unify the islands, we've got *enough* programmers, but he gave me a quote about *selfishness*.')

The escalators were working. He rode up to the top level and went around through the steel door, half open, to the bathroom where the boy and the woman were. They were gone.

He went down one level. Programmers and members holding paintings and bundles were pushing into the room that led to the tunnel. He went into the merging crowd. The door ahead was down but must have been partway up because everyone kept moving forward slowly. ('Quickly!' 'Move, will you?' 'Oh Christ and Wei!')

His arm was grabbed and Madhir glared at him, hugging a filled tablecloth to his chest. 'Was it *you*?' he asked.

'Yes,' Chip said.

Madhir glared, trembled, flushed. 'Madman!' he shouted. 'Maniac! *Maniac!*'

Chip pulled his arm free and turned and moved forward.

'Here he is!' Madhir shouted. 'Chip! He's the one! He's the one who did it! Here he is! Here! *He's the one who did it!*'

Chip moved forward with the crowd, looking at the steel door ahead, holding the gun in his pocket. ('You *brother*-fighter, are you crazy?' 'He's mad, he's mad!')

They walked up the tunnel, quickly at first, then slowly, an endless straggle of dark laden figures. Lamps shone here and there along the line, each lamp drawing with it a section of shining plastic roundness.

Chip saw Deirdre sitting at the side of the tunnel. She looked at him stonily. He kept walking, the gun at his side.

Outside the tunnel they sat and lay in the clearing, smoked and ate and talked in huddles, rummaged in their bundles, traded forks for cigarettes.

Chip saw stretchers on the ground, four or five of them, a member holding a lamp beside them, other members kneeling. He put the gun in his pocket and went over. The boy and the woman lay on two of the stretchers, their heads bandaged, their eyes closed, their sheeted chests moving. Members were on two other stretchers, and Barlow, the head of the Nutritional Council, was on another, dead-looking, his eyes closed. Rosen kneeled beside him, taping something to his chest through cut-open coveralls.

'Are they all right?' Chip asked.

'The others are,' Rosen said. 'Barlow's had a heart attack.' He looked up at Chip. 'They're saying that Wei was in there,' he said.

'He was,' Chip said.

'You're sure?'

'Yes,' Chip said. 'He's dead.'

'It's hard to believe,' Rosen said. He shook his head and took a small something from a member's hand and screwed it onto what he had taped to Barlow's chest.

Chip watched for a moment, then went over to the entrance of the clearing and sat down against stone and lit a cigarette. He toed his sandals off and smoked, watching members and programmers come out of the tunnel and walk around and find places to sit. Karl came out with a painting and a bundle.

A member came toward him. Chip took the gun out of his pocket and held it in his lap.

'Are you Chip?' the member asked. He was the older of the two men who had come in that evening.

'Yes,' Chip said.

The man sat down next to him. He was about fifty, very dark, with a jutting chin. 'Some of them are talking about rushing you,' he said.

'I figured they would be,' Chip said. 'I'm leaving in a second.'

'My name's Luis,' the man said.

'Hello,' Chip said.

They shook hands.

'Where are you going?' Luis asked.

'Back to the island I came from,' Chip said. 'Liberty. Majorca. Myorca. You don't know how to fly a copter by any chance, do you?'

'No,' Luis said, 'but it shouldn't be too hard to figure out.'

'It's the landing that worries me,' Chip said.

'Land in the water.'

'I wouldn't want to lose the copter, though. Assuming I can find one. You want a cigarette?'

'No, thanks,' Luis said.

They sat silently for a moment. Chip drew on his cigarette and looked up. 'Christ and Wei, real stars,' he said. 'They had fake ones down there.'

'Really?' Luis said.

'Really.'

Luis looked over at the programmers. He shook his head.

'They're talking as if the Family's going to die in the morning,' he said. 'It isn't. It's going to be born.'

'Born to a lot of trouble, though,' Chip said. 'It's started already. Planes have crashed . . .'

Luis looked at him and said, 'members haven't died who were supposed to die . . .'

After a moment Chip said, 'Yes. Thanks for reminding me.'

Luis said. 'Sure, there's going to be trouble. But there are members in every city—the undertreated, the ones who write "Fight Uni"—who'll keep things going in the beginning. And in the end it's going to be better. Living people!'

'It's going to be more interesting, that's for sure,' Chip said, putting his sandals on.

'You aren't going to stay on your island, are you?' Luis asked.

'I don't know,' Chip said. 'I haven't thought beyond getting there.'

'You come back,' Luis said. 'The Family needs members like you.'

'Does it?' Chip said. 'I had an eye changed down there, and I'm not sure I only did it to fool Wei.' He crushed his cigarette out and stood up. Programmers were looking around at him; he pointed the gun at them and they turned quickly away.

Luis stood up too. 'I'm glad the bombs worked,' he said, smiling. 'I'm the one who made them.'

'They worked beautifully,' Chip said. 'Throw and boom.'

'Good,' Luis said. 'Listen, I don't know about any eye; you land on land and come back in a few weeks.'

'I'll see,' Chip said. 'Good-by.'

'Good-by, brother,' Luis said.

Chip turned and went out of the clearing and started down the rocky slope toward parkland.

He flew over roadways where occasional moving cars zig-zagged slowly past series of stopped ones; along the River of Freedom, where barges bumped blindly against the banks; past cities where monorail cars clung motionless to the rail, copters hovering over some of them.

As he grew more sure of his handling of the copter he flew lower; looked into plazas where members milled and gathered; skimmed over factories with stopped feed-in and feed-out lines; over construction sites where nothing moved except a member or two; and over the river again, passing a group of members tying a barge to the shore, climbing on to it, looking up at him.

He followed the river to the sea and started across it, flying low. He thought of Lilac and Jan, Lilac turning startled from the sink (he *should* have taken the bedcover, why hadn't he?). But would they still be in the room? Could Lilac, thinking him caught and treated and never coming back, have—married someone else? No, never. (Why not? Almost nine months he'd been gone.) No, she wouldn't. She——

Drops of clear liquid hit the copter's plastic front and streaked back along its sides. Something was leaking from above, he thought, but then he saw that the sky had gone gray, gray on both sides and darker gray ahead, like the skies in some pre-U paintings. It was *rain* that was hitting the copter.

Rain! In the daytime! He flew with one hand, and with a fingertip of the other, followed on the inside of the plastic the paths of the streaking raindrops outside it.

Rain in the daytime! Christ and Wei, how strange! And how inconvenient!

But there was something pleasing about it too. Something natural.

He brought his hand back to its lever—*Let's not get over-confident, brother*—and smiling, flew ahead.

COMPLETED IN JUNE, 1969

IN NEW YORK CITY

AND DEDICATED TO ADAM LEVIN,

JED LEVIN AND NICHOLAS LEVIN

THE XYY MAN

Kenneth Royce

'The XYY Man' is published by
Hodder and Stoughton Ltd.

The Author

Kenneth Royce started writing when he was a schoolboy, using halfpenny exercise books, illustrating them, then selling them for a penny each. The war interrupted his development as a writer; later, however, after a few years in business, the compulsion to write returned. Although he has travelled abroad extensively in search of material, he finds that the most successful and rewarding source is in his own London environment. He prefers to write in longhand, which his wife edits, and he uses a pocket tape recorder as a 'notebook' for ideas. His ambition is to make Willie 'Spider' Scott the best known and most likeable character in thriller fiction.

For ANDY

hoping that you are still out

CHAPTER ONE

WHEN I STEPPED into the street and the Scrubs gate closed behind me, my first inclination was to run back to hide behind its shelter. As I had been waiting five precious years for this one moment and had verged on gate fever these last few days it was a curious reaction to say the least. Yet although fleeting, the feeling was strong enough for me to hesitate and look back at the small gate set in the larger one.

Behind those gates and others like them I suppose I had received some form of protection; three meals and a bed; no financial worries. Provided one kept clear of the strong arm boys, out of the hands of the tobacco barons and did not cross too many screws it was just about endurable but only with the knowledge of a not too distant release. The 'Moor' was the worst; if ever I had to return there I'd 'top' myself.

I walked slowly with the bundle under my arm that everyone would recognize as soon as I turned the corner. This had not been my first stretch yet I had not felt like this before. I was very much aware that I was on my own and afraid of the inexplicable. If I didn't keep clean it would be a ten-year stretch next time. I was afraid of myself, knowing that at the age of thirty-four this was my last chance. And something else nagged at me, the more worrying because I could not pin it down.

The Governor's last little lecture had been odd, almost pitying. I had the strange feeling that in some way I was up on show, an object of curiosity, and if the last five years had not blunted some of my crude perception I would have taken heed of that feeling right then. I don't know what I would have done about it but at least I would have been forewarned and on eventually meeting Fairfax would have been a little less gullible.

The good feeling of freedom did not kill my fears but it sat on them as I got farther from the gate. I'd done two years in Dartmoor before working my ticket to Grendon Psychiatric Prison. They are not nutters there, but the hopefuls, blokes they think they can do something about. I found it helpful and, by filching a confidential report, found out a little about myself without being much wiser.

The two sex chromosomes that make up each male cell in the body are tagged X and Y. At Grendon a number of men have an extra Y chromosome. The XYY man; that's me. They are all more than six feet tall and predisposed to crimes against property rather than violence. That's me, too. Clever these doctors; but had they effected a cure? When I faced the answer to that one I wanted to turn back again. I hoped I would not let them down, but had no confidence.

The last six months of my sentence had been spent at the Scrubs Hostel. You sleep in and work outside preparatory to the return to normal life—if life had ever been normal for me.

As I walked slowly away from these grim walls, my fear grew. The squalid surrounds did nothing for my morale and seemed part of the prison environs. It was late September and warm, but cloud patches plugged the sun. I had no real plans and the nerves in my stomach played spiders on my spleen. I was out—and desperately wanted to stay out, but my great dread was whether I could.

I hoped no pious so-and-so would tell me that hard work is the miracle cure. My record would show that I could work my guts out. But after a time the job would bore me, I'd want something new, another interest, and that is no way to progress.

It was going to be tough. You see, I'm a 'creeper', a cat burglar. Coppers and screws have always been surprised by this because of my height and weight. Just the same, shinning a drainpipe close to a wall has never been a problem to me.

A creeper is a loner. With one exception I'd never worked with anyone else. I've run away rather than strike someone. So during the long years in prison I was faced with a recurring problem. What would I now do if I was faced with the alternative of a ten-year stretch or of striking someone down. The answer scared me.

This was only part of my fear. There was something beyond my knowledge that nagged at me. Years ago I had experienced a similar feeling. I had entered a house by an unlatched window on the ground floor. There was a big hall with a semi-circular staircase. As I mounted the first stair, I had the most squeezy sensation of something wrong. By the time I was half way up it had grown to such intensity that I stopped, wet with sweat, and the hairs standing out on the back of my neck. I tried to go on but could not. It was my first sensation of real terror.

I was doing something I had repeatedly done yet I could not continue. Finally my 'bottle'* went, and I fled. What I now felt was the warning I had experienced on the first stair. Not sufficient to allay me, yet disturbing. I wondered what I was walking into.

The sun came out and put colour into the grey tiles and dirty bricks. I stepped out briskly and decided to make straight for Maggie's place, a nice pad in a modern block; she'd be mad at me for not telling her exactly when I was being released but I didn't want her in the shadow of these walls.

Working outside had staved off some of the surprises. Mini skirts I was already used to, but when I caught a bus up to Notting Hill they seemed to get shorter as the shops multiplied.

As I watched I vividly recalled the deep hunger I had suffered in isolation for just this. Don't lose it now, I kept repeating to

* Nerve.

myself. Don't ever give it up again, for a stark cell and a daily half-hour slog in an exercise yard.

My mind drifted to Maggie. I shall never understand why she tolerates me for she must know that I'm no damned good to her. From my viewpoint she is missing her chances and it chokes me to see such a lovely girl go to waste. During the periods I've been outside, I've done everything to try to dissuade her for her own sake. I've been as unfaithful as hell and she knows it yet she's always been there. She spoke a couple of languages fluently and worked for the United Nations in London. With her intelligence and background you'd think that she would have worked it out but I suppose like all women she is illogical. She knew I would never marry her because I could not reduce her to my level but it made no difference.

Maggie had taught me a lot; little things like cleaning my nails and sounding the 'ng's on the end of words. She had encouraged me to read while 'inside' and I did a lot, particularly when I finally became librarian at Grendon. She deserved better things but right now I was glad that she hadn't taken them.

I slipped in quietly, unheard by Maggie. There was a white blouse on the ironing board. She was carefully smoothing it over. As she bent her jet hair hung forward framing a face that should have been recorded on canvas over and over again. Five years is a long time; I thought she would hear my heavier breathing. Her mouth was unfashionably small, firm yet sensitive lips; her brows carefully pencilled in because of their contrasting lightness. As she stood I could not see her eyes—she wore large framed glasses —but I knew them to be blue green capable of almost chameleon changes dependent on mood. Maggie had always looked after her skin and from where I stood it was as clear and as petal soft as I always remembered. It was an essentially feminine yet firm face, now with a new mature loveliness that made me want to weep at my own stupidity and whisper truths that I knew I could not.

She wore a light woollen sleeveless pullover, tight over her small breasts, and the ironing board obscured her good legs. It was almost too much for me, but I managed to remain close to the door.

'Hello, love. When did you dye your hair?'

She almost dropped the iron. She stood staring, her breathing heavy. She lowered the iron but I could see she was still dazed.

'It's a wig. It's all the rage. How did you get in?' It was doubtful if she knew what she had asked. She slowly removed the wig revealing her own close cropped auburn hair. I held up a piece of stiff mica.

'I told you to change that lock years ago.'

Her lips twitched and I thought she was about to cry. Instead she said angrily, 'Take that grin off your face. You might at least have given me time to put on my make-up.'

'You look all right to me,' I said, still grinning.

'Oh Will! Oh God!'

She came to me, whipping off her glasses. Holding her was one of the great moments of my life. It was wonderful; better than the thousand times I had conjured this scene in a cell. She was warm and soft and firm at the same time and we were welded, unmoving, just desperately clutching each other. After a while she began to cry and I curbed frustration and stroked her hair and arm, wanting to prolong the emotional taste of so wonderful a moment. The tears went and passion returned like an unquenchable blaze, consuming and hungry, eager to spread and devour and gain enormous strength before being reduced to an ember.

A long, long time later Maggie gazed up at me from the cradle of my arm, one hand softly touching my chest, and asked, 'How is it your body is so brown?'

I gave her a tender squeeze. 'Been working outside, love. I can see you've been sunbathing. Glad you kept something on.' She looked down at her body and I found no difficulty in following her gaze.

'Bikinis were smaller this year.'

'So I see.'

She leaned over me, lowered her body on mine, and kissed me lightly. 'Are you hungry?'

I grinned. 'Not any more.'

'Oh.' She nudged me hard in the ribs and swung her legs over the side of the bed.

I ran my fingers up her spine and across her back. 'It's funny,' I said, sitting up on one elbow. 'When you're inside there's a lot of talk about the first thing you're going to do when you get out. Oddly enough women come second to an enormous meal of everything you like best. I was wrong, wasn't I?'

Maggie kept her back to me as she dressed but I could see her quiet expression in the dressing table mirror. 'Is that all I am to you? A woman?'

I started to get up. 'No. You're something very, very special. A nut for sticking it out, but special. Too special to waste your time on me.'

She turned to face me, zipping her skirt. 'Let's not go through that again. Not today.'

She came to me and we held each other for several minutes. Eventually I said softly, 'We'll be back on the bed if we're not careful.'

'I know.' Maggie leaned back so that she could look up at me. Her long, strong fingers were digging into my arms. 'Will, promise me you'll stay out this time.'

I tried to promise her, God knows I wanted to badly enough, but the words would not come. My lips were moving and I saw her expression change, concern and fear hardening eyes meant to be soft, yet something was stopping me. Finally I burst out, 'Look, Maggie, Dartmoor frightened the pants off me. It's a vile, putrid place, and I've no intention of ever going back.'

'That's not a promise.'

'Perhaps I'm afraid of myself.'

'You have only one real weakness which you can conquer. I'll help you. I know you to be honest in every way, bar one. If you promise I *know* you'll keep it. Please, Willie.'

'I promise,' I said, but it had been forced out. I had not the faith in it that Maggie seemed to have. I had said it to please her, not because I believed it. She gave me a peck and seemed satisfied but I felt wretched and wished I really knew why.

'You can move your things in here,' Maggie said as we entered the tiny kitchen.

I put an arm round her shoulders. 'You know I won't do that, not yet. I'll fix myself up with a room near by.'

Maggie didn't like it because she knew my motive—it had cropped up before. I had always insisted on retaining my independence mainly because I did not want to bind her to a villain. She got on with the cooking instead of arguing but was perturbed.

'Look, I want to phone Dick and Walt, may I use your phone?'

She stopped swishing the butter around in the pan and belatedly slipped on an apron. 'You *must* ring Dick, but why Walt?'

'He owes me money.' I could see trouble looming already. She removed the pan from the hot plate and faced me.

'That sort of money you can do without.'

'Look, Walt's as straight as a die now. He promised me this ages ago. This isn't bent money.'

'You mean he wants to pay you for keeping him out of prison?'

'If you like. I've earned it.' I saw this as injustice and that always made me hot under the collar.

'You've earned nothing of it, Willie. You went to prison for a crime. You were punished. Don't expect to be paid because you covered someone who should have been punished with you.'

I stomped into the bedroom and grabbed the phone. Dick is my kid brother and is as honest as I am bent. We're different sides of the fence; he's in the Metropolitan Police. We have always had a great affection for one another, something a lot of people could not understand, and he knew for certain that I would never operate in his manor. He was at home and we had a good laugh and waffle and arranged to meet. In spite of Maggie's entreaties I rang Walt Sandford and fixed a meeting for the next day.

I stayed that night and was restless. After so long I could not get used to Maggie beside me without making love to her but during periods of exhaustion I found the bed too soft. We talked a lot too, lying naked under the sheet and trying to sort out things between us. I'd be happy to drift on like this but that was a prelude to drifting back and I knew that Maggie wouldn't let me.

I took her breakfast to bed next morning and made her sit up and eat as she was. For a villain I suppose I've got some old-fashioned ideas. I've never sworn in front of a woman nor used smut. That's the way it is. With the 'boys' I'll dredge the bottom of the verbal barrel and feel right about it.

Maggie said, 'You have not lost your charm or your wide blue-eyed innocence which you can divert elsewhere while I get up. Damn you, Willie, I've never seen anyone look less like a villain than you do, so you've got a good start.'

I left fairly early and went down to Winchester to see Walt Sandford. He'd lost some of his ginger hair and was plumper but his greeting was the same; a huge smile, no airs and a warm double handshake that went on for ever. Yet he had difficulty in meeting my gaze. He opened a solid-looking safe which I eyed professionally and threw across a couple of bundles of wrapped notes.

'There's a grand there, Spider. It'll see you right for a bit.' No haggling, no magnanimity. I should explain that because I'm a creeper all the boys call me Spider; Maggie is the only one who won't use it because of its associations.

I spread the money about me. 'So it's not hot?'

'You know better. Was it bad inside?'

'It scared me, Walt.'

'Enough?' He watched me shakily, almost pleadingly.

'Yep. Enough. I couldn't go back.'

He seemed relieved, remembering his own fear.

We shook hands warmly as if for the last time and it turned out to be. I was sad and a little emotional. We had been good friends but I think the fact that I had gone up on my own played on his conscience; it didn't worry me.

I went back to London thinking that somehow Walt had lost some of his integrity and wondering how that could be now that he was no longer bent.

From the station I had the strong sensation of being followed. It may have been due to carrying so much money. But I didn't like it for I couldn't pin anyone. But who would want to tail me?

I met Dick in the Duke of Wellington in Wardour Street, well away from his divisional boundaries. We greeted each other like a couple of kids; it had been a long time for I'd refused to let him visit me inside. He told me he'd now been in the force for three years and enjoyed the work, hoping later to get into the C.I.D. I eyed him over a pint of beer which I eked out for I don't drink much. He was now twenty-six and had filled out. They tell me we both have the same easy-going grin so I suppose I was seeing a little of myself—as I gazed back at him. Like me he was blue-eyed, with a slightly snub nose, good teeth, and firm of face

and jaw, although his hair was darker than mine, almost black.
If I looked like my kid brother then I was more than satisfied and
people liked him.

'I hear Alf Bulman's with you,' I said.

'He's a good sergeant, Spider. I know you don't like him but
he is.'

'Do you know why I don't like him?'

'I've heard rumours.'

I banged my glass. 'If you ever get a promotion the same way
I'll wring your neck.'

Dick laughed. 'Watch it, I've been studying karate. Do you
really believe it?'

'Look, I met a bent copper on the Moor who had served with
Bulman. Bulman used to come to an arrangement with vagrants
and tramps. He would get them to confess to a small breaking
and entering job; they would spend the worst of winter in 'nick',
free food and lodging, and it was another arrest on his record
sheet.'

'I don't think he'd be like that now.' And then more carefully
Dick added, 'It was a mistake to tell him that you knew.'

I almost drained my drink. 'I can't stand bent coppers. Don't
you go bent, by God.'

'I only have to look at you to remind me not to.'

I stared dazedly at him and I could see that he wanted to bite
his tongue out, but it hit me hard under the belt. Who was I to
moralize. 'Sorry kid,' I said quietly.

'I didn't mean it that way.'

'Good.' I was grinning again. 'I'll buy you the other half.'

On the way back to Maggie's place I was sure that I was being
watched but I played it cooler than I felt for I couldn't understand it.

Passion wasn't wearing thin with either of us and it was some
time before I realized that she was hiding something from me.
We sat on the sofa, the lights out, the gloom relieved by filtering
street lamps and passing cars. A single kilowatt electric fire
glowed like a red hot poker, its exaggerated image showing dust
on the reflector.

But Maggie's acute honesty betrayed her. She was no politician
and truth was her only weapon even when she realized it should
not be used. She was distracted. 'Out with it,' I prompted. She
almost jumped.

'Am I so transparent?'

'Only to a villain like me. I've mixed with some of the best liars
in the world. You're uneasy. I can feel it under my fingers.'

'A man called Roberts phoned.'

I looked down at her. 'Well, what's wrong with that?'

'Please, Willie. Keep away from the boys.'

'You don't play about with people like Knocker Roberts. He

belongs to the Reisens and those boys play it very rough. They still paid their staff who were inside—and without much trouble.'

'Isn't that a good enough reason for keeping clear?'

I didn't tell her that through Roberts I had been offered a job in their strong arm mob while I was on the Moor. They have long memories and recruit carefully. And the money is in the mobs.

Maggie slipped from my arms and knelt between my knees. Her soft hands took hold of my coarsened ones and she was breathtakingly lovely in half shadow. Her eyes lost their colour in the deepening gloom but light patches caught the whites of them so that they looked bigger and phosphorescent. I'd always loved the timbre of her voice but now it was at its best, cool and pleading.

'Willie, I love you with everything that is in me. I won't preach because I know that you hate it and I understand that. I'm not pious but we both know that this is your last chance. Give up these people—all of them. Give yourself a real chance.'

I was about to answer but she gently covered my mouth with her hand. 'I know your feeling for me is not as deep as mine. I've always accepted it and I'm not complaining. I'm pleading for *you*, Willie, not for what I want from you.'

It had been a moving appeal that made me feel all kinds of a bastard. Just the same I had to say it. 'Maggie, in my book there's no one like you or ever likely to be and you know it. You know why I won't be tied down. But you must understand that these people are my friends. They may be villains but we've suffered together and I could no more ignore them than I could turn my back on Dick. You're judging me guilty already for doing nothing more than passing the time of day. It will be all right but you must give it time. Sooner or later they'll get the message and it will be *they* who will lose interest in *me*.'

The next morning I made arrangements to take over a bed-sitter, with a miniature kitchen that you could miss if you turned round too quickly. It was shabbily furnished, but light with a high Victorian ceiling. Maggie liked it because she was nuts on antiques and it was near the Portobello Road.

That afternoon I bought a four-year old second-hand 3.4 Jaguar that made a hole in my thousand pounds but refused to accept delivery until they had fitted a burglar alarm. As I left the garage there was a short, middle-aged, trilby-hatted gent looking at the used cars on the forecourt. He appeared completely innocuous until his gaze accidentally caught mine. He revealed nothing but averted his gaze too awkwardly as if he had been caught out. For some reason he roused latent fears in me. It was silly. Yet it worried me. I was certain that he knew me, although his face was new to me, the kind unnoticed in a crowd.

CHAPTER TWO

BY THE END of the week I had found a job as a car salesman. The basic would prevent me starving and the commission was not too bad. I couldn't see my future in it but it was a start.

Maggie was delighted. I didn't tell her that the garage which had employed me serviced a lot of the boys and was up to its neck in hire purchase fiddles. She thought I had only to be open about my past for employers to fall over themselves offering me jobs.

In a short time memory of cells and quarries and slopping out began to fade. I began to believe that I was out for keeps, that it could work, although I was uneasy about the feeling of being under surveillance.

Occasionally one of the boys would give me a ring via Maggie; I had yet to get a phone, but it was only for old times' sake and she began to accept it. Then Sergeant Bulman called on me at my bedsitter. Judging by the speed he rapped the door after I'd got in after work, he must have been waiting for me.

He stood in the doorway, sharp-eyed, black hair short and traditionally combed with a nice white parting correctly at one side. His nose and mouth were good and straight, and I suppose in a coarse sort of way he was good looking. He had strong brows and a nice set of teeth if he ever got round to smiling. Just over medium height, he looked up, hands in the pockets of an old raincoat over a neat blue suit. He could have been an insurance man but to me he smelled copper and that meant trouble.

'Hello, Scott. Can I have a word with you?'

'*Mr.* Scott to you, Sergeant. I'm no longer a name and number. Yes, you can have a word.'

His quick gaze darted over my shoulder. 'Can I come in?'

'A word can be said from where you're standing.'

His mouth tightened and he was needled. The strange thing is that I've nothing against the police. Screws are different but the police have always been reasonable with me, even helpful on occasion, except Bulman. There was a thing between us. He managed a lop-sided grin. 'It might be embarrassing saying it here.'

'For you or for me?'

Glancing behind him up the stairs, he said with relish, 'For you. *Mr.* Scott.' His eyes were mocking.

My stomach began to flutter and I knew that I was glaring at him. I have a conscience, you see. There are still some old jobs that have not yet been pinned on me and there is always an outside chance that they might.

'Come in,' I said begrudgingly. I made certain that he didn't nick my favourite chair. At first I thought that he was not going to sit at all but when he saw me ostensibly relaxed he carefully

sat opposite, keeping his coat on. When he began to pull out
his cigarettes I said, 'I'd rather you didn't. I'm allergic to them.
Something I developed on the Moor.'

Wearing a quiet smile he slipped them back into his pocket
without appearing put out and I knew then that the bastard
was playing with me. He could hardly wait to get it out but
was delaying it in order to savour every syllable and watch me
cringe. Inside I was fluttering like a moth, but he wasn't going to
know.

'Where were you last night between eleven and two in the
morning?' He sat enjoying himself, his gaze sweeping the room
including under the bed and I guessed it was about a job. Well,
my conscience was clear, but I was still uneasy.

'What, no caution?'

Benign Bulman wore a smile I would have liked to wipe off.
There are some people who provoke my latent violent tendencies.

'This is a friendly chat, Spider. There's no need for a caution.'

'But you will still get up in the box and swear that you gave me
one.'

He spread his hands, still grinning. 'If you think that then
you've had your caution. You don't think much of me, do you?'

'I don't like the way you became a sergeant.'

His face hardened, his gaze diamond sharp. 'Do you always
listen to bent coppers in nick?'

'Why not? I listen to them out of it.'

Bulman lost colour and his hands bunched. I was being a fool
needling him but my feeling was deep, springing from a world
and codes that I'd lived with for too long. I suddenly realized that
my directness wouldn't do my brother much good.

Bulman won the little battle with himself, and anyway I'm
bigger than he is, and he relaxed again, but there was a craftiness
in his gaze I didn't like. 'Do you know Nightingale Terrace?' he
asked.

He knew that I did. I nodded.

'Coltmore House?'

My stomach muscles started an involuntary isometric exercise.
I let them relax slowly before answering. Coltmore House was a
drum I had cased many years ago. It was a wealthy home in a
rich Georgian area fringing Holland Park.

'Not particularly.'

'But you know it?'

'I know the area. I don't know the names of the houses.'

He changed his tack. 'You know that every nick keeps a book
of addresses of empty houses—you know, people on holiday and
so on; who has the key and all that?'

I had the glimmering of where this was leading. I nodded again
slowly, my wits sharpened by caution.

'Well, Coltmore House,' said Bulman with relish, 'is listed in our book as being at present vacant, owner out of the country,'

'Has it been screwed?'

'I wonder why you said that, Spider?'

'Because it's bloody obvious from the game you're playing. And I don't like your aspersions against my brother.'

'Come on, Spider. They told me you're the non-violent type. That's a nasty temper you've got. What have I said against your brother?'

I stood up angrily, falling straight into his trap. But I couldn't help myself; it was Dick I was worried about, not myself. 'Listen, Bulman, try to pin a screwing job on me if you like, it's right up your alley, but if you try to pin my brother I'll do life for you.'

He was now openly mocking me; he'd got me on the run and held all the cards. 'I haven't mentioned your brother.'

'No? Then why mention the vacant premises book? The implication is that he supplied me with the information. Well, Bulman, even a thick-headed bent copper like you should know that I wouldn't foul my brother's nest.'

Bulman rose to face me, his expression vicious. 'You can always change your habits. But you can't change your style. This job has your handwriting all over it. Where were you last night?'

'With Maggie Parsons.'

'Convenient. What time?'

'Ask her the times.'

'I will. I'm asking you now.'

I turned towards the windows, fuming and dismayed. 'From about eight through till two or three.'

'Busy.'

I swung round while he openly taunted me to land one on him. With difficulty I said, 'My record of non-violence refers only to my customers. It does not extend to scum like you. And when you speak of Maggie Parsons swill your mouth out first with Dettol.'

Bulman was shaken at that, but he wasn't going to forget. 'You're taking too many chances, *Mr.* Scott.'

'You try to involve my brother again and you'll find out just how many I'm willing to take. And understand this, Bulman, I didn't do that job although you'd love to hang it on me. Don't try it on with me again.'

Near the door Bulman faced me. He'd won a good round even if I had come back strongly before the bell; the points were clearly his and I was still rattled. 'The hallmarks are still yours, chummy. Don't wander too far, will you?'

After he had gone I sat down broodingly. I thought I knew who had done the job. In prison it's not unusual to exchange useful information. If a man has cased a place and is imprisoned before he can screw it he might well pass it on to someone else. I had cased this one before Dick had joined the police and had passed it on to a screwsman called Ossie Jenkins. It had been a good tip, but it looked as if Ossie had got round to it at the wrong time.

If Bulman *really* wanted to nail me, he'd manage it, over the course of time. But what sickened me to my stomach was his oblique accusation of Dick. Now that really worried me because it showed too clearly his prepared line of action. I had the uncontrollable and inexplicable feeling of being pushed in a direction I had no wish to go.

I went downstairs to my car and found that a window had been forced and a small transistor radio had been nicked. It didn't amount to much but I saw it as a sign and cursed the finely tuned burglar alarm that had failed to work. Which only shows that you can't trust anyone these days.

As always Maggie pulled me from the doldrums. She said, stretching her long legs over mine, 'Why don't you go and see the Police Superintendent?'

'What for?'

'Oh, Willie. Tell him you're being victimized and why.'

It's strange but I don't think I could grass even on Bulman. There were plenty of bent coppers who needed reporting but they were protected by codes they themselves despised; that and the fact that reporting them often detrimentally involved one of the boys. So I laughed at her naïvety. Here it was again; tell the truth and all will be well. But her innocence touched me.

A few days later Bulman called with a detective constable, whom he didn't trouble to introduce, and his behaviour was much more correct. Again there was no caution; so I knew that he was groping. He wanted more details of the time I spent with Maggie and where, but this was a case of following Maggie's code —if we both told the truth it would cross check. You have to be an ex-con to know the effect of police questioning, the more so if you're now straight.

His visit was followed closely by two of the Reisens boys. They were both mobsters and they wanted me as a driver but I scared them off by telling them with bitter truth that the police were watching me. You can see why it's so easy for good intentioned villains to go back to crime; the pressures are on from both sides of the law if they think you are worth it.

I started to ease off my visits to Maggie because I knew that she was worried but that she did not really know the form. I knew what I was up against and if it was useful to lie then I lied because I have proved that the truth can land me right in it. I tried to get her to visit her parents in Yorkshire for a spell. I believe they have a good home up there, but there was her job and she was independent minded and knew what I was up to. She was worried that I might go off at a tangent.

Early in October Bulman came for me at the garage just before closing time. More than anything else it was this that really griped me. He couldn't wait another half hour until I was home. He had to make a splash of it in front of my employer and some of the mechanics.

It was a warm autumn day. I was standing outside the show-room, ready to drive some of the display cars back under cover for the night. The sun was down but it was still light. Workers were beginning to go home and the pavement was quite crowded in front of our forecourt. I was slipping some of the price cards into the cars when I saw the blue light come flashing along the road.

Traffic was fairly heavy and the black police A60 was held up once or twice—I thought it strange that the flasher was being used, yet not the siren to clear the way. Because of this I didn't connect it with me at first, not until I saw the amber eye of the left trafficator pulse on and the car swing into the kerb. I saw Bulman next to the driver and my stomach turned. The bastard took his time getting out and left the flasher going so that people stopped and stared, hoping for a bit of excitement.

'Mr. Scott?' As if he didn't know. 'Would you be good enough to accompany me to the station? There are one or two questions we would like to ask you.' He kept his voice fairly low but some of the gapers heard it just the same and I could see them nudging one another.

I kept it dignified, wiping my hands on a handkerchief because I didn't know what to do with them apart from making them meet round Bulman's neck. But two could play this game.

'Who are you? May I see your identity card?'

The pretence was crazy but he had to fumble for his wallet to produce it. I took my time, giving the swelling crowd good value.

'A detective sergeant, I see.' They'd love that. 'And why do you want to see me?'

But Bulman had to win in the end and he looked as if he knew it. 'Just a few questions——'he almost choked on 'sir', and couldn't get it out. 'We think you can help us with our enquiries.'

I looked over his shoulder. 'Do you *have* to keep your flasher going—Sergeant?'

I scored one. He looked a bit silly then called out to his driver to switch it off. While I still had a small advantage I said, 'It's inconvenient now. I still have work to do. If you think it really necessary I'll come down later.'

Then my boss put his big foot in it. His voice came from over my left shoulder and it did not sound too pleased. 'It's all right, Spider, you go off. We'll clear up.'

I did not turn round; there was no need. Bulman gave the boss a polite smile of appreciation and nodded in a friendly way, then stood aside for me to precede him to the car. It was all wrapped up. The audience went silent as I stepped forward, craning their necks to see what sort of a thug I was.

Once in the car we both reverted to type. After a quick exchange that startled the driver, we lapsed into a silence of mutual hatred. Bulman refused to give information until we were at the nick.

What happened next was all too familiar. They parked me in an interrogation room, bare table and chairs, and left me there for over an hour. I would have demanded to see my solicitor if I'd had one.

Finally Bulman came in carrying a cup of tea, for him not for me, accompanied by the detective constable he had brought round the other night. The D.C. sat at the end of the table with a notebook while Bulman sat opposite stirring his tea. To impress the D.C. of his impartiality after the fracas in the car, Bulman offered me a cigarette, knowing that I don't smoke, so I took it without thanks and slipped it in my breast pocket. I thought he was going to hit me and suddenly I felt better.

'Where were you last night?' he asked brusquely, his harsh eyes biting at me.

'Oh no. Not that again.'

'Just answer the questions, we'll do the funnies.'

'I was out.'

'We know you were. Anywhere near South View Gardens?'

'Where are they?' This could go on all night.

'Let's cut it short, Scott.' He had to have something on me to have dropped the 'Mr.'. 'You were seen near number 37 South View Gardens at one a.m. this morning. The house was entered from a first floor bedroom window at the side of the house.'

'I was nowhere near the place, as you well know.'

'You were seen there.'

'Then I insist on an I.D. parade right now.'

'You can insist on nothing.' I noticed that he didn't take me up on it.

'If you weren't there, Scott, it should be easy enough to prove. It was only last night.'

I could not prove it. In a fit of remorse I had left Maggie alone last night. To the best of my knowledge she had gone out with a girl friend. I was glad that she was not implicated in this one. In fact I had gone out on my own. As corny as it sounds, I had walked for quite a time and then gone to bed.

'At the time you're talking about I was in bed.'

'Prove it.'

'You prove I wasn't.'

He sat back sipping his tea, playing with me, enjoying it, trying to scourge his own conscience.

It went on for two hours without getting anywhere. He tried the double act with him shouting and the D.C. quietening him down and then trying the smooth technique, but they were not a good team and anyway I'd seen it all before. In the end they reluctantly let me go. I demanded a police car to run me back and that choked Bulman but he managed to dig up a driver.

By the time I was home it was too late to contact Maggie which was too bad in the event. Some of the boys might still be up though and the quickest way off this hook was to establish an alibi. See what I mean about truth? I would have to supply a good lie to satisfy Bulman. Digging up a pocketful of change I located the nearest phone booth and did the rounds of the boys, keeping away from the Reisens mob.

Finally Balls Up Balfour came to my rescue. Tug Wilson had been released that day and Balls Up and one or two of the boys had a private party to celebrate. I was given the details, times and so on, and Balls Up promised to contact the others. I knew that he would, I had no doubt of that, but he had not achieved his name for nothing. A short untidy master forger with a soft heart who was constantly broke because he was an inveterate gambler usually finishing up at the losing end of the gaming mobs, he lived over his dilapidated printing business in near squalor. Short of cash he would invariably find himself forging something for the wrong people and as a consequence nick was his second home. A master craftsman who balled things up by a weakness and inability to judge people.

The following morning I rang the nick and left a message that I would call on them at lunch time. In fairness to Bulman, he made a point of being there.

'Look,' I said sheepishly, 'I've been thinking things over. I didn't want to drag in the boys and I still don't like it. The fact is I was at a party with Balls Up Balfour and a couple of the lads because Tug Wilson came out that day.'

'I heard he was out.' Bulman was sitting opposite me again looking very satisfied. 'Didn't know Tug was a friend of yours.'

'I know what it's like to come out. We just gave him a good time, that's all.'

'Well, let's get it all down.' He pulled a notebook across. 'Stag, was it?' He asked without looking up.

'Yes.'

'No women at all?'

'There wouldn't be at that sort of party.'

'That's what I thought. Only Maggie Parsons told me that you spent the night with her.'

The coldness started in my chest. In a second I was stiff with it. I stared helplessly as Bulman began to laugh quietly, the sincerest act I had seen him make. In breaking her own golden rule Maggie had as good as locked me in and thrown away the key.

CHAPTER THREE

I WAS LIKE a man without legs, not knowing which way to manoeuvre in case I fell right in it. Desperately I said, 'You know Maggie was trying to protect me. I wasn't with her.'

'Of course she was trying to protect you.' Bulman was leaning back, his smile fixed.

'Well then——'

'Well that's it. She was trying to protect you the first time too, wasn't she?'

'No. That was the truth.'

'Come on, Scott, do better than that. I *know* that you weren't with her last night because she was out with another girl. They got back about midnight. So she lied for you. So far as I'm concerned she's always been lying for you.'

What could I say? It would make no difference now. Bulman raised his pen. 'Well let's get on with it. Those other names.'

I gave them to him, then he sat back tapping the pencil on the table and musing over the names as if they were very special emblems.

'You know, you're not doing so well.' Bulman could afford to be relaxed, he was laughing up his sleeve. 'First your girl friend lies for you, and now you present me with names of four villains who are not exactly pillars of truth. I wouldn't fancy my chances if they depended on the evidence of this bunch in a court of law.'

It was not possible to retract; on top of Maggie's lapse it would fix me for good. As it was he still had to pin it on me.

'You know,' he said conversationally, 'it's funny that this drum in South View Gardens is also listed in our vacant premises book. It's beginning to stink a bit.'

So he was still after Dick. I was feeling so morose that I began not to care. Except about Dick and I was really scared for him. Still, I tried.

'You know damn fine how it works. All any villain has to do to locate empty premises is to follow the copper on the beat and see which houses he inspects in detail. You know it but you don't want to believe it.'

Finally he had to let me go because he lacked real evidence and he had to check on Balls Up's alibi.

This time I elected a long walk before going to Maggie's. What worried me most was Dick. If they seriously began to suspect him then he was as good as out of the force and I would never forgive myself.

She met me at the door like an excited schoolgirl who'd just nicked teacher's apple. Her auburn hair spread copper tints under the light and her eyes, green tonight to match her blouse, were alive. 'I've been looking all over for you,' she gasped anxiously.

Putting my arm round her we entered the room. 'I know, love. You've been looking in the wrong places.'

'Oh, Willie, I had to see you before that beast of a policeman did.'

'You didn't make it, Mag. I've just left Bulman.'

She looked so crestfallen that I gave her a big squeeze. 'Don't worry. I'd give anything for a good strong cup of tea.' While she went to make one I spread myself on the settee, feeling bushed. Maggie called from the kitchen.

'Did he tell you I said I spent the night with you?'

'He told me.'

Maggie appeared in the kitchen doorway. 'I'm making you a sandwich too. Willie, what's wrong?'

'He told me *after* I had already told him that I'd been out with the boys.'

'Oh God, no.' Her hand went to her mouth and she lost colour. Getting up, I held her close, rocking her slightly, holding the back of her head in my hand so that her face was against my chest.

'It's all right, Maggie. It's all right.'

'I've landed you right in it.' Her muffled voice reached me like a disembodied wail.

'No you haven't. I admire you for it.' Her head jerked back.

There was a rapping on the door, and there was Dick, pale-faced, and beneath his light overcoat I could see his uniform trousers and regulation boots. By the look of him he had just come off duty. I just stood there dumbly at first, it had to be bad news. Maggie called from behind me. 'Come in, Dick, for goodness sake. I'll get another cup.' She darted into the kitchen and I closed the door. 'What's the trouble? Sit down.'

He undid his coat and fell into an armchair. His hair was ruffled as if the wind had caught it and he gazed dazedly at the electric fire. 'The Governor's had me in. He's been asking some very pointed questions about the vacant premises book. He thinks that someone is giving out information.'

'Because of two lousy jobs?' I poured out scorn. 'You know I've been in again, don't you?'

'I know. That's what it's all about.'

I didn't like the way Dick looked; it was an expression of hopelessness as if this was all inevitable. I had never felt so wretched. 'I didn't do them, Dick.'

He gazed over at me and gave a feeble grin. 'I know you wouldn't operate in the manor.'

'I've got news for you kid. I haven't operated *anywhere* since

I've been out. I don't intend to either. This is Bulman's little caper. He's so drenched in his own guilt it's warped his judgement.'

'He wouldn't much like the idea of me knowing either.'

Maggie came in with the other cup and passed it to Dick. She had heard us and now sat down beside me.

'I'm sorry, Dick,' I groaned. 'Does the super suspect you?'

'He bloody well suspects someone.'

'But our connection adds up to the obvious?'

'Wouldn't you think so in his shoes?'

Sinking back on the couch I could feel all my nerve ends jangling. 'I'll go and see him tomorrow.'

'Who, the governor? What good will it do?'

'I'm going to tell him that I'm being victimised.'

Draining his tea Dick rose and carefully put the cup and saucer on the white pine mantelpiece.

'Look,' I said, 'I know what it means to you and you're going right to the top. All the way. Commissioner.'

He grinned. 'Commander would do.'

'Right. Commander. Even if it means I have to remain straight for the rest of my life. And I can't be fairer than that.' We all laughed a bit but after Dick had gone I was in the depths of despair for him. Even Maggie's magic did not work. I rang the nick to discover what time the Chief Superintendent would be in then left a hopeful message that he might deign to see me at ten.

Maggie agreed to ring up my boss and straighten it out with him, because by now he must have been doing a good deal of speculation.

Chief Superintendent 'Mike' Cummings was grey-haired and ruddy faced with eyes that twinkled when in the mood. He is what I call straight as it is meant by a villain. I trusted him and expected a fair deal. He could not be touched with money.

I sat in his modern glass-panelled office, with its metal desk and chairs, feeling a fool. Now it seemed a sneaky, childish thing to do, yet it could affect my whole life. He sat there, half smiling, probably amused by my discomfort, and waited for me to start. I had difficulty so he encouraged me with, 'Come on, Spider. Out with it. It can't be a confession or you wouldn't have asked to see me.'

'I don't know how to put it, sir.' I was playing it humbly. 'You see, it affects my brother.'

His gaze hardened, his smile became more fixed. I'd sent up the warning light and he was suddenly all policeman.

'Look,' I burst out. 'I didn't do those jobs Bulman is chasing me for. He knows I wouldn't ruin my brother's chances. Dick loves the force and one day he'll be sitting where you're sitting.'

'Well, I hope they give him a warmer office. Go on.'

'Well, that's it. Dick's under suspicion of passing information to me and it's bloody ridiculous.'

'Who said he's under suspicion?'

'You've interviewed him for a start.'

'Amongst others.'

'No one has passed information to me and if they had I wouldn't touch it in this manor. I'm being victimised by Bulman.'

'Why would he do that?' Mike Cummings was no fool, but his easy manner was deceptive.

'I can't grass, even on a copper. But there is something he hates my guts for.'

'Even if he does, Spider, he's got to hang a case on you that will stick, and to my satisfaction.'

'Meanwhile he can make life almost impossible for me. I could easily lose my job the way he's chasing me.'

'Well, I wouldn't want that to happen. But listen to me.' Mike Cummings pushed his chair back so that he was facing me squarely across the desk. The smile had gone but his tone was still friendly.

'You've been to prison on three separate occasions and on probation before that. You're a villain and we both know it. You're in no position to demand special privileges. If you're going straight then you'll get every help from us but it's early days yet; don't blame *us* if we still see you as a possibility.

'I think I know what's between you and Sergeant Bulman but he would have got his promotion anyway. If a job is done and it bears your hall mark then we'll follow it up whether it's Bulman or any other C.I.D. officer. If there is real victimization then I'll jump on it but apart from a mutual dislike between you two, I haven't seen much signs of it. The jobs have been done—in your style. What should we do? Say to ourselves 'Spider wouldn't have done them because of his brother'?

'It can be argued that a crafty villain would want us to think just that. Now listen, Spider. You decided to go into crime. Don't start crying because things get rough. You threw the first punch, and the second and the third. You'll remain suspect all the time there is suspicion. Remove that suspicion and we'll get off your back.' He sat back, his face a little redder than before, eyeing me cagily.

'Bulman didn't have to pick me up at my job just before closing time.'

'And you didn't have to supply a very shaky alibi from some very shady characters with a lie thrown in from your girlfriend.'

I stood up wearily. He was right, of course. I had only myself to blame; it was part of the cost of being stupid.

'Thank you for seeing me, sir,' I said morosely.

Mike Cummings was too experienced to be beguiled but not

too hard to feel sympathy. 'You've nothing to fear if you didn't do it, Spider.'

I left him, sorry that I had called. I stood outside the station feeling a fool. But for my brother I would not have considered pleading my case with a police officer. As I saw it I had lowered myself to no avail and could only hope that the boys did not get to hear of it.

I walked towards my car wondering if Balls Up Balfour and the others had yet been interviewed. Somehow it no longer mattered. I must be patient, ride it out and hope time would solve the matter. That's what reason dictated. But there was no reasoning about the churning in my guts that I had suffered on and off since coming out.

So the only warning I had was animal instinct. But that's like a doctor, telling you you're ill but that he hasn't a clue what it is. It achieves nothing except a step or two towards the box. As I drew away I noticed a grey van pull out after me. When I reached the garage it continued on.

At the garage I got some strange looks. Out of courtesy I went to see the boss in his little office next to the spares stores. Never the gay type, he looked none too happy now; his black moustache drooped in mourning.

'Did Maggie phone?' I asked him. He nodded, looking up with the liveliness of a bloodhound. 'Well, I'm sorry I'm late, but I had to settle this once and for all.'

'And did you?' He had a grinding voice like an ungreased axle.

'No, not really. But don't worry about it. I've done nothing wrong.' For a while he searched my face with his sombre, not unfriendly eyes. 'I may as well come straight out with it,' he managed at last. 'I'll have to get rid of you, Spider. It's all bad for business.'

I stared at him numbly but not entirely surprised. 'But I tell you I've done nothing.'

'It's not the point, son. Look, I don't want to sack you . . . you're good at your job, but the business can't stand police enquiries. The boys who use us won't like it and I just don't want the police around here. Look at last night, I ask you; like a bloody film set.'

'They won't be coming again.'

'You don't know that and I can't afford to take the risk.'

I had a certain sympathy for him. He was really worried about his hire purchase fiddles. I nodded slowly in acquiescence. He could see that I was hit badly so he stood up awkwardly. 'Your notice would normally come on Friday so you've got an extra couple of days. Take what time you need off to scout around. I'm sorry, son. Maybe later if it all clears up . . .'

'Yeah.' He wasn't a bad bloke and it wasn't his fault. 'Thanks anyway.'

I did not want to make it worse for him so I left then to stand on the forecourt for several minutes. What now?

Later I told Maggie that I had jacked it in but she knew better. She also knew that I was perfectly capable of knocking up a steady five to ten thousand a year tax free without too much effort and it was this possibility that really frightened her. It frightened me too. This was a testing period for me for I realized how easy it would be to go back to old habits. The excitement beckoned me but I had the sense to look beyond it to the squalor and heartbreak of prison. So I reassured Maggie as best I could and went job hunting.

About this time, more from anger than anything, I decided to find out if my certainty of being watched was just the jitters or fact. I did not warrant police surveillance and I could see no reason why one of the big crime syndicates should tail me. So I was both perplexed and worried.

One night I decided to find out definitely. There are plenty of back streets in the Notting Hill area and in some of the old squares the houses are what I call back to front. That is to say that the respectable looking side of the buildings faced inward towards the grass rectangle in the square; what should have been the back doors faced on to the streets and with them the usual array of drain pipes.

I deliberately stayed late at Maggie's and left after 1 a.m. I kept to streets that were particularly badly lit. It was eerie listening to my own footsteps on practically empty streets and it is strange how late at night Old London creeps from its shell. There was a mixture of Victorian and Edwardian around here and the two periods emerged in shadowy form as if aware of their ultimate demise even in mordant bricks and mortar.

It had rained earlier and the skies were still swollen with black tumbling clouds that cut off the moon like heavy drapes over a lighted window. This was how I wanted it for good night sight was part of my equipment. I did not hurry. Nor did I stop or hesitate. I listened carefully but could hear only the rustle of wind as it swept autumn leaves from the gutter. I turned in and satisfied myself that someone was about, unheard, unseen. Whoever it was may have had nothing to do with me but someone was there.

Keeping on I chose my route carefully. The fact that I could hear nothing did not mislead me; in my profession it had been essential to move completely noiselessly even in leather shoes.

I kept my own footsteps at a steady pace, not too light, not too heavy, just sufficiently audible. Then turning into one of the small squares I decided to make my move.

I was at its narrow end. There were only two street lamps but plenty of shadows. The decaying houses reached up, pillared porticos, ethereal columns of moulded concrete. There were two lighted windows with drawn curtains, and behind one of them came the faint sound of argument.

What pleased me most was that I was as relaxed as I used to be and somehow this was important to me. Keeping close to the terraced buildings I reached the corner, turned it, kept walking at the same steady pace but now my gaze was rapidly taking in the scene. This longer stretch of the square was also empty. There were a few more lights on but nothing that worried me. I ran forward.

Gazing briefly up the stack I intended to climb I gave it a solid tug. It didn't budge and I started up, feet getting a purchase on the rough bricks on either side and my hands gripping the stack firmly. It had been a long time and yet it seemed only yesterday. I had no trouble although my breathing might have been a shade heavier than it used to be. I kept going without looking down until I reached a junction of pipes, got myself a good foothold in the angle of the two pipes, held tightly with my hands and then half turned so that I could see along the square.

Just above me to the left a light came on in a small window. There was a rough shadow on the frosted glass but I kept my gaze on the street. I was not in the most comfortable position but I could hold it for a few minutes; about twelve to fifteen feet in deep shadow above the pavement my O.P. was good.

I listened. A variety of noises reached me. Above me the water cistern started filling and the light went out. The street lamps threw bleak pools of light at their own feet as if afraid to emerge into the darkness. All told there was the sort of quietness you would expect at this time of night in an unfashionable square. And I felt good. The old tingle was back in my fingertips.

I thought he would never come but did not doubt he was there. When he did he was so good that I nearly missed him. He must have turned the corner while my gaze had been distracted by a lighted window. Even now I couldn't hear him and saw him only because the streets were wet and I caught a brief reflection. He hugged those shadows like a cat and it was difficult to judge his size because I couldn't get a really close view.

He had evidently been keeping a fair distance behind me yet he made no effort to hurry now that he could no longer hear me. I waited, ready to jump and give him the shock of his life. He still had a little way to come and I positioned myself for the leap.

In the distance two drunks began to argue then a window flew up and someone shouted at them. Above the medley of sound came another. Footsteps. The unmistakable crunch of a regulation tread in duplicate. Bloody coppers. I swore to myself. It was difficult, because of echoes, to judge exactly where they were. The sound seemed to be approaching from the opposite end of the square.

I began to sweat. They would never believe my story if they found me up here. 'A man was following me, officer, so I climbed a drainpipe to surprise him.' Christ, I could hardly believe it myself. Suddenly everything changed. The double tread was nearing the square and my man was only a few feet away. I dare not jump now in case he yelled and I certainly couldn't thump him with the law round the corner. As if to deride me further, he crossed the road just before he reached me.

He came into full view then; almost a runt of a man. I would never know him again because his dark coat collar was turned up and he kept his head down as if following footprints. I caught a glimpse of light on a dark head but he seemed almost shapeless; small, nondescript, hands in pockets and utterly silent. I had to let him go because the police rounded the corner at that moment.

Angrily I clung to my perch because I dare not come down until they were out of sight. I first prayed they would not see me. From the other side of the road there was more chance that they would than passing directly underneath me. Shining their lamps in a couple of doorways did nothing for my nerves and my perch was becoming difficult to maintain.

When they finally disappeared round the corner I shinned down that pipe like a monkey as relieved as I'll ever be. I padded quietly after the little chap but I wasn't hopeful.

The next morning I knew the tail was off. My third eye in the back of my head had stopped operating. I wondered why. Had he seen me? There was no profit in this sort of speculation so I resigned myself to being released from observation but it still puzzled me.

I didn't tell Maggie any of this, in fact I was telling her increasingly less. About my recurrent depressions for instance over not finding work and the way my bank balance was dwindling. Of course I could sell the car and I would but this was no real solution. Quite simply the number of employers willing to take on an ex-con were strictly limited. The few ideas I had needed capital backing and the only money I could raise would be bent from the boys; that I could do without, I had to. Another thing that worried me was the kick I had got going up the drainpipe. I could not pretend that I had not enjoyed it.

One night I said to Maggie, 'I'll have to get out of London, sweetheart. Go to the provinces or somewhere, anywhere there's work.'

I remember her looking at me with something like reproach and saying softly, 'There *are* jobs you could have had, Willie.' It was a sore point between us. Maggie wanted me to take anything at all as long as it kept me straight. She did not like the idea of my leaving London because we would lose touch; nor, for that matter, did I.

So I was drifting. Then Bulman called on me again, had me

down at the station, tried to break down what I had already told him and endeavoured to bluff me over Balls Up's alibi and prove that I was where I wasn't. I could see that he was just itching for the next job to come up especially if it was a house in the vacant premises book. He jibed me about having no job yet managing to run a Jag, but I let it go.

I had never felt lower. Dick called to tell me that he had been passed over for a C.I.D. course when initially he had been half promised it and the pattern was all too clear.

One morning early I had just left a most depressing interview for a job. It was pouring with rain and I was in the vicinity of the Strand. Even the pigeons had taken to the window ledges for shelter, and the recently cleaned Nelson's Column was streaming with wet patches. I was thoroughly soaked and depressed more than usual. Just then I could see no end to it.

I turned into Lyons near South Africa House for a cup of tea. Even with my early warning system it was impossible to know just what I was walking into. For that was the real start of all that followed. Had I known I would not have entered. I would have hoofed it down the Strand and broken records all the way.

I went downstairs to the self service. The rain had pulled in a lot of people but there were still plenty of empty tables; it was a little early for shoppers. I found a table opposite the double staircase and in the least crowded part of the restaurant. I turned so that I could sit with my back against the wall and disconsolately stirred my tea.

After a while I heard a chair being pulled out, vaguely saw movement on the edge of my vision. Then a cultured voice said politely, 'Hello, Spider. Another bad day?'

CHAPTER FOUR

I LOOKED UP SLOWLY, scowling. He was as out of place as champagne in a beer glass. As soon as I saw him I knew the face—vaguely, but I'd seen it somewhere. His hair was thinning, brushed back and had once been black, like his thick, finely arched brows. Sixtyish, there was no sign of age in his clear eyes, an honest grey that met my gaze and held it; they were good eyes, perceptive and, I suspected, could be ruthless or humorous. At the moment they were non-committal. His face was narrow and lined, long chin and thin, uncompromising lips. A dark overcoat was sufficiently open to reveal a Savile Row suit, white shirt and a club tie. As I took all this in he was placing his bowler hat carefully on the seat beside him and hanging his umbrella over the chair back.

'Who are you?' I demanded brusquely. I was in no mood for this. The chap looked as if he was something in the city and city gents don't accost my type with a straight motive in Lyons tea shops. I was suddenly suspicious for the wrong reason.

'Does it really matter?' he replied gently, amusement touching his eyes.

My mood was black and belligerent. If someone wanted to talk to me then he could identify himself. 'It matters to me.' He smiled, practised and charming. I briefly wondered if he was a con man. The 'Brigadier' used to dress like this before he exchanged it for government issue.

'Spider, I can assure you that it doesn't matter at all. I'll give you something to call me by if you insist.' He was pushing his cup of tea away as if he had never intended to drink it. I noticed his fine hands; they had never quarried.

But I had enough on my plate without mystery men. If he had some sort of proposition I did not doubt that I would come out the wrong end of it. A smooth bastard this one; yes, just like the 'Brigadier' who was a great entertainer on form. 'Look,' I suggested bluntly, 'why sit here? There are plenty of empty tables, why not take one and stretch yourself.'

He gazed at me, taking me in, and I wasn't interested in his analysis. His eyes had hardened a little as if he was puzzled. If he was out of place he was most certainly at ease. Without fuss he quietly retrieved his bowler, put it on to meet the faint pink lines where it had previously rested, and took hold of his umbrella. The nylon was not as wet as I thought it might have been. He rose.

'I've clearly called at a bad moment,' he said pleasantly. 'Forgive me for having mis-timed it. I'll see you during the week; one evening at your place.' He raised his bowler and was gone, leaving his tea untouched. He went up the stairs like a guards colonel in mufti. I like to see a man carry himself well.

Having half finished my tea I could see what an idiot I had been. It costs nothing to listen. Raincoat flapping, I darted for the stairs and went up them three at a time, past the bread counter and out into the pouring rain. There was no sign of him and I cursed myself. The pavement was quite crowded but almost everyone was hiding under an umbrella.

When I nipped downstairs to finish my tea it had gone along with his. I bought another and sat brooding again. Now where had I seen that face? Inside? I would have remembered. Meanwhile my stomach was doing its high wire act, red lights flashing like a petrol gauge warning; unmistakable and persistent. For the rest of that day I was preoccupied with the 'city gent'. Sooner or later I would place him.

At Maggie's that night I sat with my arm round her and we were comfortable on the couch, but there was tension between us due to the way things were. She was beginning to be afraid that it would not last, that once again she would be back on the heap. Because I did not want her hurt it made me miserable for I was never a great one for hiding my feelings. Suddenly I told her all about the city gent.

'But you would know a con man.'

I laughed. 'Even a con man doesn't know a con man; they con themselves more than their victims. But I don't think he is. Yet I know the face.'

We sat talking about it not really getting anywhere, when Maggie suggested, 'Why don't you contact the newspaper reporter you used to know. The one who showed interest after your trial.'

'Oh, wait a minute. Ray . . .?'

'Lynch, I think it was.'

'That's him. What could he do?'

'Newspaper offices have photographic files. He could arrange for you to see them.'

'There must be thousands of prints, Maggie. And anyway it's a helluva long time ago, he wouldn't remember.'

'Oh, don't you believe it. Those chaps need all the contacts they can get.'

'I'll bear it in mind. When his Lordship calls I want a stake out, the number of his car.'

'I'll do it for you. I don't mind waiting outside for two nights if it helps you. I'm perfectly capable of remembering a licence number. Don't use the boys.'

It wasn't such a bad idea. 'All right.' I came round to stand over her. 'Whatever you do, remember the three S's.'

'S's?'

'Shape, shadow and shine. Keep away from skylines and straight building lines. Merge. Keep in shadow but ensure that you are not throwing one. And don't wear anything that shines.' She nodded and mumbled a repetition.

'There's one more thing,' I said.

'Yes?'

'I like that perfume you're wearing.' I'd said it for her sake. And I made love to her for the same reason, but how can you relax when you're filled with gnawing doubts and obscure fancies?

His Lordship, as I'd named him, called next evening. There was no prior warning, just a soft knock on my door and there he was, rolled umbrella, bowler hat, immaculate overcoat and all. Doffing his hat he gave a slight bow. 'Good evening, Spider. I said I would call, you remember.'

I let him in. He stood there, too polite to gaze round my shabby room but I was left with the impression that he could still give me a fair inventory of its contents just the same. This time I liked him on sight, without necessarily trusting him. Helping him off with his coat I laid it on the bed with his hat, annoyed myself by playing the gentleman and letting him have my armchair. He had that effect on me.

'I'm delighted your mood has improved, Spider. I really do apologize for yesterday.'

'Can I get you a drink?' I asked without moving. You can go too far with this hospitality stuff. He laughed and it was a good, genuine sound that brought out my own smile. 'I know you don't drink, or hardly. And I must say I approve of your discouragement. I'll join you in abstinence.'

Pulling forward an old kitchen chair I straddled it, arms along its back. 'You *know* I had another bad day yesterday; you *know* where I live; you *know* I don't drink much. What else do you know?'

'Oh, practically everything. Look here, do you mind if I smoke a cigar? If it annoys you I won't.'

I gave him the O.K. and hooked out a tin ashtray. He got it going and I wafted away the clouds of smoke but even I could tell that the cigar was rich and pleasant. When he dropped the match into the tray there was a faint tinkle that made me realize how quiet it had become between us. He had used the time spent in getting his cigar going to give me more than the odd shrewd stare and I reflected that he spent every second in some form of observation. I was now comfortable in his presence as a person but I was highly suspicious of his purpose. I waited for him to get down to it.

'I have a proposition for you. One I fancy will appeal to your sense of adventure.'

'In or outside the law?'

'I'll answer that later. Let me explain . . .'

'You've already answered it,' I said rising. My neck was prickling in too familiar a way.

'Now don't be a chump. Sit down and listen.'

'I'm not breaking the law. Not any more.'

'Well, I'm relieved to hear you say it so convincingly. Nevertheless I think you should hear me out. It could solve your problems with Maggie and your brother's with Sergeant Bulman.'

I sat down slowly. 'This is too one-sided. You know too much about me and I know nothing at all about you. Let's even it up a little.'

He surveyed his cigar, rolling it slowly. 'Well I don't intend to tell you much about myself. Look here, I don't want to stand on ceremony, call me Fairfax.'

He took a good long pull at his cigar. 'Y'know, I haven't pulled your name from a hat. I, and others, have spent a considerable amount of time in researching your background, character and so on. There was a short list but it's to your credit that you are our choice.'

The old flannel, flattery first, I thought. I wasn't that soft.

'We know about your mother and father, how they constantly fought, how your father died and your mother just disappeared. We believe that this is at least part cause of your—er—criminal tendencies.'

I had heard all this rubbish before. 'And what about my brother? How do they account for him?'

'He is younger, missed much of what you experienced. He may have been shocked into honesty by your own dubious activities. But don't interrupt. This is all necessary, I assure you.'

I was hooked so I leaned forward over the chair back and let him get on with it.

'We think you are basically honest with this particular flaw. We know that you are loyal, for instance, and that is terribly important to us. Your word's your bond, an old-fashioned trait that many so-called honest people would envy.'

'Never mind the diplomas. Let's get at it.'

He smiled again.

'And your directness has not gone unnoticed.'

'So I'm a good lad. What is it you want me to do to change all that?'

'Tolerance is not your greatest forte. You are quick to boil against any form of injustice, no matter how trivial. Those are your weaknesses. I want you to recover something that has been stolen from us.'

'Who's "us"?'

'I could have arrived wearing a little Union Jack in my bowler.'

I laughed. 'You remind me of the "Brigadier".'

'Oh?'

'One of the best con men in the business. Once you know a con man you simply don't believe a word he says.'

'But I've made no claims, Spider. The information I have on you no confidence trickster could acquire.'

'So we come back to it. Who or what are you?'

'Y'know, I do wish you would stop interrupting. We'd get there much sooner. I want you to break into a house and recover something of immense importance to this country. It has no commercial value but it is extremely important to us all.'

He must have known that my old-fashioned loyalties also stretched to a bit of flag waving for the home base. I had enjoyed my spell in the infantry; it had been the only period when I had remained out of trouble.

'But it will still be a felony.'

He nodded gravely.

'I can't understand you,' I said. 'You can't seriously expect that I would stick my neck out for a job like this.'

'I certainly would not expect you to stick it out for nothing But, you have not properly considered it. Think. Bulman has an obsession about you. You are out of work and must be considering moving right away to obtain better luck. If you do you'll be deserting the one person in the world who is of any value to you —Maggie Parsons—a charming girl. Your brother will be free of the hazards of having you around if you move but you'll largely lose touch with him. Bulman will pass the word on wherever you go because he is that sort of person. Like you, he has a flaw.'

Well, he was right about one thing. He did know all about me.

'What are you offering that's different?'

'I can stop police persecution. I *know* that you did not do those jobs because I was having you watched. I can see that an injustice is put right over your brother's C.I.D. course. It might mean moving him to another division but he will have the opportunity he so badly wants.

'And how will I know that these things will be done? Presumably the job is soon. I won't know if Bulman will pop up again for a month or so and my brother's affairs could take as long.'

'Within three days of your agreeing to help us, Bulman will call on you to officially announce that he knows you are innocent. Within another few days your brother will undoubtedly inform you that he has been fully promised a C.I.D. course. From that point he is on his own—he can only pass on merit.'

I had to admit something else about this character. A lot *was* self explanatory. And he was infinitely better than the 'Brigadier'. I began to warm towards him and then suddenly realized that I was going mad. I had been so pleased to hear that he could fix Bulman and Dick that I had allowed myself to be carried away. What the hell was going on? 'What's involved?' I asked. I was beginning to realize that anyone willing to pull these sort of strings had a dicey job up his sleeve.

'Well, Spider, it's in your line, I can assure you. Basically I want you to burgle a house, remove from its safe a green metal deed box and hand it over to someone who will be waiting outside. The job is then done. There is no more.'

'The safe will be open of course?'

'You'll have to blow it.'

'I'm not a peterman. I've never blown a safe in my life.'

By now he had a good long ash on his cigar which he carefully removed by rolling it on the tin tray. He was eyeing me very shrewdly all the time, as if weighing my every word, every reaction. Although he was relaxed, through those eyes of his I could see that he was completely and utterly alert to the slightest nuance of tone or gesture. Because of this I became immensely wary myself. His trained intelligence was on a higher plane than mine but I had the basics, the practical experience of an animal on the run.

'That is true,' he admitted at last. 'It is equally true that you

were taught safe-breaking by the finest peterman in the country—
Larry Soames.'

'Oh, come off it,' I said scornfully.

'Taught in the welding shop at Dartmoor,' he went on, un-
daunted. Then he smiled briefly. 'You never dealt with the
tobacco barons on the Moor, did you, Spider? Too damned
awkward and independent. But Larry Soames could never get
sufficient tobacco so you saw to it that he had yours. And in return
he taught you safe-breaking.'

'It's hardly practical experience.'

'We can give you that. We can even supply you with an
identical safe to the one you have to blow to practise on.'

It all sounded nice and pat but I was crazy even to consider it.
As much as I loved my brother was I willing to face a ten-year
stretch for him? At the end of it I would still be out of a job.

He anticipated me, or rather, I suspected later, at each sign of
reluctance he timed another inducement. 'You will be paid for
the job, of course.'

'How much?'

'Enough to set you up in business. I believe you are interested
in diving work—enough for that.'

'How much?'

'Fifteen thousand pounds in a Swiss bank account.'

The shock passed through me as if the chair was electrified—
momentarily welding me to it.

'Fifteen thousand? What is it I'm nicking?'

'I could tell you anything. But I won't. It really does not
matter and has no intrinsic value.'

'You are not giving away fifteen thousand. What are the risks
and what happens to me if I'm caught?'

He shrugged eloquently; he had me on the end of a line and
was playing it as he saw it. 'I can give you no protection. If you're
caught, then I'm afraid that's it. Your brother still carries on and
you have one thousand pounds when you come out. The fifteen
is for success.'

I considered a ten stretch on the Moor for they wouldn't be
mug enough to send me back to Grendon. I knew that I couldn't
face it. I'd go mad back there and fit for nothing but crime when
I came out; which meant that most of my remaining life would be
spent behind bars. No. On the other hand my problems would be
over if I succeeded. There were one or two exciting schemes that
I could then finance. Maggie would be happy. Dick would be on
the way up. Even so—the Moor again if I failed. I would be writing off my life— if would become a living death. Even Maggie
wouldn't wait that long.

'That's only one hundred a year for every year I'm sentenced.
How could I know that the money would be there anyway.'

'You must not forget remission, Spider.'

'Your records must show that I'm not good at obtaining re-mission. I'm like a sparrow in a cage; I kick up a bit of a shindy.'

'Look here, don't you think you're taking all too pessimistic a view? You're good at it. Why on earth should you not get away with it?'

I was about to answer when he threw out yet another of his timely inducements. 'Of course, any cash that you find in the safe you can please yourself about. I'm in no position to pass judge-ment. I want only the deed box.'

I should have let it drop right then. All the warnings were at full blast but there was something pushing me on. Even so I wasn't stupid enough to agree. I said, 'Let me get it straight. If I do this job Bulman's put back in his hole, Dick gets his chance and if I deliver the box I get fifteen grand. If I'm nicked on the job and fail to deliver I'm sent up with only one lousy thousand when I come out.'

'That's a fair summary but for two points. On your word of acceptance Bulman will toe the line and your brother will get his opportunity. So you see, Spider, the trust is twofold. If you agree and then break your word you have gained something, have you not? I am entirely reliant on you honouring the agreement once entered into. You must also accept that I will pay the money.'

'It's the one thousand I don't like.'

He shrugged unrelentingly. 'This is too important to pay for failure. I am interested only in success. I am here because you are the man most likely to succeed. I am prepared to put complete trust in you.'

The inference being that I should be prepared to do the same in him. I gazed at him thoughtfully while he stared musingly back. His brain was ticking in a well-oiled, well-trained rhythm and I could see that he had himself well under control even though it was clearly all-important to him. Just how important I had yet to discover. My own thought processes were like an engine falling apart: bits were flying all over the place. However, I did have protective devices that recognized my own confusion and prevented me from making a decision at that time. I could see that there was little more to learn from him; the issue was clear apart from location.

'Where's the job to be done?' I asked, almost off-handedly.

'Do you know Portland Place?'

I stiffened. A wealthy area near the B.B.C. Too open for my liking. I nodded without enthusiasm.

'It's the Chinese Legation.'

CHAPTER FIVE

FOR A FULL TWO MINUTES I was unable to speak. The whole
crazy proposition fell about my ears. He not only wanted me to
screw a place but to invade foreign territory as well. If I was
caught inside the Chinese Legation I imagined that a ten-year
stretch would seem like a very desirable convalescence by com-
parison. They would never let me out until they had soaked,
beaten or brainwashed the last scrap of information I had to
offer. And then they would not let me go because they would not
have admitted my presence in the first place.

My God, he was crafty, this Fairfax. He had fed me a bit at a
time, led me on and saved the worst until the end. Had he
mentioned the place at first I would not have listened to the rest.
'Has it ever been tried before?'

'Not here.'

'Where then?'

'Rangoon.'

'What happened?'

'Two of our local boys went over the wall of the Chinese
Embassy.'

'Did they get out?'

'They were never seen again.'

For the next five minutes I told him what sort of a bastard I
thought he was. I was angry at the way he had done it and livid
at the ridiculousness of the suggestion. What made it worse was
the way he sat there while I harangued him. His cigar was poised
and his gaze steady through the spiralling smoke; his legs were
crossed, his immaculate creases somehow symbolizing his relaxed
yet disciplined attitude. My quick impression was of my volume
of disjointed words, curses and vehemence striking him at some
central point in his forehead, pouring into it and being compu-
terized and reduced to brief terms of sense. Certainly he did not
move or show a single sign of distress. When finally I ran out of
invective he gave a short nod of approval.

'You know you almost managed that without repeating yourself. Do you feel better?'

'Get out,' I snarled.

He rose, unhurriedly, walked to the bed to retrieve his coat.
While putting it on he said, 'Remember this number: 930-0932.
When you ring insist on speaking to me and ask for Fairfax. That
is all you need remember.' He repeated the number again twice,
then added, 'I expect to have your answer during the next two
days.'

As if I hadn't given him my answer. He had led me up the

garden path, given me false hope, and now it was worse than before as he had known that it would be.

He picked up his bowler and his beautifully furled umbrella and went to the door. For a short time he stood watching me as if trying to make up his mind but without change of expression. Then he offered his brief little smile and said, 'I can let myself out.'

And so he bloody well could, the smooth bastard. I was still seething so much that I was afraid to make any kind of move. So I watched him open the door, give an exaggerated wave of his hat, a final reminder to ring him within forty-eight hours, and then go.

Sinking into my own chair I could feel his warmth and I could have wept. The Chinese Legation, a friendly little mob who had attacked our own police with an axe and pick-axe handles. That's what they had done *outside*; I wondered what form it would take inside.

My mood of fury made me forget that I was expecting Maggie so that when she came in she took me by surprise. I just held her until I simmered down and sank myself into her presence. We must have stood like that for some minutes, neither of us stirring. Poor Maggie. I stole a glance at her face and knew that it was she who would bear the brunt of the suffering whatever I did. Slowly we sat down, anxiety clouding her features now that we had broken. She realized that something was terribly wrong but gave me time to collect my wits. What should I tell her?

'It's all right,' I said at last. 'I can't tell you what he wanted because there is some secrecy attached to it. He is *not* a villain so don't worry about it.'

'But what upset you so much?'

'He said something which I took as a personal insult. You know me. Anyway it's over.'

She was by no means satisfied but she knew me well enough to know that she would get nowhere by pushing it at this time. Instead, she gave me a piece of paper.

'What's this?'

'I was your stake out, remember? He did not come by car but by taxi. The same taxi picked him up afterwards. I don't know how he signalled it but it came round the corner just as he left the building.'

'I turned in surprise. 'You've been out there all that time? No wonder you're cold.' Leaning forward I switched on another bar of the fire. 'Stay there. I'll get some coffee.'

I was glad to get into that corner called a kitchen to turn my face and my thoughts away from her so that she would see nothing of my desperation. Fairfax had gone but his offer remained; that crazy, suicidal, utterly ludicrous offer that promised escape or eternal damnation. He had well known that my tirade would be followed by speculation. It was mad, there was no doubt of it, but it offered advantages that would not come again. Just how good was I after such a long lay-off? Fairfax did not seem worried by it. I had certainly gone up the drainpipe easily enough but that was second nature. What had happened in the world of alarms since I went inside. Advice on many of the gadgets had been passed on to me by new arrivals as the years went by. But what of those I had not heard about. The more I thought it out the more I turned away from the idea in spite of its attraction. Perhaps time had robbed me of my 'bottle'.

Even after Maggie had gone I could not stop speculating. I tossed and turned in bed, glad that she did not see me like this, so that eventually I merely lay on my back and gazed up at the darkened ceiling. The whole thing was so calculated; perhaps that was its strength. I wondered what it was that he wanted me to nick. For such a hare-brained scheme it had to be something very important. I did not know then just how much I was under-estimating its value.

Assuming that Fairfax represented some sort of British security, and the odds were heavily in favour, it seemed to me a desperate step indeed to break into a foreign legation in London. His face still played on my memory and I would have to do something about it. Once I had decided that to case the place would at least get things in perspective I managed a little sleep.

I left about mid-morning. I approached Portland Place from the Oxford Street end, scanning carefully. There were no uniformed police there and I don't know how the place rated with D.I.5. It was always possible that the smooth Fairfax had placed someone to see if I would do just this.

Portland Place is a wide street, pseudo-Georgian and bright. Although terraced the buildings varied in height and so offered individuality. A great air of respectability encompassed the place and I noticed other embassies.

There are two lanes of metered car parking in the middle of the street and I got my first real appraisal of the Chinese Legation from the island separating the lanes. A pale porticoed building, the first thing I noted was that it stood on a corner and was lower in height than its immediate neighbour. It was a good, solid, quite attractive building with huge, lace-curtained ground floor windows. I found the corner site attractive for many reasons. My first impression was good but it was not to last long.

Crossing the road I came nearer to the building, seeing the sign on the closed double doors in Chinese and English. Slipping into Weymouth Street I had my first misgivings. I had stopped just below the intersection traffic and appeared uncertain of direction. There were railings set in concrete outside the building and below them a basement. The basement windows themselves were solidly barred outside so entry that way was out of the question. There were two wooden doors, one swinging open in the gully of the basement and leading under the footpath that might be entrances to coal holes.

Casually I crossed the road to get a more complete view of this side of the building. My heart sank. I did not need binoculars to detect some of the burglar alarms; they had been painted over with the same cream colour as the window frames but to a trained eye like mine that was no camouflage. Alarms have never worried me much; they slow down an operation and thereby add to danger, but they can be tackled. What really upset me, though, was the way the windows were barred. From the first floor upwards internally across each window were huge grids, the kind seen on elevators. One set of windows was wooden shuttered and the wood wasn't three ply. And these were just the visible signs. I wondered about infra-red alarms. The more I looked the more the place appeared a fortress.

One of my earlier ambitions was to beat the infra-red system at Buckingham Palace just for the hell of it. I know I can get in because I've worked it out. To beat the system over the walls would not be too difficult. But then I knew something of the system. Here at the Legation it was different. The signs did not read 'try it', but 'God help you if you do'. It is the only place in London that I have seen so visibly barred and unfriendly. Its chill warning reached out to me. The place was no part of its surrounds. It demanded isolation and left you in no doubt. There was no sign of life but I could not help speculating as to whether I was being watched.

The building adjoining the Legation in Weymouth Street was much lower, flat-roofed and would present no problem. Incredibly a fire escape reached up from the flat roof to the top of the Legation. It was so easy an access that it had to be wired. Of more interest to me were two solid looking drain pipes which looked as if they would take my weight. But this was merely professional appraisal. As I crossed back to the main road and the traffic island I was completely despondent.

The front of the building was as utterly formidable as the side but I gave it a good casing just the same without finding anything to lift my depression. There was only one place left. Casually, miserably, I sauntered along the line of proud buildings to the other intersection, turned left down it, and first left again into Devonshire Mews. At the far end of the cul-de-sac was the rear of the Legation. To my left huddled a delightful row of mews cottages that only London can provide with such colourful charm. I could have reached the roof of any one of them without difficulty. On my right was a row of heavy-doored garages through the cracks of which I detected the odd gleaming Rolls-Royce.

Outside one of the cottages a green-uniformed chauffeur was

cleaning an olive-green Rolls which looked as if it had just been cleaned but maybe he was polishing the polish. I realized that my thoughts were becoming flippant, that I had given up serious consideration of the job.

The chauffeur looked up at me as I approached as if I didn't belong. He was right.

'Is there a way out down there?' I asked him, nodding towards the Legation.

'It's a cul-de-sac.' He did not rate me worth stopping polishing for, but he was giving too good a look for comfort. I ambled past him, the regular tripper. 'Nice, isn't it?' He didn't reply. Access to the Legation roof would have been easy from the rear. But culs-de-sac are a burglar's nightmare; a trap. I would consider going in by one if circumstances were right, but never coming out. As escape routes they were treacherous.

And yet as I made my appraisal under the unfriendly eye of the chauffeur I was strangely reluctant to move. Even as I made up my mind to tell Fairfax what he could do with his fifteen thousand I was assailed by my old malady. My finger-tips began to tingle. My blood began to race and I was fast becoming irrational. Suddenly I *wanted* to break in. It was all so bloody impossible that I *had* to break in. My mind was filled with the old urge I hoped I had left behind in prison. But now it was here and I was excited and afraid at the same time. Blast the damned feeling.

Yet it was no use telling myself that. My eyes were taking on new coverage, my mind registering a different complexity to the problems. The answers were the same but the approach was different. The place was impregnable; had been made so with cold, unfriendly calculation. If I got in and they caught me then I wouldn't get out again, certainly not alive. I knew that I was not overdramatizing, that I would merely be another case. These things happened in embassies all over the world where there was political contempt and pathological hatred of one system for another. The only difference would be that I would have entered forcibly yet freely and thus be unique. But nobody except Fairfax and the Chinese would know it.

My sudden difference in attitude found remedy. Yet a moment ago analysis had reached a conclusion of gloom and finality; now it merely provided a starting point. So the place was hopeless— right, what to do about it?

I gave the chauffeur one of my cheeky grins as I turned to leave. 'Thank you, my man,' I said as I passed him and for a moment I thought he was going to kick the Rolls as I am too big.

I felt better already. As I walked north towards the General Post Office Tower, rising like a dirty bandaged finger high above London, I was fully aware of my cursed elation. It was childish to want to break in because the Chinese clearly considered it impossible, but there it was. This was why I had seen the inside of prison walls for too long. But on a job like this I could not afford to be careless, not for a split second. There was one thing I had overlooked in the event, I could have well used a magnitude of clairvoyance.

Paying my four bob I joined the queue for the fast lift to the observation platform. Once up there, London was murky through the glass. The old town spread below in a series of grey lamps and familiar landmarks; St. Paul's, Houses of Parliament, Big Ben looking like a father figure. What I wanted was much nearer to hand. I suppose I walked about three-quarters of the way round the circular floor before I stopped. Near to the glass I spotted Portland Place, a steady stream of traffic going along it, in slow motion from this height. Reaching for the nearest telescope I dropped in my sixpence and focused down.

The roof of the Chinese Legation drew up under my eyes as if I was hovering just above it. There was an upright projection with a green wooden door on the flat roof. It was so simple that I ignored it; they weren't going to bar and wire up their windows to leave such an easy access. To the left, facing the side street, was a long sloping projection with small windows, like a built-on attic. The rooms were obviously low roofed and would be used either as store rooms or for the lowest comradely hierarchy of the all-men-are-equal-except-the-top-ones movement.

I gave the long raised attic structure my full attention. Its roof was covered in lead. Carefully I examined the rest of the roof, then possible escape channels along other roofs. Finally I swung back to the lead-roofed attic again. We were in business. I held on until the shutter clicked off.

By the time I had completed the tedious queueing for the descent my mind was working constructively, like the creeper I am, and I suppose I will always be. I despised myself for my turn of thought but the fantastic sense of challenge engulfed the feeling as it had always done. I had a brief, deeply painful regret for Maggie, but it was gone before I could dwell on it. What a place to break into, I reflected. Get in there and you can get in anywhere. Getting out again was something different so I chose not to dwell on it.

I walked from the G.P.O. Tower to Frith Street in Soho, and that's a good long walk. But I wanted time to think and I wanted to see if Fairfax had put someone on my tail.

Soho had changed enormously during my years inside. Basically its function was the same as before and it was still the biggest chunk of concentrated continental Europe inside England. And there were still some friendly faces who recognized me. But a good deal of its character had gone. The 'Brasses'* had been replaced by strip clubs which as I saw it was a sort of free advert

---

* Prostitutes.

for the former. As I heard it, the girls were doing better than ever and the cops had more difficulty in picking them up.

The smell of fresh fruit, spices, salami and roasting coffee was as good as ever as I went searching. I found it sandwiched between a strip club, or as they say, the old man's rest home, and one of those newsagents' shops with the suggestive ads painted in bold ink on postcards. It was appropriate. On the brown-painted door between the others was a shabby notice pronouncing that the 'Gainboy Studio' was on the first floor up the stairs; in brackets underneath 'Neil R. Palmer'. He was my man.

Pushing open the door I went up the narrow, uncarpeted wooden stairs. It was musty and the walls were Victorian off-white which had yellowed with age. The stairs weren't all that strong and the landing creaked even under my practised tread. The sign on the door was brighter, freshly painted, but no different in content from the one downstairs. Opening the door I faced a solid, oriental screen round which I peeped. I was in the right place all right.

The room was large. In odd corners had been pushed pieces of scenery and backcloth, old ropes, nets, curtains and unlit flood-lights. There was, nevertheless, a high density of arc lamps concentrating on a nude, heavy-breasted woman in a pose which worried me more than it did her. I decided to stay behind the screen for a bit.

A small, mincing figure of a man in blue dungarees and a white roll-neck sweater moved among the lamps like a female sparrow, quick, eager and expert. His canvas shoes made no sound on the boards and his blond, straggling hair was like a loose *toupee* of straw. There was a camera mounted on a tripod but he wasn't yet ready to use it. He spent some time on the lamps, casting shadows, multiplying breasts, arms, legs, until he had the effect he wanted.

The girl was straddling a dummy capstan against a backcloth of harbour and wheeling seagulls. She watched the man dis-passionately and did not flinch when he handled her body, easing it this way and that, moving legs and arms and angling her trunk. She well knew that she had nothing to fear and her coarse, pretty face registered a faint contempt that her voluptuous body had no effect on him.

He patted her deftly. 'You'll have to diet, darling. You're getting too heavy on top. I'll bring the lights down a bit.' And he minced away as I came round the screen.

'Bluie!'

He wheeled round holding himself in a woman's pose, his pale eyes lighting up with joy, his soft lips puckering into a pouting smile. 'Spider! Come in, dear, let's have a look at you, you gorgeous beast.'

Thinking he might throw his arms round me I backed off,

eventually offering a hand on the end of a long arm. Bluie Palmer was small, almost petite, his face pale and sensitive. I knew that his eyes could harden like old ivory; his hands were delicate and he used them expressively with speech, his long fingers performing a language of their own.

'Oh, it's nice to see you, dear. When did you get out?'

'I've been out a few months.'

'And you didn't come to see me? That's not very nice, is it?'

I winked at the nude blonde who had not bothered to move and who eyed us dispassionately. She must have caught something in my eye that she had missed in Bluie's because she suddenly appeared uncertain. When next I glanced at her she was donning an old dressing gown and watching me cagily.

'I want your help, Bluie. I want to borrow one of your cameras.'

'They're valuable, dearie. Take me out to dinner and we'll talk about it.'

'I want it now and you know damn fine that I'm not like that.'

'Really? Anyone would think that it's not legal. What do you want to take?'

'A building. Look, I'll need it for a couple of hours at most.'

'I'll do it for you, duckie. We can go together.'

'Does Blondie know what you were in for?' I nodded towards the model who showed interest.

'Spider, you wouldn't.'

'I would if it saves time.'

Bluie had got his name for producing 'blue' pictures. He had been convicted for showing and selling pornographic films. He was a brilliant photographer but had used the sex outlet to supply the money for his real photography, much of which was not commercial, and for his boy friends. For some time he explained the intricacies of a telephoto lens as long as an arm. He didn't like the idea of my having it but it was clear that this blonde did not know about some of the other models and he had a fear of her discovering, particularly as his more dubious money-making projects did not reflect his own needs. He had always been afraid of women laughing at him.

Within two hours I was back in his studio and he was developing the close-ups that I had taken. The blonde was now dressed in high heels and a mini and was on the verge of departing. She looked as if she was going back to her beat, but maybe I'm unkind.

From the studio I rang the *Daily Mail* and asked for Ray Lynch. It took some time to discover that he had left them and had moved over to the *Express*. But I did track him down and was lucky to find him in. Arranging to meet him at the Enquiry desk in half an hour, I told Bluie I would be back for the prints later on and asked him to bill me although I knew that he wouldn't; he may be queer but there was a lot of good in Bluie Palmer.

The black glass of the *Express* building had not changed and Fleet Street seemed much the same. The foyer was fairly crowded and at first I did not recognize Ray Lynch amongst the other faces. He recognized me though and came across, hand outstretched.

'Hello, Spider. Keeping your nose clean, boyo?'

'Just about. Thanks for seeing me. I hope I don't waste your time.'

He smiled. 'We're a blunt breed: I'll soon tell you.' He had changed for the worse. Bloated, dissipated almost, his increased weight strained an untidy Harris tweed jacket and the too tight slacks. The dark hair had thinned and needed combing. His face was flabby and a whiff of spirit on his breath supplied part reason. His nose and lips were firm and his bleary eyes still restless but he was a shadow of the smart, good-looking, newshunting reporter that I remembered.

His questing gaze was roaming over me as if I carried a news item somewhere about me. His speech had developed a staccato way of punctuating as if he edited his words as he uttered them. He could not yet be forty but looked more.

'How are things with you?' I asked as we moved to one side.

He shrugged a little dejectedly and his eyes shuttered out something too quickly for me to catch. 'Still reporting. They promised me a by-line, but it hasn't happened yet.'

'That's writing under your own name?'

'That's arriving, Spider.' He grimaced. 'What can I do for you, boyo?'

'I wondered if I could look through some of your press photographs. I'm trying to put a name to a face.'

Ray Lynch grinned and whatever was bugging him disappeared. 'Got thousands of them. What sort of face?'

'A well-known one. Top social, top civil servant. Someone like that.'

'You've got a job on. That all you got?'

'That's all. I'll have to wade through.'

He laughed. 'How many days have you got? Is it important?'

'Could be.'

'I'll take you along. There are six hundred odd M.P.s alone.'

'I don't think he's an M.P. But you're getting warm. He'll be backroom of some sort.'

'And the best of luck, boyo. I'll take you and leave you. If you find what you want get through to the reporters' room—I'll come if I'm still here.'

Ray was right. I almost gave it up. But after a bit you develop a knack and the boredom sets in so you automatically scud through, resisting temptation to examine the more interesting ones. The system of filing was such that it aided my cause and it took me only three hours to find what I wanted; it might have been as many days.

It was a mixed group at Ascot, morning suits and toppers for the men, expensive dresses and hats for the ladies. I knew now why Fairfax's face was familiar. This sort of photo would appear in the social columns and society magazines and most burglars read mags like the *Tatler*; how else can we select our victims?

All the names were there, Lady this and Lord that. But no one interested me except Fairfax, as debonair as ever, binocular case slung round his neck, amusement in his eyes, straight-backed and looking the world in the eye as if he owned it. Sir Stuart Halliman, Bt. I made a note of the name, thanked the keeper of photographs and went back to the foyer where I asked for Ray Lynch. He had been sent out on a job so I said I would call back tomorrow or ring.

Dick was doing a ten to six night duty so from a call box I gave him a ring at his drum. I gave him the cab number that Maggie had got for me and asked him if he could trace it. This is easy for a copper and the answers come up pretty quick.

I evaded meeting Maggie that evening. I felt a heel and she suspected something but I knew that I would give myself away if I saw her. My nerve ends were tingling and I was full of strange fears and inexplicable little warnings. But I was excited too. I pored over the blow-ups of the prints Bluie Palmer had developed for me, using a magnifying glass.

The next morning Dick popped in before catching up on his sleep. There was no such registration under the Hackney Cabs. Maggie must have messed it up—unless . . .

I went out early to the nearest call box and rang the *Express* for Ray Lynch, to find that he was not yet on duty. I told the operator that I was his younger brother and had just flown in from India after several years and could I have his home number.

I caught him at home just as he was leaving. I said in the phone, 'Ray, I found the mug shot that I wanted. You had left. What do you know of Sir Stuart Halliman?'

There was a silence, then I could hear his very faint breathing. Very softly, he said, 'Say that again, boyo.'

I repeated it and I could almost hear his struggling thoughts.

'Look here, I must meet you. Can you get down to the *Express* now?'

'I can, but who is he?'

'I'll tell you then.'

'Look, there's no story to it. I'll meet you but tell me now.'

'He's head of Defence Intelligence 5. The number one man appointed a year ago.'

The number one man of D.I.5. Dazedly I put down the phone even though I could hear Ray calling out.

CHAPTER SIX

NOT A MINION, not even the number two or three man. The number one man, the head, the fellow who controlled all the other fellows and was probably answerable only to the Prime Minister. A man with immense power; who could have someone tucked away without too much trouble; who could put pressure on the Foreign Office to have foreign dignitaries deported. What then was such a man doing with me? Why was he handling me personally? If the job was big enough for him to handle himself then it was important enough to scare me silly. Men like Sir Stuart Halliman don't personally deal with the Spider Scotts of the world; not unless they were playing it so close to the cuff that they could not delegate—dare not. And if that were the case Spider might become expendable.

I kept my promise to Ray Lynch and met him at the *Express*. He thought he was on the scent, of course, and he would have been had I been co-operative. But I could not afford to be. Because he had helped me and because I foresaw that I might need him again I fobbed him off with a story that one of the boys had considered screwing Sir Stuart's drum and I had said I would find out who he was for him. Obviously the drum would be left alone with the amount of wiring it was likely to have. It was a lousy story and Ray didn't believe it, but that was as far as he got. His eagerness was hard to believe, his whole face had come alive as if reborn. When I finally shook him off I went out into Fleet Street, walked slowly into the Strand then up to the big Post Office at the foot of St. Martin's Lane.

From a post office call box I rang 930-0932 and asked for Fairfax. A girl told me to hold on and some time later Fairfax's voice came on. I said, 'This is Spider. I want to talk to you.'

'Where are you?'

I told him and he said, 'Wait outside. I'll pick you up in five minutes.'

He rang off before I could say anything more.

I stood outside Europe's largest post office and watched the traffic snarling up round Trafalgar Square and the people popping in and out of the Press Exchange next door. An armoured van drew up outside the Westminster Bank and I idly wondered if the boys had it earmarked. Sight of it made me think that I would have been safer taking up the Reisens offer to join the mobs. The traffic came flooding down from Charing Cross Road and a solitary taxi slipped the stream to pull up on the double yellow lines opposite me. I noted the number was the one Maggie had given me. The passenger window came down and there was 'His Lordship' deigning to look my way.

It was murky and drizzle had set in. I took my time to reach the cab just to show my independence. Fairfax knew better and watched me with a smile as he opened the door for me. He sat there in his dark overcoat, the inevitable bowler and gloved hands resting on the handle of his still furled umbrella. 'Wretched weather,' he observed and as I'm not good at small talk I let it pass.

The cab moved off and I noted that the glass screen behind the driver's head was dark so that it was difficult to get an impression of the driver himself.

'You were quick,' I said. 'You couldn't have had far to come.'

Fairfax inclined his head. He turned to survey me. 'Well?'

'Fifteen thousand is not enough. And one thousand for failure is crazy. I may never come out of that place.'

'In which case neither sum will be of much use to you.'

'I want it to go to Maggie. But I want more and I need to know more.' I decided to keep to myself the fact that I knew his identity —at least for the moment.

Fairfax gazed straight ahead as if he wore a steel corset. 'I cannot give you more, Spider. Nor would I if I could. The terms are fair.'

'Supposing I'm caught? I could tell the judge and jury the whole story in court.'

He sighed. Then turned to face me quizzically. 'It had occurred to me,' he observed drily. 'But I wonder what judge and jury would make of it. Sounds a bit far fetched, don't you think? And with your record: I wonder, too, whether you would survive the eternal laughter in prison?'

I had wondered the same. I knew that if it came to a public showdown between the two of us I wouldn't be the winner and losing would not help my sentence. No one would believe me and this wily bird could probably prove that he was in Bermuda the whole time. Still it was a try.

He patted my arm briefly. 'Anyway, Spider, you are not that sort of creature. We selected you very carefully, y'know. Grassing is not your forte.'

I still haggled over terms but he was quietly adamant. To make anything of it I had to succeed and his offer was designed for success.

'You realize the job is impossible?' I tried again.

'Extremely difficult,' he conceded, 'but we have inside information that will aid you. Alarms and so forth, type of safe and its location.'

I looked at him in astonishment. 'You're asking me to rely on someone else's casing? I've got to follow my nose.'

'Then follow it. We merely provide signposts. It's up to you whether or not you heed them.'

'What's in the box I'm to nick? I have a right to know.'

"Your only right, Spider, is an expectancy of fifteen thousand pounds if you succeed. In fact it contains documents stolen from and vital to this country. It would be futile to describe them.'

I hadn't gained an inch. He was resolute in his own quiet way. He had my measure, I had to admit. 'What exactly do I do?' I looked across him to notice that we were somewhere in Holborn and had stopped by traffic lights.

'First you go to a place in Brixton to take a look at the type of safe. Incidentally as a bonus there will be an open dated single ticket to Zurich in your name. All quite straightforward.'

'Oh, dead easy, the police will be after me even if I succeed.'

'I can assure you that they will not. Your danger is *in* the Legation.'

We rode for a while in silence and I gave him credit for leaving me to my thoughts.

Then I said, 'I shall need some gear.'

'Of course. Get what you need.'

Another silence, then he turned full face and I saw the steel beneath the plastic. 'I take it that you have agreed to accept?'

I hesitated, briefly thinking of Maggie, Dick, myself.

'There's not much else to do. I accept but I won't move until the first part of the bargain is complete.'

He nodded and I think he was relieved. 'Understandable,' he said. 'But once you are satisfied then we must move very fast indeed.' And for the first time I thought I detected a subjugated desperation.

He dropped me near to my pad and I went home to mull it all over. Ray Lynch was waiting outside my door. I was surprised and disturbed because I had not given him my address and did not want reporters on my tail. There was not a hope in hell of him getting anything from me. I noticed that his jacket and hair were damp and that he carried no umbrella. Could he be that hard up for a story?

'Look, Ray,' I said as I opened the door, 'I'm grateful for your help but it was a false alarm. These things happen.'

He came in with me, those eager brown eyes of his working overtime, sweeping over my room and finishing up by gazing at me like a faithful dog. 'Give me the names of the boys who intended screwing this drum. I can get a story out of it without mentioning them, boyo.'

'Then you don't need their names. Lay off, Ray. You're making something of nothing.' I gave him a drink then told him I was moving from this district, going north job hunting. He seemed disappointed, and by the time he left his face had a pinched look of resignation and his eyes had slowed down considerably. For some reason I felt sorry for him and wondered what had happened to make him change so much.

Sergeant Alf Bulman called that evening just as I was about to leave. He stood in the doorway, refusing to come in and his words nearly strangled him. Seldom have I seen a man make such an effort. He had come to explain that I was off the hook, that he had been wrong, that he hoped that there would be no hard feelings. When he had left I did not know whether to laugh or cry but enjoyed an immense feeling of relief. Fairfax moved fast; the man had undoubted pull. It was good to have the pressure off and it was indicative that Fairfax kept his word.

I went round to Maggie's in a fairly depressed state because I was virtually saying goodbye, certainly for some time, perhaps for good. She opened the door and looked sweeter than she ever had. Candles flickered on the table and I guessed that she had prepared something special. A farewell dinner?

I felt choked and suddenly could not speak. What was I doing to her? We had slipped our arms around each other and neither of us spoke. A certain shyness had crept between us as if we had only just met and I would have to court her all over again. The truth was that I wanted this moment, just the gentle warm contact of her without passion but with something far more precious and I was certain that she could sense this. I thought desperately, you bloody fool, why risk losing her? But I knew why. I knew for a certainty that the only chance of a steady life with the kind of independence so essential to me was to do what I intended to do.

We held each other as if I was already on the way back to prison. 'You're going away, aren't you?' she whispered.

'I've got to,' I groaned. 'I must get work. I won't be away for long.'

'You won't do anything wrong?'

'You know I won't. Dammit, I don't want to go back.' She did not press the point but suddenly trembled.

I said, 'How did you know?' She looked up then. 'Oh Willie. You're so easy to read. You've been strange for the last few days.'

That night was the most wonderful yet the saddest of my life. We both wanted it to go on even when we were exhausted because we both accepted the unvoiced thoughts that this might be our last together. Daylight came on us like an assassin, silent, effective. The night had always been my friend.

The following day was dead in every conceivable way. The weather was lousy and my feelings were like the leaden clouds. I was near to reversing my decision then. There was no brightness, in outlook or mood or hope. I was pretty dead inside too.

Dick called the day after as jubilant as a puppy with a bone. He danced a jig in his policeman's boots, singing, 'I've got my course, Spider. I've made it.' And suddenly it was all worthwhile. Dick had got his C.I.D. course. Dick's progress was more important than my own and that was all that mattered—then. It cannot be

easy to put that sort of pressure on the police; just how much
power did this Fairfax wield? Where did it stop?

I rang Fairfax to tell him that the first part of the bargain had
been made and that I was ready to keep mine. He gave me an
address in Brixton to report to that afternoon. I drove to the
garage where I had so recently worked and sold my car to them
after a bit of haggling. I caught a bus to Brixton. The traffic jams
delayed me; the streets and pavements were thick with vehicles
and people and the Christmas signs were already up. The garage
was one of those old rambling affairs in one of the dingy back
streets not a stone's throw from Brixton Prison. It was a reminder
I could have done without.

So far as I could see there was no name to it. A dilapidated
showroom and a forecourt with used cars, and they could say that
again, cluttered one side of the street with a couple of petrol
pumps. It was some time before I could locate anyone but
eventually a greasy overalled mechanic passed by and I grabbed
him and asked for Fairfax.

He showed no surprise and merely nodded. 'He's in the office
behind the workshops.'

The workshops were on the other side of the street. I noticed
that either side of it were a few drab shops and beside them what
appeared to be a factory wall. The area was not ideally residential
although some terraced houses started farther up.

Crossing over I went through the workshop, cars scattered
everywhere, with more than a sprinkling of taxis, half a dozen
mechanics working and clanking among them. There was a smell
of oil and petrol and the sound of revving engines. Nobody gave
me a glance although it was naïve thinking.

At the rear of the workshop a concrete apron curved either side
of the doors, presumably for the cars to be run out and to circle to
the street. Across the apron was a dark wooden shack like a
foreman's office and I saw Fairfax through the dirty window
sitting among the rough paraphernalia, appearing completely out
of place.

I went in among the cans of paint and oil and the spare parts
lying almost everywhere. The desk was littered with stained
papers, carburettors and plugs as if it was a workbench. Fairfax
still wore his bowler and carried his umbrella. He rose as I
entered. 'You're late.'

'Traffic,' I explained.

'Then you must leave earlier. This way.'

The bargain having been struck he was leaving me in no doubt
that he had taken over. I was surprised at his annoyance but as
time went on I learned about his precision and just what it
could mean.

I followed his straight back from the hut, left along the apron
until we reached a solid concrete building that was windowless.

There were double doors and beyond them by a few feet another door as if the building was insulated by thick double walls. Later I realized that it was soundproofed.

Inside it was fairly well lit by shadeless lamps. There was no one else there. When I looked around it was as I thought a studio would be. There were cables and extinguished arc lights, what seemed to be props and the place was roughly divided into four eight-foot-high solid walls, none of them meeting the other so that we could wander around.

Fairfax took me into one of these areas. There was a long work bench and on it some boxes. Against the outside wall facing us was an old P. and C. safe. He nodded towards it. 'Try that.'

I stared incredulously. The safe was solid enough, not combination, but by no means the latest deterrent to criminals. 'You must be joking,' I said.

Fairfax was put out. He said stiffly. 'I am assured that this is the type that you will have to open in the Legation.'

'It's old fashioned. There was no need for me to come along to practise on this.'

'I'm glad to hear it. But as you're here you had better get on with it. Your requirements are on the bench.'

I went over to the bench rather mystified. 'I should have thought they would have something more up to date with all the other precautions they take.'

'Perhaps they think they are impregnable. But would it have made a difference?'

I shrugged. 'I suppose not. A difference in time, that's all.'

'That's probably their own reasoning. Is everything there?'

I never ceased to wonder at this man Fairfax. Everything was there in numbers including a packet of contraceptives when I only required one. 'Anyone could blow it,' I complained. 'You don't need me for this job.' All the time I was fiddling I was telling myself that Fairfax was playing it very close. Everything to do with me he was handling personally, allowing no one else near. I kept reminding myself that this man was answerable only at Prime Minister level. And here he was in this house waiting to see how well I blew a safe. It began to be unreal. I was slowly going off my head.

I took a contraceptive and gradually filled it with Polo Ajax, a plasticine type explosive, completely malleable, from a metal box which contained enough to blow the Bank of England. Going over to the safe I carefully pushed the end of the contraceptive into the keyhole, kneading the explosive so that it slipped in quite easily. When it was hanging down in the aperture through the keyhole I fixed a number six detonator to the open end and stuck it to the door with modelling clay. Then picked up the wire, fixed it to the detonator and ran it out on a drum to the bench.

'Right,' I said, 'we are almost ready. Are there any light points in the other sections?' I had noticed two or three with switches set above the bench.

'Naturally,' replied Fairfax, a little restless by now.

'Right then, where's the carpet?' I asked with a grin. I should have known better.

Fairfax leaned on his umbrella, eyeing me bleakly. 'I hope you will be more observant on the night,' he replied acidly.

The carpet was rolled up under the bench. Feeling an idiot I pulled it out and draped it over the safe. It had seen better days but I could hardly expect him to produce a Persian. Clipping off a good length of wire I bared the ends, keeping them separate and rolling them tight. I tucked the box of Polo Ajax and detonators under my arm. Fairfax led the way into the next compartment and I did not waste time putting the terminals into a socket and throwing the switch.

The explosion was solid and sharp and for my liking much too loud. And it reverberated. Fairfax and I gazed at each other but it appeared, as usual, that he was letting me do the worrying. We went round the wall and the safe door was hanging partly loose with a big rent in the carpet. I had a little trouble fiddling to free the lock and then the door was open.

'Good,' observed Fairfax.

'I didn't like the amount of noise. Every Chinese in the building will come running.'

He aimed the point of his umbrella at the safe cavity as if he would not deign to touch it with his fingers. 'No,' he said. 'The room you will enter is insulated with heavy carpets, tapestry and furniture. The noise will be considerably muffled.'

'They will still hear it.'

'I doubt it, but in any event I can help in the matter. We must have precise timing, Spider. Please. We will allow adequate time for you to enter, plus a safety margin of say three-quarters of an hour. During that period you must hide in the room once you have fused the safe. At an agreed time I will arrange to have a series of external explosions set off in the street. We'll provide a nice distraction for you.'

I eyed the safe, then the self-assured Fairfax who was brushing his bowler carefully with his sleeve because the dust was settling on it and I said deliberately, 'When do you want me to do the job, Sir Stuart?'

He didn't even blink. Finishing the brushing, he put the bowler back on his head, utterly straight, and there was the merest glint in his cool eyes when he faced me. 'I'm glad to find you are not a complete idiot. It gives me a little more confidence in you.'

I nearly exploded but he cut in coolly. 'Perhaps knowing of me will help you to realize just how important this is.'

'When do I do it?' I repeated dully.

'Tonight if possible. You're the expert. Let's have your appraisal.'

Leaning against the bench, I thought quickly. I wanted it over too, but I did not intend to rush it. Fairfax stood as if he was the front man of a single file and gave nothing away. It was strange how he could convey friendliness, tetchiness, impatience, without change of expression. Something in his set features conveyed these things but I was never sure what. Perhaps an almost imperceptible manipulation of his brows.

'I would prefer to do it in daylight during a thick fog. It *is* November.'

'Be realistic, man. They will be crawling all over the place.'

'I know. A moonless night. It doesn't really matter except that it doesn't help if it's raining.'

'Tomorrow night if it's dry?'

Suddenly it was on me. Tomorrow. Why not? It would give me one more chance to case the place. I nodded.

Fairfax sighed and stood at ease. It came as something of a surprise to me to realize just how tensed he was. He went so far as to undo the button of his overcoat but I guessed that was as far as he would go; he would never loosen his tie on the hottest day; so I loosened mine for both of us as it was getting stuffy. He took off his bowler and brushed back his grey hair with both hands.

'This is what will happen,' he instructed seriously. 'When you emerge with the box you will walk south down Weymouth Street for about twenty yards. You will be approached by a man in a camel coat and a homburg hat. Such a frightening combination can hardly be missed. When he raises his hat to you hand him the box. In return he will give you the number and access to your Zurich bank account, together with your air ticket. You will have to make your own air reservation but that is all. Now. Your *modus operandi*?'

I had considered it endlessly. 'All you need to know is that I'll go in by the mews and out by the low building next to the Legation in Weymouth Street.'

For a few minutes we discussed the time factor, then he produced a plan of the Legation and laid it on the bench. There was a good deal missing but it was adequate. Apparently there were two safes; the main, where all the diplomatic stuff was kept was on the first floor. The one I had to blow was in the hands of only one man, a Mr. Li Tshien. Reading between the lines, this character was their espionage head so I imagined that the safe contained a few items Tshien would not want even his colleagues to know about. We pored over the plan for a long time while I made mental notes because Fairfax would not let me sketch a copy.

When he had folded the plan away again Fairfax asked, 'I take it that you have sufficient funds to obtain your equipment?'

I nodded. 'I'll get it tomorrow morning then have another look at the Legation. You don't want any money to pass between us, do you?'

'Not even old notes, Spider. When we part this time we will not see each other again. I hope you pull it off for all our sakes. But if by chance you don't you will find it impossible to involve me.'

'You said yourself I'm not the type to grass.'

He looked me straight in the eye for some seconds but it was almost impossible to read the man beneath his present rigidity. I had the feeling that he wanted to tell me something or express something but finally his steady gaze dropped and he said, 'For all sorts of reasons people have been known to act out of character.'

If there was a message there I missed it. Then he added, 'I merely wanted to illustrate that if you are caught, mention of me will only make it worse for you. It's important that you understand that I would not only refute you but comfortably prove you a liar.'

This made me uneasy. 'You explained before,' I protested.

'I did indeed. I want to make certain that you fully understand. However, caught or not, you will still benefit financially.'

I did not like this. 'Do you expect me to be caught?'

'God forbid. I need that box badly. It is merely that in the unlikely event of failure, in the unlikely event of an attempt at grassing. I would have to be the complete hypocrite and desert a friend. I wanted you to know that it would be a hard thing for me to do but nationally necessary.'

I was touched by this. 'I understand,' I said. He had a heart after all.

He fell behind his quick freeze mask again and said with dignity, 'Good luck, Spider. I know you will succeed. And when you do remember not only the money but the fact that you will have done this old country a really good turn.'

I was a little hurt that he did not shake hands with me when he wished me luck.

CHAPTER SEVEN

IT WAS TOO LATE for shopping and too dark for casing, so I took out the photographs of the Legation roof and studied them again until I knew them by heart. Ahead of me was a long lonely evening. I had far too much on my mind to want to see Maggie or Dick or any friends. Somehow I did not feel right about the job. There was an unknown factor that nagged at me, something

I had missed. I went over the whole series of events from the time I had first met Fairfax, and even before when his men were watching me. I came back to the present step by step in great detail.

The job was incredibly difficult but it was not only this that worried me. There was something else and it was worse because I was sure I had not overlooked anything. I glanced over my shoulder and that, I reflected, was where I should keep looking. I told myself that anticipation had made my nerves taut but I knew that it was more than that.

I should have called it off then. I should have taken full heed of the warning that bugged me and telephoned Fairfax. Knowing it I made excuses to myself for not doing it. I had my pride. Fairfax had so far proved a man of his word; then so would I. Perhaps I had simply lost my nerve while wasting in prison.

The hours dragged now. I wanted to fill in time by ringing Maggie but I dare not as I was supposed to be in Birmingham and anyway she might read the signs. I had reverted to what I was destined to be—a loner. I had never imagined that I would need people until now. Just one real friend would do. I told myself I was going soft and got the photographs out again then checked my gear.

That night I barely slept and the next day dragged. I bought my equipment early and went to Portland Place to do a final casing. At nine I left my flat and took a walk. At ten I rang Fairfax from a call box. His unrelenting attitude was at least solid, something real. He did not greet me and we did nothing but synchronize watches. As it happened there was only half a minute between us but thirty seconds can make all the difference with a diversion from an explosion. He did not wish me luck and in fact his tone was so sharp that I realized he was very much on edge. And it made me feel better that in this I was his superior.

My own nerves were reaching the frozen stage, a detachment that could expel all ordinary sound and concentrate on the almost inaudible ones; a chair creaking, a brush of wind, friction of soft substances, faint footsteps, different types of vehicle engines outside, a photograph falling as I knocked it, and distant voices. Even with television on I could hear these things in my present state.

Still with time to fill I prepared my gear and produced a few old car ignition and skeleton keys and a crocodile clip. I laid them all on the bed: umbrella, nylon rope, cranium saw, short thin-bladed saw, a small drill, hunting knife, jemmy, keys, Polo Ajax, a couple of detonators, two contraceptives, a pencil torch, plasticine and a pair of light socks. To take too much or too little could be fatal. And clothes. Dark narrow slacks, dark jacket, chukka boots, dark socks, blue shirt and a *light* tie. The tie I would whip off while breaking in but it was handy and gave some degree of

normality to my dress if I was stopped by a copper. Whoever
heard of a screwsman with a light tie? Finally I coated my
finger-tips with nail varnish.

After midnight I left the flat. The streets had virtually emptied,
but there were still people about and cruising taxis. Lining the
pavement was a row of parked cars. Speed was not the attraction
and I would have to find a car to match one of my old keys. It
did not take long. A two-toned A55 Farina appeared in good
shape.

I waited, listened and looked, found the right key then opened
up and switched on. It was uncomfortable sitting behind the
wheel with the ropes wrapped round me and my tools firmly fixed
in my waist band but I preferred not to carry anything openly
except my umbrella. Explosive and detonators were in the
separate pockets of my jacket. Starting the engine I drew out of
line and eased my way forward, in no hurry.

Baker Street still had life on it. Taxis were pulling up outside
the tube station while passengers dashed in for the last train home.
There was still a fair amount of traffic.

I was fully committed. Already I had stolen without too much
thought. The jail sentence was already looming. I drove at thirty
and gave all the right signals; I could do without a breathalyser
test on this run. I kept off the main streets and the dark night
drew in like a curtain over a window in an unlit room. In that car
I formed my own prison, lights bouncing off the windscreen, the
running engine heard only by me. When I reached Portland Street
I drove up it north of the B.B.C. and parked in one of the quiet
side streets. Not too near, not too far.

It was caution all the way. I didn't open the car door until
satisfied that the street was deserted and when I climbed out did
not lock it after me but closed it quietly. Now I missed the protection of the car. I started walking slowly, swinging my umbrella
modestly. There was in fact a risk of rain, the skies were clouded
which suited me, but I fervently hoped that the rain would hold
off.

And so I stepped into Portland Place. London does nothing
for me by day, its rat race of hustle was any big city anywhere.
But at dead of night for me it came into its own. The broad,
islanded stretch of street rolled forward into the patched gloom,
its only sentinels the widely spaced street lamps. It was almost
1 a.m. and I could see nobody. That did not mean that a copper
was not having a quick drag in a deep doorway so I kept my eyes
skinned. I could hear hurried footsteps, a man, but could not
pinpoint the location. Sound and echoes travel distances at
night.

A taxi passed and I supposed it was the romantic in me that
would rather have seen a hansom cab. A good deal of this was
Regency London and night was the only time it could lose the

years and regain the posture of a nobler age. In the early hours I loved its stealth and slack tempo.

A cat jumped through the railings and for a while it trotted alongside. The air was chill enough for an overcoat but I would bear the cold rather than be impeded. My ears were out on stalks listening for the slightest sound.

Suddenly I knew there was a policeman near and I had to still my reflexes which demanded that I dive into the nearest base-ment. Homing on the warning I crossed Portland Place at an angle, my narrowed eyes scanning the intersection. There he was, standing under a portico. There was no cigarette in view but he was not taking in the scene. I kept going nice and slow, swinging my brolly a little more freely.

Coppers have a habit of stopping loners at night, particularly in London in rich residential areas. If one demanded that I turned out my pockets I was done. Clobbering him, which I was against, would not land me in the Legation, nor would running, for patrol cars would be crawling over the place in seconds. As he could still see me I turned right up the nearest side street and after a few paces, stopped.

My night London, my old noble friend, had been destroyed by the advent of the copper. In front of me, lying in the gutter under the pool of a street lamp, were two discarded disposable syringes with some bloodied toilet paper. Some junkies had taken a quick shot. It made me sick. I'd seen it before on the night streets. Doomed youth. Maybe they thought the same of my kind.

The copper's tread started on its way and it was not towards me. Giving it time, I slipped back into Portland Place, passed the Somalia Embassy, then crossed diagonally to the mid-street island. But for one or two cars the meter spaces were empty. There were very few lights on anywhere except on street lamps. I shared the empty kingdom with an equestrian gentleman of Portland stone with a flattened cocked hat who reared beside me. I could just read the inscription: Field Marshal Sir George Stuart White, V.C., G.C.B., O.M., G.C.S.I., G.C.M.G., G.C.I.E., G.C.V.O., 1835-1912. Christ! I supposed that all the 'G's' had been to remind him of his first name. It was so quiet just then that as I raised my arm I could hear my watch.

Crossing the second half of the street I faced the enemy. It stood palely in the darkness with the innocent fragility of a flower. But beneath its ethereal bloom it was solid brick and con-crete and anything but innocent. Without hesitating I swung beyond it past the array of other buildings, with other secrets to hide and then turned left. At the junction of Devonshire Mews I slipped into the nearest shadow and briefly waited. Distant double footsteps echoed but they were far off—a man and a woman. Peering into the gloom of the mews I began to move down the row of cottages with the Rolls tucked away opposite them.

The people were asleep but I had the feeling that the cars swivelled their headlamps on me all the way. I reached the end wall. This was what it was all about. Running my fingers lightly over the drainpipe that I had selected, I was satisfied. Glancing towards the Mews entrance I was straining my ears now. A passing copper would shine his torch down here from sheer routine.

Now I worked fast. I took out all my tools, keeping only the explosive in my pocket because I would not put it next to the detonators and placed the lot in the umbrella, tying the top with the stouter nylon. I tied the thin nylon to the other end of the thick and the loose end round my waist. I wanted freedom for climbing; it was too easy for tools to slip from the waistband. Laying the brolly flat on the cobbles I took a last look back and could see and hear nothing.

Just before I climbed a thought came up and slapped me straight between the eyes. I was just about to step on to Chinese soil. And I knew that if I got inside it would be as different as London is from Peking and far more dangerous. I gave the pipe a testing yank then I was going up it as if it was a flight of steep stairs. Only seconds later I was on the low flat roof of the dwelling in Weymouth Street. Quickly I pulled up the thin cord which produced the thicker, and so my gear.

Picking my way carefully across the roof I cagily inspected the fire escape leading to the Legation roof. There were two good drain pipes running up the wall and these I trusted. This was the most exposed part of entry, for once on the pipe I was visible to anyone passing in Weymouth Street. So I lay flat and took stock. It was half past one. A good time and on schedule. No sound. I started to climb.

There was nothing new in the feeling for me but it was always a good feeling. I was going up a wall like a fly in the deeply silent hour of a dark night and there were thousands within voice call. I was doing something against odds that society decreed wrong. I knew it was wrong, and I was elated. I felt good and powerful and the psychiatrists had missed out on me because I was enjoying every single moment, and I was reaching for the sky. Before reaching the top I heard the footsteps I knew so well as if they were following me up the wall. There was a nasty moment when I broke the skyline and tumbled over the parapet but I knew that I could not have maintained my position so far up.

I peered over the edge. There he was coming towards the Legation, long raincoat, lamp occasionally flashing. The nylon cord was hanging down the side of the building. Should I pull it up quickly or leave it? Either way was a risk. I decided on the old-fashioned way—no movement.

It was impossible to keep him in view without showing something of my head so I drew slowly back and listened behind the low parapet. It was agonizing this way and all I could do was to count the regular beat of his footsteps and wait for a break in the tread for I couldn't see even the flashing reflection of his lamp. At any moment I was expecting him to falter for the nylon, though thin, would be light against the wall. He had only to see it to speak into his radio and I might not know until the cars drew up.

I heard him turn the corner into Portland Place and wasted no more time in quickly pulling up my gear. My tension eased because once on a roof you are free from prying eyes: you can work all night long without interruption.

Moving across the raised roof of the attic I laid out my tools as a nurse would a surgeon's instruments. My enemies now were beneath me. Somewhere in this attic section, or possibly on the floor beneath, was the radio room and I imagined that it would be constantly manned. I had to be as stealthy as a cat.

I found I could work by straddling the raised long stretch of roof. The first part was difficult as I embedded my hunting knife into the thick lead. I had a little trouble slipping the blade underneath, but once I got good purchase the rest was hard physical work but straightforward. Lead cuts quite easily and I drew a line across then made two incisions back from the base line wide enough to take me. The sweat began to roll and I paused to wipe it off while I took a look round.

The sky was still thick with cloud. Across from me was the intriguing little outhouse with a door which must surely be wired. Regaining my breath I slowly rolled back the flap of lead until I could see the close boarding beneath. So far all to pattern. Drilling two holes through the wood I dropped one end of the cranium saw through one of them, then with stiff hooked wire ferreted for the dangling end until I could pull it up through the other hole. With an end in each hand I simply cut through. The saw was designed to go through hard bone—it found little resistance in wood. The rest was sheer routine.

When I had a large hole in the wood I drilled through the plaster until the hole was big enough to take the furled umbrella. Stuffing the jemmy in my waistband and the detonators in my empty jacket pocket I pushed the umbrella through then shook it so that it loosely opened up in the room below; holding its handle I began to saw a fairly wide circle through the plaster with my thin-bladed saw. The plaster dropped quietly into the open umbrella and there was now a hole big enough for me. Still holding the umbrella in one hand I slid my legs through the gap and listened. Then I shone my torch down.

It *was* the storeroom all right. Dusty bundles and crammed shelves lined the walls and immediately below was a stack of neatly piled files. I jumped lightly off them to the floor. I don't think I made a sound. Dust immediately assailed me for I'm

allergic to dust and fibres of almost any kind but I quietly blew
my nose before a sneeze came on. There was no door but at one
end of the room were some rough railings and banisters indicating stairs leading to the main body of the building. From that
moment the whole action ceased to feel like a burglary to me.
That old unwanted feeling came creeping up as if someone was
hiding behind the cabinets in the room. Later I was to recognize it
only too well but as yet I had not crossed that other dimension,
now so near.

Anyway there was only one thing for me to do; I was in, get on
with it, for work steadied the nerves. Picking my way through
piles of papers and wrapped parcels I reached the stairhead and
listened. Nothing; as though they were all silently waiting for
me down there. Treading carefully I reached the bottom of the
stairs, to find a locked door. I tried my skeleton keys, fervently
hoping that I would not have to use the jemmy.

The lock clicked as if I'd dropped the key. Waiting a little, I
opened the door sufficiently to peer through. The landing was
dark but at its lower edges there was a vague suspicion of light as
if somewhere below a bulb was on, its fringe barely reaching this
point. Reluctantly I had to use my torch. Its beam was narrowly
restricted, its power weak, but it was enough. There were other
doors, all closed, one with a tell tale light strip.

The radio room? Beyond it were the wooden banisters of the
main stairhead. The strip carpeting was flimsy and a little shabby
up here.

I tested each foot before putting my full weight on it; I wanted
no creaking boards. It's laborious work crossing a wooden floor
within earshot of sleeping ears. Pausing to put an ear to the door
with the light strip under it I could hear vague movement from
inside. This then was the danger point, now and particularly
when I returned. I just prayed that no one would come out for if
I was burgling a house it was a gauntlet I would hardly risk if it
involved the strong possibility of trapping myself. As it was I was
committed to meeting its dangers and I didn't much care for it.
Passing it was like locking myself in.

Committed, I took to the edge of the stairs near the wall, again
testing each step. The room with the safe was on the floor below.

Someone was patrolling somewhere beneath me. I could hear
the faint cushioned tread, regular, sinister. It was probably from
the main hall from where I suspected the faint fuzz of light was
escaping. They must maintain a regular night guard. Did they
patrol the whole building? Fairfax had not told me about the
guard and I solidly and silently cursed him. Although up here the
light was dim I could have well done without it, even so pale a
light could throw me up as a deeper shadow.

Suddenly the fact of being surrounded by Chinese hammered
me hard. I had better make a good job of getting out. I descended

he stairs in slow motion fully aware of my own restrained breath-
ng and the soft rub of my trousers. But my feet made no sound
t all. Any danger of a creak was stifled at the suspicion of its
tart; my feet were my eyes until I reached the landing, and even
hen I spent a full minute in dark silence before using my torch
gain. The place was getting plushier as I descended.

There was the door I wanted, slightly back from the landing;
. big, pale pine door, innocuous yet solid. I knew where some
f the bedrooms were, most facing the mews, but the unknown
nes were the danger.

There was a slight tremor in my fingers as I fiddled with my
eys but it was anticipation rather than jitters. Before trying the
eys I ran my torch beam round the door frame looking for an
larm. It is a fact that so many places are heavily alarmed on
xternal doors and windows but that roofs and interior doors
re so often neglected. Even so it was more than conceivable
hat Mr Li Tshien did not trust his colleagues. Nor did I ignore
he possibility of infra-red alarms being fixed to the inside frames.

Kneeling down I tried the keys; they *had* to work for I would
ever get away with a jemmy here, on the landing. Almost
mmediately I got response and the click was as heavy as firing an
mpty Colt in a cone of silence. The sweat was rolling again, and
t was no longer exertion. My hackles were up and this warning
. never ignore. For some time I remained crouched on one knee
n front of the door. When I did turn the handle the door would
ot budge. I wiped the sweat off my forehead with the back of one
f the socks. A bloody double mortice.

I got control of my breathing and turned back to the keyhole
vith the strange sensation that I was being studied by dozens of
)riental eyes, all watching my technique and merely waiting for
ne to finish. I could almost feel their hot breath through the
;looms. But it had to be done.

The lock proved awkward which it was designed to be unless I
ad the proper key. With prolonged hold-ups in exposed positions
here is always the impression that the whole place is waking
ıp and that daylight is near. I kept at it until I heard the heavy
:lick. Rising, I relieved my cramp and softly turned the handle.
ushing the door I explored the empty space with my hand,
ntered quickly, then closed the door behind me. It was total
larkness, so black that there were no shadows of any kind. I
aised my torch.

The pencil beam shot out like a groping searchlight. But the
right beam was exaggerated by the complete darkness. I would
leed more light than this. Finding a wall switch I flicked it and a
small central chandelier came on. I was carrying three folded
handkerchiefs; stretching two of them out I pressed them under
the bottom of the door to prevent the light from escaping. With
ny back to the door I took stock.

The windows were heavily shuttered and I knew there to b
grids between shutters and glass and an alarm fastened to th
window. The office was not for a junior executive. It conveye
the position of its owner. There was a solid-fronted desk; a beaut
Carpet pale green, not lush but adequate; a small, carved sid
table with a blue and white vase that could have been Ming, wit
a flower arrangement. On one wall was spread a huge, immensel
intricate lacquered fan, almost as good as Japanese.

The remaining space was taken up with dark wooden filin
cabinets to match the other furniture, contemporary chairs out c
place, a delightfully painted waste-paper basket, a long, low tabl
with a lamp and magazines including a well-thumbed edition o
the little red book. A few silk prints hung on the walls. The re
leather-topped desk held a table lamp, blotter and inkstand se
and a small pile of official-looking books on one corner. I wa
willing to bet that all the desk drawers would be locked but i
made no odds. Opposite the desk, against the wall facing me, wa
the safe resting on a solid plinth of concrete partly inset into th
wall. It formed a jarring note as if it had been deliberately raise
on an ugly pedestal so that at no time would it be overlooke
Perhaps Li Tshien did not like stooping. Before moving a step
ran my gaze slowly from wall to ceiling and wall to wall. A soli
wooden screen with dragon motif formed a secret place in th
corner to the right of the safe.

I was still standing against the wall, working it out. Wha
alarms were there? My instinct was that it could not be thi
easy. There was the safe as Fairfax had said it would be. A
key safe but solid and far too heavy to remove without tackle
What lay between it and me? I scanned those walls mor
thoroughly than I had ever done. There was an inconsistency ir
the way the silk prints were hung; two opposite each other wer
near the base wall, the others more scattered. I would have to ge
nearer.

While my mind was ranging over interior dangers my hearing
as usual, was detached to a point beyond the room boundaries
Years of practice which I had still exercised in jail; a built-ir
audio warning system. It did not let me down now. I'm not sur
whether some unknown sense made me freeze before I heard, o
instantaneously with it. What I was certain of was that I wa
suddenly rigid in mid-stride half-way to the desk, my muscle
bunched in tight knots.

My ears had served me well. The soft pad on the stairs was sc
quiet that I wonder I heard it at all. The tension brake released
and I doubt that I had ever moved so quickly. Light off, hand-
kerchiefs ripped away and a quick silent slither under the knee-
hole of the desk. There was a brief shuffle on the landing then I
heard the key in the lock. It rattled two or three times without the
door opening and I detected impatience then reluctance as the key

was withdrawn. I started to sweat as I realized what was happening. Chummy outside could not understand why the door was unlocked. The Li Tshiens of this world don't forget things like locking important doors. And now he was being as cagey as me. I did not hear the door open but a slight draught warned me. It was not easy to remain tightly crouched under the desk but I managed it. The light came on as I tried to bury myself in the wood.

CHAPTER EIGHT

HE MUST HAVE been doing what I had done except that the door was left open because I could still feel the air flow; he was just standing there examining the room. It was not difficult to imagine his thoughts. He was telling himself that he never forgot to lock the door at the same time arguing that no one could have entered. Had one of his staff asked for the key? Had he himself forgotten just this once? He didn't believe it but he could not discard it. The room would appear exactly as he had left it and that would fox him. Obviously undecided he still left the door open as he padded across the room. I heard him move the screen so he was still suspicious. There was only one other place for him to look and that would depend on whether or not he was beginning to see himself in a foolish light.

Straining my hearing to locate his whereabouts I thought I heard him moving about near the screen. I emerged on hands and knees, was about to turn towards the direction of the screen when I heard his very soft tread across the room. Changing direction, I very carefully eased my head round the side of the desk nearest the open door. I nearly drew back quickly when I saw Chummy, but training prevented me and anyway he was not looking my way.

He was short and stocky with steel-rimmed spectacles, the usual 'People's' jacket, high collared and buttoned up to the neck; loose trousers over soft sandals. From my angle he appeared balloon-faced and innocuous, but I could not see his eyes and nobody with a right in this room was innocent. I remember thinking that he worked strange hours, but so did I and I daresay his occupation was more peculiar than mine.

When he moved one of the two prints that faced one another I knew that my caution had not deteriorated over the years. This was one that Fairfax had not told me about and I would never know now whether I would have found it in time. He switched off the infra-red alarm that sent a wall to wall beam straight across the front of the safe then moved to the safe itself but out of my line of vision. I dare not push my luck too far by edging round the side of the desk.

The safe key turned and I realized that this must be Li Tshien. Clearly he now accepted that the room was empty and was probably checking his safe contents as a final reassurance that no one had been here. I crept back into my bolthole. If he came round to sit at his desk he could not miss me and I was not in the best of positions for action. I played it cool and let my ears do the work. The safe door opened, he ferreted about then padded back to the desk, placing on it something metallic. Another key turned, much smaller, and my brain began to cloud at what I must do.

The safe was open. Li Tshien stood at the closed front of the desk. I had never clobbered anyone on a job in my life. Yet now I had to. Here was an opportunity to save time, save the noise of explosion, possibly save being surprised again. My mouth was dry. But there was too much at stake to be squeamish. What would happen if *he* caught *me*? It was enough to get me crawling round the side of the desk. I came round on my side using my right elbow as a paddle and keeping flat against the wood. The size of the desk helped me for it must affect his angle of sight. Reaching the front I stopped, unsure of which way he faced and reluctant to poke my head forward; when I did my face was brushing the carpet.

He was standing close to the desk, and the only thing that saved me was that he was holding in front of his eyes a piece of white paper or a photographic print. Slowly I drew back my head, rose to my knees, and then very carefully to a crouch.

I stepped round the desk and swung at him in almost one movement. Underestimating the length of desk I bodged it. The print went flying and his glasses slewed, hanging from one ear as he half turned towards me. Instead of putting him down I had only dazed him. His chrysoberyl eyes were straining to break the haze obscuring their vision. Going after him, he fell back on his heels, dazed but not so much that his reflexes did not respond. One small amber hand groped about the desk and I suddenly saw the button. Grabbing at his jacket I yanked him away as his eyes began to clear to a murderous hardness. I saw the pinpoints of his pupils focus on me. His struggle had actually begun as I swung him round and thumped him at the base of his skull.

There was no finesse in the blow but he fell like a log, cracking his head on the edge of the desk as he went. Dashing round the desk I quickly closed the door then went back to examine him. I did not like the way he lay. The pulse was just about audible. Turning him over did nothing to reassure me; his forehead was oozing blood from a ragged gash of several inches already blue and swollen round its edges. His face was pale ochre. His soft cupid lips were open in an unconscious effort to seek air and his eyes had closed to crevices. Like that, he looked nothing, certainly not formidable, but I wasn't forgetting how he had looked on the point of recovery before I hit him the second time. As I stood he did not seem at all in good shape. Picking up his shattered glasses from the carpet I put them on the desk. This was not how it was supposed to have gone. The safe was gaping open. I glanced at my watch; ahead of schedule now that I had no safe to blow. Another speculative look at Chummy convinced me that I had nothing to fear from him for some time. Stepping over him I went to the safe. There was money, dollar notes and sterling; there were papers, sealed envelope, two small sealed cardboard boxes. There was no tin box.

When things start to go wrong they usually snowball. Hell, what now? Another search merely padded out time. If the documents had been removed from the box then which ones out of this lot were they? Looking back at Chummy I began to feel less sorry for him. What had he done with the box? And now I could see. It was on the desk where he had put it. Open. Somehow I was nervous of that.

Going over I saw a negative partly hidden by a folded piece of paper. Remembering the print I searched behind the desk where it had flown. Even before I looked at it some terrible force urged me not to and I had trouble bringing it into vision as if someone was clinging desperately to my arm. I looked, and could feel the blood draining from my face. I remember steadying myself on the desk. For some minutes my system seized up except for a sense of dread. Unexplained fear swept through me until I was paralysed. The blood had rushed back to my brain, swamping it of reason yet something was struggling to get through.

When the first droplet of thought seeped out it explained my state of shock. I knew that I had been trapped and that there was no escape. The gradual, grinding functioning of my mind threw out disjointed fragments of explanation. Fairfax had fixed me, the bastard, as surely as if he had turned the key himself.

My hand came up with the print once more as if by staring fixedly at it I was willing it to rise. And it was reluctant for it was trembling. I found myself walking to the strongest point of light under the chandelier, subconsciously hoping, no doubt, that I had made a terrible mistake. When I looked again there was no error. It was not the position of the man with the youth that had shocked me; it was the fact that I could not fail to recognize the man. It was not pretty. The Rt. Hon. Norman Corrie, M.P., the British Foreign Secretary, had been caught in a moment of abject weakness. Little wonder that Fairfax had handled this personally. I had to sit down on Li Tshien's chair. There was a nerve pain across my chest and I prayed that my scraps of thought would correlate and come up with some sane answers. Without understanding why at that precise moment, I knew that I had been betrayed. I reflected that Norman Corrie was married with kids, I wasn't sure how many. There was no whisper of him being queer

but I suppose that would make it worse if the news suddenl
burst on a startled proletariat. The Chinese were holding a trump
card if they wanted to put pressure to bear.

With more calm, I reached for the tin box and took out th
folded piece of paper. It was a letter to the Governor of Worm
wood Scrubs from the Home Secretary on Home Office note
paper. The letter was two years old and authorized the releas
from prison of Oliver Mervin Page and was signed by Norman
Corrie. I quickly thought back. I was not well up in politics bu
I had reason to remember, as I was in prison at the time, that, two
years ago, Corrie was Home Secretary. It did not take much to
realize that Oliver Mervin Page was the youth in the photograph
Corrie had already been blackmailed. Christ, I had to get out o
here quick. I had a vague recollection of staring dazedly round the
room feeling a snarl in my throat as if I was at bay. And I was
Following numbness, too many confusing thoughts assailed me
It was all too much. Burglary and its many dangers I understood
but this was political blackmail. I was a criminal yet a veritable
saint compared to those in this deadly game. I could not reason it
all out and stopped trying. Right now I had to hinge on those
things with meaning, the old reliables like the buzz of warning in
my guts to get out fast. When I concentrated on that I found it
was not so easy.

One of Fairfax's men was waiting for me. He had probably
positioned himself so that he would see me come down the pipe to
the first roof. If I came down too soon he would be alerted; the
external explosion had yet to go off and I could not go before
then; there was still three-quarters of an hour to go. Three-
quarters of an hour to stay in this place with Chummy still lying
on the floor to remind me of my first act of criminal violence. His
saffron face had dirtied to a greyish tinge as if it needed launder-
ing and the shallowness of his breathing unnerved me.

Suddenly I realized that the light would be showing beneath
the door. It might be common custom for Li Tshien to work
through the night but it might also encourage another late
nighter to call on him. I stuffed back the handkerchiefs and
locked the door from the inside with Chummy's own key.

I returned to the desk, sat down and gave my thought processes
some unaccustomed exercise. The Chinese were not going to
permit burglary and assault at their Legation without raising
hell, and I should have considered it before. They would seize on
every bit of propagandist opportunity and ensure that the Press
got it nicely blown up. They would probably place the blame on
British Security and demand blood. Fairfax had lied to me when
he had said that I had nothing to fear from the police. As I saw it
now the Chinese would howl so loud that the police would have
to move and Fairfax would craftily point the way. I was now convinced that he had already done it.

It was the fact that I had so carelessly overlooked Chinese reaction that made me certain that I had been betrayed. Had I considered for one moment earlier I would have realized that these people would not keep quiet—they would lash out hard. Fairfax would want to hush it up as quickly as possible and the easiest way was to hand me over on a plate.

This was what I had missed when I felt something was wrong. But I have not the devious mind of a politician. Only now, with the shock of what I had seen, the letter much more than the photograph, had sense struck me. I should have reasoned it before—I had not, having been carefully fobbed off.

It all began to make horrifying sense. Fairfax would have reasoned it out long ago. Once in possession of the box, he had to supply someone for the drop-out. A nice idiot of a creeper with an habitual record of crime and a recorded admission that I gained excitement by it and had often announced that I had an ambition to break into Buckingham Palace. Furthermore, I had been to Grendon so was clearly a nutter.

While I reasoned this I realized that from the moment I handed over the box I was doomed. I would be picked up that night. The work would have my trademark; I would have been seen near the Legation or stealing the car, or both. They would have it all neatly wrapped up. The way long sentences were handed out these days, they would make an example of me to pacify the Chinese. I would be old before I came out. The Chinese would know it to be rubbish but it would save face.

Hatred began to well in me. Hatred of Fairfax, of the Rt. Hon. Norman Corrie, of the Chinese and of my own inadequacies. Why me? But I knew why. What could I believe that Fairfax had told me? He had fixed it for Dick and he had got Bulman off my back. The former was my reward, the only pay-off, and I was glad of that. The latter was necessary to free me from police vigilance in order to do the job. There was nothing else I could believe. The money was a hoax for even if it was there I would not be around to use it.

Feeling sick to the depths of my stomach, listlessly I went over to the safe. In minutes life had become empty of hope and hopelessness was the great destroyer. I had no intention of rotting like a cabbage in prison. I gazed at the money in the safe and had intended to leave it there. Now I corrupted myself further and took the dollars and sterling and stuffed them about me. Fairfax had sown this seed too—he had hoped I would take the money to make it look my type of crime. I felt choked at what I was doing. But I would now need money and dare not go to my bank or my friends. From now on I had no friends. Not even Maggie. There was something else I could nick; I put the print, the negative and the letter in my inside breast pocket.

I slumped into the chair, staring at nothing. I could not help but compare myself, the tiniest of pawns, with the public image of the Foreign Secretary; my hatred of him was so intense. The bastard was probably sleeping, dreaming that Fairfax would present him with the necessary good news in the morning, while I carried the can. I sank so far into the depths of despair that I lost track of time. The explosion nearly blew me out of the chair. I listened to the rumble then heard another explosion somewhere outside and the professional in me agreed that the sound would have covered the noise of the Polo Ajax. Well, whatever Fairfax had staged, it made no difference now. I still had to sweat it out for the noise was so loud that it would have woken most people in the street. I had to wait for a while. From time to time I examined Chummy but he seemed neither worse nor better and showed no sign of coming round which worried me. If he snuffed it I might just as well stay where I was and take what they had to offer.

Time to go. The excitement must by now be over. A last look round changed nothing for me. I left the safe and the tin box exactly as they were, gave Chummy a whispered farewell and a sincere wish for his recovery for my sake, retrieved my hand-kerchiefs then put out the light and unlocked the door. I made no further move until my sight was adjusted to the darkness. Opening the door I peered out then stepped swiftly on to a seemingly empty shrouded landing.

The sensation to run was not new and I had it well under control; up the stairs with no less caution than on the descent. The light was still burning in the radio room and I could hear the pips of morse. I half hoped that someone would emerge to put me out of my misery. The door handle moved and I froze. The door opened a fraction and I clearly heard voices speaking rapid Chinese and I thought this was it. The radio pipped away while the door opened wider and I could see the back of a white-shirted man. Suddenly I took a chance and dashed past to the store room door.

Once in the storeroom I did not waste time. I knew it to be futile, that I had no chance, but I went through the motions because that's the way it is.

Up on to the stack of files, a quick clamber through the ceiling hole and out on the roof where I crouched to brush off the plaster. On hands and knees I reached the front parapet facing Portland Place and cautiously peered over. To my left, well away from the corner, a car had crashed into one of the island parking meters. The tank had burst because I could smell the aftermath of a petrol fire and see a small scrabble of dying flame around the burnt-out hulk. What the second explosion had been I could not see but a spare can in the boot would have had a good effect. A police traffic car with its blue flasher going snuggled into the kerb while a couple of coppers stood by to warn passing motorists until the breakdown van came to collect the write-off. All nice and innocent-looking like everything Fairfax touched.

It was handy too, for one of the fuzz was almost certainly the beat copper neatly tucked round the wrong corner. I supposed the traffic car had put put out the flames with its own equipment for I had not heard a fire tender. Well, that was that. I packed my gear into the umbrella and fastened the nylon to it. For the sake of Fairfax's man I still had to go through the motions. Creeping up to the Weymouth Street parapet I peered over, taking my time, sweeping my gaze into every shadowy corner as far as my vision could penetrate. Fairfax only employed the best, I reflected bitterly. Someone was down there but I could not see him.

Slipping the umbrella down on the rope to the lower roof I retained its end, for dropping it might send it snaking over the side of the lower building. It was awkward climbing over the parapet and locating the pipe and for a moment I thought I was not going to make it. I almost let go and what really made the cold sweat break out was the realization that I had almost done it deliberately. I hoped I had more guts than to give up without some sort of a fight. Evidently I had for I found myself climbing down with my old precision. Just the same I was shaken.

As soon as I was on the low roof I ducked out of sight. I was certain that Fairfax's man must have seen me but would also expect me to take extra precaution in lowering myself into Weymouth Street, so he would expect some short delay. He was going to get one. I was back in Devonshire Mews in something under a minute. I hated facing that solitary mews exit like the end of a short tunnel. It was against all normal rules to place myself in a hazardous position and the police were somewhere near the other corner.

Suddenly I was doing everything wrong. I ran silently up the mews without taking due caution but Fairfax's man would not wait for ever and then the heat would be on. Reaching the end I backed against the right-hand wall and sidled forward until I could see towards Portland Place. The police car must be just round the corner because I could see the blue reflection of its revolving light in the gloss of a solitary parked Daimler. So I turned in the opposite direction.

The umbrella was now a nuisance. I hung it on the nearest railings after stuffing the gear down my waistband, accepting that the only way I could survive was by crime. When I thought it safe I started to run, changing route, not really heading anywhere but getting distance between myself and the Legation. By now Fairfax's man would be biting his nails and the wheels would be turning.

I headed roughly south. On seeing the dull lights of the Charing Cross all-night Post Office I began to veer away, had second thoughts and headed towards them. It was now about 4 a.m., completely dark apart from street lamps and empty apart from the odd copper and prowl car which I had no difficulty in dodging. They weren't searching yet. Fairfax would assess the situation before moving and with what I carried he would have to move through the Special Branch. Once the Chinese squawked he would have no option and a good deal depended on how soon Li Tshien was discovered. But where could I go? All my contacts would be checked as a matter of routine; boarding houses, hotels, clubs would all come under the blanket.

Outside the Post Office I wondered if I was being really stupid. There was nowhere to go, nowhere to hide. I checked that I had sufficient change then went inside. Unbelievably there was a customer who looked a bit the worse for wear, having a mild altercation with a weary official. They glanced briefly my way. It was strange to see so large a place empty, like a derelict ship lost at sea, strange rustles and echoes. I tucked myself into the nearest phone booth. It wasn't the wisest of moves but wisdom had little part to play in what I did at the moment. The odds were so long that I kept getting little bursts of wanting to give myself up. I was tired, of course, but most of all disillusioned. I had offered loyalty and had been rewarded with treachery. So I'm simple. But it hurt.

Ringing Maggie was merely a desperate act to soften the blow for her and to give a final goodbye. After tonight I did not doubt that her line would be tapped amongst others. Whilst I wasn't surprised at the length of time she took to answer, I found the waiting an eternity. It took me all my time not to keep looking through the glass at the two at the counter.

'Hello! Who is there?' Maggie, sleepy and irritated.

'Maggie, it's Willie, love.' My heart was in my mouth. How was I going to explain?

'Willie! Is there something wrong?' Relief, happiness, sudden fear. It was all there. Blokes like me don't ring up at this hour with a confession of love. When I stumbled over my reply her voice became more urgent. 'Willie, what's happened? Are you all right?'

'I'm all right, sweetie. I was just wondering how best to explain. It's not easy. Look . . .'

'Are you in trouble?' she cut in, sleep finally leaving her. Her anguish went through me like a blunt sword. I felt rotten. 'Up to my neck, but don't worry. I'll be O.K.'

'Oh God.' It was a half cry, half moan. 'Don't worry. Just like that. You ring me in the middle of the night to say you are in trouble but I'm not to worry. Oh Willie, how could you?'

'Maggie, listen.' Could a man feel more wretched than this? 'If I didn't think the world of you I wouldn't have rung. It may be a very long time before I can contact you again. I just wanted to explain, that's all, so that you won't get the wrong idea.'

'But you haven't explained a thing.' I had a quick vision of her by the phone, long-fingered hand running over sagging face as the nightmare began to catch up on her. In a broken, listless whisper she accused me: 'You've done a job, haven't you?'

'Yes, but there's a difference. Listen to me. Tomorrow or the next day you'll read it in the papers. Just remember that it wasn't as it will seem. I didn't go in for money. Just remember that. The world won't believe me but it's important that you do, Maggie.'

'Oh, Willie, Willie . . .' Her voice diminished to a strained whisper.

'I had to ring you, Maggie. I knew it would choke you, but I had to say goodbye, warn you not to believe all you read. Just tighten up those lips and kick me right out of your system.' I even managed a short laugh. 'You'll find it much easier to do than you think.'

I heard her sighing very quietly. Then she said, 'You'll need—some money.'

How do you explain that you didn't break in for money but that it's stacked about you just the same. 'I'll manage.'

'Why can't you come here?' She was about to go round in circles, looking for alleys only to find each one blocked. Anyone in a trap did the same. I had. But I'd that much more time to face up to it.

'You know why. It's the first place they will look.' This couldn't go on for it would deteriorate into a hopeless emotional mess. Feeling the biggest bastard on earth I said evenly, 'Good-bye, Maggie. God bless you, sweetheart.' Before I hung up I heard her try to force words but I never knew whether she finally got them out for the phone was on the hook.

Leaning against the side of the booth it was some moments before I realized where I was. Parting from Maggie was not new but there had never been one like this. Something had happened to me this time and it shook me to realize just how emotionally charged I was. There would never be anyone like her.

Self preservation tugged at me after a bit. I didn't much care about it just then but something kept prodding me to stir. I rang a few of the boys and got a mixed bag of replies. It's educational how cautiously a villain answers the phone in the middle of the night. Once they knew it was me I usually ended up the wrong side of a flow of invective but that was only because I had made them nervous and had awakened them at a lousy hour. It was taken for granted that I was in trouble. With only two exceptions they offered me shelter. Balls Up Balfour said I could come round right away and Bluie suggested I should spend the rest of the night with him. It wasn't what I wanted for I would be picked up at once. I needed a bolthole the fuzz didn't know about. I thanked them and gave up.

Well, that was that. I could not spend the whole night in the phone booth. I had no one else to ask. Nowhere to go for even the park benches would be searched. The official at the counter had dealt with his customer but I dare not even pass the time of day with him in case he remembered me. I was back in the isolation cell. As I stepped once more into the bleak, dark night I realized that I was carrying my prison around with me and that I had been ostracized from both visitors and cons. At last I knew what real loneliness meant.

CHAPTER NINE

THE FRIENDLINESS of a London night deserted me as if it too knew my fate. The streets suddenly were not just empty but desolate. Farther away lorries trundled down the Strand to Covent Garden, so I veered towards Leicester Square, not wanting to become involved in the activity of the fruit and vegetable market.

I stopped in a cinema doorway. The square in solitude expanded from the contraction of its daytime bustle; the little green park in the middle seemed to be breathing the crisp air, bright under the crystal drops of dew. There was one more person to try. A faint chance but curiosity might prompt him. Standing back while a prowl car went slowly past I slipped out and joined the shadows back to the Post Office. Now a few people were bunched inside and from the ready quips I assumed that they were from the market.

Checking the directory I rang Ray Lynch. The number buzzed for so long that I was on the point of giving up when he came on the line.

'Hello.' Curiosity and anger mixed.

'Ray?'

'Yes. Who's that?' Undisguised annoyance. In the background I heard a woman's voice call plaintively, 'For God's sake, who's calling at this time? Hang up, honey.'

'It's me, Spider. Spider Scott.'

'For Christ's sake, boyo, why the hell are you ringing up at this hour. I was fast asleep.'

'I'm in trouble, Ray. I thought you might put me up for a day.'

'You've done a job, have you? Listen, boyo, you must be mad to expect me to be an accessory. I daren't, Spider. I've a wife . . . what have you done?' Gradual wakefulness was producing the reporter as I had hoped it would.

'The Chinese Legation.' He was going to know soon anyway.

'The *what*? You're kidding. Let me get some sleep.'

I did not answer, banking on his deepening curiosity.

'Are you serious?' No trace of irritation or sleep now. The woman called out again and Ray's voice faded as he turned from the mouthpiece to tell her to shut up.

'Do you think I'd ring you at this time for a joke?'

'Look, you'd better come round straight away.'

'You'll have to fetch me. I don't dare call a cab even if I could find one and it's too far to walk." He had a flat in Fulham.

'Christ! To hell with that, boyo.' I heard him muttering with

his hand partly over the mouthpiece and the woman shouted
something I could not catch. Then he spoke again. 'If I'm sticking
my neck out this far I shall want a bloody good story, man.'

'O.K.,' I said. 'But so far you've risked nothing. Officially
there is no announcement that I've done a job."

He ignored this. 'Where are you?'

I told him, heard him mumbling in annoyance, then he hung
up without another word. It would have been easy for me to nick
a car and drive to Ray Lynch's but that meant ditching the car
nearby and the police would be particularly interested in any
stolen cars in the area tonight.

After a while I strolled down to Trafalgar Square; even the
pigeons had not yet started fluttering. It was like a small concrete oasis with the still waters so dark that there was a completely
false impression of their depth. Instead of a myriad of palms surrounding the pools they had concentrated into one vast symbol
with Nelson at its head. What would it be like when they were all
searching for me if I had nowhere to go? Hearing a distant car I
began to head back to the Post Office, nervous, knowing that
things could break at any moment. When they did, the place
would crawl with cars and I could not understand the delay.

The car I heard was not Ray's but he showed up soon after
in an old grey Ford Consul, too light and noticeable for my
liking. It came round the square all on its own and it was difficult
to envisage the snarl-up that would follow in just a few hours.

I kept out of sight until he coasted in past the Westminster
Bank and the putty blob of his face peered out. I ran across the
road as he began to brake and had the nearside door open before
he had stopped. The sudden interior warmth made me shiver
violently and I had not realized just how deeply the chill had
bitten into me.

Ray looked across at me as he accelerated and I could see that
his straggling hair was as he had left his bed. He wore an old overcoat with the collar turned up, the dull glow from the instrument
panel added to his dissipated appearance. I could smell whisky
and supposed that he had fortified himself against the unexpected
night journey with a couple of stiff shots. 'I must be mad,' he
said and gazed back at the road.

A little traffic was creeping about although it was only 5.30.
For some time neither of us spoke but I was thinking furiously
and so would he be. He fumbled for a cigarette and I helped him
light it.

At last he said, 'You going to tell me about it, boyo?'

'Can't it wait till we get inside? I'm frozen.' I wanted time to
think.

And he suspected it. 'Now don't play around with me, Spider,
or it's out on your ear you go. I'm not sticking my neck out for
nothing. A story or the street, boyo, as much as I love you.' His

cigarette played the puppet on his lower lip as he spoke and ash cascaded down his coat. His stubby fingers gripped the steering wheel firmly, the only real sign of his tension.

Treading warily I said, 'You had better explain where your flat is and drop me off before we reach it.'

He shot me a suspicious glance, always looking for the catch. 'Why?'

'I want to case the area; know where I am if I have to make a break. And it's not fair to you if we arrive together. You can at least claim that you didn't bring me here."

He nodded grudgingly, not quite liking it but seeing the loophole for himself. 'We live in a modern block,' he said, giving me the address.

'Who is on the same floor? And are there animals?'

Another look, curious and still suspicious. 'What difference can it make?'

'A lot when you're on the run. You know who to expect to bump into, who to avoid and when.'

'Look, boyo, you're staying put in my flat until we sort it out. You're not budging.' We were nearing Cromwell Road, passing an airline bus before he added, 'Animals aren't allowed in the flats. There are only two others on our landing; an old girl opposite and a middle-aged couple farther down the corridor.'

It was hellish risky but I decided that it would have to be the old girl.

'How long will you be?' he asked as an afterthought.

'Half an hour or so. It can save me grief later. You go straight in. Wait for me to give a sharp double rap on the door.' Watching him closely I added, 'Don't worry, if I'm a bit late.'

He gave a disgruntled snort. 'Don't worry about me worrying, boyo. The first sign of danger to me or mine and you're on your own.' His restless eyes swept me briefly without compassion before he added. 'We haven't known each other long enough to be understanding friends. Each wants something of the other and provided we have that we'll not upset each other. O.K.?'

'O.K.' I had not expected him to fall over himself hiding me. I knew the risks better than he did. And I would have to give him some sort of story as near to the truth as possible. But first I must ditch the stuff I was carrying in my breast pocket.

He suddenly pulled up so sharply that I had to brace myself against the dashboard. I thought he must have changed his mind but instead he was making it up. As he leaned back, bouncing his fingers thoughtfully on the steering wheel, I noticed his pyjamas creeping out beneath his trousers.

'Round the corner is Ranelagh Gardens. It's the second block of flats along, the smaller lot. First floor.' As I opened the door he added, 'and don't forget, Spider boy, I want a good one.'

I watched him drive off, foot on the clutch, a cloud of fumes hanging like a whirling apparition on the night air. It was still not six o'clock but a lot of people rose about this time. There were already lighted windows and there would soon be more. I had little time; perhaps not enough. Already I could hear more than one pair of footsteps as I hurried after the car. I found it badly parked outside the flats filling a gap in a long chain of cars, few covered, the remainder frosted over and glittering like diamanté.

My only hesitation was in making sure that the main lobby was clear, then I went up the wide carpeted stairs two at a time. Ray could not do too badly for the place was not a dump. Approaching the first floor landing I slowed, stopped and peered round the corner. Ray's flat was to my left, a plain door with a perpendicular letter box and the number above it. Further down the corridor was the second door. The door opposite Ray's was out of sight until I stepped forward.

Pressing my ear to the door I could hear nothing and was relieved to see that I needed only mica for entry unless it was bolted inside. Some flat dwellers feel secure because there are others around them. It's a mistake. I pressed the lock back as quietly as I could, hoping that she was a late riser. If Ray opened his door now I was done.

The catch gave and the door opened. The hall night light was insufficient so I had to risk my torch to avoid knocking anything over. Nipping in I put the lock on its catch and pushed the door shut. I stood listening, as usual aware that my own breathing was too heavy and tense. I hated working quickly and against all commonsense like this. At this hour people are not so deeply asleep and it might not take much to wake her. I didn't want her screaming her head off then dying of a heart attack. Nor did I want Ray Lynch going through my things when I was asleep.

When I had controlled my own breathing I could hear the old girl snoring and in dismay realized that she slept with the bedroom door open. There is no reckoning with women; so many thought this was safer too. But at least I had located her; the door facing me to my right in the tiny hall. Immediately opposite me the only other door visible. Opening it I went in, quietly closing it behind me; the living room as I thought. I imagined a dinette and kitchen beyond it but I had no need to go farther. The close carpeting in the hall had reassured me and sure enough it was extended here.

I remember skirting a settee and was aware of the diaphanous glow of white net curtains over picture windows and of going behind an armchair for what I wanted. In one corner I knelt down, produced my jemmy and began to lift up the tacks. It did not take long to raise a flap of carpet and no time at all to slip the negative sandwiched between the letter and the print under the felt. I had only to tap the tacks back when I heard the old girl moving about and heard a switch depress. I could not see a suspicion of light anywhere; was she in the bathroom?

My frayed nerves were taking a beating for one night. I was rooted, wondering what best to do when a door opened and the light went on. It was becoming a habit and I prayed to God I would not have to clobber her—I didn't think I could. My mouth was desert dry, my neck wringing.

She must have been wearing carpet slippers for I could barely hear her. The armchair was covering me of course, and I would not be seen unless she actually came over to look. But I could not get out until she went and I had to tap the tacks back. The longer I took the more concerned Ray Lynch would become and the last thing I wanted was his ferreting about. All I could do was to stay still on my knees, head bent forward below the chair back, as if awaiting decapitation. The radio came on softly. Pop music. Then I could hear nothing more and risked a quick look round the chair. She had gone but a door was open at an angle to the windows and she had left the lights on, which meant she was coming back. Now or never. Hitting the tacks was now out of the question so I had to lean heavily on each one with the end of the jemmy hoping they would hold and not show. When I had finished I was not happy about it; a trained eye would see that the carpet had been raised.

How long would she be? The radio drowned any noise I made but it also drowned hers. I thought I heard a tap running. One second was just as risky as another. Standing up, I ran my foot round the lowered flap of carpet, trying to bed it down. Now I was playing in extra time and knew it. Skirting the armchair I took long strides towards the door. Light from the bedroom now streamed out into the hall. Taking the catch off slowly I allowed the lock to spring out against my fingers. On the landing I pulled the door behind me until the lock touched the metal inset. When I closed the door it would make a noise. Would she hear it and come chasing to the door?

By this time Ray would be wondering; there was no time left. Leaning across the corridor I rapped sharply twice on Ray's door and shut the old lady's at the same time. The click was unmistakable to me. If she had heard it I only hoped that Ray would respond first. He did and I pushed him into his own hall and quickly closed his door.

'What's the matter?' he asked, puzzled.

'You know what's the matter. I just don't want to hang around.' The layout, I quickly saw, was the same as the old lady's. We went into the lounge. Ray now wore a thick woollen dressing gown over his pyjamas, a little frayed at the cuffs and one tassel missing; there was also a cigarette burn on the breast pocket. The furniture was good contemporary stuff. The air was thick with tobacco smoke and he was smoking now. So was the

woman who appeared at the kitchen door. She eyed me at firs
with hostility then her expression became wooden as she leaned
against the door jamb.

'Er—this is Spider Scott, Sal. You know I told you about him
This is my wife, Sally.' They had been arguing about me; it wa
in the air and on their faces. Maybe I wasn't what she expected
she tried a smile and didn't quite make it. She too wore a dressing
gown, blue nylon draped over a short nightdress by the way on
lower leg peeped through. She touched her red hair sub-consci
ously as if sorry now that she had not made more of it before
appearing. She wore no make-up and although her skin wa
heavy she had once been very pretty. She was still attractive bu
had coarsened, her full lips downturned in a perpetual petulance
or sulk. There were lines under eyes that were disconcertingly
blue, and, at the moment, hard and non-committal.

'Sal, we'd better talk, Spider and I. Do you think you . . .' She
ignored him, still blatantly eyeing me and I was finding i
difficult. 'You look as if you need a hot drink.'

'Sal . . .' But Ray's protest was cut short.

'Look at him. He's frozen stiff. I'll get you some coffee.' She
turned back before I could thank her. Ray gave me a shrug o
apology but it was for himself; I needed the coffee.

'We can't talk in front of her. Wait till she's dressing.'

It suited me. I was in no hurry but I felt a little better now that
I had ditched the stuff. Ray lit a cigarette from the stub of the old
one but his fingers were strangely free of nicotine and I noticed
how carefully he held his cigarette. Was there a remnant of good
habit in the man who years ago had been so neat and fastidious?
Why had he let himself go? When I looked around more closely
I noticed the same untidiness as with Ray himself; scattered
papers, an unwashed cup, badly arranged cushions suggesting
that his wife was as bad as he.

Nodding to a chair opposite his own he sat eyeing me speculatively, impatient to question me but unwilling to do so with the
kitchen door open. By his elbow was a half bottle of Scotch and a
used glass; he poured some now half heartedly offering me one.
I shook my head. At 7 a.m.? I couldn't make him out. Unshaven,
in his shabby dressing gown and not too clean pyjamas, scruffy
hair, pouched eyes, drinking whisky in quantity, he appeared
almost derelict. Yet through his active eyes I could see his brain
working at speed, undulled by the spirit, furtively anticipating
the sort of story I might provide. He was a newspaper man, quick
to scent; yet it struck me that there was more to his zeal than
that; in the way he licked his lips and the tightness with which he
held the glass there was a quiet desperation.

Sally entered holding a mug in one hand and a small sugar
basin in the other. I noticed that she had applied a quick lick
of make-up and that Ray had seen it too; he did not look too

pleased. Feeling myself treading on eggshells it wasn't that easy to avert my gaze as she bent in front of me to put down the coffee while the front of her dressing gown flapped open. Ray was watching me, fingers on glass and cigarette momentarily frozen. Give me a cleverly alarmed window any day to this complication. With an effort of will I smiled at Ray, ignoring her until she straightened. 'The cream's in,' she said. 'Help yourself to sugar.' I said I would and thanked her.

She went out and closed the door.

It would be silly to have ignored her existence, so I observed casually, 'Pretty wife you have, Ray. The coffee is very welcome.'

'Good. Now what about it, boyo. Why the Chinese Legation?' He seemed relieved that his wife had gone but maybe it was because he was anxious for his story.

I stood up. 'Er—will she be back for a bit?'

He shook his head confidently. 'No. She'll get ready. You know how long they take.'

'It was a tip-off,' I said. To impress him and keep him quiet for a while, I took out my tools; jemmy, saws, Polo Ajax and detonator, plasticine and so on and laid them out on the settee. This removal made little difference to my appearance because my jacket was loose, but he must see that my pockets were bulging.

'Christ, boyo,' he exclaimed, rising slowly. 'Is that explosive?'

'Don't worry, it's quite safe.'

He took a gulp at his drink, interested but not sidetracked and said, 'Right. That's the how. Now what about the why?'

I grinned and winked and it took at lot out of me. 'The usual reason.' I started emptying my crammed pockets until they formed an impressive bundle on the settee.

'You mean to say you bust in for money?' He was disappointed, shaken.

'Is there a better reason?'

'The *Chinese Legation*? With the sort of precautions they take?' I tapped the pile of money. 'How many private safes carry this sort of cash? Getting in was easy enough in spite of the alarms.'

Ray was getting angry because he felt he had been cheated, this was not what he had expected. Draining his drink he poured another, his gaze darting around the implements, the money, and finally falling uncertainly on me. To give himself time he asked, 'How much is there then?'

'I haven't counted it.' I started to riffle through the notes wondering whether I had blocked him or whether he would come back at me. He went back to his chair, sipping his whisky and staring thoughtfully at me; he was too astute to accept it entirely.

'Four thousand dollars in hundreds, and twelve hundred pounds in fivers. All well used.'

Ray did a quick calculation. 'Say two thousand eight hundred pounds.'

'Not bad for one night's work.'

'With that sort of risk? You're kidding, boyo. Where does Sir Stuart Halliman come in?'

Why didn't I just tell him? Who was it had said that I had misplaced loyalties? Wasn't it Fairfax himself; so why should I bloody well protect *him*? I told myself that I was not; that in some odd way I was obeying an impulse to protect myself. I should never have come here.

'Sir Stuart Halliman?'

'You know who I mean.'

'Of course I do, but I don't . . . Oh! Crikey, you're barmy. You mean he might have tried to use me? Me—a common creeper.'

'Who better?' Ray was eyeing me suspiciously, then shrewdly as he thought of something. 'Tell me, boyo. What possessed you to ring *me* for a billet?'

'Because they would immediately do the rounds of the boys I know. This is the only safe place.'

'But you're talking as if they already know that it is *you* who did the job.'

I had seen it coming. 'I think they do. At least they will when they do a description check. My luck ran out when a car crashed into a parking meter in Portland Place. The place crawled with coppers. I was out when I was seen but they won't forget me when news of this break-in comes from the Chinese.'

'I see.' He glared at the hand holding his drink, putting it under hypnosis, for it completely steadied. He was very still indeed, then he looked up bird-like, unhappy yet still with underlying persistence. 'So you want me to be an accessory to an ordinary burglary?'

'I never pretended it was anything else.'

'By implication you did when you mentioned the Chinese Legation.'

'I'm sorry you took it that way. Look, you're right, Ray. I've no right to drag you in. I knew I'd been seen and I got windy.' Finishing my coffee I rose. 'I'll slip out.'

'No you don't, boyo.' A finger unwound from the glass and pointed at me.

'You stay here until I've made a few enquiries. If what you say is true they'll pick you up in no time.' I knew then that he did not believe me. Rightly, he assumed that there was another factor and he was not willing to let it go too easily. He also knew that had I anywhere else to go I would not be here. He went to the kitchen and returned with a transistor radio. I was shocked to see that it was almost eight o'clock. He switched on a moment before the news. It was the second item. 'Last night, thieves broke into the Chinese Legation in Portland Place . . . one of the senior secretaries has been seriously injured and a spokesman for the Legation states that he is still unconscious. Large sums of money were stolen, together with secret documents which the spokesman said can only inflame the Chinese people and hamper those working for the true cause of peace. He went on to say that there are clear signs that British Intelligence forces are directly responsible for the break-in and that it is a disgraceful violation of diplomatic immunity and an act of war on the soil of the Chinese People's Republic. So far no one at the Foreign Office has been available for comment. By coincidence, there was an accident outside the Legation in which . . .'

Ray was staring blankly at me as the voice went on and then he cut it off in mid-sentence as he flipped the switch. In quiet anger he said, 'You're quite an accomplished liar, Spider, I give you that. Secret documents and grievous bodily harm. Well, well. You forgot to tell me you nearly croaked someone.' He was tense and worried. Suddenly he was sticking his neck out too far but his persistent curiosity came out on top. Accusing me was not kicking me out.

'You ought to know better,' I chided. 'Of course they are going to say that. Secret documents; I bet if I'd taken a Chinese newspaper they'd have said the same. Look, they've been caught napping, they're going to stir it up, aren't they?'

'Maybe.' There was a strange brightness in his eyes, almost fanatical. 'I've given you shelter and you're holding out. What else did you get?'

'Look, do you want to search me?'

'Yes,' he said. 'I do.'

I stood up with arms raised in mock anger. Then you had better get on with it.'

Making no apology he searched me inexpertly but thoroughly. I smelled the whisky breath and watched his reddened eyes. When he stood back he gazed at me sullenly and said, 'Now I know why you wanted me to go on ahead. Where have you ditched the stuff?'

'You must be raving mad. In the first place, the only stuff I should have ditched are my tools.' I pointed vaguely to the settee. Secondly, if I've nicked something for Sir Stuart Halliman what the hell would I come here for? Why hide it?'

It was a good argument but he came back swiftly, giving something of himself away. 'Holding out for more money, perhaps, boyo?'

I looked at him in disgust. 'You know better than that. Is that the Ray Lynch who wrote an article about me when I last went to nick? What was it you wrote; "A curiously honest man in almost every way except a strange weakness for crime". I cherished those words.'

Something flitted over his bloated face, a memory, a brie introspection. He sat down wearily, confused, frustrated and basically angry. Just as my instinct warns me on a job, so did his He knew that there was something hidden and that he would have to go beyond me to find it.

'Look,' I suggested again. 'It would be better if I take m chances.' But he waved his hand carelessly and ash flew off ye another cigarette.

'Forget it,' he said. 'You must expect me to look for a story There's a lot that doesn't make sense, Spider. But leave it, fo now. Anyway, I must get ready for the office.' Finishing his drink he appeared none the worse for wear when he rose. He smiled a little, not very convincingly. 'When Sal and I have gone, cook yourself a breakfast. Stay here until we come back this evening.

'And then?'

'We'll have to see. Don't expect too much of me. The story you've told isn't much. Anyway you'll be safe for the day.' He went off, leaving the door open. I sat there; but I wasn't wondering about Ray, I was remembering Li Tshien and how he had looked when I had left and the B.B.C. announcement that he was still unconscious. Oddly enough the Chinese had put out the complete truth as I knew it; it was an occasion where truth was infinitely better than the usual propaganda. I only hoped that Chummy would not die. If that happened God knows what I would do. Ray would have to hand me over for certain, story or no.

Either way my prospects were so grim that I began to wonder why I had troubled to come.

They came into the room together. Shaved and dressed Ray appeared little tidier than before; his trousers needed pressing and there was a stain on the lapel of his jacket. His tie looked as if it had been tied without a mirror and his shoes needed polish. Sally was very different. Under the short fur coat she wore a beige suit with a skirt too short for her thirty or so years. Even though her legs were good still, it looked wrong. Her eyes were too heavily made up, lids vivid blue. But she was smart and cared for her clothes. They were an ill-assorted pair and I could see now that he was too short for her. She still gazed impassively at me but there was something there, perhaps in the way she held herself that was meant to reach me. I remained dead pan as they told me to make myself at home but not to answer the phone; they would be back about six unless anything special cropped up for Ray.

When they had gone I made myself some more coffee and explored the flat. One double bedroom, bed left unmade, large kitchen-cum-dining-room and bathroom. Nothing extraordinary but tidied up it would have been attractive. I stretched out on the settee, wondering, worrying, knowing that I could not last like his, that Ray would boot me out when he reached a dead end. Periodically I turned on the news.

As the morning wore on the Legation robbery adapted a different slant. The Foreign Office denied all knowledge and were appalled by the violation of the guaranteed sanctity of a Foreign Power in London. To back up their claim that they were not involved the police had now issued a description of a man they wanted to interview and it was a fair description of me.

So I had been absolutely right. I was the sap to appease the Chinese; they might not believe but they would have to be satisfied and the public would believe because most of them would not have the time or the interest to explore beyond the newspaper print. My brain was getting unaccustomed exercise; I was not used to delving into espionage and I don't think I was doing too well at it. Survival was the main thing. I had what Fairfax and the Chinese wanted; it was my only weapon and I must decide how best to use it if it could be used at all.

The next news mentioned that the condition of Li Tshien had worsened and that there was cause for concern. That got me off the sofa like I was catapulted. I was dead tired, but I could not sleep with this on my mind. I kept seeing his head hit the desk and hearing the crack. Suddenly the outside door opened and I leapt behind the lounge door, my heart thumping. It could not be Sally or Ray because it was only twelve-thirty. Yet I heard the front door quietly close and saw the lounge door open towards me. It was far too late to do anything about my tools which I had bundled on to the floor with the nylon tied round them. The door was pushed right back until one of my feet stopped it and who-ever was there stood suddenly still in the doorway, obviously feeling the resistance.

CHAPTER TEN

SHOULD I HIT HIM OR NOT? It was a measure of my condition
that the thought flashed at random. Panic. Then I had a faint
whiff of perfume and my legs weakened in relief.

'Come out, Spider,' she said, as if I hid from her every day.
Then she walked into the room. I could have killed her had I the
strength. Her fur coat was on her arm and she draped it over an
armchair as she went past, making no attempt to look back but
knowing that I was watching her. I closed the door.

'You should have warned me you were coming back earlier. I
might have hit you.'

She looked back over her shoulder, smiling, her eyes challenging. 'Ray would have been madly jealous had he known I
intended to come home.'

I sat in the empty armchair. 'Why? He has nothing to fear
from me.'

Sally sank on to the settee, slipped off her jacket, revealing a
thin, tight, fawn sleeveless jumper. She took time provocatively
fluffing out her hair with calculated movement and crossed her
legs, ensuring I got good value from them. 'It's not you he's
worried about, darling. It's me.' The endearment was a toss-away
as if she had once been in theatricals. Later I learned that she had.

'I don't understand.' I understood only too well.

She eyed me brazenly. Now that Ray was absent she made it
clear that she had made up her mind about me. I could not
understand why she was so cheap, so disloyal to Ray.

'He's not exactly a find, is he?'

I did not answer, knowing that I would be implicated if I did.
I wondered why she had married him and saw part of the reason
when she suddenly got up, went to the sideboard and returned
with a half bottle of gin, two glasses and tonic water. Before
sitting down, she produced two folded newspapers, tossing them
over to me. I had made the headlines in both *The Standard* and
The News lunch time editions. It was alarming to see it in banner
headlines.

She went past me again to sit down, every move feline, designed,
carefully enacted. She poured two drinks and passed one over.
I put mine on the floor.

'Cheers.' She relished a half glassful before focusing her very
blue eyes on me once more. 'You know why I came back?' She
indicated the newspapers. 'With that hanging over you I thought
you might like some light relief.'

'What do you mean by that?'

She stared, amused. 'What do you think I mean by it. Don't
be so bloody innocent, life's too short.'

'I have a few basic rules which I find help me get along. One is I don't sleep with married women. It may be naïve but it keeps me free of complications.'

Her glass stopped half way to her pursed lips. 'Get *you*.' Then she laughed, throwing her head back and showing a good neckline. What was it that made both she and Ray so verging on the decadent. Did they do it to each other?

'Married?' Sally laughed again incredulously. 'To him? Old tired Tim?'

'You didn't contradict him . . .'

'Oh no,' she cut in, still smiling wickedly. 'We must protect our image, mustn't we?' She gave me a long insolent look, half disbelieving what I had said. 'Feel happier about it now?'

'My second rule,' I observed coolly, 'is never to do it on my own doorstep. Whatever he is to you he's giving me shelter. And whatever I am I can't abuse it. Perhaps some other time.'

For a moment I thought she would throw the glass at me. She was unused to rebuff. 'You bloody little crook,' she said. 'You sit there moralizing while the whole blasted police force is searching for you. When you're inside with the long nights ahead of you you'll be sorry that you didn't take your chances.'

She found solace in another gin, curled her legs under her and eventually gave me a broad wink. 'Well, it'll be better for the waiting. Don't worry about Ray.'

'Why do you two go on together?'

She sighed. 'It's like a bad habit, difficult to break. There are times when we need each other.'

I took a chance. 'What happened to him? He used to be so different a few years ago.'

She swung round to face me, careless how she did it. 'Oh, he used to be quite the boy. He saw himself as a second Chapman Pincher. He was a good reporter; really good. But he suddenly got swollen headed and developed the notion that he could do it from bed with the bottle.' Sally's expression softened as she reminisced, as though things might have been different. 'When he was sent out reporting on projects, say some Government scheme or new enterprise, he would phone through a sentence or two of the official handout and prop up the bar with some of the others while the really ambitious ones went round with the officials learning something of what they were seeing. He thought he was lording it over them. Damned idiot didn't realize until it was too late.'

'There's nothing wrong in being a reporter,' I prompted.

'No. But he lost his big chance to someone else. There's a lot of difference between what he earns and what he would have got as a second Chapman Pincher. Those sort of chances don't come round too often. He started to drink. Then his wife left him. So he drank more. I guess he just lacked guts.'

She turned to me almost viciously. 'If you gave him that blood story it could make all the difference, get him back on the tracks.'

She was probably right, but there was a snag. 'The story he wants from me is unprintable. A responsible news editor would not print it without checking and when he did they would clamp down, issue a "D" notice or whatever they call it, and it would be completely unprovable. Ray would be even more frustrated.'

'So there is something then.'

I grinned at her. 'I said the sort of story he wants. The one he thinks is there. "Spider Scott—Master Spy". Why did you join him?'

'Because I was a bloody failure and I needed a man,' she said frankly. 'At that time he had not yet sterilized himself with drink. We were good for each other. We could prop up a bar and talk of our failures like other people discuss their successes, until the tears dripped into our booze. Then we would go to bed and wake up realizing that we were fit for no one but each other.'

Her third large gin was making her morbid, but like Ray she was so besotted with the stuff there was little visible effect. Suddenly she said, 'If you don't make an afternoon of it I'll make it bloody impossible for you here.'

'You already have,' I said, rising. 'I've decided to leave.'

'Oh God, no,' she cried, scrambling to her feet. 'Look, you've got it all wrong. You owe Ray nothing. He's not doing it for you, don't you see. He's doing it for himself. If he finds nothing in it you're out, darling, right into the arms of the police.' I knew it but at least he had been honest about it.

'Oh, for God's sake sit down,' she said desperately, pushing me back on to the settee. 'If you're gone when he returns he'll blame me, anyway, and half kill me.'

I had at least forced a shaky truce. I had to go for I knew that she would come back at me or in a fit of pique suggest to Ray that I had tried to molest her. But I wanted to hear what he had to say first. Taking me by surprise she leaned over and kissed me quickly. 'Don't go. Not yet,' she said hurriedly and I wondered what else I had unearthed between these two.

She prepared a lunch of eggs on toast and the taste of food raised my hunger. Afterwards she talked a little of her own life on the stage, how she had never quite made it. She had had the looks but not the talent. Reading between the lines she had probably spent most of her time on the casting couch, but a night in bed is no return for diminishing audiences and producers had seen the light. She could have done better than Ray but as she had pointed out, their combined weaknesses at least gave them the uncertain strength of the fusion of need.

Ray came in late and sullen. He greeted nobody but tossed the late editions of the evenings over to me before going straight to the whisky bottle with his coat still on. Something had gone

wrong. As he poured, he glared at me as if I had personally
arranged his downfall. Half his drink went in a gulp, then he
tossed his topcoat on to the chair that had recently supported
Sally's.

I scanned the papers. Now I had really made it. My full face
photograph stared back at me with my name underneath. It was
a police photograph; I appeared surly, awkward, but it could not
be mistaken for anyone else. It was suggested that I might be
dangerous. As it was designed to do, the police announcement
that I might help them in their enquiries tamped down the
ravings of the Chinese. The British police were on the ball,
already the suggestion that British Intelligence was involved was
being overshadowed. The country was searching for the villain. I
briefly wondered what the boys would make of it; probably think
that I had blown my top. But it was a reflex thought, an escape
for I was largely numbed.

The fact that I had been expecting it did not soften the blow.
Whatever happened there was a distinct limit to the time I could
spend here. There would be tremendous pressure on the police
to produce me. Fairfax would want to know whether I had obtained the photograph and the letter, and would want to get his
hand on them at the earliest possible moment.

And here was Ray harbouring the villain himself, a potential
scoop of a lifetime and looking very sour about it all. He sat on
the arm of a chair and swirled his drink restlessly round the glass
as if challenging it to spill; his unconscious respect for the spirit
kept it within the rim, then he swallowed hard. 'Well, boyo,' he
said, 'they've slung out a D notice on all extraneous matter
regarding yourself.'

'What's that then?' I pointed to my photograph.

'Well we can't keep the Chinese quiet and the rest is official
handout but any titbits, any inside stuff like a story out of you
will be sat on.'

'Are they so strict?'

Ray shrugged, finished his drink. 'They are since the last blow
up. The present trend is to co-operate with police and official
sources.'

'So I'm no good to you then?'

'You weren't anyway, boyo, were you? Not exactly forthcoming.
If I told my news editor that you were here he would demand
that I got some sort of story that he might be able to use later and
then that I should hand you over to the authorities.'

'Why haven't you?' I asked quietly.

'You know bloody well why. You're sitting on *the* story, boyo,
and I want it. I could produce one now from informed sources
but it's not what I want. Damn you, Spider!' He got up and
poured another drink. Sally had retreated to the kitchen and I
could hear the clatter of plates.

'Ray, you have the only story I know,' I lied. 'If another one crops up later I'll see that you get it.'

'Oh thanks a million.'

'Look, if you'll bear with me for another few hours, I'll slip out before midnight.'

'Where will you go?' It was half curiosity, half concern.

'I don't know, but that's not your problem.'

'Wait. It could be.' Ray came back to the chair arm and gazed at the floor. I suspected that his mind was working less untidily than his general appearance suggested. He ran his stubby fingers through his receding hair, his eyes bright with concentration. Slowly his fingers tightened round his glass and his puffed face came up towards mine, his gaze shrewd.

'I may be able to put you in touch with some people who can help you.'

I gazed back at him suspiciously and during the silence Sally appeared in the open kitchen doorway, an oven glove in her hands; she was as puzzled as I.

'Why?' I asked.

'For Chrissake!' Ray glared at me but beneath his aggression was tension. 'I make an offer to help and all you can say is why?'

'You told me yourself you're helping me for what's in it for you.'

He shrugged, not quite spilling his drink and disposing of half of it as he realized how close he had come. 'Later I'll get a story out of it. It won't be wasted. I'm not that much of a bastard that I'll hand you over to the police now. I've left it too late, should have done it at the outset. Meanwhile it's possible that I may have contacts who can help you get away, no more than that.'

'Don't listen to him, Spider.' Sally moved further into the room.

'Shut up, you silly bitch.' Ray glared back at her then looked sharply at me as if the first glimmering of suspicion that there might be something between us had struck him. Not slow to notice, Sally tossed her shoulders and flounced back into the kitchen.

'Look,' Ray spread his hands, his eyes screwed. 'It's just the seed of an idea, that's all. There's a bloke I know who may be able to get you out.'

'Out of the country?'

'Yep.'

'He's not likely to do it for love.'

'Oh, he'll want something for it. But you've got money.'

'Those jobs don't come cheaply. Is he bent?'

'Not in your terms. There can be no harm in talking to him.'

'I don't know. It sounds odd.'

'What's the matter with you?' Ray stood up, glass at safety level. 'What's your alternative, boyo? The police? A life stretch?

What possible harm can you come to compared with that? And the Chinese you nobbled doesn't seem too fit.'

He was right but still I didn't like it. I needed to know more but before I could speak Ray added, 'I don't even know if he's interested. I would have to ask him. And if he is you would have to sort it out between you, one way or the other.'

I must have given him an old-fashioned look for he exploded, 'Look boyo, I don't want you on my conscience. There's nothing in it for me.'

'Since when have you performed acts of charity?' I deliberately goaded. 'You made your position clear at the outset, now you've changed it.'

Instead of being angry, he shrugged resignedly. 'Take it or leave it.'

Sally had quietly returned to the door and was eyeing me intently but if there was a message I missed it. Nevertheless she had reminded me that I could not stay here. 'I suppose it would do no harm to meet him. Do I know him, or of him?'

'It's unlikely. After dinner I'll nip out to try to raise him.' He looked at me from under lowered brows. 'You don't have to look so damned suspicious. We newspaper boys know a lot of peculiar people.'

'Me, for instance.'

It took a little tension and distrust away and he smiled whimsically, his expression transforming into something wholly pleasant.

With a little time to spare while Sally prepared the dinner, Ray and I sank back into our chairs in a moody silence. I thumbed through the newspapers wondering how I could raise a question without him becoming suspicious. To pass the time I mentioned one or two news items on which he briefly commented but his mind was clearly anchored beyond this room. Then I saw what I wanted in the middle pages of *The Standard*: the Foreign Secretary was off to some conference with the Americans and Russians which it was thought involved the position of China— amongst other things. As casually as I could, paper held well up, I asked:

'What do you think of this Foreign Secretary bloke of ours. I see he's off again.' I could not see Ray's face but there was no suspicion in his tone as he offhandedly flung back, almost begrudgingly, 'One of the best we've had.' And then qualified it. 'As politicians go.'

Dare I? It seemed the right time. 'I heard he's a queer,' I said, turning the page.

'Christ, boyo. We all know that.'

He meant, of course, that Fleet Street knew it. Still he had gleaned nothing. He laughed cynically, adding, 'If we printed what we know about a good many public figures it would turn the public's stomach—apart from the laws of libel.'

I wondered if he would remain so detached if he knew that the present Foreign Secretary had released a man from prison with whom he had had an affair. I was guessing but not wildly. I knew what prison was like—the gossip, and in these circumstances the possibility of a big mouth and blackmail. I wondered what sort of a job the man had been given. If the country got to know about this one it was anyone's guess what would happen. The old country would stink a good deal more in the opinion of its enemies and would have miserably failed its friends. The Chinese had known only too well what they had been sitting on. As I realized the H-bomb I was straddling, I imagined I could feel Ray's gaze boring through the newspapers. He had informed me what I wanted to know, and I seemed to have got away with it.

Dinner turned out to be some sort of hash Sally had scraped up. There wasn't much of it for habitually heavy drinkers don't usually eat much and I was left feeling hungry. But I was not complaining; it was hot and I had a temporary roof, a refuge at a time I could hardly expect one. Both of them seemed somewhat detached during the meal, both were preoccupied with their own thoughts but Sally was apt to occasionally let hers show in a way I found alarming. Whatever occupied Ray fortunately did so sufficiently for him to miss some of the dangerous glances she cast my way. Maggie would not have taken to her.

After dinner Ray slipped on an old Abercrombie and a greasy trilby, gave me a last thoughtful look, then said he was off to see his contact, that I was not to worry. As there was a perfectly good phone in the flat which he was clearly reluctant to use I was already worried but there was nothing that I could do about it. Time here was running out fast and there would never be any-where else quite so safe.

While Sally washed up I slumped in the lounge. I should have helped but had no intention of being too near that questing body. Picking up the papers again I felt sick at the thought of what Dick and Maggie would think about it. Perhaps it was worse for Dick because of his colleagues. There was nothing that I could explain to him; nothing that would not sound false; a phone call would embarrass him, and I did not want him facing the choice of whether or not to report it. I could only hope that he would stick it out. As I sat there staring moodily into space I saw how quickly my conception of people the other side of the fence had been shaken in just a few hours. Sally finished her chores and joined me to make life more difficult. She sat opposite and was deliber-ately careless with her skirt. She never gave up but there was a wariness about her, as if she was not sure when Ray would return. I told myself that I would have to be a particular type of bastard to take advantage while Ray was out rooting for me, whatever his reasons.

'He's up to something, you know,' asserted Sally, unable to

believe that she had been rejected. I could see that she was trying
to place me; was I sexless?—had other outlets—a freak?

'Does it matter?' I asked. 'The whole country is looking for me.'

'You might come to harm.' But it was speculation, not concern. I laughed. 'As soon as I walk out of that door I can come to
harm. How doesn't really make much difference to me the way
I'm placed.'

'I could persuade him to keep you here for a few days. It could
be cosy, give you time to think something out.'

'Cosy. For him? Anyway you couldn't persuade him; he's too
much to lose of the little he has left.'

She bridled, thinking I meant her and instinctively plucked at
her skirt hem without being too successful. Reaching for the gin
bottle she began her evening stint. 'How could it hurt him? I
don't intend to leave him.'

'It would if he knew of your little capers.'

She tossed her hair back. 'And who's going to tell him?'

'Drop it,' I said, tired of the subject. There's nothing like the
threat of losing personal freedom to cramp the thought of sex. I
wanted to think of escape, not of the inviting sensuous body
opposite me.

The door key turned in the middle of the ensuing silence and
we both jumped. I moved behind the lounge door from pre-
cautionary habit. Ray came in rubbing his cold hands. He had
been out almost two hours. Dishevelled, he turned to face me.
'There's a black Humber waiting for you downstairs, boyo,' he
said; just like that.

I stiffened. 'Whose?'

Ray tried a reassuring smile that turned sick. 'It's all right.
You don't have to worry. He's not a policeman. Just sort it out
between the two of you.'

Sally, who knew him better, suddenly knocked back her drink
and reached for the bottle, her hand shaking slightly. What did
she suspect? I found myself trying to read two people I hardly
knew. Twenty-four hours ago I would have taken them at face
value. However innocent that may sound, that was the way of it.
On cue Ray went for his own bottle and as he poured he spilled
some of his precious spirit. So what played on *his* conscience. The
silence was the fatal goodbye; the lowering of the coffin into the
grave. And we all felt it.

'Does he have to go?' But Sally's appeal carried no conviction;
we all knew the answer.

I began to pack my gear about me, my mind numb, unable to
reach a conclusion. I had to walk out of the door, that I understood. I knew that outside the police and their allies were searching the country for me; at railway stations, ports and airports; in
clubs, streets and the homes of any known contacts. Already they
would have questioned Maggie and Dick, Balls Up, Bluie and

others. But what else was there? What was Ray holding back? What was it that made him have difficulty in looking me in the eye?

Yet what could I do about it? It was the sort of chance I had to take for I had no alternative other than roaming the dangerous streets.

'Thanks, both,' I said. 'I think you know I won't mention your names if I'm caught.'

Sally rose like someone out of a Greek tragedy, glass of poison held before her. I thought she was going to weep.

As I cautiously opened the door Ray called out, 'Mind how you go, boyo. Good luck.' Looking back I nodded. As I reached the stairs my stomach churned.

CHAPTER ELEVEN

I WENT DOWN the stairs quickly, hugging the sides from habit. It was nearly 11 p.m. The broad stretch of lighted foyer opened up below but I did not slacken. Hearing voices, I blew my nose as I crossed the hall and there is no better disguise for the few seconds I needed to gain the doors.

Outside it was crisp and wet. The rain had stopped but lights lanterned across the shiny road surfaces creeping into shelter. The Humber crouched immediately outside. My pace slackened considerably and I went down the stone steps to the street very slowly indeed. As yet I could see no one inside but as I approached, the front nearside door opened and I saw a hand quickly withdraw.

At the car I bent to see who was inside. A white blob under a trilby, white hands on steering wheel, the rest just shapeless shadow. 'Jump in, Spider.' An American; not too pronounced but unmistakable. I hesitated, wondering. There was a slight chuckle. 'It's your choice, brother. No one is gonna make you.' A good, cool, friendly voice, assured—and assurance was something I needed then. I climbed in and closed the door. The engine started at once and the car drew smoothly away.

I tried to get a better look at the driver but his hat was well pulled down and all I could see was a hooked nose; even the chin line was lost by an upturned collar. He drove with easy concentration. 'Don't worry,' he said. 'You'll see me soon enough. The hat and collar routine is to hide me from any other guys who might know me.' I could see him grinning. 'After all, we're pulling a fast one. The British cops wouldn't appreciate it.'

I nodded, then jumped as a voice from behind me asked, 'Cigarette?'

Turning quickly I noticed this one was hatless and fair haired but he had kept himself well out of sight. Now he was leaning on the seat back, square chin resting on forearm, hand loosely holding a packet of cigarettes towards me, one or two extended.

'No thanks.'

He nodded and withdrew the packet, smiling politely then disappearing into the shadows. I could not help thinking that the cigarette offer had been made to let me know he was there, so that it was also a warning.

'My name is Joe and that's Hank in the back. You may as well have a handle for us.'

The names were common enough to be worthless but as he said, it was something to call them by. 'I'm Spider,' I said facetiously. They laughed. Hank said, 'I guess all England knows that by now. You're a very hot potato.' His accent was much richer than Joe's, a Southern drawl. They obviously wanted to be friendly but like Ray, they were not doing it out of friendship. And they did not sound the gangster type if there is a gangster type.

All the time we weaved through the traffic, stopped at lights, caught up behind a bus or taxi I kept half an eye on where we went; the direction seemed to be north towards Highbury, Islington area. I could gain no impression about these two; they were not coppers, I was certain of that, but there was a suspicion of officialdom about them. If they were bent then I had not met two like them. So who and what were they?

Twice I saw a small Austin cruising on our tail, but being hunted sharpens perception and perhaps distorts it. Nearer to Highbury it disappeared. Joe showed no sign of having seen it. Lights flashed past. Occasionally I saw a copper or patrol car. Newspaper posters were on the subject. I was news, big news, seemingly the sole topic on the posters. It did not make me feel any better. Without taking his eyes off the road Joe said, 'You've been seen in several places. Even Scotland.' He chuckled. 'It'll keep the cops busy.' I was too numb to reply. So much for Fairfax and his straight-backed airs. I hoped he was worried sick.

The car drew off from Highbury Grove, taking one of the streets beside the green. Much quieter here and Joe pulled smoothly into the kerb outside a row of early Victorian terraced houses. We all waited by mutual consent until a young couple huddled past, then climbed out and mounted the steps to the front door. Joe in front, Hank behind me. Prisoner and escort. It made no difference.

Joe opened the door and, single file, we went in. The hall had a forty-watt bulb but it was enough to see the usual old style house; shabbily carpeted stairs leading straight up and a couple of brown-painted doors leading off the ground floor. It was the stairs for us, still Indian file, no word being spoken. We went up two flights then Joe produced his keys again and we entered a very large room. There was no shabbiness here but it was not my taste either. Very modern black leather armless settees and armchairs; white rugs, abstract paintings on salmon walls; large stereogram, television, an abundance of uniform occasional tables and a shiny cocktail cabinet which Joe promptly opened.

I gave my usual negative reply to the usual drinks question and as no one had asked me and to show just how independent I still was, I sat down, noticing that the blond stocky Hank had positioned himself by the door. He wore an American-styled English tweed two piece. His eyes were non-committal but his lips over his strong jaw line were toying with a smile—just to reassure me. His face was craggy, heavily-lined about the eyes, strong yet not unfriendly and he did his best to cover the door as if it was his favourite standing position.

Joe, on the other hand, was dark-haired and thin, features like untanned hide, hard and narrow and sharp. Now I could see that he was round-shouldered, held himself badly in a slight stoop and had the habit of running the back of his bony hand under his chin as though one of them itched.

Suddenly I stood up, resigned to this meeting under semi-captivity. 'Do you mind if I make myself comfortable?' I started ditching the stuff from my waistband. As I dumped it I heard a click, which meant locks to me and turned to see Hank walking away from the door. So he had locked it. I didn't think it would be long before I found out why. Still, for the record I did not dump all my gear. Sitting down again, Hank now joined me, eyeing me through screwed-up lids with undisguised interest; he was powerful this one.

'Go ahead,' said Joe belatedly; then over his shoulder, 'You sure you won't have a drink, Spider?' All friendly American Christian name stuff. All together for a cosy chat. About what? I shook my head and Joe brought across what might have been well-iced bourbons. He sat opposite me, Hank to one side. I knew a technique when I saw one; I'd suffered it enough at interrogation. And although I was convinced that these men were not the law I guessed another interrogation was opening up.

Unlike Ray, they did not need their drinks, they were merely props, something with which to divert attention if they needed to. Joe crossed his long legs and relaxed against the black leather, looking like a Red Indian, ill clad in a striped blue suit. I wondered at his ancestry and his very piercing dark eyes. His free hand was rubbing the stubble on his chin. 'Cheers,' he said, trying to be English as he raised his glass to comfort one and all.

I nodded. And waited. And spotted Hank watching me. Joe would do the talking, Hank would do the prodding.

'Now,' observed Joe, trying the first difficult hurdle, unsure as yet of what made me tick. 'The heat's on for you, right? Your only chance is to get out of the country?'

I nodded unwillingly. England was my home. Yet whichever way I viewed it I knew that he was right.

'Well then,' he smiled, looking even more like a Red Indian in a gaunt, proud way. 'We should have no difficulty in coming to terms. How much do you think what you took from the Chinese Legation is worth?'

Ever since we had entered the room I had been expecting it. I had a slight advantage; I was beginning to place them and mentally cursed Ray Lynch. But they could only know what Ray had told them. So I played it simple. 'About three thousand pounds.'

They exchanged glances and the silent Hank gave a faint nod.

'Three thousand,' mused Joe, still rubbing chin on hand 'That's a lot of money, Spider.'

'In dollars and sterling,' I said.

'We'd have to see the goods,' said Joe. 'They may be worthless.'

'The Chinese don't seem to think so,' I suggested.

'No. True. On the other hand they might have bleated for the hell of it. Got it on you?'

'Of course,' I said as I rose and took the money I had stolen and handed it over.

Joe thumbed through the notes then stared piercingly at me. 'What's the idea?'

'What do you mean?'

'This is all money. Where's the other stuff?'

'Of course it is. What did you expect?'

'You're pulling our leg, Spider.' It was a dangerous growl from Hank.

I turned. 'What are you on about? Ray told me that could get me out of the country; that it would cost me.'

'So you hand it all over, just like that.' Joe flapped the wad in the air and I could see a slow anger simmering as he hunched forward. Suddenly they were not friendly any more.

'Be your age,' I said. 'I'm in your manor, wanted, and there are two of you. You can take me any time you want, take all I have. By being open with you I hoped that you would be half-way to being reasonable. I'm expecting most of that back!'

Joe decided to give me the benefit of the doubt and the back of his hand came speculatively into action again; I wondered if he ever rubbed it sore. 'Money was not what we had in mind, Spider. What else did you take?'

'What's Ray been telling you? Look,' I exploded, 'I'm just a bloody burglar. What do you think I took?'

Hank got up and produced a fistful of papers, dailies, evenings. My face stared like a zombie from the evenings, and to my dismay there was a photo of Maggie. Joe pointed to them. 'In each of these the Chinese accuse you of stealing documents, right?'

'Not that again. First Ray, now you. You can't believe them, can you? You're Americans, you must know that. I'm a creeper and that's my haul. I didn't know it would blow up like this.'

'We are not going entirely on what the Chinese say. We have other sources of information.'

Fairfax would hardly tell them. And I was the only other one who knew.

'Balls,' I said.

The silence was like a current, flowing, sharp and petrifying. I had never seen two men go so still.

Then Joe gradually unlocked. He tossed the notes on to a chair and put down his glass. As he rubbed his long chin he eyed me balefully. 'So you're gonna play the innocent.' In restrained anger his accent was thicker. 'You know that we can toss you straight into the can?'

'Anyone could. Anyone with the opportunity.'

'Then what gives with you? Why play the sucker? Look,' he said, both hands coming up pleadingly. 'Let's not cross wires, huh? Maybe we started badly.' He licked his lips and his bright gaze faltered and I realized that he had not expected snags. 'We can get you out, right? But it's not money we want. We have a shrewd idea of what you hoisted and we're willing to pay for it.' He quickly looked at Hank for backing. 'We are willing *to pay you*. Now do you understand?'

'Of course. And believe me I wish I had something to sell. But this is all twaddle about secret documents.' While I spoke I wondered at my own motive for maintaining loyalty to a man who had betrayed me.

'We don't think so.' Joe stood up. He might be thin but he would know a trick or two. 'Undress, Spider.'

I saw the chunky Hank rise. 'Get stuffed,' I said. Joe spread his hands. 'Now look, feller, be reasonable. You said yourself that we can take you. Well, that's what we'll have to do if you're intent on being stupid.'

I got ready to kick his shin if he came nearer then gave up the idea as Hank joined him with a snub-nosed ·38 in his beefy hand. And Hank wasn't trying to smile any more. Their charm had been replaced with cold-blooded zeal. They did not like being made fools of.

Joe gave it one more throw. 'Look, Spider, on security matters your government and ours play it very close together. This time they seem to be holding out on us. We're just curious, that's all. We've no intention of using it against them.'

'How much is it worth?'

I could almost see him sigh his relief. A quick glance at Hank, then, 'Not less than eight thousand dollars, not more than twelve, depending on what it is.'

'That's a lot to pay for curiosity,' I said, rising. Before his anger could move I started to strip.

They went through my clothes like the experts they were, using a powerful light on the hems of underwear and shirt. Nor did they forget my shoes and socks. Then I was treated to further indignities and I was examined as if I was secreting drugs in nick. They even combed my hair with a flea comb. They knew their onions but weren't too pleased at the end of it.

I dressed and sat down again. So did they. Joe actually reached for his drink and sipped at it; the prop had become medicinal. And they stared at me hostilely yet thoughtfully, as if by this alone they could penetrate my secret. I certainly wasn't telling two Americans the secret indiscretions of our Foreign Secretary, who by now was doing a bit of sweating himself, I suspected.

Good. I had to suffer. And it would be *my* jail sentence. I wa
bound to finish there.

'May I have a drink now?' I suggested.

They did not answer, still giving me the silent stare. Then Joe
made one of his observations. 'The fact that you are holding ou
makes it the more interesting. You'll talk eventually, Spider.'

'Torture? I didn't think you people went in for that.'

'Listen,' snarled Hank, and because he spoke so seldom it wa
more effective. 'You're a two-bit hood the police would give their
eyes for right now. You've embarrassed your own country. No
one will shed tears if you're roughed up a little before we hand
you over.' Which was probably true, so I shut up. Then I went
over to the drinks cabinet and poured myself a bourbon because
there was no Scotch. I did not like bourbon but I needed the
warmth and temporary strength it could give me. They made no
attempt to interfere for they were mulling over the problem. Joe
obviously made the decisions and his face had the ascetic quality
of sharp intelligence, even so it seemed that he required the
physical strength and automatic backing of Hank to finalize.
Right now he probably wanted to talk it over with Hank but
would not do so in front of me nor did he want to leave me.

'Would you like me to wait outside?' I asked facetiously. They
glared woodenly. Let's face it, they had a problem; they could
either beat it out of me or try to trick me. It depended on how
important it was to them.

But while I was putting on the face, doing my own private bit
of flag waving, I did not feel so cocky myself. Where was all this
leading? Fairfax had sold me out. Ray wouldn't have handed me
over for nothing. Could I survive from night to night like this?
I knew that I could not. Everyone wanted a return. Soon I would
be on my own, on the streets; watching shadows and running from
those that moved. And it would not be long after that before I
was running from those that did not move. I could not survive,
not in winter because I could not even take the refuge the tramps
took.

I sat down and looked at the two Americans who were now
giving the matter due thought. More sanely, I suggested, 'I have
the money. Why not make the best of it? You say you can get me
out—well I'll pay. That was always my idea.' And what would I
do when I was out? But I refused to dwell on it.

'We don't need your money.' I could now see a red weal on
the back of Joe's hand. He needed a shave. 'Spider, we might up
the price, appreciably. But we must have some inkling of what
you took from the Chinese. God dammit, we know you haven't it
on you so why are you worried?'

'Well, I'll tell you. I can't read Chinese so I put it all back. In
the safe. I probably got their papers mixed up so they squawked.'

'All right, have it the hard way.' They both stood up.

'Look,' I said hastily. 'Why don't you talk it over in the next room?'

'We don't need to. And I don't think our lock will hold you. Right?'

'You can't tell. Some of these locks . . .' But Joe cut me short.

'And if the lock did hold you, why you're a pro, Spider. You'd simply hack out the door frame. Right?'

I did not reply. They had made up their minds. I rose rapidly.

'I'm sorry, feller, but you've only yourself to blame. If there was some other way . . .' They began to close in and I let Hank have my bourbon straight in the eyes. It was a mistake. He came in like a tank with its visor down. Blindness did not stop him. He was on beam and gave me a swipe which I half rode but which nearly took my head off. I fell sideways over an armchair, dazed and in pain. I kept rolling from sheer instinct. Wobbling to my knees I saw a pair of blue clad legs and swayed as one of them drew back.

Trying to collect my senses I rolled again and swung my legs out to catch Joe off balance. I shakily reached my feet as I heard him crash. The room was swimming as if I was in a fish bowl being moved about. In the middle of the wavering bowl I saw Hank wiping the spirit from his eyes and trying to peer round for me at the same time. I was still too dazed to take advantage of Joe's position and he was up on his feet before I could move towards him.

His head was clear but his pride was hurt. He came at me like a scythe, a fast chopping movement that thumped my shoulder and momentarily paralysed my left arm. My knees began to go but I conjured that little extra and kneed him in the crotch as he grabbed me to make the final cut. As he jack-knifed I thumped him hard on the jaw, almost breaking my knuckles. Grabbing him as he began to fall I thanked God he was skin and bone for I could see Hank advancing with his ·38 drawn, and deadweight even Joe took some holding.

But I did hold him and kept him close to me as a shield from red-eyed angry Hank. Making a supreme effort I managed Joe with one hand and groped under his jacket with the other. Finding the harness I reached the butt and pulled it out. By slipping my gun hand under Joe's armpit I was able to increase my support of him at the same time aiming at Hank.

'Drop it, Hank.' I sounded like one of them, but he got the message, realizing that he would hit Joe if he fired. Yet he hesitated.

'I've nothing to lose, Hank. Everyone's after me and I face a life sentence. It wouldn't be any extra for snuffing you.' He worked it out, saw logic and dropped his gun.

'Move back from it.'

He wanted to get his bare hands on me but he moved. While

he was still backing I dropped Joe in a heap and quickly scooped up the other gun, not moving my gaze from Hank's blazing sore eyes.

'Unlock the door, Hank, and leave the key in the lock.' Hank wasn't arguing any more. His training was against him; he was far more certain than I was that I would fire. He unlocked the door and moved aside when I waved the gun. Backing on to the door I slipped out the key.

I made him move over to the far wall, then went to pick up my money from where Joe had tossed it. I also picked up one or two of my tools, leaving the nylon behind.

'Now I'm going out, Hank, and I'm locking the door behind me. If you rush the door while I'm still the other side of it I'll empty this gun at you.'

He did not say anything. Backing to the door I opened it, slipped through, and quickly locked it. I ran down the stairs and was out on the porch in seconds. For some moments I stood there in shadow. They had not handled me too well; their blatant offer of money for a sell-out had been made without real knowledge of me. I was certainly no saint but I was not a traitor either; the old country still meant something to me, although I couldn't tell you why.

From under the portico I took in the wet, bleak scene; it was drizzling again and the lines of parked cars huddled for protection. I was back on the streets with nowhere to go and was reluctant to move. The weight of the gun in my hand made me realize that I was still holding it. In the shadow I opened the cylinder and dropped the bullets then did the same with the other gun which I had stuffed in my pocket. Firearms had no part in my life of crime so I stepped forward and dropped both guns into the basement.

There was no one to turn to this time, so I took the steps to the street slowly. I suppose part of me was on the look-out but right then I did not care too much. I could try breaking into a church; might snatch a few hours' sleep if I could bear the cold. And then what about the next night—and the next?

With a full day's growth on my chin I must look a thug. I was grateful then for the indifferent street lighting. Turning up my collar against the rain, pushing my hands into my trouser pockets for a little warmth, I hugged the shadows and strolled slowly north. I was feeling sorry for myself but I reckoned I had good cause. What worried me most was the desperation I was feeling; I would have to eat and drink and that meant more stealing for I dare not show my face.

Hearing the suction of tyres on a wet road behind me, I pulled in as far as I could. Was it seeking parking space? Turning round, I could see its approaching black shape beyond the line of parked cars. There was no police light on top but it might be a Q car.

When it passed a parking space I began to run for I knew that I had been seen. Behind me I heard the car accelerate slowly. As I lengthened my stride someone stepped from the shadow and put out a foot. I went flying, hitting the wet pavement and skidding along it on my face. The pain in my knees was worst, but some-one saw to it that I did not suffer and tapped the back of my head with a blunt instrument.

Oblivion solved my problems for some time. During the black period I did not dream at all and in a way was robbed of its com-fort for I knew nothing. It was when the darkness began to recede, light vacillating through my heavy, fluttering lids that my prob-lems began. Hearing my own moans bore oral confirmation that the pain had returned; my knees, hands, face—and my head—were broken, my brain swelling through the cracks in agony. And I felt sick.

I had learned another language for I heard myself talking without understanding, then realized that there was another voice. But the realization was thin, unconsciousness still almost complete. Recovery was something I tried to fight off with the return of feeling. Oblivion was what I needed but the will to discover was too strong. I struggled back feeling very sick indeed, vaguely wondering why I bothered.

I tried to feel my head but my arms would not move. This more than anything made me strive for consciousness. Anything that smacks of retardment or shackling immediately reminds me of nick and how I loathed it. So I fought back, trying to concen-trate through the great agonizing thump in my head. Before I finally came round I knew that my arms were tied behind me.

They had me in a basement. The rough brickwork came swing-ing into vision before all else. Then I smelled damp and even-tually could see it staining the walls in dark undulating patches as I finally focused. A single bare bulb dangled on a dusty flex.

Two men loomed into sight. Always two of them, I thought. But not the same two.

CHAPTER TWELVE

I WAS WEARY, sick, and in great pain. Being bound to a chair
in the middle of a filthy cellar did not raise my morale either. I
was tired of being a tennis ball, passed from player to player
especially when the players kept changing identity. And I was
utterly tired of being used.

They approached slowly and with prison cunning I did not
reveal that I had come fully to and let my head droop sideways.
The way I felt it wasn't too difficult. I was catching on hourly to
the fantastic situation I had landed myself in. These two looked
the Russian equivalent of Joe and Hank.

There were differences; they were older for a start; late forties
or early fifties; they appeared more experienced and had certainly
fixed me from the outset. And there were similarities; the
pudding-faced, thick-set one had not Hank's pleasant looks and
needed only a cloth cap to appear the typical revolutionary, but
he had the same bleak determination, and in the hard brown
creviced eyes was utter ruthlessness; this man was harder than
Hank, much harder, and he was not restricted by any reluctance
to strike an Englishman. He had a way of quietly staring as if I
was a specimen object and not a human being; he emptied me of
hope. This man would respond only to his own impulses or an
order from a superior.

The other man was obviously a higher official; well groomed,
in a beautifully cut suit. But for his handsome, high-cheekboned
Slavic face, he might have come up from his country estate. He
was a grey man; clothes, thick waving hair, eyes like hard glazed
early Chinese porcelain. Even his fine brows were grey and his
tie which should have contained more contrast. But he was a
gentleman to his manicured fingernails, if the definition is
accepted as breeding and poise. Tall and elegant, a quiet hypnotic
charm exuding as he neared me, a reserved smile playing with
firm lips, eyes crinkled to reassure but the porcelain brightness
untouched by its props.

I prickled, unable to take my eyes off him; he had a demanding
presence and held his holdered cigarette in the Western fashion.
Something about him chilled me through. Evil? That's how it
reached me, veiled behind a compelling urbanity.

Whether it was accident or design I don't know, but already he
had used a psychological weapon against me. To an old lag the
space of the cellar represented possible freedom for I was planted
right in the middle, but my pinioned arms and legs meant I would
have to pay for it. This boy knew his stuff. I sat there, feeling
trapped, frustrated and a bloody fool on exhibit.

Matey approached nearer and I was left with no illusions that he would have fitted in with the court of St. Petersburg at least as well as with his present masters. Cold efficiency would be his métier, his sources of direction immaterial.

'Good morning, Mr. Scott.' A marked accent but complete fluency. 'Let me apologize for your discomfort. I would rather untie you, especially a man who has suffered so much confinement, but your rather rugged treatment of the two unfortunate C.I.A. men led me to take reluctant precautions. Under any other circumstances I would naturally take your word that you would not attempt to escape.' He smiled with complete conviction and this was his strength. Women would go for it if his interests leaned that way.

You polished bastard, I thought. Still simulating half awareness I wondered how he and Fairfax would react to one another. It would be interesting for their approach work was quite different. My mind must have wandered for a bit for I suddenly heard words I did not catch, then I received a tremendous flat hander round the ear and crashed sideways with the chair on to the rough stone floor.

My ears had a high-pitched whine in them and my body was a series of private battles. I could not move even if I had the will, but someone, Pudding Face for his Highness would not spoil his manicure, roughly righted the chair with me slumped heavily in it. I don't know which of them had hit me, it had been so fast and unexpected.

'I trust that cleared your head?'

I gave up acting asleep.

'A useful remedy, the hard slap. Doctors will tell you. The delivery was purely medicinal and I can see that it has already worked. Good. Can you hear me clearly now?'

I nodded and glared balefully at him. That had settled it; they would get nothing out of me. Russian gits. I was angry but knew little about them or I would not have been so confident.

Matey smiled at me. 'You look as if you would like to kill me, but you shouldn't, y'know. I want to help you and believe me, you are nothing without help; quite doomed.'

I tried to loosen my wrists but gave up.

'Li Tshien is dying. You remember him? I am told that you smashed his head against the desk. There is also a complication, although it will make no difference ultimately to the poor man; it will, however, harden a judge's and a jury's heart against you— some of his smashed spectacles are embedded in his eyes. So he is blind, too.'

I thought back desperately. I remembered the smashed glasses. My stomach heaved and I wanted to be sick. I had not smashed his head against the desk, but I would not get far denying it.

'There is nothing in the papers about that,' but my voice did not sound my own.

'You mean the English papers? I can assure you that it is in all European newspapers, and the Chinese and our own. It does not read very well and the stigma on British Intelligence has never been worse.'

'What have they got to do with it?'

'Oh, my dear fellow. Really. Sir Stuart Halliman must be exceedingly disturbed. But why did you do it? Did you belatedly realize that he would betray you? If you did you were right. We all know the crass hypocrisy of the English gentleman.'

He was trying to trap me of course, hoping I would burst out in some kind of defence and thereby betray myself. It was clear that nobody but Fairfax and the Chinese knew for certain what had been in the box. The inclination was strong in me to retaliate but I held back with difficulty.

Matey was watching me intently behind his smile. '*We* would not betray you. We look after our people. Always. And they are well rewarded. Do you believe that?'

'Yes,' I said, truthfully.

'Why do you believe it?'

'I can read.'

'You are thinking of Blake and others? They are only the obvious ones, Mr. Scott. Our success is based on complete honesty to those who help us. It is the only pattern for success. If I say that we will smuggle you out you can accept without question that that is precisely what we will do. We are very good at it.' He raised his brows modestly but was not boasting. 'You will be well looked after.'

'I'm not a communist.'

'That does not matter. We will find a good use for you. You have talent and attributes which we can use. We may not pay as much as the Americans but you would be safer. In any event, you would not want for anything.'

'You are offering this for free?'

'If you help us.'

'What am I supposed to do?'

This was the crunch. Very carefully he removed the stub of his cigarette, dropped it and ground it out with a precise movement. He blew carefully into the holder, wiped it and with a handkerchief inserted it into his breast pocket. I am certain that his mind was working in the same calculating way. His smile had gone and it made a chilling difference to his gaze. I was afraid when I stared back at him, but pride would not allow me to drop my gaze.

'I think you know well enough,' he answered coldly. Now that the crisis had arisen he showed no pretence. 'Let me have the documents you stole from the Chinese and I promise that you will have no further worries.'

He was better at it than Joe and twice as deadly. His offer was probably genuine. I believed that they had kept their promises for the reasons he had given. Word gets around. It was tempting. Politics meant nothing to me; politicians had the gift of the gab, skins like rhinos and as much real ability. They were greedy, vain and useless. So what did it matter whether I was operating under the Russians or the British. I needed security. But was I the type ever to get it? I wanted to know more, and there was only one way of seeing how many faces Boris had.

'Everybody seems to think I stole documents because it was the Chinese Legation. You've searched me; you know what I stole. I wouldn't have the first idea of what documents to steal.'

'If you were sent in for them you would have been briefed.'

'Who the hell would send me in with a record like mine?'

'Mr. Scott, I have no time to argue, particularly with a man who seems determined to secure his own downfall. Let us consider your position. The whole British police force is searching for you. Without our help they must find you. The Chinese have made such a fuss that you will get maximum penalty and soon the additional charge of murder will be made. Do you want our help or don't you?'

'Of course I want it.'

'Then where are the documents? They are the price of your freedom?'

'There aren't any. Not that I took, that is.'

He looked much as Joe had done but in a more frightening way. When his charming smile left him it was like gazing at a death mask. Pudding Face stood by in a completely subservient position but I would hate to see him given his head. Boris was not staring at me to determine whether or not I spoke the truth. His mind would not have dwelt on it, he was accepting that I was lying because he decided a long time ago that everyone did under interrogation. What he was now deciding was what would most effectively make me change my mind.

'I was hoping,' he said, 'that you would be helpful without undue pressure. Voluntary co-operation is more valuable than the screaming confession of a tortured man. There are more refined ways of making you talk but they take time and of that we have precious little. However I have protected you so far from something you will now have to know.'

Turning to Pudding Face (he called him Fyodor) he rattled off some Russian and the hatchet man ran out on the double. Matey walked up and down in front of me with his hands behind his back, not giving me a glance as if he was very sure of what he was doing and had no doubt at all of the outcome.

But the interlude offered me no hope. I began to see my earlier resolve as plain wishful thinking, and I was sick to the stomach at the thought of Li Tshien. I could not remember about his eyes but I remembered well enough his deathly pallor.

Fyodor returned with an open cardboard box and gave it to Boris who promptly held it out for me to see. Inside were two ·38 pistols which had a vaguely familiar look. He knew how to excite my nervous system all right. The guns were all too ominous.

'Do you recognize them, Mr. Scott?'

I began to sweat. He took a pencil from his pocket and lifted one of the guns out by the trigger guard, dangling it under my nose. 'Can you smell cordite? You should, they've been recently fired.'

I could smell it all right and that wasn't all that smelled. You bloody bastards, I thought.

'We had been watching the house for some time. The C.I.A. can be very careless. It can be proved that you were there. Mr. Lynch of the *Daily Express* called earlier. Then our American friends left with him and returned with you. I don't think that Mr. Lynch would hold out for long under police pressure, do you?'

It was strange how he became more English as he neared his objective; his accent was now barely audible; his gestures more casual.

'What are you getting at?' I did not feel so good.

'The opportunity was too good to miss. We saw you discard the guns in the basement and drop the ammunition. It was a foolish thing to do in any circumstances. So we collected them ourselves. We found eight of the twelve rounds but they were more than adequate.'

I had suddenly stepped into an icebox. I cannot recall a spasm of cold so intense as this one. I tried to stop the shudder but he could not have missed it for it hit me like a shock. And then he made me wait knowing that at last he had me on a piece of string. Dread addled my brain. It was all leading to a point where I had no choice left. Closing my eyes shut out his face but brought the horror of reality nearer and bloodied figures with hollowed eyes loomed up behind my lids. The pain I had felt before had gone, dramatically anaesthetized by a gripping fear. Before I had at least had a bizarre hope, now I had none.

Opening my eyes again, he was smiling, at last genuinely with a touch of sadistic pleasure. Fyodor still wore no expression at all. Matey stood with one hand holding the box and the other dangling the gun. He was rocking gently on his heels, well satisfied. 'It must be unusual,' he taunted, 'for the spider to be caught in his own web. You are quick to perceive. I give you full marks.'

I held my tongue because only the ripest blasphemy entered my mind and it would be wasted on an atheist like him.

'You realize why I hold the gun like this?'

I realized but said nothing. He would keep it up now, pushing me all the way.

'Your fingerprints are all over it. And the other one, of course.'
He turned to Fyodor with a smile and I saw a flash of gold teeth.

'How would you like me to return these guns to the room where the two dead Americans still lie?'

'You cold-blooded Russian bastard,' I yelled. 'Why did you kill them?'

'But didn't I explain? An opportunity to blame someone else is all too rare. They were of no great importance, those two, not even to the Americans; they were of the lower order of the C.I.A. and they bungled the handling of you which I won't do, I can assure you. They did not really warrant killing but the chance to do it without taking blame was too tempting. You are an ugly killer. You blind people before they die and you shoot people dead. There is not a person in the world who will not believe these things once you are captured. Even the charming Miss Parsons will believe, because the weight of evidence will be so strong. Regardless of what it does to you it will certainly break her heart. It cannot be easy for a decent-minded girl to eradicate from her mind that she has been made love to by a triple killer. Imagine what that will do to her.'

I did. I began to wonder how he knew about Maggie then remembered that a couple of newspapers had tried to interview her and had taken her photograph. I fervently hoped that she would do nothing silly. Boris, here, knew how to turn the knife in the wound all right. I rubbed my wrists raw struggling with those bonds. All I wanted to do was to get my hands round his neck and squeeze the life out of him. I struggled so hard that I crashed over on my side and only then did the real frustration taunt me. Tears of rage pricked my eyes because I could not get at them and they just watched impassively, doing nothing to help me up.

My temper began to abate as they knew it would and I could feel blood trickling on to my hands where I had seared my wrists with the rope.

'You're a very emotional man. I always understood the British to be level headed.'

'You murdering bastard,' I snarled.

He laughed unpleasantly. 'You have it wrong. *You* are the murderer—you must learn to accept the idea. After all we have only anticipated the inevitable on the one hand and applied a little backing on the other.'

As I began to cool off I felt drained. My spirit was at its lowest. I was already in a bad enough fix before this bastard got hold of me. My pains returned slowly as if under the direct control of Boris. There were new ones in my arm and shoulder as I lay. 'Can you get Fido to help me up?' A last sling of bravado.

'Is that how you see him? A dog? I don't think it will disturb him. You can stay there until I have some sense from you.'

He looked taller from ground level and I could see how brightly polished his shoes were. At last I detected colour in him; he wore red socks. Well, that figured. 'What's the deal now?' I groaned.

'Once I have the documents I will dispose of these guns.'

It was damned difficult eyeing him on my side so I stopped trying and spoke to the far damp patch on a level with my gaze. 'What about getting me out?'

'That still stands. We will see that you will be beyond British justice.'

There were two ways of taking that and in my present morbid state I did not like the sound of it.

'Are you going to kill me afterwards?'

He hesitated and obviously had not expected the direct question; I made the effort to gaze at his face but it did not help me.

'You deserve it. You have behaved idiotically. But no, you won't be killed if for no other reason than that bodies are not easily disposed of and I don't like hasty plans. If you were found dead other governments would then know that we or someone now held the documents.'

'These documents aren't what you think.'

'We will judge that. If the Chinese had them they should be interesting enough. But I see that you at last have the sense to admit their existence.'

I stayed silent for a bit. It was the first time that I had admitted it to anyone, and I felt wretched. They had sprung the trap so tight that I was left with no alternative. Also, Maggie had enough on her mind and I couldn't see Dick remaining in the force as the brother of a triple murderer. I had no illusions that Boris could and would make it stick. He was a professional, a hackneyed word these days, but he was one, every fibre of him. It was the only thing in him that I appreciated.

He spoke in Russian and Fido got me straightened without too much strain. I was glad to be upright but they had no intention of my getting too used to the idea.

'Where are they?'

I had a pang of resistance followed by hopelessness. They would get it from me in the end. 'I hid them in someone's flat.'

'Where?'

'Look,' I said. 'You can't go barging in on some old lady. It will frighten her to death and it won't do your image any good. I'll have to get them myself.'

'Exactly where are they?'

Again I toyed briefly with the idea of lying to him, then I saw the gun box and realized it was useless; there was another reason —I was convinced that Boris never missed a lie. Like I sensed danger he had his own highly sensitive lie detector. He might miss the truth on occasion but never the lie. So I told him, hating myself and listening to my own voice with great humility. I did not want to know myself.

He listened carefully then mulled it over after passing the gun box back to Fido, who trotted off.

'I think you are right,' he said finally. 'You are a trained burglar, a good one to break in on the Chinese like that, so I accept that you get them back. While you are in her flat, however, we will not have our eye on you. That worries me.'

I shivered as he fixed me with a special laser beam stare that went through me so that I felt it. 'I'm only going because of the guns and what they can do to me and my friends. You'll still have those, so what are you worried about?'

'You've shown yourself to have misplaced loyalties.'

'So I've been told. They won't help me now.'

'No. But I intend to ensure that you are in no position to act foolishly. I'm going to see that you are robbed of some of your energy and strength. You must be slowed down. You're not a good risk.'

I did not take too much heed of this. He was being ultra cautious. Fido came back and Boris gave him a quiet instruction to unfasten the bands holding me to the chair. My hands were still tied but I was now able shakily to stand up.

I stood swaying a bit, then I stretched to ease my limbs, breathing deeply. Fido hit me in the guts in the middle of my intake. My breath burst like a blow-out and I doubled in an agony that left me helpless and sagging on my knees. The pain had all my concentration, my lungs were rasping, then a white hot carving knife went through them as he struck me with incredible force between the shoulder blades. The hatchet man was getting a reward for being a good dog.

Sprawled now on my face I was trying to retch, breathe and ease the pain at the same time. There was no retaliation I could give for it was taking everything I had not to flake out. If I had had any sense I would have let myself go, but I was cursed with a stubbornness that had got me into more trouble than not. That silly little Union Jack shot out of my head because I was not going to let a bloody Russian see me as chicken. For the same reason I would not cry out though God knows I wanted to as his boot nearly stove in my ribs.

Christ, I thought as the pain engulfed me so that I curled up like a hedgehog, if it goes on I won't be able to do the job. But the dog had to have his bone and I was punched and booted around that floor until the sheer agony of it made me wish I was dead. When I vomited I nearly choked myself and the excruciating pain in my straining guts made me throw up again. There was no way I could wipe my mouth and I wanted to beg them to unblock my nose and windpipe. But I said nothing, biting down a fantastic swelling hatred. In a few minutes I was sure I would lose consciousness.

Half choking I took what he had to give me only because I could avoid none of it. Not once did he touch my legs, arms or face. Pain became my sole sensation. Death, I thought blindly, would bring relief. Save my friends. Always my friends. I would be out of their way; no further embarrassment to them. Do them all a favour. Spider. Die. You're nearly there. Just let yourself slip. The pain will stop and they'll have to do their own burglary and might bodge it and get caught.

Then into my wondering mind came a floating vision of the old lady I had not even seen. If she got in the way they would kill her and it would be my fault. And if I died the bloody sadist who was kicking me to death would live to kill again. By Christ I'd fix him some day. Hold on, Spider. Hate him with everything you have. Concentrate on it. Hold that thread and you'll eventually get him.

Voices. Somewhere, but on a limbo. In Hell; it couldn't be the other place, not for Spider. A command. It must have been, it was sharp, cutting through space. Silence. Void. The earth spinning, as I rolled away from it towards the sun, feeling its increasing heat all over me. Put the brakes on quick. Can't stop. Heat overwhelming. I'm on fire. I rolled and rolled, trying to back away from the tremendous heat until I realized that it was part of me. I *was* the sun. It was me. Red hot, holding the earth to my magnetism. The blue planet. But it wasn't. It was changing colour, yellow. Stationary. Strange shape. And glaring, glaring until it blinded me.

I opened my eyes more carefully. Still the glare but not so bad. It was nearer. No cloud. Dust layers and I could see the bright glow of the earth's centre glowing hot from this distance. I looked again. Very, very carefully, for even moving my lips sent spasms through me. God. The light bulb.

Had the kicking stopped? He had left me with a body of inflamed nerves, and grossly bruised muscles. On top of everything I had tremendous cramp in my arms and slowly realized that I was lying on top of them. Rolling sideways I was sick again. So sick that I did not want to move ever again. Convulsions ran through me. I wanted to stop them because each bore more pain. But I had no strength and was on my last ebb of resistance. They had timed it to the last vicious kick. Experts; professionals; bastards.

I heard a choking rasp and realized that I was gasping for air. Suddenly I was being lifted as if a crane had hooked me through the arm. When I realized that my arms were free I nearly wept with relief, would have done, but although I could not see them I knew they were there.

Someone was still holding my arms, then they let go and I

crashed to the floor. I was left there, but I could use my hands now and after a while began to push myself up, first on to my knees where I stayed for some time, and finally, very shakily, on to my feet.

I stood swaying like a drunk, the coarse brick walls moving through mist. I was not sure whether I would not be better on the deck. The agony would be about the same. Deciding to stay where I was did not help me put a foot forward so I stood rooted, weaving like a reed in a wind, holding my guts with both hands.

Then came the voice; sharp, authoritative, loathsome: 'Come, dear fellow, you are not hurt that badly. Pull yourself together.'

The stupid fool. He had let Fido go too far. I had no strength to answer.

'Walk.'

He might have shouted, 'By the right, quick march.'

Taking a step I felt myself going, gasped in agony, righted myself, and took another as if I was in a bog. I tried opening my eyes wider. Things steadied a little. My breath was still rasping and belatedly I realized that I could now reach for a handkerchief so I wiped my nose and mouth and it did me good.

They were standing in front of me. Fido did not even look as if he had enjoyed himself. Maybe he was one of these freaks who get no satisfaction until the victim is screaming for mercy; maybe it made no difference anyway.

They were near but were not exactly risking life and limb. Had I reached out for them I would have fallen. I had not the strength of a baby. So this was slowing me down? I took another tottering pace like a child learning to walk with my arms raised for balance.

'We must hurry. We have not all night.'

I focused on Boris and tried some words through gluey lips and a swollen tongue.

'You think I can manage like this? You're mad. I couldn't rob a money-box.'

'Walk round the room. Come now.'

I suppose it was less painful than having the sadist at me again, but only marginally. I set out round the walls like a doubled up tortoise. I wanted to vomit again but there was nothing left and my empty stomach heaved against ruptured muscle until I had to lean against the wall. There was no question of playing against time. I knew that the job had to be done in darkness and I wanted it over. If it was left to the following night Boris might take it into his head to slow me down again. Anyway I wanted an end to the whole business; I wanted out and away from these shores where I could sit and lick my wounds. So for my own sake I set off round the cellar again, trying to make progress. I think Boris realized it for he kept quiet. One thing was for sure; I would not be able to break into a run and that was all he was worried about. Just the same, when I stared over at him I caught a quick specula-

tive expression as he wondered whether for once he had mis-
calculated. At least he was concerned enough to explain:

'Your head, your legs and your arms are untouched. So you
should be able to think and use your limbs. I'm sorry that it was
necessary to beat you, but I'm prepared to take no risks. Drugs
would have affected your whole body and I want your fingers and
wits alive. Now we must hurry.'

Have you ever tried using your limbs when your body is
roughed up? Every step hits at the stomach, every arm movement
tightens the pectoral and back muscles. Breathing was difficult. I
gave it three more slow marches round the exercise yard, finding
myself a very special isolation prisoner guarded by two screws
who could teach our screws a thing or two. They would have
the Mountbatten Committee on these boys in no time.

I was half dead but ready. Giving Boris a nod of acquiescence
produced a black scarf from Fido and for a terrible moment I
thought he was going to strangle me as he approached. Backing
off, Boris called out to me that he would merely blindfold me and
my relief made me realize that I no longer wanted to die. The
regular masochist, that's me.

Between them they helped me up some worn stone steps, one
on each arm. Although I could not see a thing through the thick
scarf my sensitive feet detected the wear. Not that it helped at
all. It was hard going up those steps and I gave the odd groan
to remind Boris that he had overdone it. Certainly they were not
rough in their handling of me now. They needed me.

We stopped on level ground; a key rattled in a lock; double
mortice. But it was instinctive appreciation of a situation. I had
no one to tell these little gems of wisdom and they would merely
clutter my brain with a lot of other useless information. Still, it
kept me in trim and told me that my mind was functioning
again. . . .

Cold air suddenly blasted in, grasping my overheated body
with icy tendrils that sent shudders through me. More steps, open
on one side I detected, and leading to street level I guessed. Iron
gate swinging back. Silence. Making sure the street was empty?
Then I was bundled forward and gasped with pain as I was forced
to bend to get into a car. Once in it was not too bad but I was
cold and could not stop shivering. Car doors banged, someone got
in beside me; nothing was said. No wasted words with these boys.

We moved off. During the first few minutes we took so many
corners too fast that I was flung around until I howled at them to
cut it out. I knew that they were trying to fox my directional
sense but they did not have to be so stupid about it. Then the car
slowed, my bandage was whipped off and I was not surprised to
find myself sitting next to Fyodor.

It was all right for me to look now so I did not much bother.
We were in suburban London and the streets were still empty and

wet. I looked at my watch; almost three-thirty. I had left Joe's place I suppose about midnight. In three and a half hours flat these boys were well on the way to getting what they wanted.

Boris issued instructions from the driver's seat without looking round. 'When you have the documents, return with Fyodor to the car. We will then keep to our part of the bargain. Oh, and I have arranged for some of my men to be strategically placed round the block of flats.'

That was not what worried me for I would have expected it of him. Boris would write his own name down daily in case he caught himself lying. 'What's this about Fido? I don't want him with me. I go into that flat alone.'

'Oh no. Fyodor goes in with you.'

CHAPTER THIRTEEN

THIS THREW ME. It was going to be bad enough without such a complication. 'I'm not working with him breathing down my neck. The old girl sleeps with her bedroom door open; you're pushing your luck.'

Boris was undisturbed. 'Fyodor will silence her if she wakes. He can help, you see.'

My body was not hot any more. The cold was like sudden cramp. To my dismay when I looked out we were nearly there.

'I'm not doing a job worrying whether Fido here is going to croak the old girl and then pin yet another one on me. I'm not *that* much a bloody fool. I never work with anyone; take it or leave it.'

I was not feeling brave; I was worried sick. Boris was quiet for a while and his preoccupation was apparent from the way he drove round the block of flats three times before gliding into a side street not too far away. The manoeuvre was partly observation of course but I knew that I had thrown him a bit. Slipping into a parking spot he pulled up and switched off his lights and engine. We sat there silent in the darkness while he made up his mind.

'All right,' he said. 'You go into the flat alone. Fyodor will wait outside the flat door.'

I still did not like it but knew that was as far as he would go. 'O.K.' Getting out of the car was no more painful than getting in and my breath caught me like a skewer in the lungs. From Boris's standpoint the beating made good sense for they could have overtaken me with no trouble at all had I tried to run; the thought never crossed my mind for it took me all my time to cross the road. Fyodor padded along beside me and I suddenly realized that I had not heard him speak.

Not quite four o'clock; about the quietest hour of night when sleep is at its deepest. Sleep? What was that? I had not had any time for two nights, though strangely I was far from it at this time. It was a simple enough job I had to do but underrating it could be disastrous; one good penetrating scream is more effective than a burglar alarm.

I did the blowing my nose routine as we crossed the lobby and Fyodor sported a well-pulled-down trilby making him more thug-like than ever. The porter was either making his tea or having a quiet doze somewhere, for my searching eyes couldn't find him. The stairs brought my stomach muscles into play and I suffered. The pain slowed me down and twice I had to stop. Now that his master was not in sight Fido's gaze showed that he re-

gretted not doing a proper job on me. We reached the first floor
and stopped.

Getting my breath I relaxed so that the worst pains ceased and
took note of the two doors. I wondered if Sally and Ray slept with
their respective bottles by their bed. Because of my condition
Fyodor had carried my gear under his jacket and I now held my
hand out for it. I only needed the jemmy, torch and the mica. He
handed them over with reluctance and I briefly considered
thumping his head with the jemmy. But apart from the fact that
it would probably ruin the tool I've no doubt that he would use
some fancy grip that would send me through the wall. When he
tried to follow me to the old lady's door, though, I risked putting
my hand on his chest to stop him. It was like trying to push a
barrel of lead.

'One more step from you and I'll go back and tell Boris.' He
did not understand a whispered word but he got the message. For
a few seconds I looked into the empty depth of his eyes then felt
his pressure relax against me. He was not so dumb that he had not
weighed it up. Frankly it made me nervous that he was there at
all, he was too exposed.

Creeping to the old lady's door I opened it, heard her heavy
breathing, then looked back at Fido. He was standing by the head
of the stairs watching me. Resisting the temptation to give him
the soldier's salute I went in softly, closing the door quietly
behind me.

Regular breathing came from the bedroom and I was glad that
so far she had been spared the drama going on around her. With
luck she would never know and it was better that she did not. A
quick beam showed the lounge door closed so I crossed to open it.
To block off sound I closed it behind me. Now I could use the
torch more freely, provided I focused on the corner I needed.
Behind the armchair I found the carpet as I had left it so I raised
the half-bedded tacks with no trouble and flapped back the
carpet.

There they were, the cause of all the trouble. The letter, the
print and the negative. It was like finding them for the first time.
The same fears hit me. My hand trembled; the print glistened
animatedly in the torchlight. I was weak and in pain but that was
not the cause of my tremor. How could I be any more certain
that the Russians would keep their word than I had been of
Fairfax when faced with these same documents.

My uncertainty was real. Boris did not trust me but he might
consider it necessary to get me out as he had promised. Yet why
should I trust any of them? They were all treacherous liars
behind suave manners.

Finally it was not my fears that persuaded me. I stick to that to
this day. It was the photograph of Britain's Foreign Secretary
caught in a moment of weakness that obliterated all other facets

of his character; that and the letter which must have caused
an agony of mind for him to succumb to blackmail. Maybe I
gave him too much credit. Perhaps I felt it as a national shame
when in fact it might have meant little or nothing to him except
now when he was again under threat but this time by people
more ruthless than himself. Why the hell should I cover for him?

Kneeling in that corner, my fading torch lighting up the glossy
print as if it were an obscene play being spotlighted on stage, my
thoughts and fears were confused. Only of one thing was I
increasingly certain. I could not let a bloody Russian see this—
and then use it against my country, even though I represented
nothing but its criminal element. To allow a Russian to see it was
letting the lot of us down. I could not do it.

So what should I do? Burn them now? Fix the lot of them—
myself included? No imagination was needed to guess at the
sweet revenge Boris would mete out.

Automatically I gently tapped back the tacks then slipped the
photos and letter in my inside pocket. Carefully, with the aid of
the chair, I straightened, barely resisting a groan. I was not fit
enough for profound thought but I had to make up my mind
quickly with Russians outside and Fido keeping the keyhole
warm. And where the hell was it all going to get me? Each step I
took landed me deeper in it. For the first time since becoming
involved with intelligence agents I began to think like them.
Propping myself against the wall I allowed my mind to wander up
the devious paths that Fairfax, Joe and Boris had followed. It was
hard work for me for I was not used to conniving but the only way
I might beat them would be by using their own methods. They
were well practised and I was a beginner at this sort of conflict but
I could try. I'd had enough of being their punch bag and had
little more to lose. Each one I had encountered had pushed me
further in the mire; as sweet a bunch of sadistic hypocrites as you
could meet.

To get back to realities, I wondered whether Boris had men
outside or was he bluffing. How could I get out without Fido
knowing?

Carefully picking my way to the net curtains I pulled them
aside to note French doors leading to the small balcony outside. I
opened the doors, stepped on to the balcony, made sure the curtains were as I had found them, then closed the doors. The chill
air got me again and I huddled back. The humps of other blocks
and buildings reared up like a kid's brick game. The isolated early
riser had switched on the odd light. Above me a baby bawled.
But the streets were silent as yet. Where was Boris down there?
And his men? Was Fido worrying yet?

Looking right and left I noticed that the nearest drain pipe
was out of reach and the balconies were too far apart to cross from
one to another. Remembering another dark night in another town

when the police had almost got me, I glanced up to the balcony of the flat above forming a canopy over my head. With the body Fido had left me I was in no condition to try what I had in mind. Yet I had to if I was to survive. If my strength went or if I could not bear the agony then the drop to the pavement was enough to fix me for good.

I took some deep breaths to test the pain factor. Even that I had to do carefully. I would never make it. I considered Boris then the photograph and decided I would have to discover my weaknesses the hard way. So I went to the edge of the balcony to look down into the damp street, and its rugged line of wet car tops.

The easiest way would be near the wall so I stepped back, suctioned the wall with the flat of my hand and raised my knee to the top of the balcony rail. Had I been fit I would have put my foot on it but as it was the spasms gripped me. The only way I continued was by telling myself that I would get used to it, not notice the pain so much, as I forced on. In the sense that as I pulled myself on to my feet on top of the rail I nearly passed out, I suppose I was right. I toppled forward, overhanging the street at a dangerous angle, but my reflexes saved me and both hands now held desperately to the wall. Releasing one hand I reached up and with relief obtained purchase on the base of the upper balcony. Before the beating I would have pulled myself up with ease; now I had to find the least agonizing position.

By now I had both feet on the top of the balcony rail and both hands gripped the balcony above me. I was stretched to the limit and not too comfortable. The test would be when I pulled up and my back and stomach took the strain. Fido was probably getting nervous and it was a good incentive although I dreaded moving. I braced myself. Get it over quickly.

I heaved with the full power of arms and shoulders and my feet left the balcony. The movement was quick, the agony acute, but I slung up one hand and got a grip on the top rail of the upper balcony. It had to be done in one movement, for I knew that I could not survive a second attempt. My arms did well. It was when I crooked one leg to obtain foot purchase that my body started to resist. Suddenly I was saturated with sweat and I began to tremble. I clung on with hands that were fast losing feeling. The back of my eyes began to burn as the blood pounded in my head and I thought I was blacking out.

Part of me went out for I don't remember too much except the sheer pulsing torture of it. Most of my actions must have been the instinct of survival, or plain cussedness. Whatever it was it worked. While I was unaware of working at all. Luck too came into it. My balance was right and I must have got my foot lodged first time. Conscious thought returned when I found myself doubled over the upper balcony, my feet outside, my dangling hands touching the floor. From there I literally dragged myself over while the moist salt blocked my eyes and trickled into my mouth.

For some time I lay on the concrete balcony in a huddle listening to my breathing and unable to move. Victory is a good tonic; I had made it. Laughing a little light-headedly I recalled in a sort of daze that the last time I had done this I had managed all the way to the roof. Well that was out. I got up and staggered. I had left the jemmy on the lower balcony because I could not carry it and cope. If the old lady had no more problem than wondering how it got there then she would survive. I doubted that Fido would try to break in; he probably would not know how without an axe. Finding the French doors latched I slipped through the mica and lifted the catch. Inside I gave it a couple of minutes. No sound. Shone the torch. All doors closed. I negotiated the furniture, noted the odd but explicit combination of a pipe and a pair of crumpled nylons on a low coffee table then passed into the hall and listened. Whoever was in the bedroom had been claimed by sleep or exhaustion for there was no sound. Leaving the flat I went wearily to the stairs and started to climb them.

I was exhausted but the stairs were like an escalator compared with the balcony climb. At each landing I had to rest but I was also looking for something. I did not find it until the fifth floor and by this time I was in slow motion. There they were, the burglar's invitation cards; two bottles of milk and one newspaper.

Whoever lived there had been away only this day or was expected back this day; it was a bit late for the latter so I took a chance and let myself in. Stale air informed me that all windows were closed. No sound of breathing. One by one I silently tried the doors and with a discreet use of the torch established that the flat was empty. There was a chain on the front door so I put it on, knowing that I would have a little warning if someone came.

Searching the flat produced a few pointers. Articles in drawers, cosmetics on dressing table indicated a man and woman association; a letter revealed that they had gone away for two days to visit mother who was not expected to last. They were tidy people; the flat was spotless, too clean to expect a char. I helped myself to cold meat and cheese from the fridge, some wholemeal bread and milk. I did not worry about leaving fingerprints for I did not think it mattered any more.

After that I relaxed on one of the two single beds to sort things out. I did not intend to sleep. I went out like a light.

I awoke cold, aching and in daylight. Sitting up quickly, pain shot through me and I slowed down. Shivering, I think it was the cold that woke me with the drop of metabolism. My head was pounding and I shakily went to the bathroom, found some aspirin and took three with water. I felt terrible yet I had slept for nine hours. It had been a stupid thing to do. Someone may have called, the occupiers might have returned. My original idea was to snitch a blanket and sleep on the roof.

The central heating had been switched off but I stopped the shivers by having a cold water wash and a painful shave with some kit my unknowing host had left behind. I did not remove my moustache. The time was now 2 p.m. Not wanting to leave in daylight I pushed my luck and decided to stay at little longer. I made some tea and never was a hot drink more welcome. Afterwards I washed up and put things back as I found them, tried on a couple of suits in the wardrobe, but found them much too small. I was still in a bad way but at least I was beginning to feel human.

By early evening I was becoming a little nervous knowing that I was pushing my luck by staying. It could not last. At six o'clock I was restless to go but wanted to contact Maggie and she would just about be home. I gave it a few more uneasy minutes expecting someone to come to the door at any minute. Back in the comfortable lounge I rang Maggie and waited breathlessly. The sense of guilt in my simple act was tremendous; my mouth went dry. She answered, weariness and dejection seeping out in the offering of her number.

'Which number did you say?' I tried to keep the tremor from my voice not wanting anything to mar recognition. Her immediate hesitation told me enough. She made the mistake of sharply drawing her breath then she slowly repeated the number. I could feel the tension from where I stood. If someone was listening, would they detect it? 'I'm sorry,' I said. 'I've got the wrong number,' and put the phone down.

Would she remember? It was an old prearranged distress call I had used on her many years ago. Was it fair to expect her to? It was a chance I was prepared to take. I listened at the front door before opening it and slipped through on to the empty landing. On my slow way down the stairs I wondered if Boris was still around with his merry men or whether he had given up the ghost. I reasoned two ways; that as I had disappeared so completely he would expect that I had fled; two that if I had not fled I would hardly be stupid enough to use the front door. I decided to be stupid.

My handkerchief act across the hall got me through the doors and out on to a fairly crowded street. My only disguise was a two-day growth on my lip; it wasn't much.

It was a long hike from Fulham to Maggie's drum and I had no intention of making it. Boris had put back most of my belongings except the two thousand eight hundred I had taken from the Chinese but I was in no condition to be angry about it.

It was a strange unnerving experience walking the street with so many people on them, almost all of them having see my face in a newspaper or on television. So I kept to the insid pavement, dabbing at my nose with my handkerchief whe I thought it prudent. Eventually I called a taxi, giving th address behind the same prop and getting into the cab out c of his sight almost immediately. Boldness sometimes pays bu taxi drivers are not idiots and most of them keen observers. I sa directly behind him so that he would have to screw his head o to see me.

Before we reached Notting Hill I assessed the fare, added to i told him to pull up and passed his money through the opene glass panel behind his seat. While he was counting it I was ou and away, the crowds much thicker here. Walking to the neares cinema I paid, handkerchief still up while I had a fit of coughing and went in. I sat through three hours of films without reall seeing a thing. If the taxi driver had recognized me and the fuz had expected me at Maggie's then they would have expected m some time ago.

It was hard on Maggie but I was hoping that she would under stand.

I came out just before the crowd. The streets had thinnec considerably. I trod more warily now as I neared Maggie place. Sticking my head into this noose could not be worse tha those I had so far survived. Back to shadow hugging, crossin when I spotted a copper, changing direction at the approac of a prowl car. There was an outside chance that they ma have finished with Maggie, that they would not expect me t leave it so late to go to her. There was also a matter of routine precautions. Coppers are not fools and Dartmoor is full enougl to prove it.

The nearer to Maggie's the more I used the back doubles Fortunately the block was stuck off the main road but that gav the law a better chance for observation. Entering the long stree which contained the flats farther down I had the unmistakabl warning of coppers.

The street was not well lit but I was not the invisible ma either. There were two entrances and the fire escapes were rounc the back but if one was watched they all would be. Difficult. Ove each entrance was a nice big light so that residents would not trip over the steps. Stepping back in shadow my radar told me not t go farther.

It was late but not sufficiently late for the streets to be empty A good half of the flat lights were still on. A patrol car turned a corner and started cruising along nice and slowly so I took to the nearest portico. After it had passed I ventured out to see it stop on the opposite side to the flats. A man was leaning over talking to the driver's mate from the pavement. So they were still at it.

My word, Fairfax wanted me badly. Yet I could not let Maggie down now and there was another reason.

I had to get in. Climbing would not help me this time even had I been fit enough. And the place was obviously crawling with coppers. Maggie's flat was on the third floor in a side street so I could not tell whether or not she was up. I should have put a bit more thought into it while in the cinema. What would Fairfax do? Boris? I walked slowly away from the flats and down the usual line of parked cars. I had to walk some way and it took two cars to provide me. And I had to be very, very careful with the torch.

A Morris 1100 is an easy car to open. Slip a piece of mica or a penknife down the straight side of the louvre and you'll knock down the catch. With the louvre open slip your hand through and open the door. I nicked an umbrella, a hat, a raincoat and a seat cushion. By this time I was some distance from the flats. In a doorway I loosened my jacket and stuffed the cushion down my back. Trying on the raincoat almost split it but by leaving it unbuttoned, a necessity because I could not make it meet across my chest, it was at least bearable in spite of tightness under the armpits. Having a normal sized head I was luckier with the hat.

With furled umbrella I set off. A stoop took away my height and the cushion made me a semi-hunchback. The hat hid my hair and shadowed my features. The umbrella was a prop but it was well furled and gave dignity—and a weapon if I needed one. The raincoat fitted badly but it was a good one and I hoped the whole effect would be rather eccentric.

Eccentrics do not hurry, at least that was how I saw it. That was the hardest part, toddling along, tapping my umbrella like a blind man for I could not swing it with my stoop. When the flats loomed up again I needed all my nerve. I had evaded the fuzz often enough but I had been fit and fast and I had been going away from them. Never had I tried to dodge them by walking straight at them.

The police car had gone.

The greatest difficulty was in keeping my pace regular, to resist the almost overwhelming urge to run. When I had my copper on beam I crossed the road unhurriedly, knowing that I was now under surveillance by at least one pair of eyes. The block loomed up but I had my head down as part of my stoop. Strangely enough my position eased my stomach pain.

Reaching the block I plodded on. There were probably two of them this side and as the street was at the moment empty, they would be watching me with interest. The first entrance came in sight and I hoped I had sufficient bottle to go through with it. Deliberately I went past the first entrance and it took all the nerve I had. I was not proving something to myself or being stupid; I merely saw it as insurance. If they were not already on to me my action would help to throw them.

But the space between the two entrances was the longest walk of my life. The hair on the nape of my neck prickled all the way as if someone was aiming at my back with a rifle. At the second entrance I turned without change of pace and plodded past the strip of lawn to the open doors at the head of the stone steps. My mind was so much on the eyes boring into me from across the road that I tripped over one of the steps. I did not fall but it shook me, reminding me of every muscle. Turning round slowly I tapped the step with my umbrella, upbraiding it as an eccentric might. Then I passed into the hall, under the glare of lights.

I should have taken the lift; it would be the natural thing to do. Yet I had a great fear that someone else might get in from the first or second floors and my feeble disguise would not stand close scrutiny. So I took to the stairs. An eccentric might well have done but it was unlikely that someone as seemingly handicapped as I was would do so. I knew it; I made my decision.

Stairs were becoming part of my life and I had learned to take them slowly. There had been at least two people in the hall as I crossed it but they had been shapes on the fringe of my vision and I had not turned to look. Reaching the third floor without incident, I rested for a while against the wall; I wanted to be breathing normally when I rang Maggie's bell. Now I was here I had different fears; afraid of her and what I had done to her. Had I the right to take for granted that she would want to see me? I was dead nervous when I rang the bell.

She opened the door almost immediately. We stood staring at each other for several seconds and I felt the biggest bastard on earth when I saw the lines of anxiety etched on her face in only two days. We clasped each other tight and silently and I knew that it was still the same between us. Taking my hand, Maggie closed the door.

A little life had returned to her face but she still looked drained; there were no tears and I was left with the impression that she had already cried herself dry.

'You're still dressed,' I said, as we sat clasping each other as though expecting to be torn apart at any moment and that was the size of it.

'Of course. When you telephoned I knew that you would come.'

Dear Maggie. I told her exactly what had happened, leaving out the violence. It was important that she knew and I did it to sustain her. There was little time. 'I have some clothes here, Maggie. These I am wearing have been too well described.'

She went to the bedroom and came back with fresh slacks, a sports coat, underwear, socks and a shirt. 'Take your shoes off,

Villie. I'll clean them while you change. Would you like a
bath?'

'Wouldn't I half but it's too risky. I mustn't be caught with my
pants down.'

I was already stripping fast, not thinking, so that when she
cried out, 'Oh God, look at you,' it startled me. 'Look at your
body,' she cried in anguish.

I had not seen it myself. Looking down, it shook me a bit, but
my thoughtlessness needed quick covering. I grinned. 'I'd be all
right in a multi-racial society.'

Maggie picked up my shoes and hurried from the room, not
trusting herself to speak. While I finished changing I thought
about the police. Maggie had already checked a few times with
the light out and had seen no sign of extra cars and men arriving.
They would have been here by now had they recognized me. She
had told me about their constant visits and the tremendous
harassing she had suffered from all sorts of people, some of whom
sounded like Fairfax's men.

She returned with the shoes and I slipped into them. We had
not yet faced reality but I could see it coming when she sat
opposite me. When she adopted her probing pose I was always
uneasy.

'What happens next?' Maggie was good at ferreting my lies
so I had to be careful. Since I had decided to think like those
other conniving so-and-so's I took a bit of practice and talked
round it.

'I have some sort of plan,' I replied. 'If I go on as I am it's
only a matter of time before I'm picked up. I know I can't last,
Maggie, but please believe in me for a little longer. How's Dick
taking it?'

'Not very well. He feels—let down. He's talking of resigning.
He worshipped you, you know that.'

The past tense did not escape me. I felt rotten yet reminded
myself that a good part of the reason for the fix I was in was
due to trying to help my brother. When the chips are down
people can be bloody self-centred. Except Maggie. Her loyalty
and love had not changed, but I had expected Dick to have more
faith.

'Don't worry about it, Willie. He'll come round.' Her hand
squeezed mine and it made up for a lot.

'Whatever happens don't let him resign,' I pleaded. 'Don't
tell him we've met. Don't compromise him, but try to persuade
him to hold out a little longer. I know how it must be, the side
glances from his mates, but try to stop him resigning.'

'I already have.' She rose and looked sadly down at me, 'I
suppose you're off again? Did you come—just for the clothes?'

I nodded. 'But more important for Balfour's address. I can't
remember it and I know it's not under that name in the telephone

book.' It was difficult to explain without hurting her. 'You know
I wouldn't call to see you, Maggie, I wouldn't put you in that sort
of danger if it could be avoided. There is just a very, very faint ray
of hope but to exploit it I must be mobile and that means different clothes.'

'Your moustache looks terrible,' she said, trying to remain
composed. 'They said on television you might try to grow one.'

'Oh, hell.'

'Hold on, I've something that might help you.' While Maggie
was gone I transferred the photo and letter to my clean jacket.
She had not seen them nor had I explained the details of the
cause of all the the trouble; she had enough on her mind without
national secrets.

When Maggie came back into the room she was blonde. It
took me by surprise. The transformation was so marked that at
first I thought another girl had sprung out on me. She whipped it
off and I was left floundering at the remarkable change.

'Try it on,' she said.

'Wear a girl's wig? Me?' Taking it from her I must have
stared at it in horror for she laughed briefly and it was good,
God, if only things were different.

The cut of the hair was what I call chopped; a razor cut I think
they call it, but still clearly for a woman. She read my thought.

'I can trim it. Put it on.'

It was a strange feeling for me. There were them and there
were us. Suddenly I was becoming one of them and I did not like
it much—even though long hair was the rage with the boys. I
did not fit.

'Come here.' Maggie fiddled about with it on my head and
finally taking it off carefully, snipped up the back. 'Try it again
but pull it on carefully or it might split up the cut.'

It went on nice and tightly. I looked at myself in a mirror.
Blimey. I never thought I'd see the day. But it was good, if
damned effeminate. When I turned round Maggie had produced
a dummy head which she fitted the wig over and went to work
with scissors. 'I'll make it look more like a man,' she explained.
'Put these on.' She handed me a pair of large-framed spectacles.
Putting them on I felt one side give as the hinge went but it did
not fall away. 'I've broken them.'

She looked up. 'Never mind, they'll hold for as long as you
need them. Can you see all right?'

'A bit fuzzed but they'll do.'

When she had finished the wig I was no more comfortable
about it but I certainly accepted its possibilities. I shaved off my
moustache, because of its contrasting darkness, with the kit she
kept at Maggie's.

'You look quite different,' she said with obvious satisfaction.
'Nothing like your photograph or description.'

We were in a state of semi-elation when the door was knocked and wiped the excitement straight off our faces, freezing us solid. The silence was so complete that the clock sounded like a metronome. Then another discreet knock that puzzled me. I signalled Maggie.

She went to the door. 'Who is it?' she called.

'Tell Mr. Scott that if he does not act sensibly I will inform the police that he is here. Within seconds the building will be surrounded.'

Boris. I had underestimated the bastard. I stared at Maggie in despair.

CHAPTER FOURTEEN

THERE WAS little time to think. Boris would not break in; it was too risky; too much adverse publicity in the offing. But he would anonymously call the police out of sheer vindictiveness if he did not get what he wanted. I mimed instructions to Maggie.

'Mr. Scott has not been here for days. If you don't go away I'll call the police, whoever you are.' Maggie was still close to the door.

I could imagine Boris's expression of disbelief. 'Miss Parsons, don't waste time. I followed him here, I congratulate you, Mr. Scott, on your impromptu disguise. Ingenious. Unfortunately I saw you adopt it.'

He was speaking close to the wood in order not to arouse others.

'What shall we do?' Maggie silently mouthed at me. Personally, I was for letting him in and clobbering him. Then what would we do with him? It would not be fair to Maggie. I really needed time to talk it over with her, to discover the alternatives. Boris knew it too; did any man know more completely the machinations of a deperate human mind when faced with one of his ultimatums.

'You have sixty seconds from now, Mr. Scott. Hardly time to leave the building, I think. And you cannot move too fast, can you?''

I shrugged helplessly at Maggie. 'I'm coming out, Boris,' I called. 'You'll have to extend your time limit, I'm only half dressed.'

'Fifty-two seconds.'

Giving Maggie a sudden savage kiss, I pulled open the door before she could protest. Boris was smiling quietly in triumph as he stood leaning casually against the wall. His assurance faltered when he saw the change in me. Fyodor stood like a statue on a plinth mislaid halfway down the corridor.

Boris raised his grey homburg at Maggie and turned on his plastic charm. 'Good evening, miss. I am sorry to disturb you at this hour but Mr. Scott and I entered into an agreement.'

Stepping out into the corridor I turned to speak to Maggie but she had rushed back into the room. Meanwhile Fyodor came up behind me and we dropped into the prisoner and escort routine again. Then Maggie was back in the doorway, her face deathly white. 'The police are here,' she announced almost inaudibly. Boris frowned and I was startled. We all stood there in silence, then Boris snapped, 'You mean police reinforcements?'

Maggie pointed helplessly to the window behind her. 'Car loads of them.'

Both Boris and I dashed past her into the room to stand either side of the window. A common enemy had temporarily drawn us into reluctant liaison; it would be a great embarrassment to him if he was stopped or held by the police. Diplomatic privilege would protect him, but not against his superiors or if the Foreign Office requested his withdrawal.

'Maggie,' I hooked my arm at her. 'Stand in front of me here then pull the edge of the curtain back slowly.'

Standing behind her as if to remain out of vision, I peered over her shoulder until my lips were touching her ear. Below us, several cars had pulled up. No flashers were beaming but the unmistakable exodus of uniformed police could not be missed. They were surrounding the entire building. A mouse would not escape. In my softest voice I whispered, 'As we go down the stairs, thump Fido over the head with a mallet. He's the one outside.' My arm was round her waist and she gripped it tightly. I had asked a lot of her but I did not think I was endangering her at this stage.

Boris said, 'Why have they come? Had they seen you enter they would have been here long ago.'

I was up against it anyway, impossibly so. It was good to see Boris concerned. 'If D.I.5 had a man out there he might have recognized *you* and *Fido*. He added two and two.'

'You appear so different that we will have to bluff it out.'

'Do you think I would get by, Maggie?' I held her by the arms for she was half dazed by the turn of events, and I was not happy myself. She looked back with glazed eyes. 'Your clothes and hair are different. I think it might work, but only if they did not know you. I don't think it would fool someone like Sergeant Bulman.'

In Boris I saw the slightly lesser of two evils; maybe I could fix them both. I turned to him.

'If I'm seen with you it will put the lid on it.'

I could see that he knew it too, yet he dare not let me go. 'We will go down the stairs together. I will then walk out alone while you stay with Fyodor. If I get through without incident you and Fyodor will follow. And don't try anything foolish again. Your only future is with us.'

I shrugged an acquiescence, then he added, 'It will be natural, I think, for us to take an interest in the police behaviour. To try to walk through them as if they are not there will be madness. It is a danger we cannot avoid.'

Well, it would get him out of Maggie's hair and that was what I wanted. 'Goodbye, Maggie. Thanks for everything.'

Boris tried to be the cavalier. 'Do not worry, Miss Parsons.' He smiled, raised his hat again. 'Good day.' He led the way out of the flat, I followed and Fido tagged on as we left the room.

To distract I asked Boris what he had done with my stolen

money. Reaching the head of the stairs he did not look back, but
told me over his shoulder that it would be returned to me once
the deal was complete. Everything was so plausible with Boris;
I was sure that he could convince anyone of the necessity of putting a bullet in them. We started down the stairs in single file and
then there was a sickening crack behind that paralysed me into
inaction.

I wanted to turn but was afraid to. Boris wasn't. He began to
spin round and his movement triggered mine. With a snarl I
smashed my foot in his back and he crashed down the stairs. Not
waiting for him to stop I spun round to see Fido swaying on the
top step, his flat gaze glassy, non-seeing as he gripped the rail to
steady himself. Jumping the two stairs between us I hit him under
the jaw so hard that I swear his feet left the carpet. Something
cracked; judging by the pain it might have been my hand but
later I discovered it was not. As he crumpled I helped him on his
way with my left foot and he rolled like a hedgehog to join an
unconscious Boris on the lower landing. From the way Boris was
huddled he must have hit his head against the well.

Looking up I saw a very shaken Maggie holding a broken
French Empire candelabra. I could have wept for her; it was
mercurial gilt, one of a pair. It had taken her years to find—at a
price she could afford. There was no time to commiserate. My
body racked me as I reached Maggie and bundled her back into
the flat.

What more had I done to her? Maggie, who had never used
violence in her life and who abhorred it. Removing the bent
candelabra from her clutching hands I tried to stop her shaking.
'You did not kill him,' I told her. 'You didn't even knock him
down. His head is like iron.'

'Look at your hand,' she said helplessly, shocked near to tears.

It was already swollen, black and blue, the knuckles split. It was
worth it. Fyodor had got his and he would remember it.

'Maggie, love, they'll be up here any minute. Please listen.'
I shook her gently and she snapped out of it.

'Who's immediately upstairs?' I asked urgently.

'It's empty. You could use it.'

'That's the first place they'll look; all the empty flats. Is there
anyone you know?'

'I have a friend on the floor below. Shirley Ames, number 21.'

'Is she the hysterical type?'

'I don't think so. She's been very kind to me while you've
been away. Shall I ring her?'

I did not trouble to explain that I thought the phone was
bugged. She realized it herself but her thinking was not yet
straight. She looked up sharply. 'Willie, please don't frighten
her.' Then suddenly she was all action as the extreme precarious-
ness of our position brought her back to reality. Before I knew

what she was at, she dashed off to the bedroom and returned with a spray.

'Take off the glasses and hold a handkerchief over your eyes,' Maggie instructed. I heard the soft hiss of spray and felt the wetness on my eyebrows.

'Open them. Give me the handkerchief.' She wiped around my brows. 'Now look at yourself.'

My brows were now blond like the wig.

'It's for putting coloured streaks into hair.' I hardly recognized myself. But it was effective. The fire escape was outside the darkened kitchen and I hurried towards it. It was too late for the stairs.

'Tell the police you know nothing about Boris and Fido. Never seen them. Clear all trace of me, sweetheart, they'll be here any moment.' She was already bundling up my old clothes.

'Is Shirley Ames' flat to the right or left of yours?'

'To the right. Please go, Willie. God knows I don't want you to but the whole place must be surrounded by now.'

I gave her a wink and stepped out on to the fire escape. The block formed a square with gardens in the middle and two big gates leading to the street. This side would be as closely watched as the front but it was dark; they would not see me on the escape until I got lower down or made a noise, and as silence was my trade I was not too worried about that.

Just the same I went down that escape testing each footfall. I could hear movement below; there were so many of them that their silence had become unnecessary. I had never known such a cordon. I had not explained to Maggie because of the time factor and anyway it was best that she did not know; I reckoned that all the flats would be systematically searched once they found I wasn't in Maggie's. Boris and Fyodor's bodies would give them food for thought but it was not going to help me.

I crept down feeling trapped yet inspired by the ridiculous challenge of it. The odds were hopelessly against me. It was doubtful if there had ever been such a manhunt. I suppose I was resigned to being caught and it had made me philosophical, yet a temporary freedom was my only hope. I needed time. I made no sound on the escape and caused no tremor of its structure.

Reaching the platform on second floor level I squatted against the wall and waited. I could smell them down below me in the courtyard. Waiting too long could be as disastrous as lack of caution. I expected to see heads pop out from Maggie's kitchen at any moment. A torch was out of the question. I fiddled in the kitchen door lock with one of two bent hair-curler clips that I had taken from Maggie's. The inside key was on the slant so I had to manipulate to straighten it. Of all times for it to happen the bloody moon came out like a night light and I huddled as tight as I could, my face to the wall. Was there a mat behind the door

or was it lino? As I pushed the key through I cringed, waiting
for the tell-tale ringing that might attract a sharp police ear or
wake Shirley. There was nothing. A mat. Phew! More fiddling
before the door clicked and I froze.

Whether or not I liked it I could not open the door with the
moon shedding its light into every corner. From below the iron
platform I was on gave me good cover but an opening door might
be seen. So I waited, cramped and anxious, expecting a sudden
shout to go up. They were taking their time but they would make
sure that all the gaps were closed before moving in. So what space
did that leave me?

A chunk of cloud came up like a hand over a torch. Still
crouched I turned the door handle, hoping that there were no
bolts, and pushed. I was in on hands and knees, knocking the key
on a rough mat and sniffing the smell of cooking. Closing the door
in slow motion, I put back the key and turned it. If the flat was
similar to Maggie's I would find my way around.

Beyond the far door was a short corridor, bedroom to the
immediate right, lounge straight ahead. I did not use my torch
which had little life left, but picked my way carefully. At the bedroom door I listened and could not hear a thing. The sudden
dread that Shirley Ames might still be out and would walk in at
any moment hit me like a thunderbolt. Her scream of fright went
through my head. Then I pulled myself up by the chinstrap and
entered the lounge. From there to the front door was no problem.
There was no hall but a sort of recess used as a mini study.

That was it; the moment of truth. Opening the door I stepped
boldly out, straight into two coppers.

I don't know who was more surprised. Shoving my head back
round the door I whispered loud enough for them to hear:

'Goodnight, Shirley. See you tomorrow, darling.' And I turned
round grinning at the two rosy young faces under the big
helmets. 'What's going on?' I said, upping my accent to meet
the demands of the flats.

'Your name, sir?'

I hastily recalled which visiting cards I was carrying in my
wallet. 'Certainly, but why? What's the fuss?'

'We're looking for someone. Your name, sir.'

I could not believe what was happening. A change of hair,
eyebrows, spectacles and not least of all clothes—incredible. But
careful how you go, Spider. 'James Cummings. What's he done?'

'Have you an identity on you?'

'Only a card.' I dished it out; representative of the Marlon
Group Limited.

He looked at it as if it meant something. 'No driving licence,
sir?'

'Not on me.' I held out my hand for the card. He returned it.
'I take it I can get out. I must catch a cab.'

He nodded. 'I'm afraid you might get stopped again, sir. The place is surrounded.'

'Good Lord. Who are you after, Jack the Ripper?'

They gave me a grave nod in unison, very important looking, and I started down the stairs blessing young, inexperienced coppers. I reminded myself that some coppers would recognize anyone under any disguise—just a few who knew the small points about bone structure and so on. And they had a nose like mine in reverse. I'd have to try to stay away from them. Even so it had been a reasonable test.

That was how I felt before I reached the hall. When I took the turn of the stairs, my stomach dipped. The hall was flooded with them, plain-clothed and uniformed. How I kept my legs going I don't know but I dare not hesitate. Suddenly I felt an abject fool walking into their arms like this. So many pairs of eyes turned in my direction when they heard my footsteps that I damned nearly ran back up. My mouth was dry again and my legs had disappeared.

Two plain-clothed men detached themselves but to cut it short I went straight up to them. 'It's all right, officers, I've just seen your men on the second floor.'

'Really, sir? How do you know we are policemen?'

'Come now,' I said in my best Oxford and gave them what I hoped was a sweet smile. 'I gather you're looking for someone.'

'About your height, sir. Dark hair, clothes. Seen him?' He whipped out my photograph and flashed it under my nose like a warrant card. I stared down at my own sullen face and how I refrained from making a break for it I'll never know. They must surely see the sweat and the fear in my eyes. Yet I heard this strange posh voice reply, 'That's the man they showed on television. Is he here?' I could feel my voice quivering yet it *sounded* level. I was dazed. Coppers were turning to look at me then turning back to natter among themselves when they noted I was taken care of. In the back of my mind was the dread that Fairfax might enter and if I fooled him for ten seconds it would not be for longer. I had to get out of here before I gave myself away.

'I take it you haven't seen him, sir?'

Answer, you fool. Don't forget your accent. 'Not here. I mean not in the flesh.'

Christ, there was Alf Bulman in his inevitable raincoat on the far side of the hall talking to a uniformed man. They would have dragged him out by very virtue of the fact that he would never forget me. I was facing him straight on. I rubbed my nose and thought, well this is it, get ready to run. But how would I get through this lot? I had yet to realize how many were outside.

'Which flat have you just come from, sir?'

When would the idiot let me go. 'Number 21.'

'Do you live there, sir?'

I noticed that his colleague had a register in his hand and was looking down it. 'No, I was visiting a friend.' Bulman was nodding his head as if terminating a conversation.

'What is your friend's name, sir?'

How desperate did I have to get before I belted him one and fled. My nerve could not hold up under this, it was not my forte.

'Shirley Ames.' The one with the register nodded; in the near distance Alf Bulman glanced casually over.

'Social call, sir?'

'Don't be impertinent. Use your imagination.' My anger was not feigned, I was running out of bottle. Yet it had the right effect. He grinned sheepishly; man to man.

'All right, sir.'

I took it that I could go. Try walking through a scattering of coppers who are all looking for you. *You* know that you're you and you're just waiting for *them* to realize it. Your legs are melting rubber and you reckon you begin to smell like it. Eyes watch you, casually, but shrewdly, and you walk slowly through stares like criss-crossing searchlights of variable strength; but you are the focus. You want to reduce height, hide your face, turn up your collar, run. Yet if you are to survive you will walk straight at full height, chin up, taking the interest in them that they would except. If you can do that knowing that every one of them is there because of you, then your nerve is good or you've been touched by madness.

My nerves were shattered and the blood was racing round my brain. At this stage, I really had little conception of what I was doing. From the corner of my eye I saw Alf Bulman and as casually as I could, turned my head away. Surely they must be in Maggie's place by now? Would she have the nerve to delay them. They must have found Boris and Fyodor, and Fairfax's men would have some idea of what had happened. I was hoping that all Fairfax's D.I.5 men were upstairs. The presence of the two Russians would satisfy them of my own presence.

Just as I was nearing the big glass doors two pairs of footsteps broke out behind, hurrying towards me, but by now my legs could not have broken into a trot. They came up either side of me, but just as I was about to struggle they carried on past not even holding open one of the doors for me. I caught the door as it was swinging.

As I passed outside the roar from Alf Bulman remained in his throat or he simply had not recognized me. I was out into the air.

On the other side of the street, a row of uniformed men stretched out at intervals and between them and me were odd bods in plain clothes with a couple of higher-ranking uniformed types. No one approached me and I guessed that the fact that I had been allowed through was good enough for them. I stood on the steps looking about me because it would have been unrealistic to do otherwise. It was impossible to gauge the size of the cordon thrown round the building, but I reckoned that they must have run into three figures counting the detectives. Which made me a pretty desirable commodity.

I stepped on to the pavement as a taxi came sliding up. At first I thought nothing of it and as it began to pull up to disgorge a passenger I almost hailed it. I was stopped in my tracks by its registration number. It was Fairfax's special cab. Nipping smartly behind it as it came to a halt, I felt the warmth of its exhaust fumes on my leg as I crossed the street and started to walk in front of the spread-out line of the law, as if I was a general inspecting troops. I did not feel like a general. I felt like a crook on the diciest run of his life.

All those eyes bored into my back, but in fact at this stage I doubted if they took much notice of me at all. I kept walking until I rounded the corner, heading for the main streets. Afraid to look round I kept going, too tense for relief, still not believing that I had escaped the net.

I was not yet out of the woods. Once they realized that I had fooled them, they would recall the tall blond bloke with the tatty haircut and would scour the streets. Meanwhile, the wig still had its uses. I hailed a late cab and gave him an address near to Balls Up's place. If I could fox the police I knew that in the dark I did not have to worry too much about a cabbie. Later on he would remember so I gave him a point that would leave me a fair walk the other end, so that they would not connect my dropping-off place with Balls Up.

It left me with little time for the net would encompass any spots where I had been seen. As I sat back in the cold leather I reflected there was an outside chance that Maggie would convince them that I had not been there; she was not a good liar and if they thoroughly searched, they must find the other stuff. There was no danger of Boris telling them because he would deny all knowledge of an association. Right now, Boris would be faced with some of the problems I had just missed and this pleased me.

I dropped off in a dark area not too far from Wormwood Scrubs so I was quite at home. I did not expect to be followed but I made sure for my life depended on my next few moves and I only hoped that I was capable of seeing them through.

I walked for half an hour before I came to a shabby narrow street with hardly a lamp in it. Nineteenth-century London. The whole damned lot needed blowing up, scouring and rebuilding after a decent disinfection period. Right now it was just what I wanted. Coppers moved in pairs and were more easily seen and heard.

There was no name above the drab printing shop. Once there

had been paint on the woodwork. An antiquated printing mach-ine hid behind a dirty sheet glass window with rude words fingered out of the dust. The shop itself cringed back between a junk shop and a small tobacconist's, just a shade cleaner than the print shop. Yet Balls Up scratched a living, did a little better than that when the boys called on his artistry and not so well when he operated for the wrong people and finished up inside.

The door was locked, the whole area in darkness. Balls Up was too trusting for a villain; no bolt was on the door so I let myself in and started up the worn, bare-boarded stairs; he could afford carpets; he merely did not see the point in buying them. He prob-ably kept his money under the floorboards. Passing the room where he so often had his all-night gambling sessions I opened the next door.

Stale air and sweat assailed me and the noise of erratic snoring. Only one person there. With my back to the door I switched on the light; no shade, low-wattage lamp, bare boards but for a couple of grubby Indian scatter rugs that had probably fallen off the back of a lorry. A ball of grey hair stuck up from a bright red counter-pane like an unwashed mop. Then he shot up in bed, eyes wide, his right hand groping down the side of the bed searching for something to hit me with. I did not feel like grinning but I needed his confidence and his help so I managed one, then whipped off the wig and glasses.

'Christ! Spider! You bloody idiot, why'd you come in like that, mate?' Then, as sleep left him. 'Why come 'ere at all? Old Bill* has been round 'ere, looking for you. You're in it, mate; right above your eyes. And they've put a price on your 'ead, fifteen thousand.'

'And you're going to help get me out of it, Balls Up,' I said, still grinning. He hadn't shaved for a week and looked an old, creased man.

'Oh, no.' He swung his legs out of bed; he had been sleeping in his underpants. 'You can't stay 'ere, mate, they might pop up again any moment. They've put me through it, I can tell you. What did yer want to screw the Chinks for? Any other time, Spider. They say the Chink's dying, I can't risk it, mate.'

I put him out of his misery. 'I'm not staying, Balls Up. I wouldn't do it to you or any of my mates. I've got a job for you to do; dead urgent and you could do it on your head.'

It was half past two when I left Balls Up and went searching forlornly for a cab. I was not exactly in the right area for finding one but I kept going, heading all the time towards Soho. In the end I had to nick a car and use my crocodile clip because time was running out. I left it in Shaftesbury Avenue before cutting up Dean Street into strip club land.

If there are going to be people about in London at the dead of

---

* Police

night, then a good proportion of them will be in Soho. And the coppers and cars are not short there either. So I was in a highly nervous state. There was additional worry; my normal description was all over the country but should I now remove the wig? Was it going to be an aid, or my downfall? Did the police yet know about it? The other thing was Balls Up's mention of a price on my head. This was something new. Apparently some donor interested in Anglo-Chinese relations had put up the money as a measure of diplomatic goodwill. Fifteen thousand pounds. It was an amount with a familiar ring and I had no doubt that Fairfax was behind it.

It meant that I could not even trust the boys. Fifteen grand tax free was a sizeable sum and I might well have made a mistake by going to the inveterate speculator, Balls Up. He was a good bloke, basically, but like anyone else he could justify himself by saying I was doomed to capture anyway so that he might as well cash in. That's what they would all say. Ray Lynch must be hard at his bottle for not hanging on to me a little longer. If I was isolated before I was now in solitary and yet it was essential to communicate whatever the risk.

When I tried to break into the Gainboy Studios I cursed Bluie Palmer for bolting his door. There was no ground floor window that led to his place and I did not fancy using a jemmy on a street door even if I had one. Stepping back I looked up but his studio lights were out and the floor above that where I believed he lived was also in darkness. Hearing a policeman's tread I had to push off to return a few minutes later.

This time I rang the bell, leaning against the button and hoping like hell that it worked for I couldn't hear a thing. A man and a woman passed me, slightly drunk and very amorous; I heard the man ask her name so he wasn't doing too badly on short acquaintance. The trouble was that there would be plain-clothes men around here and I was pushing my luck.

Hearing a window open above me, I stepped back and saw a pale face leaning out staring at me. 'For goodness sake, what do you want at this time of night, darling?'

His tone told me that he had not recognized me and his lack of interest suggested that he might have someone with him. It was a complication; I had half expected it.

'Bluie, let me in for God's sake. I must talk to you for just a minute.' My loud whisper carried. Odd things happened in this area but recognition could be fatal.

'Oh dear!' His plaintive whine informed me that he had recognized my voice. 'You really shouldn't have come here, Sp——'

'Let me in,' I snarled, cutting across my name. 'For one minute, that's all. I won't stay.'

The window closed and I stood hopefully. I knew how he felt. I was not being fair by implicating him, yet that's what mates were for—to help out. When I heard his soft tread on the stairs I was relieved. The bolts shot back and I was in.

'You may be gorgeous, darling, but I'm taking a frightful risk for you.'

I followed the green, short, silk dressing gown, the bare legs and the strong perfume up the stairs. From the studio floor upwards was richly carpeted and when Bluie led me into his lounge I could see at a glance that he made a lot of money from his dubious photography. There were flowers and tassels and drapes and the whole room had the touch of a fussy woman; Bluie's own touch. But there was nothing wrong with his Scotch and for once I had one, large and neat.

'Keep your voice down, darling,' he said as he motioned me to an old gold cushioned chair. 'I have a friend staying with me.' He smiled sweetly, looking me over appraisingly and I had to keep my feelings deep within me; I needed this man's help in a way I hoped would take his fancy, might even excite him; so I risked it and smiled back. Gradually I was learning the diplomatic game and began to disgust myself. Patience, too, I was learning as Bluie cooed. 'The wig looks heavenly on you, ducky. It's definitely you. You know it's lucky for you that I don't need the money and that I'm fond of you; they're offering ever so much for you. What *have* you done, you naughty boy?'

The only way I knew how to handle Bluie was the old way but I had to swallow it. I dare not upset him by as much as one word. So I aroused his professionalism and when I did that his interest centred on what I was saying. Just the same, I had yet to meet a well-breached man who would close his ears to the offer of another easy pile of bunce. Just how fond of me was he?'

What do you do when there is a price on your head so that you dare not let even your friends see you and you are faced with several hours of darkness? It was cold and I was without an overcoat so even a quiet kip in a hidden doorway was out of the question. With what I had in mind I would have rung up Ray Lynch again but I reckoned that fifteen grand would be too tempting for him.

The first thing I did was to get out of Soho and that is not easy to do unobserved, day or night. After that I kept walking. Even this did not bring warmth for there had been a sudden drop in temperature. I was tempted to jump the railings of the National Gallery and prop myself behind one of the big Corinthian columns for a rest and sleep but the cold kept me going. I was grateful then for the long sleep I had taken in the empty flat.

I could not walk and let my mind wander so my plight was with me all the time which meant that every second was like a minute and time dragged. I must have dived into a score of recesses, doorways, alleys, at the approach of foot coppers and patrol cars. Suddenly there were more of them and I wondered if the call had gone out and a new hunt was on.

There was nothing pleasant about London's dawn. A wet greyness crept over the buildings, giving them a shadowy drabness that matched my own mood. As the light increased I maintained my wig on the basis that although the police may know of it, the general public might not. With the increased light came more people, vehicles, danger. I kept walking.

The sun came out and with it some warmth. When the morning was really humming with crowds I dived into a news cinema and bought myself a couple of bars of chocolate. Sitting at the back I snatched a little sleep and stayed there for three shows. The chocolate made me thirsty but I could bear that. If only I could listen to the news I would know what to do about the wig unless the police were playing it crafty.

Back on the streets I played the police long range. The far sight or glint of a helmet was enough to send me another way. No one paid attention to me except some of the oldies who gave me the glare reserved for blond long hair-dos.

Two o'clock was the deadline. I had to hang around Charing Cross Post Office where there are usually police around. But it had to be somewhere near enough to Soho without being in it, and not too long a walk for Bluie. I spotted him crossing the road, green velvet jacket, red tie, tight check trousers, swaying his way with a large envelope under his arm. He went into the Post Office up to one of the writing counters and put down the envelope while he filled in a form. Sidling up next to him I started to fill in a form, changed my mind, screwed it up, threw it in the nearest bin, picked up the envelope and left.

On the run you are safer in crowds especially in London where you have to be beautiful or a freak to attract a second glance. The police weren't so indifferent and the number of coppers they had called out during the night was not for an exercise; their ears would be burning today, their eyes sharper. So I took the greatest care crossing over to St. James's Park.

In spite of winter, the park was not deserted. I buried myself as far from the Mall as I could and sat on a cold park bench to study the contents of the envelope. They gave me a lot of food for thought. I considered Fairfax and the low trick he had pulled on me; of the C.I.A. and the K.G.B., of Li Tshien. Of them all Fairfax did not come out of it too well and in my hands I had the means to strike back at him. I decided to contact the Chinese.

CHAPTER FIFTEEN

THEY WOULD WATCH the main stations, so it meant the hazard of crossing Trafalgar Square again to the Charing Cross Post Office. It seemed that I was beginning to live there. There were unhappy moments waiting for a phone booth to become vacant but a place like this is always busy. Eventually I was in.

Before phoning I searched my mind for another course and reluctantly decided that there was none. The ringing tone went on for so long that I thought they were not going to answer, then a clipped, sing-song voice came on the line and I asked to speak to Li Tshien. There was silence, background voices, then a guarded 'Who is speaking?'

'Tell him it's the man who took the letter and the photographs.' This slayed him. The voices became so rapid that they sounded like a tape being played at too fast a speed. Then another voice, more authoritative, no less guarded.

'What do you want with us?'

'I want to do a deal, to return what I stole except the money.'

'Then you come round at once. Straight away. We talk.' I could imagine them doing their little tricks and me doing all the talking.

'Don't take me for stupid,' I said. 'Are you interested in talking or not?'

'Yes. We talk.'

'Then meet me in half an hour on the wooden bridge in St. James's Park.'

'Not possible, half hour. Two hours, maybe three.'

'You won't find me there. The police will have me by then. And the stuff. Half an hour or not at all. One man on his own. If I see signs of others, I'll be off.' They wanted time to discuss it of course and I did not intend to give them any.

More gabbling, high-pitched and argumentative—it was all Chinese to me. Eventually, 'We come now.'

I snapped, 'I said *one.*'

'Yes. One. We come now.' There was one thing about the Chinese; I did not have to worry about them telling the police.

I stayed in the booth with the phone at my ear until someone else wanted it, then got out quick in case he started to study me.

I strayed back to the park with plenty of time in hand. The envelope contents were distributed about my body in various pockets. Reaching the wooden bridge, I leaned on it and watched the ducks and swans. An old lady close by was throwing pieces of bread to them.

Half an hour was a long time on the bridge with a cold breeze rippling the water. This was one of the times I would have preferred an overcoat but it's impossible to work in one and to run with one is to carry an anchor. I was not sorry when I saw a Chinese approach; a short, thick-set, Mongolian-faced man, pale in an English winter, muffled with a thick woollen scarf, heavy Crombie overcoat, thick gloves and a trilby hat. He wore steel-framed spectacles and was altogether an image of too much reminiscence. He stopped on the bridge and looked about him, giving me barely a glance. Waiting for the old lady to finish fattening up the wild life I said, 'Are you looking for Mr. Scott?'

He gave me the inscrutable look that pins men to walls and ignored me.

'I'm Spider Scott,' I said. 'I've changed my hair.' He took more interest in me then, but was still highly suspicious.

'Would you like to hear me describe Li Tshien's room to you? Tell you where your radio room is?'

That helped. He came up beside me and we both leaned over the bridge, as unlikely a pair as you could meet.

'You have the things with you, Mr. Scott?'

'Some. I want two thousand eight hundred pounds for them.'

'That is ridiculous. That is the amount you stole from us.'

'And the Russians stole it from me. That's what I want and I want it today.'

Surprisingly he pulled out a crumpled bag in which were some broken biscuits; crumbling them he tossed them to the birds and a series of concentric pools broke out on the water. 'How much did British Security pay you for stealing what is ours?'

'Everybody thinks that,' I said. 'If they paid me I would not be selling now. The C.I.A. offered me money and escape. The K.G.B. offered me escape and money. But I have a conscience about Li Tshien. I did not mean to hurt him. I'm willing to sell them back to you at the price of replacing the money I stole. Plus one other request which will cost you nothing.'

'I must be sure that you have them to sell. Remember that they are ours—our property that you are demanding money for.'

'Can it,' I snapped. And in case he did not understand me, 'Who did *you* steal them from? How much did *you* pay in the first place. If you took the photograph yourselves you certainly pinched the letter.'

'I will speak to my superiors about the money. May I see what you have?'

'If you are not empowered to negotiate you are seeing nothing.'

'All right. All you bourgeois think of is money. I will see that you have it.'

'At half-past four o'clock. I'll ring you at half three to tell you where we'll meet.'

'That is not enough time.'

'Take it, or leave it. And while we're talking of money all you

Communists think of is bloody blackmail. That is what you want them for, isn't it? I'd sooner be a thief.'

He was biting his tongue to get back at me for I had cut a wound in his indoctrination. The cold murder left his almond eyes and he said, 'Show me.'

I produced the letter and handed it to him. On its own it was useless; only coupled with the photograph was it devastating evidence. He put it in his pocket and I made no attempt to stop him.

Then he gave me a very special look that was a complete examination, penetrating, as if he had managed to focus inside my head and knew how my mind was working. It made my flesh crawl. This fellow wasn't going to forgive me, ever. I struck back.

'Any tricks and I'll do one of two things; I'll send what I have to a news agency and start the biggest scandal of all time. We'll lose a good Foreign Secretary and maybe a government. But you will lose most. There won't be a paper in the Western world that won't publicise the slimy, degrading tactics of the representative of the Chinese People's Republic. Or I can sell them to the C.I.A. or the K.G.B. As you hate them both, I leave you with the thought. What I'm asking is chicken feed.'

He nodded almost imperceptibly but there was no fear in him, only unadulterated, undisguised, fanatical hatred. He shuffled off, looking miserable from the rear.

Taking the subway at Cockspur Street, I went into the Gents' and shut myself in a cubicle. It was claustrophobic, too much like solitary, but it was safe for a few minutes. So I had now been reduced to hiding in toilets. I gave it as long as I dare then it was back in the cold and over once more to the Post Office. I did not expect to find Fairfax's number and address in the phone book so I rang Ray Lynch at the office. He was out. I did not know where Sally worked so I took a chance and rang her at her flat. She was in and suffering from a cold. I was touched at her relief on hearing from me; one day hardly constitutes a friendship but she was sincere. I asked her how I could get in touch with Ray. She did not know where he was. Did she know Sir Stuart Halliman's address? She said she would look in Ray's special address book. She came back and gave me an address in Eaton Terrace, Belgravia, then she asked, 'What are you going to do, Spider?' And 'What happened to Ray's friends?'

'They weren't too friendly, but don't blame him.' I was about to tell her to take a stiff drink and go to bed with her cold then realized that it would be fatuous advice. So I said, 'Tell Ray I'll give him a scoop. I mean it. Tell him to get off the bottle and wean himself back on his job. I can make it for him.' Hanging up, I reflected that Fairfax was going to pay for what he had done to me.

At four o'clock I rang the Chinese Legation. I was half an hour later than arranged but I wanted their resistance down. My cunning line of thought began to appal me. They would be thinking too and that more than worried me; they would put their heads together with one thought in mind; how to fix me for fixing them. I was expendable in all their eyes, even my own. So I was not too confident when I demanded that the same man was to meet me at the same spot as before.

This time I arrived late at the bridge and had developed eyes all round my head. If they were going to make a move it would be now or after he had left. That's why I had made certain of daylight with the night not too far ahead. There was no bounce in me when I went to join him on the bridge. There were plenty of people in the Mall and a few on the park paths. There were also two policemen but a good distance away.

He raised his eyes to me, but not his hat. I still did not like what I saw. 'You have the money?' He nodded. 'You have the photograph?' I nodded back, then took another good look around the park, particularly at two parked cars on double yellow lines opposite the ugly lump of the Admiralty Citadel.

'How's Li Tshien?' I asked, dreading the answer.

'Do you not read the newspapers?'

'I'm not in a position to buy one. He's still alive?'

'Is that important to you?'

'Yes.'

'Then I will not tell you one way or the other. You must sweat it out, Mr. Scott.'

You bastard, I thought. Let's get it over. I passed him the positive face down, ashamed to look at it with him. On the other hand, he turned it over and gave it close scrutiny, finally slipping it inside his overcoat.

'The negative, please?'

'The last time we met I said that there was something else I wanted from you.'

Those flat suspicious eyes warily roamed mine and I hoped I had the nerve to carry it through. I told him what I wanted. At the end of it, he gazed blankly at me and said, 'I am pointing a gun at you. I can shoot you, take the negative and run to waiting friends or you can give it to me now.' Then, 'I promised you the money, nothing more. I have it here.'

'Shoot me,' I challenged. 'You might be doing me a favour. But you won't, because you dare not risk the scandal; there are too many people about.' He had a gun all right. I could see part of its shape through his overcoat pocket. 'If you do as I ask I will guarantee the negative through your letter-box tomorrow morning.'

'You are a thief. Why should I trust you?'

'You are a blackmailer, which is why I don't trust you. Look, Wong or whatever your name is, you have the letter and the print;

enough to work on. I agree that the negative is proof that the positive is O.K. You think I can still do a deal with someone else with the negative. So I can. But they cannot do for me what you can do. I'm in your hands. Anyway, I wasn't stupid enough to bring the negative with me.'

He nodded too quickly as if making up his mind halfway through what I was saying. 'All right. We will then be back at the beginning minus a little cash. All right, Mr. Scott, I will have to trust you.' He handed me a packet which I opened. I was not going to count it there but there appeared to be a very substantial amount. When I looked up he was already walking away in his unlikely gait. I reflected that it had all been *too* easy. I looked around and noticed the cars still there.

Time was back on my hands. If I could last out another twenty-four hours there was a little hope; if I was captured before morning there was no hope at all because everything depended on keeping the negative out of official hands until then. There was no certainty that the Chinese would do what I asked them. There was absolute certainty that if I was captured before they could move they would make no move at all and I would be landed with a life stretch.

I moved slowly through the park away from Trafalgar Square and towards Buckingham Palace. Turning suddenly I noticed that one of the cars was moving down the Mall at a snail's pace; the other had branched off at right angles, so that they could form a pincer movement at the end of the park.

Apart from being in bad nick I did not want to run, for it would draw attention. Their chesslike minds would have figured that out. So I about-turned just to confuse them. The car in the Mall pulled up sharply and a cruising taxi driver almost rammed it. The two passengers in the back seat of the car shot forward on the seat and I caught a long-range glimpse of them.

They say all Chinese look alike but that's if you haven't clobbered one of them and have every reason to remember his face. Pain or not I risked a jog across the grass before they U-turned in the middle of the Mall and drew the biggest chorus of motor horns for the day. The car survived but if they tried that manoeuvre too often the cops would get them.

My sight of the passengers had not been all that good but my heart had thumped out. One of them had a strip of adhesive diagonally across his forehead and had looked remarkably like Li Tshien, glasses and all. The sight had startled me. The bastards. And if it was Li Tshien that made Russian Boris a bigger bastard. Blinded and dying! The relief weakened me and I plumped down on a bench, my head between my hands. It had to be him.

The cars, of course, were there to follow me until such time as their occupants could pounce. They knew that I had no shelter, that if I popped into a cinema I would have to pop out again.

They knew that the only place I could hide would be in the darkest loneliest alley or derelict house so that all they had to do was to keep me in sight and wait for the streets to clear when they could safely scoop me up. If the Chinese got hold of me I would lose on every issue.

I got walking again and headed for the Strand, the one-way section that terminated at the traffic lights outside the white bulge of South Africa House. Their Chinese minds should have considered the one-way systems and unless they knew their London they would burst a gasket as they watched me walk against the traffic.

Cutting down Villiers Street I turned under the arches and came back into Northumberland Avenue. They would cruise around, but provided I could lose them early, my chances increased. What spurred me on was the thought that they wanted *me* as well as the negative; they would not want the police to question me, it might not help their image.

The office workers were beginning to pour out of blocks around the Strand and the traffic was thickening noticeably, buses spurting to avoid the rush-hour crowds. This was better for me; people were too intent on getting home to notice. Diving into the News Cinema in Grand Buildings at the end of the Strand I spent a couple of hours there mulling over my next step. I had to be sure that I had shaken off the Chinese because if they saw where I was going it would destroy everything.

When I left the cinema it was dark with a near December nip. Crossing Northumberland Avenue and Whitehall I headed down the wide stretch of the Mall with the park on my left; it was almost empty, just odd people taking a short cut.

I don't know why I turned; normal precaution, perhaps, but when I did I went dry.

A blue Ford Consul was idling just behind me. I recognized its number plate first. How had they got back on to me? I stood and turned; people walked past me giving me curious stares that I could have done without. There he was, diverting across the park at my sudden stop. It had to be he, a well-muffled Chinese. I had been so clever in slipping the cars that I had overlooked the elementary risk of foot tails. He was in touch with the cars with a small transmitter like the police use.

I cursed myself for negligence and for being stupid enough to mention the Americans and the Russians to the Chinese. I had frightened them so they were staying with me. And they had me on an open, fairly isolated stretch. The nearer I got to the Palace the quieter it would become.

Again I retraced my steps. At the corner of Cockspur Street outside the Canadian Pacific building, I dived into the subway, sprinted along it and took refuge in a cubicle in the Gents'. I did not stay long enough for them to conclude that was where I was.

After a couple of minutes I left and there, at the exit, two Chinese waited for me. They were both young, in dark overcoats and both ignored me as I came out.

I went up to the nearest one. 'What do you want with me? I'll keep my word if you do what I ask?'

He looked blankly at me but did it with such indifference that the message was clear. Then he gabbled in Chinese as if he hadn't understood, looked at his colleague and shrugged. My stomach turned; the way I translated the message gave me the impression that I would not translate many more. They were biding their time and that could only mean one thing.

There are four exits from Trafalgar Square subway. I could not see that it made any difference which one I took. So I took the Strand; that was where most people and most of the lights were. At a time I would prefer to keep away from lights I was being forced under them. I needed light to keep the Chinese at bay, darkness to dodge the police. I supposed that if I handed over the negative the Chinese would leave me alone but if I did that I might just as well cut my own throat.

Occasionally I saw the blue Consul, sometimes the other one, a green Mini. Once I saw them both at the same time, one behind the other. Always behind me was at least one Chinese, no longer trying to hide the fact. I kept going; there was no one I could turn to and I did not delude myself that the Chinese wanted the reward money. They wanted to kill me and they only had to hang on to succeed.

Friendlessness took a new dimension. Crossing the Strand I entered the forecourt of Charing Cross Station, passed under the arch and bought myself a ticket to Clapham. It came as no surprise to find my oriental friends forming the short queue behind me. I heard one of them ask for a Brighton ticket, as I turned away; they were taking no chances.

At the departure board I idled about. It was an awkward time; too late for rush hour, too early for the theatre first houses to turn out. Quiet, yet with sufficient people around.

I made my move, not rushing, no sudden dive for a departing train. Through the barrier and into an empty compartment which was easy to find at the time. I sat in a corner away from the platform side so that my escorts would know that I had no intention of jumping back on to it. They arrived just after me, seating themselves opposite one another on the platform side so that I was neatly sealed off.

It was strange how they ignored me, casting not even a glance. A patient pair awaiting a grim opportunity. They might even try it on this train but not in the station. They chattered away in a range of high-pitched pings, so animatedly that they might have been arguing about a football match. No one else got in our compartment which was probably carrying more than most.

A few whistles, a clatter and we were pulling away. Next stop Waterloo, just over the Thames. We reached the bridge and I had my door open and had jumped for the track in something like my pre-Boris speed. It was a dicey move dropping between electrified tracks but it was better than waiting to be killed. I took a tumble and rolled from the huge wheels gathering speed. Then I was up, shaken and hurt, but mobile.

Something, a pebble, shot through my hair and then something plucked my jacket and spun me round so that I almost fell into the passing train. They were shooting at me.

Bundling myself between the tracks I tried to make myself invisible as I saw the shape of someone leaning out of a lighted, disappearing window. A shot whined high over my head and another ricocheted off the granite chippings with a big exploding spark. God, they were desperate.

As the last coach trundled past I crossed the tracks, very careful to avoid the live ones, to the steel barrier that separated the railway from the footbridge the other side. The thought of my friends having a radio link with each other was enough to spur me. I was shaken as I awkwardly climbed the gridded barrier. They intended to make sure that no one got that negative.

On top of the barrier I waited until it was clear, then dropped to the footbridge. None of this did me much good but it was no time to complain. With two cars both ends of the bridge would be covered. Taking my chances I jog-trotted towards Waterloo. The motion half killed me but that was preferable to the real thing so I kept going. The lights of Festival Hall spilled across the Thames and farther up the river a ship's siren blasted a warning.

After a while I had to slow to a walk and was disgusted to find myself still unnerved. Being shot at was an unhealthy experience. That was another score to settle with Fairfax.

At the end of the bridge I stopped to view the huge court-yard of Festival Hall spreading to the river's edge. From the number of people there was obviously a concert on.

Slowly I descended, pushing the padding back into my jacket where the bullet had caught it.

They were waiting for me at the foot of the stairs, not the same two, but with the same look about them. They were hanging on grimly, knowing that eventually I would wear down and their turn would come so that they could finish me calmly and not panic as they had done on the train.

Taking a lesson from them I walked past as if I hadn't seen them. I had my pride, even if it took all my effort to show how much I didn't care. They tagged on. I stopped; they stopped. There was a lot of movement outside the Hall. I went to examine the posters. To this day I could not tell you what was on them. I waited; they waited, I used to be good at giving the police the slip but Fyodor had done too good a job on me.

I was afraid to leave the vicinity of the Hall. Behind it there were too many dark passages; in front was only the river and the bridge I had just crossed. One of my escort was careless in the use of his transmitter and I saw him talking into it inside his overcoat. Whistling up the others I supposed so that there would always be someone on to me. It had not been funny from the outset; now it was nightmarish. Just then I could think of nothing more to do.

As if knowing it too, my escort looked over at me at that precise moment. One even smiled slightly; not humorously; it was the reflex of victory; of his prey being irretrievably cornered. I couldn't manage a smile back. I tried a prayer.

CHAPTER SIXTEEN

THEN THINGS WENT CRAZY. Suddenly. Unexpectedly. Where the foyer had been practically empty, the doors leading to the stalls burst open and were held back as crowds of people emerged. Through the great glass doors I saw them coming, all seemingly talking at once and then they burst around and beyond me, pouring out in their hundreds. It was the end of the concert.

Feeling a brief pang of excitement I fought against them, bustling my way towards the stalls, murmuring apologies as I went. 'I'm sorry, I've left something. I'm sorry, madam, pardon me, I've left my hat.' Taller than most, I had no doubt that my Chinese shadows would initially visually follow my blond top, but once inside the auditorium I knew that I was out of sight.

The gangways were packed with orderly people shuffling towards the exits. I had to fight my way back, offering my inane apologies repeatedly until I deemed it time to dive into one of the now empty rows.

Dropping to my knees I poked around under the seats, out of sight of everybody. Tearing off my wig, I left it as a souvenir and put the glasses in my pocket. For a couple of minutes I watched the stream of passing legs then risked it and rose. Of all the chances I had taken I reckoned this one reasonable. I had to get back into the mob before they tailed off too much. There were other exits but I gambled on the way I had come in. I reckoned they would not expect me back the same way. Allowing my knees to sag a little my height was reduced by an inch or two and people were packed all around me; people who had just heard a thundering good concert and were still talking about it, thank God.

Out in the air, groups were breaking up, people making for the car park or the station. I immersed myself in the biggest stream towards the cars. I saw nothing of the Chinese largely because I was intent on keeping myself hidden; there might be more of them now though and I wondered how they were positioned.

I decided to nick another car. I could not do it with all these people about and I did not want to land in a traffic jam. So I tagged on to a group who seemed to be making for Waterloo station. It was nicely dark and my friends were probably still looking for a blond top.

With luck they were going frantic.

The traffic streamed past for some time but the moment of danger arrived as it eventually thinned and the footsloggers had diminished around me. Then I saw a Consul strategically placed facing the oncoming crowd so I sidled inside a loose group of four, developed a limp and lost height.

Once past the car I risked a quick look back and all seemed

well but they might be cagey with so many people about. Taking a chance, I dived into a darkened side road—in the hope of finding a car. One or two people had obviously parked here rather than near the hall for I could hear footsteps ahead and behind me.

Passing under a street light, dim in this old part of London but not dim enough, a light shone straight in my face, blinding me. Too late I smelled copper. How could I have missed him? Instinctively I kicked out at the lamp and the beam swung up like a searchlight as I caught his wrist. He swore and the lamp crashed to the ground, the beam pivoting like a demented lighthouse.

Still half blind I tore into him as he tried to draw his truncheon. It wasn't his fault that I caught him so easily. He probably had a fractured wrist where I had kicked him and how they can move at all in those bloody great overcoats has always baffled me; his truncheon was not half-way out of its special pocket before I thumped him on his jaw. I had a vague glimpse of his open mouth, then he was sagging to his knees. I didn't wait to help him down. There were shouts behind me and I was off.

Someone half-heartedly stepped in front of me. I could have swung past him but in that fraction of time I saw he had been opening his car. He wasn't too young but there was nothing I could do but belt him. I tried to pull my punch and went for his body. He doubled and gasped, falling back against the wall.

The car door was open. It was a Jag, and would have the acceleration I wanted. As I jumped into the driver's seat I realized with a shock that a woman sat petrified in the passenger seat. She was young and white-faced, and stared at me in terror.

I switched on as the police whistle shrilled and there was a pounding of footsteps. The old boy was still doubled up holding his stomach. I felt bad about that, worse as the girl beside me suddenly unfroze and rained blows at my head, screaming that I had hurt her father. It wasn't my night. I rammed the automatic gear lever to Drive and did the tyres no good the way I pulled away from the kerb.

With one shoulder hunched and face half averted against her sudden attack I managed to pull out without hitting anything, then switched on the beams. My passenger had gone berserk, which wasn't helping my driving or my face so I chopped one of her arms hard side-handed and she fell back numbed and clutching it. Before she could move in on me again I said, 'Try anything more and I'll strangle you.'

She was frightened enough but the threat terrified her into defeat. She started to cry. 'You've injured my father; he's an old man.'

I kept my eyes on the road. She seemed a nice kid and I did not want to scare her.

'I only winded him. He'll be O.K.'

'Please let me out. Let me go.'

I risked a quick glance. She was pretty. Violence had suddenly entered her world. She had read about people like me. Now it was happening. 'I can't stop now, love. They'll be after me.' I was feeling the excitement of a good car under me. 'As long as you sit there you'll be all right.' Had I told her the truth it would have sounded ludicrous; that I did not want to ditch her in this area at this time of night on her own. It might have given her a good laugh.

I can never drive with my windows closed and it was no different now. That's how I heard the first police siren. I could see nothing. There was other traffic now but the sound was somewhere in front. The copper must have been active on his little radio; they were too popular, those damned things.

I had to get to Eaton Terrace as fast as I could. Having been so bent on initial escape I had gone for distance but now it was time quickly to collect my bearings. Hell, I was heading towards the Oval. Swinging into Kennington Lane I spotted the blue flasher cutting through the light traffic towards me and tried to brake to normal speed. As we passed each other I saw his brake lights come on in my mirror, right indicator on, then he was skidding in a U-turn to chase me. I watched my mirror like a hawk, let him come screaming up behind me, thumped the brake sharply and U-turned in a movement that made the girl scream and the traffic concertina to a stop.

I had judged it nicely to the fraction of a gap. The police car could not follow immediately. It braked again, but by then I had my foot down overtaking in a way that must have roused the mildest driver to a frenzy of invective. The girl was having a bad time of it too. She was crying quietly in a pathetic, resigned sort of way, hands up to her face.

I kept going, making enemies all the way, hearing the siren some distance behind me. Aiming at Vauxhall Bridge, I kept my foot down. The police radios must have been hot for another siren sounded ahead of me and the old blue bobble blinked away as a car drew out of an intersection making an effective road block straight across the road.

There was traffic in the facing lane, too much to try to ride against it. If I stopped I would have had it. The pavement was clear just there so I swung left past a lamp post, brushed it, pulled over as I mounted the kerb with a jerk that kept the girl busy with her fears and did nothing for mine, took the police car on the inside, just avoided going through a shop window then swung crazily back on to the road.

We rocked a bit but she settled while the police tried to get after us from an awkward angle. We roared over the bridge like we were taking off, careered straight up Vauxhall Bridge Road,

did a couple of left-hand squiggles and finished with a scream o
tyres in Lupus Street, heading west.

My violent manoeuvring had finally subdued the girl into a
terrified silence. I sensed more than saw that she sat rigid, clutch
ing her bruised arm and waiting for the crash.

There was not so much traffic round here in Pimlico which was
just as well, for I was not looking for No Entry or one-way traffic
signs. I took the turns as I needed them and prayed that there
would be nothing coming the other way.

In spite of my breakneck speed, the sirens were closer but they
had the advantage with their hooters and flashers clearing the
way; I had to rely on other motorists quickly spotting a madman
and making the best they could of it. We did a beautiful drift into
Sutherland Street but still Eaton Place seemed at the end of the
world.

The flashers were now in my mirror. Ahead of me another
appeared coming my way and swinging over to cut me off. He had
yet to get the tempo of the chase; keeling the other way we
circled each other between the parked cars, passing each other on
the wrong side of the street in a frenzy of movement that induced
a motor-cyclist to jump off and pull his bike into a space by the
kerb.

There were so many flashers behind now that they seemed to
be playing musical chairs as they juggled for position. The sirens
were baying like hounds closing in for the kill.

I had to give a touch of brake before crossing Buckingham
Palace Road heading towards Ebury Street, beyond which lay
Eaton Terrace. Almost there but more sirens were sounding.

It seemed to me that there was one sound in the world,
the whining sirens wailing in agony; the engine noise was an
integral part of me, without it I would feel deserted. The local
residents must be having the time of their lives speculating on
this massed police activity. The luck could not stay with me; a
little earlier or later and the traffic would have been much more
dense.

I entered Eaton Terrace in a wide skid and not knowing how
the numbers ran. The howl was around me now and then the
worst happened. Two prowl cars cut me off at the top. Braking
too quickly my rear end swung but I kept the brake down hard
while we swayed between the rows of parked cars. Bold figures
showed themselves on one of the big pillars of a portico; they
weren't the numbers I wanted but they were a guide.

My rear was sealed off as the chasers came roaring up and
windows began to open and curtains were pulled back. The din
was terrific. And then, the sirens were switched off one by one
until they tailed into silence, with the blue lights blinking out
each end of the street.

Car doors slammed, heavy footsteps approached as the coppers spread across the street in opposite approaching lines. We had stopped in the middle of the street but I wasn't worried about a ticket for parking.

'Cheerio, love. You'll be all right now.' I opened the door and stood beside the car. Then I yelled out, 'Stay there or I'll give it to the girl.' They did not know whether I was armed or not; they pulled up. Which way did the numbers run? It was a fifty-fifty chance.

Suddenly the girl broke loose from the car and fled to the nearest row of police, her footsteps at that moment the only sound. Police lamps shone down on me like floodlights on a stage. They must have seen that my hands were free. Without an instruction they came bearing down at me again. Once they had the girl they came much faster narrowing my space to move.

There was no time to work it out. I ran hard across the road heading beyond the boldly numbered house and towards the upper line of police. They must have thought that I was going to break their cordon for they slowed and hunched like a group of wrestlers. Behind me the second row came pounding up and I expected to be seized at any moment.

There could have been little space left when I veered towards one of the houses and raced up its steps just as someone's hands clutched at me. Wriggling away I kicked backwards, heard a grunt, then reached the top of the steps. There was no time for the door. As I climbed the railings the police momentarily halted, thinking I would either fall back or crash into the basement.

I did neither. Crouching on the railings I gave myself all the impetus I could muster and hurled myself like a ball straight at the plate glass window of the ground floor, arms round knees, head tucked in. I took the break somewhere across my shoulders. The sound of shattered glass triggered a vibrator alarm and as I crashed on to the floor I knocked something over.

It was one of those pulsating alarms, something like a siren with a sore throat. On top of that there was a hammering on the front door and somewhere inside the house a bell was ringing its head off. There was such a cacophony of sound that wealthy Belgravia would have a topic to shock sensitive minds for ever.

I had fallen heavily and I collected more bruises. As urgent as it was to get up I could only do it slowly, unwinding like an old man. Glass crunched under my feet then the light came on and there was Fairfax, straight-backed and expressionless, in a woollen dressing gown with some crest on its pocket and a ·38 pointing nice and steadily at my middle. I must have looked a wreck standing there with the cold air sweeping around my back and the insistent cry of coppers yelling to be let in.

'I saw you coming,' he said as if we were in the middle of a conversation. 'Why couldn't you ring the bell, that window is going to freeze the room.' It seemed that he could hear nothing of the frantic clamour particularly of the alarm shooting straight through my head.

'Look,' I snarled at him, pointing to the broken window, 'if you want your stuff delivered get that bloody pack of bloodhounds off my back.'

He stared briefly, made up his mind, nodded and slipped the gun into a pocket. 'Stay here.'

As if I had a choice. He left the room and I could hear voices at the front door; some were raised angrily. I stepped out of the draught and was not surprised to find this a period room. On the way in I had knocked over a stone bust on a white marble plinth. The thick carpet had saved both them and me from serious injury. Glass lay scattered about but I was too weary to do anything about any of it. Suddenly the alarm switched off and the relief was enormous.

Fairfax returned, severe-faced and angry about the eyes. 'I had to telephone the Police Chief to make them see reason. The Superintendent outside thinks it extremely odd that I don't hand you over immediately and I really cannot blame him. They insist on leaving men outside. Now let us get out of here to somewhere comfortable. Dammit, I'll never live this down.'

He led me across the hall into a more spacious room hung with small gilt-framed oils and a collection of miniatures. Without a word I sank into a deep-seated armchair. He went to an old Tudor chest. 'Don't go to sleep, there's time for that later.' He poured two large brandies, handing me one. 'Don't tell me you don't drink. You need it.' He sat opposite, shrewd eyes puzzled. 'Now what the devil did you run out on me for?'

He was right about the brandy; it was stoking my depleted central heating system.

'Because you sold me down the river, you bastard. You set me up as a scapegoat to pacify the Chinese. They would have banged me away for life.'

'Oh, come now. We'd have had you out in two years.'

I could only stare furiously at him; no denial, no suggestion of an apology for treachery. Blasphemous words stuck in my throat.

He blandly went on, 'Well, where's the stuff?'

'The same bloody question from you all; C.I.A., K.G.B., the Chinese, and now you.'

'I thought the others might have a go, it was too good an opportunity for them, that's why I was so concerned.'

'Concerned for what I carried? Not for me?' He was getting under my skin again.

He permitted himself that brittle smile of his over his brandy goblet. 'You are evidently well able to look after yourself, Spider. Well, where are they?'

'I've sold them back to the Chinese.'

I had to hand it to him; there was a momentary stiffening of fingers on glass but otherwise no sign. Then his expression slowly changed and he gazed at me as if I was his closest friend and had let him down.

'Then I was wrong about you.' His words came slowly as if his disappointment was at being wrong in his assessment, not that I had gained revenge.

'What did you expect me to do? Hand myself over for a lifer because you had stabbed me in the back?'

'I don't care for your analogy. The money is in Switzerland although you have clearly decided that it is not. Once the Chinese had received their face-saving gesture from us, after a couple of years you would have been free. As it is, you are still wanted and will have to take the full consequences. There is nothing that I am prepared to do for you.'

I said, 'Don't come the aggrieved stuff with me. You got yourself a tuppeny-ha'penny creeper and decided that I was expendable; I didn't matter; I was a villain with a record. You didn't mind using me provided you could get shift of me afterwards in the quickest possible time.'

Fairfax sighed slowly and put down his glass. He rose, and for once he was not quite so straight-backed. Only then did I realize the strength of the blow I had given him. Going to a Georgian display cabinet he removed a beautiful porcelain figure, gazing at it with affection and pain. 'The trouble with you, Spider, is that you have a chip. At no time have I regarded you as petty or small or a villain. I needed your prowess, it is true. But I also needed your integrity. It never occurred to me that you would discard it.'

The old bastard had this way with him of always making me feel in the wrong. It was *he* who had ditched *me*, I kept reminding myself.

He held out the porcelain figure to me. Taking it I considered it a piece I would not have missed had I been out on a job.

'Know what it is?' he asked.

'Meissen,' I said. 'I could get a fair price for this from a fence I know.'

'I dare say,' he rejoined dryly. 'I stole it during the war from a German museum in Cologne. That and others. Quite a few of us were at it.'

Handing it back I did not know what to say. He had let me see something of his fallibility behind his rigid mask of self-respect. He had equated himself with me and he need not have done it. A bit slowly I climbed to my feet. 'Can I use your phone?'

'A condemned man's last request? You may.'

'I want this person to ring me back. You will want to know about it.'

I moved over to an antique phone that the G.P.O. insisted they

would not connect to their systems; again it revealed the position
of this man.

He said, 'You'll see a number embossed on the side. Tell them
to dial it back. It's not the real number but it will be relayed here.'

I got Ray Lynch out of bed; he was drowsy, half drunk and
irritable. When I told him who was speaking he half sobered and
became attentive. 'I'm giving you a scoop, Ray. Listen carefully.
Ring Li Tshien at the Chinese Legation. Tell him that you have
spoken to me, that I am safe and not in police hands; and if they
want me to stay out of them, this is their last chance to do it my
way; that I'll call in the morning if he gives you the story. Then
ring back here and report.' I gave him the number.

Fairfax, re-seated, was watching me curiously but I wasn't
ready for him yet. He was trying to weigh me up again as if
acknowledging that he had made a mess of it first time.

'While I was with Boris and Fyodor they told me that they
had killed two American agents called Hank and Joe who had a
drum in Highbury. They had done it so that it would look like
me.'

'Boris? Tall, aristocratic with his chunky muscle man? Yes,
it's typical of his style. There would be no point in killing the two
Americans. The police might be fooled but other espionage
agencies would not have been. The Russians are very good at
blackmail.'

'So the Americans are alive?'

'One dark, Indian appearance, the other a fair-haired, all-
American boy?'

'That's them.'

'They were alive this morning. They knew that the Highbury
place was blown; in fact they left there today.'

'That bastard Boris had me sweating over it.'

'Colonel Kransouski. Impeccable manner. Very good at his
job. I'm surprised that you did not sell out to him.'

'I very nearly did, but I . . .' I suddenly realized my mistake.

'Go on.'

What the hell. Taking a good look at Fairfax I saw that he had
wilted in the short time we had been together. He considered he
had insurmountable problems; might even lose his job with the
certainty that the Foreign Secretary would lose his, with accumu-
lative repercussions that would echo down Whitehall and up and
down the country. I wished Ray would ring back. He did as I
finished my brandy.

'Boyo,' he howled down the phone, 'you're a bloody marvel.
I've been on to the newsroom, everything is set. Thanks, Spider,
my old boyo. This one we'll celebrate. You can explain then.'

I would have to contrive an acceptable story. When finally I
put down the phone, I turned to Fairfax. I knew that I was grinning but my whole body was trembling and I could not stop it.

Seeing my uncontrollable shakes, Fairfax brought me another brandy. Before sipping it I dived into my inside pocket and produced the print, the negative and the letter, throwing them down on the inlay of a Sheraton table.

One at a time he picked them up and I saw the tremor in his fingers. He looked at me with immense relief and for once I felt that the feeling was *for* me and not for what he held.

'I got two of the boys on the job,' I explained. 'One turned out the letter, the other fiddled the photo. He retook the positive, deleted the head on the negative, then reinserted it so that both the print and negative cannot stand expert scrutiny. It will look as if the head has been placed on someone else's body. The letter will also show up as a forgery if the chips are down. All the Foreign Secretary need do is call their bluff.'

His relief was tinged with concern as the possibility of a new danger entered his head. I could read his mind on this one. 'You needn't worry,' I said, ' you must know that the letter on its own is valueless. The bloke who faked the photo would see nothing wrong in it if you get me. Anyway he's not a blackmailer. Strange how villains had to straighten things out for you, isn't it?'

'Well, well,' Fairfax muttered, clearly delighted but not willing to show too much. 'I thought I could not be *that* wrong about you. What of the phone call?'

'Tomorrow's headlines in *The Express*. 'Li Tshien, Chinese diplomat who was brutally assaulted, has regained conciousness to emphatically deny that the person who attacked him is the person wanted by the police and displayed in newspapers and on television. Representatives of the Chinese People's Republic cannot stand by to see such injustice . . .' and so on. 'The person now described by Mr. Li Tshien is short, stocky, and fair-haired . . .' Have you got someone like that you can tuck away for a couple of years?'

Fairfax smiled; it was almost full-blooded. His features began visibly to relax as I watched him rub one eye. 'Look here,' he said, 'you must ring Maggie to let her know that you are a free man. Then I suggest you go to her, bath, change, and we can meet tomorrow evening for dinner.' Then, in frank appraisal, 'I was not wrong about you, Spider. You are the only one to come out of this creditably.' He sat back, completely relaxed. 'You know, I have a colleague who could use you. On a different basis, of course. Better than drifting back to crime, what?'

The old blighter had already put it all behind him. He mused over my name. 'Spider Scott. You wouldn't do anything foolish like putting your initials on your issue briefcase, would you? Tell me, have you ever been to Japan?'

I couldn't leave him quite so self-satisfied. 'By the way,' I said. 'I promised the two lads two thousand quid each for the forgeries. I knew that you wouldn't mind paying; cheaper than the reward

—tax free, of course. And you can pay for a car hire to take m
to the Chinese Legation to deliver Bluie's fake negative in th
morning.'

The cigar was choking me, but as Fairfax had given it to me a
dinner I'd finish it if it killed me.

'This is the life,' I spluttered to Maggie who sat right close to
me on the settee in her flat. We both had our shoes off and ou
feet up on the bed stool in front of the fire. Maggie was gazing a
the ceiling relaxed and happy, still wondering about it all.

'Have some more lemonade,' I suggested, reaching for the
champagne bucket, another gift from Fairfax.

'No thanks.' She squeezed my hand.

I didn't blame her. This high living is overrated. The back o
my throat felt like an incinerator from the cigar and the cham
pagne was dry and flavourless on my palate. If I'm going to drink
I'd prefer beer. Still, it was free; I kept at it in the hope that
might get to like it. The dinner had been good, though; I could
cultivate a taste for good restaurants without straining myself.

I was richer by seventeen and a half thousand pounds. Maggie
knew that I was richer but not by how much. The story Fairfax
and I had contrived very vaguely reduced me to the role o
inadvertent decoy, the innocently involved bystander who had
received a little handout by way of compensation. I was content

Pulling Maggie closer I drew on the cigar again which resulted
in a violent fit of coughing. When I recovered I leaned back again
still wheezing. I eyed the cigar like an enemy but refused to dis
card it. 'This is the life,' I said again.